THE SINS

D0505541

Frank Delaney was b... ... ...
His non-fiction include... ...rk on the Celts, James Joyce,
and Dr Johnson. He also works as a broadcaster – with
the BBC for whom he devised the Radio Four
Programmes 'Bookshelf', and the language series 'Word
of Mouth', and as presenter of 'The W. H. Smith Book
Show' on Sky News. He has lived in London since 1978.

'A powerful and compelling novel. Beautifully written
and richly described.'   *Prima*

'It's a five-hundred-page page-turner, a big story told in
detail . . . Delaney's got you hooked completely, and
you turn the last page wishing he'd get up a bit early in
the morning and hurry up with the next instalment.'
                                                    Sunday Press

'We have barely relaxed our nerves when we begin to
sense the scarifying shades of François Mauriac.'
                                                    Irish Times

'Frank Delaney excels at depicting the contradictions of
his quicksilver subject.'   *Daily Mail*

'A big story, bringing together themes of political
bitterness, the power of the Catholic Church, ideas of
redemption and atonement.'   *Sunday Tribune*

'Formidably accomplished first novel.'   *Annabel*

'An engrossing read.'   *Irish Press*

FRANK DELANEY

The Sins of
the Mothers

HarperCollins*Publishers*

HarperCollins*Publishers*
77–85 Fulham Palace Road,
Hammersmith, London W6 8JB

Special edition 1995

Published in paperback by HarperCollins*Publishers* 1994

Previously published in paperback by Grafton 1993
Reprinted three times

First published in Great Britain by
HarperCollins*Publishers* 1992

ISBN 0 286 15127 8

Set in Times Roman

Printed in Great Britain by
HarperCollinsManufacturing Glasgow

For Susan

Spring 1925

1

A mile from the village, the bus entered a tunnel of trees and dense hedges. The young woman turned her head to search for her reflection in the darkened window beside her. Peering, she opened her mouth a little, and ridged the back of her teeth with her tongue. The image of her face in the glass faded as the bus crested a small hill into a whiter daylight. She turned back again, and shifting on the hard wooden seat, craned her neck, fidgeting to see the road ahead past the driver: the fog still divulged only dripping trees looming over the high formal stone walls on either side. As *The Princess* crested the second hump by the New Quarry, the conductor, who had been leaning against the door, straightened up, readying for duty. The young woman withdrew her right hand from her pocket where her fingers had been secretly praying on a rosary; she touched an eyebrow, nudged her brown cloche hat in an unnoticeable adjustment.

Minutes earlier, as it did four days a week, the bus had driven past the verge of a damp forest where this morning, alarmed at the noise of the engine across the silent lands, a deer slipped on soft earth – the edge of a shallow grave. As the animal staggered and then recovered, drawing its fastidious hoof out of the stumble, another tiny shred of flesh slid from the decomposing corpse wrapped in the remains of a greatcoat beneath the ground.

The village materialized, a single one-sided street of low houses. Chimney smoke plumed upwards. Within, the villagers moved quietly, and the older people, their bodies slower to grow warm, still wore their night attire under such heavy coats as they owned. The bus engine vrammed and rattled; a black and white mongrel cat loped back from some small chill expedition in the hedges and squeezed under the planks of a warm barn in one of the yards. The curtains of the village twitched, yet doors remained closed.

The young woman on the bus massaged her forearms in the damp cold, then gathered her hand-knitted gloves and a small leather attaché case. At the helmeted pump, the dingy *Princess* halted with a gulp, and a bicycle on the roof spun one of its wheels; it looked a little like an insect's wings whirring slowly.

Her name was Ellen Morris. As the bus door slapped open, she stepped down briskly and innocently, and then jinked from the grass verge to the hard pavement beyond.

The driver took his time, did not immediately engage his gears.

'She could be foreign though, couldn't she heh?' said the conductor, the door still open. 'If it wasn't for the accent?'

Both men leaned over to watch where she went; they gazed at her shoes, her coat, her legs, and the driver puffed, 'Phwhoo-hoo then?' when Ellen headed for the only non-domestic building in the place: single-storey, uninspired, grey, municipal; two chimneys, and a small slate plaque on the porch wall: *Deanstown National School*. The bus driver returned to his steering wheel, the conductor forced the stiff door shut, and *The Princess* cranked itself together and pushed away.

Ellen Morris pressed the small gate into the tiny yard and knocked on the door. A child opened, and Ellen asked, 'Is Mr Kane here?' by which time Mr Kane was already striding down the classroom from the fireplace. Before he could say a word, she spoke again, not quite blurting.

'I'm a day early, I'm Ellen Morris, you wrote to me, after I applied to the advertisement.' Ungloving her

10

hands, she began to arrange the attaché case on her hiked knee. 'I couldn't come tomorrow but I didn't know that until yesterday, there's no bus I think on Tuesdays.' She thumbed the metal catches. 'Or if there is, we thought it might be too foggy to travel. But if I'm too early, or if it isn't all right . . .' From the attaché case she handed him a letter addressed, 'To Whom It Might Concern'.

The child who had opened the door returned to her desk shrugging her shoulders in curiosity and mouthing the whisper, 'A Mistress?'

The Princess, out of sight by now, stopped at the statue down in the hollow where the fog thickened; the conductor picked up the loose bale of empty jute sacks left there, inspected the string-tied label and then the bus clattered onwards to the east end of the parish.

Mr Kane said, 'Come in, so. Are you frozen with the cold? You're Miss Morris, so?'

To which she replied with the words, 'Both. Yes,' and he smiled. She walked so directly through the door that he had to lean aside, and with none of the tentativeness of a stranger she stepped right in, as far as the classroom's edge between the squat, flaking pilasters of the school porch.

'Well. Now. Right,' he said, turning the letter back and forth in his hand, but not opening it.

He said, 'You're very welcome.' Stowing her gloves under her arm, she placed her attaché case flat on the windowsill, and said, 'How do you do. Mr Kane, is it, I suppose?' shaking his hand.

He stooped his head a little to walk through the inner door, waited, and when she had picked up her attaché case, he steered her into the body of the school and up to the fireplace.

'I can't give you a cup of tea or anything until later on. I didn't know about the buses. On Tuesdays, that is. Is today, what, Monday, yes, it must only be in the winter

11

they do that, although I thought they go past here, but of course, yes, they only go as far as, yes.' He looked doubtful but polite.

He stopped and looked down again at the letter in his hand, then at her face. 'The Canon is expecting to. To interview you. But that's tomorrow. But sure what harm? Can't we go and see him today, he's there, I know.'

Ellen Morris had begun to organize herself: attaché case on the nearby table near the Globe of the World.

'Were there many on the bus?'

'Only myself.'

She swivelled her head confidently, looking around at the schoolroom: maps on the walls, *Mercator's Projection of Europe* and, shiny, new, *The Counties of Ireland in 1924*; the clock over the fireplace, *Made by Kneeshaw 1894* inscribed across its open, friendly face with the black Roman numerals; Breughel peasant paintings in profuse blues and yellows; *Curwen's Modulator* singing-lesson chart; on the easeled blackboard, chalked in careful, tall, joined lettering, 'Neither a Borrower nor a Lender be'; spreading stains of old damp by each of the three windows. Across the light blue, thick, flaking walls of both rooms spread the turquoise roundels of the twelve months, with their rhymes – 'January brings the snow; Makes my feet and fingers glow; February brings the rain; Thaws the frozen lakes again.' Turning to the attaché case in afterthought, she clicked it open again, and carefully handed forth a large envelope to which had been pinned an advertisement clipping. *Qualified Assistant Required for Two-Teacher National School: to take charge of Low Infants, High Infants, First Class and Second Class. Higher Diploma not Essential but Desirable.* She held it forth before her, as if displaying a firm certificate to him. Mr Kane looked at it, then at her, then down again.

'My references. There.' She stabbed a finger at the letter in his hand. Then she presented the advertisement to him:

her duties discharged, she held her hands out sideways to the fire behind her and flexed her fingers like a pianist warming up.

Mr Kane placed the letter carefully behind a tall box of loose chalks on the mantelpiece, then read the advertisement, and lifted it to see whether she had pinned anything beneath.

'Yes. Ye-ess. A copy of your letter. Ye-ss. H'm-h'm' – on a rising inflection. He opened and closed the fingers of his free hand to the general heat of the fire.

'I believe you speak French,' she said to him in her sudden way. 'Isn't that very unusual?'

He stared in the bright coals a moment, and then with his free right hand began to stroke his chin, leaving a fleck of chalk on it. The children in the desks looked on, a miniature audience, one or two whispering with giggles to those behind them. He rubbed the tips of his fingers back and forth together to loosen the ingrained chalk dust.

Mr Kane said slowly, 'The job here is for. A teacher. So you might. Well, I suppose, teach – for a bit.' Then he queried, 'H'm?'

She replied, 'You mean what an Inspector would want me to do?'

Winter sunshine began to illuminate the interior of the fog, and by the school window a woman walked into view. She wore a man's coat and a headscarf, and carried a bucket to the pump for water, her breath adding little punches of further mist.

'My references.' Ellen again indicated the letter on the mantel. She began to open the buttons of her coat, and loosened a little the cream silk scarf at her neck, tucked into her blouse like a cravat. The moment her eyes left his face as she attended to these easing tasks, he looked her up and down.

'Now,' Mr Kane said, in an air of turning to something new.

He faced the class. In one corner of the room hung an askew door, the entrance to the Juniors' room. Mr Kane had a tiny piece of food caught between two of his longer teeth. He rapped the front desk with a knuckle.

'Attention. Quietness please. Sit straight up and fold your arms.' The children's whispers, which had risen almost to speech, faded at the severeness, and the desks clattered metallically as they all turned.

'Continue with this headline. Do it three times. I'm taking our visitor into the other room. D'you want to bring your – ?' He indicated the case and gloves on the table and led the way down the open aisle, stooping slightly to say softly, formally, 'At the most we have about sixty-six. That's with a full attendance, and it usually works out. About fifty-eight or -nine, and nearly half of them in this room. This is the Low Infants, the High Infants, the First Class and the Second Class.'

'As advertised,' she confirmed.

The door rattled lightly when opened, to a room where a fourteen-year-old girl stood in front of another fire.

'We never call it the Babies' Class. Miss Harrington, who retired, that's why the vacancy. She thought it offended them to be called "babies". Especially when they're big enough to go to school.'

Rows of little children at tiny desks were counting out small polished sea-shells.

'That's all right. Angela, you can go back to your desk,' he said to the girl who had been caretaking. 'Now –' he addressed the small ones, 'Quietness, please – this is Miss –' he paused, 'Morris, and she's to be with you until lunchtime.' To Ellen he murmured, 'I've been sending them home at half-past twelve every day. Until a new appointment is made. When the weather is *in*-clement. [He pronounced 'inclement' as two words.] I think I might send them all home early today. The fog and that.'

She said again how sorry she was, but felt it better to

14

arrive a day early than not turn up tomorrow and have everybody waiting.

'No matter, no matter. All yours, so.'

Mr Kane gave her the classroom with a stern wave of his hand, and left, scraping the rickety glass-panelled door across the floor to close it behind him. She placed her attaché case and gloves on an empty, much wider table covered with a soft green baize loose cloth, took off her coat, but retained her scarf and hat, and said to the children, 'Hands up who can guess who I am?'

A hand or two crept up, then one or two more, then slowly the rest followed, until soon all the hands except one or two stood straight up in the air like a sweet little forest. Ellen looked all around, and then picked out a boy who had not raised his hand, and who sat looking down at his desk. She pointed to him and said, 'Now, what is your name?'

All the other children laughed, and Ellen said, 'Quietness, please.' The boy looked at her and his face reddened, and he looked down, and said nothing.

'You can put your hands down,' she told all the children. 'Are you going to tell me your name at all?' The little boy blushed deeper, and Ellen said with a smile to him, 'All right. All right. We can get your name from you later.' She stood with her back to the fire, and clapped her hands, 'All right. Since you all had your hands up you can tell me at the same time. Who am I?'

The children sang, 'A new Mistress, Ma'am.'

Ellen smiled and asked all to say together, 'The name of the Mistress you used to have?'

'Miss. Harr. Ing. Ton, Ma'am.'

Then she asked them where Miss Harrington was? This question produced no unison. One girl put a hand up and said, 'Re, re, re, re-something, Ma'am.'

Ellen nodded and, inviting them to 'repeat it after me', mouthed the word 'retired' several times. Next, with their sing-song help, she counted the children, twenty-one of them. When they had finished, she said, 'Now. What's the nicest prayer you know?' at which they fell over themselves to answer, 'Ma'am, Ma'am, Ma'am, Ma'am, me, Ma'am, me, Ma'am, me, me,' all except the same boy again, who, in the corner of her eye, said nothing.

'All right so,' said Ellen. 'We'll say the *Hail Holy Queen*. "Hail Holy Queen, Mother of Mercy. Hail, our Life, our Sweetness. And our Hope."'

They sang along willingly after her. 'To thee do we cry. Poor banished children of Eve. To thee do we send up our sighs. Mourning and weeping. In this Valley of Tears.'

Ellen tented her hands together like the roof of a toy church, and bowed her head up and down with the rhythm of the prayer.

'Turn then. Most gracious Advocate. Thine eyes of mercy towards us. And after this our exile. Show unto us. The blessed fruit of thy womb, Jesus.'

Ellen looked down, then thumb-wiped a small fleck of wet dust from the toe of her brown court shoe.

'O Clement! O Loving! O sweet Virgin Mary. Pray for us, O Holy Mother of God. That we may be made worthy of the promises of Christ.'

The children, with no vocabularial difficulty whatsoever, romped through the prayer, but although the little boy's lips moved, no actual sound appeared to emerge. Without looking at him directly, Ellen, during the praying aloud, next began to walk back and forward across the floor, and up and down between the rows of desks, bending to hear the words coming from sundry mouths, stopping subtly a little longer each time near him, sometimes behind him, sometimes a little in front with her back to him. His hair and ears had some congealed grease; he wore a hard, cheap jumper – as did most of the others – and although he held his hands obediently on top of his desk, he had scrunched them tight together. He had not been washed that morning, nor perhaps for a number of mornings.

Fourteen miles away, in the next town, *The Princess* bus had reached its morning destination, and to warm themselves, the driver and conductor addressed mugs of tea and slices of currant bread in *The Criterion*, where they told Miss Cronin about Ellen.

'She have a kind of a flat nose. Like she looks foreign.'

Miss Cronin when being shrewd dropped her voice to a stage whisper. 'That Harrington woman retired; she was left a farm in Waterford; that might be a new one, so, that must be it, isn't it, lads?'

'She's well shod, whoever she is,' said the driver. 'Well shod, yeh.'

'She looks like a Protestant,' said the conductor.

When the *Hail Holy Queen* ended, Ellen said, 'Now another prayer. Remember. All prayers go up to God.'

Again hands shot up. '"The Our Father", Ma'am.' And, equally breathlessly, 'Ma'am. Ma'am, the "I Confess".' Ellen again called them 'Very good'. She clasped her hands.

'The proper name for the "I Confess" is "*The Confiteor*". The what?' They struggled, and eventually managed with pride, 'The Con. Feet. Ee. Yor.'

She started them, as if pushing a cart until it picked up speed. '"I confess to Almighty God. To the Blessed Mary ever Virgin. To Blessed Michael the Archangel."'

Continuing her journey through the desks, she again chose at random to bend down beside a reciting child, chanting with it, nodding her head in good approval. 'To Blessed John the Baptist. To the Holy Apostles, Peter and Paul.' By each desk she inclined in order to listen, sometimes down on one knee, accompanying the child's chant with a mouthing of the prayer through an encouraging smile. 'And to all the Saints.' Her intention materialized: she wished to approach unalarmingly, and from the front, the silent boy, who mouthed a little, but definitely made no sound.

'That I have sinned exceedingly. In Thought, Word and Deed.'

The little boy, who until closer examination had a merry face, avoided her eyes, and then looked down. Ellen stooped low, continuing the prayer.

'Through my Fault.' She knelt. 'Through my Own Fault.' She placed her hand on the cheek farthest from her, and turned his face gently so that he faced in her direction. He screwed his eyes shut, and began to cry, the tears falling from one eye. 'Through my Own Most Grievous Fault.'

On his desk lay a matchbox. Ellen opened it, saw a moth inside give a tiny flutter, and she closed it gently. She gave the boy a secret, exclusive smile, and placed her hand on his hair.

Nodding to the rest of the class, and making her face into an encouraging expression, she stood straight again, and began to mouth the prayer exaggeratedly as she spoke.

'Therefore I beseech. The Blessed Mary ever Virgin. Blessed Michael the Archangel.' The boy's second eye oozed a tear, and she patted his face: he was no more than five years old, with, beneath the grease, fair-to-blond hair.

'Blessed John the Baptist. The Holy Apostles, Peter and Paul.'

The little boy did not open his eyes; nor did he move his lips.

'And all the saints. To pray for me. To the Lord Our God.'

The classroom yelled a great 'Amen', and Ellen walked

to the head of the room again, having given the boy a final gentle tug on the hair.

Mr Kane opened the door of the classroom and announced that a break might be taken, but if they wished to go into the yard to play, they had A, to put on their coats and B, to keep running all the time.

'Who is that child?' Ellen asked, watching the released boy grab his matchbox, scamper into the porch and out through the door. Mr Kane beckoned her in the direction of the fireplace in the Senior room and, removing the tall brass mesh fireguard, stood nearer the coal glow.

'I should tell you a bit about the history of this place,' he said, 'before you meet the Canon, and before you make up your mind that it's a place like this you might want to work in. That is, if he offers you the job. Although with those references. Well, anyway.' He stopped short of the imminent compliment.

He said, 'You're probably used to swankier. There isn't anybody here worth a lot, they're a far-back crowd, the ones here. Some of them aren't, the big farmers' children, they're all right. But most of them are cottiers' children; we even get one or two of "no fixed abode". That young fellow, the one who won't talk, that you were trying to get to join in' – he ignored her eyebrows' acknowledgment that he had been watching and listening – 'they're as poor a family as you'd get anywhere in the world. There's fourteen of them in the house, and the father a bit of a – well,' and he never finished the sentence.

Ellen went to the window and looked out, where the children's breath condensed on the air, and Mr Kane said nothing for a moment or two.

'He doesn't seem to have any coat,' she said. 'That boy.'

Mr Kane looked down and ascertained the white handkerchief folded in the breast pocket of his tweed jacket. He patted it, then asked, 'The Canon? How would you like to make up your mind – if, I mean, the job is offered to you?'

She walked back to the fire, and said she didn't know. 'But I suppose I wouldn't have applied for it if I didn't want to take it. They're scarce enough, jobs like this.'

To which he replied, 'So are the right candidates.'

Mr Kane went to his tall, sloping desk, took out a speckled fountain pen, wrote a note on careful blue paper, folded and enveloped it, called in the girl Angela, the one who had been keeping the Junior classroom quiet, and sent her down the road to the Canon's house.

'How far away is the church?' asked Ellen. 'I mean, do they say Mass every morning here? Is it near enough to go?'

'Look. Look,' interrupted Thomas Kane, his head lunging forward gently towards the window-pane. 'That's the father. The boy you were asking about.'

Wearing a cap and a navy-blue, shabby overcoat, a heavy man pushed a bicycle ahead of him across the green, then clambered up and cycled away. Although she would recall that moment with great clarity, and prove capable nearly two years later of describing every facet of the man's appearance, and even the manner in which she herself stood when she first saw him – one hand on her hip, other hand still fiddling with her scarf – she now registered only cursory interest. Returning to the fireside, Ellen Morris at last removed her hat.

'That's nice,' she said. 'Who did that? Yourself?' With a knuckle she touched the drawing of a black and silver eel pinned to the wall.

'No. There's an itinerant artist. He comes around every few years. Some of those eels live to twenty years old.'

Ellen straightened the corner of the drawing.

'His full name is Jeremiah Anthony Williams. He's a bit, well, you know, a bit . . .'

As they walked down the hill under the dripping trees, Mr Kane did not finish the sentence, and Ellen did not press. He returned to it.

'Don't mind if he's a bit on the – rough side. What I mean is – coarse. He may be a Canon, but he hasn't ever been outside the county hardly. Except maybe to Dublin, once or so. He's capable of asking questions that he shouldn't. I mean, the sort of things he might ask in Confession.'

Ellen laughed, trying to keep up with Mr Kane's tall stride. Her coat brushed on a shrub along the Canon's avenue, wetting the upper sleeve extensively, although the light water merely sat glistening on the fabric. Inside, she sat alone in the tiled and musty hall, waiting to be called; and among the stale geraniums in brass pots she shivered in the cold. The housekeeper had ushered Mr Kane in to meet the Canon somewhere in another cave of the house. Soon, Mr Kane reappeared and, still wearing his coat, beckoned with one finger. Ellen rose, put her attaché case in her left hand and drew the glove from her right, prepared for handshakes.

'Oh,' said Canon Jeremiah Williams, when he saw Ellen. 'The last one was like a hairpin,' he said to Mr Kane.

They shook hands. The Canon, even lankier than Mr Kane, and with a ridge where his hat had been sitting on his hair, said, 'What's a good cure for the scour?' Ellen, with the air of someone who had not fully heard, begged his pardon; he did not acknowledge, and continued, 'Two of them calves have that hell's curse white scour and I can't pluck one single thing from a hedge anywhere in Christendom that'll stop the flow. They have the fields scuttered.'

Looking at Ellen's bosom – she had opened her coat: an oil heater formed the apex of their three chairs in the large, heavy room – he continued, 'There's some women say they can't eat turnips if they're feeding a child, and God Almighty, we gave the cows turnips last week for the first time in years, and their milk is as hard and as yellow as dung.'

Mr Kane did not look at Ellen; she, seeking stability, began to assess the room. *Robert Emmet's Speech from the Dock*, a stained coloured print, hung above the mantelpiece, the young rebel, his hair black and plastered like a Napoleonic *beau*, standing defiant and poignant before a hostile courtroom a century earlier.

The Canon followed her gaze and misquoted Emmet's famous epitaph, 'Until Ireland takes her place among the countries of the world. Ah, yes.'

The housekeeper came to the door and said, 'Well, Canon?' He nodded his purplish face, and continued, 'Then and not 'til then let my epitaph be written.' To Mr Kane he said, 'Did you close the school early, that fog? Will you drink a glass of sherry wine, any of you?'

Ellen sat there and rubbed her hands to warm them, looking politely from one man to the other, then looking ahead when they seemed to ignore her.

'Do you know that Canavan man at all, Mr Kane?' the Canon asked, with no sign of interest in an answer. 'Do you know what he's after doing? He's after burying another wife. And the Curate has bronchitis again; I had to say the two Masses yesterday again.'

In the next hour, the housekeeper, who murmured unceasingly to herself, laid cloth, cutlery and surprisingly elegant napery on the bare table at which they had been invited to sit; she set forth thin soup dregged with rice; mutton slices on which white grease had been allowed to form like wedges of slush; turnip and mashed potato; and the Canon drank at least six minuscule glasses of sherry, while Ellen, feeling a little dizzy, resisted after two. Twice she had to ask the housekeeper for cutlery; the men had started eating before Ellen received, first her soup spoon, then a fork.

In a while, she asked venturesomely, 'Has the Curate been seeing a doctor for his bronchitis?'

'Mr Kane, I suppose the car is going great?' said Canon Williams. He wiped his mouth on his sleeve, kept up a stream of comment, observation, enquiry, never once referring to Ellen or acknowledging her.

'I found grand wild thyme the other day,' he said, 'down the Fourpenny road. That Curate of mine hasn't a penny to his name, the collections aren't enough at all. Do you know mountains called the Paps of Anu, down in the west, they're named after some pagan woman.'

Mr Kane ate in silence, his back straight; his food had a tall distance to travel from plate to mouth: he administered every spoonful and forkful with poised carefulness.

'I had a letter from the Bishop,' said the Canon. 'The Confirmation is going to be a month earlier next year, at the end of April; the Bishop has to go to Rome.'

Mr Kane said, 'We had better start the paperwork, soon, so.'

The old russet dog snuffled occasionally in front of the heater. 'That Coughlan woman,' said the Canon. 'I declare to God she's after having another child.'

Ellen, during a silence, asked, 'Do you have a big orchard here, Canon?'

The Canon threw back his head and laughed. After a moment or two, opening yet another new subject, he said, 'That young McCarthy lad is coming on well, isn't he, Mr Kane? He'll be on the senior team in a few years.'

The housekeeper returned. Ellen whispered to her, 'Where is the necessary?'

The housekeeper, very much more loudly than Ellen had spoken, said, 'You'll have to use a chamber-pot upstairs.'

Ellen half-folded her napkin and, ignoring Canon

Williams's intense stare, left the table. The housekeeper showed her into a bare upstairs room where one shutter remained closed. In the gloom Ellen saw that at least eight chamber-pots stood around the floor, some of china, some the standard white enamel with blue rim. She had cause to wrinkle her nose.

The housekeeper said sourly, 'I'll empty it after you. That's what I do.'

She stood there. Ellen looked at her.

The housekeeper said, 'I'll wait outside the door.' She halted briefly, then spoke back into the room. 'There isn't any paper, so you'll have to go easy.'

A smile on her face, Ellen chose a pot with a bright bunch of flowers on its floor.

When Ellen returned, the Canon stopped mid-sentence and looked at her, following her with his eyes from the door to her chair. He said to Thomas Kane, 'Did you ever hear of a song called "Barbara Allen"? D'you know that song was composed near here, up in Ballintemple. This is the centenary of it, 'twas written a hundred years ago next month. A famine emigrant took it to America. 'Twas John Quirke told me that last week.'

Abruptly, after a last, smacking spoon of lukewarm semolina and milk, the Canon said, 'The bus will be soon,' and rising from the table, left the room.

Mr Kane held Ellen's coat towards her shoulders and arms, and she whispered, 'Isn't he going to interview . . . ?' His headshake prevented her speaking further.

At the gate, as they began to walk back up the hill to the village, she said, 'Was that an interview?' Mr Kane laughed and told her that it was as much an interview as she would ever get.

'What was that he was saying about a song?' Ellen asked.

Thomas Kane said, 'A complete invention. He makes things up to please himself. They sound nice to him.'

'The Robert Emmet. Shouldn't it be "the nations of the world"?'

'Of course it should, wasn't that the whole point, Ireland a "nation", it is already a "country"; that's Jeremiah for you, always gets the most important bit wrong.' Mr Kane shook his head regretfully.

Neither said another word, and, audible for a long way through the leafless trees, the dank *Princess* arrived.

As she climbed aboard, he said, 'Goodbye now, Miss Morris. Can you start next Monday, please? We're very shorthanded, as you can see. I'll fix up lodgings for you.' She looked at him and nodded.

'Thanks very much,' she said.

The conductor sloped down, edging with his hip between the empty seats.

'You have a ticket, Miss, haven't you, since this morning?' He punched it.

Ellen Morris looked back at the receding village and saw Mr Kane standing by the little gate of the drab school. She settled down, bulking the tails of her coat beneath her to comfort the wooden seat.

Opening her attaché case, she took out a notebook and fountain pen, and trying to wedge her writing elbow to her hip to prevent the bus shaking her hand, she began to write. 'Monday, 2nd February 1925. Deanstown. I could not see the place for fog.'

New mists for the coming night began to form in the fields behind the walls.

2

Her father said, 'They had a lot of trouble out around there, that place was very active y'know. The Irregulars were out in force there.'

Her mother said, 'How far away did you say the church was?'

'And that whole place out there,' said Bob. 'They all went against the Treaty, every single one of them.'

'Is the Curate young, even?' said her mother. 'Two old men, dth, imagine. A young priest is often better I always think.'

'I believe 'twas vicious out around there,' said Bob Morris. 'Vicious, by all accounts.'

In a week of buying and labelling, Ellen put together two suitcases, one large, one small, and a trunk. Her mother wondered about it all, and Ellen said, 'Mama, it is only thirty-six miles away. It isn't the far end of the world.'

On the Thursday evening, three days after her first visit to Deanstown, and three days before she was to take up residence out there, her father said to Ellen, 'Ellen girl, will you walk me down to Ginger Hill, I have to drop a letter into Tim Taylor's office?'

He paused from time to time to rest. 'This old damp. This time of the year.'

Bob always waited to speak until late in an opportunity. Climbing back up Ginger Hill, past the railings on Sarsfield Buildings, he said, 'I'm going to miss you, Ell.'

'Ach, Dada, it mightn't be such a gaudy place, but it isn't the North Pole I'm going to.'

'I was asking around about him,' said her father, 'your

26

Mr Kane. And the great thing about him, they say. D'you know that he quit the Troubles? He did indeed. Gave it up. Left it all. The great thing was. Mind you, he was a hard man, as hard as Collins himself, Kane was. But they say the great thing about him was. That not as much as a pellet did he fire once he quit the Troubles. At the Irregulars nor the Free Staters. Neither side, not a pellet. Not one.'

He lifted Ellen's hand, tucked it under his arm, and they returned to Brunswick Square.

The Canon, as School Manager, wrote to Ellen with her Letter of Appointment. It came enclosed in a note from Thomas Kane who arranged to meet her on the Sunday afternoon in Mooreville, not in Deanstown.

Bob Morris said, 'No, no, 'tis the least we might do and you going off like this,' as Ellen thanked him again for the car he had hired.

'Here, dab of Holy Water,' said May Morris, flicking her wetted fingers in the vague direction of her daughter's forehead, and both women's hands fluttered into the Sign of the Cross automatically.

'Now d'you know who's out there?' said the driver, who talked all the time. 'That Kane man, maybe you don't remember about him, he's the one did the big ambush at Tankardstown in 1919, d'you remember, a bunch of them, they took a man off the train and he heavily guarded? Oh, aye, he's the one, he's your man.' The driver wore a cap which he kept lifting and replacing on his bald spot. 'Aye, that's him. The train had a stop for only one minute. And yer man – he was on there as quick as wink, and a pair of guns on him. And came off it without a scratch. There was a Sergeant Enright killed in it, a distant cousin of my own sister's husband. Oh, aye.'

When Thomas Kane walked across the street to meet

27

Ellen, as arranged, under the Maid of Erin statue, the talkative driver fell quiet and touched his cap. While Ellen shook hands and opened the conversation, the driver hauled out the cases alone, and then, a silent transaction, the two men together stowed Ellen's trunk in Mr Kane's car.

She sat bolt upright in the front seat, up and down the hills on the narrow roads, in air brilliantly clear with frost. 'It seemed best,' he said, 'to meet you in here. So that you can get an idea of the general area.'

As they drove, he pointed out sights: significant trees, one struck by lightning; he skirted the triangular beginnings of the forest: 'It is claimed that owls nest in there. Although I have to say I haven't ever heard any'; he showed her a house in which a man hanged himself; he drew attention to the blueness of the mountains: 'They say it is a sign of rain when the mountains seem near.' The ivy gleamed on Deanstown Castle, a spreadeagled, ruined *château* on old southern terraced slopes far from the road, and he told Ellen she should 'make sure to see the place when the weather gets fine'. Whatever the crispness of the air, he did not himself wear gloves, and she looked at the backs of his hands on the steering wheel: each hand had a thickset blue vein meandering upwards to the middle knuckle.

'He's very precise,' she said to her closest friend the following week-end. 'You notice it about him every day. He's not like my father, Leah, he's not a man I imagine everybody likes. He has a sharp cut about him, do you know what I mean?'

Leah, the wife of Herbert Winer: Jeweller and Watchmaker, said aloud on that Sunday night, 'What time is it, Herbert? I suppose Ellen is installed in her lodgings by now.'

Leah drew a picture of a dress she thought of trying to make for herself; she copied a drawing from a Butterick's

28

pattern book. The caption beneath began, '*When fashion suddenly goes topsy-turvy, and ordains such things as waistlines and busts that have long been hidden*'. She wrote 'topsy-turvy' twice, and then beside it began to sketch a profile of her own bosom, looking in her bedroom mirror to do so. Sideways in the small cramped room, briefly dropping the wool wrapper from her shoulders to her waist, raising her arms above her head to improve the profile, shivering, her nipples cold and edgy in the air of the wintry room, Leah Winer dressed again, and called out to her husband in his home workroom down the passageway, 'D'you think she'll be all right out there, Herbert? A girl who was never away from home in her life?'

'Now that'll all help you to get your bearings,' said Thomas Kane. 'And here we are.'

He chugged into the yard of a good farm. 'We're about a mile from school. This woman is very clean.'

She appeared in the low doorway, shading her eyes against the descending winter sun.

'Hallo, Mrs Greege.'

'Hallo, Master. Is this her?'

Two awkward young men appeared behind their mother and came to the car to help with the suitcases and trunk. Mrs Greege surveyed the luggage as it passed by.

Ellen's room – not quite as large as the one in Brunswick Square, but what was? – roamed pleasantly beneath the roof, a long room, whose three windows, on account of the house's design, were at ankle level, and they looked out on the farmyard and the road gate. The room formed a square shape, with a little long neck right in the centre of one side; when writing home, she made a drawing of the room; 'it looks like an over-balanced, fat "T", a bit like a square tennis bat with a stubby handle,' she wrote. She loved the tobacco-brown rafters; the old chest on which she could stand a bowl of flowers; and above all

29

the writing-table and chair: 'I find the room has a serene atmosphere.'

Ellen sucked a tooth as she gazed at the huge old newspaper engraving celebrating *Lord Roberts at the Relief of Kandahar in 1880*: 'But I suppose I will have to put up with it,' she wrote. 'I have plenty of storage, anyway.'

Just inside the door at the foot of her little corridor, a splendid wide space opened where her trunk and cases would dwell unencroachingly.

Ellen stooped to a window, watched for a moment the last flicker of gold in the evening sky: it caught the green paint of Mr Kane's car as he nudged out of the yard and turned left down the narrow hill. She stood and began to unpack. One by one, she opened the drawers in the heavy tallboy: the top one, which was above her eye level, stuck.

'I see,' she murmured aloud, and reaching into her lemon-coloured washbag, took a piece of soap and rubbed it along each upper edge of the drawer until it opened and closed with a smooth action. As she knelt to lay cardigans and skirts on the floor of the big bottom drawer, she glanced through the window again and understood that the distant house she could see must be that of Mr Kane, because as she watched, he opened his gate, climbed back into his car and drove through, lost to sight behind some tall evergreens.

Downstairs at supper, the two sons sat shyly, and ate very carefully. Ellen rounded the corner of the wooden stairs into the kitchen: Mrs Greege made a comment upon the knitwork in Ellen's cardigan.

'Did you buy that? Really? In a shop? Do you knit at all yourself? There's a very good woman over in Camas, cable stitching and that.' Mrs Greege spoke quickly, yet the words filled her mouth in clods.

Ellen said, 'No, but I do needlework.'

=

Thomas Kane padlocked the wooden door of the lean-to garage he had built with his own hands when he bought his car the previous year. He raised his head to admire the evening star in the bright sky, and walked across the gravel to his front door.

'This is lovely,' said Ellen Morris, referring to the cold bacon. 'Now, what are your names?' she said to the two young men, neither of whom answered.

'That's Liam, my eldest, and that's Shamie,' represented their mother, 'and did you meet Lily when you came in? She's my sister's daughter; she came over here to keep me company when my husband died, she's from the next county.' The aproned girl at the end of the table smiled at the two youths, but did not look at Ellen.

Ellen asked the sons, 'Did you go to school to Deanstown?'

Liam blushed, as he always would whenever Ellen addressed him, and as would his brother, and stumbled, 'Oh, aye. To Master Kane.'

'Wasn't he the man that was hard on them too, the same Master Kane?' said Mrs Greege. 'Wasn't he though? He put the fear of God in them all. Did you know him before?'

Ellen answered that she had not, and Mrs Greege said, 'Well, I'm the one to be telling you all about him.' She added, 'I suppose you'll be doing your own washing?' and moved on into another topic.

Ellen Morris, tolerant towards the newness of her situation, bit her independent tongue recurrently throughout this first conversation. Crockery clinked with cutlery: wood on the fire spat. Lily at the end of the table choked on a crumb and coughed herself vigorously to tears, releasing the boys' grins. After supper, the boys lifted the table and set it back against the wall; Lily cleared the utensils into a white enamel basin with a blue rim and took the unsteady pile – 'Lazy man's load,' called Mrs Greege – into a rear scullery, from which then came the sounds of washing-up.

'No wife, yet, the Master,' said Mrs Greege, 'and he what? Forty, I suppose, forty-one?'

Chairs scraped across the floor to the fire; wordlessly, the younger brother, Shamie, created a place with cushions for Ellen on the settle. All present in the semi-circle looked into the little flames, and little was said. Ellen's tentative questions, regarding farming, or the sports played locally, or the priests, met with either embarrassed monosyllables from the brothers, or increasingly intrusive observations from their mother.

Finally, Mrs Greege asked, 'Does the Canon know you brought all that style with you to wear?'

Ellen frowned and said, 'Style?'

Mrs Greege said, 'He's against style, the Canon. I don't think the man was ever in a city in his life.'

Soon after this, Ellen said, 'I think I'll start to get ready for bed,' and stood.

'Good God Almighty, but you're the early bird entirely,' said Mrs Greege. 'At eight o'clock in the evening only?'

'I have all sorts of things to do,' said Ellen, climbing the stairs. 'Good-night to you all.' Murmurs answered.

In her room she took out paper and pen and began her letter.

c/o Mrs J. Greege,
Mantlehill,
Deanstown.
8th February 1925,
Sunday night.

Dear Dada, Mama and all,
    Well, here I am, hardly able to believe I am here. This is my address, and it is a farm, with hens in the yard and

the cowshed within earshot and nostril distance! I am
about a twenty-minute walk from the school, and I am
quite excited about it all! Mr Kane met me off the bus
with his car, 'the ninth car in the county' he informed me
(a Singer, Dada and Jim). They all seem nice out here,
very quiet, but I think some of them are going to be very
inquisitive. The country is lovely, big fields and a lot of
woods, and a wide, quiet river, and an old castle.

Ellen stopped, sat back and looked all around the room.
She reached for a corner of the quilt and inspected it,
front and back, stroking a piece of velvet she found among
the patchwork. Rising from her chair, she then inspected
the embroidery on the pillowcases and the edges of the
sheets, and the satin bindings on the heavy wool blankets.
She caught sight of her face in the mirror-stand on the
tallboy, and turned her hair a little in her hand. The oil-
lamp's glow embellished the brass minarets on the bed-
posts. Returning to her table, she took an envelope from
her leather writing-case and scribbled on it – 'Questions
to ask Mrs Greege: 1. Ironing? 2. A larger heater?' then
returned to her letter, and her little diagram of her room.

An hour later, she began to unpack the heavy trunk,
typically methodically – if much more slowly than she
might have done at home. Fumbling in the pocket of her
coat hanging on its hook behind the door, she found the
burgundy-coloured leather purse of her rosary beads and
knelt in prayer, her hands across her eyes, forehead
bowed; 'The Five Joyful Mysteries of the Rosary,' she
began, 'the First Mystery, The Annunciation.'

Fifteen minutes later, she concluded. 'Dearest Lord,
gaze down upon me, Thy servant, and teach me the
strength to change the things I can, the fortitude to accept
the things I cannot change, and the wisdom to discern the
difference.' Finalizing with the Sign of the Cross, she rose
stiffly and stretched. Partially undressing, shivering in the
cold, she washed sparingly in cold water from the tall

china ewer, put on a nightdress, drew her underwear out from underneath it, and climbed into the stiff bed.

Down the hill a mile away, Thomas Kane sat reading *The Idylls of the King* by the fire in his underfurnished and sere house.

'This is the only chair I could find in the county,' he told his sister some years earlier, 'that is tall enough to lean my head back against. Look?' He demonstrated. 'It comes right up. Whereas most of them only come up as far as under my shoulder-blades.'

Once, he rose, and poured the ageing tea into his mug from the pot sitting inside the fender. He looked at, but did not wipe clean, the ring of tea-stain the pot had made on the white fireplace tiles. When the clock on the mantelpiece reached exactly eight o'clock, he put the book down, rose and went to the table, where some papers lay near the lamp. Taking his speckled fountain pen from an inside pocket of his jacket, he unscrewed the cap and began to write in large, perfectly-spaced handwriting:

'Motion: That – if a National Teachers' Organization is to be formed, it should be for the entire country, and with a full-time Representative and Staff.' He underlined *the entire country*, and then wrote, '*ISSUES: 1. Pay and Conditions; 2. Accommodation including the Right to Buy (Residences); 3. Pensions. 4. Compassionate Bursaries.*'

In a writing-box on the table, two buttons from a military greatcoat jingled when he reached for a new sheet of paper. He wrote at a steady medium pace, as if he had long ago measured the use of his time and knew how to fill stretches of hours. Twice, he took from under the sloping lid of the mahogany writing-box a list of names, and ticked off one or two. After two hours, during which he rose once to fix the fire, he replaced the cap on his pen at exactly ten o'clock. He tidied everything away and turned the small key in the lock of the writing-box. Stretching his back and sighing through his nose, he rose and left the room, taking the lamp with him to the hallstand: to his annoyance, the wick's quick flare blackened the clear glass globe. From his front door, he walked the twenty yards to the green iron gate at the road, and checked its clasp firmly. He stepped back from the shade of the *macrocarpa* trees and looked at the sky. Weak light from the hallway fell on the gravel. In the summer, dogs barked at night, cows lowed, and bicycle tyres swished by as people cycled home from dances or public houses, sometimes talking quite loudly; last autumn nearby, a family of foxes some-times barked. In the winter and the early spring, however, not a sound was to be heard from inside the house, only the scratching of a pen on paper, or the startle of coals resettling themselves on the fire. In the silence, he listened for the noise of the weir four miles away. Back in the house, he took the clock from the kitchen shelf, wound it, checked the bolt on the back door, turned the thick key in the front door and climbed the stairs to bed, holding the lamp ahead of him carefully.

By the mirror, he took off his collar, wetted his finger on his tongue and rubbed at a small dark mark where the stud had pressed. Hauling off his shirt, he examined the cuffs, and then laid shirt and collar aside to wear in the morning. He wore only a long vest underneath, and having removed his black shoes and socks, climbed into bed and blew out the flame of the lamp.

As Miss Morris arrived next morning, Mr Kane met her at the school door and asked, 'How did you get on at Mrs Greege's?'

She replied with a smile, 'I think I'm going to be talking to myself a lot there.'

He nodded pleasantly, and took out his watch.

'Well. Half-past nine,' he said, as he did every morning. Thus, they began to work side by side five days a week in the small, insalubrious two-room school, with no other adults present, and most of every day a shared experience.

'Now – who gives out the plasticine?' Ellen asked, and all hands shot up.

'All right, all right. This is how we'll do it. This week the front two desks here, then next week the front two desks here. And then every week a different two desks. But. Before that. I want the names of every one of you. Who's first?'

They looked at each other and hunched their little shoulders. Nobody raised a hand. They giggled.

'Oh!' She swooped on them with a big mock of a smile. 'So you have no names?' They grinned wider.

'Oh, you're like sucky-calves, are you? They have no names either?' – which freed them to laugh openly.

'So,' she pressed on, 'I want to hear each of your names. Out loud. And I'm going to write each name on the board. And the names are going to stay on the board all this week. So you can look at yourselves. Like a mirror. I'll start with my name,' and she wrote 'Miss Morris' in firm letters in bright green chalk.

Their words tumbled out. Kitty. Joanie. Angela. Mattie. Mickey. Eddie. Mary. Paddy. Nellie. Dan. Mary. Jimmy. Gussie. Mary. Danny. Tim. Patie. Mary.

'The alphabet goes largely untroubled around here, I see,' she observed to Thomas later, as he looked at the board. 'Not to mention the Litany of the Saints.'

When she came to the small fair-haired boy, he of the great reticence during her first visit last week, again he said nothing. Two children in front turned and giggled, and she rebuked them with her first curtness. She walked across to the head of the row in which the boy sat – dressed exactly as he had been a week earlier – and said, 'I don't know your name at all, so how can we talk to each other?' He put his head down on his arms.

'All right,' mollified Ellen. 'All right.'

To the boy sitting beside him she said, 'Now what is his name, because I am certainly not going to leave him off the board?'

A number of voices answered, 'Timmy Quinn, Ma'am,' and another piped from somewhere, 'Ma'am, he don't talk at all.'

In the same green chalk and in equally large letters Ellen wrote 'Timmy' on the blackboard. All the names completed, she then occupied the rest of the morning having them make small baskets from plasticine, and adding to their vocabulary the words 'fruit', and 'wicker', and 'weaving'.

Shortly after their break began it rained, and all rushed back in. They sat in throughout lunchtime, and Thomas Kane murmuringly guided Ellen around the school cupboards: the ink supply, in large black carboy bottles; the pencils, bought by the gross every August; the Progress Record. He instructed her in the school's meagre architecture. A waist-high wooden partition, surmounted with bright glass panes to the ceiling, separated their classrooms. The polished wood, a glossy light-brown oak, had married beneath itself, or else represented some kind of official apology, compensation for the general shabbiness of the building. In a corner of the partition, on the Senior classroom side, a knot-hole had dropped open in the wood many years ago; the children and the teachers traditionally used it as a mailbox, or last resting-place, for broken pens. 'The nib graveyard,' he now remarked to Ellen – and made her smile by wondering whether the cache accumulating daily on the floor within the partition would prove of great eventual interest to archaeologists.

When classes resumed, she had all her charges walk slowly around the boundaries of the room, hands behind their backs, saying 'One and One are Two. One and Two are Three. One and Three are Four', until they reached

Twenty; then she marched them all back again in the opposite direction and took them to Forty. As they scrambled to get back in their desks, the little silent boy stood beside the board, and looking askance up to Ellen, drew a finger under his own name.

A moment or two after that, she started at a 'whh-ikk' sound from the outer room. As she looked through the glass of the partition, Thomas Kane, wielding a long-ish ash stick, gave a lanky boy four hard strokes across his palms outstretched. Each time the boy stuck his hand impersonally out from his body, the teacher steadied the uncouth young hand, lined it up for aim, and whipped the stick down: the arm bounced with the force. The boy stepped back to his desk, hands squeezed tight in his armpits, avoiding the eyes of his classmates, and Thomas Kane mundanely returned the stick to the grooved slot that ran beneath the blackboard and was designed to hold sticks of chalk. Ellen turned back to her task: for a moment she lost her place in the counting game.

Ellen's classes finished at half-past two and in the abandoned echoing classroom she began to rearrange the little drawings of farmyard animals, the large old paintings of flowers, and to make notes of what needed renewing. The Senior room evacuated at three o'clock, two senior boys and two senior girls remaining behind on a weekly rota to sweep the wooden floors. The Roll Book finalized, her basket rearranged for the walk home, the fires made safe – it all would take until twenty-five- or half-past three each day.

With the rain clearing, and the sky now a blue miracle, that Monday, her first day, brought again one of February's glorious, sunny promises of spring. Thomas Kane closed the cupboards, turned the key in his desk, checked the window latches, replaced the fireguard, then reached for his coat.

'I have to make a list,' she said, checking her sleeve for her handkerchief, and taking her gloves from her basket, 'there's an awful lot to be done.'

'Gorgeous sunshine.' He drew the wicket gate behind them. 'I'll walk on a bit the road with you.'

As they turned to cross the green towards the pump, curtains in two cottages flickered in little tics.

'That must be her,' the hidden voices of the village houses told each other. 'Look,' they called to those by the fireside, 'there's the Master and the new Mistress.' The village's eyes saw a pair of formal walkers: Thomas Kane and this very small woman with the new Red-Riding-Hood basket over her arm, and her gloves and her hat.

'Ha, boys-oh-dear, well, well?' said Mr Hand to nobody in particular in the kitchen of his pub. His wife said that night, 'D'you know what it is? She looks like a Protestant. A'course, she's a townie, isn't she?'

On the left ran the limestone wall of the Castle demesne, a circuit of three miles in all.

'Look at that?' Thomas Kane indicated the letter-box, now painted green since the Treaty, set in the wall outside Hand's public house.

'Do you know what they say? They say that was installed by Anthony Trollope himself. He worked for the Post Office all around here.'

Beyond the wall, wide fields stretched, tufted in the sporadic growths of winter.

'Even this time of the year,' said Mr Kane, 'the fields never lose their colour, the green is nearly blue, like they say about Kentucky.'

The mountains were pocked with little snows. On the right, they passed one last village house, painted ochre, and with leaded dormer windows; when their gardens flowered, he said, 'the cleanest of these houses could be on the lid of a chocolate box. They built the village like a toy, or an ornament – to make the estate look good. The Prince of Wales rode through here, did you know that? Everyone came out and lined the road and shouted their wishes to him that he get a good wife in Ireland, and he's supposed to have said to Dublin Castle later: "Rather a long way from getting shot by the Irish, don't you think?" That's what he's supposed to have said.'

He slowed his pace down to allow for Ellen's shorter steps; he then contrived to walk a foot behind her, looked at her face to view her in his surroundings. They walked past the Teacher's Residence, which he indicated.

Ellen said, 'Yes, I noticed it this morning. I can see it from my window. It looks quite new.'

'It is. The old one was burnt down.'

'Oh?' she said. Had he known her better, he would have recognized her inflection as a request for amplification.

A glossy crow flew off a wall; a flight of rooks swept out across the sky.

'Do you like the countryside?' he asked her. 'Do you know land at all, or fields. Hedges, and the like?'

She replied that she knew rural life mostly from books: when they went on holidays it was always to the sea, but that this place was lovely, really lovely. Without any context he said, 'It gets a lot of flies sometimes here in the summer. There are forty million species of fly in the world.'

'Well, so,' he said, his last remark as he turned from Mrs Greege's gate, and, with a serious nod, walked his fixed measured pace back down the road to his own house, remaining within sight. She glanced after him, and then, preparing her demeanour for Mrs Greege, went indoors.

'I am, thank you, yes, settling in fine. Yes, he seems very nice, a very nice man, and a good teacher, yes, very good.' Ellen answered the questions on the move, climbing the stairs.

Her skin glowed in the dimness of her room: too early to light a lamp. Since her first teaching job, a few streets away from Brunswick Square, she habitually changed after school; now she put on a white wool blouse, a heavy woollen red jumper which always went well with the dense blackness of her hair, a heavy tweed skirt and thick stockings: the larger oil heater she requested had not yet arrived, although she noticed that she had acquired a hot-water bottle. She sat on the bed to rest.

The room fell silent inexorably. She stared through the window to the quiet farmyard below. In a while, she looked around the room, seeking work, but she had now unpacked everything, had even rearranged her writing-case and her sewing threads. She sighed.

'Miss,' said Mrs Greege at supper two hours later, 'if you lock your door while you're out, Lily can't clean your room.'

'Yes, I suppose so.'

Thomas Kane sat at his kitchen table. A red-faced man seated opposite him had brought with him a form for the Master to fill in, declaring an interest by kinship in a Will advertised in the papers last week.

'He was the wife's cousin, first cousin, Master, their fathers were brothers. The wife could tell you herself. That man's father married secondly, and this man who died went to Delaware when he was a young fellow, and he made money out of making iron.'

The Master wrote carefully on the solicitor's form, 'Mrs John Guiney, of Cappadun, Deanstown: first cousin on Paternal side.'

He said to Mr John Guiney, 'Has your wife any proof of the family connection?' and Mr John Guiney brought from his pocket a very old and large envelope.

'She had letters from him, Sir, and a photograph and two Christmas cards.'

The Master said, 'Oh, that's excellent, John, excellent.'

John Guiney left, and Thomas Kane boiled two eggs and made tea and cut three slices of bread, heaping butter on them.

By the end of the week, Ellen had reorganized many of the boxes of chalks, counters and reading primers in the Junior room. She opened a 'Food Notebook'.

'Will they mind,' she wondered, 'if I ask them what they eat?'

He sawed at his chin with his fingertips. 'It might be a bit . . .'

'Suppose I make it a game?' she asked. 'Suppose I say we will do it so that we get to know all the kinds of food in the world? I have pictures of Africa somewhere.'

On each of the first four afternoons he walked with her to Mrs Greege's. On the fifth, the Friday, she caught the bus at a quarter past three from outside the school, her smaller suitcase in her hand.

'They'll think you're gone for good,' he smiled, and furtively indicated the village windows, 'when they see the suitcase,' and indeed the bus conductor asked the predictable question.

'No. Only for the week-end,' she smiled back.

'I'd say all the same 'tis a bit lonesome out around here for a city girl like yourself?'

'Everybody's very nice,' she riposted.

At half-past six, she walked from the corner by the railway station, down the sloped pavement past the railings of the park in Brunswick Square: shopkeepers in the by-streets had begun to plank up their shutters for the night. Sailors came to this park sometimes and smoked pipes, talking loudly in foreign languages. Many of the railings, particularly around the bandstand, had been manufactured, everyone said, from the cannon captured at Waterloo. The oaks on the western side were planted by a gentleman in honour of each of his early *amours*; later, the sole elm tree for his wife. Children tried in vain to measure with string the annual subsidence of 'the Sinking Church' at the lower end.

'Who's that, it can't be Ellen?' Her father slanted the newspaper outward. 'And how are you, girl?' standing over her in big affection. 'They're all out. Your mother is gone over to the Jesuits to say a prayer. Rina is down at Maud Joyce's house, and Jim is out, maybe with Mary Rose.' One of his large eyebrows rose to conspire with Ellen's amused nod. 'We got your grand long letter.'

Ellen colonized the hall table, chair and floor with gloves, hat, bag, suitcase, notebook, umbrella.

No matter what the time of day, Bob Morris always wore a suit and a stiff collar and a tie. His wife said he would have 'to undergo a surgical operation to remove them'.

'Your mother should be soon.'

He waited on her, as he had done since her birth. They sat at the kitchen table. A step fell in the hall.

'What's this? What's this?'

Coming through the door with some arms-raised business towards a hatpin, May Morris kissed Ellen who murmured 'hallo'.

May laid her hat on the kitchen's side-table.

'Have you no food in front of you? Bob, did you ask the girl has she a mouth on her, and she travelling?

'I'm just after talking to Father Watson,' her mother said, heading for the meatsafe. 'He was asking will you call and see him?'

Ellen said she would, but she wanted 'a quiet time', that settling in at Deanstown had been 'very tiring'. She stood and fetched a towel from the hot cupboard in the scullery.

Her father followed her to the hallway and whispered to her, 'D'you know what? You're getting to be a real handsome woman, a – a – smasher. That's it. A smasher.' She grinned at him over the baluster, hand on the rail, as she ran upstairs.

May called up the stairwell, 'If you're going out, 'tis going to rain. I'll have your tea here in a minute.'

Opening a door at the top of the stairs, Ellen, with the pleasure of renewed acquaintance, ran her hand along the side of the bath.

'Now, tell us all your news,' said Bob, elbows leaning in eagerness on the table.

'Bob, you're unseemly, wasn't her long letter enough for you?' said May. 'Did you find out about Masses?'

'Not every morning, except in Lent,' replied Ellen.

'What's the lodgings like?'

'Oh, Dada!' Ellen laughed. 'If you met Mrs Greege! She's like a bony wasp, she creeps around and stings.'

'Who is she herself?' asked May. 'Who are her people?'

'Farmers, there's pucks of money there, I mean all her clothes are good, and she keeps a very clean house, but she's always criticizing me.'

Ellen did an imitation of Mrs Greege's accent.

'Huh, Miss, where'd you get that shtyle from, you're like a doll that walks and talks and shtands, aren't you, huh?' – and they all laughed.

'She has her hair tied around her head as if it was a wreath stuck on, but I saw it one night when she was getting ready for bed and it was down to her waist and black and grey. She's the boniest woman I ever saw; she makes Mrs Halpin look fat.'

'Imagine!' said May. 'Mrs Halpin look fat.'

'And him?' asked Bob. 'The Kane man, what's he like? I was asking about him the other day; d'you know that Newman man from Newcastle West, he knew him slightly in the old days, don't you know? And he said, I'll tell you what he said, he said, "Thomas Kane is his own man to the power of three, Bob." That's what he said.'

'He's that all right,' replied Ellen, 'and – I don't know. He's – he's what I'd call "formal". They're all afraid of him.'

'But you're not?' asked Bob.

'Pwit,' said Ellen, 'no fear.'

'D'you know the story about him, do you?' asked Bob. 'He was Collins's man out there, he was the driving force, they said, and then, all of a sudden, he upped and left. Oh, in 1920, or so, as early as that. But I mean, he was the genuine job, so he was, there was a reward out on him, d'you know?'

They talked until half-past ten.

'Are you getting Mass in the morning?' asked May. 'Father Watson is saying a half-past ten, because he's going away tomorrow night so he won't be saying a Sunday Mass.'

'Oh, that's a good idea, are you going, Dada?'

'No, I'll be sane and wait for Sunday like the rest of the country,' said Bob, and Ellen punched his arm with her fist.

Thomas Kane spent Saturday cleaning his house from top to toe; he even cleaned the windows, and washed old dishes. A parcel containing two books arrived in the post from the mail-order booksellers in London. Slowly he opened the knots, rolled the string into a tiny hank secured in the middle by a bow-knot, and then placed it in a corner of the kitchen table drawer. Turning the parcel from side to side, he eased off the brown paper, and folded it into a neat rectangle which he placed on top of the glass-fronted bookcase in the corner of the kitchen. He clicked his tongue on his teeth as he saw in the bookcase, and took down, a book whose coloured jacket had been torn on the spine: two young men smiled at each other in a sylvan setting: *Under the Greenwood Tree*. Thomas tore a scrap of paper from an envelope in his pocket, wrote on it, 'Get some stamp paper and fix this,' and slipped the note inside the frontispiece of the novel.

He returned to the parcel on the table, still wrapped in heavy tissue paper from which he finally undressed the new books: *Moths of the World, A New and Important Compilation*. Taking it into the bay window, he made it fall open at 'L'. 'The Luna Moth (*luna*: the moon) is pale green in colour. *Actias luna*; it is predominantly found in North America where it has the reputation of great beauty. Very soon after the females emerge from their cocoons they begin to emit a radiant which attracts mates from up to four miles away.'

Thomas turned the book over and over in his hand and opened several other pages, still standing at the window. Then he returned to the table and exchanged it for the other book: *In Brightest Africa* by Carl Akeley. At random he read, 'The phenomenon of elephants helping each other when wounded is not general by any means. Only a few days after shooting the big bull, I had an instance of elephants abandoning one of their number that was wounded and not very badly wounded either. I had gone into the forest again, and had come upon another bunch in very thick country. I could only get little glimpses of a patch of hide or ivory once in a while.'

Beside the armchair in the bay window sat a small item of furniture, about two feet high, funnelling gradually outward from bottom to top, and covered in turquoise, yellow-flowered fabric, a gift from his aunt. She regularly obtained butter-boxes from her local creamery and covered them with furnishing materials – but she lined the inside in white cloth too thin to conceal the original black stencil: '56 lbs (Avoirdupois)' of the waxy yellow, soft, strong butter from the creamery. On the padded lid Thomas now set down his two new books, within hand's reach of his armchair.

John Watson, S. J., came swishing up the side aisle in his black soutane. One or two people still knelt in prayer: the sacristan, everybody said he had gone bald too young, doused the tall candles with his hooded stick. John Watson took Ellen's hands in his and whispered, 'Your mother said to expect you.'

'Do you know what?' Ellen once said to her father. 'He's the only man small enough for me to look in the eye,' and they laughed, but not unkindly.

In the porch, the noise of the outdoors allowed them to raise their voices a little.

'Oh, Father John, I have so much to tell you.'

He beamed. 'When I saw you at the Communion rails, I thought, dear Ellen, what a shame I have to go to Cork tonight, otherwise we could have had one of our walks tomorrow.'

'One walk wouldn't be enough, Father John. All I have to tell you.'

'Are you liking it out there? Is it exciting? You're not going to be buried out there are you, Ellen?'

'Oh, Father, there is so much to do. With those children.'

'I'll be listening out to hear will your accent change?'

Ellen laughed in a whisper. 'It will do no such thing!'

'Oh, I don't know, do I detect a slight broadening of the vowel sounds, do I?'

'Mind you, Father John, I have this landlady, Mrs Greege, and if you heard her? She might infect me all right. Especially as the place is so quiet out there.'

'Oh, but you'll be able to keep up with your reading?' They moved into the yard and raised their voices further, to normal. 'I thought of you the other day, and that grand essay you wrote, I was teaching Wordsworth. "I travelled among unknown men" . . .'

Ellen interrupted him and quoted, '"In lands beyond the sea" – ' She laughed again. 'Father John, go away out of that, I'm only thirty-six miles away.'

'I thought that'd rise you. So now, you see, I told you. Janesborough is the hub of the globe after all!'

They laughed.

'Come in for a quick cup of tea,' he said. 'I suppose you'll be going round to Mrs Winer, will you, I met her the other day, we said hallo.'

'Tell me, Father John,' asked Ellen as they walked round the high brick building. 'Have you by any chance a copy of that other essay you asked me to write, d'you remember in the holidays years and years ago?'

'"The City of Janesborough"? I have indeed, do you want it?'

'I want to read it to the children. Because I wasn't much older than them at the time.'

'Oh, yes, oh, yes, I can see that,' he said. 'Now.' They sat down. 'Let me have a look at you.'

In the austere drawing-room, under the dark oil painting of Saint Ignatius Loyola, he spilled tea again on his chin, and apologized. 'I'm getting old, my hands have the shakes.' They laughed. 'Do you know, Ellen, I'm eighteen years a priest next week?'

'Hah!' she teased. 'I can guess your age now!' She mock-counted on her fingers. 'You don't look a day over a hundred to me,' she grinned.

'Close,' he said, 'close.'

'I'll tell you one thing, though, Father John, if ever I'm to be holy, I'll be holy out there; I think I'm saying two rosaries a night there, there isn't anything else to do. Although they only have Mass on Sundays.'

He left the room to fetch the essay for her, and returned reading it aloud.

'Here it is. "The City of Janesborough, where I was born and where I live with my parents and my brother and sister, has a population of forty thousand people. Most of its trade comes from the fact that it has a wide river port, and boats sail up and down. They come from Amsterdam and Genoa and Bordeaux and they carry jute and flour and wine. My father is a printer. He prints boxes and calendars and notices and advertisements." Now, wasn't that very good for, what age were you, eleven?'

'Stoppit, you'll make me blush, Father! Oh, and I have worked out your age.'

'You haven't.'

'Yes, I have. Eighteen years a priest, you said, and fourteen years before that in the seminary, from the age of what, eighteen?'

'Smarty!'

John Watson laid the school jotter on the table between them and, switching to seriousness, said, 'I hope we're not going to lose you to them out there, Ellen, are we? I hope some strong countryman . . .' He leaned back, as a painter does to get a perspective on his canvas. 'Oh, now! Are you blushing, what?'

When Ellen left the Jesuit residence, Father John Watson climbed two flights of stairs to his room. For several minutes he stood at the window watching her walk the length of long Catherine Street; he stroked his face, drawing both hands from under his blond sideburns down to the point of his chin, where his fingers met each time in a brief praying tent before resuming their stroking. Turning away, he sat on his bed, took off his shoes and began to polish them.

Along with the parcelled books, the postman, always late on Saturday morning, brought Thomas Kane another of the letters he had been receiving for over two years. He opened it with a 'Dth' of mild annoyance. He had kept them all, when other recipients might have destroyed such correspondence.

'Never forget. I liked you the minute I saw you, and I will always feel like this. Signed. A Secret Admirer.'

He swept the backs of his fingernails in a tapping motion across the notepaper.

'I know who you are, Missy,' he said aloud, and half-grinned.

The writer, a handsome, often distressed woman, never dated her letters and often carried them around, sealed, in her handbag for days, even weeks.

Thomas Kane spoke to the letter in his hand; 'I danced with you a few years ago, so I did, Missy.'

Leah's bangles jangled against the table.

'Is that fresh air I see on your cheeks?' she asked. 'Come in, come in. Your letter, all that news. Let me look at you.'

Ellen sat on the little window seat, completely relaxed, content to let Leah's warm breezes blow.

'How do you like my blouse? I copied the embroidery. From my sister. Oh. But what can be done. She owns the blouse I copied from. But will she lend it to me? No. No, no, no. I have to go there, and sit there. I saw your mother, did she tell you?'

Leah put the teapot on the table and made a sucking-inwards noise, a reverse whistle, as the over-hot handle caught her hand.

These women made friends fifteen years earlier, and would remain steadfast until death. Ellen had called at the Winer house when, aged ten, she was collecting for the Cathedral Building Fund, and Leah, a young wife of twenty, curly-bobbed and lively, laughed at the bright girl and said, 'Didn't anybody tell you that you shouldn't collect from us? But come in anyway.'

With a sweet home-made drink she told the fascinated child about Judaism, and then on the way out gave her a shilling for the collection. When Ellen tried to protest, Leah said, 'It all goes to God, doesn't it? You see to that, you see to it that God gets it, that the priest doesn't put it on an old racehorse.' Her laughter, and her colours, and her curls, stayed in the little girl's ears and eyes, and one day the following week, as if in secret and a little timidly, Ellen called again.

Ellen's mother disliked Leah intensely, 'for reasons'.

'I know your reasons, Mama,' said Ellen. 'Your reasons are the same as everyone else's. This city hates the Jews.'

Ellen's father liked Leah, and said so in glances.

'Leah,' Ellen said once. 'You have what I call "a bonanza personality".'

'Bonanza. Bonanza!' Leah sang the words.

'The Jews always look after their own,' sniffed May.

'Sure why shouldn't they?' asked Bob. 'That's fair enough.'

Herbert Winer, as withdrawn as Leah was vivacious, also came of a Russian pogrom family, and now made a living as a jeweller, with a speciality in engraving silver pocketwatch-cases.

Ellen often said to Leah, 'Whatever Herbert says, he makes it tell. I always remember the things Herbert says.'

Herbert had given Ellen one or two of her favourite watchwords, such as, 'Always wait until a man has stopped smiling before you do business with him.' And – 'Never live in a house from which you cannot see the weather changing.' 'I love his advice, Leah,' Ellen said.

He had many more: he imparted them as sparingly and thoughtfully as a chess-player's moves, in his thin, very slightly accented voice. 'What is bad is not people being bad. It is people being bad and pretending to be good.'

'Where do you get these sayings from, Herbert?' Leah would ask again, and then, turning to Ellen, answer her own question. 'He is his grandfather, they say, his very grandfather, down to the laces of his shoes.'

In private, Herbert found the anti-Semitism of the city unendurable.

'If they came and spat, I could understand,' he whispered to Leah, his voice sad on the pillow. Unlike her neighbours, who received deliveries, Leah always had to go out to shop.

'I don't mind, I like the walk, I meet people,' she protested. Yet she received cheerful shouts from breadmen, milkmen, the lot: 'Ah, how'ya, Mrs Winer, how's the children?'

'Explain to me,' said Herbert, 'if they are so friendly, why are we the only ones they won't deliver to? If only they remained silent,' said Herbert. 'It would be honest.'

The doctors alone did not treat them with that cutting edge of slight difference.

'You know why that is, don't you?' murmured Herbert. 'Look at what the Jews started in this country by way of maternity medicine?'

'So?' Leah settled now with the teacups. 'What. Is. He. Like?'

'Who?' asked Ellen.

'Ah!' Leah burst out. 'Who? This man, this what is his name?'

'His name, I told you, in my letter –' Ellen wore her patient teaching tone '– is Thomas Kane, Leah, and he is very. Very.'

'Very what?' asked Leah.

'Well – very. Very strong. In himself, I mean.'

'Is he now?' sipped Leah.

Thomas would grin to Leah months later, shortly before all their frightful days set in, that Ellen gave the impression of not observing him much on that first afternoon drive.

52

'No,' Ellen would butt in, 'I wanted to see the town, and all the places on the way out to the village. And you can't say I didn't notice anything, what about that lovely, fine-wool plaid rug you gave me for my knees? Herbert, he even has a spare pair of gloves for passengers.'

'It's beautiful countryside out around there, Leah,' she said.

'Oh, is it now?' mocked Leah, 'beautiful countryside, indeed, well, I didn't ask you about the beautiful country-side, I can see beautiful countryside anywhere, Miss Ellen Morris,' and she arched her eyebrows.

'All right,' Ellen caved in. 'I'll tell you four things about him.' She splayed her fingers. 'One, he doesn't look his age at all, more like a man in his early thirties.'

Secondly, she said, he has a voice and accent the likes of which she had 'never before heard. Kind of soft and hard and deep. And quite countrified, but he makes you listen to him. Thirdly, he is in a way quite frightening. He has, what is it? I don't know. He often seems so cross, nearly angry, impatient, and at the same time, he's slow and actually patient.'

And fourthly, Ellen warmed to her subject, 'How did such a man come to be in such a small country place? Leah, I'm not joking you, he was dressed like a tailor's dummy, like he came out of a bandbox. He had a blue striped shirt. And a lovely grey overcoat, grand.'

Ellen concluded, 'And another thing. He seems like he doesn't talk much, Leah, but he's talking all the time. But not inquisitive. He didn't even ask me as much as one question. Stop looking at me like that, Leah.' Ellen swiped a glove at her friend.

Coming back across Brunswick Square from half-past nine Mass next morning, Bob said, 'The thing is, Ellie, the thing to remember is – the thing people say about him is, he never fired a shot in the Civil War, that's the thing.'

'Dada. Stoppit. The man is my Principal, not anything else. And stop saying things out of the blue.'

'You're just like your mother. Ooh, well,' breathed her father. 'What age is he?'

'I don't know, now I'll get cross with you. Mrs Greege says forty or so.'

Bob rested on the doorstep.

At breakfast Ellen said, 'The night is very quiet out there. He –' she called Thomas 'he' in all reports to her family that first week-end – 'he says that in the hills above Deanstown there are people who only come out once a month, to shop down in Mooreville, and they never travel farther.'

'What do they do for a doctor?' asked May in wonder.

'Only if they're dying, I suppose.'

Her father said, 'Don't be too surprised if the people are suspicious. Strangers, you know. They mightn't warm to you straight off.'

'Dada, sure I won't be threatening them?'

He said, 'Ah, no, Ellie, but you have to think what they've been through, five years of gunfire, and then the whole Anti-Treaty business?' He pursed his lips and blew his breath out, a wry, summarizing noise. 'Sure, look. Brother killed brother. There was father against son. That's only two years ago.' He nudged the cat out of his way with his stick.

'Isn't it funny now that a man his age . . .' Bob did not finish the sentence, a habit that infuriated his family, and he moved on to another musing. 'I'd love to know some time why he gave up Collins and all that . . .'

'Dada!' said Ellen crossly. 'Stop grunting to yourself. And for once in your life, stop repeating yourself.'

3

In the beginning, they stood off from her. 'Sleek,' they said; and the clothes: 'all that style. Dth, dth. And poor people going hungry.'

Other things, too: 'the walk of her'; Mrs Leamy said to Mrs Hanafin, 'Isn't she very sure of herself altogether?'

They said, 'Them city ones.'

After some weeks, one ameliorating observation passed around: 'At the same time, she was very devout at Mass, did you notice that?'

Naturally, Ellen never guessed what they said: had she known she would have relished the content, if not the tone; to her Training College classmates she had insisted, 'Why shouldn't we have minds of our own?' To John Watson she had said, 'Oh, Father, I'm perfectly aware that I confuse the nuns, perfectly aware of it. If I was only independent by itself, they'd understand me, but the fact that I . . . that I –'

He interrupted to say it for her: 'That you are obviously devout? Yes, Ellen, it confuses them, what a revolutionary you are!' and they laughed.

The village roughed her up a little. On a morning when Thomas Kane had gone to a Diocesan Teachers' meeting, Mrs Leamy called to the school and rapped hard on the window.

Barging through Ellen's pleasant enquiry, 'And who are you now?' Mrs Leamy said, 'Joanie, my Joanie, Joanie Leamy, doesn't want to sit beside Danny Heaphy.'

Ellen said tartly, 'If you're so concerned about the way Joanie spends her days, why don't you wash her a bit more thoroughly in the mornings?' – not a retort Mrs Leamy could easily report to a neighbour.

Mrs Hand, from the public house, called to complain that the children were learning too many prayers.

Of her, Ellen enquired with some aggression, 'Who is responsible for the welts on the back of your child's legs? Because whoever it is should be reported.'

The children in her classroom raised no such boundaries. By the middle of Ellen's second week, their traditional morning reluctance had disappeared and they set off for school cheerful, returning in a mood of happy ease. To her Principal, Thomas Kane, Ellen said, 'Is it all right if I make some adjustments in the classes? Some of those children are not the same age as their class and they should be.'

And soon, while still keeping their distance, the parents began to speculate on the effect 'the New One' would have upon their aloof Thomas Kane. Late February sun warmed the village, bringing lemon light to the skeletal beeches.

The *Distinguished Monologuist*, Mr Val Vousden, sat in a room of Mrs Heffernan's, the house in which he was lodging overnight, and began writing down the words of a new recitation. He said aloud rhymingly, 'My many days,' and then, 'my worn-out gaze.' Licking his pencil, thereby leaving a thick dart of its blue lead on the front furrow of his tongue, he began to write on the rough thin paper of a school jotter, 'My son has brought me over to end my many days.' He sat back and said slightly aloud, 'Dah-da-da-Dah. Dah-da-da-Dah. Dah-da- my worn-out gaze.' Mr Val Vousden stood up, went to the door of his room and opened it, and putting his head into the next room, a kitchen, asked was there any way at all the woman of the house could dry a pair of socks for him for the morning?

56

'D'you remember that big puddle I walked into, Mrs Heffernan?'

'Of course I'll dry them, Mr Vousden. Give them out here to me.'

'O, thanks very much, Mrs Heffernan.' Val held the socks out, lanky arm like a pallid semaphore, towards Mrs Heffernan's comfortable apron.

No man can go on onstage with a cold like this, Val Vousden whispered to his mirror, and sniffed and wiped his nose on a corner of the sheet. He moved to the door again and called, 'Mrs Heffernan, would you by any chance have another blanket?'

Back came the promise that she would bring it to the room in a minute, and he climbed into bed to anticipate her care.

Mrs Heffernan, when he first knocked on her door, did not fully disguise the thrill of meeting him, and with relish advised him not to venture out until he was better. Nonetheless, he began to place her in a considerable dilemma. His shirts proved no problem, she knew she was a good washer and a great ironer, and not just in her own estimation; and a little drop of paraffin would take the heaviest stains out of his swallowtail coat – but should she iron them narrow trousers? He said they had no crease in them, they weren't meant to have, but, in the name of God, who ever he   of trousers without a crease? Her Billy wouldn't go to Mass on a Sunday, God be good to his soul, without a crease in his trousers.

Within a quarter of an hour of his arrival, she had him comprehensively under her care. Now she brought the blanket, and then another, and tucked them in heavily from halfway down – nothing too encroaching – to the foot of the bed, where she heaved the mattress and folded them underneath.

'They're good Foxford blankets, the nuns make them up in Foxford.'

'You can't beat beef tea, Mrs Heffernan,' said Val Vousden from his bed, strewn papers around him, looking over his spectacles at her.

'I s'pose you're only passing through? Imagine anyone lining the pockets of a pair of britches with purple?' Mrs Heffernan held up the trousers and said, 'Isn't that very grand?'

'Well, the truth is, I'm here on a bit of, well, research I call it, Ma'am.'

'And if you don't want a crease in them, Mr Vousden, well, well? D'you go to Mass yourself, Mr Vousden, Vousden is an unusual name?'

'I have God in my imagination, Mrs Heffernan.'

'D'you know what, Mr Vousden, I never dream of God at all, I'd think it wrong of me.'

Val Vousden said, 'Did you ever hear, Mrs, of a famous brass band called *The Deanstown Brass and Reed Band*?'

'Ah, I did indeed, Sir. My father walked behind it. I'll tell you now,' she said, and was glad to rest on a chair for a moment, a good woman at sensing a conversation approaching. 'The man who knows about the Deanstown Band, now, is a schoolmaster out there. You'll know the name the minute I tell you.'

When Ellen stepped through the puddles to school on Monday morning, some agitation seemed to be taking place just inside the circle of the schoolyard wall. Thomas Kane, still wearing his coat which he never removed until both fires had begun to blaze truly, stood at the door, his hands raised in front of his chest, in a gesture of warding off, or pacifying, or dismissing – or, it turned out, all three. A girl of about twelve leaned back against the school wall, clean and neat, but confused: a woman in a hat implored.

'No, I can't, Mrs. I have a day's school to teach. Look. There are some children here already.' He began to step back into the porch.

Ellen, steering herself to the door, gave a glance of enquiry, and the woman turned to her.

'Will you ask him, Ma'am? You're the new Mistress, aren't you? He'll do it maybe if you ask him.'

Master Kane clapped his hands twice, and the crack resounded fiercely enough to make Ellen jump.

'Miss Morris.' He looked straight ahead and spoke sharply, 'improving' his accent. 'I would go straight into school if I were you.' Thomas moved aside to let Ellen pass.

'Ma'am. Ma'am.' The woman put out a hand that pawed the air, like an infirm dog. 'You ask him, Ma'am.'

Ellen stood, looking keenly at the young girl, who wore a fair-isle jumper and green skirt under her best coat. She addressed the woman.

'Ask what?'

The woman pressed forward as if to reach the Master physically. He stood there, rigid and unpleased, frozen into grey steel. Even Ellen recoiled; then she stepped out into the morning again, and interposed between Thomas Kane and the strange woman. In a voice of quick decision, she flattened the air with her hand: 'I don't know what this is about, but whatever it is, it seems to be too important to talk about in a hurry. Why don't you come back after school today when the Master has more time?'

Again she looked enquiringly at him; he raised his hands in a gesture of hopelessness.

'And bring the girl with you. What's your name?' Ellen turned to her.

The girl dragged the flat sole of her foot along the wall behind her, but said nothing. A little mollified, the woman asked, 'What time would that be? Three o'clock or so?' and upon receiving Ellen's affirmation walked away, the girl following.

Ellen asked, without bothering to smile, 'What's . . . ? Who's that?'

Thomas Kane, jerking his head upwards, and already turning away, said, 'Ask me afterwards.'

Ellen watched the woman and the girl as they walked towards the gloom at the edge of the village. A dark cyclist overtaking them swished a little puddlewater towards their legs. Closing the school's outer door, Ellen did not pursue the matter: this was the day on which she had decided to show the very small children how water worked, and she needed all her energies and concentration to stop them from soaking themselves, while teaching at the same time.

At two o'clock, too early, the woman and girl returned, and hung like ghostly birds around the school walls; they peered in occasionally to see whether Ellen had finished with her classes. The last words of Ellen's last lesson consisted in the children chanting 'These are. The Four Cardinal Virtues. Prudence. Justice. Fortitude. And Temperance.'

'Now, what are the Seven Deadly Sins?' She intoned with them through the short aggressive litany. 'The Seven Deadly Sins. Are. Pride. Covetousness. Lust. Anger. Gluttony. Envy. Sloth.'

When they tumbled out and homewards, she settled her hair quickly, a pin or two in her teeth, her little mirror propped on the narrow metal mantelshelf, and went to the door to encounter mother and daughter. Mr Kane came down the Senior room quickly and tried to intercept her.

She shook her head. 'No. Not yet.'

Having failed, he stopped abruptly, with a brief glare.

'Now what's your name?' Ellen asked the woman. 'And what's your story? Step into the porch.' The girl followed, still silent, and to her Ellen said, 'I'm going to talk to you later.'

In the porch, the woman rested against the high sloped lid of the wooden box which housed the turf and coal for the fires, beside the chipped enamel handbasin on the wire trivet.

'Ma'am, we're McAuliffes, from over outside Millerstown. I want the Master to do a job for us, he's the only one in the world can do it, and we were sent here to ask him by Father Shine, the Curate in Urlingford. He knows the Master well, and he says the Master is the man.'

As she began to speak, Ellen heard the heavy footsteps start again on the planked floor, and quickly she closed him off by shutting the door leading from the porch into the Senior classroom; the footsteps stopped, then receded: his baritone drone resumed as he returned to his class.

'The man for what? How do you mean? What is the Master the man for?' Now the girl edged forward, looking only at her mother.

'Ma'am, my husband. Things out around here. The Irregulars and the Free Staters. He was caught up in all that thing.'

Ellen asked, 'How do you mean?'

The woman said, 'I mean, Ma'am, what General Collins called the Civil War. And, Ma'am, my man hadn't a thing to do with it. The Master would know that.'

Ellen said, 'But Master Kane. He had nothing either – to do with "it"?'

To which the woman replied, 'Sure I know, Ma'am, sure I know, isn't that the very thing Father Shine was saying, Father Shine over in Urlingford. That the Master's the very man. That he hadn't a thing to do with it and that's why. But didn't he know General Collins well?'

Ellen said, 'But General Collins is dead this past three years nearly?'

The woman unhooked her spectacles and rubbed them on her coat. Her naked face stared like a moon at Ellen.

When she wished to become more authoritative, Ellen stiffened her back and chin, a trick they had been taught in *Teaching Discipline* class.

'Now, Mrs McAuliffe. You will have to make yourself plain. Come on now.'

'Sure, I'm trying to, Ma'am, and I will with the help of God. My husband, they said he was a Free Stater, sure he was nothing. He had no politics, and they said he was a Free Stater spy and he wasn't. Ma'am, sure he couldn't spy on himself. He was a bit of a talker, maybe, when he had drink on him, you know what that's like.'

Ellen drew her prim line across her mouth. 'No, I don't actually, but go on.'

'Ma'am, you remember them "Orders of Frightfulness", don't you? D'you remember, Ma'am? 'Twas when De Valera's side, the Irregulars, said that nearly anyone on the other side, that anyone who agreed with the Treaty, that was General Collins's side, should be shot. Well, anyway, my fellow, Sean, was taken from the house about six months after them Orders of Frightfulness was given, and we never seen him since. He was a distant cousin of Sean Hales.' Ellen nodded, recognizing the name of a government brigadier assassinated in Dublin. The girl fidgeted more and more.

'But,' said Ellen to the mother, 'that was nearly three years ago, those Orders? How does this affect the Master?'

The woman reached out, and Ellen now permitted her touch.

'Ma'am, they said my husband came into them Orders, because it was applied to a whole lot of people, and that's why he's gone. Nobody ever told us, 'tis only hearsay, like, but we never seen him since. He was working in the court office over in Johnstown. And this poor child, she can't sleep since, nor can I, there's only the two of us, and we haven't a pinch of money, and if we knew where he was . . .'

Ellen patted the woman's arm, releasing her tears. Mrs McAuliffe took a clean handkerchief from inside her cardigan and coat-sleeves, and began, not to blow her nose, but to wipe her cheeks. Her hat had come slightly askew.

'So. You want the Master to find out. Where he. Where he, where your husband. Is?' Ellen looked from mother to daughter, and pursed her lips with approval at the cleanliness of the child's hair. The child nodded, her first animation.

Outside, on the road, *The Princess* bus snored metallically by, at least twenty minutes early.

'Ma'am. They came in the evening,' said Mrs McAuliffe, 'and he walked with them, they didn't drag him nor nothing, and the worst sign of all, they came the next day and took his coat off the nail on the back of the door. That's the worst thing.'

Ellen opened her mouth to ask, almost formed the words, 'Why is that the worst thing?' – but held back.

Mrs McAuliffe continued, 'Father Shine keeps telling me not to fear the worst, but sure, Ma'am, he was never married himself, how would a priest know? Don't you know that yourself?' Dropping her voice to a whisper, Mrs McAuliffe said, 'Ma'am, we can't hold a wake nor nothing. There'd be a widow's pension, if . . . if . . . if . . .'

The girl tugged at her mother's sleeve, in a half-tearing, half-striking motion, and made a worried noise.

'Now,' said Ellen, turning fully away from the woman to the girl, 'what's your name?'

The mother said, 'She's called Hannie, Ma'am, Hanora. After my own mother.'

Ellen patted the air between herself and the woman and said, 'No, Mrs McAuliffe, let her tell me herself.' She turned more fully to the child. 'Now, Hannie, what is your name?'

No reply. The porch door burst open: three o'clock, and the children from the Senior room began to tear out.

'Quietly. Quietly. You're not elephants,' called Ellen. Turning to Mrs McAuliffe in a way that the girl could not see, she mouthed the question to the mother, 'Stutter?'

The woman, looking at the child, nodded.

When the stampede of children had passed, Ellen led mother and daughter into the lower half of the vacated classroom. The Master sat at his high desk, writing up the Progress Record, a task he and Ellen had agreed they hated.

Mrs McAuliffe called out, 'Sir.'

Ellen shushed her swiftly, placed a finger over her own lips and whispered, 'No, Mrs McAuliffe. Leave this to me. I'll talk to him. You sit there,' directing the woman to one of the long benches by the wall. She placed the girl in a desk and sat facing her from the desk immediately in front. At the top of the room, Mr Kane continued to write, a hand now held laterally to his forehead like an eyeshade. Aware of his earshot, Ellen began.

'Hannie. Put your hands flat on the desk in front of you.'

The girl complied.

'Good girl. Now lift your chin. High. High. Higher. Good.' Ellen counted the motions, one, two, three.

'Good. Very good. Now, turn your head around like this. To the left. To the right. Good. Good.'

The girl looked terrified.

Ellen said to her, 'Hannie, you have a very nice face. Now. Put your hands on your jaws, each side. Like this. So that you can feel this. And this.'

To demonstrate, Ellen felt each of her own jawbones.

'Good girl. Now. Open your mouth and close it again. So that you can hear the click of your jaws. And feel it. Yes. Yes. That's it. Good girl. Now put your hands flat on the desk again. That's it.'

Ellen put her own hands over the girl's, and said, 'Now, Hannie. I want you to say, with me, these words. "Miss. Morris." And "Hannie. Mac. Auliffe."'

The girl shook her head.

'Yes, of course you are able to say it. Try saying just "Miss Morris" first. That's me by the way.' She stabbed her own chest with her finger.

Ellen laughed, and thereby stirred half a smile in the girl, whose mother sat mute.

'Now, come on.' Ellen grew brisk again. 'Mmiss. Mmorris.' The girl began with tremendous hesitancy. 'Mm.'

Her nostrils dilated and she blushed with embarrassment.

'Mmm,' Ellen said. 'Now that is very good. Very good. Just say. Miss. Mm. Issss.' She tightened her mouth, then widened it open in accordance with the syllabic exaggeration.

The girl said, 'Mm. M. Mmm. Mm.' Then, with what seemed like a surprised expression, she said, 'Issssssss.'

Ellen nodded in affirmation. 'Yes. Yea-ssss. Good. Good. Now. Quickly. Try Morris.'

The girl tried immediately. 'Mmmaurr.'

Ellen said, 'the "-isss" is easy. You already said it.'

The girl went, 'Isss.'

'Quick, quick, while you have it,' said Ellen, 'Morr. Iss.' The girl repeated, 'Morr. Iss.' Ellen applauded. 'Now. The whole lot together,' she said. 'Miss Morris. You know. Just normally. Like me. Come on. We'll say it together.'

With some repeats and efforts the girl said it. 'Mmm-iss. Morr. Isss. Mmmiss. Mmmmmorrr. Isss. Mmiss. Mmorrriss.'

Ellen nodded approvingly each time, more and more enthusiastically. The girl said finally, 'Mmiss Mmmorris.'

'Oh, what a good girl you are, Hannie,' said Ellen. 'Now I'm going to give you something for that,' and she reached up and took the lavender ribbon from her hair and gave it to the girl.

'Wash it before you wear it,' Ellen laughed, and received a thin smile.

'Now, soon you won't be at all afraid of talk,' said Ellen. She rose and crossed to the mother, who anticipated the question.

'Ma'am, she's like that ever since the night her father went. She was normal before that, fine, you couldn't shut her up. But she was her father's dote. Never left his knee when he sat in the chair. She's an only child. And she's stuttering that bad ever since.'

Ellen said, 'Do we know your address?'

'The Master has it, Ma'am,' she said pointing: he clearly heard, but ignored. Shadows drifted across the school.

When the McAuliffes left, Ellen put on her coat and hat and assembled the contents of her basket.

'We have to talk,' she said over her shoulder to the austere, sitting figure. Then she turned to face him fully, and said, 'I have to say. You should have talked to that woman more kindly.'

She blushed as she said it, and Thomas Kane, after a moment's hard survey of her face and eyes, smiled and smiled. 'Yes,' he said, thoughtfully. 'Yes.' From next morning he called her 'Ellen', although never, of course, in front of the pupils.

One evening later in the week, standing by the mirror in her room, Ellen counted off the days she had been in Deanstown.

'The first Monday doesn't count. From the day I came, Sunday night, Monday night, Tuesday, Wednesday, Thursday, that's five, home on Friday, back on Sunday night, that's six, then Monday, Tuesday, Wednesday and tonight, ten nights.'

On her bed sat a small pile of clean clothing; in the scullery an hour earlier she had completed her ironing, with Lily watching her silently – and blushing whenever Ellen said a word to her.

Outside, darkness had begun to fall. She reached for the matches, shook the lamp slightly to make sure the oil reached the wick, took off the clear glass funnel and struck a match, then sat down to write.

'Insect' book for school.
Ask Thomas K. about shopping in Mooreville.
Get my own hot-water bottle.
Ask Leah about 'Voller Corsets' advertisement in last week's *Daily Mail*.
'Small' towels.
Ask Thomas K. about cobbler: mend brown shoes.
Piano anywhere?
Ask Miss Humphrys about teaching children with stutters.
Ask Father John for loan of *Imitation of Christ*.
Bring Janesborough essay to school.
Ask Thomas K. about houses to rent.
Get new vests from Cannocks.
Ask Thomas K. about McAuliffes.
Get dance book for the children?

Lily called up the stairs to say tea was ready. Ellen checked her hair and face and went downstairs. Mrs Greege, in one of her silent moods, dominated the morose table. Ellen made three bright efforts, and each one foundered: none of the others, the sons or Lily, had the capacity to break Mrs Greege's mood, which was expressed in gazing sourly down at her plate, and sighing at length from time to time. Ellen fell silent, too.

In school next morning, after the eleven o'clock break, Ellen inadvertently left the stiff door of her classroom slightly ajar. After some minutes, she realized that Thomas had been standing outside it, pretending to 'post' an old nib in the knot-hole, but actually listening to her. In the midst of telling the children about the suffragette movement, she stopped abruptly.

'No, Miss Morris.' He opened the door. 'Carry on, I didn't mean to interrupt you,' and he withdrew.

At lunchtime he said to her, 'That was very interesting.'

'Did you think so? You didn't think it was too much, or over their heads?'

He said, 'I found out in Belgium that no age is too young for education. Children can take in more than we think. And especially the way you told it. You shared it with them. As a great story, as a play, nearly.'

He stood by the window watching the children cavort outside.

'Of course.' He stopped.

'What were you going to say?'

He resumed slowly, 'If they were your own children instead of somebody else's.' He stopped again, and she waited.

'My brothers and sisters always say I never stop trying to teach them.'

She asked, 'How many have you?'

'I'm the oldest of nine.' Then he murmured, 'And one in Heaven.'

'Aah,' she said, 'that's a pity.'

He did not turn to look at her.

'Yes, it is a pity. That's what it is. A pity.'

After a pause she asked, 'What were you doing in Belgium?' He said, 'I was looking for a man whose picture had been painted by somebody famous, a Scotchman. But that's another story' – and accomplishedly left no room for further enquiry.

As school concluded, she enquired, 'What is Mooreville like for shopping?' and he offered to give her a lift there the following day, then reminded her, 'Now remember the Burkes on Sunday,' an invitation for both of them to visit one of the well-to-do farmers.

'I have to find out from you some time,' she said, as he

rattled the school door to check that the lock had taken, 'about the Orders of Frightfulness.'

'Ah, yes,' but he closed down the mood, so that asking further questions would have felt uncomfortable.

That evening, Mrs Greege said directly after eating, 'I wonder, Miss Morris, that floor in the passage out there is very dirty.'

'I beg your pardon?' Ellen froze at the table.

Mrs Greege raised her head and said, 'Every woman around here does housework.'

Lily, on a nod from Mrs Greege, fetched from the rear kitchen an empty bucket, a scrubbing brush and some cloths. She filled the bucket from the huge black pointed kettle on the range, and, head held to one side, deposited bucket and steam, cloths and brush, on the floor beside Ellen's chair, but would not meet Ellen's eye. Ellen put a hand to her mouth; everybody except Mrs Greege left the kitchen. Without turning around, Mrs Greege pointed: 'Start from inside that door.'

An hour and a half later, Ellen sat on her bed, looking at her crinkled hands. She began to grieve. The small bowl of greenery she had assembled earlier in the week, culled from hedgerows and evergreens on the way home from school, lent the room a tiny glow. Ellen sat on the bed in a position where she could observe herself in the lamplit wardrobe mirror. She blew her nose and straightened up, rose, washed her face in cold water and sat down again.

27th February 1925,
Friday night.

Dear Father John,

It was very nice to have that cup of tea on Saturday. I forgot to ask you if by any chance you have a spare copy of the *The Imitation of Christ* you could post out to me?

I'm not going home this week-end so that I can get to

know this place a bit better. As I was saying to you, the children are very backward and I feel I should stay here for a year anyway to get them started. The Principal did his MA in Dublin and says he knew some Jesuits in the University. I wonder if you knew any of them? Remind me to ask you the next time we meet.

If you get a chance, call around and see Dada some time as I feel he may need the company, too. If you get another letter from me in a day or so, then you'll know things are truly lonesome out here! Keep remembering me in your prayers, as I will you.

> God bless.
> Your affectionate friend,
> Ellen

She sealed and addressed the envelope and began her next letter.

My dearest Leah,

I wish we had had more time last week-end, but I'll be in again soon to see you all. Things here are desperately quiet. At the moment if I stop writing and listen, I can't hear a single sound, except the odd creak from the house, or the rafters above my head. I have a Valor oil heater at last, and it is throwing diamonds of light on the wall, like a little picture-house.

Mrs G. here is terrible, and I don't know what to do about her. She made me wash the floor this evening, and I didn't know how to say 'No'. Thomas Kane, the Principal I was telling you about, found these lodgings for me, saying it was the cleanest house in the parish. Now I know why it is! Maybe I'll ask him what I should do about her. He is the oldest of nine children, and he is proving very easy to work with, and very nice. He's actually quite gentle behind that terribly stern face he has, and he's giving me a lift to the town tomorrow to show me where the shops are. I haven't eaten an apple since I came here, and I need some things of my own. He's also taking me out to an invitation for our tea on Sunday, local farmers who want to meet the new Mistress!

I have to go to Mass here for the first time on Sunday

morning and I'm dreading it a bit, going on display with a capital 'D'.

Leah, I miss you and Herbert and the girls, how are they all? Something very unpleasant happened at school the other day. A woman visited, whose husband has disappeared since the middle of the Civil War, and she asked Thomas K. to find him, but he won't agree. I'll tell you this and other news when I see you.

My best to you all.
Your affectionate friend,
Ellen

Finishing the letter, she began to weep a little again, then straightened up, put on her coat and went out for a brisk walk, startling the sitters around the Greege fireside as she slammed the front door shut. A half-moon sailed quietly and slowly behind orderly clouds. Ellen, familiar with the road, walked down the hill towards the village. Thomas Kane's house had no lights shining as she walked past. A cyclist without a light grunted behind her, and made her heart jump, as did the little dog trotting behind the bicycle. One or two small yellow glimmers lit curtained windows in the cottages. Defeated by the night she turned home quickly.

In the room, she took off her scarf, opened her coat, sat on the bed for a moment. Then, kneeling, she murmured, 'Friday, yes,' then began, 'The Five *Sorrowful* Mysteries. The First Mystery. The Agony in the Garden. Thou, O Lord, shall open my lips, and my tongue shall announce Thy praise.'

Thomas called at noon, the car's roof glistening with the recent shower. Black spots of rain dotted the brim of his hat.

Above the noise of the engine, she called out to him as they drove, 'Could I rent a house locally?' He shouted yes, if she could find one.

'Should I buy a bicycle? Although I have an old one at home, I could bring it out on the bus.'

In Mooreville, he introduced her to *Careys, Tea, Wine and Spirits Merchants*, where the manager, Mr Gilsenan, in his brown apron breathed on her: 'This is the busiest day, the world and his mother come in of a Saturday'; she saw the Post Office and the banks, the bullet marks on the walls of the church, and *Wilkinson's*, the bicycle shop. She wrote everything down in her notebook. Thomas showed her the New Town, with the wooden slatted houses, built in the Land War: 'The tenants refused to pay rents any more to absentee landlords.' Sheltering in a doorway, he looked over her shoulder and corrected her on features of local spelling.

When a second shower began, Thomas steered Ellen into the *Mooreville Tearooms*; one other person sat there, a young woman wearing a scarf tied around her hat as if she too had been motoring. Thomas nodded 'Hallo' to her. The young woman had just finished and stood to leave: she looked at Ellen inquisitively.

'Ernestina Stephenson,' said Thomas, when the door's bell clanged closed, 'you know – the stud farm, that high slope up behind the school?'

'Oh, with the red roof?' asked Ellen.

'Protestants, naturally,' he said.

Nobody else came in while they sat there. Unawkward, comfortable from the experience of sharing breaks and lunchtimes at school, they drank tea and ate buns, two for him, one with jam for her.

She broached the subject. 'That McAuliffe woman?'

'Yes,' he said.

'Is there anything to be done for her?'

'I don't know –' he seemed to go no farther. Then, considering, he back-handed the crumbs from the corner of his mouth. 'The whole thing is . . . peculiar. Look.' In an outburst he continued, 'What is most known around here is the least talked-of. The more a thing is common knowledge the more secret it is. And the other way around. Do you know what I mean?' Not giving her a chance to answer, he forced a change of subject. 'I have to go to Outrath, would you ever mind coming with me, it's only a few miles out the road?'

He explained when they got there, 'This is a co-operative creamery, and I'm on the Committee; we're applying to the Government for a grant. We have to get some of these new separators, I have to drop in a form there.'

She sat in the car, watching the rain pour down. After ten minutes or so, he came striding back, seven-league-booting over the puddles in the cart-ruts.

'Ah, no, don't apologize,' she said. 'I enjoyed waiting. I like looking at the rain. You never see the weather in a city.'

Just before he got out again to start the car, he peered through the windscreen to assess the wide circle he would have to turn in the creamery yard.

She said suddenly, 'There's something you might know what to do about. I don't know what to do about something' – and in full detail told him about Mrs Greege and the scrubbing of the floor.

He clipped his words, 'We can't. Have that. You're the Teacher. They try to do this to authority around here.'

'What could I do about it? I feel that if I go to live somewhere else, she will talk about me all over the place. And I don't have enough. Enough . . .' She hesitated.

'Enough what? You have plenty of energy, anyway.'

'No, not that.'

'Enough experience, maybe?'

'Maybe.' Ellen took the rope he threw her. 'Yes, enough experience. To stop her.'

'Well.' He spoke in a straight line. 'I could interfere.

But I don't want to. The best thing is to show her you'll not put up with it.'

'And how do I do that?'

'By saying to yourself, "I won't put up with it." You might have to say it over and over again. I had to take a decision once that was very difficult, and I decided to do what I did on the basis that what was going on – was doing me harm. Inside myself.'

Another quiet and tense night for Ellen. She sat in her room all evening, asking Lily to bring her meal up on a tray.

'Ma'am,' said Lily, desperate with embarrassment, and manoeuvring the tray clumsily, 'my aunt says are you sick or something, because there's not trays in this house, she says, no one waitin' on anyone?'

'Never mind, Lily,' said Ellen. 'Thank you, anyway, I'll talk to your aunt. Don't you mind. And thank you for the tray.'

Next morning, among candles and silence and the smell of mustiness, and maps in damp on the walls of the church, Ellen Morris and Thomas Kane had their first opportunity to observe each other in public.

She walked to Mass: camel coat, brown hat, black shoes – brown shoes still not mended. Outside the church, a long line of men formed in chatter against the wall; inside the yard, women conversed animatedly. Ellen walked through, returning a 'Hallo' here and there. One woman came forward and said, 'You're very welcome. I hope you'll like us,' to which Ellen said with her lovely smile, 'I do already.' The men all looked at her legs.

She dipped her finger in the marble font, made the Sign of the Cross patiently, chose an empty pew about a third of the way back from the altar, genuflected and knelt. A quarter of an hour early, she prayed on her knees for five minutes, then rose and sat back.

Mantlehill's sacristan always tolled rapidly: he blamed a heavy rope on a light bell. The church began to fill: folk joined Ellen's high-backed pew on each side, nodding to her in seeming recognition. A few minutes before the due arrival of the priest, she saw Thomas: he walked up the aisle to her left and took a seat a little ahead, licensing Ellen to scrutinize him. Then she concentrated on her prayers once more.

At Communion, Ellen went to the altar-rails first. She passed abreast of him on the way up the aisle; he viewed her hips and legs, then folded his hands. On her way back, since she had her head down in an attitude of devoutness, he could gaze at her from the front without being observed in return.

Thomas went last to the altar-rails, almost in a shepherding and summarizing role, and as he walked back, his eye caught her looking at him: he did not smile, that would have been unseemly.

Outside Mrs Greege's at five o'clock that afternoon, he said to Ellen, 'There's a great stretch in the evenings now,' and held open the car door for her: he wore the clothes she had seen on him at Mass.

The thatched farmhouse, long and powerful and low and pink, lay at the end of a mile-long avenue with pot-holes and occasional gravel.

Ellen offered to open the many gates, but Thomas refused and stepped down each time, bending his head to avoid the canvas roof of the car. One of his fingernails had a little residual stain underneath, as if he had failed to remove oil. Fixing the stiff catch on the windscreen, his hands tensed.

Mrs Burke, Thomas said, 'had ideas about herself'. She

also had silver hair and a lazy eye, and a bone-breaking handshake, and pictures in the hallway; 'That's my son the engineer, the Master here taught him; he has a great job now over in Wolverhampton, but he'll be back one day, please God. Now, what'll I call you, Miss Morris? Your mother, now, is a friend of Mrs Joyce, who's married to a cousin of my late brother-in-law, they're Burkes over in Croom.'

They stood on the smooth flags of the big glistening kitchen and Mrs Burke said, 'Oh, we're not sitting here, you have to come into the parlour, the parlour,' and led them along a dark and tidy passageway to a room of lace, and peacock feathers in tall green vases, and small brown cameo photographs in huge black frames; men with starched moustaches, and women with blouses made of chilled linen, standing formal and stiff, or sitting on large chairs, the couples never looking at each other. A fire roared before a table set with china, and a tier of three plates stacked up on a silver rack: sandwiches, scones and small plump buns in filled, fluted-paper cases.

'Now, my husband.' Mrs Burke began every sentence with a firm statement of the subject matter. 'My husband Martin is a distant cousin of W. T. Cosgrave's wife. In fact, he'll be in in a minute, he's dying to meet you, but I won't ever let Martin into the parlour in workboots, you know what the men are like.'

Thomas told Ellen afterwards that in Mrs Burke's boasting of her husband's family relationships, she conveniently left out the fact that the Burkes 'were on the Irregular side, they were very bitter too; they'd never vote for Cosgrave now, no matter what she says about him.'

Martin Burke, quieter and graver than his wife, came silently in, still buttoning a clean waistcoat, a small man, with his highly polished brogue boots.

Mrs Burke said, very kindly and approvingly, 'They tell me you have great style, Miss Morris, that you've a different outfit for every day of the year. I suppose a single girl can afford clothes these days, 'twasn't like that in my day, although not that my father stinted us for a thing, not at all. You see this?' She fingered her own cream silk sleeve. 'That was my grandmother's.'

'Very nice,' said Ellen, who watched carefully Martin Burke's thoughtful respect as he shook Thomas's hand, and then accepted the introduction to Ellen.

The talking began. Would Mr Burke be 'taking any con-acre this year?' (The more prosperous farmers, and Thomas 'definitely' included the Burkes, rented extra land most summers.) He might, but last year he got 'a bit of a sickener. I took eighteen acres from the Horans and the river flooded up into it, d'you remember that heavy rain we had in May, and I never got it dry 'til 'twas too late.'

So there was not to be a new Sergeant after all, which was just as well, as 'the man in the Barracks, didn't he know everyone and wasn't that the main thing?' said Mr Burke.

Peggy, in a black flowered print crossover apron, brought in plates of bacon, black pudding, egg, glistening glands of sausage and kidneys; later, to much acclaim, a wide apple pie arrived, in a deep dish, not a round plate.

Ellen tasted and asked.

'That, now,' said Mrs Burke, 'is my grandmother's own invention, extra cloves and, mind you, brown sugar; she was an O'Connor herself, her nephew, Surgeon O'Connor, is very well-known, very well-known.'

Peggy left with the hot-water jug, and Mrs Burke said to Ellen, 'Did you know that Parnell stayed in this house?' Ellen discussed, very interesting, Mrs Burke's pronunciation of the name, her mother's aunts argued about it, but her father always said that the man himself liked it pronounced 'Parn-l' and not 'Par-knell'.

Mr Burke nodded, 'Your father is exactly right. Exactly right.'

Mrs Burke said, 'That woman. Dth. Such an awful thing to happen to a fine man that he falls in with a bad woman.' She fussed on. 'Of course, she didn't stay with him in this house, not at all, he was on his way to a meeting in Cork and he stopped here. I can show you the very bed he slept in, but he sat in that chair the Master is sitting in now. He made a joke to me, that at least he wouldn't trouble me for hot water to shave in, you know, on account of the beard. "I won't be any trouble to you, Mrs Burke, for hot water in the morning anyway," he said.'

As they stood on the Burke doorstep, clouds flying unthreateningly across the waxing moon, Mrs Burke said to Ellen, 'Now you're as grand a girl as I met in a long time. If I can ever do anything for you, you just get the Master to drive you up here and we'll have a good chat. Martin, isn't she an awful nice girl?'

Mr Burke shook her hand diligently, and Ellen, half-buttoning her coat, blushed a deep red.

Thomas hummed a ditty in the car. 'Oh, Kitty O'Shea. Oh, Kitty O'Shea. You're as black as the night and as bold as the day.' Cattle snorted unseen in the fields as he opened and closed gates. Ellen drew the rug around her knees. At half-past nine, they reached Mrs Greege's gate and Thomas turned off the engine.

She asked, 'Did Parnell really sleep there?'

'He did. But what was unusual was that for all his politics, Parnell usually only stayed in Protestant houses, and that's another reason why the night in the Burkes' house was such a noted episode. And Mrs Burke nearly had a heart attack of delight. She walked like a woman on stilts up the church the next Sunday.'

Ellen told Thomas that she liked Mrs Burke. 'I didn't mind the snobbery too much. I mean, if you knew my own mother?' She added, 'You have a great appetite.'

Thomas had eaten the apple pie almost singlehanded.

'What did you think of him?' asked Thomas.

'A nice man. Genuine.'

Ellen said, 'You know – for years I never knew what the Parnell scandal was, because nobody would say he was brought down by a woman. All my father would say was, "and just as he was going to govern Ireland and get us Home Rule". That's all.'

The lamp steady in the quiet bedroom, Ellen wrote in her notebook, 'Mr and Mrs Martin Burke, The Red Farm. The walls of the kitchen are about three feet thick, and the windows have deep shelves wide enough to hold the sewing machine. The poker in the fireplace in their parlour is the biggest I have ever seen, with an eagle's head.' Then she wrote underneath, 'Thomas Kane'; and again, 'Thomas Kane'.

She stood up, moved the lamp to gain a better light from the mirror of the wardrobe door, angled her body sideways and smoothed her figure, from her shoulders down her breasts, finishing with a flourish, her hands flying off her hips. Capping her pen, she put the notebook away, and stood directly in front of the mirror, this time mouthing words, like an actress rehearsing lines. Then, walking downstairs very slowly, she rounded the corner into the kitchen and drew a deep breath. Mrs Greege, alone in the kitchen, was sewing under the lamp.

'Mrs Greege. I want to say something to you, please. I am the new Mistress in this parish. As such I must, and will, have the respect of the people. I am not your maid, and I never will be. As long as you know me, never think to ask me to do a menial chore again.'

Ellen gripped the end of the balustrade. The woman in the black clothes half-leaped from her chair beneath the oil-lamp. The wick flared and Ellen walked back upstairs;

shaking and with eyes closing and opening repeatedly, she reached her room.

Next morning, Monday, Thomas handed Ellen two brown paper bags: one contained ginger snap biscuits. 'You might like them for your lunch. I have a bag too many of them.'

In the other brown paper bag he had placed a small silvery stone, with a tiny white fossil embedded in it.

At lunch he said to her, 'Here, this is what they were talking about' – and handed her some verses of a monologue written out in his own hand. Martin and Bella Burke had recalled a gathering at which Thomas memorably gave them a recitation; 'D'you remember, Master, what was it, Percy French, wasn't it, "The Four Farrellys".' All had smiled; Mrs Burke conspiratorially assuring 'Lovely, lovely' to Ellen, who, later, had asked Thomas for the words.

> In a small hotel in London I was sitting down to dine,
> When the waiter brought the register and asked me if I'd sign.
> And as I signed I saw a name that set my heart astir
> A certain 'Francis Farrelly' had signed the register.

At three o'clock, as the last children left the school, it began to rain, and at the window she said, 'That's bad, now. I have no umbrella.' They sat by the fire in his classroom for almost two hours, and he showed her the Roll Book which went back to the school's foundation in 1847.

'In all that time,' Thomas often pursed his lips between one sentence and another, and Ellen, when he talked, rarely took her eyes off his mouth, 'in all that time, hardly one family in this half of the parish has ever gone on to Secondary Education.'

The rain still fell; it fell and fell, on the fields, the trees, and on the ochre, leaded-windowed, gabled houses of the village.

'One or two boys or girls from farmers' houses,' said

Thomas, 'like young Burke, went on to the convent or the secondary school, and I had one lad who was as brainy as you could ask for, and we even got him a scholarship, but the parents took him out of secondary school after a year or two, and sent him working, to England or Dublin, or somewhere. He's a barman now, over in Kent, when he should be a barrister or a surgeon. Oh, and we had one priest. But the rest of them are in shops, or working for farmers. Or doing nothing.'

The rain slackened a little, and they quenched the lamp and locked up. When they had left the village, the rain intensified again, and Thomas said, 'Here. Put your head under my coat,' and held it out high to her for shelter, which drew her in close to him. Within sight of Mrs Greege's, although by now it had grown fully dark, he took the coat's wing back gently, saying, 'You know what they're like if they see us.' Yet they stood in the shade of overhanging ivy on the demesne wall, talking for another hour. Nobody passed by, not a bicycle, nor a cart, and still the rain quietly fell.

'It rained like this the night my father died,' Thomas said, 'my brother nearly got pneumonia on his way to get the priest.' Ellen's shoulder touched Thomas's arm as they stood in the growing cold. Abruptly he stopped speaking – then after a moment's silence, said, 'If you don't go home next week-end, we might go out for a drive.' They parted.

Two days later, on Wednesday, when the children went out to play at noon, Thomas walked into Ellen's class-room; he held something behind his back, and was smiling. He handed it to her: an egret's feather.

Ellen rhymed in delight, 'Oh. Oh. How did you know?' and told him that her mother's two aunts had always admired one lady 'of their acquaintance but not of their knowledge': they said of her that 'she was never without an egret-feather hat'.

Next morning, he handed to her a book: new, carefully covered in brown paper, and with Ellen's name in his handwriting on the cover: *In Brightest Africa*, by Carl Akeley. On the way home, walking with her as far as Mrs Greege's, he said, 'March is coming in like a lion.' On Friday afternoon outside his house he said, 'Wait a minute,' and he reappeared with a cushion cover of black satin embroidered with tea-roses; it had never been taken out of its original tissue-paper. 'My aunt sent it from San Francisco.'

That evening she jotted down a snatch of poetry in her notebook:

> When the winds are breathing low
> And the stars are shining bright.

Browsing through her possessions, she sought her old notebook from Teacher Training College, the one with the Morocco thonging along the binding, and smiled at notes she had taken from Miss Humphrys: *The Modesty of the Person*:

All daytime clothing must hang loose, no belt, nothing tight: nowhere on the body must the wearer be alerted to the flesh. Undergarments must also flow, never knowing constriction or pressure, only the loosest of cords. Even in the gymnasium, nothing of the body may perform in public; the legs must not be divided by pantaloons or bloomers. When taking a bath or a shower, always wear swimming costume in order not to give offence to yourself.

Throughout the week-end it rained and blew, too wet almost to go to Mass: Ellen got soaked: nowhere did she see Thomas in or near the church. For the rest of the day, although not quite sitting at the window waiting and watching for him, Ellen realized that Thomas had not appeared for the drive he had suggested. On Monday morning he told her the car had broken down again.

82

4

A bugle blast rings out. Then another blast, then another, too musical and varied for an ordinary hunting horn, and besides, no hunt is meeting anywhere nearby. The children in the Senior room jump; the Juniors have left already. Thomas cranes his body aside to see through the open door. When the bugle rings again, followed by cheers and 'Halloos', Ellen moves to her window, then looks back through the glass-paned partition at Thomas, who by now has begun to move quickly.

He shoos the Seniors out: they raise a little cheer in the porch: he shouts at them in an angry voice Ellen has not previously heard.

Wheeling in sharply by the pump and the handball-alley, into the space between the green and the school, swings a *caravanserai* of one rickety motor-vehicle, neither a coach nor a truck, and two gaudy carts drawn by flighty piebald ponies, behind which trot a further two such animals tethered on halters. These carts bear high piles of mysterious boxes, crates and flat folded objects, all painted in blue and red and yellow. At the head of the procession rides a man on a motorcycle wearing a leather helmet and goggles pushed up on his forehead. He is the bugle-blower, and he also leads the 'Halloos', and waves his bugle arm aloft vigorously while shouting.

Across the handlebars of his motorcycle he has fixed a placard reading *'Joe-for-Yells'*. The last high horsedrawn cart has a message across the front, *'Emily-for-Laughs'*, and the motor-waggon's side bears the curly legend, *'Mrs MacReady's Famous Travelling Herbal Show – If You Suffer from Coughs or Threatening Notions. We'll Kill*

You with Laughs or We'll Cure You with Potions. Two Shows Nightly – Sunday Matinee – Many Cures Worldwide – Only Natural Herbs Used from the Fields of Our Own Fair Land.'

'Oh, my God,' says Thomas. 'Oh, Jesus Christ!'

Ellen joins him at the door, stepping on tiptoe in a hopeless attempt to peer over his shoulder. The parade halts.

'Good day to you, Sir,' shouts Joe-for-Yells, and blows on his bugle again. The motor-waggon's horn toots a vulgar, louder toot, and someone on one of the carts screams a loud whistle. A boy jumps down and bangs cymbals.

'What in the name of God is this?' asks Ellen, finally getting past Thomas's hips.

'What is it, Thomas?' repeats Ellen, but observing Thomas's agitation. He does not answer, makes an 'I'll tell you later' sign, and, racing back up his classroom, begins to put away into the tall glass-fronted cupboard some objects he normally leaves out all the time: his gleaming ebony ruler; his own private brass-capped inkpot; his pens; his box of good writing paper; the ivory set square and protractor on the windowsill; the Roll Book and the Progress Record.

His hands tremble as he locks away his compass; and an old silver watch he uses to demonstrate the mechanics of clockwork in one of his beloved *General Knowledge* classes; and the music-box he bought in Bruges and is always promising himself he'll try to mend some day. As he locks the drawers beneath the glass cupboard doors, he looks over his shoulder and sees the children outside, talking and laughing with the people from the travelling show.

He rushes past Ellen and reaching the door again shouts, 'Home with you! Stop hanging around here! You're slow enough to get here in the mornings! Home now!' He turns back into the classroom and looks at Ellen, and he is trying in vain to slow down his responses.

'Isn't that a bit harsh?' she says. 'Children always love a circus.'

He takes the clock down from the wall and puts it into another cupboard, the key of which has always lived in the lock, but now he pockets the key.

'Good day, Sir.' The laughing voice outside again, followed by another blast on the bugle. The man comes to the door, a seedy fop with missing teeth and a drowned, lank-haired complexion, then calls a third time. 'Good day to you, Sir.'

Thomas stands with his face to the wall beneath the blank patch where the clock has been. All of this has happened within the space of two or three minutes, all of it frantic, and to Ellen, still unexplained, and she now grasps Thomas's arm, and repeats her enquiry urgently.

'Ellen, this is trouble. This is trouble.' He will not turn around. 'This is bloody trouble. These fellows are scavengers and hooligans. Put away everything you have.' She looks mystified, and begins to make some resistance.

'Look.' He holds up a hand, and his authority has returned. 'This is what has happened. Who is the School Manager? Who is the Manager of this school? Not me. Not you. The Canon, isn't it?'

Ellen makes no objection, simply listens.

'What does the Canon do in his spare time? What is he famous for? What? What do you see him doing on Sunday afternoons and on other occasions, you even asked me about it just after you came here?' Still he does not let Ellen speak.

'He gathers herbs, doesn't he, the Canon? And he "cures" people with them, doesn't he? His famous "cures". That bunch out there – they belong to that same fraternity and they have him hoodwinked. They persuade the Canon every few years to let them use this school

85

every night for a while, for their herbal cures and their vulgar shows. They put on sketches that are blue.'

Mrs MacReady, hair white and powdered and pomaded like a third-rate Regency portrait, rouge on her cheeks, with the nose of a crone and the step of a dancer and filth beneath her fingernails, comes out from behind the motor-waggon. She raises a hand dramatically in the air.

'We took Wicklow without firing a shot. Our *Colleen Bawn* was the best show they had ever seen. Emily is a *tragédienne* as well as a *comédienne*. But Carlow gave us our best cures. We cured half Carlow and all Tullow in one evening.'

Ellen wrinkles her nose as Mrs MacReady jinks forward.

'Where is that fine man?' she cries. 'Let me see that fine Mister Kane. The Man all the women want. The Man with the Motor-car.'

Thomas turns from the porch in disgust, but Ellen catches his jacket and he turns back.

'How long will you be here for this time?' Thomas calls out, with all the charm of a writ-server. One of the horses on the halters rears and whinnies. Joe-for-Yells blows his shattering bugle again.

'Who knows? Who knows? The Gaiety of Nations. Until cockshut time. I am Napper Tandy's fancy. Oh, I met with Napper Tandy and he shook me by the hand.' Mrs MacReady raises her skirt like a little girl and does a small waltz to accompany her snatch of song. 'We have wintered in Wicklow, my dears, but here we may spring. The Cat, the Rat and Lovell the Dog.' Children appear behind her, followed by a girl of about Ellen's age, mid-twenties, in a black jumper and stained jodhpurs.

Ellen turns to Thomas and begins to joke. 'Soap and water in short supply.'

He shakes his head angrily, and comes forward from the door to halt Mrs MacReady's progress.

'You will have to give us a few minutes to get the school to rights,' he says. Ushering Ellen ahead of him, he shuts and locks the door, stranding the noise outside. She asks for explanations.

'The Canon gives them the right to camp out there and use the school outside of teaching hours to put on their shows. They make a holy mess of the place. This is the fourth time. Oh, this is desperate, this is desperate. They leave it filthy. You can see what they're like.' He hits his desk with his fist making the lid jump. 'They stole two of my best fountain pens, they tore pictures out of my books to decorate the walls during their sketches. The smell of that stuff they call medicines. Uegch!'

Ellen draws up a chair, and sits him down.

'Have you complained to the Canon?' she asks calmly. 'Have you ever done anything about the missing things?'

Thomas tells her the Canon would never hear a word said against Mrs MacReady, he believes her to be 'saintly', and 'a near genius'. When Ellen asks what they should do now, Thomas replies, 'There's not a thing we can do. Not a thing. We have to give them the key and go.' He tightens his mouth to a line like the edge of a slate.

Ellen says, 'That's not good enough for me. I'm going to come and see their show.' He argues that if she does that, it will be seen as supporting them.

'Not if their show is as bad as you say it is. That will give me something to say against them.'

Through the school window Ellen sees a pony-and-trap draw up on the road near the pump. A young woman sits watching the circus. It is Ernestina Stephenson, and Ellen says irrelevantly and involuntarily to Thomas, 'Lovely pale complexion that Stephenson girl has.'

At seven o'clock that evening, in drizzle, Ellen returns from Mrs Greege's to the school, and in her handbag she brings notebook and pencil. A crowd has gathered, already over a hundred people. Mrs MacReady sees her, and says, 'There's no room,' but Ellen has bought a ticket from one of the children in the yard, and she pays a further five shillings to book a medicine 'exclusively' later: this fact unmans Mrs MacReady's initial opposition to Ellen's attendance.

All the desks have been removed, and piled high in Ellen's room; in the process her blackboard with tomorrow's letters on it – the junior infants have reached 'J', 'K', 'L' and 'M' – has been knocked half off the wall, and the surround has been cracked. One or two people smile at her and say, 'Hallo, Miss', or 'Hallo, Mistress': many others nod, point, whisper.

A wide canvas sheet, with mountains, snow-covered Alps, and waterfalls daubed on it, some of the paint now crazed and chipped, hangs across the front of the room, from Thomas's dais to the maps above the library boxes and science cupboard. It has been fixed to the ceiling with nails, around which spread huge jagged coins where the plaster has been broken. On Thomas's blackboard easel perches a large placard. *To-night. Joe-for-Yells and Emily-for-Laughs in The Rose of Killarney. Star Attraction. From the Stage of London and Vienna. Madame Rose MacReady in a Selection of Dramatic Roles.*

Ellen takes out her notebook and squeezes along the second row of benches. The globes of the oil-lamps, kept pristine by Thomas who polishes them every day with a special duster, have already begun to blacken with uncontrolled smoke. A smell of sulphur fills the room.

'Jayzes,' she hears a flat anonymous voice behind her say, 'Kane'll go mad in the mornin' when he sees the cut of the place.'

Somewhere a pair of hands claps twice, a whistle blows, then cymbals bang, then a bugle calls. From behind the Alps, quick as a foxtrot, springs Joe-for-Yells carrying an enormous accordion on which he begins to play a jig. He

dances across the open space of floor in front of the first
bench, swaying the huge gleaming box, pressing its buttons, punching its keys, and dancing, dancing. From
behind a waterfall comes the girl, in a green and white
peasant blouse with shamrocks all over it, and as the oooh-
ing room says, 'Aaaah!', Emily-for-Laughs sings,

> *'There is not in this wide world a valley so sweet,*
> *As that vale in whose bosom the clear waters meet.'*

Ellen makes a note: 'Words of song wrong. "Bright"
waters, not "clear".'

> *'Oh, the last rays of feelings and lives shall depart.'*

Ellen writes: 'Wrong, too: "of feeling and *life* must
depart". She sings "of feelings and *lives shall*".'

> *'Ere the bloom of that valley will fade from my heart*
> *Ere the bloom of that valley will fade from my heart.'*

'Not "*will* fade", it should be "*shall* fade"': Ellen notes
down eleven further errors in the remaining three verses,
including 'Sweet Vale of Have Woke You' for 'Sweet Vale
of Avoca'. The attendance, still piling in, claps, cheers
and joins in the singing. A child blows out one of the
lamps. In the dramatic shadows Mrs MacReady
materializes, her head hooded in a wide Kinsale shawl,
black, lined with red, 'heavily patched,' Ellen observes,
'hence the dimming of the lamps.'

Mrs MacReady comes forward.

'A dramatic recital. "The Traveller", by Walter de la
Mara.'

> *'"Is there anybody there," said the Traveller,*
> *Knocking at the moonlit door,*
> *As his horse in silence chewed the grasses*
> *Of the forest's leafy floor.'*

Ellen's pen races. 'Not called "The Traveller": the poem's *correct* title is "The Listeners". Not "de la Mara", but "de la Mare". "Chewed" should be "Champed". "*Ferny* floor" not "leafy".'

> '*And the bird flew up out of the tower,*
> *Above the traveller's head;*
> *And he smote on the door a second and a* third
>   *time,*
> "*Is there anybody here?*" *he said.*'

In the spellbound room, the racing ferocity of Ellen's pencil almost becomes audible. '"Turret" not "tower". Where did she get "a third time"? It doesn't even scan.'

To cheers and applause, and heads turning wonderingly to their neighbours to share the enjoyment, Mrs Mac-Ready takes her bow.

'Here's a riddle,' shouts Joe-for-Yells as he bounds into view. 'Riddle me this. Johnny had a long thing. Mary had a hairy thing. Johnny stuck his long thing into Mary's hairy thing.'

'Wee-heeeeee,' the hard men at the back shout. 'Waaayy-haayy,' and others laugh nervously. 'Yeh dirty things,' shouts Joe-for-Yells. 'Answer – a man putting a handle in a brush.'

Ellen leaves, and the room falls silent as she walks out. By doing so, she misses *The Rose of Killarney*. In the darkness she hears footsteps coming towards her along the road, and she recognizes them.

'Is that you, Thomas?' He says he has been coming to ascertain that she is all right, and he walks her to her lodgings, asking anxious questions about the condition of the classrooms, the blackboards, the desks. She gives all details.

'What is the point,' he asks – of himself, not of Ellen –

'in fighting, in struggling all the time, to banish ignorance and vulgarity?'

She removes a glove and gives him a warm handshake.

'You'll get it all right again,' she says.

In her room, Ellen began a long letter to Leah, but she never finished it, nor did she ever post it. In the letter she asked questions such as, 'What was it like when you met Herbert? How did you feel?' and – 'When are feelings morally wrong, Leah?' and – 'Before you married, Leah, did you ever feel very excited just in thinking about someone?' She did not sleep, her mind racing between the problems of the MacReadys and the excitement of Thomas Kane.

Next morning Ellen finds both classrooms clean and tidy.

'Did they clean up after them?' she asks Thomas, and receives an askance glare.

She returns that night. Mrs MacReady greets her. 'You missed *The Rose of Killarney*, so we're putting it on first, and you never collected your medicine. Isn't Joe-for-Yells a scream? Sometimes he goes a little too far; I have to say to him, "Joe-for-Yells, tone it down, tone it down, there are ladies present," but he gets so excited he doesn't hear me.'

She preens in front of Ellen, pink lipstick and a high-necked frilled blouse with stains all around the collar. 'Do you know who's coming tonight? Mr Val Vousden himself, he's in the area and he sent word to Emily-for-Laughs, aren't we honoured? Oooooh, did you hear about last night, two of the boys outside got very excitable, oooh, excitable, and they did not like each other. A bit too much of the other medicine, maybe?' and she winks.

Ellen makes a note when she sits down, 'Ask about two "excitable" boys? Drink taken?'

A squeezing strain on the accordion comes from behind the Alps; then a tune, soon recognizable as 'Believe Me if All Those Endearing Young Charms', then the voice of Joe-for-Yells:

> '*O, believe me, if all those endearing young charms,*
> *Which I gaze on so proudly today.*'

Ellen's pen flicks into action. 'The correct word is "fondly", not "proudly".'

Mrs MacReady's voice announces, 'Ladies and gentlemen. MacReady productions, in memory of the late Mr MacReady, have pleasure in presenting the romantic drama, *The Rose of Killarney*, by the late Mr John MacReady.'

A child appears, a little fair-haired girl, in what had long ago been a sweet black velvet dress. Wringing her hands she says, 'Oh, if my Daddy would only find a pretty wife, because my Mammy has gone to Heaven.' The packed room moans a soft, 'Aaaahh!' From behind the waterfall on the other side of the room, Joe-for-Yells appears, singing again the first two lines of 'Believe Me if All'. Ellen notes, 'Are they the only two lines he knows?' He takes the little girl by the hand and says, 'Never mind, my darling, we will find a lovely new Mammy for you. Look, who is that over there?' By the window, Emily-for-Laughs stands on a bench, and rubs her head as if washing her hair. 'Oh,' says the child, 'it is a beautiful lady.'

Ellen said to Thomas next morning, 'And it went on like that for about twenty minutes, it was awful. But everybody clapped like mad when it was over and I looked around and there inside the door clapping hardest of all was the Canon. Then she took out this medicine, and she called it "sycamore oil", from the leaves, she said, "of the biggest sycamore in the country", and she claimed it cured boils, and coughs and baldness. How could any one thing do all that?'

Thomas said, 'Look.' He pointed to the door of his cupboard; someone had tried – and failed – to force the lock. 'I'm going to come down here tonight,' he said. 'They've been using the side wall outside as a lavatory.'

At darkness, he walks to meet Ellen; about halfway between her lodgings and his Residence, he hears her footfall, stops, turns about, then falls in step with her.

'The Canon won't be there anyway,' he says. 'He's gone to a meeting over in Rosegreen, I met the housekeeper on the road. Of course, she's going to the show as well. Wouldn't miss it, she said.'

By the time they reach the village they have to push through the crowd, and by then all seats have been taken. Thomas stands there, all the authority of his school stripped from him. He and Ellen move to a standing position by the wall; Mrs MacReady avoids them, hugely busy with bottles for people around the room.

'Did you keep that stuff you bought?' whispers Thomas. 'I'm going to take it to a chemist.'

Emily-for-Laughs appears, and announces in her glum way, 'This evening we're going to begin with a medley of songs and jokes from –' she gestures dramatically towards the canvas backdrop – 'Joe. For. Yells.' So far, whispers Ellen to Thomas, Emily-for-Laughs has not smiled once.

Joe appears; tonight, ribbons flutter from the huge accordion, his flattened hair glistens; a red spotted cravat at his thin neck, he sings, switching lithely from verse to verse, pieces from many songs, all of which either Ellen or Thomas, comparing notes long afterwards, recognize, and thereby know that in most he has the words wrong. Then, after the applause, he begins to tell jokes.

'There was this woman. And she wasn't backward in

coming forward.' He makes an explicit gesture with his hands to shape a large and pointed bosom. He makes the gesture again, and amid the sporadic laughter he sees Ellen turn her head away. Joe-for-Yells prances over to her and, addressing the audience, his finger aimed almost in Ellen's face, chants loudly,

> *'My dearest dear and dearest monkey,*
> *Your face is like the Divil's donkey.*
> *With your awful hands and your cloven feet,*
> *You stole out of Hell while the Divil was asleep.'*

He raises his hand with a flourish and says, 'Yerra, give us a kiss, Missus.' Ellen pushes his hand away, and Joe-for-Yells, backing a step into the centre of the 'stage', makes the bosom-outlining gesture again and winks sideways at the audience.

The quick hush in the room suggests that Joe-for-Yells has gone too far. Something whisks past Ellen's shoulder and hits Joe, just on the ear beside a sideburn, and he staggers back against the canvas Alps, an urgent wheezing groan coming from the accordion; something hits him again, and splits his nose as he straightens up. He does not fall, but holds the accordion out in front of him. The flying right fist of Thomas flashes out a third time, but connects with the accordion. Women in the front benches squeal and lean away, and a man whom Ellen has seen with Mrs MacReady's group, attending to the horses but never appearing in the performances, comes out from behind the canvas, an unwieldy length of planking in his hand. He tries to reach beyond Joe-for-Yells to hit Thomas, but does not get quite that far. Thomas, gleaming in the lamplight, his face as grim and hard as a miner's at the coal-seam, tears forward now, picks up Joe-for-Yells who has fallen to his knees, pushes him to one side, drives towards the man with the plank and kicks him viciously on the knee. The people at the front of the room begin to back away: the men at the rear try to see what is happening; Mrs MacReady stands on Thomas's dais by the far window, shouting. Thomas hits the man with the plank twice, hard, in the face, and when the man falls to his knees, Thomas kicks him in the face, knocking him backwards. He then reaches down to Joe-for-Yells and, grabbing him by the hair, begins with great speed to drag him to the door. People scatter, clearing a pathway, and some run out under the night sky, as Thomas drags Joe-for-Yells across the little yard, out through the small gate, to the motor-waggon, hits him in the eye, very hard. A bystander says, 'Jayzes. Them travellers eats nearly nothin'. You'll kill him.'

Thomas turns to him, 'Are you looking for something, too?' The man backs off, 'No, Master, Jayzes. No, no.'

People pouring out of the school run back in again to get out of Thomas's way as he returns. The second man, much shorter than Joe-for-Yells, has risen to his feet, and Mrs MacReady is standing by him. Thomas picks the man almost right off the ground by the hair. The man screams, and Thomas runs him to the door and flings him into the yard. When he returns, Emily-for-Laughs comes at him, shouting, 'What are you after doing to my husband?' Thomas hits her with the flat of his hand across the cheek, and she staggers sideways. He grabs both Emily-for-Laughs and Mrs MacReady by the upper arms, and hauls them to the door. Two of the children run after them, weeping. It all takes place within two minutes.

Ellen comes forward as Thomas returns. He motions her with his hand and hisses, 'Don't. Move.' As he rips the canvas curtain from its moorings, little showers of plaster fall from the ceiling. Wrestling the painted canvas into a large, crackling ball, and gathering some other bits and pieces – a 'magic wand', with a star on top; the top hat of Joe-for-Yells; the black, patched Kinsale shawl – he goes to the door again and throws them out over the wall of the yard in the direction of the parked *caravan-serai*. Nobody has left the vicinity: all stand around with no wish to interfere. On his last ferocious errand Thomas picks up the accordion and, almost running, launches it hard against the motor-waggon where it crashes near the head of Joe-for-Yells.

'Master. Ah, Master for Jayzes' sake . . .' Another bystander appeals. Thomas walks to the man and raises his fist. This man also backs off.

Thomas stands on the doorstep of the school. 'All of you,' he shouts. 'Go. Home! Now! You. Mrs MacReady! I'll give you five minutes. If you're not out of here in five minutes, I'll set fire to the lot of you!' He goes inside the school.

The people begin to slope away. Some move a short distance from the school and stop to confer. Those still inside drift out: one or two say, 'Good-night now, Master, good-night, Miss,' to Ellen, who stands by the door. In the distance, the door of Hand's public house opens with a yellow glow.

'Those children are frightened,' Ellen remarks, and moves towards the MacReady *entourage*.

Thomas holds up a hand. 'Don't go. Near them.' She stops instantly.

Returning to the schoolroom, she picks up her basket diffidently, and, as Thomas, breathing hard, begins to tidy up, she moves over near him, strokes his arm briefly, slips out and walks quietly home through the darkness, avoiding the two or three little knots of people who stand around the village in dumbfounded conversation.

As she draws near Mrs Greege's house, she looks back and sees approaching from behind her the unsteady lights of a procession. Under the dark trees Ellen cannot be discerned, and the motor-waggon and the carts rumble slowly by her in the night. She watches them until they vanish into the dip at Hogan's Bend.

5

All next day, Thomas said not a friendly word, not to Ellen, not to any of the pupils, not even the ones he liked particularly. Systematically, he recovered the objects he had locked away. Standing on a chair, he measured with a ruler the plaster damage in the walls and ceiling; he tried to remove a 'medicine' stain from the white window-sill; he had not polished his shoes, nor had he shaved well.

He taught at his most impersonal. Taking a piece of light wire he said, 'Look at this. If you have a perfect geometric shape, then you can bend it into any other perfect geometric shape. In other words, a perfect square will also make a perfect rectangle, a rhomboid, or a perfect circle.'

After school, Ellen said, lingering at the doorway, 'I'm off, so. Are you finished yet?' and he shook his head, bending to the dais.

Next morning at ten o'clock, she heard raised voices, and rushed to the door. The Canon, standing in the porch, pecked his walking-cane hard on the floor; 'Mr Kane. That woman is a saint. I know it. She's . . . she's a . . . a scientist. A pure scientist. And a pure saint. She was here at my invitation. This is a very serious matter. I'll have you know.'

Thomas said, his voice louder too, 'I told you before, Canon Williams, that those people are dirty and danger-ous and I will not have them corrupting my school.'

The Canon replied, '*Your* school? I think you're forget-ting yourself, Mr Kane. *Your* school?'

Ellen, walking into view, said, 'Canon, I was there. I saw everything.'

'Oh, good morning, Miss. Good morning.' He raised his tall-crowned hat.

Ellen said, 'And it was very serious. I was here three nights of that show, and those people should not be touring the country.'

The men backed off in different directions. Ellen continued.

'Canon, I made notes of what was going on, and it was nothing short of disgraceful. They had every song wrong. Every song. Completely wrong. I was going to visit your house after school tomorrow. With my notes of what went on.'

Thomas folded his hands behind his back, but fidgeted with his fingers. The Canon half-turned away, then came back at Ellen.

'What kind of a Miss . . . a Miss – a "Miss Prim" objects to people getting the words of songs wrong?' The Canon stalked off.

On the road home, Ellen, her hand pumping up and down, spoke insistently to Thomas.

'I am going to tell him that teaching here is also about setting some standards, that we try to teach the children how to learn to live decent lives, and to say their prayers and to speak cleanly.' Her head bounced in emphasis. Thomas made no comment.

The Canon himself opened the door. As she sat down, he said, addressing a point above her head, 'I have a touch of lumbago. They tell me elderberry wine is very good for it? Do you know anything about it?'

'I'm afraid I don't, Canon.'

Hands trembling, Ellen took out her notebook, and stiffened her neck, held her head up high.

'Right. Now, Canon. Mrs MacReady.'

98

'Of course, my mother had it, like a martyr. To see that poor woman getting up out of a chair.'

'Canon, I made a note of what they were doing. In a school. Where people are supposed to be taught things the right way around.'

The Canon coughed. Then he coughed again, and made the bout of coughing last, until it rang as hollow as a false laugh.

He poked the dog with the toe of his boot, 'Out, Rusty, out, out. He's fourteen this year. Or is it fifteen, that'd make him, what, a hundred and five? One of the dog's years is seven of ours. Did you know that?'

Ellen said, 'Do you know that they damaged the school building and tried to break into cupboards?'

Canon Williams folded his arms tight across his chest and looked out of the window. Ellen pressed on.

'Did you know that one of them began to molest me in front of the whole parish?' Canon Jeremiah Williams stood up and turned away, his lips wet.

'Canon, you called me "Miss Prim" for worrying about the words of songs. What words would you like me to teach wrongly in *The Apostles' Creed*? Would you like me to teach, "I believe in God the Father Almighty", and leave out, for instance, "I believe in Jesus Christ His only Son our Lord"? Is that what you'd like?'

'You don't understand the country people. The past goes away here slowly. The people here need the bit of entertainment. Look at what they're used to. 'Tisn't that long ago since the Famine. And the Troubles. And the Irregulars. You're trying to say they have no past. They're entitled to their ballads. You should have joined in with the songs instead of correcting them. Miss Prim.'

'Canon Williams, I'm a teacher.'

'What songs anyway?' asked the Canon surlily.

'*The Wearing of the Green*.'

He turned round to face her, full of interest; 'How in

99

the name of God did they get that wrong?' he asked. He pursed his lips. 'Could you teach them the right words? If they came back?'

Ellen shook her head. 'I want your assurance as our School Manager that they will never be allowed back. The Department of Education wouldn't like it, would they? Grants and that, for school repairs.'

After a long silence, Ellen eventually rose, gathered her coat and her basket, and moved to the door. The Canon followed, and in the stained-glass porch, pointing to some withered plants in brass pots, said, 'Did you ever grow geraniums?' Then, he said, 'You're a lot older than your age. And you're not married at all, they tell me.' He had closed the door behind her before Ellen could blush.

Ellen stopped at Thomas Kane's gate, but found it closed; the house looked empty.

'Herbert,' said Leah. 'Do you know who I met on the street?' She often leaned against the jamb of his workroom door when the girls had gone to bed. 'Rina Morris. She was in her school uniform, she's a good deal taller than Ellen already. She has a year to go at Privet Hill, and then she says she doesn't know what she wants to do, but she doesn't want to teach.'

Herbert nodded. Leah went back to the kitchen and began to clear the table, and sing. Thinking of something else, she returned to Herbert's door and said, 'She's very observant, Ellen's sister. Do you know what she said to me? I asked her had they heard from Ellen, and she said the letters were getting full of the man Ellen is teaching with, that Kane man.'

'Ah, yes, yes,' said Herbert, in that facilitating tone of voice which always left Leah guessing whether he intended a comment, or was merely acknowledging her remarks.

=

Lent began, with Evening Devotions at the church on Wednesday and Sunday evenings, and Ellen declared to Thomas her intention of attending every one. 'It will get me out of Mrs Greege's. A bit of a nice sound in the evening, at least.'

In the silver glitter of the altar, and yellow light of the candles, and the high, raised gold of the starry monstrance, the *Tantum Ergo* echoed. On the frosty Sunday night, he waited outside the church, and said, 'I didn't bring the car, 'tis such a fine night. My God, the Canon can't sing.' She laughed.

He walked her to the top of the Norman motte-and-bailey near the church, and said, 'From here you can see the moon at its best,' which proved true; solemn and bright, it lit the surrounding countryside so clearly that houses and woods quite far away could be picked out.

'Who was that woman in the camel coat?' asked Ellen, as they walked down the slope.

'With the headscarf? Thin?'

'About four seats back from the altar-rails?' asked Ellen.

'I think,' said Thomas, 'she must be the new Doctor's wife.'

'She reminded me,' said Ellen, 'of my grandmother, she had the same cut about her. The famous Helena.'

Thomas said, 'What was she famous for?'

'She was a character,' replied Ellen. ''Twas from her I got the clothes, I mean the interest in them. She had a bombazine mourning skirt for my grandfather's funeral. A woman used to come to the house with a basket and a brown paper bag. Patterns. They had to open out the dining-table, all the leaves extended. Then the famous Helena climbed up on the table.'

Ellen did a mimicry.

'I will wear my black silk blouse. Will my emerald brooch be too much? Too frivolous for the dead? I can

101

never bear to have no colour anywhere.' Thomas laughed.

Ellen continued, 'So the dressmaker – and her mouth spiky with pins – said the custom in some places was for women in mourning to have a scarlet, or a cream silk waistband on the skirt, "on the inside, of course, Madam". And I wasn't let go to the funeral but I wore a nearly-best dress. I still have it, green organdie, with red flights of ribbons on the edges of the sleeves, made by that same Mrs Moody and her pins. And then when they all came home from the funeral, my grandmother, when no one could see, winked at me, and turned her back to the crowded room, and twisted her waistband inside out quickly, to show me the red lining. She had lovely long legs.'

Thomas laughed again. 'She sounds a character. Did you hear what they're saying about Mrs Doctor Hogan? That she has no luck because she wears green, very unlucky, and that that's why she and her husband are always arguing.'

Matters had altered in Thomas Kane's life. The silent watchers of the village behind their curtains saw and understood. His homeward stride had changed: now he paused to talk further to his new teacher, and if he did not always walk as far as her lodgings with her, he detained her outside his own gate with one more comment, or walked a few steps after her to call her back and say one last word. Mrs Greege observed Ellen Morris at close quarters, saw her switch between excitability and introspection, watched her walk out from the house most fine evenings and return flushed not long later. Did she meet someone? Mrs Greege, an accustomed and experienced watcher, did not need to ask, knowing that time would reveal everything, and in any case, she had a clear understanding of the nature of the inevitable. However, she did make one comment to test the waters of Ellen's affections.

'Didn't I tell you he was a hard man, the Master? They're all talking about him and the way he gave them MacReady men a hammering?'

She watched Ellen's colouring face carefully; 'Any man would do what the Master did. They were wrecking the school. The filth of them. They didn't respect anything and when that man offered me offence – well, what would any gentleman do except what the Master did?' But by now Mrs Greege knew her young lodger well enough to recognize the furrow of anxiety when it cut into Ellen's forehead.

On Friday, Thomas waved a letter excitedly after the postman had gone: he came to her classroom door laughing with pleasure.

c/o Mrs Nancy Heffernan,
Ballinagown.
Wednesday,
1st April 1925.

Dear Master Kane,

I am trying to find out about the famous Deanstown Brass and Reed Band that won the All-Ireland Championships in 1897 at the Royal Dublin Society Showgrounds in Balls Bridge.

How many men were in the band, and is it true that they played for King Edward the Seventh when he was over here as the Prince of Wales? And for the Count de Jarnac the day he left to become the French Ambassador over in London? The reason I am asking is that I am arranging a new series of monologues for my Summer Tour, and I want one to be about famous musicians who are now forgotten, on account of nostalgia, etc., etc., always such a potency, as I'm sure you know.

I am staying here at kind Mrs Heffernan's, having been infirm etc., for some weeks now, but recovering very well, thank you. Then I have to go off for about a month, to Dublin and that, but I'll be back in these parts in the first week in May. If you would do me the esteemed favour of writing to me, my address is usually, 2 Pavilion Terrace,

Patrick's Hill, Cork City, County Cork. I would be ever so grateful for the courtesy of an answer. Thanking you in advance,

> I remain, Sir,
> Yours truly,
> Val Vousden (Mr)

Thomas said, 'Well, well, well.'

Ellen had a letter too, from Father John Watson; no more than a note, on the white paper with the jet-black address;

> Dearest Ellen,
> I have only one copy of Thomas à Kempis, but when next I'm in Dublin, I'll get a copy especially for you. So sorry to have missed you. Your Mama tells me you are settling in well. When are we going to see you again?
> Yours in Christ,
> Father John

Thomas took the calendar from the wall under the clock and held it out at arm's length; he had left his spectacles in his coat pocket. She walked the length of his classroom.

'That new chalk. It is easy to break, if you lean on it the slightest bit.'

He said, 'Use shorter lengths. Break the stick in half.'

'Oh,' she said.

He asked, 'Are you going home the week-end?'

'I don't know yet.'

Ellen began to give Timmy Quinn little tasks to do. He handed out pencils; and knobs of plasticine – she encouraged each child to recognize the piece they had been using yesterday – and the small pictures that formed numbers. When she needed to demonstrate something such as height, and tell them feet and inches, she stood Timmy beside her. His hesitation at singing stopped; he yelled with the rest, and Ellen said to Thomas, 'I feel I'm making some progress. I wish I could say the same with the young McAuliffe girl.'

They had returned to the school twice, Mrs McAuliffe and her daughter. The child's demeanour had deteriorated; the mother's anguish increased. Ellen managed to pin Thomas down, and extracted from him at least a clear picture of the difficulty.

'The talk is,' Thomas said, in unease, 'that Sean McAuliffe got in with the wrong crowd. He had a job in the courthouse and of course it gave him plenty of information. And it was a bad time to have information. He wasn't the only one who disappeared.'

Ellen asked, 'Why won't anybody talk about it?'

He said, 'Your father would probably tell you why. People don't. I told you. They never talk about the truest things. Too dangerous.'

Then, dismissing it, he said, 'Look. This all came up two years ago. The same thing. Her brother asked me. The Sergeant said not to do a thing about it. And he said the Superintendent said the same.'

'And who will?'

Thomas said, 'Nobody.'

'But the poor misfortunate woman?'

Thomas shrugged his shoulders.

'Can't somebody? She can't get a widow's pension or anything?'

Repeatedly, Thomas pinched his lips with his hand. 'The people responsible are still around. I mean – very around. Local. If a body is found – well.' In finality he said, 'The gun isn't gone away in this country yet.'

Thomas scrubbed and scrubbed: the blacking had lined the pores and wrinkles of his hands, even if the range did glow. Next he explored each paper-wrapped item in the large cardboard box he took from the cupboard in the corner of the kitchen. In a clean basin of water, he washed each new cup and saucer and plate, polishing their thin gold edges. From a flat, rectangular parcel which had lain in a drawer for two years, he shook a clean white damask tablecloth: the creases had become so folded they seemed almost grubby. Spreading this cloth on the parlour table, having moved all his books and his writing-box to the sideboard, he set the table for two people. He checked a circular cake-tin; in it lay, like a trove, a dark, glistening thick fruitcake with almonds and currants on top, set like nuggets.

Ellen leafed through *The Leader*, to a large drawing of the plans for the new boat club at Athlunkard which would have 'a sanitary annexe and chamber'. *The Coliseum*: Wednesday, Thursday, Friday and Saturday, twice nightly at seven and nine o'clock: *Moon of Israel* by H. Rider Haggard. 'Greatest Drama Ever Screened. A critic reports: *The production has been made on such a truly stupendous scale as to leave us gasping with wonder and admiration. A Picture of Artistic Splendour, Magnificent and Enthralling. The Crossing of the Red Sea and the Drowning of Pharaoh and his hosts is but one of the thrills, Matinee Thursday and Saturday at 3.30 P.M.*'

A horse whinnied in the yard and a woman's voice called Mrs Greege. If people stood beneath the eaves talking, Ellen could hear every word.

'Ah, hallo,' said Mrs Greege. 'How's Ernestina today? Won't you come in out of the rain itself?'

Ellen stooped to the window. The girl in the pony trap wore a man's hat and coat.

'No, I have to hurry. Can Shamie come up to help? We've two pigs to kill. Would you like the puddings?'

'Of course he can, sure that'd be grand. Are you sure? Sure, a cup of tea out of your hand is no harm, on a day like this?'

'I can't, I can't.' The girl spoke briskly and in a loud voice.

'Aw,' said Mrs Greege, 'sure that's a shame, sure the man who made time made plenty of it.'

'Not for me. Is Wednesday all right?' asked Ernestina.

'Grand, grand. Tell me is it true you're getting an engine up there?'

Ernestina barked. 'Oh, my blessed brother. Whick! Whick!' she said to the pony, and hauled the reins around. 'Stay, boy! Stay, boy! And he says he's going to plough with it, did you ever hear the likes of that?'

At supper, Mrs Greege volunteered, 'There's a great row in that Stephenson house, she's entitled to half the place but if he marries she mightn't get it, and he's after one of them Merrigan girls. From a cottage.'

Hearing a loud noise passing by on the road outside, Ellen perked up. Mrs Greege noticed and said, 'There's more than the Master with a car, the new doctor has one.'

Ellen changed the subject. 'Do you know a Mrs McAuliffe at all?'

Mrs Greege replied, 'Everybody knows that old story, that woman has people tormented looking for pity.'

It was Thomas's car. After school he had driven to Kilgobnet to see Stewart the tailor, to collect the new suit. Stewart, a Scot, had been in the Army.

'I was lucky,' he said to Thomas. 'Most of the officers were tall men like yourself. Very hard to make clothes for a small man.'

Eight weeks had passed since the dank fog of the February morning through which Ellen first peered at Deanstown. Two days later, her life changed for ever. On a Thursday afternoon, just after her pupils had left, Thomas gave her a packet tied with a ribbon. It contained papers bequeathed him, he said, by an aunt: an account written both in letters, and in some unpublished articles, of the life of one of his ancestors, a man called Timothy Nash.

'He was a great-grand-uncle of my mother, he was a hedge-schoolmaster,' Thomas explained.

'But this is an heirloom?' said Ellen.

He smiled. Ellen could not forbear, and dipped into the pile there and then. The first document she opened, a brief 'history' of Nash attempted by Thomas's aunt (also a teacher), outlined the relevant history in general.

In the days of the Penal Laws, Catholicism was banned. Only a few priests were allowed to continue in their parishes: other priests went on the run, saying Mass across the country at Mass Rocks, convenient tables of natural stone set in remote places from which any arriving soldiers could be seen a long way off. No ordinations were permitted, therefore the Church secretly arranged for boys wishing to become priests to flee the country and be ordained in Irish Colleges abroad, such as Salamanca, or Louvain, or Paris, or the Irish College in Rome. Most of these men never returned, choosing instead, for safety's sake, to work in the country of their adoption; many thereafter annealed their angry souls by writing virulent and seditious tracts. A few, not as many as a hundred or so, came back in disguise to Ireland and went into hiding. They roamed the country, saying their secret Masses, and also, since all education was equally forbidden, teaching the Catholic people and their children. Under the trees and the hedgerows, in isolated smallholdings and broken farms, on the sides of the hills, they held lessons in religious instruction, and in Virgil and Plato and Horace.

Timothy Nash was one of those hedge-schoolmasters, and he taught for several years before going to England. For a detailed account of his early life, please refer to the other papers in this box which I have collected from my own father and my aunt, especially the words of Mr Nash himself. I will just give a short account here for the moment.

He was born in a house on the edge of the woods near Bruree, not far from the route of Sarsfield's Ride. His grandfather had been a well-off farmer whose family lost the farm under the Penal Laws to Timothy's uncle, who became a Protestant and added an 'e' to his name to indicate that he had changed his religion. The original family kept the dwelling house, however, where Timothy grew up, and it can be seen to this very day, a pleasing enough house.

The letter went on for several pages: Ellen folded it and put it away to await reawakening.

'Can I take this home?'

'Oh yes, 'tis yours,' Thomas said.

The packet's bulk filled her basket. A slightly closer scrutiny told her that one piece in particular seemed to have sources of all kinds in it, notes on books, translations and brown newspaper cuttings and official-looking documents. Ellen asked Thomas how much he knew about Timothy Nash: he could only offer that people said he 'carried the Nash looks'. They had, in any case, been a colourful family, the Nashes: one of them had been with Sarsfield at the Siege of Limerick, and may even have been on Sarsfield's Ride, or Hogan's Ride, some people called it, the famous midnight break led by the Rapparee, Galloping Hogan, to blow up the Williamite siege train at Ballyneety.

That night Ellen discovered among the papers, as she spread them out on her writing-table, a tiny folded lace handkerchief which smelt of ancient flowers: she read on:

Timothy was admired as a child for his intelligence and as a result the parish priest, a Father Tobin, took a special interest in the boy, and gave him lessons on the quiet. Timothy proved a very good student, and showed what Father Tobin called 'a true thirst for knowledge'. Father Tobin therefore approached another family in the next county who still had money and who were well-disposed towards educating Irish boys, and told them that he had in his parish a boy of unusual cleverness who would make a very good priest. This family put up the money and

Timothy, aged fourteen, was smuggled out of Janesborough port on a boat going to Spain, to join the Irish university in Salamanca.

Two nights after he left, obviously acting on the tip of some informer, soldiers called to his house and took away Timothy's father to the barracks in Kilmallock. He told them the boy had run away, and they tortured him but could not get any more information out of him. They hung him upside down and kept dipping his head in a bucket of water, holding him down long enough to make him think he was drowning. Still, he gave them no information. They let him go, and he returned home, walking, even though they had taken away his boots and never gave them back to him. Mr Nash (Senior) never recovered from this and his health grew worse. Timothy was never to see his father again. A year and two months later Mr Nash died, and when the word was brought to Timothy in Spain he did not react in the way the priests who had charge of him expected. He did not weep. Instead he flew into a terrible rage and had to be held down. It took, they said, two full-grown men to restrain him. He was a very tall young man.

Next day, Thomas said to her, 'I have to slip home early,' and he muttered words which sounded like, 'something to do. So would you ever lock the door and drop in the key to me?'

He greeted her at his house in a new suit and dazzling white shirt.

'Come in, come in.' She had only stood in the hallway once before; now he ushered her into the right, through a doorway to a room where a fire blazed, and a table, with white linen and cups and saucers, sparkled.

'Oh,' she said. 'Are you expecting somebody, I shouldn't be here?'

He smiled. 'I am, I am expecting somebody. Take off your coat.'

She blushed deeply, and with never a question, and with a meek air, sat in the chair he pulled out. He poured tea for her, and sliced cake, then sat opposite.

Desperately she blurted, 'Those papers you gave me, they're very interesting, but, they're your family, I can't keep them. I mean I'd love to read them and that, but they're your family belongings . . .'

He looked across the table. Her eyes diverted – to the ring of white stain made by a glass or a cup on the dark piano, which had one candlestick missing.

'I hope you'll be able to keep those papers,' he said. Pausing, he then continued, 'The reason I asked you here, was is there any chance you'd marry me?'

She put down the piece of cake she had picked up and looking at her plate said, in perhaps the quietest tone he or anyone had ever heard her use, 'There's every chance.'

'Does that mean you will?'

'It does.'

They said nothing more about it, or about anything else, for several moments.

Eventually, he said, 'Good,' then he said again, 'good.' He exhaled, and would not stop looking at her, no matter how she looked away.

'You'll have to understand,' she said, as if in sudden, new thought, 'this is whirlwind. I mean, I don't mean, I didn't expect and I didn't, I'm not surprised. But I know nothing at all about being a wife, and they'll all say you're an awful lot older than me.'

'They can say what they like,' he said. 'And anyway, what does anybody know before they get married? Sure everybody has to learn.'

'But. I've never even walked out with anybody much, I was always at home,' she said.

'Same here, I mean I wasn't always at home, but.'

'You've travelled, though,' she said. 'And you were out a lot in the world . . .'

'Is it too sudden for you?' Thomas asked.

'Oh, no, no, no.' Then she stopped. 'No.'

'I was at the hare coursing the other day,' he said, 'and

111

when I saw them let the dogs off, I thought. That's what I felt when I saw you first. I was like a dog racing out of a box to get to you before anyone else did.'

Ellen's eyes filled with tears.

They probably exchanged no more than a hundred words in the next half-hour or so. She finally said, 'I'll have to go. If anybody saw me come in, then I'd better go before dark.'

He said, 'I know.' Then, 'Hold on a minute.' He left the room: she heard him climb the wooden stairs, and return, something hidden in his large hand – a small, square, high-domed red box, of fading leather: he stood above her as she opened it, and she found inside a ring: small diamonds clustered inside a circlet of tiny pearls.

'It used to be my mother's and her mother's,' he said.

She put her hand to her mouth. 'I suppose – I shouldn't wear it yet. Until everybody has been told.'

'I suppose that's right.'

She sat in the chair, looking at the ring in the box, inspecting even the jeweller's name in gold lettering on the white satin. 'Kneeshaw's,' she said. 'The same as the clock in school.'

He said, 'Here,' and she looked up. He bent down and kissed her, and the force, not just the physical pressure of his face, left her gasping. When the kiss ended, he clasped her hand. She stood and put her head on his shoulder and said, 'I want to walk back, please, Thomas, I want to sit quietly by myself, and think quietly.'

'You're sure,' he asked, 'you won't change your mind?'

'Oh, no. Oh, no!'

Inside the door, as she put on her coat, he said, 'I have enough money for us to live very comfortably. I have, in the bank and the post office together, about . . .'

She shook her head. 'My mother will ask you anyway. I won't.'

Then she said, 'When – did you have in mind?'

He said, 'June. Just at the school holidays.'

'That's an ideal time. You mean this June?'

'Yes, this June.'

'What will they say?'

'No matter.'

She talked to herself the whole way home up the hill, in breathless gabble, with an occasional laugh.

'Oh, God, Lily,' she said merrily to Mrs Greege's niece in the kitchen, 'do you think your aunt would ever install a bathroom in this house?'

'She won't, Ma'am, nor hear of it, she thinks 'tis bad for one.'

The dying sun caught the tips of the trees in a distant hillside wood where a deer nuzzled a young green shoot at the base of a tree. The deer shook its head to free its teeth from a piece of heavy cloth inching a fraction above the surface.

Summer 1925

6

Mrs Greege herself called up the stairs to announce breakfast. Ellen clunked firmly down.

'So 'tis a big day for you, today?'

Thomas was calling for Ellen at twelve, then driving to Janesborough to meet the Morris family.

'And I have those black puddings you like.' Mrs Greege bent to the long scrubbed deal table. Ellen cocked a suspicious head at the good china: she did not have long to wait, not even until the second cup of tea.

'Will there be many coming to the wedding?'

Perhaps the white teapot picked up light and threw it on Mrs Greege's face, or perhaps she just sat in a shaft of morning sun; in any case the grey tufts of hair in her nostrils appeared as never so clearly before. Thomas said Mrs Greege planted them there deliberately, to give her face drama, or for the greater glory and honour of God. Today she wore a heavy skirt of grey twill: the geese hissed in the yard at some sudden agitation.

Ellen deflected: 'We haven't finished the lists yet; there's a lot of family.'

Mrs Greege served fat speckled quoits of black pudding – and angled again for an invitation.

'I suppose linen is always an acceptable wedding present?'

Thomas had said that he would with his own two hands throw Mrs Greege out of the church if she turned up.

'Or a bit of silver, it always brings good luck, Miss Kneeshaw was saying the other day? Kneeshaw's sell a lot of it for wedding presents, or a clock? But I suppose ye'll get plenty of clocks, the Master being such a man for keeping good time?'

A breeze stirred, then suddenly billowed the lace curtains; a shiny red-brown hen raced briefly across the yard to flee a hostile scurry, and wound to a halt clucking in dust and indignation; the yellow morning began to warm up – by noon it would be hot again today, beaten gold.

Ellen decided to collude with the conversational mood; 'Mrs Greege, who do you think will end up marrying us, the Canon or the Curate, they're fussing over which of them should do it?'

'What about that friend of yours, the priest?' Mrs Greege sawed at the soda bread. 'Lovely clothes.'

Ellen looked down, smoothed her blouse into her light skirt, with an expression on her face of not-quite-grasping Mrs Greege's compliment.

'D'you mean Father Watson? Sure, this is an old skirt, I have it five or six years; I always think the summertime is the only time you can wear yellow.'

Mrs Greege's skirt creased as she hoisted one long knee across the other. 'I had a cousin whose sister ran off with the man she was going to marry. Is that his name? Watson? What is he, is he an Englishman or something? No, I meant the underclothes.'

'He is not an Englishman, he's a Dublinman. What?' Ellen's tone sharpened as it dawned. 'The underclothes? What underclothes?'

It burst like a shell.

'But they were in a parcel,' she snapped. 'Addressed to me!'

Mrs Greege spoke in a flat tone. 'I opened it by mistake.'

Ellen picked up her knife and put it down again. 'And it was you who re-tied it? Is that what accounts for it?'

Not even Mrs Greege with her great gifts of obtuseness could mistake the chill in Ellen's face and voice.

'I suppose you could never let yourself be married by an Englishman, could you?'

'He's not an Englishman, he's a Dublinman, I said. And besides Father Watson is a Jesuit priest. If you don't mind?! Irregardless of that – what business had you opening that parcel? What else have you opened? That is an offence under the law.'

'If a parcel comes to my house, I am entitled to open it. That's the fact,' said Mrs Greege, tough of face and voice.

'It was addressed to me!'

'Care of me.'

'I'll report you.'

Mrs Greege handed Ellen the breadboard, with the fresh soda bread on it.

'What have you to be ashamed of? Sure you'll never wear them again anyway. 'Tis an overall you'll need to run a house.'

Ellen fell into the trap. 'But I'll still be teaching.'

Mrs Greege, having won the information she sought, snapped the trap shut. 'Hach! Isn't the Master the crafty man? Two salaries coming in, his and your own.'

Ellen, defeated, rebelled into monosyllabic answers, finished her breakfast, returned to her cool, dim room and washed her face again with the corner of a damp towel. She locked the door, and lay on the bed for five minutes: still an hour and a half before Thomas would call.

Had she looked out the window in the direction of the Castle, to the south-east, Ellen might even have seen the black figure speeding through the fields towards Thomas's house.

'Completely charmed, completely charmed.'

His hand worked like that of a man at a stiff water-pump. Thomas, stripped to the waist as he shaved in his

119

bare bedroom, had first caught sight of him in the mirror, then for about fifteen or twenty minutes watched him from the upstairs window, this extraordinary creature beetling down the morning fields from the Castle, the tails of his coat flying out behind him, a hat in one hand and, over the opposite shoulder, a kind of large leather satchel, which bounced off his hip as he hurried. Thomas sometimes counted half-aloud the strokes of the razor on his face: he paused in mid-count. As the man drew closer to the house and Thomas stepped back to one side of the window, lest he be seen watching, it became apparent that the man talked to himself all the time, and gestured, sometimes half-stopping to make a wider gesture. Where his white hair receded on the dome of his forehead, sweat shone in the light; the perspiration also made little rat's-tail curls at the other end of his hair, which had been allowed to grow into flowing locks. Patches of damp appeared at the neckband of his shirt which he wore without a collar and he had opened the buttons of his waistcoat: the thin legs of his stovepipe trousers clung and wrinkled.

'How on earth did you happen to come from across the fields?' Thomas asked with a smile.

Mr Val Vousden apologized with a little rueful face for the wind he had just broken in Thomas's hallway, and said, 'I am not accustomed to such exertion, and I ate rather well last night. That lovely black pudding. Somebody killed a pig.'

His voice see-sawed in a warm tune.

'I stayed with the O'Donnells and you know them, I'm sure, they certainly know you, so you know full well what their hospitality is like, and it was their suggestion to come across the fields, and it was grand with me, the morning is when I compose.'

During the night, a full bladder had awakened Thomas and he decided to go downstairs and outside. True darkness had never fallen; the wall of the house still had some heat to his touch. The leaves of the sycamore rustled above his head.

'Would you like a cup of tea or something, you're an early bird?'

Val Vousden stepped out of the hallway again, into the sunlight, and with another tiny, quick slap-wheeze of escaping wind, 'Oh, pardon me again,' sat on the green iron-and-wood garden seat under the bay window, easing his hands with downward strokes along the shins of his trousers, while through the window came the noise of cups and cupboards and the clank of a kettle's lid. Val Vousden raised his nose and sniffed, and said in a loud voice, 'Honeysuckle,' and to this remark, Thomas's voice called, 'What was that you said?'

He repeated, 'Honeysuckle. Or is it eglantine?' and from within, in polite momentum, 'Oh, yes.'

Thomas emerged through the hall-door, a cup and saucer steadied gingerly in one hand, in the other a plate with a small stack of thick-sliced bread and butter and jam.

'Oh, gracious,' said Val Vousden. Thomas went back to get his own breakfast, and Val Vousden shuffled along the seat to make room. The two men sat in the sunlight eating, and then leaning forward and down almost simultaneously, to pick up the heavy blue-banded cups resting in their saucers on the gravel at their feet.

'I. Fmlst.' Val Vousden swallowed a bite suckingly, and began again. 'I fmlsts say. I.' He sprayed some crumbs. 'Must say.' More crumbs and a swallow. 'How much I enjoyed. Our correspondence. You write a great letter, Master.'

Thomas coughed. 'I don't think I'm a hundred per cent clear. On what you want.' He blew out his cheeks, puffing after a mouthful of tea. 'Is it that you want to start the band up again? They didn't play for the Prince of Wales, by the way. And that story of them – ˙ coughs ˙ – playing for the Comte de Jarnac?˙

Val Vousden pointed wordlessly with a finger at the privet bush in front of them where a dewed cobweb glistened like a crystal snood.

Thomas paused and took it in, nodding and continuing.

'What they did was. They played at the Union Farming Society Show, and it so happened it was the last one where the Comte de Jarnac was the President, because he left not long after that.' Thomas flicked crumbs and jam from his fingers fussily. 'A thrush nested in that bush last year, and she used to dive at me every morning I came out. I had to start using the back door.'

'No, I didn't think at all about restarting the band,' said Val Vousden, 'but what a lovely idea. I only wanted to write a recitation about an old musician who retires, and who comes out of retirement for one last glorious marching day.'

Thomas said, 'I have a few bits and pieces for you. An old programme, and a thing from the newspapers, and there's something one of the bandsmen wrote. Now there is a fellow, he's down there in Boss Glen. Called Egan. He played in the old band. He was in the Munster Fusiliers.'

Val Vousden traced his finger along the rim of his still-steaming cup and said vigorously, 'Oh, imperial echoes. Imperial echoes. I remember the military bands well when I was a child, I was always following them.' He started. 'Oh, I suppose, of course, maybe I shouldn't . . . Be talking about the military to yourself, Sir.'

Thomas smiled. 'Oh, nonsense, man, nonsense, there's nothing as good as a military band, not at all.' He smiled again. 'Not at all.'

Val Vousden said, 'This man, Egan?'

'Now he'd know a lot,' said Thomas, 'you see, several of them were killed, the Somme and Ypres and places. I had an uncle killed there myself. But I know for example that some of the Band's uniforms are still around, I don't know who has them, or even if they're still more or less intact.' He rose and went indoors. 'I'll get you those papers.'

Val Vousden stuffed them carefully in his satchel and shook hands as if with an emperor.

The postman came.

Dear Mr Kane,
Is it true? They are saying you are great with that new teacher. Say that it isn't true. I have been asking you to leave a message for me on your pew in the church, and then I'll have the courage to meet you. You know my feelings. Have you any feelings for me? If you met me you would have, but I can't make the arrangements, it is the man has to do that. Please. Please.

Your Admirer

P.S. I feel like tearing her eyes out if it's at all true.

Ernestina and Cyril Stephenson agreed that the best day might be Sunday, 26th July.

'Rory will be here, and will Constance be home? In which case, we haven't much time, we'll have to start writing soon. Mama,' continued Ernestina, 'always said politeness demanded eight weeks before a summer party, twelve in the winter.'

Her brother said, 'Yes. Yes.'

'Cyril, you are certainly not going to invite that bloody little domestic of yours, that shop-girl or whatever she is.'

'You shouldn't swear.' Cyril yawned.

'I'll do more than swear if you try that on. That little bitch,' she said. 'If we hadn't Mrs Cullen coming in every day, she'd be washing your bloody shirts by now. That's how they connive, those dirty little Roman Catholics. And don't you dare sell that bloody yearling either without telling me.'

Cyril yawned again. 'We have too much meat,' he said. 'I knew we should only have killed one beast. We'll soon have no more left to kill.'

Ernestina snapped, 'Well, we have to kill our own, we owe the butcher too big a bill. And when are you going to fix the greenhouse, you'll have to do it before we have any party?'

Cyril whistled a tune.

'You said ages ago you'd fix it. If it rains what'll we do?'

'That sky. It won't rain for a month. Anyway, you can't fix that glass until the laburnum is cut back.'

'I'm not touching that laburnum! You cut down the one in the yard.'

'It was poisoning the horses.'

A brown terrier ran across the lawn and disappeared behind the high brick wall, yapping. Ernestina leaned forward and opened the window wide. Cyril toyed with a chess-piece from a board that had several of the pawns missing. A light breeze through the window stirred the yellowing newspapers on the chair.

Ellen jumped with relief when she heard the car, and stooping to the low window, saw the lovely brass lamps, like two wonderful ancient helmets. Thomas had taken the hood down. Ellen ran downstairs. She never replied when Mrs Greege called out, 'Aren't you going to ask the Master in?'

Ellen climbed into the car, even though he had begun to clamber out of the other door. Up the road, beyond Hogan's Bend, he stopped the car to listen to the underclothes story.

'From now on,' he summarized, 'and 'tis only for a few weeks, try and have every parcel sent to the school.'

Ellen put her arm in his, and placed her head upon her

new favourite resting-place, the top of Thomas's arm, the broadest, hardest part, just beneath his shoulder.

'I get very confused.' She pressed her head tighter to him.

Children gathered around the car, haw-ing their breath to make condensation on the brass lamps; Ellen's father opened the door and came to the front of the top step, beaming. In the hallway deep behind him, a figure moved.

'This is him, Dada,' said Ellen, as she stood with Thomas on the street, looking up.

'Now, how are you?' said Bob Morris, as pleasant as ever. He held his hand out to Thomas, and turned to Ellen, saying, 'No wonder you were hiding him from us, an ugly man like that.' All laughed.

'Come in. Come in.' He called to his wife. 'Mama! Mama!'

Nobody moved. They stood in shadow, as the sun had not yet westered sufficiently to reach their side of the square.

'And you drove in?' he asked.

'No, we walked,' said Ellen, and they laughed again.

'Come in. Come in,' said her father again.

Ellen's mother came forward, making actions as if she had just taken off an apron, which she had not; and then other gestures to fix her perfectly all right hair.

'Mama, this is Thomas.'

May stepped forward, then back.

'Well, I declare to goodness. Let us have a look at you. You're very welcome to our house.' She spoke emphatically, and then began to blush – from the neck up, and it spread, and spread, and spread, until it reached her under-chin, then her veined cheeks, and then her forehead. She shook Thomas's hand; then stumbled backwards and led the way in. 'Jim and Rina are both out, they'll be in in a little while, are you famished with the hunger, isn't the weather lovely, if it keeps up like this for the wedding we'll all be blessed.'

'Father Watson left a note,' said May to Ellen. 'He's gone to Dublin for his annual Retreat, you know, Rathfarnham Castle.'

Thomas admired the stuffed fox in the glass case, and as he put his hat without forwardness on the pegs of the hallstand, enquired politely as to the identity of the powerful lady in the large studio photograph – Ellen's great-grandmother, Bob Morris's grandmother, an eagle of a woman, portrayed beside a pillar with ivy. May led the way to the drawing-room, where the piano gleamed and the smell of furniture polish rose warmly with the sun's heat. Tall cream plumes of pampas grass, and a large basin of pinecones, filled the fireplace, now empty for the summer.

'I hope you don't mind my asking,' said Bob Morris, 'but is that a Harris tweed by any chance?'

Thomas, looking down, plucked the cuff of his rust jacket.

'It is actually.'

'Did you offer the man a drink, Robert?' said May. 'You'll think we have no manners at all,' she said to Thomas.

'I'll get it, Mama,' said Ellen, and to Thomas, 'we have Locke's, or a Paddy.'

'Or some of that good Midleton whiskey, give him some of that, that's very good altogether,' said Bob. 'D'you know you can't get Harris tweed in this city. They used to bring it in, but you can't get it for love nor money. And 'tis a thing you have for the rest of your life.'

May had already left a glass jug of clear water on the tray, and Ellen brought it to Thomas's chair, along with the round heavy tumbler.

'Dada?' she asked.

'I will, girl, special occasion.'

'I got this in Glasgow,' said Thomas, again inspecting his sleeve.

'Glasgow?' said May. 'Imagine! Ellen said you're very travelled.'

Ellen perched on the wide arm of her father's chair. The four people sat disposed around the room, and the sunlight caught as yet just one corner, where a tall black lacquer screen, inlaid with mother-of-pearl birds, stood behind an empty chair. Thomas crossed his long legs.

'How old is this house, as a matter of interest?'

Ellen looked at her father, and Bob responded with practised knowledge.

'This house was built by the grandfather of that lady in the picture in the hall, he'd be my great-great-grandfather; he'd be what? Three greats to Ellie here. He was a Morris from over Carlow direction, they had mills and they came here when paper started to come into real demand. Now he was born in 1725, two hundred years ago this year, he put his date of birth on the deeds of this house, and he bought the site, this was green fields –'

'Imagine,' said May.

'– and he built the place in 1750; it took two and half years, and d'you know, the roof has never needed a bit of repair, and still doesn't; there was workmanship for you. And not a bit of rot, or a thing.'

'Well, well,' said Thomas in approval.

'But that's not the most surprising thing,' Bob continued. 'The most surprising thing of all is the age of the man when he built it, he was only twenty-five years old.'

'Imagine,' said May. 'Of course they were Protestants. The family converted afterwards.' She always affirmed religious good news with a little bob of her head.

'He did a lot for a man his age,' said Thomas.

'Who's that?' sang out May as the front door opened.

'Rina,' said Ellen.

'My younger daughter, Catherine. She arranged that,' said May, pointing to a bowl of roses.

'Very nice,' said Thomas, 'very nice. How old is – Catherine – Rina?'

'Seventeen,' said May.

Thomas got up and they shook hands, Rina's gloves half-on, half-off. She sat down, blushing.

'Did you see any sign at all of Jim?' asked her mother.

'He'll be here,' said Bob; 'he said it when he was going out.'

'But will Mary Rose be with him, that's what I want to know. I don't know how many we're to cater for?' said May.

'I always say 'tis easy to take a name out of the pot again once you have it in in the first place,' said Bob.

May opened tall double doors and they moved to the dining-room.

'I have to keep those blinds down all this summer, or that table would fade entirely,' said May as they sat.

A leg of cold ham had been carved into huge slices, which lay on a willow pattern dish in the centre of the long table.

'Now those napkins were Ellen's grandmother's; she bought them in Vienna. Imagine,' said May. 'Now, d'you like cold chicken or cold turkey or cold goose with your ham?'

Glass shell-shaped dishes of preserves paraded down the tablecloth. 'I pickle my own apricots,' said May. 'There's a man out there in Ballysimon, he bought a very old house, Bob knows him, and he has an apricot orchard, imagine, and we go out there every August and come back with baskets. The plums are our own, look you can see them there under the blind, on that far wall, reams of them.'

Thomas lowered his head and shoulders, and gazed

politely, then turned back to the table and, with the tentative decisiveness of good manners, chose cold goose and cold turkey, and some of the apricot and plum preserve, then accepted the large bowl of soft green lettuce leaves with sliced tomatoes and sliced hardboiled eggs.

'Hallo, I'm sorry I'm late.' A red head poked around the door, followed by a cheerful face. Thomas rose and shook hands across the width of the table, amid smiles.

'Are you on your own?' said May.

Jim sat down, and said, 'She couldn't, she had to help her aunt or something, their stall.'

May said aside to Thomas, 'We have our Bazaar tomorrow, for the church: 'tis a pity you can't stay for it.'

'Ach,' said Bob, 'the man must have seen a hundred bazaars.'

Ellen said to Thomas in front of Jim, 'He won't tell us whether it's serious with Mary Rose, but he's been walking her out for the past four years.'

Jim laughed and said, 'The less you know.'

Cakes had been both baked and bought, and scones, and cream for the tea, and home-made jam and apple jelly. Thomas's performance at the table drew admiring comment from his prospective mother-in-law, 'There's nothing like a man who likes his food.'

He amused them with stories of the neighbours in Deanstown, and made Ellen's father laugh more than once with descriptions of the children's remarks in school – how, for instance, he could not get one little boy to come into school on time. Finally when he asked him why he was late, this child, the youngest of a large and very poor family, simply stammered, 'H-ha-h-had I a spoon, had I?' Another, when sent to the pump to wash his face, inevitably returned with what Thomas called 'a high-water mark on his forehead', and when asked why he didn't wash all his face, replied that his shirt-tail would 'only reach so far up'.

'D'you know what?' said Ellen to Thomas, as they walked slowly to Leah's house later. 'You subdued Mama. She was. No, not frightened exactly. In awe, I suppose. And as for Dada, well – I never saw him like that before. So excited.'

'You'll come back, won't you,' asked May, 'and have a cup of tea out of your hand before you go?'

Leah, when introduced to Thomas, held on to his hand after the handshake, and looked at Ellen, saying over and over, 'My, my. My, my.'

After that initial response, Leah's restraint took Ellen aback a little. The girls giggled and ran off; then the three of them sat and talked for a little less than an hour, then Leah had to shoo them out because it was the Sabbath and she had to prepare the house. In the hallway – Thomas had gone to the bathroom – Ellen whispered, 'But – do you like him?'

'Yes, yes, of course. Such a big man, so distinguished, and you are really going to marry him? This is dramatic news, dramatic. Your letter. I was amazed.'

Thomas returned at the moment observing that they must persuade the Canon to put running water and electricity into the house.

'Now, you have to come back soon and meet Herbert, my husband,' said Leah. 'He's out at his prayers.'

Ellen said, 'We'll have to be here several more times before the wedding, anyway, there's so much to do.'

Late on Saturday afternoon, Ellen travelled with Thomas in the car to the outskirts of the city, kissed him goodbye at a place where nobody could see them.

'I meant to tell you,' he said. 'I had a dream about you last night.'

'Aaah?' she said.

'I dreamt. Do you know that cat on the marmalade jar? The one that sits looking in at the fire in a lovely homely room? I dreamt that we were sitting together on the sofa behind the cat.'

In the evening sunshine Ellen walked the mile or so back to Brunswick Square.

'What are you doing?'

Rina lay on the drawing-room floor copying an address from an American magazine. 'Sending away for something.'

The *Ladies' Home Journal* offered a Hickory Shadow Skirt. 'THOSE FRESH CRISP LITTLE VACATION FROCKS – keep them smooth and wrinkle-free! The Hickory Shadow Skirt of cool lingerie fabric, and light, fine rubber. It prevents body warmth and perspiration from reaching your dress. Wrinkleproofs and shadowproofs perfectly. In flesh color. As low as $1.50.' (The item never arrived: her father said it fell over the side of the ship into the Atlantic and was floating away somewhere near the Azores.)

'You missed the Leonards,' said Rina. 'They brought that.' A brown paper parcel, large and flat and tied with strong white twine, lay on the table. 'Mama says 'tis sure to be linen.' At which Ellen moaned.

'Mama says you can never have enough linen,' said Rina.

Ellen sat at the piano and played a halting piece of minuet.

'Where's everyone?' She turned on the piano stool and twirled the full three hundred and sixty degrees.

That night, Leah said to Herbert, 'But it is all very fast. "Marry in haste, repent at leisure." I don't know, Herbert.'

'She's very intelligent, Ellen is.'

'Yes, but is her heart intelligent? I mean – too much determination can be a bad thing too, and she seems very determined, but she has no experience of the world at all, has she? What do you think, my dear?'

Herbert put down what he was doing. 'If Ellen wasn't a teacher. Say if she was something else. Say she – what? Say she painted pictures or something? What would she paint? I often ask myself that about other people. What would they paint?'

'Not big bright colours, like I would,' said Leah.

'No, no.' Herbert mused on.

'Very small and neat? Is that what you mean?'

Herbert said, 'I think they might surprise us. I think they'd be neat, yes, but I think they might be more baby-ish than we think.'

'Should I talk to her, Herbert? I'm uneasy.'

'No harm in writing to her. I mean. Behind that very – that very organized exterior of hers, I mean?'

Leah said, 'That's what worries me. I know she's very warm, but she's very cold as well, and I think she's doing this without taking everything into consideration. I mean, he's an awful lot older than her.'

When Thomas met the bus next evening, he suggested a drive and a walk. Where the river forks two miles from Deanstown, people gather and sit on the wooden seat on summer evenings, when the senior men of the farms and the cottages discuss the county's prospects in the championships, while watching the hardy boys from the farms cavort in the cool water after a day's dusty work. On occasions, one of the men brings a fiddle, someone else a deck of cards. Tonight, the old makeshift seat beneath the willows, completely obscured from view – except from the water or the woods on the far bank – was empty: a football match in the next village had attracted everyone. Thomas glissed a flat stone along the water, one-two-three-four, then it died.

Private in the remote open air, they held hands, they leaned shoulders. Ellen wore a cream dress and took off her short coat, too warm, turned it inside out and folded it to make a cushion on the wooden seat. Thomas kissed her at dusk and kissed her again, and then, with no objection from Ellen, he put a hand up under her loose clothes and quite easily felt her – all over, thighs, knees, hips. His hand came to rest for some time, flat like an offering, on the plain of her stomach just beneath her waist, and with tenderness covered the soft plateau completely. Ellen looked straight ahead, at the dark sluggish water of the river, at the swirling reeds. Her face seemed grim; an expression she wore when concentrating, or requiring a moment of courage. She turned her face inwards to Thomas's lapels, and just once more, very slowly, those strong fingers, that hard palm, swept slowly over her again. Raising her head and looking out across the dark water and sedges, Ellen sat perfectly still, neither accommodating nor impeding, blinking very fast at first, and then closing her eyes, and swallowing like an excited child.

She added one prayer at bedtime, not habitual in her repertoire, except after her Confession on the first Saturday of every month. 'O, my God, I am heartily sorry for having offended Thee. And I detest my sins most sincerely, for I have sinned exceedingly. In Thought, Word and Deed. Through my fault. Through my own Fault. Through my own Most Grievous Fault. Therefore I beseech. The Blessed Mary Ever Virgin. Blessed Michael the Archangel. Blessed John the Baptist. The Holy Apostles Peter and Paul, and all the Saints. To pray for me to the Lord Our God. Amen.'

As the weeks passed by, they stayed behind in the school, eating sandwiches, drinking tea from a flask, or red lemonade from the village shop. Ellen made her final bridal lists, and Thomas enlightened her with snippets from the newspapers, local and national.

JUNE ROSES

June has come. The first day, at all events, brought us a little sunshine. Hope it will continue and that straw hats will be more in evidence than umbrellas. The latter, though not invented by an Irishman, suits our Irish climate. After the initial miraculous weather, cold bitter showers and lowering skies marked the end of May. Soft, fleecy, wool-hued clouds hovered to the north and north-west. The nip in the air reminded us that icebergs were breaking up, perhaps, in the Gulf Stream.

'Icebergs?' said Ellen. 'As my mother would say' – mimicking May Morris's accent perfectly, 'imagine.'

O, HOW THE WHEEL BECOMES IT

The Whitsuntide demand for Raleighs has exceeded all previous records. It is a modest estimate that the Whitsuntide holiday saw not less than twenty thousand fresh Raleigh bicycles and their riders on the road.

When she first mentioned that her grandmother had a household ledger, Thomas told Ellen that he would buy her one too – when they went to London on their honeymoon. In anticipation she clipped various pieces – domestic use, recipes, gardening or cleaning tips, advertisements, or simply items of interest.

Fancy! A man still living who saw the great Napoleon. And a hardy old fellow for his 140 years. He is Haji Tahir, an Arab, born at Mecca, who went to Palestine

134

in the year 1799, at the age of 14, when he saw 'Bony' who was then operating on the Syrian coast.

* * *

BUTTER! BUTTER! BUTTER!
We are open to purchase this Season as usual large quantities of Unsalted Butter at Highest Market prices. Butter will be bought on Thursdays, Fridays and Saturdays throughout the Season. Highest prices will also be paid for Fresh, Clean Eggs. Edward Ryan & Son, Ltd, Brewery Stores, Thurles.

Deanstown,
Friday.

My dearest Leah,
Thank you for your long letter. The weather here is still lovely. Please God it will keep.

You will be pleased to know that your letter did make me 'think again' – although it would be a bit late in the day to change my mind! Not that I want to.

Yes, it is 'a plunge' – and 'a whirlwind romance', as you say. But without any doubt Thomas *seems* very good to me (as your letter generously said) and also *fond* of me, and I have to take things for how they affect me. What other, fuller knowledge do folk have? Although you didn't say it, you might have been wondering how much I knew about him before deciding to give him the rest of my life. The only thing I can say is – what can anyone know about anyone else?

I think I must have exaggerated to you in my letter about that fight with those travelling show people. Yes, I did ask myself – Was this a very violent man I had agreed to marry? But as you know, Dada had told me that Thomas never got involved in anything bad after the Troubles, and even then he left the Flying Column in the height of things, which I think showed great courage. When he attacked those show people Thomas was provoked, and

135

he was nearly even challenged to fight; those people would have stopped at nothing, and they had ruined the place, and I must say that I was very proud of the way he dealt with it. Even though I think any woman would be frightened of how strong he was with his fists, I don't think he'd ever be that angry with me, or use violence towards me.

I know you think I'm probably too young to be getting married, or that this is too short a courtship. But isn't that what married people always say to those who are getting married?

Dear Leah, I'm only teasing you. Naturally enough, though, I have worries, but I feel that I can get enough of my own way with Thomas. He makes me feel very good, it is not like marrying a man my own age who has still to grow up. He says that this is what he always wanted, a wife he can devote his full attention to, so that really I have to do very little, it will all just happen, which is lovely for me.

The thing I find, no matter what you say about my not having walked out with enough fellows so far, is that it seems very easy to get men to do what you want in any case, and Thomas is always around me, always near me. The other odd thing is that I don't find anything at all strange in the notion of sleeping in the same bed with a man, even though I hated it whenever we had visitors at home and Rina and I had to share. Maybe I'm not shy, or something.

Leah, soon I'll be 'Mrs Thomas Kane'. Imagine! I keep practising the name, and wondering what it will sound like when people say it to me, although around here I suppose they'll only call me 'Mrs' or 'Ma'am', or 'The Mistress'. You must write to me immediately after I'm married, so that I can see what the name looks like on an envelope!

Will the girls be coming to the wedding after all? Your letter never said. Because I need to teach them how to stand a little back from me at the altar.

I have lots more things to tell you, only I haven't the time now, as Thomas says we have to go and look at some furniture. I won't let him buy a thing without my seeing it first.

Thank you again, dear Leah, for your dear sweet letter,

and I didn't take offence. You have always meant well towards me.

Your affectionate friend,
Ellen

On her last visit to the city before the wedding, Ellen had a conversation with Father Watson.

'Have you prayed for guidance?'

'Oh, Father John, endlessly.'

'Well, if you have no doubts?'

'Father, when you meet him, you'll see.'

They sat in the grounds of the Jesuit Provincial House.

'Have you doubts, Father? About me, I mean? As a candidate for marriage?'

He thought.

'Have you, Father John?'

'There's one thing, my dear.' He hesitated, then hastened. 'But I may be wrong!'

'Oh, Father?!'

'No, no, don't get alarmed, more alerted is what I mean you to be, dear Ellen.'

As she reported to Bob later, few people could be as thoughtful and kind as John Watson when he tried.

'What crossed my mind, Ellen, was this. You recall that you told me about this – travelling show, what was it?'

'Oh, I know what you're going to say, I know what you're going to say! Thomas's violence, isn't it?'

'No, no, my dear, not as simple as that. Just – well, we've had very odd, very hard times in this country. I get told strange things on the few occasions I hear Confession, morbid things. But if you're sure.'

'Father John!' Ellen turned to face him. 'You're not jealous or something?' For a second before he laughed, just for a second, no more than that, the priest looked away. When he turned back, he asked, 'And how's your Mama enjoying the preparations? She must be very excited?'

137

7

There seemed to be ribbons everywhere – the handlebars of the bicycles, the lamps on Thomas's car, on the hats of the girls. A young teacher, from Ellen's Training College class (she too was to marry a teacher) chased a red ribbon that had fallen and was being swept by the breeze across the yard of the church, and she tied it to the straps of her handbag and everybody laughed. Men jingled the coins in their trouser pockets; smiling, they held out closed fists to the children and made them prise open the big knuckles to find the sixpence inside. Little Rachel clung to Herbert's legs, and although she smiled up, and even chatted, would not come out. Mrs Martin Burke buttonholed May Morris in the porch, and the two women had a wonderful, competitive conversation about whom they knew and to whom they were related.

One of the Kane boys had brought a small handbell, and sitting on the saddle of his bicycle outside the church gate, under the trees, rang it like a giddy town crier to get the procession started. Ill Uncle Denis, not seen at a family function for something like seventeen years, had a complexion like prison pallor. The three priests gleamed together as they accepted the envelopes of the bride's family.

Pushed by a dozen playful hands, the car lurched forward: Thomas had had the foresight to reverse into the church gateway. Ellen clung to her hat and veil with one hand, her bouquet with the other, and everyone squealed as the cheering men finally slapped the back of the departing car.

Along the road, people stood waiting at the doors of

138

their houses; they smiled and waved, and relished a full, uninhibited stare. Some had slipped into the back of the church to watch the ceremony, and they now stood on the hilltop gazing down. Even when the parade of two motor-cars, many, many bicycles and two pony-drawn traps went out of sight into the tunnel of thick hedges down at Hogan's Bend, those up at the church could still hear the cheering, and the halloo-ing, and the singing, and the merriment of the handbell. Then the sound freshened again as the road swung back into view, and the colours, not yet so far away, could be seen: the purple, the bright green, the blues and the reds, and white.

Four of Thomas's brothers rode their bicycles along beside the car like furiously happy outriders, on a day so hot and sunny that the road threw up dust which puffed every time a brother hit the shiny paintwork with his cap. In a pony and trap behind – the car only held two, Thomas and Ellen – came the bridesmaid and best man: Rina and Thomas's brother Arthur, back from America for the wedding, and his sister Margaret, who did not want to be called a Matron of Honour, so could hardly decide whether she was an attendant or not. The Morrises had hired the car of the talkative driver, and Father Watson travelled with them: Canon Williams and the Curate would cycle.

Thomas stopped at the crossroads to accept the greetings of a line of carts on the way home from the creamery; they had all been at the village pump filling their empty churns with water for the livestock: in the ferocious heatwave, many streams had gone dry: even a famous well was threatened. The men in their waistcoats and collarless shirts, some even wearing overcoats notwithstanding the sun, raised their caps to Ellen, and said, 'Well, now,' their indelicate teeth beaming and gapped.

In this vivacity, among the men who got down and crowded around the car, nobody took much notice of a walking vagrant, a strong, thickset and quick man. As ten farmers and their labouring-men shook hands with Thomas and Ellen – 'I hope you'll have all luck, Master. And yourself, Ma'am' – this hobo, unseen until too late, reached in towards Ellen's bosom and twisted and wrenched away without any difficulty the gold cross and chain she was wearing, and then he ran.

Too late she called out, or, rather, too late Thomas heard her in all the din: the man was gone.

'Thomas! Look!' she cried, pawing the top of her breast-bone, and looking around her awry, but Thomas turned too slowly from his pleasant outreached handshaking, and Ellen, although half-rising from the car, did not know the man nearest her, and could not ask him by name to follow the tramp.

She pointed with her finger, and Thomas, not compre-hending, asked, 'Who is it?' Everybody looked, but nobody moved.

'Thomas, Thomas! He has my cross! My good cross! He's after whipping it off me!'

'Who? Who?' asked somebody else, but another horse and cart drew up outside, further cutting off any quick pursuit.

'That man, the one running, he whipped off my cross, Aunt Bridge's cross!' cried Ellen, pointing. The cross and chain had been in the family for at least a century, perhaps two. Aunt Bridge, still hale, was coming along to the wedding later. 'She says she's seventy-five,' in Ellen's words: 'You could add five years to that and not be uncomfortable.'

Thomas had admired the crucifix: knew how old it must be: the cross had a Penal Laws motif, Christ on one side, Mary on the other, comprehensive worship in one image, to be treasured in the days when the next Mass might be six months away, and then only out on a secret hillside.

Thomas started the engine. The running tramp, hearing,

140

looked back, and rushing to the demesne wall, climbed into the fields and disappeared. Ellen should have cried out more significantly. Thomas should have taken more notice of the short outcry she did make. Between them it fell: nobody, upon later enquiry, knew the tramp, or had ever seen him before.

Earlier at the altar of the church Canon Jeremiah Williams celebrated Nuptial Mass, assisted by the Curate and Father John Watson. Thomas wore a dark grey suit, his head held as correct as an officer, bowing only to put the ring on Ellen's finger: both looking straight ahead exemplarily.

Intoning the prayers with the Canon, John Watson's long hands fingered the Missal as if it were sheets of music.

'You know how much I like him,' said Ellen to Thomas, 'but he has little oddities about him. He never bought me a cup of tea in my life. I know priests have no money, but . . .'

She said nothing about a certain lack of personal fastidiousness, Father John's ears, and clothes, not always what they might be, the opposite of the things she liked so much in Thomas and unusual too in a countryman.

When Ellen fell in love with Thomas, she described the intensity to only one person – surprisingly not Leah. Obviously she did not go into detail; not even to her notebook could she express as she thought.

'Oh, Father John,' she said to him about Thomas, 'I laugh at myself when I think of it, but his voice is like fire in my ears. Wouldn't you think I was suffering from calf love?'

'Of course, the problem, Ellen my dear, if problem it be, is that you have the mind of an intelligent woman and the innocence of a girl.'

Since she first came to know Father John Watson, she

found that he often made a remark which took her days to decipher. This, and a difficult balance between intimacy and reserve, led to her fashioning devices of conversation: for example, she used questions as a means of trying to tell him what she felt. Did he know or had he ever encountered sudden instant attraction between people? What were the moralities involved, by which, she hastened, was it all right to feel you wanted to give your life completely to one man, even at the expense of what you knew were certain gifts you had? What were the dangers involved in spending the rest of your life with a person, even one to whom you felt so committed? Should not a person experience several such relationships before committing herself finally to one partner for life – 'I mean, Father, of course, observing the norms of chastity and so on?' He never answered directly.

Thomas did not meet the Jesuit until yesterday, in the rush of last-minute preparations.

'Aha,' said Father Watson looking right up at Thomas, 'the man we've all been hearing about.'

'And which of us is that, now?' asked Thomas agreeably, but the pleasantry did not ignite. Nor did the priest take it wholly genially when Thomas completed a quotation for him: Father Watson, looking at his watch, said, 'Well, we'll have to hurry or we'll tire the sun with talking and send him down the sky,' and Thomas, again intending amiability, murmured, 'They told me Heraclitus, they told me you were dead.'

'Oh! The classics out in Deanstown,' recoiled Father Watson a little. 'Well, Ellen, you never told me.' Whatever Thomas noticed, she certainly caught the edge in the Jesuit.

In the preceding weeks and months, however, Father Watson had been assuring her that, yes, what she seemed to feel for Thomas could accurately be described as love as known to humans, and desired by God so that people could bring themselves to Him, and if it expressed itself, as he hesitantly put it, 'in a sacred way', that was part of God's desire too, and that the love of man for woman was created by God, but that love of the mind must also be a part of Christian marriage, just like love of the flesh. Ellen said, 'It often makes me a bit uneasy' – but did not elaborate on the images and curiosities that flashed through her mind whenever she thought of Thomas, or the heat that made her mind's eye blink whenever he touched her: 'Father John, you always make me less confused.'

At the altar during her wedding, she looked at the little Jesuit again, his head bowed a little, the glistening chin: who would ever think he was nearly ten years older than Thomas?

'What I feel is not exactly . . . affection for him,' she struggled to explain to Thomas more than once; 'I mean not the way I am towards you; what I like is the respect he makes me feel for him.'

Father Watson, by arrangement with the Canon, gave the briefest of sermons, without a text.

'Dearly beloved brethren. Thomas Kane and Ellen Morris are two people we see this glorious summer morning at a moment of important ritual in their lives. Both have the intelligence, and the sensibility, not only to rise to the individual importance of the occasion – but to observe this ritual. And not just observe it for themselves, but on behalf of all of us. All of us who love them. All of us, their families. All of us, their dear friends. And perhaps even more importantly, all of us, all of you, the community they serve as teachers and leaders.

'As teachers and leaders, Thomas and Ellen, now Mr and Mrs Kane, they each know, both by instinct, and by education, they each know the importance of ritual in our small communities. They each know furthermore, and I know they have discussed this, that they both feel a part of our emerging nation. Our nation which so badly needs ritual and leadership.

'When God's own ritual, such as the Sacrament of Matrimony, is consummated as suitably as this at local level, ritual will pervade us, and our new nation, at national level. And thus we will heal all the wounds of a generation which has seen three wars – the War of Independence, the Great War and the sad Civil War.

'My dear brethren. It is our great pleasure to meet here this morning as witnesses to this loving union. I happen to know that Ellen takes a particular spiritual pleasure in reading that wonderful work, *Of the Imitation of Christ*, and therefore, I salute her and her new husband, Thomas, by quoting another Thomas – Thomas à Kempis himself, who said: "Would that we had spent one whole day well in this world."

'"Well", my dear brethren, "one whole day *well*": I feel we will all look back on this day, and see how we have indeed spent this "one whole day well". Spent it *well* observing this inspired wedlock between two remarkable people.'

When the couple and their best man and bridesmaid went around the back of the altar to the sacristy to sign the register, the congregation barely managed to maintain the decorum of silence in church. Children swung from the high peaks of pews, or scampered along the aisles to inspect some curious, or winking, or playful, beckoning man or woman. May Morris, long embroiled in attention-seeking indecision, had chosen light grey: 'Dear God,' she whispered now to Bob, 'how could Auntie Neenie be serious about that lilac frock? On a woman her age?'

The glee was at last released in the church porch and soared outwards among relatives who had not met since the last family funeral or wedding. They used these occasions to record the passage of time on each other's

144

faces and bodies, to run comparisons on ageing, to measure family competitiveness and progress. 'And I hear Ally is doing great? Isn't that great?' to which a gratified mother would say of Ally's new-ish husband, 'Of course, he's a very steady fellow, Sean is, he doesn't drink nor smoke, and he takes con-acre every year of his life.' No mention made of the age difference between Sean and Ally, nor Sean's resident old mother who was still holding on to the rights of the farm, nor the baby every relentless year. They all greeted each other in the friendly impersonal mode, as when Auntie Neenie hove in view: 'And how's Rina at all? Are we getting a bit stout, are we? Sure we all had puppy fat' – this to a seventeen-year-old girl enduring remorseless shyness.

All on Ellen's side, first intrigued by the resonance of his difficult fame, had been more or less captivated by Thomas; 'Even "herself",' said Ellen: – 'And God knows, to be perfectly straight about it, she's a "b" with an "itch", that's what she is.' The said Auntie Neenie clamoured that she had at long last met a man who could make her change her mind 'about the married state', the reason she herself never married being, of course, that she never found a man who 'would come up to my expectations'. (Causing Ellen's father's famed observation: 'Nothing to do with the port-wine stain on her face.')

The families differed widely. All the clothes on Ellen's side matched; Thomas's people had broader, open-air complexions. Ellen's people talked a lot; Thomas's, fewer, smiled more than they spoke, hung back farther than Ellen's relatives, waited until approached. The women, formidable and with great jutting roundnesses, dominated Ellen's family: the men seemed more prominent in Thomas's. To his brothers, with both parents long dead, Thomas was their father, their hero, their point of reference, their good security. The four boys looked up to Thomas, crowded around him, laughed at his jokes, teased him about his suit as they had long begun to tease Ellen, revelling in her friendly gullibility. 'Now – you have to polish his shoes every morning. He likes his egg boiled soft. And whatever you do, don't ever bake him a caraway seed cake, it goes straight to his head and he falls down in fits.' In the future, whenever any one of them appeared at the house, they consistently brought some present for Ellen: a salmon, or a pheasant, or eggs, or some plant or shrub.

To the Kane brothers, Leah's presence at the wedding was as exotic as a little carnival, or a dancing clown. When Ellen introduced them just outside the doors of the porch, they loved her, and her good humour, and her fun. Leah, delighted to be surrounded by so many men and all so much taller than her, and taller than her husband Herbert, laughed and joked with them, and got Herbert to explain his skull-cap to them, and asked them their names, and whether they could dance, and whether they had girls? None of them had, and she chided them, saying she knew girls who would come and chase them if they did not make a move to marry soon. They loved it all, and later that day they each danced with her. With two out of the four, Leah had to do the asking – but then each one of them swung her around the room, laughing out loud at her stumbling, breathless dizziness.

Given that the marriage took place 'on Thomas's territory', as Ellen's mother put it, they came to an arrangement. Contrary to custom, Thomas would attend to all the day's costs: Ellen's parents would spend their daughter's wedding money on furniture for the happy couple. Thomas conferred for weeks – mysterious meetings with farm women in faraway corners of the parish.

An army of wives provided hot and cold food. Most guests, given the weather, opted for the salads, white-and-gold hardboiled eggs, harems of gleaming beetroot everywhere; the huge baked hams like sweet babies, the long pink salmon, the cold turkeys and chickens. He even had cold pheasant, taken as a great favour from the old ice-house at Moore Abbey – but nobody ate it: 'Hot pheasant is bad enough,' one man murmured to another. Drinks of all kinds stood on every table, bottles of whiskey and brandy, and forests of black stout bottles: Arthur devoted himself to pulling corks. Ladies drank wine and sherry, huge jugs of orange squash with the slices of orange floating in them (prepared by the Misses Harpers' niece who had spent some time in London). A long continuous table reached from the back wall of the parlour, making a causeway out through the bow windows (frames removed for the day) as far as the privet hedge, so that half of the people at the feast sat indoors in the shade, and the other half, although at the same table, sat outside in the bright light. A pigeon swooped into the high *macrocarpa*, and out again quickly. The men hooked their caps on the sides of the chairs; the women placed nests of handbags beneath the table. An accordionist and a fiddler played on and on and on, their notes squeezing and scraping across the wall of fifty conversations.

Thomas and Ellen sat on slightly raised chairs, backs to the piano which was covered with cloths, and dishes of cakes, opposite the mantelpiece, across from the picture of *Vesuvius Erupting*.

'How are you?' whispered Ellen. 'I've hardly had a minute to say hallo to you?'

He whispered back, 'Do you think everything is going all right?'

'Oh, grand, grand! Look at them, look at the way they're enjoying themselves?' Then she whispered with a chuckle, 'What about Auntie Neenie?'

'She gave me a big kiss,' said Thomas.

'Oh, God! How did you avoid the birthmark?'

They dissolved into laughter.

Ellen said, 'I don't think I'll be able to eat a thing.' and devoured a plate of cold meat and salad.

Five speeches: the Canon; Ellen's father; Arthur Kane, the best man; Thomas; and Father Watson. The Canon blessed the wedding.

'I'm the lucky man today,' he said, and everybody laughed.

'I'm the Manager of the school and now the school has a great wife. And the Pope can't say a word agin it.' More laughter. 'And what's more,' he said. 'As any man should be with a wife – I'm afraid of my life of her.' They roared.

Outside, by the road, three of the older boys had captured a six-year-old cousin: they threatened to take his trousers off and send him in to all the girls. The boy wriggled away and ran off, and from a safe distance began to call them names again, hoping for another chase.

Ellen's father reminisced: Ellen in her mother's shoes and hat; Ellen on a rug in front of the fire; Ellen learning to read; Ellen growing up; Ellen on long walks: 'I can tell Thomas one thing. He'll never find a better listener than Ellie.'

Arthur, like a showman, made everybody laugh with stories of sharing a bed with Thomas when they were little and how Thomas would never cut his toenails, but said he was leaving them grow long to torture Arthur, 'and he used to rake his nails up and down my legs. I hope he's changed. People buying a horse look at the animal's teeth. Ellen, you should have looked at Thomas's toenails; you've probably discovered an addition to the Impediments to Matrimony.' Much laughter and cheering.

Thomas stood. He made a speech full of kindness and tenderness, towards his brothers, towards his dead parents, towards all their past, hard life together.

'I think of my father often, I think of where he came

from, and sometimes I see him in my mind's eye. On fine Sundays he used to ride out across the country on a horse he borrowed from our neighbours. Just for pleasure, the way other men go for a walk. And my mother would see him coming back, and go out to meet him, and so would we, and he looked great.

'And I think of my father's life, and how he was as a young man with his own brothers, some of whom are here today, Uncle Matt, Uncle John, the two of you are so welcome. And I think of how he was as a young man, how he was lively and good, and all his folks up there in the north of the county, a big, bright crowd of people. He liked my mother very much altogether, and I thought of them many times in the last few months when I was walking out with Ellen. And how they would have liked her.'

Stillness and affection had fallen on the room, as Thomas continued, unaware how he moved them, these his guests and friends and kin. Any spoor or chill which his person may have carried from his own history had evaporated; he stood as a man who had put awfulness behind him, and who now looked to his future with warmth, and confidence, and a friendly sense of safety. When those who had proved ambivalent about the role and purpose of the Flying Columns overcame their diffidence, even hostility, towards the more prominent individuals, they lionized them, especially in the glow of hindsight: from this latecoming adulation Thomas now benefited, and their faces turned up to him ready to like and admire.

'My father and mother gave me a valuable gift, and it was this. They told me many times that I never had to set out to do anything to please them deliberately, that I did not have to think of pleasing them, that my being there and just trying to be good and decent, that was enough pleasure for them. Now I have married Ellen, they, to my sadness, are not here to see her, or to dance with us all,

149

and even though I would not have been marrying Ellen to please them – well – I know they would have been delighted.' Around the room, Thomas's family could not look at each other; the girls sniffled and blew their noses; the boys looked downward.

Thanking everyone, Thomas began praising Ellen.

'I told her myself, and she knows what I'm going to say. When she came out here last February, I know what the fellows around here are like. And I was like a greyhound out of the traps.' They roared.

'And I know I speak for her when I say, that anyone of you here is going to be welcome under our roof at any time of the day or night. Only, try that you don't all arrive at the same time.' He sat down to cheers, laughter and applause.

Father Watson, the last speaker, then rose. He said, 'I had a speech prepared, and I wanted to give it. I wanted to talk about the sanctity of marriage, and what a man must be for his wife, and what a woman must be for her husband. I've known Ellen Morris for ten years and I met her through circumstances where she behaved with great compassion to a child who was dying. Ellen befriended her –' May Morris could be seen nodding, and mouthing to her neighbour, 'That's true, that's true' – 'and Ellen made that little girl's last days bearable and cheerful. I know therefore that she is utterly capable' – his Dublin accent, and mannerisms, and phrases sounded foreign in the long room, and his trained speaking voice rang out into the air – 'utterly capable of being all the things a man could wish for in a wife. I hope for a lasting and vivid friendship with Thomas, and now that I have heard him speak here today, anything I have to say about the prospects for a marriage between these two exceptional people would be superfluous.'

Many of the people in the room did not quite fully comprehend the meaning of the word 'superfluous', and would never have used the word 'utterly' – but they knew that this 'odd little man' was paying their Thomas and their Ellen a huge compliment, and they applauded him sincerely.

'Quick,' whispered Thomas, 'that photographer is going to be drunk if we don't get him working now.' They stood in front of the door, in a rotation of groups and poses. 'The nick of time,' murmured Thomas, 'he's well on already,' as the man had difficulty unfolding his 'sticks'.

Tables were pushed back. A piper arrived, and the other two musicians cleared a space in front of them. Arthur rushed over and grabbed Ellen. Everybody shouted, 'Yeee-ow, go on there, Arthur!' Dancing furiously, Ellen pawed up to feel the cross and chain flying at her neck, and missed it. She danced on. Uncle Michael, her mother's uncle, looking on and, tapping his old feet, said to his wife, 'You used to have a bosom like that.'

Men and women and boys and girls drifted here and there. Aunts admired the peony roses on the tables. Cousins talked about jobs in Dublin. Lavatory arrangements became informal; the small shed at the side of the garage (Thomas had whitewashed it the previous Saturday) had people standing beside it, therefore men walked into the acres near the house: others walked deeper into the fields. Girls on tiptoes, and with fat bottoms and ribbons, giggled and skipped a little up the road, in the opposite direction from the village, then slipped in past the hedgerows in twos and threes. Ellen was called by a cousin to attend to a tearful Rina: she had torn the hem of her dress when she caught her heel in it, and feared her mother's wrath: a needle was found, and Leah helped. Aggie O'Carroll, the girl from the Training College, gave Ellen an illuminated scroll the nuns had given her: *The Housewife's Prayer*: Ellen read the first lines:

> *'Lady who with tender ward*
> *Didst keep the house of Christ the Lord,*
> *Who didst set forth the bread and wine*
> *Before the Living Wheat and Vine;'*

'Oh, this is lovely, lovely,' Ellen squealed. 'Thomas, stop them playing for a minute. Aggie – read out the rest of it.'

Aggie, not at all shy, stepped over near the lulled musicians and read on,

> *'Be beside me while I go*
> *About my labours to and fro,*
> *Speed the wheel and speed the loom,*
> *Guide the needle and the broom,*
> *Make my bread rise sweet and light,*
> *Make my cheese come foamy white;*
> *Yellow may my butter be*
> *As cowslips blowing on the lea . . .'*

– and when she came to the end,

> *'To me Thy gracious help afford*
> *Who art the handmaid of the Lord'*

– and after the word-swooning and clapping had died down, Ellen exclaimed, 'Oh, I'm going to have that framed the minute we get back from our honeymoon.'

Thomas and Herbert met for the first time at any length; previous encounters had been fleeting (all on Saturdays), and now they could not be prised apart. In the corner of the sitting-room they sat, Herbert, with his quiet courtesy, questioning Thomas intently late in the afternoon.

'I've always wanted to find out about Collins.'

Had Ellen heard, she would have caught her breath, knowing Thomas's astringent reticence on the subject of his own past.

'And tell me, was he a big man?'

Ellen had tried over and again, in an effort to break through the mist of dropped hints from the people of Deanstown. All she had really gleaned, apart from the fact of their connection, was that Thomas and Collins had quarrelled violently. When the news came through of Collins's assassination – Mrs Burke had passed on this nugget – Thomas, shopping in Mooreville, knelt in the street, as people did all over the country, and wept. He let it be known that he would lead a candlelit vigil to the church the night of Collins's funeral, and the whole parish turned out, irrespective of political affiliations.

'Not as big as people think,' he told Herbert. 'About five foot ten or so, or eleven. And he had a curious way with him. Whenever he met somebody, say you were in one of his Command Units, and you came to see him, and he was fond of you, and he hadn't seen you for a while, the first thing he'd do was wrestle with you until he over-powered you down on to the ground.'

Herbert then pushed back the lock of fair hair dipping down into his spectacles, and delivered the next slow but passionate question; and from their first moment, the two men discovered their mutual, if passive, commitment to politics.

'Oh, undoubtedly, undoubtedly,' said Thomas, when Herbert asked him if Collins would have gone into politics had he lived. 'God, to think of it. What? Thirty-one? And all he had done? Where were you when you heard of his death?' It was to Herbert, and to Herbert alone, that Thomas revealed the extent of his involvement with Collins, and only in that roundabout way did Ellen ever come to hear of it, and only then in the most appalling of her days a year and more later.

When Herbert first asked, Thomas brushed down each arm of his new suit thoroughly, five brisk strokes, then fixed the cuff of each sleeve. He patted the front of his jacket, and straightened the pens in his inside breast pocket. He transferred an envelope from one side pocket to another. After these comforting preliminaries he began.

'Well, we had three ferocious years, him and me, I sort of worked alongside him. My house, the Teacher's Residence, was burnt down by the Black and Tans while I was away doing the Master's degree. Although I was never suspected of any involvement. It was burnt in reprisals for an ambush I set up, and they'd have burnt down the whole village if it wasn't for Captain Johnson. He was a retired Army man, India, that type of thing, and he stopped them. The Sunday week after they burnt the house, Collins involved me in a series of things in Dublin which I'm sure you remember, a lot of shots and that.'

Herbert asked, 'Bloody Sunday?'

Thomas said, 'Yes. Anyway, to cut a long story short, I began not to be able to sleep, and a few weeks later I got notification that I couldn't go back to the school here, because the Inspectors had decided to close the school until the Teacher's Residence had been rebuilt.'

Thomas concluded his tale. 'I was finished the thesis, and I wasn't going to be examined on it until about August, so I saw my chance and I went to see Collins. I told him I was out of it, that I was out of it altogether, that I couldn't do any more the things he wanted. We met in a room in Aungier Street.'

Thomas sat up straight: Herbert leaned forward.

'Why? Why were you out of it?'

'I can't do that sort of thing. I never wanted to. I mean – I agreed with the principle, the Cause itself, and in the beginning I agreed with the actions we had to take. But it got too much for me.'

Herbert nodded. Rachel came over, shaking both her legs. 'Dadda, wee-wee, wee-wee?'

Herbert said, 'Look, my love,' and pointed, 'there's Mamma.'

'No, Dadda, you. You!'

Leah rescued.

Thomas smiled after them, and after a moment resumed. 'Anyway, I said more or less the same to him as I'm after telling you. And do you know what he did? He hit me. Across the face. He had these brown leather gloves he used to wear, winter and summer, cycling, and he hit me with them. This was the middle of June. I said if he hit me again I would . . .'

Thomas stopped, then continued, 'Anyway. The upshot was he threw his arms around me, and said I was to go with his blessing. The following night I left on the Mail Boat with my bicycle. I was in bits. I went off to Antwerp and places.'

Both men sat and reflected.

'But will we all fit?' asked Leah.

'Of course we will,' said Bob, 'won't we?' he asked the driver.

'Bit of a shqueeze, Sir, but you will, I'd say.' Bob smiled at his own mischief, knowing May's opinion of Leah. Herbert sat in first and the girls, asleep, were handed in to his arms.

The end of the day had come slowly and good-humouredly. At ten o'clock or so, as twilight gathered, people began to leave. It had become known that the couple were to spend their wedding night in their own house – but Thomas had successfully sealed the stairs.

'They'll make us a French bed if we don't watch out,' he laughed to Ellen.

Together, the Morrises took their leave of their daughter. Bob shoved a roll of notes into Ellen's hand; 'For something nice in London.' Father Watson, formal once more, made promises to visit the pair when they returned.

Thomas's brothers stayed until last. They hung around until all other farewells and laughter and goodbyes had floated away on the dusk and then, one by one, they came and shook hands with both Ellen and Thomas. When the youngest brother, Des, aged twenty, tall and lanky, with fair curly hair, came forward, he burst into tears. 'Ah, Thomas,' was all he could manage to say, and Thomas caught his arm with one hand, and with the other pulled his hair gently, and then they all slipped away into the darkness, crackling their shoes on the gravel, their low conversation fading down the roadway amid the clanks of bicycles.

Thomas turned to Ellen, and said, exhaling, 'Des. I often think of him. He's the one I reared, really.'

They went in and sat down among the happy debris of their own wedding.

'A pity to have to close the doors such a fine night,' said Thomas, 'but the cats will get at the turkey. Or the ham.'

'Or the salmon,' said Ellen. 'We'd better put the milk in the pantry. What time are the women coming in to clear up?'

'Twelve. What in the name of God is that?' asked Thomas, pointing to an ungainly brown paper parcel with angles sticking out of it.

'Auntie Neenie's present,' said Ellen. 'Diamonds the way she was going on. Open it' – a set of five washboards, from tiny to large – 'for everything,' said Ellen, 'collars up to sheets. You can hang them up for me when we come back.'

'Look at this.' He held out to her a stiff brown envelope: she opened it and took out an old newspaper. 'Your mother gave it to me,' he said.

'Heavens above!' said Ellen. 'Well. You are privileged.'

It contained a newspaper advertisement from 1811 – the Notice of Sale of the farm by whose purchase the O'Kellys, May Morris's people, became rich.

They stood. Thomas said, 'You looked grand. All day.'

'The funny thing is,' Ellen said, as if thinking aloud, 'I'm not a bit tired. And I thought I'd be exhausted.'

8

Ellen inched her head towards him, to lay it beside Thomas's shoulder, gently touching, yet not waking him up. Sunlight slanting down at a tangent through the cream net curtains made patterns on the wall; dust danced in the beams of honey light above the dressing-table. Ellen stretched carefully, easing each leg. On the back of her neck she fingered a small line of soreness where the chain of the cross had cut into her skin when the beggar whipped it away outside the church; it had broken easily, and at the wedding the incident was a nine-hour wonder.

She touched the back of her teeth with her tongue. Her ears began to focus; Thomas's breathing; the birdsong, every trilling a separate and energetic sound; a calf 'mwaaah'-ing for, or at, its mother. She eased up on her elbows and began to look at Thomas. 'He has hairs on his chest!': his new pyjamas, blue stripes, a stubble, mouth slightly open, a hint of saliva, like a tiny tide-mark of foam; face peaceful, the black brows a fraction away from meeting; one tooth at the side slightly broken.

Ellen scanned the brightening room. On the mantelpiece stood a small photograph of a man in uniform. Uncle Eddie, he told her last night, died on the Somme, 'for the defence of small nations,' said Thomas with sarcasm. Two brass candlesticks held the white coiled remains of last year's candlegrease.

Ellen lay back again, slowly raised her arms in straight parallel lines above her head, studied the satin ribbon on the little puffed sleeve of her nightgown, looked at her hands side by side: a thin, thin gold ring.

'Marriage,' she whispered. Then, 'Married?'

157

Quiet as a mouse she sat up. In the side mirror of the dressing-table whose angled glass held the window in its reflection, she could see the branches of the sycamore, and in the distance the forecourt and gate of the Castle, lit brightly aslant by the morning sun.

'Married. Ellen married?' she said in the smallest of whispers. She put a hand beneath her hair and lifted it out from the back of her neck and let it fall twice, three times, held her hands out again for inspection, turning her head to one side as if preparing to paint or draw. She dropped her chin, stiffened the back of her neck, raised her head and yawned with her mouth as closed as she could keep it; she leaned forward and stretched her hands down along her sheet-covered legs towards her ankles. On the marble-topped washstand not far from her face, inside a wide matching basin, stood a large white jug with blue flowers. The soap dish of the set nestled beneath the shoulder of the basin. Several towels hung from the mahogany rail beneath; she had folded them herself last night, in heavy layers, blue, and striped blue-and-red, and plain white: wedding gifts, all. Ellen stretched her legs and thighs, moving her stiff hips with pleased caution. Leaning forward she could see the small clock with the bright open face on Thomas's little bedside table, half-past five. She lay down again softly, but still woke Thomas, who half-smiled.

'Ahunhh.'

Ellen placed her face fully into the folded joint of his shoulder and arm.

'Good morning, Mrs,' said Thomas, sleepy and good-natured. 'And how are you this morning?'

In a series of large wiggles of her body, she moved closer, pushing her face up to the hollow of his neck and jaw.

'I was just wondering.' Thomas stopped and yawned. 'Heeaannh, I was just wondering. Who was this stranger in my bed?' He brought his right hand over and began to stroke her head and hair.

'Listen to the birds,' said Ellen. They lay for a moment, Thomas slowly waking up.

'God in Heaven, this room needs a coat of paint,' she remarked.

Thomas yawned, 'Aisle. Altar. Hymn.'

'You and your old jokes,' said Ellen. She rubbed her itchy nose on his arm with a 'nnnnn-hing' sound.

'Different altogether,' said Ellen, her finger twisting a vacant buttonhole on Thomas's pyjama jacket.

'What's different?' he asked.

'Different skin, different muscle, different shape.'

Thomas yawned again, blinked his eyes as slowly as a frog several times, then did reverse blinks, opening the eyelids as far as he could. He eased his jaw away from Ellen's head, brought his other hand up behind her and began to stroke her shoulder.

'The pigeons,' said Ellen, 'listen to them. Listen.'

They lay in the bright room. The curtains began to blow a little as a morning breeze dropped by from somewhere, then subsided ever so quietly.

'Different what did you say?' asked Thomas through a yawn, pushing air from the sides of his lips. Ellen rolled the back of her head on to his hard forearm.

'You aren't awake yet, are you? I think – the shoulders. Different from women, from girls. Men's shapes. I taper. You're more. Rectangular.' She sat up, hanging her face down so that her hair fell forward. The hand with which she propped herself touched his and he closed his fingers over her.

'The raven's wing,' he said. 'Black is blue, isn't it? Your hair.' She lifted a hand high above her head, then placed it on the pillow.

'I'm always telling you. I have a flat nose. Like a boxer,' she said. 'And freckles.'

He lifted her hand and kissed it, throwing her slightly off balance. She looked down at him without turning her face fully.

'My legs are stiff,' she said. She began to whistle a little. 'Wasn't the dancing great?' She put her hands behind her and bounced her ankles on the bed beneath the single sheet.

'Is it the dancing made your legs stiff?' Thomas asked in a whisper, and with an expression of tender roguery. She looked at him quickly through the side of her hair, then looked away, then turned around sharply and pressed her head down on his chest, her arms reaching up to his shoulders.

'Thomas.' She moved her face from side to side, as if feeling his chest with each eyebrow. 'Thomas. I wish.' She raised her head, looked at him very seriously and put her head down again. 'I wish the word "tender" were longer and had more letters in it. And had more "n's" and more "r's" in it, and a few "l's". Soft letters. For a soft word.' She began to spell it. 'T.E.N.D.E.R.'

A small bird, robin or sparrow or something, landed briefly on the windowsill and fluttered away again quickly. Ellen's face lifted and dipped on the swell of Thomas's breathing.

'Ellie?' She grunted in response.

'Nothing,' said Thomas.

After a few more moments Ellen bounced out of the bed. She went to the window, parted the net curtains and raised the lower sash to its fullest height. Leaning far out, she gazed all around her, at the sycamore, at the currant and gooseberry bushes in the garden, and the tall green-white pampas grass on the lawn, and the red-hot poker flowers, and the two apple trees. 'One sweet, one sour,' Thomas had said, 'like myself.' They had closed the gate last night, and a white glistening cobweb of dew had formed on the latch.

'Somebody left a bicycle.' The saddle had large shiny spots of bright black, from the dropping condensation on the leaves of the sycamore. 'There's Blackie.' The cat crossed lazily from one privet hedge to a corner growing sunnier as the light moved around. Ellen half-turned to Thomas, rubbing her arms.

'Are you getting up, or what?' He canted himself over to one side, and stretched, then put his feet on the rug.

'Come over here. You look like an Algerian girl in a painting,' he said. 'Come over here and sit down,' patting the bed. Without looking at him she backed across the room from the window.

'Yes, Sir?' she said, in mocking obedience. He ran the back of a hand down the side of her face, caressing, then back up again, then traced the shape of her head.

'Yes,' he murmured. 'That's right. An Algerian girl.' She flounced off the bed and went to the door, saying back over her shoulder, 'If you knew I took size seven shoes would you have married me?' and continued to the room that Thomas said they should make into a bathroom if they ever got running water, a bare-floored room, where he had kept the chamber-pots and some spare kitchen chairs.

'I'm only putting on second-best clothes yet,' Thomas called after her. 'We're going for a walk.'

She answered, asking what time the train was?

'Not 'til twelve. We've nearly six hours. Are you hungry?'

She closed the spare room door behind her.

They agreed to just a slice of bread each, with butter, and honey from a new comb, and have full breakfast later. Standing in the kitchen, plates and bottles and glasses everywhere, she walked over to Thomas and put her head on his chest, then stepped back again. Then she dusted the white soda-bread crumbs and flour from her fingers and walked out into the small cobbled yard.

'I'm wearing no shoes,' Thomas said, following, 'it'll be a bit cold at first, but not for long.' Stepping gingerly on the gravel, he held the gate open for her. Ellen took her shoes off and left them on the wall.

'The Mathews had these stones mortared in here,' said Thomas, as she climbed, and rested on the wall, 'like the steps of a stile – so that they could get on to the road easily when they came down from the Castle for a walk.' Cautiously, she got down the other, steeper side, and stood on a little grassy mound waiting.

'When my father first visited this parish,' said Thomas, 'all these fields were filled with trees; there was a whole forest here, sloped down to that long hollow, see that –' he waved a hand – 'that was the Castle's ornamental lake.'

Ellen shaded her eyes with a hand and looked. They set off together, walking a little apart.

'I didn't sleep very well,' she said, 'but I'm not tired.' She took his hand briefly, then let it go. 'Though I suppose with the journey ahead of us I should have stayed in bed a bit longer.'

Under the beech tree Thomas broke off a small branch and handed it to her, the leaves gleaming in the light.

'Here.' Ellen snatched it and deliberately bumped him with her shoulder, then swished the leaves like a fan. She looked up at the sky, and turned all around in a circle like a child playing dizzy.

'Look. Look! The moon.'

A faint, fading disc hung high to the west, soft, benign. Thomas began to sing in a low voice. 'Then awake 'til rise of sun, my dear. The sage's watch we shall shun, my dear. For in watching the flight. Of bodies of light. He might happen to take thee for one, my dear.'

Reaching the ditch that led into the big broad expanse of fields sloping up to the Castle, Thomas led Ellen to a sturdy hazel, showed her where a gap opened if she pushed the lower branches, and she scrambled through.

'Now that bush, d'you see it, up there?' – he pointed to a stunted dwarf tree standing all alone in the middle of the fields ahead of them. 'That's standing on what used to be the bank of the ornamental lake, and that bush never grew. Because the nurserymaid from the Castle let the only son and heir drown at that spot. The child was only two. She was out walking with him. And she let him wander away. They jailed her. And she put a curse on the place. That it would only become a nesting-place for rooks and jackdaws. And that is exactly what it is.'

From the edge of the sunken fence, and then farther up, by the ramparts, they could see for miles in a circle, and he talked in his quiet deliberate voice, breaking up his sentences for emphasis, as he did habitually.

'That house off there. No – there.' He redirected her pointing arm. 'The man in that house. He was in the Crimea. A groom. Best man with a horse for miles. And the worst temper.'

Ellen's eyes picked up the flight of a small dipping bird from the point where it took off on a turreted gateway, and traced it down, down the fields, until it became lost against the foliage. Behind them, far away, the mountains in this light seemed as compact and precisely located as if placed there in a great toy – tidy foothills, orderly peaks. In the near distance, the light caught two farmhouses and a hilltop copse; much nearer, beside the Norman motte, stood the church in which they married yesterday, and far, far beyond that, Ellen could see, as Thomas promised she would, the spire of the cathedral in which she had been baptized, a full thirty-six miles away. Down on the big Castle pond, waterfowl screeched and flustered; Thomas said swans lived there, on a large high knot of earth with rushes in the middle; and migrant geese came.

'Oh, by the way,' he said suddenly. 'Val Vousden. He

wrote. Do you know what he told me? And I forgot to tell you in all the excitement? He has traced most of the instruments of the old band. Their banner, everything. The uniforms, some of them are still all right, lovely, blue and gold jackets, the county colours. The blue of the sky, the gold of the corn.'

Ellen looked at Thomas as he talked quietly on. She had developed a way of standing dutifully while listening, hands held simply behind her back. If sitting down, she nested her hands in her lap, or rested them folded on the table or desk in front of her. In this pose, she had the capacity to listen for a long, concentrated period, and she tried diligently not to interrupt, even when questions coursed through her mind. She told Thomas frequently how much she liked hearing his stories. Now, when he finished telling about the band, and the number of members it once had, and a meeting he might hold to try and have it revived, she moved away a little and looked at him.

'Thomas Kane, I am going to do something especially nice for you one day soon. No. Don't ask me what it is. I'll think.' She looked away. 'Perhaps . . . perhaps I will plant a greengage bush for you and make you some greengage jam? But you mightn't like greengage jam, of course.' She looked at the Castle walls. 'Ooh, Thomas, look, that face, what is it?'

She pointed to a scowling, bearded head carved in white limestone above where the door had been.

'That, Mrs Kane – how d'you like being called Mrs Kane? – is a riverine god. It is the head that represents the spirit who lives in the river Nore. There's one for every river, but the stonemason who did that one, it was supposed to be a different river, he only knew the Nore.' He strode on. 'If it's greengages you're after, here, come on.'

She followed, watching her feet make footprints in the dew.

'It looks Greek, that head,' she said. 'Like Zeus or one

of those, Poseidon, or the one always changing, that one. Proteus.' Then, 'Good God above! I never said my prayers, last night or this morning. I'll have to say them later. Isn't God very good to us, this weather?' She chattered on like this from time to time, a detail in her that Thomas loved: soon, he would particularly come to enjoy standing quietly outside the door in their house before he entered a room, eavesdropping on his young wife talking to herself.

They emerged under the arch of the tower gateway, the east entrance to the Castle, and turned down the Bell Walk towards the wood. Nobody in the world had yet awakened; they might have seen foxes or badgers, so early had they risen. Not even the cattleboy from the farm, nor one of the farmer's many daughters, had yet come to call the animals in for milking, and the cows grazed in the fields away down near the main road, placid brown-and-white miniatures. Ellen ran in across the old terraced, formal Viennese gardens with their repeating circles of tall, pointed box trees set on gravel beds. She skipped from tree to tree, disappearing from Thomas's view, reappearing, smiling, waving, squinting one eye closed against the sunlight as in her later photographs. He leaned against the crumbling parapet, arms folded, watching, pleased with her. She slowed her cavorting, then walked in procession along an aisle of the trees, bowing to him as she approached, and they grinned at each other, then covertly eyed. So began their marriage, governed by reticence in the face of intimacy, obligation at the head of their community, filled from the beginning with the decorum of their religion: the transactions of the night would never be talked about, never discussed, and if hinted at by either, would be greeted with oblique humour, or embarrassment, by the other.

Distance had softened the village's dinginess, and restored some of its old calendar prettiness in the early light. The

165

yellow ochre, the leaded panes, the pointed gables gleamed.

'They diverted this stream, you know,' Thomas said, as Ellen splashed her feet, stretching her toes in the thin friendly mud and the watercress. 'It used to come in over there, just under that bank, but they changed the direction of it so that it could flow over a course of stones in here, behind that wall. And the Castle kitchen servants used the stones' – he cupped a hollow with his hands – 'as a little flat, square box in which they kept the milk fresh in the summer. Now. There you are. There's all the greengages you could want, Ellie. They're wild, now, of course, but they were properly cultivated. I suppose those are over a hundred years old.'

Ellen went forward, with Thomas watching her. He looked at her legs, and her shoulders, and her behind; he stood with his legs apart.

'*Espalier* plums, Thomas, look. Pears. A red-currant bush. This place is a bower.'

Thomas sat down on a broken stretch of the brick wall, and Ellen picked her barefoot way over grass-covered stones and masonry. She peered at each new discovery, making pleased sounds, ran her hands around the shape of a small and pretty window. 'This must have been a pantry or something,' she called out. Then, head down, concentrating on placing her feet carefully in the brick-strewn long grass, she made her way back to him, looking up with a dazzling smile just as she reached him. He held out both hands for her to grip and hauled her up near him, kissing her hair as she drew level.

'Do you know what I have at home?' he said. 'I have the original planting-map, and the drawings, of this kitchen garden. I'll show it to you.'

'At home,' she said, immensely happy. She let him kiss her on the mouth. Climbing down from the bricks, she stumbled on ahead. Back in the fields, and heading diagonally towards their house which had never been out of their sight, she said, 'Thomas?' paused, resumed, 'Are we blessed or something?'

He said nothing, walked beside her as she swung her arms, and they reached the two white, overgrown posts that marked the entrance to the old avenue. When he helped her over the wall and then down on to the road, her skirt caught on the wall and revealed a thigh, and he looked away.

'Yes, you're right,' he said, 'blessed.'

Inside the door he caught her arm, and began to say, 'I think . . .'

She hunched her shoulders and leaned towards him, making shushing sounds, and then followed him as he walked ahead of her, through the kitchen.

9

Ellen looked out of the window towards the distant Castle, on whose terraced slopes the white paths of the gardens intersected in broad-ribboned cross-hatchings; black specks, crows, sat on the tattered dovecote. Her breast touched the windowpane. She wore a skirt, and had draped a towel around her shoulders.

Thomas sat up and said, 'I'd better shave,' then stood. 'Look – new razor, in honour of you,' and held the blade up, swishing it, a small rectangular scimitar shining in the light. 'I'll go and get fresh water,' and as he went she shivered in the sudden cold air coming through the door, and quickly, before Thomas returned, put on a bodice. She continued to hang clothing in the wardrobe, fetching things from suitcases they had left in one of the empty rooms.

When she had fully dressed, he, wiping his razor, observed that she looked different in the mirror, that he had never noticed it before. He stood behind her as she straightened her waistband before the long glass in the wardrobe door. The back of her head came up to the middle of his chest. He kissed the crown of her hair, and placed his fingers where he had kissed her. Then, with her wide eyes watching their reflections in the mirror, from behind her he ran his hands slowly all over her, touching first her hair, neck, ears, eyebrows, and mouth; his fingers stroked her throat, shoulders, armpits, lifting her arms a little to do so; the large hands roamed slowly over her breasts, down lazily to the ribcage, hips, then stomach, down through the valley of her pelvis into her thighs; and kneeling, he touched her shins, her ankles, caressed her feet over and over. She turned around to face him as he stood, and kissed his chest.

'Thomas, I want to talk about this.'

'Yes?'

'To make sure. Of . . . That there isn't anything wrong in any of it.'

'We're married.'

'Yes. That is true. That is true.'

He stroked her hair, then ran his thumb along the side of her breast by her upper arm, then with his fingernails softly raked her side from armpit to hip.

She said, 'But we could. We could be more, more – enlightened, about it, and all of it, and that. Know more.'

She had once asked the question in the Training College in biology classes, why women were not given more information about their bodies?

'Because there is none,' the embarrassed doctor had said.

'None?' asked Ellen. 'None at all. You mean, none in England, or in France, or America?'

'We're not in England or in France or in America,' she was told. 'We are in Ireland. This is a Catholic country, and these things are not discussed.'

'But why not? They're our bodies,' she persisted.

'You had better take that up with Mother Agatha,' the doctor said, a decent enough man, middle-aged and with a large family of his own.

She did take it up with Mother Agatha, or rather Mother Agatha took it up with her. The conversation only led into the usual *cul-de-sac* of authority, which always happened when Ellen tried to create some innovations, such as dramatizing history, or discussing feelings.

'That is not the way this College is run,' she was firmly told.

=

Thomas asked her hesitantly, 'Have you ever talked to anybody about it?' He took the towel from over his shoulder and rubbed his face and neck.

'No.'

'Not even Leah?'

'Not yet.'

'And how did you know . . .' He tailed off.

'There was a book they gave us in Teacher Training, written by a priest. It had diagrams.' Then, taking his hand, she asked, 'Have you ever talked to anybody about it?'

He answered evasively. 'Men talk. A coarse sort of way.' He did not elaborate – on the fact that men in the country, on the farms, workmen and the like, discussed women in crude terms as 'mares', good for 'a ride'; or in terms of dogs and bitches; or bragged of what they wanted to do to local flighty girls in terms of 'bulling' them.

He said, 'We should get going. Arthur will be here soon.'

He hummed a tune, then looked out of the window.

'I have all kinds of good ideas in my head,' Thomas said half to himself, and pulled on his new waistcoat.

Arthur came cycling in through the front gate.

'Hallo, Mr and Mrs Kane!' he called upwards. Thomas and Ellen both put their heads out of the window.

'Where's the car? 'Tis going to be a very hot day again.'

'In the garage,' said Thomas, 'but we'll have to push it out, there's no room to turn the starting-handle, I left it too close to the wall. Hold on, I'm on my way down.'

'The two of you look like a framed picture up there,' called out Arthur. They laughed and withdrew.

The train, almost empty, passed through the woods where Thomas's grandfather had lived, and he pointed out to Ellen the thatched roof of the family house, barely visible through a swoop in the trees. Somebody walked past the First Class compartment, stopped in the corridor beyond their door, walked back again, stopped on the other side, and passed the door a third time. Gazing out of the opposite window at the sunny morning, neither of the newlyweds paid attention. A sharp rap on the glass made them jump, and the compartment door opened. A woman stood there, in a white dress that had gathered smuts from the engine and the flying steam. She held a straw hat in her hand.

'Oh,' said Ellen recognizing her.

'I just came in to wish you all the best,' said the woman. 'You were married yesterday, weren't you?'

'Oh, hallo,' said Thomas.

'And you had a great wedding, we could hear the music, we nearly joined in.'

'You'd have been very welcome,' said Ellen in stout hospitality.

'But we'd have had to bring you a present,' said the woman. 'How and ever, here I am now, and I suppose you're off on the honeymoon.'

'You're Mrs Doctor Hogan, aren't you?' asked Thomas.

'Miriam's the name. After Moses's sister. Watch me,' said the woman, who spoke in little tunes. She put her hat on the empty seat, opened the compartment door wider so that they could see her and, singing loudly, waltzed up and down the corridor, her arms held out in a meeting curve as if dancing with a partner.

> *'Oh, the days of the Kerry dances,*
> *Oh, the ring of the piper's tunes.*
> *Oh, for one of those hours of gladness,*
> *Gone, alas, like our youth – too soon.*
> *When the boys began to gather*
> *In the glen of a Summer's night.'*

She stopped and bowed. Picking up her hat she lilted airily, 'People should dance for other people's weddings.

I'm off now.' She closed the door and they heard her lurching back along the corridor.

Thomas and Ellen looked at each other and laughed.

'Was she drunk or what?' asked Ellen.

Thomas said, 'Did you know whether she had the words right?' – and Ellen thumped him, and they laughed again.

'Well. We heard she was a bit odd,' said Thomas.

They saw Miriam Hogan again at Kingsbridge, hauling a suitcase to a porter and asking him to lift it, then arguing with him when he refused, fanning him threateningly with her hat.

At the Mail Boat quayside, a difficulty arose. Although Thomas had booked and paid for a full cabin, the boat in service had no berths. Thomas could not improve the situation, and he began to rage. Ellen took his arm.

'Thomas. This is a lovely night. We can wrap ourselves up warm and sit out on the deck.'

'That's not the point, Ellen.' He jerked his arm away. 'That's not the point. We booked and paid for . . .'

'But they're giving you a refund.'

'I don't want a fucking refund.' He stopped suddenly. 'I apologize, I swore to myself I'd never swear in front of you.'

'It's all right. It's all right. Come on, it's all a strain, a wedding is.'

She calmed him, led him aboard: Thomas fidgeted in guilt. When the boat had cleared the intricate harbour, a sailor brought them tea and biscuits on a tray, and offered them a drink which they both declined. They went out on deck, and still holding the teacups, stood at the rail. The night beamed on them, a starry sky with a white moon rising.

'We're like the pictures of romance in the magazines and on the book covers,' she said.

They walked a little, then leaned over the rail watching

172

the rush of the water by the dark keel. Sitting in the stern's lee, they looked backwards at the receding lights, and then up at the sky.

'God!' muttered Thomas. 'Look.' At the far end of the deck, Miriam Hogan walked up and down with a sense of drama, a cardigan thrown across her shoulders. Upon disembarkation, she also boarded the smoky, jerky London train.

In the hotel, Thomas looked at everything; inspected the light switch, the brass taps on the bath, the ceramic waste-pipe hood; the curtain-pulls; the lights. To Ellen's confusion of embarrassment and delight – although she made no remark – he wandered in and out of the bathroom while she bathed, and talked to her easily, even though he seemed to avoid looking at her.

In the tall bedroom, she said to him, and in a moment regretted it, 'You scratch yourself a lot?'

'Yes-I-do' – in a short tone.

In the next ten days, he seemed to Ellen to have brought a lot of money; he kept it in an inside pocket the flap of which he secured with a safety pin. She said, 'Thomas, aren't you spending a lot of money on me?'

'No matter. I'm a very prudent man.'

Sitting in the hotel dining-room, he turned back the tablecloth and looked at the wood beneath.

'Mahogany, I'd say. Not white deal, anyway.'

'Prudent? Lovely word. Yes, you are, Thomas, you are prudent.'

'We ate no meat in our house for several years, except at Christmas; my mother's widow's pension was one shilling and sixpence a week, and a houseful of us.'

Ellen said, 'When you tell me something like that, it dawns on me that I don't know you at all yet.'

He grinned. 'Plenty of time now. Look.' He pointed out to her a man sitting alone reading a newspaper. 'The thing he's picking his teeth with. I'd swear it is made of silver.'

In Selfridge's he bought her a 'gown', as the saleswoman said, a good grey dress; and another for wearing at school, so that as he looked at her through the glass partition he would be reminded of their honeymoon. Back at the hotel, she asked, 'Thomas, do you feel very proud of doing all of this?'

'Proud?'

'Well, you know, coming from where we do, and here we are like big people.'

He said in a quiet voice, 'We are big people. We are ordinary human beings like everybody else. That's big people.'

Unhooking garments, she asked, 'Will you ever tell me? I mean one day, about – the things you were involved in?'

He generated silence in the room by standing still.

Ellen said, 'Nothing. Sorry.'

The days followed in heat and movement. A train to Bath, to see the Roman Springs. To St Paul's Cathedral. To the British Museum. To Kensington Gardens.

'Did you know,' said Ellen, 'that Queen Victoria had a plaster cast made of Prince Albert's hand? At her dying request it was placed in her coffin.'

In Oxford Street, she bought a straw hat with a maroon ribbon: 'The money Dada gave me,' she said.

One afternoon, after they had lain in bed late, he said, 'We are going for a long walk and a surprise.'

She saw him ask directions from the hotel porter, note them down carefully on an envelope, and they set off. They crossed a bridge going south, and entered a neighbourhood of small streets and burly warehouses. The children looked at them and shouted things, and Thomas and Ellen smiled, agreeing that in their hats and finery they must have looked unusual. Soon they came to a row dominated by huge tanks, and Thomas, checking his notebook, said, 'Down here.' As they stopped outside a funny little, long, two-storey building, he said, 'This is where we get your housekeeping ledger,' and grinned at her.

At the sliding glass panel he asked the girl, 'Mr Alton, please?'

'Who wants him?'

'I do.'

'No, I mean the name' – she pronounced it 'nime'.

'Mr Thomas Kane. I wrote to him.'

'Aren't you the dark horse?' whispered Ellen.

He replied, 'You said you wanted one.'

'But I thought you forgot.'

At the end of a room with long, long tables, where men measured card, and glued book bindings together, Mr Alton, ageing and ingratiating, showed them a variety of ledgers: the very large, with many columns for cash entries; or the more compact, cash-book type. Ellen looked and looked, at over twenty in all.

'What kind of business are you in?' Mr Alton asked.

'Teaching,' said Thomas.

Finally she chose a large book, measuring twenty inches by twelve – 'like the school Roll Book' – with a mauve cover staked out by red, deep corners, like large photograph angles. Inside, past the lavishly marbled endpapers, the pages, though ruled in part into little boxes and squares, also had enough lines to write upon. She needed a book she could organize in a way that permitted her to paste in recipes, cuttings and any other items on the box-ruled sections, while leaving room to write the captions, such as the date of the newspaper from which it came, or any other observations. She hefted the book in her hand, measured it side to side, end to end, spread the covers out as if writing in the early pages, then the middle pages, then the end pages. Mr Alton admired her rigorousness, and proudly pointed out to her how the spine, their own development, their own invention, had been deliberately made flexible so that a user would not have to wrestle with the pages; with most such ledgers, he informed them, comfort in writing only came as one drew close to the centre of the book, but in this case comfort was 'assured the whole way through'.

Next, Ellen sat with the ledger, as she might if writing in it, to ascertain that the top of each page came within her easy reach, that she would not have to stand up, for example, when writing at the beginning of every page, and then she judged the distance between the bottom of the page and the bottom of the book itself, so that her hand would not have an awkward struggle when writing on the very bottom line. Then she gauged how it would be writing overleaf, assessing that the paper proved thick enough not to allow even a heavy hand's ink to show through.

'Almost vellum, almost vellum,' Mr Alton kept repeating. 'Three hundred and sixty pages.'

She decided to take it but worried immediately about the weight of it, but, Mr Alton said, 'for another shilling' it could be sent by Royal Mail. Then Thomas and Ellen had a discussion as to who should pay for it; Ellen felt strongly that she should, and Thomas, although he had established that he had wanted to make her a gift of it, gave way. She paid Mr Alton in cash, waited for a receipt and, thanking him, they left.

They crossed the river again, and by now the afternoon had grown very hot. Thomas asked Ellen to wait for him outside a public lavatory on a busy street. She took off her hat and began to fan her face with it. A small-ish man unstretched himself from railings where he had been leaning and, unnoticed by Ellen, walked towards her. She only saw him when he first stood in front of her, and she strained politely to hear what he was saying, could not quite catch the words.

'Are you on, love?' he repeated.

'On?' she asked.

'Come on, love,' and he reached out and touched her arm and then squeezed. Ellen, baffled, looked down at the hand, then drew back a little. He reached out again, and only then did she say, 'Stop, stop,' and somewhat comically began to swat at his hand.

'Come on, love, stop pretending,' the man protested.

'Pretending what?'

'Come on, come on.' He cajoled, but in a tone which grew more determined. Stepping beside her he attempted to put an arm around her shoulders, while grabbing her left hand.

Bewildered, Ellen said, 'What do you want?'

'Well, what do you think?'

A heavy woman approached, a puffy face rouged.

'Hoy,' she called. 'Who's she?' The man tightened his arm on Ellen's shoulders, and began to try and walk her forward. Ellen resisted.

Thomas appeared at the top of the steps under the blue 'Gentlemen' sign, looking around pleasantly for Ellen. He stopped, puzzled, then pressed forward and grabbed the man by the shoulder. The man shouted, released Ellen and struck out at Thomas, partially connecting. Thomas tried to lift the man off the ground, and the shouting intensified, with Ellen joining in and Thomas shouting abuse. Thomas tried to slam the man's face into the high railings around the lavatory stairwell. People walking by stopped, and stood back. The man wriggled out of Thomas's grasp and began to run. Thomas ran after him but stopped when he heard Ellen calling. The puffy woman drifted away.

177

Another woman, seeing Ellen's shock, had stopped to sympathize. Thomas came back. 'Are you all right?'

'Yes, yes.'

'She shouldn't have been standing here,' a man said to Thomas. 'This is a beat.'

'Why not? What's a beat?' Ellen and Thomas asked in bewilderment.

'Where are you from?' asked the sympathetic woman.

'Ireland, we're on our honeymoon,' said Ellen.

The man said quietly to Thomas, 'This is a beat. You know, tarts.'

'Prostitutes?'

'You got it.'

'Oh, God,' said Thomas, looking shocked. He stopped a cab. At the hotel, Ellen sat on the bed, clinging to the brass rail, her face buried in her forearms, beneath her drifts of hair. She rose and filled the bath. He sat alone in the bedroom, and she emerged silently. After some slow pottering, she asked, 'But I don't look like one of – "them", do I?'

'How do you know what "they" look like?' his voice grey.

'We used to see them on Dickson's quay when a new ship came in. Tight skirts and bosoms.'

'This place,' he said, not unbitterly. 'How can people live here?'

'I thought you were going to kill him,' she said.

'I would have done.'

'I was frightened –' she began, but whether at being accosted, or at Thomas's response she did not specify.

Ellen stretched cautiously on the bed, wrapped in towels and a dressing-gown, and Thomas, still fully dressed, lay beside her; they confessed to feeling shocked, and drifted off into a sleep, a knight and his lady lying side by side on their naïve slab.

At dinner in the hotel dining-room that evening, Ellen,

more forthright by then, told Thomas that she was 'really frightened' when she saw him picking up the man who had accosted her, and he said it was no more than his husbandly duty.

'Do you remember before we were married – ?' They had returned for a last walk to Kensington Gardens.

'Those are nice words,' he interrupted.

'Aren't they? Do you remember before we were married –' with a wide smile '– we said. You said, I could ask you any question.'

'Yes?'

She had begun to emphasize, an indication that she found a subject uncomfortable. 'We said that we could talk about – being married.'

'Yes.' This time he did not look away.

'Did you ever hear of a woman called Marie Stopes?'

'No.'

'She's a woman in her mid-forties, she's a sort of doctor, interested in women and marriage.'

'And?'

'Well, she has a place here in London where people can get advice about marriage.'

'Advice?'

'Advice about, you know, what we've been doing.'

'Advice?' Again, Thomas shifted.

'No. I mean deeper information, knowledge, babies, so on. I know nothing about all that.'

'How do other women manage?'

'I suppose they talk to their friends and sisters or whatever. But I want to find out more. About myself. About you.'

'But what more is there to find out? Don't we know enough? Do you want to go and see this woman?' he asked apprehensively.

'No. Not really. But I thought we might get one or two

of her books. She wrote a book called *Married Love*, we could get that. There's another thing.' Ellen blushed and brought it out in a rush. 'My father and Jim, they wear cotton pants beneath their trousers.'

Thomas also blushed.

They bought postcards in the bookshop too, and to Leah Ellen wrote, 'Weather and hotel and everything lovely. Hope you enjoyed the wedding. See you soon.'

Thomas remarked that the postcards would probably travel on the same mail train and boat they were taking home. In the street they opened *Married Love*, glanced at one or two of the pages, and then put it in Ellen's handbag. As they began to walk, a photographer persuaded them to stop, and Thomas paid him to send on the photograph.

10

'I'll tell you one thing,' Ellen said.

'What's that?'

'I don't feel the need to go to Confession at all. Even though I know we're all supposed to. But I've nothing to tell.'

'Same here.'

From the date of the end of their honeymoon, they had seven weeks of settling down before school reopened in September.

In tiny Deanstown, with its farmhouses, cottages, the school, a public house, a pump and a village green, the grass still grows voluptuously in the summer, and still, as Thomas once upon a time repeated so fondly, in a shade closer to blue than green.

When Thomas Kane and his wife Ellen, née Morris, settled down there in the first weeks of July 1925, the population was larger than today. Most of the gabled, yellow-ochre cottages have long fallen into disrepair; Hand's pub closed a long time ago; the long demesne wall has been breached many times by the fences of new farm owners; several ornamental gateways here and there throughout the locality, those beautiful, hand-cut lime-stone pillars, have simply keeled over into the grass.

The drays of the farmers no longer rumble through Deanstown every morning with aluminium churns bound for the creamery two miles away in Silverbridge on the river: lorries, from farther away, collect the bright sweet milk. Six miles to the west, the town of Mooreville then provided all of the Kanes' immediate needs: groceries,

181

stationery, some books, a selection of clothing: it still could. That summer, the helmeted pump plunged out cool, lead-dark water which Thomas fetched at least twice daily, a bucket lugged gently spilling at the end of each arm. The distant mountains, as ever did, gave them their weather forecast.

For a while nothing touched their charmed lives. Their bodies moved in the warm space around their house and garden, in their busy marrying of each other, in their sweating, thoughtful beginnings of mutual understanding. Their fingers and thumbs and lips found new muscles, a new language; in each of the partners, new people came to dwell, unquestioning, and free. That summer the weather proved extraordinary, as if it intended to heat up the air in anticipation, or warning, or premonition. Not more than five years ago, Thomas had hidden in these fields, lain in these hedgerows, his peaked cap turned backwards, a gun in each hand, waiting to kill. Now, in the tremendous silence of a different urgency, his hips and his back ached similarly – as did those of his new wife. With a not dissimilar savagery, he surged towards her bringing her life, as he had lunged towards others bearing them death.

Yesterday (reported *The Leader*) **was so far the hottest day in the county since the heat wave began. The mean temperature was 106 degrees, but at 2.55 it reached 112 degrees in a confined area. The temperature at 1.15 today was 102 degrees in the sun. Barometric and other indications, we are informed by an authority on the subject, point to a continuance of the present fine weather.**

Ellen cut out the report, and pasted it into her ledger, the first record of their married life. Thomas, tapping the glass at midnight, marvelled at the temperatures. Ellen, wearing a light nightdress of lawn cotton, bought in London, could not sleep. Over and over again, they drenched themselves in perspiration wordlessly, and then achieved brief, deep sleep before the morning light and the birds awakened them. Each came to know something of the rhythms of the other's body, whether the other lay awake or had fallen asleep. If Ellen awoke first, she lay perfectly still, or tried to look down at his face. If Thomas had been awake, he turned to her as she stirred; after his own sleep, he reached for her the moment he opened his eyes. The summer had rendered the nights bright, and some light always hung in the room. Profound stillness could be heard through the wide open windows; inside, the walls and timbers ticked, contracting after the expansion of the day.

When they met around the house or the garden, they always touched. She wore the minimum of clothing beneath the lightest of dresses; he stripped to the waist and wore cotton trousers and plimsolls, and they kept the gate closed to discourage visitors. Sometimes through the day, she went upstairs, undressed and sponged her legs and torso with a cold flannel. One afternoon, when she sat with her ledger beginning to shape its future, Thomas came and sat opposite her. She smiled up at him and pasted in the cutting from the *Irish Independent* very carefully, using a paste of flour and water mixed in a large egg-cup.

HINTS THAT HELP

Rub new boots with a slice of new potato, and they will then polish as easily as old ones.

When stewing meat be careful not to put in too much liquid.

Tablecloths and shirts should be taken off the line

before they are quite dry, folded smoothly, and laid on one side to be ironed the next day.

An excellent aluminium polish is a mixture of borax, ammonia and water. Apply with a soft brush.

If, instead of a hard carpet-brush, a damp cloth is used to clean the stair carpet, the nap will not come off and it will wear twice as long.

Do not put away for any length of time linen that has been starched. It is apt to crack. Rinse the articles free from starch, dry, and fold in blue paper. The latter keeps them from turning yellow.

Every time she could, Ellen went and stood near Thomas. Through the window she often watched his bare back bent working in the garden.

Thomas smiled at her all the time. He looked down on her face, called her 'wife' in a teasing way, stroked her hair, held her hand if they sat out in the evening, on the bench in front of the bow window. He looked like a man who had just encountered great fortune; he indulged her, and when she did ask the occasional awkward question, like querying his violence towards the porter on the Mail Boat when they had no cabin reservation, or raised again the immense force he had threatened towards the man who had accosted Ellen on the street in London, Thomas smiled and said, 'Another time,' or 'Eh-yeh,' and went on stroking the back of her hand, or twisting her wedding ring softly round and round: she never returned to the MacReady affair, and he ever evaded her enquiries regarding the missing McAuliffe man.

Their intimacy, now flying high in all its sensations and urgency, became to both a business of assumption, rather than spoken agreement, and developed into a matter of great, silent importance. Only once did Ellen ask anxiously, 'Thomas, is this all right, is it all right for us to be like this?'

He replied with a smiling question, 'Married love?'

The process of Ellen's joining the local community now began in earnest. Numerous invitations came: tea on Sunday afternoons; to join in farmers' wives' guilds; the Canon asked her would she play the harmonium in the church? Where previously she had respected Thomas's exalted place in the community, now she relished it as part of her own life; she took pleasure in the parish deference now embracing her.

The Stephensons held their garden party – a hundred people on the lawn in front of the paddock. Thomas and Ellen walked there, up the long shaded avenue, past the woods Captain Johnson had planted years ago. Ellen wore a notable red dress.

'I'd love to see the inside of the house,' she murmured as they drew near. A table held bottles and jugs and teacups and saucers. Old wicker chairs reposed under trees, and a croquet mallet. The tablecloth flapped a little in the breeze. Nobody came to host them, or take them around. They greeted a farmer they knew, who stood on the edge of the crowd awkwardly, and with him, holding cups of tea Ellen had fetched, they drew back a little.

'That's the brother.' Thomas pointed out a large, heavy slow man, in his late twenties, wearing a thick tweed check jacket.

'He'll roast in that coat today,' observed Ellen.

'You'd need a magnifying glass to see the sandwiches,' said the farmer standing with them, and abruptly left.

Thomas and Ellen stood under a wide spreading tree.

'Who is that in the warlike yellow?' asked Ellen. 'Oh, that's, that's . . .' She struggled to recall the name.

'The daughter,' said Thomas, 'Ernestina.'

'How in the name of immortal God,' said Ellen, 'could she let herself go out of the house in that dangerous colour of a frock?'

'And,' said Thomas, 'she's no oil painting at the best of times.'

They gazed, absorbed. Most people there had passed the age of fifty, and had dressed as if for winter; a few women wore light skirts and blouses or thin coats, but many wore tweed skirts and tried not to perspire. Their heads bobbed as they listened closely to each other and they never stared at anyone else; they wore old brooches.

A tall, thin man, with a stoop, came to where they were standing.

'Now who's this pretty girl, I thought to myself?'

Ellen shook hands.

'I'm Henry Wallace, I'm the uncle you will have heard about. The Indian one.'

'You're not an Indian, are you?' Ellen asked, much less shy than Thomas.

'No, no.' The man laughed. 'I lived there. Bombay. My sister married in here. Dead now, I'm afraid. What are your names?'

Ellen replied, 'Mr and Mrs Kane.'

Thomas added, 'Only just.'

'I'm Ellen. He's Thomas.'

Henry Wallace said, 'Thomas Kane. Kane. Oh, I say. I know who you are. You're quite famous. Although I s'pose I shouldn't be saying that here.' He giggled, and indicated the party over his shoulder.

Ellen saw Ernestina advance to a few yards behind Henry Wallace, look very hard, intercept a passing woman by the arm, indicate Henry Wallace, and say something. The woman stopped to look, shading her eyes against the sun, then murmured to Ernestina, who waved a hand strongly, as if shooing her forward.

Henry Wallace said friendlily, 'I always wanted to meet you, Kane. You were a great gunman, weren't you?'

Ellen winced. 'Oh, Mr Willis, I don't think . . .'

Thomas looked down at the cup and saucer in his hand, and shook his head a little.

'Wallace, it is. I think I've said the wrong thing,' said Henry Wallace. 'Haven't I? And I think I've got it wrong right through, haven't I? Oh, dear. Look. I mean it. I am genuinely interested in what you fellows did. I always felt we got it wrong our end. I used to be a soldier, just like you.'

This seemed to surprise, and even mollify, Thomas.

'I say. Would you like to talk about it some time? I'd love to hear how it was all planned.' Henry Wallace leaned forward in a kind and eager way.

The woman to whom Ernestina had spoken materialized in their group. Smiling tightly at Thomas and Ellen, she said, 'Henry, Ernestina needs your help.' She obliged him to wade off.

'Well, that was a bit of a surprise,' said Ellen.

'I normally hate those fellows,' said Thomas.

They drifted a little, had a conversation or two with people of similar unease. One man, a veterinary surgeon with a moustache, said, 'Of course we're a Republic now, we have the Catholics here as guests. And the Sinn Feiners. You can't beat that for fairness, can you?'

Ellen tugged Thomas's arm. 'He said it to rise you. Take no notice.'

Thomas leaned towards the man. 'It seems we had too few bullets,' he said with a smile.

'Oh, now!' said another man in outrage. 'Oh, now! Really!'

An anxious man chimed in, 'We all have to get on now, don't we?'

They saw the Canon, and, under the mulberry tree, Miriam Hogan: she waved a hand at them and munched on a pie or something. When they made a move towards her she turned her back.

'God, she's odd,' said Thomas, 'look, she's talking to no one. And eating everything she can get her hands on.'

Ellen said, 'She's very handsome, though.'

The Canon came over to them and said in a loud voice, 'Haven't the Protestants very dry old faces? And 'tis no wonder they're thin, did you see the size of the sandwiches at all? And the tea. Holy Mother of God! Like water. You could baptize a child in it.'

Thomas and Ellen left, walking down the drive under the trees.

'That crowd,' said Thomas. 'Whatever they have they took from us.'

'But that was all long ago,' appeased Ellen, 'and we have most of it back now. And at least they're educated.'

'But we're not, I mean, the people around here.'

'They will be,' soothed Ellen.

'I doubt it,' said Thomas.

They turned back for a last look: Henry Wallace waved a farewell.

Ellen and Thomas went to Mass every Sunday morning in the car, the hood down in this glorious weather. Their arrival always seemed an important moment, and for the first few weeks people came across to introduce themselves, and congratulate the Master on his good fortune, and then add a word to Ellen about how it was 'high time a good man like that got himself a decent wife'.

By tacit understanding their pew, halfway down the aisle, was reserved for them alone. The Master and his wife led the movement to the altar for Communion, and their joint demeanour, dictated by Thomas, set the standard for outward expressions of devoutness among the rest of the congregation.

They dressed for Mass with great care, Thomas in a

dark or a grey suit, Ellen in grey or navy, always with hats: he removed his in the porch, she affirmed hers in place with a long and powerful hatpin. They sat erect during the sermon; the Curate short and sweet, or the Canon, rambling and interminable.

Mass-going brought Ellen information and advice. She wanted hens, chickens, pecking beneath the apple trees. Wives outside the church door on Sunday gave her cuttings from the papers, the long weekly lists of providers, some of which Ellen had already clipped. In Herbertstown, Grouselodge and Ballingarry she could buy Rhode Island Reds, White Leghorns or White Wyandottes, as well as Indian Runner ducks; in Killeglass and Broadford and Doon she learned she would find Brown Leghorns, some geese and what seemed like a larger, more vigorous strain of Rhode Island Reds; she pasted these and related matters in her ledger.

CHICKENS! FOWL! YOUNG TURKEYS!
Thousands cured of Gape or Pip by the famous 'Pipu-line' Dusting Powder 1/3d, postage 9d extra. H. Bell, Ltd, 62, Quay, Waterford. For discoloured heads, drooping, etc., use Bell's Liver Tonic Powder; a great cure, 2/6d; smaller size, 1/6d. Postage 9d.

'I have to have a messenger,' said Ellen to Thomas. 'I'm going to catch the first schoolboy I see at Mass.'

Outside the church porch she asked Michael Quinn, 'Will you come and do some jobs for me?'

'I'm left school, Ma'am.'

'I know that, but the Master says you can run quickly.'

'All right, Ma'am.'

'Drop down today after dinner.'

'All right, Ma'am.' She neglected to tell Thomas.

=

The Misses Harper befriended Ellen, sent her little notes from the large grey Georgian house, The Rectory; their late father while still the Protestant minister had bought it outright from the Church of Ireland. The spire of his church stood down by the river in Silverbridge, among trees populated with rooks. They called their boxer dog Marcus, and they spoke with pronounced English accents. Called Georgina and Judith, they cooed over Ellen.

'You look as if you just arrived off the boat from Dresden.'

'You are a china doll, dear Mrs Kane, of great value, great value.'

Recipes, preserves, flower-arranging tips, crochet patterns – they offered all of these with enthusiasm and courtesy, with flourishing delicacy and charm. On various Saturdays, Ellen learned how to transplant the corms of flowers; how 'difficult' dahlias could be; how to prune a rose bush; how to make damson jelly; why to split the end of a beech twig before putting it into water: 'The leaves stay fresh longer.'

When she walked to their house, they strolled, sometimes arm-in-arm, to meet her – letters had, of course, been exchanged – and the meeting on the tree-hung road was a model of good manners and some incongruity, the little bright-eyed, refined, fulfilled, pretty teacher, and the two tweed-skirted spinsters, one with tinted spectacles and the other with a permanent straw hat. Georgina told harmless jokes, such as the one about the man who remarried somewhat hastily after his wife died, and justified it by saying, 'The light of my life has gone out – but I have struck another match.' The Harpers had a brother who never appeared in public, said to be 'a little delicate', and whom neighbours had come across on many mornings early, sitting stark naked in the reeds by the river, playing a violin.

The sisters relished Ellen's company; she had come

from a city, and therefore must know about fashion and society. Ellen loved their naïve good manners – and their polished accents suggested that the wider world might after all be introduced safely into this worryingly closed, however idyllic, community.

On several afternoons of this unprecedented hot spell Thomas and Ellen cycled, or sometimes drove, to the river, to the place where they had first walked, where Ellen had worn her cream lace dress, where Thomas had first 'laid hands' on her (as she once called it). Down in the dark water they delved, gasping cold at first, then delightful. Ellen learned to swim properly under Thomas's guidance, and in a blue swimsuit and little white rubber cap she waved her hands slowly like fronds, up and down, up and down, to the fork where the tributary joined the big swifter river, and back again.

Nobody else ever came there by day, only the waterbirds, some coots, and a crane. In the near fields they heard corncrakes: in the distance, always in the distance, a cuckoo. Nearby, Chadwick's Well, a round, deep, bright structure of white cement, sparkled full of turquoise waters.

In the early cool of the evening, before they ate, they often walked the fields – sometimes to the Castle again, of which Thomas never tired, sometimes to the old kitchen garden where the ancient *espalier* pears and plums, and the greengages, were ripening, much to Ellen's anticipation.

The food she prepared surprised not only Thomas but herself. She had natural taste and a flair for cooking, even though she stuck to what she had learned in Domestic Economy, and what she had scantily gleaned from her mother or now picked up from local women. She made him 'Fancy Lady', an Irish stew, but using brown gravy and a tablespoon of sherry; all over and around the chunks of meat hewn from chops, she packed potatoes from Thomas's garden, and his hard, fat onions from the hanks inside the back-kitchen door. Once they even had wine, a bottle Thomas had been given at a Teachers' Conference the previous year. They drank some of it on a Sunday at lunch, and put away the rest in a cupboard where it lived for five years – and when Ellen eventually found it by accident she burst into screaming tears.

On the last Sunday in August, with a week to go before the opening of the school, Ellen, having arranged herself carefully, sat down to begin reading the heirloom Thomas had given her, his aunt's inherited papers and letters about Timothy Nash, the hedge-schoolmaster. The handwriting was steady and elegant.

> I began assembling this in 1882, and hoped to expand it wider and wider, but as I found out more and more about my subject I felt that I should stop.

Ellen fingered the pile and methodically began to rearrange the package. Under the heading 'The Life of Timothy Nash' she made five notes on her writing-pad, '1. Rearrange all the papers in chronological order. 2. Buy folders at Hickey's, and labels to keep the parts separate. 3. Ask Thomas for the name of a good Irish translator. 4. Call to library in J'borough.'

She looked at the clock on the mantelpiece, counted out forty pages, enough, she reckoned, to occupy two hours, and began to read, skipping the illegible bits until later.

The original writer, from whom Thomas's successive aunts had inherited, first described Timothy Nash's classes:

> . . . lying in a sunny meadow surrounded by impoverished children and their bedraggled parents. Most of them had

once been wealthy, before being displaced by Yorkshire or Somerset yeomen families planted into their lands. In his hedge lessons Nash took these dispossessed Catholics into other worlds, the realms of gold. These poor, miserable people, deprived of learning, and of land, and of living, encountered the ancient writers, Horace and Livy and Virgil . . .

Some of these hedge-schoolmasters died in the open air in the wintertime because they were always on the run . . .

We used to see Mr Nash coming across the fields to us, always down the same pathway by the headland of the Hill Field, a long black coat down to his ankles, and a fading black hat like an Italian priest. He came to our house about four times a year and we took turns to watch for the soldiers who hunted him if they thought he was in the area. He would either have been dragged out of our house and shot on the spot, or hanged after a quick trial. By that time, there was nearly as big a price on the head of a hedge-schoolmaster as there was on a priest, and we were always afraid of informers . . .

Sometimes, if it was raining, he taught inside, and he made us chant *Amo, Amas, Amat, Amamus, Amatis, Amant*. He told us about Euclid and Pythagoras. In the open air he was at his best, and out there in the haggard field, most especially when the grass was long and there were buttercups, he taught Latin poems.

Ellen made notes. 'Go and see the Nash house over near Bruree. Look up the Penal Laws and see the details regarding education. Find out what the population of the Irish Colleges abroad was. When was Salamanca founded? What regiment would have been stationed nearby in 1770?' She read on through the details of Timothy Nash's scholastic career, which, it appeared, had dazzled the whole College.

At the back of an account of his brilliant capacity to translate sight unseen from the Greek, she found another page, folded in four and pinned tight; the pin had long rusted. Fearing blood-poisoning from the rust, she did not handle the pin directly: she forced it from the pages with the corner of her writing-case, opened the paper and read in the same hand.

> He was disciplined several times for [two words that looked like 'moral insubordination'], and on four occasions for [was it 'excessive' or 'extreme'?] and unnecessary violence, resulting in one student [the ink had splodged: perhaps 'needing the care' or 'cure'] of the College's physician. He struck a tutor with an [Ellen could not make it out: it might have been 'oar', but boats had not been mentioned] and rendered the man ill. [A following line had been heavily scored out, and the passage concluded with the words, 'concern but not astonishment'.]

Ellen sat back, thinking deeply, then shivered. She stood up, walked to the bay window, fiddled a moment with the long lace curtains, touched the fronds of the palm, and turned back again to the table. Delving further into the package of papers, she took out the ones in Timothy Nash's handwriting and held them up to the light as if examining banknotes; she turned them over, moistened a finger and touched the black, insect-like ink until one word ran a little, then laid the papers back on the table with a little shudder.

At supper – cold beef and tomatoes, with Thomas drinking a glass of stout – she said, 'Thomas, what kind of a man was Timothy Nash? I mean was he a violent man?'
'I have no notion,' said Thomas.

Michael Quinn came almost every day to the house.
'Michael, you're going to be invaluable to me.' She addressed him more as adult than boy, and invited him to bring his little brother, the unspeaking Timmy – who, on his first appearance, hung around the gate, peeping in like an elf, with a big beaming smile. Ellen lured him forward with a slice of apple pie. Timmy's nose ran permanently.

Michael cleaned Ellen's bicycle; he helped her wash potatoes; Timmy followed her around the house, always a few steps behind. Once, she grabbed him unexpectedly and washed his face in warm water and soap. After a first quick struggle, he stood, caught between embarrassment and pleasure; she held her own good handmirror to him, then let him take it in his hand; he stroked the back, trying to touch the lace inside the glass.

Michael worked beside her at the scullery table, topping and tailing the gooseberries, taken too late from the garden and quite squashy, and he willingly entered into her games to help Timmy speak.

'Goose. Gog,' Ellen said. Michael repeated it equally slowly.

Ellen procured from her mother discarded shirts which had once fitted her brother Jim, and gave them to Michael. She showed him how to clean windows, she inside, he outside, and made him go over smears again and again. When Timmy climbed on the chair behind Michael, Ellen teased him through the glass by pretending to speak, but uttering no sound. This brought forth a number of words from Timmy.

She praised Michael, gave him apples, and paid him in half-crowns.

'That's too much, Ma'am.'

'No, Michael, the labourer is worthy of his hire.'

She said to Thomas, 'That Michael – there's something very endearing about him. He's invaluable to me.'

'His father's a bad egg,' Thomas grunted.

'But you should see how nice he is to the little fellow. He plays with him, and talks to him.'

'Eh-yeh.'

Thomas and Ellen went back to school on the first Monday of September.

'I have a sudden craving for an orange,' said Ellen, then

continued, as they stood watching the children play, 'Isn't it extraordinary? How much has happened? Since last February.'

Arms folded, he merely smiled.

'I love all the new books,' she said, 'and the chalk from last year's boxes and the smell of the ink – I know it isn't last year, but you know what I mean.'

Leah arrived the next Friday to stay for just one night, a rare treat, Herbert had given her 'a Sabbath off', even though she had, dutiful wife, as she said, prepared everything before she left: the food; the children's clothes; the prayer books; Herbert's suit and shawl. She stepped off the bus in the middle of the village, a wonderful, coloured creature, with a suitcase that would have sufficed for a four-week stay. She wore a bright pink coat, and a hat of curved feathers, and high heels.

Thomas and Ellen both met her, Thomas carrying her almost empty case the few hundred yards to the house, Leah's heels sinking in the soft tar of the road. Eventually, seeing how her shoes might be ruined, she took them off and walked along the grass borders of the road. Thomas, looking at the shoes, said, 'You can take that tar off with butter.'

Ellen said, 'Can you? Leah, Thomas knows everything: I'm going to put that in my ledger' – and proceeded to tell Leah about the recipes, the household hints, the short poems.

'She even cuts out the advertisements,' said Thomas. They all laughed.

After school, Thomas had to go and help a farmer fill forms for a drainage grant. Ellen and Leah took their cups of tea out to the garden bench which, during the summer, Thomas had moved under the sycamore tree at the side of the house. The women began to talk.

'You look very well,' said Leah. 'And happy. It is

196

possible to be happy living with a man, although with Herbert I often think I have to make the happiness, he worries so much.'

'Leah, tell me something,' said Ellen. Leah sat up, sure in her wisdom and experience that something 'interesting' was about to be addressed.

'You know, when you and Herbert got married first.'

'Ye-es?' asked Leah.

'Ah-m.' Ellen halted. A breeze stirred. Ellen put a hand to her mouth.

'I read. I read in this book we bought in London. Well, no, in a magazine Rina got from America. That married women should always consult a doctor.'

They murmured for half an hour, obliquely, thoughtfully.

Leah, earnest and quiet, summarized, 'They don't talk about things like this in our religion, either. Although we seem to understand more – more about, I suppose, about – joy.'

The leaves in the tree rustled. Leah shivered, pointed to the sky, to a cloud moving slowly over. 'I told Herbert the weather would break. He said it would probably never rain again, there would be no crops this autumn, and did we have enough packages of food laid in?'

Ellen smiled, and Leah continued.

'I can't afford any of those things in packages. Do you know, Ellen, I can get skim milk for a third of the price of real milk, and the children don't notice it in their tea, and if Herbert does, he doesn't say anything.'

'The next time we're going to see Mama and Dada, I'll make sure Thomas throws a bag of potatoes in the back of the car for you,' said Ellen.

They took the cups in and the rain came. It poured all night; Thomas came home soaked to the skin but very pleased that the ground would have water. He and Ellen lay in bed listening to a sound they had never heard before together, the rain on the slates of the roof.

Next morning, being Saturday, they slept a little late, and then downstairs could hear Leah moving about and singing in a sweet voice. Thomas lifted the window high and put his head out, breathing the air.

'Oh, the coolness.' He turned to call Ellen and found her leaning against the dressing-table. She had grown very pale and looked disturbed, shaken.

'What's wrong?'

'I don't know, I'm feeling terrible, I can't swallow, I'm all dizzy.'

'I'll call Leah.'

'No, she'll see the bed, how tossed it is.'

'She's a married woman.'

He went to the door.

'Leah. Leah!' and she answered from the hall.

'Ellen's feeling off.'

'Off?' Leah climbed the stairs. 'Not off, surely? How can she be off?' and quite unabashedly sailed into the room. Leah felt Ellen's forehead, sat her on the bed, then made her lie down. Turning to Thomas, she said, 'A glass of water, or a cup of tea and a rest, I think.'

Thomas hurried downstairs and Leah said, 'Dear Ellen. You are going to have a new little person in this house, I think,' and counting on her fingers, starting, 'August, September, October, November . . .' she said, 'And in May, I think.' Outside it began to rustle with rain again.

'Don't say anything to Thomas,' asked Ellen.

'If you're all right,' said Thomas later, 'we could go to the pictures when we take Leah back. There's one on at the *Grand Central* called *Sinners in Silk*. I'll read it out to you. "Featuring Eleanor Boardman, Conrad Nagel and Adolphe Menjou. A highly dramatic and unusual story of Life. And then – Realization – comedy and interest. The

Rejected Woman. In seven parts. Featuring Alma Rubens." Would you like to do that?'

Leah said, 'Ooh, I like Adolphe Menjou.'

Ellen, still lying down, said, 'Thomas, I don't think I want to go into Janesborough today.'

'No,' said Leah, leaning against the jamb of the bedroom door, 'I will get the bus.'

'No, Thomas will drive you, won't you, Thomas?'

'Certainly.'

'No.' Leah put up a hand with the air of somebody who would not lose this argument. 'I will go by bus.'

Thomas stood at the door, looking out at the rain. He whistled a little.

Ellen said, 'Leah thinks I might be going to have a baby.'

His hands hung by his sides. Then he rubbed his mouth.

'Well, well, well. That's great news.' He said no more, and did not look at Ellen, who fiddled with her hair. 'Great news,' he repeated.

In a moment, he strolled downstairs. First he stood by the bookshelves, then went into the parlour and rearranged the small clock on the mantelpiece, then back to the kitchen. He opened the drawer, took out some stamp-paper he had been saving, fetched down the copy of *Under the Greenwood Tree*, and began to repair the torn jacket. When he returned, undressed and climbed into bed, Ellen had begun to drop off to sleep. His hand found her forearm, which he clasped.

Autumn 1925

11

Ellen suggested they take 'nature walks', so that she could learn about the countryside.

'With a heart and a half,' Thomas said, and, not un-wryly, continued, 'I know every stick and stone of these fields.'

Laying it out like a campaign, he planned that they walk every second day or so, with varied moments for the different sights: pastureland in the morning, marshland at evening, woodland by day during the week-ends, and he taught Ellen the values and liabilities of each field. He showed contempt for farmers who allowed moss to grow; plucked blades of silverweed for her; identified the different fescues and clovers in the opulent aftergrass of the summer's meadows. She learned boys' lore: how to stand motionless if glimpsing the rarity of a fox; where to sense a nest in the grass: 'Go to where the bird has flown from, not to where she seems to be leading you'; how to find downwind on a seemingly calm day: 'Put your finger in your mouth, until it is wet and warm, hold it to the air: the side that gets cold first – that's where the wind is coming from.'

'I wish we had owls around here,' said Thomas, 'an owl can eat nearly twice its own weight in mice of an evening.'

'Aach!' said Ellen.

'Or wouldn't it be lovely if we had nightingales? "Thou wast not born for death, immortal bird,"' quoted Thomas.

'But wasn't Keats an immoral sort of fellow?' asked Ellen.

Together they admired the slender form of the lark, and its flirrup-flirrup of flight away from them; analysed the difference between an occupied badger sett and a disused one, according to the freshness of the earth at the entrance; what will put off a thrush's attacking dive as it protects its nest?: 'Wear tall-ish headgear, like a hat, not anything flat, wear something with a crown to it'; that she should never, ever approach a nesting swan – 'A swan can break your arm with the beat of a wing'; where to find the variety of wild briar that smells like roasted apples: 'At a stone wall, and facing south or south-west'; the impression of a shod hoof, complete with nails, the twig formation from which the horse chestnut got its name; how a trapped bee or wasp sent down a rabbit burrow will have the same effect as a ferret. Thomas captured a dozen or so wasps in an unwashed empty jamjar, and sealed it with a punctured lid: 'They can't get out but they still get air.' They walked to a warren near the Castle ice-pit, and arranged themselves on either side of the entrance. Waiting several minutes – 'Give the burrow a chance to calm down' – Thomas threw some jam down the earthen hole as far as it would go, then opened the jar and shook the wasps out. He smiled across the grassy bank at Ellen, as her eyes widened when she heard the thumping. Next, a posse of rabbits galloped out of the burrow, raced to a few feet away, their noses twitching unstoppably, then seeing Thomas and Ellen raced farther and urgently. They were followed by a slower thumping and tiny, hairless, sightless bodies rolled out, down the earthen hillock, as two large females heaved out baby rabbits hardly two days old. The adults climbed over them, began to haul at them, then they too raced away in several directions, abandoning their young to the humans. Having inspected the babies to their satisfaction, Thomas ostentatiously led Ellen away, far down the field until they had moved out of the territory of the burrow. There they hid behind hazel trees, and could see that the adults had returned and engaged in some transaction, presumably returning the babies to safety, or, as Thomas believed, 'either sniffing them to decide whether to abandon them, or moving them to a safer place.'

'Isn't that cruel of us,' she asked, 'disturbing them like that?'

'No, it's only animals,' he said. 'Wait 'til the spring, 'til you see the hares kicking.'

They returned from these walks exhilarated and breathless, and Ellen found that Thomas, no matter what chore was about to preoccupy him, seemed never far away from the bedroom as she went upstairs to change. He sat on the bed, talking, or listening: one afternoon she asked sharply, 'As a matter of interest – do you mind me looking at you while you're dressing?'

He fidgeted. 'I don't know. I mean . . .'

For some days he avoided the bedroom when she went there, until, on two successive occasions, she called to him, and when he arrived, engaged him in conversation, and the issue was soon smoothed over.

Mrs McAuliffe and Hannie came again to the school.

'I can tell, Miss, that you're not someone who has much time for people with a sad story.'

Only for the sake of the child did Ellen hold back a sting of her tongue.

Mrs McAuliffe now said to Ellen, in Thomas's presence, 'You know, Miss, they all told me the Master here wouldn't help, but Father Shine said that wasn't the case at all, no matter what people said about Master Kane.'

Ellen said, 'Now, Mrs McAuliffe, you shouldn't be talking about the Master like that. We're here to help. You know that.'

'He did a very good turn, the Master, a couple of years ago, didn't you, Master? For a man whose hay burnt down. The Master got every farmer for miles to give a small bit of hay of their own, until the burnt barn was all filled up again. Didn't you, Master? Ma'am, the pension and all that, I have to clean houses for people; the eggs I sells only brings in a few shillings.'

'I'll tell you what,' said Ellen. 'The Master and myself will be making enquiries about . . . about your problem. Will that do for the moment?'

'Ah, Ma'am, it won't do, no,' said the woman. 'Sure, how am I to know anything, we've no funeral, nor wake, nor nothing.' She looked again at Thomas and said in an accusing tone, 'Master Kane, you should be doing something.'

Thomas reddened, not in embarrassment; in anger.

'Now that's enough,' he snapped, 'that is. Enough.' He walked back into his own classroom. Ellen shepherded the woman out, running back to get a book, *Stories of the Saints*.

'Here, Hannie, there's a present for you.'

'Ma'am, I'd rather give her her father back.'

Ellen returned to Thomas, and asked with vehemence, 'Does that woman think you're supposed to know about something?'

Thomas said, 'Look, I spoke to the Sergeant. That is a bad case. That man is dead. The people who killed him and buried him are still around. And nearer here than you'd think. I told you that before. If they find out that anybody is looking into that case – well, there's danger in it. Now leave it alone like a good woman.'

Ellen said, 'But – that's terribly unjust. That child is missing her father. I'd take it as a great favour if you did something.'

'No, I won't.'

'I think you should, Thomas.' She bobbed her head. 'It would be a kindness, and a good act, and a fine example. Why should such bad things be buried? Besides, isn't it very clear that she thinks – and so must other people –

that you were involved in things like that, and you should show them you weren't.'

Thomas closed the lid of his desk.

Ellen pressed. 'I'd think a lot of you if you did.'

He looked at her with a statue's sightless glare.

Ellen asked, 'Did you know her husband?'

Thomas said, 'A little useless scut of a fellow, but he had one good point, he was very reliable. If you asked him to be somewhere to do something, he'd turn up as promised, not like most people, but he was useless when he got there, as lazy as sin.'

They walked to October Devotions, and prayed and sang before the white-and-gold altar of the church. On crisp evenings of moonlight and frost, Thomas pointed out the stars to her on the way back. They could hear their footsteps echo, and now she also longed for an owl, never having heard one. Sometimes he stopped and hushed her, and they listened to a scurry in the roadside, or a cough not far away – a badger. One Wednesday evening she stopped.

'Euch!' she said, 'what's that smell?'

He sniffed the air. 'A dead animal probably. There's a dead beast inside the ditch somewhere.'

Ellen turned to the list of contents in the handwriting of Thomas's aunt, and found the Flora Callaghan letters, four in all. The first one, addressed, 'Dear Miss Kane' had been written in 1850, and said,

> As you suggest, I am writing herein my memory of the first time I saw Timothy Nash. I have taken the liberty, and I am sure you will not take offence at it, of consulting my brothers and sisters so that a full picture of the unfortunate man may emerge.

Unfortunate? Ellen sat up. She flicked through the other letters and then stopped herself, thinking that the story must unfold in its own natural way, that she must not jump from source to source. Her bladder was full: would the Canon ever be persuaded to install running water and electricity?

'"Unfortunate"? Timothy Nash "unfortunate"?' she queried half-aloud, and read some more of Miss Flora Callaghan's first, very long letter.

My father had arranged for a hayloft above the cows to be set aside as a place where Mr Nash could sleep and teach. Mr Nash had no slates like the modern schools do, all he had was a curious, very large leather bag out of which he took many books, small volumes that must have travelled a long way. At the beginning of every class he would arrange these in a neat pile and throughout the lesson he would read from them in turn, telling us about the people who wrote them.

We never thought of laughing or giggling in his class because he had a severe nature which rendered children quiet in his presence.

He wore linen that required much attention, and a blue bandanna at his neck which also deserved washing. He had a waistcoat the colour of burgundy wine and he frequently smelt of a smell I knew later to be strong drink. In appearance he was a tall man with dark brown, nearly black curly hair, which had a little grey in it. He had a flared nose and eyebrows which met in the middle, and gave the appearance of a handsome, erect man who could be most distinguished if he chose.

When he read to us he would rise from the palliasse on which he had been sitting, the same upon which he had slept, and stand as if acting the words, the book held out at arm's length, reading in a strong voice.

Ellen exclaimed half-aloud, 'But that's just like Thomas!'

My father once asked him whether he thought it could prove more prudent to hold classes in softer tones, lest passing soldiery or an indiscreet servant be attracted to this unusual sound, and Mr Nash's reply left no room for further discussion. He was a strong man, of large physical

208

capacity and fiercely-held opinion. He had difficulty once or twice with some people of my father's acquaintance to whom he showed extreme violence . . .

Ellen exclaimed to herself, 'Oh, my God!'

and I feel certain that his very forthright demeanour played no small part in the unfortunate continuation and outcome of his life, but his love for learning could never have been gainsaid.

I cannot think what assistance my poor recollections may be to you, dear Miss Kane, but I will write again and see if I can offer something more illuminating than this humble meal from my memory.

In the meantime I would be grateful if you would convey my simple affections and notice of regard to your brother and his wife, and to your respected self

> I remain,
> Yours Most Truly,
> Flora Callaghan

'Thomas, this sick feeling won't go away.'

He looked over the top of his spectacles. 'I told you. You should go and see the doctor.'

'Leah says there's no need. Mama says there's no need, they all say 'tis perfectly natural in the first six weeks, even three months.'

Upstairs, she took off all her clothes and stood in front of the mirror peering intently at her stomach. She rubbed a hand over it and turned this way and that watching the candlelight reflect from mirror to mirror, and did not hear Thomas step softly into the room behind her. He put his hands gently on her bare shoulders from behind, kissing her neck.

'You look like a painting,' he said. 'You look like a picture in a gallery.' For the first time ever Ellen did not attempt to cover herself in his presence.

=

After school in the evenings, Michael Quinn came to do his chores. Ellen asked Thomas to show the boy how onions should be plaited into a hank: Thomas did so with scant grace.

'Don't be so gruff with him,' Ellen hissed when Michael had gone to the pump to fill the bucket.

The boy showed Ellen how to wash a bottle clean: put a handful of little gravel pebbles in the bottom, some water, then shake it hard, and all the scum of the old cream will disappear. One afternoon, Thomas walked into the kitchen while the boy was sitting there at the table, having tea and a piece of apple tart, with Ellen reading to him from *Treasure Island*. Thomas walked out again.

At supper he said, 'I'm telling you, Ellie, there is bad blood in that house.'

'Well, Michael's all right, you have to admit that. And he's very useful to me.'

Thomas said, 'I have taken to putting certain things out of sight.'

Ellen flared. 'Now, isn't that very pompous of you? Look at the way that boy protects Timmy from that father of theirs? Look at the nice way he talks about that hopeless mother of theirs?'

Thomas retorted, 'You see? You're saying it yourself. They're a useless tribe.'

'Thomas, I'm surprised at you. That poor boy – he walks as if expecting a blow on the back of his head all the time. Where is your compassion? I'm very fond of him, and the more I see of him, the fonder I get of him. He's completely trustworthy, and he's very willing to learn.'

The following Saturday, Ellen and Thomas drove to Janesborough. They called to Brunswick Square first, just before noon. Ellen's father had decided not to go into the printing works that day, and they found him in the little front garden behind the railings, lifting bulbs. He had in mind, he said, to clear that ground for some standard roses from now on, only he did not know how far back from the railings he should put them, and did he have enough room?

'Did you go to the doctor yet?' whispered May in the kitchen.

'I'm just going to go, Mama.'

Thomas said to Ellen's father, 'The thing I'm thinking is, it solves one problem, at least I'll have something comfortable to call you now. I can call you Grandda or Granddad, or whatever the child says.'

Mr Morris said, 'Right enough, I never knew what to call my own father-in-law.'

'Yes, you did,' cut in his wife. 'You used to call him "the oul' shite".'

'But not to his face,' her husband replied, and everybody laughed except Ellen who protested, 'Mama! Really!'

Father Watson greeted Ellen in the dark-brown camphor-smelling drawing-room.

'And how is the wonder-man?'

'You mean Thomas? Fine, Father John, he's grand,' she replied, too preoccupied to catch – or perhaps ignoring – the edge in his voice.

They decided to go for a walk, with Ellen realizing that somewhere on the way she would be buying him a cup of tea, and probably something to eat.

When they had swung on to the parkway path towards the river, she told him the news about the baby. He took her arm briefly, squeezed it gently and said how pleased he was.

'Birth is a miracle,' he said, 'though I have always thought that death is a miracle too in its own way.'

'Does that baby know anything now?' she asked, stopping to take a piece of the cinder from the path out of her shoe.

'Not knowingly, not until it begins to experience life. But of course it is life, it is part of you and Thomas, part of your joint being.'

'I don't remember anything before I was born.'

'It is not given to us to know anything before birth.'

'How do I know I shall know anything after death?'

'Because the Lord has said so, we have the evidence of Christ Himself and the Gospels and the whole Testament. But I take your point. If you didn't know anything before you were born, it may not be given to you to know anything after your death. Therefore – what has the whole experience been for? That is what you are saying, is it not?'

'More or less.'

'That, Ellen,' and he laughed, 'is what centuries of theologians have discussed. I have a simple view. This child of yours and Thomas's, he or she will grow a little like you, a little like Thomas, with your eyes, perhaps, or Thomas's curly hair; he or she will copy a gesture of yours, or walk like its father. That is the root, is it not, of Christian belief, that God made us in His own likeness? Is it not also a kind of immortality, a kind of eternal life, that one day, if we had family portraits, your descendants would see that one of them would look exactly like you? That's why rich people have portraits painted, especially non-Catholics, because they have no safe after-life.'

He asked Ellen how she felt about the baby, about how she felt spiritually.

She said, 'I feel in two minds about it. I have a kind of natural joy, but I also have a kind of fear.'

'Apprehension?' he queried.

'Is that the word?'

'Yes, it's a natural enough feeling. It probably comes

from wishing to protect the new life, Ellen dear. How is Thomas feeling about it all?'

'Well, naturally he's hoping for a son.'

'Naturally.'

'And he says he's very pleased, quite excited, but of course he has reared children before, he had to be the father to his brothers and sisters when his own father and mother died. And I think he feels the responsibility.'

'And –' Father Watson cleared his throat as if embarrassed, then looked off to the distance, as far as he could see, before planting his spike: '– And, Ellen, he is not too worried, I take it, about the marital quietude?'

'How do you mean, Father John? What's "marital quietude"?'

'I mean, he is not upset at the loss of marital rights?'

'What loss?' Ellen blushed, and stopped to face the priest. Behind them a pilot boat set out down the choppy river to guide a cargo ship in from the sea.

'Well, my dear Ellen –' the priest put on his most serious tone and raised himself to such height as he possessed. 'When a woman is bearing fruit, it is of course the Natural Law, and therefore the law of God, that congress must cease.'

'Father John,' said Ellen, consternation growing, 'you are not serious? You are not serious? You mean we could be committing sin?'

'Yes, I'm afraid I do. I admit the Church, the teaching is a little hazy, but it has been a generally-held belief that this is a sacred time for a woman, for you, in this case, and must not be profaned.'

They had reached a café on the edge of the park, where a busy street ran down to the water. Two drays and their horses and carters stood by the kerb, thudding barrels into a public house cellar, the street grille of which had just been raised. The priest and the pretty young woman skirted them and entered the café: he ordered tea for them

213

both, and bread and marmalade for himself, and then a jam roll.

Ellen could not look at him for a moment or two, then raising her eyes and staring him in the face, said, 'Father John, can you make sure about that. Please?'

The priest's face darkened and then grew embarrassed.

'Ellen, I said it was a confused issue. But it is there, in Canon Law.'

'Father John, you know I like everything very clearcut, no shadows, no doubts, I want no possibilities of being anything other than on the right side. If there is any doubt I find it, even if I have to dig it out, and then it worries me even more.'

'Yes, Ellen, yes. But you do not need to have scruples to get by in life and to stay in the sight of God. God doesn't want you to be perfect.'

'I do!'

'But that's impossible.'

'Father, would it be a Mortal Sin or a Venial Sin?'

'My dear, I don't know.'

'Yes, you do, I know by your face. It is grave, isn't it?'

'Well, anything like that is grave. Yes, I have to tell the truth, it was supposed to be a Mortal Sin, but I don't know if it still is.'

'Things can't shift their ground like that, Father.'

'Ellen, I spend my life dealing not with moral certainty, but with moral uncertainty. I'll do all I can to establish the certainty in this. The point is. Congress between man and wife has as its intent the procreation of children. Once conception has been achieved, anything thereafter according to Canon Law is no better than bestial.'

'Bestial? For something God Himself has blessed? Bestial?'

'Well, that's what they say. A bit strong, I grant.'

'And in the meantime?' Ellen leaned forward, clearly in anguish: the serene and passionate bedroom she shared

214

and so adored with Thomas had just been invaded uglily, confusingly.

'Ellen, if you don't know something is a sin, then you can't be committing one. And you don't know this is a sin.'

'You've just told me it is!'

'I've just told you that it was once regarded as one. I don't know what the most recent thinking is, that is what I'm going to find out. In any case,' he continued, 'think of the good fortune you have now created for this child by choosing such a fine man as Thomas to breed with.'

'He isn't a racehorse, Father John.'

The priest laughed. 'He may not be, but there is some very interesting thinking going on over in Europe right now – about people choosing ideal partners, for the purposes of producing even higher strains in their children, ever finer types of child. All lawful and above board. Though I can see where some doubtful morals might creep in.'

'Does it follow that they will also inherit . . . ?' Ellen did not finish her sentence, said instead, 'You've confused me terribly, Father John.'

She reported to Thomas immediately they got in the car. He looked at her aghast. 'You talk to him too much. Why the blazes did you say anything at all to him?'

'I didn't mean to,' Ellen said apologetically. 'He actually said it to me. We were just talking about birth, and then he asked me how you felt about this.'

'What do you think yourself? Do you think it'd be sinful?'

'I don't know,' said Ellen, angry and wan at once. 'I'm up and down and in and out about it. I don't know what to think.'

'Feeling is sometimes better than thinking,' said Thomas. 'What do you feel? Do you feel it would be a sin?'

'I won't know until –'

'Until we do it again?' He grinned, seeking to ease matters. 'So I get one more go, do I?'

'Oh, Thomas.'

That night, she saw him go to the bookcase and take down *Married Love* by Marie Stopes. When he saw her glance of enquiry he laughed and remarked, 'Just fighting fire with fire.'

'There's nothing in it about all this,' Ellen said.

'How do you know?' Thomas asked suspiciously. 'Were you looking for it?'

'No, but I've read it from cover to cover.'

A page fell open. 'What's this?' asked Thomas, and began to read. '"This little crest, which lies anteriorly between the inner lips round the vagina, enlarges when a woman –"'

Ellen snatched the book out of his hand: he chased her and they wrestled but she would not give it up, and they concluded in laughter.

When, hours later, they climbed into bed, Thomas said, 'It is not a sin, it can't be a sin,' he said quietly, and with all his authority, 'for a man and his wife to be married. Remember what the Canon read out at the altar. "With my body I thee worship." Ask the Doctor when you go to see him.'

'But will we be punished?' she asked.

'Punished? For what? That's a strange God that would do that,' Thomas said. 'How would he punish us?'

'Perhaps the old stories, you know, the birthmarks, maybe that's what it all means?'

He grimaced in the dark: nevertheless he bundled her up in his arms and rocked her, holding her head on his chest.

In the church the following morning only Thomas noticed the hesitancy in Ellen as she rose to go to the altar-rails for Communion.

12

Dr Morgan said, 'You left it long enough. What are you, three months gone?'

'About that.'

'When did you get married? Late June? Ah-ha. Honeymoon job. Well, well. And no complications of any kind?'

'None.'

'Good man, good man. At the same time, why didn't you come earlier?'

'Well, isn't it very selfish to pay myself such attention?'

He said tartly, 'Well, you went to school to the nuns, that's for sure.'

Examining Ellen very carefully, he checked her eyes, her ears, her pulses, made her undress completely and drew a blanket over her; piecemeal, he unveiled her as he continued his examination. He became brusquer still when she did not raise her legs to the required height and angle. She lay as still as a peaceful animal, her face peering up at him from the rim of the white blanket, hands held above her head, never taking her eyes off his, a direct response to her own embarrassment, while inspecting his matter-of-factness as if to learn how he achieved such a manner. When the examination had been completed he invited her to dress and sit at his desk, and he began to ask her questions.

'Now do you know what happens to a woman when she is having a baby? The reason I ask is that if you sat here at my desk day in and day out, you'd be amazed that anybody ever got born.'

Ellen, typically, summarized, as if in a classroom, what she had learned, what she knew, about conception, pregnancy and childbirth. Though amused, he was pleased that she had taken the trouble to learn so much, and then burst out laughing when she mentioned Marie Stopes.

'Where did you hear about her? You'll get yourself excommunicated from the Church if you mention her name.'

'But there's a letter from a Jesuit printed in the preface of her book?'

'Yes, but that's only window-dressing. D'you remember what the letter said?' Dr Morgan reached for the shelf behind him and took down his own copy of *Married Love*, grinning at Ellen's surprise. His hands shook a little.

'Listen to this. This is the Jesuit, what's his name, Father Stanislaus St John, though I suppose he pronounces it "Sinjen", this is what he has to say: ". . . the case you give of the worn-out mother of twelve. The Catholic belief is that the loss of health on her part for a few years of life and the diminished vitality on the part of her later children would be a very small price indeed to pay for an endless happiness on the part of all." Blah. Pure blah.' Dr John Morgan grinned.

Ellen smiled. Then leaning forward, suddenly urgent as if her life depended on it, and as earnest as a child, she said, 'Doctor, I have a problem – raised by a priest too.'

The benign man blew through his yellowing moustache. 'You're not the first and you won't be the last.'

'No, seriously, and by a Jesuit as well.'

'They're the boys for the problems. Don't I know it, wasn't I at school to them?'

'A friend, a Jesuit, an old friend, told me that it is a mortal sin for my husband and myself to go on –' she stopped.

'Having "connection"?' asked the doctor.

'Yes.'

'Did he now? Envious old buggers, the priests.'

218

'Is it?'

'Is it what? A sin? I don't know. There's all kinds of superstitions about it. Did he tell you the baby will have a birthmark?'

'He didn't, but I heard it.'

'That's the sort of thing,' said Dr Morgan, 'there's a basis in superstition, and sin has a lot to do with superstition.'

'He says,' Ellen pressed on, 'that the purpose of the relationship between man and woman is to have children, and once that has been achieved, then anything else is sinful until it is necessary to try again.'

'Yes, I know. And that's all designed to keep the Catholic Church growing in numbers.'

'He says people will grow in strength towards each other through their self-denial.'

'You mean,' said the doctor with a snort, 'if I deny myself my little night-cap every night by the fire, I will come to like whiskey even more? More old blah!'

'He says' – when Ellen got the bit between her teeth she was difficult to shake off – 'that Thomas and I must stop immediately, that we are committing sin every day and every night.'

'What does your husband, Mr Kane, what does he think?'

'He hasn't said much, so far, but I know he's upset.'

'This is awkward. And 'tis awkward for me, as well. I'm supposed to be a Catholic doctor. If I tell you anything, or say to you anything that contradicts Catholic teaching, and if it gets back to a priest or a bishop or any of those boys, they can – and will – make a complaint about me. But I'm also a man who has travelled a lot, I have seen a lot of the world. My wife is German, I have a daughter nearly your age, I was in the British Army in the Far East – this bloody malaria –' he held out his shaking hands – 'and I have my own views on this and other matters. But

219

I can't tell them to you, but neither can I condemn you or anybody like you for disagreeing with the official line. A nod is as good as a wink to a blind horse. The reason there are superstitions, and the reason why people made it into a sin to have marital relations while a woman is expecting, is probably a social matter too.'

'How do you mean?' asked Ellen, who sat on the edge of her chair all through this conversation.

'I mean a matter of protecting the woman and the child in her womb.'

'How so?'

'Pweh!' said Dr Morgan. 'Listen to me. I have women coming in here from all over the county and the city. I had a woman here the other day who couldn't, she thought, have children. But, she thought, it might be her husband was at fault, but of course she'd never be allowed to say that, the man's pride must be kept intact. And not only that, but every effort to have children nearly "tore her apart", she said. I asked her a few blunt questions.'

'I bet you did,' interposed Ellen.

'I certainly did. I asked her was her husband's member big? And she said, "What'll I compare it to, Doctor?" What could I say? A bull? A stallion? A sheepdog? A ferret? Anyway, we worked out some rule of thumb – literally' (he glanced across to see whether Ellen smiled: she did) '– and then I said to her that maybe her own private parts were too tight. She lay down there where you were lying a few minutes ago, on that couch, the poor innocent woman took all her clothes off without a blush, that's how desperate she was, and I examined her. D'you know what was wrong? I'll tell you what was wrong. No matter what feelings she had for her husband, or where she had them, the man ignored her, and insisted – these two were married eight years, remember? – he insisted on going in the wrong entry. Up her backside, if you don't mind me being blunt.'

220

He leaned back. 'Yes, of course, you may look shocked, but he had never seen it done any other way, or so he thought, from bringing the cow to the bull. Or watching the dogs in the yard. Going to a stud farm, I suppose, was his education.'

'The misfortunate woman,' said Ellen.

'Haven't you married women friends you can ask?' said Dr Morgan, bringing the consultation to an end.

'There's one, but it's different,' said Ellen.

'Different how?'

'She's a Jew, different faith.'

'Isn't she alive?' asked the doctor sardonically.

Thomas asked her, 'How was Dr Morgan?'

'Mind your own business,' she snapped. He looked at her and flared.

'I am minding my own business. You're my business. Or aren't you?'

He got out, slammed the door of the car and walked down the street out of sight. Returning five minutes later, he swung the starting-handle viciously, climbed back into the car and said nothing.

She said, 'I didn't mean to say that.'

'You did!'

Then they both spoke together: she said, 'What I meant was, he was talking about . . .'

He said, 'Ever since that blasted priest got his hooks into you . . .'

She said, 'He hasn't got his hooks . . .'

Thomas shouted, 'What the hell right has he – ?' then clammed his mouth shut, fixed his hat, chugged the car out in the middle of the street and set off for home. By the time they reached Deanstown, both had calmed down at least into silence, although he spent at least half an hour in the garage, doing some chore or other with the light of a lamp. Indoors, Ellen had fried liver and onions, one of his favourite meals, and when he came in to wash his hands, the table looked calm and likeable: she had taken down the milk jug he liked, with the broad blue band around its belly.

That night she pleaded a headache and invented some nausea, and allowed Thomas to walk alone to the church. The moon shone clearly as she stood at the door to see him off, and he took his walking stick and hat and gloves. She could see his tall back in the long shaft of light thrown from the door as he walked down the gravel to the gate, disappearing into the night, and she stayed there for several moments until his metallic footsteps on the hard road faded completely.

AD MAIOREM DEI GLORIAM

The Provincial House,
The Terrace College,
Janesborough.
Sunday, 15th November 1925.

My dear Ellen,
Perhaps I should also address this letter to Thomas, as it vitally and intimately concerns both of you, and I hope you will share its contents with him; in fact you must. I know you have been waiting to hear from me, and I apologize for the delay, but the matter seemed so vital I thought it best to obtain the fullest possible spiritual advice.

You will recall that while we walked and talked, the question arose over the sacredness of birth and its preludes. We considered whether in the sight of God it would be morally unlawful for man and wife to continue to engage in congress once a wife had conceived.

Although Canon Law is unclear as to the actual or precise dimensions of sin on this specific point, we may infer the moral stance from clearer points on related issues. The Church says quite clearly, and this is dogma, therefore handed down by God and preached infallibly by the Pontiff as Christ's Vicar of Rome and Visible Head on Earth, that the purpose of congress must be directed exclusively for the procreation of new souls. Once this objective has been achieved, any other form of such intimacy is obviously licentious.

Therefore we may assume that any other form of intimacy includes congress after the event of proven conception – which is your question, dear Ellen, is it not?

Therefore we have to assume that, once conception has taken place, congress between married couples is grievously sinful. Obviously before conception has occurred it may be of an unlimited, though always of course respectful, nature, as this is the Lord's way of ensuring our continuity in His image and likeness.

If such a ruling may initially seem to cause distress, then I can assure you that in the eyes of the Church the spiritual reward accruing to both parties on account of their willing and loving abstinence, is far greater; and it is of course of a temporary nature, as relations may resume once the child has been given the gift of birth.

I am sure that this restraint will only strengthen the love between you, dear Ellen and Thomas, and I send you all my best wishes and blessings.

Yours sincerely in Christ,
John Watson, S.J.

Thomas took the letter from Ellen. He looked confused, blinking as he read it.

'What does that phrase mean?' he asked, pointing to 'we may infer the moral stance from clearer points on related issues'. 'Oh, yes, I see,' and he read on.

'Ellen, do you believe him?' he asked. She nodded.

Thomas stood back. 'But that means we can't hardly touch each other any more, or until the baby is born, I mean. And that's not 'til next May?'

Neither seemed to know what to say.

Thomas looked into the distance, the letter floating in

his hand. The school break for play had already run on too long. Thomas blew on his whistle.

In the afternoon he found her in tears.

'I'll make a bargain with you, Thomas,' she said, barely able to speak. 'I'll let you touch me with your hands, but that's all.'

He said, 'No, that's no sort of a bargain.'

They spent the evening avoiding each other at home, ate an almost soundless meal, and that night in bed, as they lay side by side, he asked in the dark, 'Is it even wrong to hug you? Can't we find out more about this? There's another six or seven months before the baby is born.'

An invisible wedge parted their bodies in the bed, from shoulder to ankle, a high, thick, hard, cold wedge, reaching from the soft warm mattress up to the ceiling as surely as if it had been a gigantic version of the steel-blue wedges Thomas used to prise a cord of timber apart before he split it finally with the axe. Within days, another wedge, even thicker, and colder than ice itself, and flecked with blood, would prise them farther apart.

Winter 1925

13

Whenever the District Court sat in session, Thomas, on account of his standing in the community, frequently appeared as a character witness. The visiting judges also called for his impartial opinion, providing 'extra knowledge of the circumstances', and he rendered other services, such as the explanation of implications in various cases. Although serious violence had generally dwindled, the Land Division still rankled: when some estates were distributed among local people after the 1922 Treaty, a few inevitably claimed unfair treatment. Civil War revenge occasionally played a part in an assault, or a shooting at a house: Thomas usually knew both parties, or their kinfolk. The visiting judges liked him because he gave his opinion very forthrightly, without fear.

He owned a special, dark, double-breasted suit which he kept almost exclusively for court: many of the officials, both the locals and those who travelled with the judges, told him repeatedly that he should have been a lawyer, not a teacher. He enjoyed the compliment, and if time permitted he stayed in court listening to the cases, even when his duty had been discharged. Some of the judges sought his company afterwards for conversation and local history, and he was one of the chosen few nominated to accept guns, handed in by those availing of the gun amnesty. When no criminal cases came before a Sessions, it sometimes fell to Thomas to buy the traditional white gloves presented by counsel to the bench.

His status, his forthrightness, and his reputation for strong discipline brought with them a task that Thomas never relished: he was asked to birch offenders. On the two required occasions he carried it out with punctiliousness: both of those assignments had been requested of him by Mr Justice Hipwell (whose wife had a club foot: they were known as 'Hipwell and Hopwell'). Justice Hipwell sat again in the first week of December.

Thomas received a notice of the charge-list the previous evening, handed in to the house by the Sergeant. The letter lay unopened until he had finished his chores and washed his hands.

'You like the court business, don't you?' asked Ellen with pleasant interest.

Thomas said, 'Look at this.'

She leaned over his shoulder.

'Oh, my God! Oh, Thomas, no. Why didn't he tell me, he was here on Saturday? Awww!' Ellen squealed. Michael Quinn had been charged with theft.

'Thomas, you'll have to get him off, you'll have to vouch for him.'

Thomas said nothing, other than, 'We'll have to see how it is.'

'Thomas,' she charged, 'you knew about this, didn't you? You must have known?'

Leaving Ellen – by agreement with the Canon – in charge of the whole school, Thomas hoped to return to the classroom by lunchtime. Tuesday morning, however, vanished in licensing renewal applications, at which Thomas gave some testimonials as to the good character of two pub owners. After the brief lunch adjournment, awaiting the Quinn appearance, he listened to two further hearings.

One concerned a man from Rosegreen who was apprehended, according to the charge, 'while drunk and shouting at the sky'. The man was bound over to keep the peace and fined three shillings and sixpence. The second hearing concerned the larceny of a tree from the yard of the

Church of Ireland. The man who took it offered no explanation: he was fined two shillings and sixpence and ordered to retrieve the tree from his own garden and replant it in the church grounds at Silverbridge.

The third hearing began. Michael Quinn had allegedly stolen two watches from farmers' jackets at a sports day the previous summer. Late delivery of the charge sheet had given Ellen no time to see the boy. She had handed to Thomas a letter of good character, and in it she offered the court her services in the boy's hoped-for probation.

'Thomas, I implore you. That boy tries to look after his brothers and sisters, and he has nobody to look after him. Now you know I'm especially fond of him. Please, Thomas.'

When Thomas re-entered the courtroom he saw the Quinns, father and son, sitting at the back, in the narrow public benches waiting to be called forward. He went across to them, to say an encouraging word, that he would volunteer to appear as a witness on the boy's behalf, that he had been talking to the court solicitor. The boy's father – the man whom Thomas had pointed out to Ellen the very first morning she came to Deanstown – turned on Thomas abusively.

'You're all part of this crowd, you're all the same sort of Free Stater crowd, your justice was never any good for anyone.'

The boy, white-faced and edgy, looked away in distressed nonchalance. Thomas rested his hat on the seat and indicated his desire to help; the man knocked the hat to the ground.

'I know you of old, Kane. You were a Collins man. Keep your help. We don't want your help.' The boy's father spoke savagely, yet in the kind of hushed whisper he might have used in a church.

Michael continued to try and look uninterested.

229

The hearing began: the boy, his arm taken firmly by the Sergeant, stepped forward into the dock, and stood there white-faced against the wooden grained panelling.

'Are you Michael Quinn?'

The Sergeant nudged the boy, who answered. Mr Justice Hipwell asked the clerk where exactly did this alleged crime take place.

'I know it was at the Sports Day in New Inn, but where, which field? Was it during the running? Or the three-legged race? Or what?'

Nobody knew. Two farmers gave evidence and said that they found their watches missing out of their pockets; they had laid their jackets on the ground during the tug-of-war. When they went to the pub later they heard that a boy had been down at the stalls outside the church gate trying to sell a watch to a tinker.

The boy said only 'Yessir' and 'Nosir' to the judge's questions: 'Did you know this was wrong? Did you mean to steal these watches? Isn't it wrong to go around the place like a little thief taking things from people's pockets?'

Thomas gave evidence.

'My wife in particular knows this boy and feels that he is a good boy, that he is not a criminal. The boy left school a year ago at fourteen, he is not really strong enough to work for the farmers.'

He handed in Ellen's letter: Mr Justice Hipwell read it and only commented, 'Oh, Mr Kane, I forgot. Congratulations on your marriage, I wish you all the best.'

Thomas told Ellen later that he tried to build a picture of 'difficulty requiring leniency', in sentiments that, as he pointed out, he did not fully feel. He appealed further on the boy's behalf – that he diligently brought the younger children to school; that he looked after a mother who had much illness, she had lost several babies. He, Thomas, had taught the boy, had never known him to give trouble, could even give a guarantee about the boy's future behaviour.

'I take your point, I take your point.' Justice Hipwell always nodded in agreement with Thomas, and then asked whether the boy's parents had come to court. With Thomas still at the wooden rail of the witness box, the father rose from the rear. He shouted at the bench that no justice would be forthcoming in this court, that all this country had done was exchange one system of discrimination against Irish people for another, and that the court had no power anyway in his eyes, it was 'Free State fraud'.

Mr Hipwell gave the man a choice – he could leave the court, or be arrested and bailed to the next session on a charge of contempt: he chose to leave – noisily: Justice Hipwell sentenced the boy to twelve strokes of the birch.

The Court Clerk asked – whom would the judge nominate to administer the punishment? Normally a parent was commanded by the court to do so: here the court found that the relevant parent had shown himself to be unsuitable: what was to be done?

The judge deliberated, whispering it further with the Clerk. Thomas saw them looking at him and, by now back in the well of the court, he began to slip away towards the exit. The judge called him back.

'Mr Kane, you've helped in a similar matter in the past. You'll oblige again? The court would be in your debt.'

As Thomas opened his mouth to protest, the judge continued, 'And as you know the court can actually command you to do so, though I am sure that will not be necessary in your case. If you have a word with the Clerk he will inform you of the necessary forms that have to be filled in, specifying time, date, witnesses, etc.'

The court rose; Thomas had no more influence in the matter. He went forward to the Clerk's desk, and gathered the forms. The Clerk said, 'I know 'tis a bit hard to have to do it, but the Justice is very grateful, and I suppose your wife might want to be the official witness.'

They parted, and when Thomas turned to go, Michael, still standing in the dock, stared at him across the empty room. He rushed out of the dock and half-ran across the courtroom to Thomas and stood there, not saying anything. Thomas quite simply did not know what to do and turned on his heel and left. The boy, quite a tall boy for his age, but, as Ellen was fond of saying, 'woefully thin', followed to the car and stood again.

Thomas had to attend a committee meeting at Outrath creamery at half-past four, and by the time he got home at seven o'clock, Ellen already knew the verdict of the court, and that Thomas had to carry out the punishment. She had intercepted Michael on his way home, had taken him in, given him tea, consoled him.

'Why, Thomas, why?' Ellen stood shaking in front of him, shaking as if cold, and rubbing her hands, screwing her eyes in pain. 'Why did you agree to it?' She tugged each cuff of her cardigan. 'You won't do it, will you? You'll pretend, won't you?' She came around and stood before him each time he turned away.

No matter how patiently he tried to explain – 'Will you listen to me, Ellie?' – she interrupted.

'But if you do commit contempt of court, if you don't whip him, that's only a fine, that's all, isn't it? Even if your standing in the court is affected, what matter? And anyway what's your standing, compared to that poor boy's wellbeing? You have standing. You'll always have standing. He'll probably never have standing. Or wellbeing. Thomas, he hasn't a pick of flesh on him, you'll cut him if you whip him.'

Patiently, Thomas said, 'It isn't "whip", it is "birch", I can't avoid doing this task.'

'But it could be. This is like you being a hangman.'

'Now, you're going to get yourself upset, Ellie.'

'Thomas, please don't do it. Go back and tell the court . . .'

'The court is gone now, for another two months.'

'Tell the Sergeant, Thomas.'

'No, Ellie, there's a duty.'

'You never liked Michael, you never liked him.' She turned away and said, 'This is terrible, this is terrible.'

He said, again patient, 'This is not terrible, this is the way it is, this is the law.'

Ellen burst into tears and hugged her arms tight across her bosom. 'You can stop it. You can! You don't have to do it. You don't have to be so high and mighty to that child.' She waxed. 'You're going to like hitting him, aren't you, like you like hitting everybody, like you like slapping the boys in school? What's this you call them, "paw-warmers", isn't that what you give them on their hands? I see you at it every day.' She backed away and crashed into the kitchen table behind her.

He said, in a very cold voice, 'You have a child inside you. You should be calmer than this,' then walked out of the room, left the house and went firmly to the school, where, with candlelight, he sat at the high desk and read for two hours.

When he returned, all the lights downstairs had been extinguished except in their bedroom. From the hallway he heard Ellen climb into bed. He undressed on the landing, hung his clothes over the banisters, put on pyjamas, climbed into bed beside her and lay in the rigid, cold silence.

Thomas had agreed with the Sergeant to have the boy fetched to the school on Saturday morning. At eight o'clock on the night before, Ellen, sitting alone in the kitchen waiting for Thomas to come back from a nearby farmer's house, heard somebody shuffling across the gravel to the front door. She scarcely waited for the knocker to be lifted; three figures stood outside, like waifs and strays from a sentimental painting – Mrs Quinn, and Timmy, and one of his sisters.

'Won't you come in?'

They refused and asked for Thomas.

'He's not here,' said Ellen; 'he won't be home for a while.'

It transpired that they knew this; the Quinn children had been watching the house.

'You are very thin,' said Ellen to Mrs Quinn, who wore a coat that had once been fawn, and the children had no coats on this freezing evening. 'You'll have to have a cup of tea.'

Mrs Quinn refused and made her request straight out.

'I can't,' said Ellen. 'I can't. I don't like it either, but I can't stop it; the law's the law, the Master says.'

The woman stood looking at Ellen, then looking away, then looking back. To her next remark Ellen replied, 'No, he's not a hard man. The Master is a fair man. Very fair. Everybody around here knows that. He's only doing what the Judge asked him to do. The Master is a Justice of the Peace, and Justices of the Peace often have to do things like this.'

Mrs Quinn ignored her, talked through her, and Ellen stepped back. 'If you want to come in and sit down and talk about it, do. I don't know when the Master will be home.'

Mrs Quinn muttered something and turned away.

Ellen stepped after her. 'Don't curse me. Do you hear? Don't you put your curses on me. I've looked after your young fellows and I will continue to do so. So don't you curse me.'

The little girl looked up and said, 'Sorry, Ma'am.'

Timmy waved a little hand as he walked away.

Thomas came home, having seen the departing trio. 'Oh, God Almighty.'

Ellen did not reply directly; she arranged the table for supper. After a few minutes she said, 'What do you expect? And now I find myself having to defend my husband. She said you were a hard man. What could I say?'

In the discomfort and hurt of unaccustomed silence, they began to eat. Rescue came in the form of Miss Harris, the poultry instructress, to whom Ellen had written. Miss Harris was one of the great talkers of the world, untroubled by the necessity of context.

'There's a girl from Broadford, that I was with last week, who was in the same class as you, Mrs Kane, she's marrying a vet from outside Croom, he's a fellow with a hare lip, you might know him, every old stocking meets an old shoe, his mother is a big stout woman, he has a whole lot of sisters, a Maguire man, the vet, his mother is Mrs Maguire, there's a great row, he's not getting the farm on account of him having a job already as a vet, they're dividing it up between the five sisters, achh, the commotion that's going on, 'tis a fine place, there's nearly three hundred acres, though some of it is boggy, what harm sure even a tin knocker will shine on an empty door.'

Miss Harris's volubility enabled Thomas to slip away to bed early. Next morning, Ellen had risen long before him and he found a note at nine o'clock: 'Gone to the school to light a fire. Somebody has to do something *kind*.'

Thomas dressed in the court dark suit, and his best coat and hat. From the front door he turned back to get gloves.

Smoke rose in a blue unwavering plume from the school chimney; the Sergeant's bicycle stood against the wall, and he, in a heavy coat, the silver buttons shining against the dark blue fabric, stood flapping his hands at the fire.

'Hallo, Master.'

Ellen was bending near the grate, in coat and woollen hat, foraging in her large canvas shopping bag.

'I s'pose I'd better get him, so, Master.' Thomas nodded. The Sergeant walked across the planked floor, his boots making a pleasing ring. He turned.

'Master, what'll you use?'

Thomas looked up, looked out the window, looked carefully at Ellen, rubbed his chin.

'I'll get the lad himself to cut a stick.'

Ellen drew a breath, was about to say something, stopped, blushed, turned away, bobbed her head hard, and frowned. The Sergeant spoke again.

'Two lads of mine, Sir. Out of the barracks. They're gone to the house to stop the father coming here. D'you know, like?' Thomas nodded.

When the Sergeant had gone, Ellen looked at Thomas and half-smiled.

'I think,' she said, 'I have a solution. I brought this bag. Now any noise made hitting that with a stick will sound like a beating. And I brought this too.' She took from the bag a long, quite thin alder cane. 'I broke it last night off the tree near the back door.'

Thomas shook his head.

'Thomas, if he cuts it himself –' Ellen now spoke in the voice of someone trying a different tack '– will you mind if he only cuts a light stick. Otherwise isn't that very cruel? I mean, proverbially cruel, "cut a stick to beat yourself"?'

Thomas told her that was precisely his point, that the punishment was likely to have greater, more lasting effect.

'Thomas, is there anything I can do, that will . . .'

He told her kindly and carefully that he felt obliged, felt it important. 'I need your support in this, Ellen; we have a joint place here. They look up to us.'

She opened the door, from which one could see down through the village, down to the end of the long sloping hill past the Canon's house. Soon the frost would begin to drip from the gaunt trees. Figures appeared, materializing

236

as two adults and two children: the Sergeant wheeling his bicycle, Mrs Quinn, the little daughter and the boy Michael. Thomas and Ellen, disregarding the cold from the open door, watched them. They stopped; the Sergeant said something to the boy and they started forward again, much more slowly. Down to a snail's pace they reached the school wall and stopped again. As the Sergeant began to make some arrangements with them, Ellen stepped outside, her breath billowing white. She heard the Sergeant explain to Mrs Quinn that nobody would be allowed in; Ellen reinforced this, and told the woman she would take care of the boy, warm him, make things as easy as possible.

Michael refused to come in; the Sergeant began to drag him. Ellen took over, and led him gently in through the door, and walked behind him up to where Thomas stood.

'You know why you are here?' Thomas asked. The boy nodded.

'You have to answer me,' said Thomas, 'that's part of it.'

The boy, on Ellen's prompting, answered a 'yes'.

'You have a choice,' said Thomas, not looking at Ellen, 'I can either use this,' indicating the ash stick with which he kept discipline in the class, 'or I can send you out to cut a stick.' The boy pointed to the stick lying in the chalk-groove beneath the blackboard.

Michael had no coat, and still wore short trousers. He had socks and boots, not in good condition, and the suit, bought very cheaply for his Confirmation four years before, had been much worn since, winter and summer. He wore a shirt with a collar, very unclean, and nothing else, no underwear.

Thomas, having asked Ellen to close the door, said to Michael, 'You have to turn around and bend over that front desk.'

Ellen went to the door as if she had become a wind-up

toy, little bobbing mechanical movements, and almost ran back.

'I am supposed,' said Thomas, 'according to the law, to birch your bare flesh; you are supposed to lower your trousers.'

Ellen made a tiny, whingeing noise, and clenched and unclenched her hands with great rapidity, and hammered them in the empty air by her hips.

'But,' continued Thomas, 'on account of the *in*clement weather, I will let that pass. Now you know that you are to receive twelve strokes for stealing other people's property.'

The aspect of a beating which most surprises, and which people often most remember long afterwards, is the noise of the first stroke. Ellen rushed her hands to her ears, then spun her head around. Last night's frost had the whiteness of light snow; the breath from the cattle rose like a nativity in the fields across the road; a bird nipped past the window.

Thomas struck again, the firelight catching his face as he lifted his arm. The boy shook each time. The third blow seemed especially severe and the desk clanked.

Ellen had by now begun to tremble in her entire body: her shudders punctuated each blow. Thomas never moved quickly, but had he ever moved so slowly? At the fourth blow a new noise started, a pushing of air from the stifled calls of Michael who seemed to wish to get up from his doubled position, but did not dare. Thomas struck again, changing direction this time, and by laying the stick flat across the thin body, he caught new angles. Michael screamed. Ellen began to breathe like someone in heavy exertion, and now was almost spinning on her feet. As a small child when severely agitated she seemed determined to change the orbit of the world by spinning against it: she repeated this movement now, drumming her shoes on the boards of the floor, turning a full circle, her hand to her mouth.

The door burst open; the little girl had escaped from the Sergeant. 'Mikey! Mikey!'

The Sergeant's huge hand reached in and grasped her, 'Sorry, Sir, Ma'am. Carry on,' and he closed the door.

As the sixth stroke descended, Michael twisted and Thomas missed, catching the boy's thigh. He yelped appallingly. Thomas paused, which seemed almost crueller to Ellen than anything else he had done. At the seventh stroke, Ellen saw a trickle of blood on the boy's thigh and said, 'Thomas, Thomas,' and pointed to it. Thomas made a helpless gesture and laid on three more strokes. By now the boy squirmed so much Thomas had to hold him down tight with his left hand, and he became so angered by this, that when he might have eased off, he intensified his efforts. The last three blows, Ellen afterwards said bitterly, were harder than the first four. Outside a scream had begun and they could hear the Sergeant saying, 'Now shut up, will you, shut up now, you're disturbing the peace.'

Michael's thigh blood became a wider trickle. Thomas stopped, out of breath. He laid the stick along its groove, took his coat from the hook, and his hat, and walked from the room, hands deep in his pockets. Outside he nodded to the Sergeant and walked in the direction opposite to home.

Ellen eased the boy up from the desk: he could scarcely move.

'He didn't hurt me that bad, Ma'am, the Master.' He had to stop, lacking breath. Tears leaked into runny lemon mucus from his nose. Ellen stood him carefully at the tall mesh fire-guard and fetched three hot-water bottles from her large bag. She emptied one of them into a basin and from a towel unwrapped soap, a face-flannel, a jar of ointment.

'You'll have to help me,' she said, trying not to be embarrassed, 'you'll have to turn around and let down your trousers.'

When he did so, she cried for the first time, wept hot tears. It seemed as if she could count ten different stripes, red, and red-blue, mottled at the edges, and not a few of them had opened and begun to bleed. Nor was the boy accustomed to any basic hygiene. Ellen dipped the face-flannel in the warm water and as gently as cotton wool patted the angry stripes. The boy all but fainted; his mother came in, the Sergeant held on to the sister outside. Mrs Quinn stood helplessly by.

It took almost an hour and the other two hot-water bottles before the boy could actually think of walking. Ellen emptied the basins out of the back windows so that the little girl would not see the bloodstained water. Ellen talked to herself all the time, heaped coal on the fire, gave the boy sweets, soothed him, 'It will never happen again, don't you know that?' held his hands and rubbed them, and finally wrapped him in her own coat and saw them off. She then mopped the few small bloodstains from the floor beneath the desk and stood by the fire, and wept like a child. After some minutes she dried her tears, then remained for a long time looking into the flames.

'What is this all about?' she asked herself, over and over again, aloud. 'What is this? What is this all about? What kind of man am I married to? What is this business, this business of marriage, supposed to be? Is this what marriage is like?'

She blew out the lamp, doused the fire as much as possible, locked the door and walked very fast down the three hundred yards to the house, coatless and carrying her shopping bag. She flapped her free hand repeatedly. As she reached the gate, she heard the swish of a bicycle behind her and turned as the sound came to a halt right by her heels. The Quinn boy's father, to whom she had never spoken before, loomed over her. Ellen, a hand on the gate, said to him, 'He'll be all right, Mr Quinn, Michael will be all right.'

'Ma'am,' said the man bitter as acid, 'anyone who'd do that to a child should get a taste of the same himself.'

'I understand you, Mr Quinn,' said Ellen, piously and impetuously. '"He who takes the sword shall perish by the sword." Isn't that what the Bible says?'

'That's right, Ma'am,' said the man. 'That's right.' He shook his fist in the air, turned his bicycle around, and Ellen opened her front door. She knelt at a chair in the kitchen, as close to the black, shiny range as she could get without burning herself, and, of a sudden more uneasy than she had ever felt, began to pray.

When Thomas walked from the school he intended to stay out all day. His pace increased as he left the village and turned along a deserted by-road; he walked maniacally fast, sometimes clamping his hat tight to his head. Once or twice a cyclist or a horse and cart passed by; he did not return their greetings. Reaching the abandoned bridge at Griffinstown, a full six miles from home, he ducked under the parapet and crouched in the flood arch, under limestone which kept out the cold. The water flowed by, black and sluggish, and he hunched there, staring at the river. When he came home, walking much more slowly, in the dusk of the late afternoon, he called in a quiet voice, 'Ellen? Ellen?' as he took his coat and hat off in the hall. She did not answer, and when he opened the kitchen door, it took him a moment or two to pick her out in the gloom, by the glow of the range.

14

Thomas provided the means of recovery from their dreadful *impasse*. He did not relent upon what he had seen as his duty; nor did he apologize for having done it. Ellen did not address him nor provide food for him for eight days, during which he behaved as he had always done: lighting the fires; closing the shutters at night; bringing in potatoes from the pit; cleaning the globes of the lamps and nipping the wicks of the candlesticks. He helped himself to bread and butter and tea and eggs; he fried bacon.

On the Sunday, a week and a day after the birching, Thomas walked into the kitchen after Mass, his coat still on. Ellen stood by the tall cupboard, folding her scarf, and putting it away.

Thomas said, 'Ellen. Enough is enough. Do you understand me?' He said it slowly and clearly, and only once, then turned to the hall, closing the door behind him. She stuck her tongue out at the closed door, and when Thomas returned to the kitchen some time later, she said brightly, 'Wasn't that a useless sermon the Canon gave this morning?'

Thomas said, 'What would you expect from a pig but a grunt? He hasn't what you'd call a silver tongue.'

Ellen laughed. 'Made of lead, more like.'

From this time, questions of Thomas's violence became part of the daily swirl in Ellen's mind, causing her affection towards her husband to undulate erratically. Always a great enumerator, she was sometimes observed by Thomas as she stood gazing without looking, and silently counting on her fingers. If he offered a penny for her thoughts she said, 'Nothing': but what means could she

242

have found of telling him that in the silent counting on the fingers of one hand she was listing the violent incidents she had witnessed of him: the MacReadys; the bad language to the boat steward; the man in the street in London; the birching of Michael; the casual use of the cane in school? All Thomas knew was that after such a bout of introspection he could never expect closeness or friendly warmth from her for several hours.

At other times, she overwhelmed him with tenderness. That Sunday afternoon, for example, standing behind his chair she began to stroke his hair, then leaned forward and wrapped her arms around his chest, making a complete mess of his newspaper.

He had grown reconciled, though with difficulty, to the Church's 'intervention', making only one bitter remark, a cutting reference to the fact that she had taken to keeping her underwear on beneath her nightgown: 'Most people take clothes *off* when they go to bed.'

Otherwise, he remained constant, saying, typically, in the bedroom that evening, 'You've no idea what I think of you,' and he held her hand and pinched her cheek with gentleness: she butted his chest tenderly with her head. Looking down, she saw a bruise on his thigh, and learned that he had bumped off the edge of the gate.

'It looks just like the bruises on poor Mi –' she began, and stopped, and her mood went cold.

When the next huge tweak of her worries came by, she displayed a little more calm and, in the face of what seemed to her further evidence of the cruel strain in Thomas, she did not panic – but afterwards, she flinched for days if he touched even her hair.

An old chest of drawers had been one of the few articles salvaged from the night the soldiers set fire to the previous Residence. Never usable again as domestic furniture – blackened, and with the splats of huge heat blisters – it

243

had been kept, almost for old times' sake, by Thomas, in the farthest of the three sheds leaning against each other to the new house. There, Ellen found Blackie, in a drawer, while actually giving birth, the round, wet spheres plopping to the old blanket scraps on which she had nested, and the cat licked the wet gossamer filament off the five kittens, one after another.

Thomas went along with Ellen's excitement, and discussed progress every day for over a week, until the kittens' eyes had opened and their crawling changed to endearing fluffy-scrawny lurches.

'But we have, how many? Ellie, we have one, two, three cats already, and Blackie four, we can't have another five cats. Give them away if you can, but I'm telling you, this parish has more cats than people, and you'll not get takers.'

She did not enquire into an alternative solution, and subsequently reported with glee that several children next day shot their hands up when she asked, 'Who here would like a kitten?'

Thomas advised that she should wait until they returned with permission from their parents. Next day, all fell by the wayside: not one parent had agreed: all had too many cats or other domestic animals already. Ellen did not report this to Thomas until asked.

'What did I say to you?' He reached for the butter. 'Some of them can't feed themselves, let alone pets.'

Animals strolled all over Deanstown. A loose cow, a mad jennet, two bad-tempered geese, several ducks, mangy dogs, innumerable cats; all were dirty, mucky from the passageways between the houses, or the dungheaps of the yards. Only Mrs Greege's hens had any scrap of decency about them, but she might well have polished them, for all anybody knew.

Two days later, Thomas raised the subject of the kittens again. Ellen ducked it, saying she would discuss it later, and in school tried the children once more, with no success whatsoever.

On Saturday morning he said, 'Ellie, those kittens.'

'I know, I know.' She looked flustered.

He asked, 'What are we going to do about them?'

She replied, 'Would you run me to Camas, to the vet, and see if he'll take them?'

'Ah, woman,' he said, half-amused, and a little irritably. 'The vet has more to be doing than dealing with a few kittens. He'd put the run on you if you walked in there like that.'

'But the kittens are animals, too?'

'If you walked into a vet's yard,' said Thomas, 'with a litter of kittens under your arm, he'd give you a strange look.'

Ellen asked, fearfully, 'What do people do with kittens they don't want?'

'What do you think they do?'

That afternoon, averting more than fending off Blackie's half-hearted, mewling defences, Thomas picked up the five kittens one by one and plopped them into a potato sack. Ellen did not appear: Thomas had told her very clearly that he intended to remove them 'before they get any bigger'.

'New life,' she said. 'It's not fair,' but she put up little fight, other than a last suggestion of giving them away as 'Christmas presents. Or couldn't we keep one for our own baby?' He merely looked at her over his reading spectacles.

Thomas left the house and walked diagonally across the Castle fields; in one hand a shovel sloped gun-like over his shoulder, the other hand held the squirming sack stiff-armed out from his side to avoid little soft poking claws: the piled-up kittens mewed, tossed in the brisk walking motion. He followed the muddy cowpath by the Castle

245

stableyard walls, until he came out into the open ground under the plane trees, and soon reached the sluice at the old pond.

In summer, the pond, replenished from a small underground source, fed the stream from which farmers watered their cattle along the way for eight straight miles until, a minuscule canal, never widening nor deepening, like the lives of its neighbours, it reached the river. The sluice-gate, therefore, though by now the colour of rust, always worked: its hinges were kept well oiled. At the point in the pond where the sluice wall dammed the water at the stream's beginning, gathered a small black pool, a yard square, but as deep and threatening as a filled canal lock.

The winter sun came out, low in the sky, and weak, and Thomas raised his face to it. He laid the sack on the pond shore, crushing small sedges, and walked around the field, intently examining the ground, bending almost double here and there, prodding the earth with the point of the shovel's blade. This narrow section, generally infertile, and too neglected even for the farmer to slash the 'Thistle, Ragwort and Dock' in response to every year's notice in the police stations, had turned into a cemetery for unwanted, small domestic animals drowned by their owners at the sluice. Thomas found the site of a recent burial, and tracing its lines, eased the turf sward off the old grave. The traces of a rotting sack appeared. He then worked the shovel into a space beside the bits of jute, availing of the softer weakened ground to dig a new, equally shallow hole.

Returning to the sack he picked it up and measured the new trench with it, then dug some more and continued to measure it with his sack's volume, until the little pit would completely accept the entire bundle. Then satisfied he stuck the shovel in the ground, leaving it to stand erect, stepping on the blade's shoulder to make it fast. He picked up the sack again, at which the kittens mewed afresh. Thomas strode over to the sluice-gate and, squatting on the wall, lowered the sack into the water, dousing the mewing. He angled the sodden bag in such a way that it caught under a jutting ledge just beneath the surface. The sun continued to shine, warm on his neck, and a bird fluted, unseasonably pert. From the sack in the water came a brief, puny thrashing, then a series of small bubbles rose to the surface.

Thomas secured the neck of the sack to the sluice wall under one booted heel, fumbled inside his heavy coat and drew out a watch. He gazed at the mountains, so near and welcoming and mysterious in the winter light, and referred to his watch once or twice. After five minutes or so, he returned the watch to its pocket, lifted the inert load from the sluice, and evading its plashings and cascades, stepped nimbly from the wall to the shallow grave, and buried the drowned kittens.

Had he raised his head from his labours and looked back in the direction he had come, he might have seen his wife. Standing by a haw bush on the height of the sunken fence, a distance of about two hundred yards away, she had a clear view of all Thomas had been doing. By now, she knew him well enough to feel safe following him across the fields: an intent man, he rarely looked back while walking, and in any case she had travelled by a different field. She stuck her gloved hands deep in her pockets joining them across her stomach; afflicted, she went home along another diagonal path on which the woods would shield her. Not a word did she say when he returned: she accepted casually the cup of tea he made. Later, sitting reading in the kitchen, he remarked, 'I notice you didn't ask me anything about the kittens?'

She said, quite slowly, 'No. I didn't.'

'Don't you want to know what happened to them?'

No reply.

He lowered the newspaper further, and looked kindly. 'What I want you to know is – two or three of those kittens would have litters of their own in a few years' time, and then two or three of them; all the females would have litters and so on, and we wouldn't be able to feed them all, nobody would. Much kinder to get rid of them. So I drowned them. Up at the Castle sluice, and then I buried them. These are small laws. It's not like humans.'

She said, 'I know, I know,' thoughtful and pacifying in her tone. 'I suppose these are things I'll have to learn. I was wondering – if I lived alone out here, would I be able to do it myself?'

He replied, 'My mother never managed it, one of us, or my father before that, we always had to do it. How will you go about killing the turkey?' They laughed. Next day, however, Ellen relapsed into one of her worried silences. He joshed her once or twice, but getting no response, occupied himself elsewhere.

It poured with rain the week before Christmas, and Ellen – who had used her own money, as she pointed out to Thomas – had to dash from the car each time, to the doors she visited with the parcels of sugar and tea she had been buying, thick string-tied paper bags, blue and large for the sugar, brown and smaller with the bags of tea. Briefly bewildered children, or their mothers, opened their latched doors and saw their schoolmistress standing there, her hat heavy with raindrops, and bowing her head as if sheltering under their eaves, and thrusting forward these parcels, saying, 'Just something for the Christmas.' All accepted, except at Quinns where the father opened the door.

'No, I don't want them.'

'But they're only for the Christmas. And the children.'

'I don't want them. I've enough for my own family.'

'No, but really,' Ellen pressed again.

He said, 'I have enough for my own family. I'm in work the whole year.'

Ellen pushed a little past him and placed them on the windowsill inside the porch.

'It's Christmas,' she said. As she left, he tossed the parcels in a small arc after her: they burst open either side of her feet, spilling the white sugar and the black-brown tea in the puddles. Not knowing what to do, she bent for a moment, then realized nothing could be picked up, and she reached the safety of the car.

'Did you see that?' she asked Thomas breathlessly. 'Did you see that? He threw them at me.'

'Did he hit you with them?' She shook her head. Thomas drove away, saying, 'I told you not to go in there. He's unreliable, that's saying the best about him.'

'But the example for the children?' protested Ellen.

'Ah, God help your head, Ellie,' said Thomas. 'People think you're giving them charity, and they mightn't like that.'

She said, 'I haven't seen him around for ages, not since . . . Oh, God . . .' As if about to confess something, she bit her lip. Thomas did not press; in any case, she would not have told him what she had just remembered: the pious 'Perish by the sword' remark she had made in the heated aftermath of the birching.

All week, especially when the weather improved, people visited with gifts. Mrs Mahony brought a pair of geese; 'The Master loves a goose, Ma'am, doesn't he?'

Ellen replied, 'Is that why he married me, d'you think?' but the joke may have been too sophisticated. Denis MacLoughlin's wife brought a large ham. 'We cures this ourselves, Ma'am, and we smokes it.'

'We cure. And we smoke,' said Ellen, unable not to correct.

'Do you, Ma'am, isn't the Master blessed so. I thought,

saving your presence, a city girl wouldn't know anything about that class of a thing at all.'

'No, no, it isn't that,' said Ellen and, recognizing that she was about to get hopelessly lost in the intricacies of colloquialism, gave up, rescuing herself by getting from Mrs MacLoughlin details of how they cured and smoked the ham.

'The bad thing is, Ma'am, wet turf is good for it, but it'd kill ourselves with coughing, and Denny's always saying we have to kill ourselves to cure the ham, like. But the good turf, it ed not make enough smoke, like.'

Ellen said to Thomas as they ate, 'Mrs MacLoughlin, where's her accent from?'

'The planet Mars,' said Thomas. 'I never know a blind word she's saying. Ask her some time about the flowers in her garden? She'll tell you she grows "chrystantrums", and "germaniums" and that when she got married, her aunt gave her a present of crockery, "the finesht set of bowels in the county". When I met her first, I needed an interpreter.'

'But very good-natured, though?' said Ellen. Thomas nodded.

Mrs Quinlivan brought two porter cakes still in their tins. 'Don't eat them now, Ma'am, keep them for the Confirmation, or something, they keep grand.'

Thomas said, when Ellen reported this, 'What a shrewd piece of advice, in case you were going to dig them out of the tins there and then, with a trowel, and tear into them. What else did Mrs Quinlivan say? Any funeral news?'

Ellen turned from the washing-up: 'Now why do you ask that?'

Thomas laughed. 'Go on, tell me. Did she say anything about a funeral?'

'Well, she did, as a matter of fact.'

Thomas asked, 'Was she just back from one?'

'She was. How did you know?'

Thomas asked, 'And did she tell you how old the unfortunate man was, how many children he left, what he died of, and who he left the place to in his will? And how in the name of the good God above in Heaven will the widow manage at all, at all?'

Ellen replied, 'Yes, more or less, that's nearly exactly what she said. How do you know? Did you meet her on the road? Because if you did, why didn't she give you the cakes?'

'I didn't meet her at all. But going to funerals is her hobby. That woman has been known to travel fifty miles to a funeral. Her husband the same. D'you remember that train crash? The one at Tarr's Bridge? Her husband went to the scene of the accident, and he got around one of the ambulance men to get him the dead train-driver's boot-laces and he brought them home as a souvenir. Mind your feet, Ellie.'

The rain of the past week had raised the water-table all around the house, and Thomas was laying armfuls of straw on the weeping stone floor.

On the eve of Christmas Eve, the weather changed for the better. Ellen finished the last Christmas pudding and vowed to Thomas that henceforth she would have them all made by October. He laughed and told her his mother always said that too, but 'was always up to her elbows in candied peel the Sunday before Christmas'. As Ellen took off her apron, she smoothed her stomach, and said, 'Have I begun to look anything yet?'

He turned her in an angle to the light. 'Oh, you certainly have,' he said. 'Although in clothes it's hard to tell.'

With the burst of speech that always signified intense anxiety in her, she blurted, 'There's something worrying me. That I want to say to you,' and sat on a kitchen chair: he leaned against the table.

'D'you know the way the Stephensons breed their

251

horses, you know, the thoroughbreds, a good hurdler, or a good filly for the Guineas, or whatever the race is? Well, I was wondering – Can the same be done with human beings, the same breeding?'

'You mean are we going to enter that child –' he pointed at her stomach '– for the Derby?'

Ellen did not laugh. 'No. What I mean is – will it, can it, will it bring forward, in it, as part of it, exactly what we, you and me, are like?'

Thomas said, 'I don't know. I suppose, not all of it, and not exactly any of it, maybe. It will have to be – itself. Why, what are you driving at?'

'Well, you won't talk about it, but if it is a son we have, and if he turns out to have your temper . . .'

'You mean – my violence? Don't you? Now who were you talking to this time? Not your "dear Father John" again?'

He spread his arms impatiently. 'The night after next is Christmas night, tomorrow night is Christmas Eve night, and I'm not allowed to have connection with my own wife in my own bed; she even wears her knickers when she goes to sleep, and we're not allowed even to question it. How, so, do you expect me to talk about something that's only an indefinite, when there's an urgent definite that we're not allowed to discuss at all?' His voice rose.

'But there isn't anything to discuss, we know it's a sin while a woman is expecting.'

Thomas barked. 'On one man's say-so. We don't know for certain. What I do know is a sin is – denying kind friendliness, that's a sin. It goes on all around us, has for years, and we're adding to it here, privately, between us. No wonder it spreads.'

'Oh, Thomas, I don't deny you anything, look around you, look at the house, look at the baking I've been doing, look at the shine of the place, and the way I pray for you. Come on, Thomas, be fair.'

Since he had begun the long and difficult attempts to control his anger and his physical violence, Thomas avoided provocative situations, and now he walked out of the house, into the yard, and then through the leafless hedge into the empty, quiet garden and its ridges of last year's drills.

On Christmas Eve, the houses of the countryside drew into themselves. Men finished last tasks at noon and changed into Sunday clothes, in order to do some last-minute shopping, or drink in crowded public houses. Wives tried where possible to accompany them, in order to prevent excess. Shopkeepers gave extra measure, or a cake, or a bottle of something in gratitude for the year's custom (and carefully drew attention to the gift). Spouses did not exchange presents: Santa Claus came to see many of the children; some, from the poorest cottages, avoided meeting playmates for several days, or pretended Santa Claus had indeed come and brought them sweets which by then they had eaten. By seven o'clock on Christmas Eve, apart from stragglers – swaying on carts, or walking unsteadily along the dark roads wheeling bicycles – all had come to rest indoors, and in each home the youngest lit the Christmas candle in the window to guide the family wandering towards Bethlehem to a friendly light.

Ernestina Stephenson envied the Catholics that tradition. Certain that nobody would enter her room – the house had fallen silent: her brother must have gone 'carousing' – she put her bedroom lamp in one of the windows for a short time. She scraped her hands violently through her hair – 'He's a fool! He's a fool!' Dr Hogan was a fool: telling her that the way she felt now might not necessarily be the whole truth: the last few days she had been feeling much better: she might even go for a drink on New Year's Eve to the Harpers. And the nightgown and bedjacket, ordered from a magazine – why not? Why not a Christmas gift from herself to herself?

'You will never get me inside a hospital door,' she told Dr Hogan. 'Never.'

'All serene, so?' he asked. 'All serene?'

He said the same words to his wife.

'No, Jack,' she snapped. 'No. Not all serene. You can cook it.'

She stood in the kitchen, arms folded tight, her coat still on, face red after her long walk.

'And by the way, when are we going to change the name on this house, why does it have to be "The Dispensary"? Why does it have to have a name at all?'

'It was called that when it was built, Miriam. You know that.' He rubbed his hands. 'The car was freezing. Would you like a cup of tea?'

'You're always making tea. No wonder you get on so well with my mother, Jack.'

He put the kettle on, still rubbing his hands, and poking the stove.

'Where did you put the turkey anyway, Miriam? Even if you're not going to cook it?'

'Down a manhole, Jack, where do you think?'

He took it as a joke.

At the crossroads, as the bus approached, casting a rectangle of shaky yellow light, Val Vousden raised his hand, and manoeuvring his precious Gladstone bag, accepted the respectful greetings, and acknowledged the smiles of the Christmas homegoers. Through the dark bus windows, he could see tiny lights here and there in the hills, each one signifying a window and a home. The bus dropped him at Patrick's Bridge; Val walked briskly to Shandon, and began the slow climb up the hill to his sister's house. He never understood their family's tradition of having

Christmas dinner on Christmas Eve: it was an odd, old custom: they should have dropped it years ago: 'The bells of Shandon. That sound so grand on. The pleasant waters of the river Lee,' he hummed to himself, out of breath by the time he reached the door.

'There's a parcel here for you,' said his sister.

'Oow, ow, ow,' yelped Val, 'is it Mrs Heffernan? It is! It is!' shouted Val, feeling the crinkle of careful paper inside. He opened it and spread it out on the table for all to see, and held it up against himself.

'Isn't it splendid?' he said. 'Isn't it splendid?'

In the gaslight the blue of the blue uniform, and the gold of the gold, seemed to him made of precious metal.

'Ow, Ow!' he yelped again, sheer delight.

The father of the Quinn children drank all day, and then he attempted to drink all of the evening, going from the earliest closing bar to a later, then a later, then a later. He greeted all and sundry, and only those who did not know him – and there were many – returned his greetings. However – nobody refused him a drink: not on Christmas Eve, and in any case he had long since learned only to drink in bars that did not care what colour his money was. He did not grow violent under the influence of drink: he grew mellow, and with his huge frame he could drink an enormous amount. On the carrier of the bicycle he had tied a large paper bag; it contained sweets and biscuits, and small dolls and toys. To a little girl sitting in the corner of one pub, waiting silently for her father, he handed a packet of biscuits and a sixpence.

'Happy Christmas,' said Leah Winer to her neighbours, for which she encountered Herbert's mild protest.

'It doesn't matter. It is their festival. Yes, Herbert, I know they don't greet us on ours, but if they knew when our festivals were, they might.'

'We have a festival every week,' he said.

'Herbert, do you want everybody going around saying "Happy Saturday", do you?'

'Didn't the church seem extra golden?' said Ellen as they took their coats and gloves off after Mass next morning. 'People don't shake hands here at Christmas, do they? They don't even say "A happy Christmas", do they?'

Thomas closed and locked the gate, as if to give the impression they had gone away for the day. An overcast sky darkened the house, so they secured the shutters at noon, lit all the fires and lamps, and spent the day in peaceful, fond quietness with each other. Thomas gave Ellen a piece of especially beautiful cut stone he had found in the Castle ruins and had polished by the monumental mason in Mooreville; Ellen gave Thomas a wide, warm scarf, with tassels at the end.

'I was going to give you gloves but that's unlucky,' she said.

He read to her as she prepared their dinner; *The Gifts of the Magi* by O. Henry, a story of lovers making sacrifices to give each other Christmas presents; the story made Ellen sad. As he finished eating he said, 'You should be praised to the skies for that food. To the skies.'

She had put hot-water bottles in the bed. As she finished her prayers and climbed in, Thomas raised himself on one elbow and reached out his arms. She drew back. 'No, Thomas, no. I promised God and His Blessed Mother at the altar this morning, and at the very moment the Canon put the Host in my mouth, that I wouldn't give in to temptation.'

'Oh, Jesus, Ellie, I'm not temptation, I'm your husband.'

Ellen shrieked from the kitchen next morning.

'You thief, you thief!'

One of the cats had hidden overnight, and made inroads into the remains of the goose. Thomas laughed as Ellen wailed. 'Now I can't even use the carcass for stock. I've a good mind not to give the rest of it to them.'

'Come on,' argued Thomas, 'they've earned it.'

At noon they decided to walk to the ploughing championships at Ross: the frost had hardened the fields sufficiently and, as Ellen said when she closed the door, who could resist the brilliant sunshine? Thomas did not act as a judge, but should a dispute arise, especially in the measuring of a plough's deviation within a drill's length, they turned to him for an adjudication and his word was final.

'It's not that I'm a ploughing judge, or that,' he explained, 'it's more mathematics really, measurement, and it's not even that, it's really a sort of court of appeal and to stop them fighting. Anyway, it's a good thing, because they'll stop betting if I'm here.'

The first competitor was calming his horses as they arrived, and ploughing began within minutes, watched by a scattered crowd of absorbed, talking spectators.

'Each man has to open two headlands,' one of the organizers explained to Ellen, 'and do seven drills each turn, and each turn is measured. And the marks are given for the cleanness of the headland and the evenness of the drills and the evenness of the turns between the drills.'

'And does the whole field get ploughed?' she asked.

'It does, Ma'am.'

'Very handy for the farmer.'

Another man who was listening laughed. 'Ah, now, Ma'am, sure he'd pay a man to plough it ten times for what he'll spend on the drink today above at the house afterwards, but don't tell the Master that.'

Thomas, overhearing, said, 'What was that, Paddy, I didn't hear a word you said,' and they all laughed. He wore his new scarf. They kept moving, slapping their hands together, and Thomas showed Ellen what to watch for as the brown earth heaved behind the blade in thick slices.

'The real experts never look behind them to see what they have done, they concentrate on what they have to do, on what's before them. Look at that drill. He couldn't do that cleaner with a razor.'

Ellen dropped on her hunkers beside Thomas, and wonderingly traced the clay where it met the old unploughed land, a hard and straight edge. Gazing up the length of the rising field behind the man with the two horses, watching the satin back of his waistcoat shine in the sunlight, and seeing the powerful steel silver of the ploughshare make slabbed earth waves through the loam, she asked Thomas, 'Why does the plougher walk to one side instead of directly behind the horses?'

'That's another sign,' he said. 'A good ploughman never ruins his own work by treading on it. I remember an old fellow from Callan, over near the Kilkenny borders, telling me once that a good furrow should look as if God Himself reached a knife down and whipped it along the field.'

In the event, Thomas was not called on for what he called 'any Solomon business'; they declined the offer of a drink up at the house and walked home, their noses and cheeks glowing in the twilit frost.

On Tuesday, school reopened, and the postman brought a rough and mysterious parcel, crude handwriting, yellow binder twine, higgledy-piggledy postage stamps. Thomas winked at Ellen and said, 'I can guess what it is, and don't ask me 'til we get it home.'

As he unwrapped it that afternoon, his meticulousness – balling the string, folding away the paper – made her jig with agitation from foot to foot, and she even tried to snatch the parcel away, but he laughed and fended her

258

off easily. When he removed the thick inner layers of newspaper, a salmon lay disclosed, raw and pink like some newborn, mythic thing. No note, no letter.

'I know fine well who this is from,' Thomas said, 'and I know how he came by it too. That's my Uncle John, so it is. And his good strong net. Now that's a great compliment to you. He was always promising me one, but it never arrived 'til this year.'

For an hour or so that night, in the yellow light of the lamp, Ellen settled down to *The Story of Timothy Nash*. She had chosen a separate notebook: selected carefully with stiff covers and one hundred and twenty-four pages. Having discussed it with Thomas, she intended to write it like a dissertation. The story began to emerge quickly and clearly in her large careful writing.

> After a long period of education in Salamanca (see note) (*here Ellen turned to the back of the notebook and made a detailed note about the Irish Colleges in Europe and the Penal Laws which provoked their existence*) Timothy disappeared from the College, seemingly inexplicably, shortly before he was due to be ordained as a priest. It is believed that he spent some time working for farmers in Spain (by then he had a fluent grasp of the language), and then made his way into France and down into Italy. From his own papers it is clear that he spent some time in Rome, though his existence there may not have been an edifying one.
>
> We encounter him most interestingly when he appears in three southern counties, Limerick, Cork and Waterford, in the year 1786. He found a patron, a wealthy farmer named Callaghan near Mallow who, the father of a large family, changed his religion from Catholic to Protestant in order not to lose his farm and livelihood. But James Callaghan secretly continued to worship as a Catholic, and therefore engaged Timothy Nash to educate his children. The first document from outside the circle of Nash's relatives is a letter from the late Miss Flora Callaghan (deceased 1860 approx.) describing the encounters her brothers and sisters had with Timothy Nash. I shall quote.

Ellen fingered through the papers, copied several passages of Flora Callaghan's letters, and opened out a large family tree, showing where Nash entered the family. The dates of each member had been entered beside their names, as had the places of birth and death. Beside Nash's entry stood an asterisk, referring to a footnote.

As you will note, Timothy Nash is the only member of the family so far to die outside his own parish.

Ellen checked the place-name beside Nash's entry: 'Beaumaris'.

'Thomas! Where are you?'

'Yes,' he called.

'Where's Beaumaris?'

'Never heard of it. Is it in Italy?'

He came through the door. 'Check the atlas.' They searched futilely.

In the weeks after Christmas, Ellen ate more and more: ever larger plates of porridge and cream for breakfast; six, eight, nine potatoes, at a time: 'Ah, Ma'am,' the solicitous women at Mass said when she told them, 'sure why wouldn't you, sure you're eating for two.'

'Thomas, I'll be fat,' she said.

'When the baby is born, all the fat will go,' he said.

'And I hardly feel the cold,' she said.

'But you must be careful if the roads are slippery,' Thomas warned; 'sometimes you can't see that ice.'

This time, Ellen opened the letter.

28th February 1926.

Dear Mr and Mrs Kane,
    Isn't it a good job this isn't a Leap Year, or that last year wasn't either, otherwise I'd be claiming my silk gown, and I'd be using it now as a shroud, not for myself,

260

though, but for someone else, and her little head of black hair would ornament it fine. Too sweet to be wholesome, that's what they're saying about you, Mrs Kane, although everybody should be calling you Miss Morris still, because you came in here and took what wasn't rightfully yours, namely one of our men, and our best at that. But I have my eye on you, Miss Morris, and I watch you wherever you go, at the ploughing, or coming out of Carey's with your boxes of messages, and the boy from the shop running behind you like you want all the men to be. The law may say you're married to him, but I don't.

Yours watchfully,

Through the glass of the partition, Thomas saw Ellen reading the letter, and raced towards her.

'Give it to me.' She followed him to the school porch where he stood reading it.

'Ah, dth.' He seemed more exasperated than angry.

'What's that about a silk gown?' Ellen asked.

'Oh, just an old joke around here. If a woman proposes to a man during a Leap Year, and if he refuses her, he must buy her a silk gown. This woman – if it is a woman – is sick in the head.'

'I'm frightened,' said Ellen, arms clinched shivering to her bosom. 'I never saw an anonymous letter before.'

Thomas dismissed it. 'They're always going on around here.'

'Did you get some before?' asked Ellen.

'Several.'

'Oh, Thomas, if you showed them to me I wouldn't be as frightened, maybe.'

Thomas said, 'Let me think about it.'

Ernestina Stephenson sat on the long window seat, her breath frosting the glass, watching two of the men fork hay across the fields for the cattle.

261

'You, dear brother, have no intention of marrying your little Roman Catholic. Isn't that right?'

Cyril gulped from a mug of tea.

'You shouldn't be saying things like that,' he said, in an unconcerned tone. Ernestina did not look any less anxious.

'But she has every intention of marrying you, and that's what's worrying me, you know what a fool you are.'

Ernestina had a gruff, abrupt way, mannish, and her thick spectacles repelled people even further.

'I could confront her,' said Ernestina.

'What?' said Cyril.

'If you were a man, you'd tell me what your intentions were.'

'I'm going to the hunt tomorrow,' said Cyril.

'Yes.' Ernestina looked at him. 'Yes, I bet you are. Listen, can you give me money? I have none.' Cyril reached into his pocket and took out two notes.

'Ten pounds?' said Ernestina, 'that'll only do until Friday. Is that all you have?'

Cyril reached again.

'Twenty. A bit of an improvement. Another fiver, please? I hate these Irish notes.'

'If you had enough of them you wouldn't,' said Cyril.

'Would you ever think of saying something new or original?' asked Ernestina, as he drank some more tea.

Ernestina said, 'If you're not going to tell me what your intentions are towards little Miss Merrigan and her dirty little family – her dirty big family – I'll ask her myself.'

'Off you go, so,' said Cyril.

15

The frost lasted for six weeks, right through to Saint Patrick's Day. Ellen, though large, had expected of herself a greater ungainliness, but instead spoke of being limber, of wishing to walk.

'Although I think I'll draw the line at climbing walls,' she said to Thomas, 'and can't we go by the gate anyway?' The schoolchildren had told him the Castle pond had frozen solid, fit for skating, and Thomas decided, 'I'd better check it for safety.'

'Oh,' said Ellen blushing as they walked through the fields, 'I forgot one little detail.'

Thomas laughed and said, 'I'll wait for you. And I'll watch out to see there's nobody coming.'

She disappeared behind some bushes, and when she caught up with Thomas who had strolled on, he said, 'I never saw such steam.'

The tease took a moment to register, and then she punched him.

Two boys careened, yelling, on the slide the locals had made down the length of the pond: when they saw the Master and the Mistress, they drew themselves to a halt by drifting off to one side where the rime of the frost sat like light snow.

'I'd love to but I'd better not,' said Ellen, 'you have a go.'

Thomas said, 'I'd better test it first,' and stood with all his weight on the closest edge. He had brought a chisel, and began to lever the ice away from the sedges.

'Look,' he said, 'frozen solid, right enough. Did you hear about the Stephensons' engine? Stuck. On the field.

They can't budge it. Everyone's laughing.' He stepped on the lake, bouncing, bending and flexing his knees. 'Look. Not a give. Not a trace of a give.' He walked gingerly outward. 'It's six feet deep here.' He bounced harder. 'Ellie, this is extraordinary. Look.' He drummed his heels on the ice. 'I can't even make a crack.' Taking the chisel from his pocket he attacked the frozen surface. 'Not a mark.' He strolled-skated over to the little island at the very centre, while Ellen watched clapping her hands in the cold.

'Aah,' he called out sympathetically. 'There's a water-hen.' He bent down, struggled with something in the reeds and stood back having failed, then began to return to Ellen. 'A water-hen, dead,' he called out, 'it got caught or something, frozen to the ice. Stiff as a board.'

The whiteness of the landscape lit his face reddening from exertion.

'Thomas, you're a disgrace,' she said. 'Anyone would think to look at you now that you were no more than twenty-five years of age.'

He took her arm. 'Come on. I'm going for a skate,' he said, and they walked around the shore.

The two schoolboys stood back in sheepish respect, as Thomas had a run at the slide. He took off by locking his feet and whizzed by Ellen, waving to keep balance. Then his arms began to windmill and he fell crazily, crashing on to the ice and spinning a little on his hip. The boys laughed, and Ellen had difficulty in not joining in. When Thomas picked himself up, he held his elbow gingerly and made his way slippily to the bank.

'What are you looking at?' he asked the boys. 'Go on. Skedaddle.' They looked at each other, then slunk away.

'I've hurt my blasted arm,' he gritted. She inspected, turning the arm a little this way and that, making him squeak with pain.

'Come on,' she said, 'we'll go and call in to Dr Hogan.'

It'll be an excuse to meet him.' Thomas had previously remarked that the same new doctor had not had 'the manners to come and introduce himself in the last six months', but Ellen pleaded the stranger's case, saying the man was still settling in.

He himself answered the door of the Dispensary, younger than they expected, but still almost Thomas's age, and wearing something Thomas hated, a bow tie. Nevertheless, Dr Hogan immediately disarmed Thomas, when he exclaimed, 'But you're the man with the Singer car. I have an Austin Seven myself.'

Thomas asked, 'The green one?'

'Green is right.' He ushered them in. 'Green for glory. With a nice little yellow stripe. Here. Sit down there. Don't mind the mess. It'll be better than this, I have to do a lot myself, the wife is very busy. You know the Tierneys, I believe?'

'Which Tierneys?'

'From Glaslyre.'

'Oh, I do well,' said Thomas.

'We met your wife on the train,' said Ellen. 'And she was on the boat.'

'She has cousins in England,' said Dr Hogan. 'And the Tierneys are cousins of mine, that's how I heard of this job. What happened to us?'

Thomas said, in quite a short tone, 'I fell; I slipped on ice.'

Ellen laughed. 'Tell the man the truth. He was playing on the slide up at the Castle.'

'Slide?'

'The schoolchildren made a slide on the pond,' said Ellen, 'and Thomas was playing on it.'

Thomas said, irritably, 'I had to make sure it was safe.'

'Are we able to take off our coat?' asked Dr Hogan, and helped Thomas out of it. 'Funny, I was going to call to the school and say hallo on Monday, but sure you brought yourselves to me here.'

'What is your wife busy at?' asked Ellen.

'Ah, she's always doing some old thing.' He stood examining Thomas's coat before laying it on a chair. 'And our jacket. Oh, we drew blood a bit, that's hopeful. I'll tell you one thing. You have a lively bit of life around here. Did you hear about your rabbit-catcher?'

'What's up?' asked Thomas.

'The Sergeant called this morning, see if we can lift our elbow a bit higher. They can't get into the house. They're gone away to get a crowbar. Higher.'

'Ow!' Thomas winced and jerked. 'Crowbar? I'll get in there. What do they want to get in there for?'

'Now the other way. When are you due, Mrs Kane?'

'Early May.'

'A good time, child'll grow up in the warmth of the summer. The fresh air. Watch out for the wasps, though. Now back this way. I see. Does this hurt? Whose patient are you?'

'Dr Morgan's,' said Ellen.

'Hah! I did a locum for him about six years ago. Ex-Army, yellow moustache.'

'The very man,' said Ellen.

'"Malaria Morgan" we used to call him. Now does that hurt us? H'mmmmm. D'you know what it is? I think we have a chipped elbow. Was it our elbow we fell on?' He turned about and speculated towards some half-prepared shelves.

'We'll have to fix that up for us, that's no good.' He began to hum.

'Are you musical?' asked Ellen.

'Love it,' said Dr Hogan. 'Balfe is my man.'

'Because I'm getting a choir going,' said Ellen.

'I'm the wrong man for that, I'd never turn up,' said Dr Hogan. 'And anyway, d'you see, I'm no good in a chorus,

I'm a great man for the *tour de force*, that's what I am. Here we are.'

He unwrapped an awkward package and took a yellow slab of hard cloth from it. 'This is what they call a plaster, it has plaster of Paris in it, I don't know how they do it, and it's supposed to be very good. Now we have to hold our elbow like this' – he bent his own elbow three-quarters of the way closed, then stood over Thomas's elbow and eased the plaster on, while Thomas winced again.

'And we'll have to wear a bit of a sling. The scarf'll do lovely. Well, well, a Singer Roadster. About ten days, I'd say, and we should be all right, 'tisn't a bad chip.' He hummed again, and, the sling finalized, washed his hands in a basin. 'What about the rabbit man, d'you see? I s'pose we should go and see him?'

He invited them to squeeze into his Austin Seven, and then had to go back to the house for the starting-handle.

Thomas, staring straight ahead, murmured to Ellen, 'Look at the top window.' A face pushed aside a net curtain and Miriam Hogan stared down, dark-eyed. She withdrew when Ellen saw her, and the net curtain flickered back into place.

On the edge of Deanstown, where the trees ended, the Sergeant flagged down the overloaded green Austin Seven. Johnny Halloran's house was known locally as 'The Hotel', a building of acute dishevelment, noisome and broken-paned.

'Oh, the very man yourself, Sir,' said the Sergeant, when he saw Thomas. 'Hallo, Doctor, there's a great stretch in the evenings, isn't there? Hallo, Ma'am.'

Thomas squeezed out of the car, wincing, and the Sergeant began to explain. Nobody had seen the old man of the house for two to three weeks: the son had been evasive. The son's wife had seemed more than usually 'off the main road', as the Sergeant put it, and had barred entry

to the nurse who wanted to 'put ointment on the baby'.
Now the Hallorans had refused to open the door at all.

'Could you give them a shout, Master?' asked the
Sergeant.

Thomas walked to the door, knocked, then tried it: the
latch shifted but not the door. He knocked again.

'There's someone in there,' said Ellen, who saw movement in a curtain of newspaper at a top window.

Thomas retreated several paces and tilted his head back
to address his voice upwards.

'John Halloran, come out of there! At once. Do you
hear me?'

Dr Hogan looked aside at Ellen, raised an eyebrow and
bulged his cheeks at the force of Thomas's authority. The
door shook under Thomas's fist. 'Did. You. Hear. Me?'
He stepped back again.

The door opened abruptly and the infant scrambled out,
followed by the distraught man.

'I didn't do nothing, Sir. Sir, he was that way for days
before we copped on.'

The wife followed, barely dressed, talking to herself.

Thomas beckoned the Sergeant who went in, and after
a moment came out holding his nose.

'Jesus. Begging your pardon, Ma'am. No, Sir, don't go
in,' he said to Thomas, who pushed past – and who
returned just as quickly holding his nose with his un-
slinged arm.

'Phewack,' he said. 'You're needed, Doctor.' Jack
Hogan shrugged and entered.

Returning, a white handkerchief pressed to his face, he
asked, 'Sergeant, what do we do for an ambulance around
here?'

'We haven't one, Doctor, usually the Master's car, and
that's no ambulance, that's a job for a hearse.'

'No, we have to determine cause of death, Sergeant.'

The Hallorans stood by the wall, where Ellen had gone

to hold the small child's hand: a little boy, he was naked from the waist down, and wore only a flimsy vest. Dusk gathered, and a flicker of snowflakes.

'We have to do something before this child gets his death of cold,' she said briskly.

'I'll take the woman and the child into the hospital,' said the Doctor.

'Master, don't be hard on me, I didn't do it, I didn't do it,' said the husband.

'Johnny, in the name of God how many rabbits have you in there?' asked Thomas.

'I don't know, Sir.'

'Didn't I teach you to count?'

'You did, Sir, but I forgot again.'

'How long is your father dead in there?'

'I don't know, Sir.'

'Well, when was he last alive?'

'I don't know that ayther, Sir.'

Thomas drew him away from the knot of people and began to talk to him quietly. Ellen helped the wife and child into Dr Hogan's car, and smiled at the way he looked forlornly at the hitherto clean seats.

'Ma'am, no, Ma'am, I can't let you in there.' The Sergeant moved too late: Ellen had already reached the edge of the kitchen, and just as quickly she slapped a hand to her nose and mouth. She could make out the many shapes of rabbits hanging all around the dim room lit by a small oil-lamp, and a flameless fire smoking heavily up the chimney. On a low mattress lay a figure, but her eyes did not wish to register the condition of the skin on the face beneath the matted grey hair, and she fled.

The old man had died over a week previously. Lacking the intelligence or the will to move him, the family sat there looking at him; the child even rambled across the corpse, playing 'horse-y'. In milder weather, rapid decomposition would have set in earlier: it had just begun.

'What happened,' said Thomas back at home, as they dried their hands, and stood in front of their kitchen range, 'was that the father died, and Johnny had no money to pay for the funeral, and he didn't want the indignity of a pauper's grave for him, so he thought he'd wait, and with luck the frost would break and the ground would ease, and he'd sneak him up to the graveyard one night, across the bar of the bike or something, and bury him himself.'

Thomas laughed. When he went to throw the water out into the yard he held the back door open and called Ellen. Together they stood and looked at the snow falling.

'Well, that's the end of the frost,' said Thomas, 'rain next.' The snowflakes, like millions of soft tumbling insects, fell into Ellen's eyes and pleased her, as she looked up into the night sky. They bolted the back door.

After supper she asked, 'How bad is the elbow?'

'Ah, the blasted thing is a nuisance,' said Thomas. 'Good job it isn't my right arm. At least I can still use the chalk.'

She went to the parlour, and returned with a bottle.

'You deserve this,' she said, getting a glass.

'I always thought port was red,' he said; 'this is black.' He sipped. 'Sweet. Well, goodness, I never knew. D'you want a taste? I'll get a glass for you.'

'Oh, Thomas, in my condition.'

'Arrah, woman, half the infants in the country were carried floating on a pond of Arthur Guinness.'

She drank equally wonderingly.

'Isn't this nice?' he said. 'I wonder how it'd go with onions?' and she giggled, the port, and the fire, and the pregnancy flushing her face. Thomas had another glass, but Ellen declined. He sang her a little song:

'If I were a blackbird I'd whistle and sing
And I'd follow the ship that my true love sailed in.

And on the top rigging I'd there build my nest,
And I'd pillow my head on her lily-white breast.'

'You changed the words,' she accused happily.

As eventually they stood for bed, he gave her a large gentle hug with his good arm, curving his hips out backwards to accommodate her pregnant stomach.

'You made all the difference to me when I met you,' he said. 'All the difference in the world.'

As Ellen undressed, Thomas held the candle to the mirror, casting light farther into the bedroom. At a chosen moment he turned around from the reflection to the reality. As she stood by the basin undressed to the waist, he walked towards her, skirting the end of the bed, his scarf-sling incongruous against his pyjamas.

'I want a kiss. That's all,' he said.

'And you can have one and welcome to it.' He drank from her mouth. She moved back and said, 'You are lovely. You are great.' Reaching out, his right hand traced across the blue veins on top of her breast, as a child follows a map with its finger.

In school next day, Thomas called out a boy and made him stand at the top of the class. Drawing the ash stick from the groove beneath the blackboard, Thomas told the lad to hold his hand out straight. Out of the corner of his eye, he saw Ellen appear right up close at the partition, watching closely. Thomas gave the boy one reasonably mild slap across the palm and put the stick away, telling the amazed boy to return to his desk. Nevertheless, Ellen frowned.

The snow had begun to melt under soft rain. Leah came to spend the night, complete with her big suitcase. The schoolchildren looked at Leah with wonder and she smiled at them all, shaking the drops from her umbrella like a swimming dog. Thomas sent the Senior room home early, and he and Ellen walked home, with Leah between them trying to shelter all three with the umbrella, and getting all three of them wet.

'Now, we're going to have a real good chat,' said Ellen, as they drew their chairs to the fire Thomas had lit in the parlour. 'I'm going to make a cup of tea, and Thomas is going out, he has a meeting.'

'Are you off, so, be careful,' she called to Thomas from the hall, 'what time will you be back? He won't be back until late,' she tossed to Leah, and closed the hall door.

'Did you see this?' asked Leah, and handed Ellen a cutting, who read it, and said, 'Great! But, Leah.' She halted. 'Sure how will I know what size I'll be?'

Leah said, 'A first baby? You won't change too much.'

Mrs Gleeson, who is retiring from the Drapery business, having disposed of her Winter Goods, is offering her last Summer's Stock at exceptionally low prices. Wonderful Value in Ladies' frocks from 75/6d, Latest Style in Ladies' Costumes and Coats from 20/-. Children's Frocks from 2/6d. White Voile and Silk Frocks in great variety for 4/6d. Wreaths and veils from 2/-. Ladies' and Children's Hats from 7/6d. Children's White Shoes from 7/6d. Blouses and Jumpers from 2/-. Cardigans, 6/-. Underclothing of all descriptions marked less than cost. Boys' suits from 8/6d. Odd knickers from 2/6d.

A TRIAL WILL CONVINCE.

'Now how are you?' said Leah. 'Is everything all right?'

'I'm fine,' said Ellen, 'just fine.'

'And Thomas?'

'He's fine too. Oh, Leah, I have so many things to tell you I don't know where to begin.' She leaned forward and touched her dear friend's arm, and they smiled broadly at each other for no reason other than pleasure at the prospect of several uninterrupted hours together.

Their history of friendship permitted them a shorthand language, the mutually understood references of common ground: children, neighbours, fashions, households.

Leah asked again, 'And how are you, I mean – how are you? Herbert said to ask.'

Ellen said, 'Well, grand, really. Everything fine. A cake collapsed yesterday, you should see it, Leah, I had to throw it out. The waste, I think I put in too much fruit, and there was an awkward breeze down the chimney, the fire in the range was irregular.'

Leah looked at her and said, 'Your complexion is lovely – but are you a bit peaky?'

Ellen said, 'Well, I had a bit of a blow this morning, in the post –' and when Leah looked startled, Ellen said, 'No, I mean, no bad news, but not good either.'

She began to tell Leah the story of Timothy Nash: that Thomas had never really looked in the heirloom papers: that it had proven fascinating: but that beneath it ran a great undertow of anxiety.

'He so reminded me of Thomas, Leah, and it worried me.'

'But the letter this morning?' asked Leah.

Ellen said, 'Well, I'll tell you. Thomas's aunt had written out a whole family tree, and in it, it said that Timothy Nash died in Wales, in a town called Beaumaris on the island of Anglesey. We thought it was in Italy. So, to cut a long story short, I wrote to the local authorities there, to see if I could get some information.'

Leah said, 'Ah, why didn't you leave it alone?'

'You know me, Leah, I can't drop a thing once I start it. Anyway, I had this very peculiar letter back this morning, which said should I "wish to pursue any further details of Timothy Nash, who died in Beaumaris in 1806", I should "write to the Courthouse". I haven't told Thomas yet.'

'Hold on. Hold on. What is worrying you about the Courthouse?'

'I don't know, but I have a very bad feeling.'

Leah asked, 'Why, Ellen, are you so interested in this hundred-years-ago man?'

Ellen took another deep breath, and said, 'The thing that worries me is that I never expected Thomas to be so, so rough. I don't mean rough, and not to me, he's not, I mean –'

'You mean violent?'

'– Well, yes, I suppose so. And I'm frightened of it.'

Ellen's dam of tears burst. 'I've never said it to anyone.'

'But he has never hit you? Or has he?'

'Oh, God, no, nothing like that. But it is there in him, and children might have it in them, and what will I do if I breed a murderer? I'm serious, Leah, I'm serious. You haven't seen him when he's like that, I have.'

Ellen recounted again in greater detail than ever before, the MacReady incident. 'Leah, we could have lost our jobs over that.'

She told Leah of the birching of the Quinn boy. 'The unfortunate lad's bottom was cut and bleeding.'

Leah opted for a cool position.

'Do you seriously feel threatened by the way you have seen Thomas behave?'

'Not for myself, no,' Ellen said. 'But this worry won't go away.' She told Leah about the honeymoon incident, and the intensity of Thomas's behaviour on the street in London seemed to have the same resonance as Nash's violence to a policeman who almost arrested him.

'It is all there, in the papers about Nash, Leah. And of course, the whole "Canon Law" thing doesn't help,' said Ellen as an afterthought.

'The what?'

'Oh, nothing. I mean, I never told you. I thought it was too – too private.' Ellen unfolded the story.

Leah sighed. 'I wondered, I must say. I mean – it isn't the first time I heard a story like that with the Catholic Church. But if you want my opinion –'

Ellen cut in, 'Oh, Leah, don't confuse me any more than I am already.'

Leah halted, changed her direction. 'You've been worrying too much,' she said. 'You married a good man, then you stopped being a wife to him, all for the sake of your religion. Do you know – Herbert hinted to me that something like that might have cropped up, and he wanted me to ask you.' Leah sighed. 'I should listen to him more often. He's always right.' She continued, 'And then you saw Thomas being very angry and brutal, and you thought you'd made a big mistake, and now you find you think he has bad blood in him, and that your children will carry that bad blood.'

Ellen asked, 'Wasn't that what your letter was about, do you remember – before the wedding?'

Leah reached forward and took Ellen's hand: 'No, that was about things you should really understand, every girl should understand, before marrying.'

Ellen said, in a bitter little tone, 'I know, I know, "Marry in haste. Repent at leisure." I know.'

Leah gripped her friend's hand. 'Oh, Ellen, no, I feel for you, I feel so sorry, what you've been worrying about. And telling nobody about it. You'll worry the baby too, you must stop. Thomas is a good man. Herbert says so, too.'

'But, Leah, you know that Thomas did a lot of. Things. You know, Collins and that. The Troubles, I mean – for God's sake, Leah. He was a gunman!'

'I know. Herbert told me. He told Herbert.'

Ellen said, 'He never told me.'

Leah said, 'He told Herbert in detail. And if you're this

frightened, aren't you glad he didn't tell you? Look – why don't you let the baby's placidness just – just take you over?' They sat in thought for a moment.

Leah asked, 'How much of all this has there been lately?'

'Almost none. And in fact, I wonder if he isn't trying to get "it" under control.'

'There you are. People can change, Ellen, and we must not so much help them to, as allow them to. If Thomas changes, don't say anything to him about it, just find other ways of rewarding him. But the point is – he is violent, he probably is truly a violent man. That doesn't mean that your life will be the worse off for it. I mean – there are things about me that Herbert hates. I flirt, he says, and he hates me flirting, says I shouldn't be "cocking my back-side" he calls it, at men. And there are things about him that I think are wrong in any human being, I mean Herbert is quite mean with money, Ellen, and keeping small things to himself around the house; he buys himself little treats that he doesn't share – but that doesn't mean that I can't live on and on with him.'

'But, the fear. Won't go away.' Ellen provoked another fit of weeping in herself. 'And I have no choice in the matter, that's the real difficulty.'

Leah reached a handkerchief across, clean from beneath her cuff.

'I knew I was right to come out and see you. I said it to Herbert. Now you've cried enough. You don't want the baby crying too. Has all this been bottled up in there for months?'

Ellen snuffled. 'It's not so much bottled up, as much as it feels as if it is all in another room, and when I open the door it all comes tumbling out.'

Leah read silently the letter again from Beaumaris. 'Do you really want to follow this up? You'll only be a month or so off the baby?'

'It'll ease my mind, Leah.'

Leah poured more tea. 'But Thomas seems thrilled with the thought of the baby, doesn't he?'

Ellen leaned back and closed her eyes.

'And you love each other, and he's very tender to you? Despite everything? I see it in his face. And is that all that's worrying you? I mean, you're not worried about Thomas being a father? Forty-one or forty-two isn't young for a man to learn these things?' Leah wore her 'fishing' expression, but she caught nothing.

'No,' Ellen lied, 'that's the thing I'm really worried about,' and touching upon a greater concern, said, 'I mean, Leah, if you'd seen that poor Michael Quinn's bottom after Thomas birched him. I can't get it out of my head.' She did not mention the 'Perish by the sword' remark, by which she frequently felt haunted.

Ellen subsided, her eyes closed. Leah said, 'Take a little sleep there, I'll wash up these cups. I always felt weepy at this stage before the girls were born. By the way, what happened to that poor woman whose husband disappeared?'

'Oh, nothing.'

An hour later, they said good-night on the landing. A few moments afterwards, Ellen nipped back downstairs, took down a fresh pot of the Miss Harpers' prize gooseberry jam, that she knew Thomas loved, and set it on the table for his breakfast: she was fast asleep by the time the car's lamps floodlit the front of the house.

Val Vousden came offstage at the Opera House, thrilled with the reception: they wanted him back for another curtain call, and then another, oh, my! And another!

'Home was never like this,' he quipped to Willie Crosbie in the wings.

'Go back again, boy,' said Willie Crosbie; 'they can't get enough of you.'

Val bowed low, reversing his twirling legs sideways. Val pranced forward again, obeying to the letter the trouper's rule of curtain calls – on quickly, off slowly.

'He wouldn't milk a herd of cows better,' said Willie Crosbie to Geraldine, his favourite usherette.

Val darted out one more time, bowing lower than a weeping willow and twice as flourishingly, then straightening high, the high dome gleaming, and kissing his hands, and mouthing 'thank-you-thank-you-thank-you-thank-you-thank-you-thank-you-thank-you-thank-you-thank-you-thank-you-thank-you-thank-you-thank-you' he bravely stepped up and quick-marched off, his back view releasing the audience from their rapture.

Val had a wonderful gesture of imploring, both hands held out palms upwards, like a prince pretending to be a beggar.

'Aren't they great, Willie? And they loved "The Deanstown Band".'

'You see,' Willie said. 'There you have it, boy. Brand-new material. They love a new recitation.'

'Ah,' said Val, 'I thought as much.'

'A great piece, Val. The best piece you've done with a long while.'

> 'In the blue of sky and gold of corn,
> They marched their glittering uniforms,
> With fife and drum and bright trombone,
> They played the tunes their folks could hum.
> This little band of village men,
> Of humble birth and lowly breed,
> Made music fit for Count or King,
> To gladden hearts of every creed.'

'Great stuff,' said Willie, leaning against the wall, reading it.

Val snatched it back, signed it and gave it to Willie, 'personally autographed'.

Val entered his dressing-room and shook hands with the tall young man there, who brown-haired and shining-eyed, congratulated him.

'Bernard, I have great plans. That band, you know –' and Val closed the door.

In the corridor, Willie read on for a moment or two, then, with Geraldine, vanished through an emergency exit like a rabbit.

Spring 1926

16

Hushed, the church heard the lists.

'Monday, the 12th of April – John Ryle, Lackendarra: Tuesday, the 13th – John Tobin, Piercestown: Wednesday the 14th, Spy Wednesday – Michael Connors, Newtownbeg; Thursday, the 15th, Holy Thursday – John Relihan, Kiltynan. This parish is very honoured [the Canon pronounced it 'onnurd'] to have Easter Stations this year, it being a Confirmation year. And it being Holy Week, I needn't say –' The Canon paused for emphasis – 'there will be none of the usual practices, that is to say, there will be no drink. And no card-playing, but there will be a dispensation in each house for the day, and the usual Lenten fasting of only one meal and two collations will be lifted.'

On the way home, Thomas explained. 'The Stations are regarded as a great honour because the Blessed Sacrament comes to the house, 'tis like the church coming to the home, but most people find them very difficult. Because the Canon won't announce them in time, that misfortunate Mrs John Ryle won't have a minute to get her house clean, or food in, before the Canon and a whole crowd of people descend on her tomorrow morning. Everywhere else in the country, they get several months' notice, but he thinks here it will stop them having the time to buy in drink. The opposite is the case, they need the drink after all the fluster.'

'Are we going?' Ellen asked.

'We're expected to go to at least one. Our Station is on Thursday, at Relihans.'

=

John Relihan's house in Kiltynan lay within a long walk's distance, but Thomas decided to drive, on account of overcast skies and Ellen's largeness and occasional breathlessness. Wednesday, closure day for Easter, was her last day at school: an untrained deputy would take over until September.

'It is a bullock you have in there?' the Canon asked Ellen after Mass, looking at her stomach.

'Subtlety and delicacy,' sighed Thomas afterwards, 'Canon Jeremiah Williams's hallmarks. Known for them from here to Timbuctoo.'

Ellen was greeted with warmth, and chose a chair at the back to kneel against: that way, she could view the whole proceedings.

'Ah, Ma'am, sure you mustn't kneel, never mind the knees, sit up, sit up, sure if God'll not forgive you now, He never will.'

The women pressed around her, in her small celebrity.

'God bless you, look at the complexion of you, nature's boon.'

They intended to make her as welcome as they knew how.

'Ah, Ma'am, you have a sheen on you, that'll be the healthy child. And the lucky one. And the Master looking great? I never seen a man look so well. Sure every man needs a wife, don't they?'

The Station, essentially a Mass celebrated at the farmhouse kitchen table (which had been elevated on four butter-boxes), brought the ceremony closer to her than Ellen had ever felt, and, almost excited, she said to Thomas later, 'I never enjoyed anything as much. I never felt so devout.'

The Station Mass ended; the Canon intoned, 'God bless all here. And the crops for the market and the house. And the beasts for the fair and the table. And the women for

284

their children now and the future. And the men that they will have strength and health and purpose. Now and in all the times to come, Amen.'

The fifty or so people there shuffled to their feet. John Relihan, as head of the household, moved forward to the Canon and put an envelope into his hand, the cue for neighbours to do the same. Connie, the sacristan, took the vital packets one by one as the Canon handed them to him, and when this ritual ended, the Canon moved off up the house to the parlour to disrobe, followed by Connie who would count the cash. The men lifted the table from the butter-boxes, and redistributed the chairs; the women began to assemble the tablecloths.

Neither Thomas nor Ellen took any part in this. Fittingly, as host, the head of the house, John Relihan, a stocky man with short black wiry hair, whose face shone, engaged Thomas, next most important guest after the Canon, in conversation: Thomas stooped as he listened, his hands behind his back, his head inclined away.

A stout woman approached Ellen, and introduced herself, John Relihan's sister-in-law, married to his brother.

'Tell me now, is your time good?'

Ellen did not fully comprehend.

'I mean, were you sick at all in the morning, or did you have wind in the stomach? I have a great cure for wind in the stomach.'

Ellen said, 'Oh, hold on, hold on, I'll write it down,' and from her handbag came the ever-present note-book.

'This is it. Now. You take a cupful of milk, that's about half a pint, and you boil it well [she pronounced it 'bile'] and you let it cool down to drinking heat.' Ellen wrote quickly, the pad on her knee. 'Then. You take four tea-spoons of soot.'

'Of what?' Ellen looked at her.

'Four teaspoons of soot. Soot from the chimney.'

'You do not!?'

'You do, Ma'am. Four teaspoons of soot.' Ellen wrote it down, but slid in a question mark.

'And you mix the soot well into the cooling milk and you drink it.'

'But doesn't that taste terrible?' asked Ellen.

'It do, Ma'am, but sure anything is better than the wind.'

Ellen looked up speculatively, and from the far end of the kitchen saw a thin, handsome, young-ish woman staring at her, who quickly looked away. Thomas beckoned Ellen over.

'Do you know John Relihan at all?' The man shook her hand heartily. 'I'm sorry I missed you when you came in. You're very welcome. How are you settlin' in here with us all, at all?'

Ellen replied, 'Oh, sure I'm nearly a native, I'm here now, what? Over a year.'

'Oh, sure, one of our own. One of our own. And you have good news on the way.' He also indicated Ellen's stomach.

'Well, I hope so, I hope so.' Ellen noticed both the man's shyness and the determination of his courtesy in acknowledging her condition.

'I have five myself, Ma'am, and one in Heaven, and sure we liked every one of them.'

'And one in Heaven? Aah,' Ellen said sympathetically.

'Ah yes, Ma'am, sure the little thing was dead before 'twas alive, sure that's the way.'

Conversation continued: neighbours, the Land Commission rulings, boundary fencing, arguments over inheritance in families: Ellen loved these conversations and listened avidly, barely tearing herself away when 'breakfast' was called.

She gasped when she saw the table. One of the reasons why people such as Thomas condemned the Stations had to do with social rivalry: householders, even those who could scarcely afford it, outdid each other with food. The Canon returned to the big kitchen, and said, 'Glory be to God' when he saw the feast, raising his right hand and making the Sign of the Cross over it all.

Along the centre of the main table ranged seven large, long dishes in a row, three by three, a leg of pork, a leg of mutton, a leg of beef, each huge: Thomas and Ellen would get a fortnight's eating out of any one of them. On the next three dishes, a turkey, a goose, and a pair of chickens. All the meat was cold, mostly cooked the night before: in the middle of the seven sat the largest dish of all, a huge pink ham: 'There's a quarter of a pig there,' Thomas whispered to Ellen. All around these sat little satellite plates: sliced hardboiled eggs; sliced onions; bowls of cold potatoes; dishes of glistening chutney. The two adjoining tables had been packed even more tightly: two large glass bowls of cream; Ellen counted nine varieties of cake – Madeira, chocolate, sponge sandwich, two seedcakes, a fruit cake, Swiss roll, lemon layer cake and a wide flan covered in cream, with slices of orange layered across it. No fewer than five apple tarts, circular and golden brown, had been baked, in dishes more than a foot in diameter: a further eight plates contained small buns in cases; cream horns filled with home-made raspberry jam added to the cream; small apple tartlets with pastry striped across them in an 'X'; large, hot plump currant scones, that had been opened, buttered and closed again gently and the butter oozed out; another plate of soda scones, no currants, had been opened and spread with butter and home-made gooseberry jam; on the sixth plate a little arrangement of jam tartlets, with gooseberry, raspberry, blackcurrant and loganberry jams, all home-made; the seventh plate bore slabs of dark cakes, long and with smooth chocolate spread along the top; and on the eighth sat lordly, high buns, the tips of which had been slit and filled with blobs of cream. Around these, several small dishes had been laid out, with all the available home-made preserves Mrs Relihan commanded, from herself and her relatives and neighbours who, in the previous rushed days, had arrived bearing gifts.

The Canon sat at the head of the table, John Relihan on his right and Thomas on his left. No woman joined this sitting, with the sole exception of Ellen, given a place of honour at John Relihan's right hand. Fifteen people ate at this first serving: two more sessions would follow, and at the end of it all, the servant-girl of the Relihan house, and the others lent for the morning, all of whom had tea and sandwiches standing up in the rear kitchen, would clear everything.

Amid exclamations, the men were given heaped plates, the Canon's, Thomas's and Ellen's the most heaped of all. Other than the declared hierarchy of Parish Priest, his Principal Teacher and the head of the house, no social lines were drawn: men from cottages sat alongside the men on whose farms they worked; any guesswork regarding the strata in which people belonged would depend entirely upon the quality of their clothing and the grades of sheepish shyness on their faces.

For once Ellen listened rather than talked, and briefly, out of the corner of her eye, she saw again the long, handsome woman, this time having put on her coat, and making her excuses to Mrs Relihan, preparatory to leaving. Ellen tried to catch Thomas's eye and indicate the woman, who inexplicably made her feel uncomfortable, but the opportunity passed, and through the window she saw the woman mount a high bicycle and ride away. She reconnected with the table's conversation in time to hear the Canon say, 'The Mistress, there, is a fearless woman, I'd say.'

'What was that?' Ellen smiled.

Thomas told her, 'We were talking about which is braver, a man or a woman?'

'A woman has more to lose,' said Ellen. 'That is, if she has children, she has to look after them.'

'Fair point, fair point,' said the Canon. 'But would a woman use a gun?'

'What about the Countess Markievicz?' asked Ellen.

'Ah, sure what was she?' said the Canon. 'A Protestant woman from the west of Ireland caught up with ould romance, and parading the streets of Dublin in 1916 with a gun in her hand; sure she never fired a dangerous shot. They tell me her gun was never fired at all.'

All eyes except the Canon's turned on Thomas. He said nothing, and chose to concentrate on a wedge of pork. Mrs Relihan poured tea in his cup.

'Not the case,' Thomas told Ellen on the way home. 'Her gun was fired. Several times.'

'Their teeth are generally very bad,' said Ellen, 'aren't they?'

They had developed a habit of sitting in the car when they reached home, talking there for several minutes. Ellen now said, 'Who was that tall, good-looking woman?'

Thomas asked which one, and Ellen continued, 'She had her hair drawn back from her forehead; I was expecting it in a bun, but it wasn't, it was cropped at the back. She had a black cardigan.' They climbed out of the car. Thomas had taken to coming around to Ellen's assistance. 'I saw her looking at me very hard.'

Thomas replied, 'You're still something of a curiosity, they haven't all seen you yet.'

'No,' said Ellen, 'no,' but she was not replying to his observation. 'Who was she, Thomas?'

'Her name is Edel Crowe.'

=

'I told you I would,' said Ernestina to her young brother, 'but you never take a blind bit of notice of anything I say. So I'm going up there now. This minute.'

'To the house?' asked Cyril? 'You're not going to the house, are you?'

Ernestina said, 'I certainly am.'

'In your best bonnet?'

'I don't wear a blasted bonnet. Who do you think I am? Little Bo-Peep?'

'No time like the present,' Cyril said, although he looked less than contented.

'I wish you would stop trotting out those proverbs of yours.'

Ernestina went to the hall. Cyril called, 'She won't be at home, she'll be at work.'

'No, she won't. Thursday is her half-day.'

'You know everything.'

'I do and I know something else, brother dear, I know that the gig is tackled.'

A pony and trap awaited in the yard.

'Are you too lazy to walk?' called Cyril.

'I'll leave that to you for the night-time, you'd know your way there blindfold by now,' said Ernestina, who knew perfectly well she might want to leave quickly. In the yard she halted, her breath catching – again: she winced in pain.

Ernestina drove fast, the Stephensons were known always to have a good pony. One skilful hand slapping the long leather reins just on the stinging point of the pony's shoulders, she rested an arm along the mudguard of the trap, whose yellow wheels flashed in the sunlight. Thomas Kane stood at his gate as she drove by, and he saluted her: she raised a hand.

Her destination – a high-peaked cottage, a woodsman's in the days when the Castle precincts had been extensively forested. As the Land Commission divided the estate after the 1921 Treaty, the Merrigans were given permanent title to the cottage on a peppercorn annual ground rent, plus five acres of land on which they grazed one cow, and some goats. Nothing distinguished the cottage, no flowerpots, nor bright colours, nor pretty curtains. Ernestina drew the pony to a halt, and took off her thick spectacles to polish them. She shouted.

'Hallo! Hall-ooo!'

The ajar door opened back fully, and a girl stood there.

'Hallo,' Ernestina called, 'Joan, is it?'

Joan Merrigan stepped a little farther forward, and said a tentative 'Hallo'.

'I wanted to have a word or two,' said Ernestina, in what Cyril always called her 'as nice-as-pie' voice.

Joan Merrigan answered, 'Yes,' and walked towards the trap, taller than Ernestina, and quite heavily built. 'What do you want?'

'Just a few words,' said Ernestina, in whose hands the initiative trembled.

'I want to know what . . .'

Ernestina stopped as the girl laid a hand on the back door of the pony-trap.

'I was wondering,' said Ernestina, still sweetly, and now in a lower tone, 'about you and . . .'

'About me and what?' Joan Merrigan spoke neither enthusiastically nor surlily, but with no overwhelming respectfulness, either.

'About you and my brother. That's what,' snapped Ernestina.

'What about it?' asked Joan Merrigan, who wore a pink butterfly slide in her hair.

'Well. What is it you're doing with him?'

'When?'

No give whatsoever from Miss Merrigan. Ernestina blinked vigorously; those bloody glasses again, how often she cursed them.

'When what?' she asked.

'When what what?' came the Merrigan reply. 'What are you going on about?'

'I'm talking about you and my brother,' said Ernestina, 'and I want to know what you're doing with him?'

'And I'm asking you when?'

'How do you mean "when"? What I mean,' said Ernestina, reverting to her 'reasonable' tone, 'is what your intentions are to my brother, who after all is a considerable citizen. I'm Miss Stephenson, by the way.'

Joan Merrigan looked at Ernestina.

'Ah, would you come down and look at yourself above. "Miss Stephenson".' She withered further. '"Miss Stephenson". Your brother may be a "considerable citizen" but he's not above shifting around here. "Miss Stephenson". We're not anybody's tenants any more, are we? Why don't you ask your brother?'

Ernestina said, 'I thought that, well – as women . . .'

Joan Merrigan looked at her once more, walked away from the gig, and went into the cottage, not even bothering to close the front door.

When Thomas saw Ernestina pass by in her trap, he was preparing to walk down the road to the school: Ellen had taken to bed for a rest. The postman had forgotten the dates of the school closure for the holidays, and had lazily pushed some letters under the door. One marked URGENT, came from the Department, a most unusual occurrence, and Thomas opened it immediately: it contained not a letter but a promulgation.

A virulent, and often fatal disease, thought to be but not yet confirmed as, a strain of contagious poliomyelitis, has been reported in Thurles; a second suspected case has been reported in Ballingarry. Experience in other countries has shown that this disease spreads like wildfire if contracted in a small community: children of schoolgoing age are particularly exposed, especially if

292

undernourished. Accordingly, the Medical Officer of
Health has ordered that the schools in your area must
not reopen after Easter until further advised. Your School
Manager has been informed, and it will be announced at
all Masses on Sundays and Holydays in the interim.

Thomas spread the notice out and read it again. He folded
it carefully and put it in his inside pocket for Ellen to read
at home. The second envelope had that deadly, familiar
handwriting, and, although addressed to Ellen, he slit it.

I have now seen the whites of your eyes, Ellen Morris,
you who call yourself Mrs Kane. Your child, whatever you
say, will be born a bastard, because you came in here
and stole that man.

Thomas read no more. Snapping the letter shut, he said,
'That's enough! That's enough,' and sat down. After a
moment or two, he unlocked his desk and took out a black
metal oblong box with Japanese designs on it: long ago it
had held fancy biscuits. In it he had put all the other
anonymous letters and now he spread them out, one by
one, on the floor, too numerous for the desk, and he
forced himself to re-read them, from the very earliest,
passionate declarations of love, to this, the most recent
and most poisonous.

'Always look for a pattern,' was Collins's phrase when
analysing military operations against him: Thomas now
took out a sheet of paper, and, kneeling, began to make
notes. He noted down phrases in common, or repeated
word usage, from letter after letter – there had been
eighteen in all over three years – and he noted the dates,
if dated, and the frequency, and then made a note to try
and trace where he, and then he and Ellen, had been
immediately before a letter arrived. He looked for any
pattern of mood in the writer, which would authenticate
them as genuine, and not some hoaxer; he compared the
lengths of the letters, counting the paragraphs in the

longer ones, the words in the very short ones, and he wrote every finding in his tiny, immaculate handwriting. He even marked the two letters he knew Ellen had seen.

A rap on the windowpane alarmed him. The face peering in shaded its enquiry with a hand in order to see better: Dr Hogan, in a different bow tie. Thomas, not thinking quickly enough in the small sudden fright, went straight to the door and admitted him, then realized he could not cover up the letters spread out on the floor.

'I saw you through the window, did I give you a fright? Did you get the Department notice?'

Dr Hogan spoke rapidly, and sent a hand over his thinning sandy hair.

'How serious is it?' asked Thomas.

'Ah, it is bad. I'm after coming from a meeting of Dispensary men, and apparently there's a case nearer home, a Carroll girl from over Scullystown.'

'God, that's a bit close. I know that family, they're originally from here.' Thomas whistled. 'How old is she? And how is she?'

'Nine. Hard to say. She has two of the symptoms, and vomiting a lot. The mother is nearly out of her mind, and I told them nothing about the others, and when you see a mother worried like that, you always know. The thing is, if she hasn't been that well-fed, she'll go like a light'; he snapped his fingers. 'By the way, there's another Department promulgation on the way, and I think you might be best to keep it to yourself. I advised they shouldn't put it out at all, except to the afflicted relatives, because it's going to cause havoc.'

'What is it?'

The doctor sighed. 'It's about burial. D'you see, it has to happen immediately a doctor certifies, within twelve hours if possible and with no attendance other than the family at the funeral. People are going to find that very hard.'

'And very alarming. Like the Black Death or something,' said Thomas. 'What eejit thought that promulgation up?'

A sharp clip-clop rang on the road, and the men turned to look through the open school door.

'The Stephenson girl from the stud,' Thomas answered the doctor's enquiry.

Dr Hogan turned around; 'Ernestina?! What's she doing out? She should be at home. Bit of bother there.' He looked down at the floor. 'Were you working?' he enquired, indicating the letters. Thomas took a deep breath, looked at Hogan, took a decision.

'Will you keep a secret?'

The doctor said, 'Isn't that what I'm paid to do?'

Thomas, by example, invited him to get down on his hunkers, and began slowly to tell him the story of the letters. The two men stayed there for over an hour, Thomas soon lighting a lamp. After thoughtful conversation filled with pauses, the doctor finally took away several of the letters in his pocket, wrapping them carefully in unused notepaper Thomas had given him.

'The weather seems very settled,' Ellen said, sitting up in the half-darkness. 'Would you do me a favour,' she asked, 'and hand me over that,' indicating a white squat jar with blue lettering on the cover. She sat up and began to rub the hand-cream into her palms in a slow circular motion. 'Do you know, I know I look heavy, but I don't feel heavy yet. Leah was saying it won't really bother me until the last week or so. That's dreadful about that Carroll girl. Do you know them?'

Thomas said he did, and after some other desultory conversation, Ellen rose, and Thomas lit a second candle to give her light by which to dress.

'I hate tomorrow,' he said. 'I've always hated it. I hate

that whole idea, fields of skulls, that, Haceldama, all of that, field of blood.'

'Oh, I love Good Friday,' said Ellen. 'It's the only day of the year I wear lipstick, because it reminds me of the blood and passion of Christ. Why don't you do what I do on a day I hate. Do something nice, something that you enjoy.'

'Well, I can't do that, can I? You and Mother Church and Canon Law won't let me,' replied Thomas, with spirit. Ellen, despite herself, laughed.

'No, no, that's not what I mean, do something else that you enjoy. I'll tell you what you'll do. You know how you like honey? Why don't you walk over to Connells and see if they have any combs of honey left? It'd be good for me too, with the baby.'

Thomas sat beside Ellen on the bed as she brushed her hair and began, pins in her mouth, to make a small rampart of it high on her crown.

'Whatever I say,' he began, 'I can't wait for that little thing to come into the world. Did you notice John Relihan's remarks at the Station? No matter how rough a man is, a baby will move him.'

He held Ellen's hand for a moment, and she allowed her hair-piling to be interrupted, sitting quietly, looking straight ahead where the mirror caught the dim reflection of them in their moment of quiet, she in her large white nightgown, he visible by the face only, his dark clothes augmenting the shadows.

'There is such a thing as religious mania,' said Thomas. 'I've heard it.'

'You're mocking me again, Thomas,' sang out Ellen.

'No, I'm not.'

'Yes, you are!'

'No, I'm not. People get it, and they foam at the mouth.'

'They do not. I've never heard of it.'

'I saw you at the altar, Ellie, and you were nearly in a trance.'

'How can I help it if I love God, too?'

Thomas was opening a sack of seed potatoes. 'I think I'll start putting these in. Seriously, Ellie, do you really feel as strongly as that religiously?'

'But isn't it a lovely feeling?'

'I always feel anxious when I pray too much. It opens up things I know I can never reach.'

'But isn't that the point?' Ellen put two cups, saucers and plates on the table. 'Do you want milk in your tea?'

'Don't I always have milk in my tea?'

'But today . . . ? I'm not having any.'

Thomas straightened up. 'Penance or no penance. Mortification or no mortification. Good Friday or no Good Friday, you are to have your nourishment.'

'But.'

'But rubbish, Ellie. How d'you think God will thank you for not looking after your health right now.'

'My health is fine.'

'Good. Make it finer.'

She laughed to take the small head of steam out of things. 'Thomas Kane, for a sensible man you're ridiculous. Come on, sit down. You have to go and get that honey.'

Thomas had always wanted to write, and had achieved a small distinction with anonymous book reviews, some local history journalism and, for a national newspaper, an account of Dean Swift's visit to Deanstown: Thomas wrote it in 1917, to coincide with the 250th anniversary of the Dean's birth, submitted it to the editor and received a cheque for three guineas. This encouraged him, and at the time he further reasoned that any such literary or journalistic activity would offer perfect cover if questioned by the military; nevertheless, not one other piece was accepted, and he gave up, through a combination of disappointment and the pressure of his 'extracurricular activities', as he privately called them.

When he returned from Belgium and France, in the autumn of 1920, and settled into the newly-built, empty house at Deanstown, he tried again. This time the failure had nothing to do with editorial rejection: as if a huge boulder had been put in his pathway he found any free direction forward blocked, and no matter how he pushed and heaved with his mind, he could not run ahead as he wished. After a few paragraphs the light darkened, and he could not make it bright again. Everything he wrote seemed to him slight and thin, hollow: he tried writing doggerel, to see if that would loosen things: he even copied out paragraphs from *Under the Greenwood Tree*, a book he particularly liked. He made lists of the matters which interested him, and even wrote nature notes for himself, recording the bird life in the garden during that winter. Once, recalling assiduously all the things that had made him laugh, he attempted to write humour, but found that the most difficult of all and gave up.

His habitual control of the details in his life meant that all these attempted pieces had now been assembled in two large notebooks, so cohesively gathered, and in such uniform writing, that a stranger might at first assume his eye had fallen on a journal of sorts. Thomas had never shown them to Ellen; in some sort of hope, he looked at the notebooks from time to time, and when he did, he inevitably turned to one page, the only piece in the entire collection which half-pleased him. One wet Sunday afternoon he had made a dart for freedom around that boulder blocking the cave of his imagination – he wrote, quite quickly, and without labour, an imagined description of the Castle as it must have been had he visited it in the mid-eighteenth century, when it had the reputation of being the finest demesne in the land.

Seen from the road to the village, a belt of ornamental woods in a circle formed a fringe very like a ruff, above which rose the Castle in all its spires and grandeur. Through these woods several paths have been cut radially, each path opening on to the shore of the ornamental lake, from the far bank of which terraced fields rise in a parterre to the sloping lawns immediately before the Castle door. On the left, as I walked up the fields, my hat in my hand, a long line of exquisite trees and bushes culminated at each end in a gate: this was the Bell Walk, so called because Grand George Mathew, the owner of the Castle, had hung it, his main avenue, with bells which tinkled to warn the Castle of approaching guests, so that he might welcome them as warmly as he hoped to do.

Where the Bell Walk ended stood a sunlit wall, decorated with ivy and flowers, and along this wall in alcoves stood a number of brilliant white statues and busts of famous figures and gods. In the distance, I saw a maze, reached by a gravel path along each side of which grew tall sunflowers like columns, each taller than a six-foot man. As I approached, a servant in a blue apron and a large white wig called out, 'Hallooa' and walked down the sloping green lawn to greet me, offering me wine and biscuits from the silver tray he carried.

Although he liked to re-read this passage, it also made Thomas a little uncomfortable, principally because he had never developed it, and also because he knew that he had not entirely originated it all, that some of the description had come from local word-of-mouth, and from the written descriptions in the library at Thurles, recorded by an English visiting clergyman called Campbell, who had called to Deanstown in 1775. Nevertheless, Thomas found some pleasure in the thought that one day he might find the freedom to pursue this strange man with the hat walking up the fields to the Castle, a figure that he, and only he, had invented. He played with the notion now and again, and especially every time he walked to the house of the Connells which lay a good two miles on the far side of the Castle.

On Good Friday afternoon he drank tea there. Brother and sister, both unmarried, the Connells complained strenuously of the Canon's appeals for money, and told Thomas something he had heard rumoured but never confirmed. One of their workmen had caused trouble with a gun: 'that Quinn man. I never felt safe with him around the place,' Nora Connell said, and her brother chimed in, 'That fellow's – well, he's not good, not good.'

Nora Connell said, as Thomas stood up, 'Now that honey'll do the Mistress grand, now, and her time so near.'

'Sure how would you know?' asked her brother humorously.

'Don't I talk to people, don't I?' she riposted.

Thomas took a different route home, heading for a high brake of trees from which the widest and highest view of the surrounding countryside could be had, a full three hundred and sixty degrees of the landscape he loved. No cowpath wound this way, and he walked over the new grass, tussocking already in the mild spring weather. The last climb to the coppice was always the steepest and, holding out the string shopping bag gently so as not to break the eggs he had bought, nor damage the honeycomb, he scrambled up the bank and leaned his back against the outermost tree in the group.

Facing first to the west, he saw the spire of Ellen's cathedral, in the shadow of which Leah and Herbert lived; in shorter focus, on the nearest, next highest hill, beside the motte-and-bailey, stood the church in which they had married. To the south, the mountains had changed to velvet. Suddenly, Thomas heard behind him in the distance the rattle and chink of a cart. He turned to face east, and down below, caught in a late shaft of sunlight, sat the small cemetery of all the scions of the Castle families, their private burial ground.

As tiny and whitened as a graveyard in a Mexican story, it had fallen more or less into disuse, and although some local families had claimed rights to be buried there, no funeral had been taken to it for at least two to three years. Beyond it now, and approaching the gate, on the wide, almost overgrown gravelway, a cart approached, drawn by a large pony, rearing its head. Thomas stood, transfixed, recognizing the family: on the cart sat a man holding the reins, and across from him a woman wearing a black head-scarf. Dangling his legs at the back, but with bowed head, sat a schoolboy of about twelve years of age. In the centre of the cart lay a medium-sized coffin with a white cloth partially draped over it.

The cart reached the gate of the cemetery, and the man jumped down, followed by the boy. Thomas could hear the sound of conversation, but could not discern its content. With some difficulty – a stiff lock, and overgrown grass – the man and boy forced the little gate open, and spent some minutes as if looking for something in the near corner of the graveyard. The boy returned to the cart, and while the father began to uproot great bunches of grass with his hands, the boy fetched two shovels and a pickaxe.

While Thomas watched, they dug, toiling and grunting, their heads bent. After a time they removed their jackets and piled them on the coats they had already spread along the little white wall. The sun had begun to set and a small mist could be seen, vaporous and white-grey, a foot or so above the ground: tiny steams rose from the bent working backs. The boy rested for a moment.

Without warning his mother jumped from the cart, ran to the cemetery, wrenched the shovel from the boy's hand and began to dig furiously. The man restrained her, argued with her, and eventually she handed the shovel back to the boy and retreated to the rear of the cart, where she put her head down on her hands and began to sob: the sound carried, it seemed to Thomas, for miles.

Soon the grave was complete: the man and boy approached the cart, and took the coffin, half-sliding, half-lifting it, on to their shoulders. The woman led the way, praying. In a slow, crouching, and obviously taxing movement, the man and his son lowered the coffin into the ground and stood for some minutes in prayer. The boy began to weep, and then the man: the woman walked over to both and comforted them, an arm held out to each. They filled in the grave much more slowly than they had dug it, and replacing some green sward, and then some fistfuls of grass, they closed the gate of the graveyard; the man and boy took their coats and jackets from the wall, donned them, and joined the woman on the cart.

The pony wheeled around and they left. Thomas made the Sign of the Cross, spoke a small prayer almost aloud and stood there, growing cold, for several more minutes, until he could no longer see the departing family in the gloom, and then until he could no longer hear the strong creak of the cart.

Ellen met him at the door, had heard his footsteps.

'Dr Hogan called,' she said. 'That poor Carroll girl, Thomas, she died.'

He replied, 'I know.'

17

'If I don't get these potatoes in,' Thomas said next morning, Holy Saturday, 'we'll have nothing to eat for the winter.'

He moved into the farthest corner of the garden, over beyond the blackcurrant bushes, where, at the cherry tree, the hedge began separating the Teacher's garden from the Quarterground, the village allotments. Ever methodical, he had two buckets which he carried from the sheds to the drills. One contained the seed potatoes, innocent tubers, sitting there like little babies: the other bucket bore Thomas's measuring stick, exactly a foot long, cut from a straight piece of ash; another longer measuring stick, flat, the handle of an old hurling-stick, two and a half feet long; his 'line', made of two pointed pegs wrapped together in a ball of binder twine; a sharp penknife with a pearl handle, and a two-pound bag of lime. He returned for the spade and the fork.

Ellen appeared, pulling on her coat.

'Thomas, there are Confessions in the church from eleven o'clock, aren't there?'

He stuck the spade in the ground. 'Do you want me to drive you?'

'No, the walk will do me good.' He did not comment on her red, swollen eyes.

In a corner of the prepared ground, where flat, well-dug loam glistened brown, Thomas stuck down one of the pegs with the binder twine. Unrolling the other from it, he walked backwards until he reached the other corner. Measuring with his eye, and using the hedge as a general marker, he stuck the other peg in the ground.

Using the line of cord as his guide, he then took the old hurling-stick and laid it flat on the ground, one end just touching the 'line'; and at intervals up along the cord, measuring all the time, he made marks in the earth. Looking back, he had now delineated the first drill – the cord 'line' would form the right-hand side, and the marks, two and a half feet from the cord, the left-hand side. Between those two parameters, he dug with the spade a narrow trench. He then took the fork, and from the heap of farmyard manure in another corner (acquired with compliments from Michael Connors's cowsheds and delivered by cart) filled a wheelbarrow and returned to his drill, which he filled with manure to a point level with the general earth of the patch, so that he had a long narrow trench comfortably plump with straw-flecked cowdung. Taking one of the buckets, he next flung with his hand, all along the drill, little fistfuls of the lime from the paper bag; the lime made puffs of white in the air, and coloured the shins of Thomas's blue dungarees.

'Bless me, Father, for I have sinned, I am three weeks since Confession.'

'Yes, my child?'

'Father, it isn't that I have any great sins to tell, but I need help and advice.'

'Yes, my child.'

'Father, do you believe in Original Sin coming down through a family?'

'How do you mean, my child?'

'Father, do you believe that a grave flaw in a parent may be passed on to a child?'

'Do you mean like – madness?'

'Not so much that, I mean – more a characteristic?'

'Do you mean – contrariness or meanness? Like a nose, or the colour of a pair of eyes?'

'Ye-ess, Father.'

'I've never heard of it, my child, do you want to tell me any more?'

The old head in the dimness behind the wire mesh grille shook itself awake: the Canon sat up. He astonished Ellen with his kind, almost mellifluous manner.

The postman, skidding his bike to a halt outside the tall hedge, brought four letters.

Dear Master,
    Regarding that matter we were talking about, I have some information that might help. When it suits, will you walk up to see me? I hope the Mistress is fit-and-well.
               Yours faithfully,
               Jack Hogan (Dr)

'Father, I married a man who for part of his life, before he met me, was involved in the – in the . . .'

The priest waited. Ellen tried again, hesitating, like a child pre-emptively telling of an undiscovered misdemeanour.

'Father, I am very worried. My husband . . .'

'Yes, my child.' No voice could have sounded more sympathetic. Ellen began once more.

'Father, I am married to a fine man.' The Canon inclined his head, only in encouragement, not to give any sign that he already knew: the Seal of the Confessional extended to preservation of identity.

Ellen said, 'But he was once involved in the Troubles, and I know that he had to do things then. And now I've discovered that there is violence in his breeding, and once or twice since I came to know him, I've seen him behave very violently, and I don't know what to do, and I'm expecting a baby next month.'

'And you're afraid this will carry down to the child?'

'Yes, Father' – careful not to call him Canon, to use the universal address instead.

'Dear Madam,' the letter from the registrar at Beaumaris had said, 'Further to your enquiry of the 9th inst., the person regarding whom you write, one Timothy Nash or Nashe, was tried on counts various (see below), and sentenced at Beaumaris Court on 28th March 1806, sentence being carried out seven weeks later, on 17th May.'

'You say you believe he's a fine man?' asked the voice of the confessional.

'Oh, yes, Father, and everyone looks up to him, respects him. People consult him.'

'And he goes to Confession and Holy Communion?' – again, the fine line between knowing and asking.

'Oh, yes, Father.'

At the bottom of the standard form, Ellen had read the words: 'Nash or Nashe, T.; (Irish): Charged with: (1) murder of a policeman, one R. A. Edwards at Chester on 29th January, 1806; (2) bodily harm to a warder, one T. Bowen, Beaumaris, on 2nd February, 1806: (3) serious bodily harm to a policeman, one R. Hampson, Beaumaris, on 2nd February, 1806: (4) actual damage to Crown property, Beaumaris, on 2nd February, 1806: Sentence: hanging: executed Beaumaris Jail, 17th May 1806; confirmation H.M. CORONER, E. A. Bolton, cert. 17th May 1806.'

The Canon asked, 'Has he ever been violent to you?'

'Oh, no, Father, never.'

'Nor ever shown signs of it?'

'No, Father. Quite the opposite.'

The Registrar at Beaumaris had attached a note, in wide, looped handwriting.

Dear Madam,

Like you I have an interest in local history, and was pleased to receive your enquiry. This sketch of Nash or Nashe, made by a Beaumaris artist in the courtroom during the trial, became very popular in this town, as Nash's name became a byword for villainy. The local newspaper printed it and postcards were made of it. I hope it assists you.

Yours truly,
N. S. R. Hughes

Ellen gasped: the face in the picture might have been Thomas's, only less composed. Just as cruel, though. It had the wide cheekbones, and the strong black hair, and the looming black eyebrows meeting in the middle, the straight line of mouth, the unpleasant dimple in the chin.

'Thomas, if he walked in here now, people would say he was your older brother.'

'Do you fear him, my child?'

'It's not that, Father. What I'm afraid of is – with the help of God we're going to have several more children.'

'Please God,' murmured the priest.

'And I would be terrified if one or more of them turned out to be. Murderers.' Ellen gasped the word out.

Thomas, his thumbnail black with clay, recognized the writing.

My heart is broken. You knew how I felt for you. Does your 'wife' know about your past? If you do not meet me I will start to inform her, and perhaps she won't any longer look at you with the sheep's eyes she has been making at you. This is your last chance.

'How long have you been worried about this, my child?'

'Just a year or so, Father, since the first time I saw my husband being angry, although he wasn't my husband then. It was very frightening.'

'But you married him?' the priest said.

'I did, Father.'

'And since then?'

'Well, there were other things. On our honeymoon, he beat somebody who insulted me.'

Setting out for the church, Ellen had said to Thomas, 'It'll be very odd going to Confession to a priest I know.'

On her return she reported, 'It wasn't odd at all, it wasn't like talking to a person.'

As if to a stranger, Ellen said, 'Father, it feels as if I'm confessing what I think are his sins.'

She told about the birching of Michael Quinn.

The old voice countered, 'But he did that in the line of duty?'

'Yes, Father?'

'And when he was involved in the Troubles? Duty again?'

'I suppose so, Father.'

'Was he excommunicated during that time, my child?'

'I don't know, Father.'

'And he attacked somebody who offended you? In public I take it?'

'Yes, Father.' She stopped. 'But there's something else, Father' – and plunged into the story of Timothy Nash.

When she had digested the letter and the etching, Ellen asked, 'Thomas, did you know any of this?'

'Now that you mention it, there was a bit of a cloud,' he said.

'That's a bit airy of you.'

'Ach, Ellie, if we were to dig up and drag out everything in our past, we'd spend our time killing each other,' he dismissed.

=

Ellen tried to peer harder through the wire grille of the Confessional. The voice said, 'And no man is responsible for what his ancestors did, if that was the case we'd all be in queer street, wouldn't we?'

Ellen's lips pressed on each other as if putting on lipstick.

'My child, your story, although you may not think so, is not unusual. A number of women worry greatly about what their husbands and sons did in the last ten years or so. But they were hard times. God forgives men for hard times.' He straightened.

Thomas opened the other two letters: a formal note from the Canon confirming the date for Confirmation, unless 'the current poliomyelitis outbreak affects it'. However, the fourth letter contained a new promulgation from the Department, saying that if, to all intents and purposes, the outbreak seemed to have passed locally, the countrywide experience suggested it might be safe to reopen the schools in ten days, making a closure of four weeks in all. Coal Money should be adjusted in the annual budget, etc., the Progress Record should be marked thusly, etc. 'Eth! Don't they know anything?' cursed Thomas, then put the four letters in the inside pocket of his good coat hanging on the hallstand and returned to the garden.

'Is there anything else, my child?'

'There is, Father, there's this other thing I want to ask you.'

She outlined Father Watson's advice, and the outcome of it, the abstinence. The voice sighed. Ellen could smell him, a combination of tobacco and what might have been slightly sour milk. He sighed again.

'My child, aah. This is a matter of. Well. This is not something.' He stopped. 'My child, I'm an old man, and I don't keep up with things. But I'm no heretic. I believe in the love of God. That is why He gave us all the wonderful herbs that grow in the fields and bushes.'

Ellen smiled in her mind.

The Canon went on, 'And your friend the priest, who advised you regarding Canon Law, is correct, within the laws of our Holy Mother Church. He's right. So, how can I advise you in a way that is contrary to Canon Law?'

Ellen bent her head, fumbling in the darkness, looking for a handkerchief, quiet as dust. The old priest shook himself, as if at a sudden chill.

'My child, this is my opinion. There are Laws of God, and there are Laws of Man made in honour of God. The Laws of God move within us with a natural force. The Laws of Man made in honour of God have to be learned specifically and applied. That may only be a simple man's view, but I, for one, would never do anything to interfere with the flow of goodness from one human being to another, especially when blessed within the sanctity of marriage.' He slumped back, and Ellen thought he had finished speaking. Then he began again.

'I would say this to you. If you and your husband, when you discovered you were expecting marriage's greatest blessing, that of a lovely little babby, if you and your husband . . . If you and your husband while you were expecting – provided there was no danger.' The Canon had slowed down to less than half his usual snail's pace. 'If. You. And. Your. Husband. Well, do you think God would cast you out if you stood before Him at the gates of Heaven? Ah, no. Ah, no. Not at all. Canon Law is a thing for priests to debate. What would your husband think?'

Ellen said, 'He would agree with you, Father.'

'Then, my child, go in peace and above all, in love.'

The priest raised his hand, and began, '*Te absolvo. In nomine Patris, et Filii, et Spiritus sancti.*'

Ellen interrupted, 'Father, you haven't given me any Penance?'

The priest replied, 'Aren't you after doing Penance enough, if all this was bothering you? You're about to bring a young life into the world. I see no need for Penance. Go in the love of God.'

Turning to the bag of seed potatoes, Thomas crouched, opened his pearl-handled Sheffield steel penknife, and began to cut them in half. In this small but complex manoeuvre, he could not slice at random across the tuber: he had to ensure that each half bore a quota of 'eyes', the black points in the tuber through which the potato propagated itself. This completed, he took his bucket and, walking in a crouched position, his buttocks almost tipping the clay beneath, he planted the potatoes in the ground, on the limed manure, precisely a foot from each other: he measured the separation by the short ash marker which he pressed down forward from each tuber. When a full row had been completed, he stood and eased the ache in his back, and checked with his eye whether any of the little white-faced half-tubers had tilted over in his wake. With his hurling-stick he measured two feet from the outer edge of the drill and then re-set his 'line' and from it, with the fork, dug the earth and smoothed it over the newly-made drill – and then began the whole procedure all over again.

Ellen reached the house. She said to Thomas in breathless half-amusement, 'You know, when I start out walking, I'm fine, and then I start to waddle like a duck. Oh, I'm so fat, Thomas.'

He looked closely at her face, and, heeling off his boots, walked upstairs in socks and silence behind her.

In the room, she took off her hat, looked with a sigh at her puffy face in the mirror, frizzed out her flattened hair with a hand, and turned to Thomas. She walked over to him, took his two hands and wrapped them around her shoulders like a cape, so that she could lay her head on his chest. For several minutes, she stood there, saying nothing. She began to weep, and, still holding carefully his hands clay-ey from the garden, he sat her down on the bed and knelt beside her.

She said, 'Thomas, it is all all right, it is all all right.' She repeated it over and over, and then recounted everything she had said in Confession.

Thomas sat on the floor, like a boy, looking up at her. For that brief period the relationship had changed, and Ellen became the leader. Thomas accepted every detail of her great affliction, even when she implied that she had been believing he would breed a race of murderers.

'Thomas, I have something else to tell you.' At that moment his eyes filled with tears.

'I asked him about Canon Law.' Ellen hung her head and looked up from beneath her black brows.

Thomas laughed. 'Jeremiah makes his own Canon Law. I bet he gave you short shrift?'

'No, he's a different man in Confession altogether. He's not nearly as crude.'

'That's what I said to you beforehand.'

'He said the Law of God was what mattered.'

They both laughed and cried at the same time.

Thomas laid his head on Ellen's knee, and she stroked his hair.

She said, 'Here, do you want to feel my stomach, it's moving a lot.'

He said, 'I wouldn't. No. I wouldn't think it right.' She bent down awkwardly and laid her cheek along his face raised towards her. He took her hand and twisted her wedding ring around and around.

'When my sister died,' he said, 'and when I had to put her body in the coffin. Ellie, she only weighed a stone or so, she was so wasted, and a child of seven weighs about three stone. They brought the wrong size coffin, they brought a grown-up coffin, we had to pack it with blankets. I took the best blankets and sheets in the house, so that she didn't shift around inside the coffin. And I remember saying to myself, and I said it over and over during tough times later, I said, "I'll never be happy in my lifetime, I know it, never." And I was wrong.'

'Oh, you were. My dear man.' In half an hour or so, after whisperings and silences, Thomas went downstairs and laid the table, and fried eggs and black puddings for lunch, and then boiled potatoes.

Thomas had to flee the April showers, and indoors he stood at the window, near Ellen, his dirty hands dangling by his sides, and in peaceful silence looked out at the rain, and the clouds sweeping over from the west. When the sun came out again, he returned to his task.

At nine o'clock, unusually early, they prepared for bed. When he climbed in beside her, Thomas discovered that Ellen wore no nightgown, her stomach large and almost blue in its whiteness. Thomas, in pyjamas, lay beside her.

'Thomas,' she said, 'if it were medically safe, and I feel it isn't . . .'

'Shh,' he said, and laid a hand on her breast, stroking it, and repeatedly sending his palm smoothly across her rubbery nipple.

'There were times, in the early days,' he said, 'when I thought that – if we hadn't stopped – I would somehow pump strength into the baby.'

'I often thought that, too,' said Ellen. 'But I even thought that was a wrong thought.'

'Will you say anything to Father Watson?' asked Thomas.

'I don't know. I don't know. I suppose he acted in good faith.'

313

'I'm not so sure,' said Thomas, 'I'm not so sure. But we won't talk about that.'

He arranged his shoulder so that Ellen's head could rest on it, and there she fell asleep, and slept without moving, while Thomas stayed awake for hours, looking into the darkness. Eventually, he could bear no longer the numbness in his arm and shoulder, and he moved Ellen with infinite gentleness, and settled his own head to sleep.

18

'A bit erratic, d'you see. Is that what you mean, Mrs?'

'Well, yes, what I mean is – don't pay any attention if Miriam is a bit of an oddity from time to time.' Mrs Gardner's other daughter, Alice, had married a vet from Reynoldstown. Miriam, at home with her mother, did little except play the piano and go for long walks; the worse the weather the longer the walk.

'She was immensely attached to her father, God rest him, immensely, and I always say that a good daughter makes a good wife,' says Mrs Gardner. 'And her father doted on her; I never told Alice, because she'd rightly think it unfair, but their father left bigger provision in his will for Miriam than he did for Alice. I suppose that was because Alice was married, and well married too, before her father died, God rest him. So don't ever breathe a word to Alice, will you, we never thought . . .'

She stopped just short of saying, 'We never thought anyone would want to marry Miriam.'

In the drawing-room of the house near Mountshannon, on the heights above the river, watching the dark stream reflect the clouds overhead, Jack Hogan grew besotted with Miriam Gardner. He watched every movement. At a meal he observed her every bite. Across the room he never took an eye off her.

Earlier in the afternoon, unobserved, Miriam looked in through the side window at the pair drinking wine.

'She's very pale. Is she a bit on the anaemic side?' Jack asked.

'No, Miriam was born pale, I think,' said Mrs Gardner.

'Will she marry me, do you think?'

Mrs Gardner smiled, and tried again to settle a wisp of grey hair.

'I like a man who worries about winning a woman's hand in marriage,' she said. 'Miriam's father was afraid of his life that I wouldn't marry him, and in the event we had twenty-eight good years together.'

'When will I ask her?'

Mrs Gardner gazed down at the Shannon, and at the gigantic rhododendrons, and at her adored cypresses, and the row of willows by the steps far below.

'I'm playing whist tonight, here at home. We have a card drive for Father Cooney. We play in the large dining-room, the one we only use at Christmas. If you and Miriam sit in here, by the fire, you'll not be disturbed, and she'll feel safe with all those people around. I'll make sure Madge makes us all a good supper first.' Mrs Gardner looked at her garnet ring, and breathed on it, then polished it on the cuff of her grey cardigan.

'D'you drink much?' Miriam stretched her long legs by the fire.

'I learned it in the Army,' said Jack Hogan. 'It was almost *de rigueur* in France.'

'*De rigueur*. That's nice. *De rigueur*. As a matter of rigour': a lazy way of speaking, sometimes halting completely in the middle of a sentence: she fascinated Jack.

'As a matter of necessity,' said Jack. He consumed the long hair, the small but obviously hard breasts, the green stockings, the plaid skirt.

'I've never had. A drink.' Miriam moved her head from side to side as if exercising a muscle in her neck. 'Were there nice girls in France?' All those rising inflections.

'Would you like a sip of my wine, Miriam?' he asked. 'No. And certainly, Miriam, none as nice as you.'

'Tell me about babies. Mama said we all took the pledge and we're not allowed to drink.'

'Oh, I see,' said Jack. Then, nonplussed, he asked, 'About babies?'

'Yes. You're a doctor.'

'What do you want to know?'

'How to get one. Mama won't tell me. And Alice won't tell me.'

'Well.' Jack took another drink from his glass.

'Mama said, if I got married I'd find out.'

'If you married me,' said Jack, speaking more carefully than he had known he could, 'I would tell you.'

'I will marry you,' said Miriam. 'Mama said you were going to ask.'

'May I kiss you, then?' asked Jack.

Miriam held up her face. Jack rose from his sofa, almost missed his footing, put down his glass, crossed the fireplace to her sofa, and bending over double, kissed her cheek for a long time. She never moved. He moved his face around and kissed her mouth, and she never responded. He returned to his sofa.

'Is that settled then?' he asked.

'Yes,' said Miriam. 'Will you look after me well?'

'Oh, very well,' said Jack. 'Oh, very well, indeed.' Then he grinned, and said, 'You're a terrible chancer, you know all about babies, don't you?'

Miriam rose and pirouetted in waltz-time, singing, 'I'll be your sweetheart. If you will be mine.'

On their wedding night in the Shelbourne Hotel, she thumped him on the shoulder as she climbed into bed, and said, 'Shove over, don't lie so close to me. And go to sleep now. Go on. Move over. Turn your back to me.' In Geneva, she made him book two rooms, one each, before she would agree to check in. He called to collect her for dinner downstairs; she had locked her door, and he had to stand in the corridor waiting.

At dinner, he said, 'Married people are supposed to . . . to have a relationship that is . . .'

317

'Shhhhhh,' she interrupted. 'I know. I heard. I read about it.'

Later that night, he entered her room after knocking. She sat at her dressing-table, still apparently fully dressed, the buttons of her blouse open down halfway. A pool of cream satin lay on the floor. She pointed to it and warbled, 'I always simply step out of my underclothes.'

As she scratched vigorously at her shoulders and upper arms, she continued, 'I have a rash.'

'Let me see it, Miriam. Maybe it needs a bit of ointment.'

'No fear. You're not my doctor.' She laughed. 'Isn't that a scream? You're not my doctor. You are, but you're my doctor husband.' She stood. 'Stay where you are, Jacko.' In front of him she undressed completely. 'Have you red hair down there, Jack, or are you going thin on top there too?' she chortled, and climbed into bed so quickly he had to shift from where he sat.

'Miriam, you should be putting ointment on that rash, your arms are bleeding.'

'Good-night, Jack. Switch out the light when you're going.'

She tore at her shoulders with both hands. He closed her door and slipped back to his own room. Miriam's dowry, handed to Jack in a bank draft by Mrs Gardner, was much, much larger than he had ever considered, and there were stocks and shares to follow.

Ernestina Stephenson, although very different from Miriam Hogan, née Gardner, had some characteristics in common. The tendency to 'fly off the handle' without warning; the abrupt change of direction in conversation; the unexpected little shows of force; and Jack recognized them from his own wife, and also from the conversations he had been having with medical colleagues in Cork. One significant difference appeared clear, however – Miriam had been like that almost as of nature: Ernestina had become that way through fear. Only thinly could she answer Jack's questions on that very first evening she allowed him to examine her.

'You'll have to tell me everything as clearly as possible, Errr-nestina,' he said. 'D'you see?'

She sat there, like a frozen person.

'I need,' said Jack in a tone gentle enough not to frighten Ernestina, 'to see what these bumps, you call them, are like.'

'Why?' asked Ernestina. 'Don't you believe me?'

'Now,' said Jack Hogan. 'I'll make a note or two. Date of birth?'

Ernestina said, dully: 'Thirteenth of November, eighteen ninety-four.'

'So that'd make you, what? Just gone thirty-one? Parents alive?'

'Both dead.'

'Ah, that's tough.'

'No, it isn't. I hated the two of them.'

'I have to ask, you know, family history, what did they die of?'

'Father a bullet. The war. Mother cancer.'

'Were y'ever ill before?'

'For a while.'

'Since when?'

'My father had a jacket like that.' Ernestina touched Jack's check cuff. A tear rolled out of one eye. 'I started bleeding all the time three months ago. Non-stop. I started getting very much thinner, and I'm eating nothing. And then the other day, I found.' She stopped abruptly.

'Found what, Errr-nestina? The bumps, is it?'

She sat looking straight ahead, her eyes closed behind the thick spectacles, the same lone tear rolling, rolling downward. As if choosing a place on a map, Ernestina pointed one stiff finger to her right breast; then, to Jack's

319

horror, to her left. Her misery accentuated her plainness.

Jack said, 'I'll have to have a look. Why don't you sit here on this armchair, but you'll have to take off some of your clothes. You'll have to let down your straps.' Ernestina had been sitting on the bed, then she rose, and Jack turned away to his bag, taking some time to fetch his stethoscope. After some rustling, he heard her sitting in the chair, and she said, 'I'm ready.'

He turned around, and without yet looking at her, showed her with a smile how he warmed the gleaming disc of the stethoscope between his hands, 'So that it won't make you jump with the cold of it,' he said. He knelt on one knee beside her, and she sat with her arms draped on either side. Her body, Jack noted, had greater beauty than her poor face: ah, dear, the number of women who were like that, if the world could only see.

He listened at her breastbone, then made her lean far forward, and he listened at her back.

'Now,' he said, 'show me where you found the bumps.'

'They're like eggs,' she said, and again her mapping finger pointed out, on the right breast, one, two, three, four and on the left, one, two.

Jack Hogan said, 'I'm going to have to see what they're like for myself. Guide my hand.'

She took both his hands and, laying them flat on the surprisingly firm tissue, introduced the planes of his top three fingers to each lump in turn, one, two, three, four, five, six – and he found number seven. One was large, hard as eggs: others the size of a hazel-nut. Jack sat back on his hunkers, then stood up, uncoiling the stethoscope from around his neck.

'Now this bleeding, Errr-nestina? How heavy is it?'

'I've used up all the small linen towels we had in the house. I'm down to table napkins. I throw them away. Or I'm cutting up towels into squares. I have cardboard boxes of them hidden around the house.'

'Oh God, girl, you should be in the hospital.'

'I told you, I told you. I can't go to hospital.' This time a brace of tears squeezed out. 'If I go to hospital, that little Merrigan bitch'll be in here behind my back, washing his shirts, and I'll be ousted. She's after my brother.'

'Whooo-phooo!' Jack Hogan let out a long exhalation of breath. 'Well, you have to go to bed, Errr-nestina. And you have to go now. You're to take a good rest.'

'You're the only man who was ever nice to me,' said Ernestina, looking away from him in a panic. 'Your wife must be very lucky to have you.'

Jack Hogan said, ''Tis very easy to be nice to you. You're a very nice girl. But you're not well, and you have to rest. Now, are you in any pain?'

'Sometimes.'

He promised to call again in two days – 'to see how you are.'

Ernestina dressed again and lay on the bed. As Jack folded and clasped the lugs of his Gladstone bag, and prepared to leave, she held out a hand and shook it.

'Thanks very much,' she said. Jack went.

Cyril strolled in. 'What did he say?'

Ernestina said, 'That I have to rest a lot.'

'Well, I must say. The things some people will do to get attention.' About to leave the room, he turned and remarked, 'Imagine you having a Catholic quack? H'm?'

In the week before Confirmation Day Thomas came home in despair.

'Ellie, what in the name of all that's high and holy are we going to do? They know as much about Catechism as a pig knows about a holiday.'

Eleven children were going forward from the school to be confirmed, and Thomas had a high reputation for the preparedness of his pupils.

He said, 'I think I'm just going to have to say to the

321

Archbishop that on account of the polio scare we couldn't get them ready properly. But you know perfectly well what they'll all say all over the place, "Hah, the new Master must be too busy with the new wife." That's what they'll say.' Thomas's rough mimicking of the local accent made Ellen laugh.

'How's Miss Kellett shaping up?' asked Ellen, regarding her temporary replacement.

'Useless. She doesn't know "B" from a bull's foot,' said Thomas.

Ellen said, 'Why don't you send the children down to me at lunchtime. I'm doing nothing here. We've ten days left.'

Every day the eleven candidates straggled to the house, and Ellen arrayed them in the kitchen, taking them through the Bishop's likely questions.

'What is chrism?' Blank faces again.

She led them into the answer, beating her tuning fork on the air as if teaching music.

'Chrism is the anointing oil for Extreme Unction, the Last Rites of the Church.'

'Good,' Ellen nodded. 'Now, what is chrism made of?' and without waiting for them not to know the answer, she began another chant, beckoning them like a choir-mistress to recite with her: 'Oil of olive mixed with balm and blessed by the Bishop on Holy Thursday.

'Where is chrism applied? Anyone? No? Very good. You'll know it yet. Don't worry. Come on now, after me. Chrism is applied to the Five Senses: Seeing, Hearing, Smell, Taste and Touch. First the priest puts chrism on the eyelids, then on the lobes of the ears, then on the edges of the nostrils, then on the lips and then on the palms of the hands and on the soles of the feet.'

The house rang with the young, thick voices, led by Ellen's spoken melodies of instruction, as she sat there, voluminous in a powder-blue smock and a pretty blouse:

Blackie, sleepy, sat on the folded-down table-top of the sewing-machine in the bay window. Ellen told Thomas that for the last three days those children should spend all day with her, and she would continue the instruction, and slowly but surely she took them through the greater part of the curriculum.

'For a sin to be a Mortal Sin, what must it have?'

'It must have Grievous Matter, Perfect Knowledge and Full Consent.'

'Full Consent, what?' They stared at her and at each other.

'Full Consent, "Your Grace"; it's the Archbishop you're talking to, so you call him "Your Grace". You must end every answer with "Your Grace"; if it was a Bishop, what would it be? It would be "My Lord". Not what a boy I taught once called the Bishop, he called him "Our Lord"' – which made them laugh.

'Name the Nine Choirs of Angels?' By now she had them all chanting together in a kind of unison which at the end of the week would shine under her polishing.

'Cherubim, Seraphim, Thrones. Dominations, Principalities, Powers. Virtues, Archangels and Angels.'

To their great surprise one day, Father John Watson called, stepping out of a shiny car which someone else drove. He did not stay long. Ellen greeted him warmly, and Thomas distantly, but with perfect good manners and offers of hospitality, which Father Watson refused, saying he was *en route* to somewhere else, and when he realized how near he was he thought he had better call and say hallo. He knew Ellen's time was coming up soon, and standing on the gravel in front of the house, he twisted his hat in his hands, saying, 'Remember how splendid your wedding day was here? Your dear parents are well, Ellen, and very excited. I met Rina the other day, and she is thrilled at the prospect of being an auntie.'

'Now what was that in aid of?' asked Thomas, policing the car out of sight.

'I'm not criticizing you, Thomas,' said Ellen, 'but I'm sure he felt your coldness towards him. I certainly did.'

'I hope he did,' said Thomas. 'He can stew in his own juice for a little while.'

Ellen smiled. 'It doesn't trouble me too much,' she said; 'the two of you will become great friends one day. You're both too intelligent not to.'

> '*Faith of our Fathers living still*
> *In spite of dungeon, fire and sword.*
> *How our hearts beat high with joy,*
> *When e'er we hear that glorious Word.*'

Ellen, her huge pregnancy obliging her to sit far back from the keyboard, pumped hard at the pedals of the harmonium. Each member of the congregation sang at their own individual tempo, in their own personal key.

'I could have been playing *The Mountains of Pomeroy* for all they cared about accompaniment,' she said to Thomas afterwards, 'or a polka.' The church was packed, and sixty priests – 'A record,' claimed the Canon – attended.

'Why was the Canon so nervous?' asked Ellen afterwards.

'Can't you guess?' said Thomas. She shook her head. What she called her 'boxer's nose' seemed flatter, and like a snub-nosed child's, and her complexion darkened with the restfulness of placid days.

'Jeremiah was afraid,' said Thomas. 'Didn't you threaten at the time of the MacReady business to report him to the Bishop?'

'Oh, I had forgotten all about that,' said Ellen.

'But he hadn't. These people forget nothing.'

=

The choir began the second verse, so slowly that Ellen doubted they would reach the end in decent order.

> *'Our fathers chained in prisons dark*
> *Were still in heart and conscience free.*
> *How sweet would be their children's fate,*
> *If they like them could die for thee?*
> *Faith of our fathers living still*
> *We will be true to thee 'til death.*
> *We will be true to thee 'til death.'*

The Archbishop, beneath the yellow and white Papal banner of the Papal Tiara and Crossed Keys, raised a hand to the congregation.

'I'll say this for the Archbishop,' said Thomas on the way home. 'He's a great blesser. I haven't felt as blessed in years.'

'The grammar in those hymns.' Ellen shook her head. 'Awful.'

The other half of the parish, Silverbridge, hosting the Confirmation this time around, had priority, which meant that the Deanstown children were the last to be examined and confirmed. Ellen picked at her fingernails. In perfect acoustics she heard each question, and her tutored ones rattling off the answers. 'Oil of olives, mixed with balm, and blessed by the Bishop on Holy Thursday. Your Grace.' One by one they sparkled haltingly, the boys' hair slicked down with oil, the girls' hands twining behind backs, bunching their gloves into a ball. One by one, the Archbishop patted them on the face, and nodded.

The potentate of an alternative empire, this fat-faced man had a great, semi-secret power. Archbishop Edward Ahern governed the Archdiocese, and thereby controlled every moral detail of every Catholic existence within his territory. He had the right to pronounce on everything, and be sure of receiving at least profound respect, and usually unquestioning obedience. Above reproach, any man who became a Bishop, still more one of the country's four Archbishops, lived a notable life: the Guest of Honour wherever he appeared; the focal point of all gatherings; never a second fiddle, except perhaps to the President himself, or the Cardinal.

Parallel to the civil authority, the Church worked as a political entity, unacknowledged as such, and with the ultimate freedom of having to declare responsibility to nobody other than its own God. Committed only to a Master whose existence was not even provable, obliged to nothing other than the great intangibles of faith and morals, it had appropriated unto itself the cleverest kind of power – that created by impressive doctrine and decree, based on the abstract rather than the concrete. Using prayer, ritual and cloth-of-gold ceremony, it preyed upon the workings of the human imagination; it capitalized upon Man's oldest need, for some force which both acknowledged and warded off personal fear, while at the same time guaranteeing the eternal survival of the primal force, the force of life itself, and by corollary, the defeat of death. In return for no more than responding to the Church's guidelines, the Catholic human being was granted the opportunity never to die. By offering to every person in its fold, no matter how humble, the promise of such Eternal Life – and within the sight and favour of God Himself – the Church achieved its greatest power among such people as those in the parish where Thomas and Ellen attempted to educate: simple people who never challenged in spiritual matters, and who belonged as of breeding, in a continuity of superstition. And, lest learning interfere, the Church had seen to it that the clergy controlled the schools.

Most of all, in the same way as any elective civil power needed to garner votes, the Church needed births among its faithful, the numbers had to be kept up; and the greatest blessing a couple could bestow on their country, and the greatest benison they could bring unto themselves – and so they were told repeatedly – was the gift of a large family. Domestic economics did not enter Church doctrine.

Accordingly, there sat Edward Ahern in Silverbridge's rural-baroque little church. A tall arched mitre of white silk, of gold thread and scarlet lining, was fastened to his plump head: a pair of wide grosgrain ribbons fluttered down to his shoulders: atilt in his left hand stood a tall crozier of gold and gilt: a giant episcopal ring squatted like a big, brilliant insect on his finger. He wore white-and-gold slippers made with the love of duty by the nuns, who also washed his white socks. His vestments gleamed with the power of tradition: were it not for the general knowledge that this was a man of the cloth, a man of God, and barring some dreadful personal secret, surely destined for the ranks of the august in the next world, he might have been taken for some kind of visiting Sultan, here to levy from his homageous people. No property, emotional or intellectual, of any other human being in the vicinity, assailed him.

Edward Ahern had risen – from a poor cottage in the north-west of the next county – through acquired skills: an ability to hide his shrewdness behind a mask of seeming *naïveté*; general good-natured *bonhomie*, tempered with the steel of authority which he had learned to flash at just the moment, and for just the appropriate length of time, in convocations such as a Diocesan Schools meeting, or some such other useful stage.

He built an impeccable career path: an exemplary seminarian; then a young and zealous pastor who did not cause his colleagues the discomfort of competitive piety – although he was very devout, of course, and with a particular devotion to the Blessed Virgin Mary. Next, he taught for some years in the seminary which bred him; whence he was appointed Secretary to his predecessor;

then bishop in a smaller diocese, and now lord of his own land – a model Churchman.

His astuteness burgeoned with status. He led men well, capable of a not-too-familiar joke; astride the sporting references; author of competent Lenten pastorals; he could even take a glass of stout on occasion, and above all, when voices had been raised calling for the excommunication of Collins and the other guerrillas, Edward Ahern was remembered for nothing, for no kind of controversy whatsoever.

In his public appearances, in which a Parish Confirmation ranked high, he paid very considerable attention to his demeanour and had been thoroughly, if informally, instructed by English and French churchmen encountered in Rome. From them he learned the little tricks of good presence: grooming; an impressive watch; excellent shoes always and, extra touch, a discreet white scarf in winter with the very best clerical black overcoat. Nobody, not even those close to the personal side of his life, speculated at a secret vice. In any case, he had none.

This morning, His Grace pronounced himself well pleased with all the states of learning in every candidate for Confirmation. For his text, he chose one of the Beatitudes, his favourite one, 'Blessed are the meek for they shall inherit the Earth'. As a seminary teacher, he had been fond of telling his future pastors that in their preaching they could find the finest outlets for expressing themselves.

'When you find God in your own life – and He is there, He is there everywhere – tailor your sermon to the importance He has for you, and then you will speak with the courage of your own experience.' Edward Ahern understood that politics – called by whatever name – began in the personality.

He concluded. 'My dear people of the parish of Silverbridge and Deanstown. I promised not to keep you long on this sunny and blessed morning. This is your day, not mine. I am your servant here. I am God's servant here. I am your servant and God's servant here, in this parish, among these fields where you earn your bread.

'This morning, we have had the pleasing spectacle – and how it must gladden the heart of Christ and His Blessed Mother Mary; how it must cause delight in the alcoves of Heaven – this morning, we have had the pleasing, the holy, spectacle of young people being confirmed.

'Let us lastly examine the word. Confirmed. Confirmation. To make firm, to say something with determination. With authority. With pride. But, my dear brethren, I am not the one confirming. I know we use the phrase "the Archbishop is confirming". Or "The Archbishop is holding Confirmation".

'No, I am not. Just as we say, "the priest married a couple", the Canon "married John and Mary". But the priest, my dear brethren, does not marry a couple. You are surprised. But marriage is a holy sacrament, and yes, of course the priest is there. But – it is John and Mary who marry. The sacrament is entered into by you, the faithful.

'Today I have been privileged to officiate at Confirmation. By young people. By these young people – who confirm that they are willing to become strong and perfect Christians, and soldiers of Jesus Christ.'

As he began the telling phrase, Ellen's lips synchronized with him: 'Strong and perfect Christians and soldiers of Jesus Christ.' She moved her buttocks on the wooden pew and the baby kicked – awake again: the woman next to her tried not to yawn. Ellen could see Thomas in the church ahead, sitting at the outermost edge of the front left-hand pew, the place of honour for the teachers. His head – and she had never remarked upon this before – showed not the slightest trace of baldness.

Many people stood, leaning against the walls; the sweat

329

on the Canon's forehead picked up the light from the candles and the sanctuary lamp; on the right-hand aisle, the rows and rows of priests in their white surplices and black soutanes sat still and comfortable in their accustomed professional environment; the altar boys, three on each side, squatted at the foot of the altar steps, and tried not to fidget.

Ellen looked at her watch – a quarter past twelve; at this rate they would be finished, what, about half-past one? A slow Communion – probably for every human being she could see, except the very young children, although several priests would minister, then the procession to the statue, all before they would be finished. Half-past one, at least. Craning slightly to see others, she recognized – with a lurch – a headscarf. Mrs McAuliffe. Ellen sat straight again, easing upwards and outwards to take the pressure off the small of her back, and giving a small 'Kehh' of release.

'Why aren't you blushing?' Ellen teased Thomas when she met him at the church door after the procession. The Archbishop had included some unexpected remarks.

'Lastly, my dear brethren, I want to bring to your attention something for which we should all be grateful. I am a child of this Archdiocese as are all of you. We have all lived through terrible turmoil. We are now building our own country after eight hundred years of oppression. In this pattern, one member of our society will be, and already is, of the utmost importance – our Teacher.

'The moulding of the young mind: the building of the young character: the making of the young Catholic. In this we are especially blessed to have the likes of Thomas Kane, who since I was last among you has married and, I am told, Mrs Kane is an equally splendid teacher; we have been able to judge the fruits of their work today. And they themselves are about to be blessed, with the help of

God, with the beginnings of what I hope will be a large family, and I want you all to think of them in your prayers.'

Thomas said to Ellen, 'That's only his way of keeping us in line.'

In the crowd they were separated. Ellen went to congratulate her young stars, who stood more or less in a bunch, creaking in the stiffness of their clothes, gloves and hair-oil.

'You were great, the lot of you, you gave him the best answers he ever had.'

They, naturally enough, did not know where to look, and one or two shrug-hunched their shoulders and allowed themselves a grin. People greeted Ellen, and gathered around; the women wishing to know when? and how was she? and what she was hoping for?

'I don't care, so long as it has ten fingers and ten toes,' laughed Ellen.

'Errah, Ma'am, didn't I dream once I had a litter of pigs,' said a woman with very quick speech, and everyone cheered her.

As she left that group to find Thomas, someone plucked her sleeve. Ellen turned, and her smile died when she saw how haggard Mrs McAuliffe had grown, suddenly an old woman.

'Ma'am. You won't forget, will you, Ma'am?'

Ellen patted her stomach. 'Well, we're very busy at the minute.'

'Ma'am, has the Master any news for us at all?' Ellen could see Thomas, head bent, listening to a couple of elderly priests, but she couldn't catch his eye.

'Ma'am, I know we're awful trouble to you, but – we can't even mourn the man. And sure every Christian creature has the right to mourn.'

Ellen looked down at her shoes. 'That's true. That's

true,' she murmured, and looked up again, blinking in the sunlight to try and catch Thomas's eye. She scraped her lower teeth on her upper lip again and again: Thomas emerged.

The woman clutched her.

'Ma'am. Aw, Ma'am.'

Thomas came over, and decided to pacify. He bent his head to speak to Mrs McAuliffe; to tell her that he had had a number of conversations with the Sergeant; that the police assured him they had made exhaustive enquiries; that he could see no sensible means by which he could assist. Ellen, too, murmured soothing words: together she and Thomas affirmed their own remarks; both nodded their heads repeatedly.

Sean McAuliffe had been shot with, unnecessarily, two bullets; the first had gone straight into the head from the back and it never emerged; the second, half a moment later through the side of the head, burst open at the other side. He never felt either shot, all happened too quickly: what he felt was a kind of fear he had never even heard about: he looked straight ahead, and saw one man standing on his left, in a heavy old navy-blue bodycoat, and felt the presence of another, his wife's brother, directly behind him.

'Lads, listen to me, listen to me.' He whimpered. 'Look, I said nothing to no one.' He begged. 'Lads, I'm neutral, I'm neutral, I'm neutral. I was only at the door of the dance, selling the tickets.' A clandestine member of the Anti-Treaty Forces had been at the dance when Free State soldiers called: they could not have known him: someone had to have identified him.

They had held McAuliffe the previous night in a cottage from which the occupants, relatives of one of the two men, had been asked to depart for forty-eight hours. McAuliffe's mood went through many changes – from innocence to defiance to truculence to despair and back to blandness again, then once more through the whole cycle.

'If it wasn't serious,' said one of the men, 'would you be here?'

'Or tied to the chair?' said the other.

When they left him alone for some hours, although absolutely secured in his bonds, he began to hope that they might have intended him to escape, and he rocked the chair back and forth, back and forth – but he only succeeded in falling over and bruising himself in the process. On their return, he pretended not to recognize that the coat they carried belonged to him: he put it on, thanking them for the warmth.

'Did you tell herself, or the child, did you tell the child I was safe?'

'We didn't. You're not.'

In the sequences of little actions that make up cold-blooded murder, where both parties have become incontrovertibly aware of what is about to happen, logic drifts away. Time, the most important factor in the all-round equation, loses its texture and its tempo, and becomes an elastic matter. Noise is altered: a cough sounds different, a whistle unreal; every infinitesimal movement, every sound, every sight, is promoted to a stature never normally attributed to it; men already hard, indurate themselves further in order to carry out their deeds. Those holding the weapons handle them with extraordinary casualness, even, for instance, scratching themselves with the gun, finger already inside the trigger-guard. Those about to be killed choose one of a number of courses of response. They soften uncontrollably and become jelly, helpless; they dignify themselves with a last raising of the head; or they weep quietly; or they struggle to the last; or they rail and curse their executioners; or they beg captors to forgive them; or they offer bribes, or try to strike deals, to divide and conquer with promises; they speak incessantly to themselves as if to rationalize the awfulness of what is happening; or they soberly ask to have a last message delivered to loved ones; or they give themselves up to the arms of sheer terror, every black thought and innate fear realized, every night-time spectre of fear from their tenderest childhood stored away to roar out of the cavern at this moment; or they join the ranks of the mobile animate insensate — rigid and uncomprehending.

When the trio had been walking for ten minutes or so, in the later stages pushing awkwardly under low branches — several scratched his cheeks, because with his hands tied behind his back he had no way of keeping them from slapping into his face — McAuliffe saw the freshly-dug pit, the brown earth and leaf-mould against the dank wood's floor, and began to scream.

'Shut up,' said one of his captors, 'or I'll shut you up,' and hit him on the back corner of the head with the heel of his hand.

'The priest! The priest!'

'Where was the priest for Tony Lawlor?' they asked, referring to the soldier for whose betrayal they had abducted McAuliffe.

In the lifetime of Thomas and Ellen Kane, and of McAuliffe's young daughter, Hannie, and for the rest of the life of Archbishop Edward Ahern, and ever there-after, very few people in Ireland would ever, ever, even in private, discuss the events of the Civil War, the secret, livid dreadfulness of field and valley and night-time and river bank and woodland, as these beautiful places were defiled with revenge and death. The whole vast, mutual crime went unpurged.

'Aaah.' Half a scream, half a sigh. 'Oh, Jesus. Jesus. Jesus. Oh, my God, I am heartily sorry . . .'

They took McAuliffe's bonds off, then took off his coat, turned it inside out, put it back on him; he stood there unbound and made no attempt to escape. His eyes tried desperately to weep, and failed.

Up close, gunshots seem never as loud as reputed; the crack too thin, too narrow, a plank of sound rather than any fat explosion. When fired close to the skin, so swift is the sound, and so short-lived, unless the local acoustic breeds a long echo, that the rip of flesh and the crack of bone may even be heard, and if there is one, the burble of flesh. The birds whirred away, more of them than the winter's day seemed to have been hiding, and some deer stampeded. The men, one at the back, one at the side, one, two, used two handguns, a Colt and a German gun, the one they called 'Peter the Painter'. Only a little smoke hung in the air, grey-blue, mingling with the condensation from the breaths of three men, now two. Both men instinctively held their noses, though not through a distaste for the smell of cordite: McAuliffe's last bodily action had been involuntary. He did not fall quite accurately into his grave, they had to adjust him to it, before with grunts and pantings they shovelled with their feet all the loose soft earth piled around.

In the thronged church precinct, when seen from a distance without being heard, when observed by one other pair of eyes on the edge of that good-humoured Confirmation mêlée, the Kanes, especially Thomas, looked like people giving full help and information to someone in distress. Regrettably, Thomas pointed to the west – but a watcher out of earshot would not have known that he had only been telling Mrs McAuliffe that he himself, at the time, had helped the police search all those fields and woodlands for her missing husband. His bodycoat slung over the handlebars in a loose bale, and tied with the belt, the watcher in the crowd, the heavy man with the cap – who continually beat his small boy until the boy had

difficulty in speaking, although Ellen's efforts in school
had helped – cycled away.

At home, Ellen, by now climbing slowly and resting halfway, went upstairs. She opened the wardrobe door to put
her hat on the top shelf, then unhooked the hooks and
eyes at the back of her maternity dress. As it hung loosely
about her, she reached to adjust some of the garments in
the wardrobe. One skirt had not fitted for ages, and she
took it out, saw that the buttons at the waistband had
forced a little of the fabric apart: she must have worn it
too long before switching to smocks, and she put the skirt
on the chair to stitch later.

Turning to the mirror, she held a jacket up against her
swollen bosom, and turned this way and that. She sat on
the bed in fatigue, looking down with pleasant aimlessness
at the garment in her hand. Bought in Todd's a month
after she had met Thomas, with that nice braiding, not
too much, on the revers, a darker effect, same on the
cuffs, with that little dart there at the bust. Should it have
had buttons covered with its own cloth? Or, maybe, even
shiny buttons, not full brass, no, too like a blazer. For
several minutes she sat there examining the cream piece
of clothing, running her hand along the shoulders, puffing
the sleeve a little, tugging it, straightening the satin lining.

Summer 1926

19

'How is it spelt? C. A. U. L.? Or W?'

'"U",' said Ellen, looking again at the letter. Thomas had left his spectacles upstairs and held the dictionary at arm's length, the page slanted towards the light of the window. 'Cattle. Well, we know what they are, anyway. Caudex.'

'What's that? Caudex?'

'Shh. Stop interrupting me. It's the stem, it says, of a plant, a palm. Caudicle. Cauk. Caul. Here we are. "A kind of close-fitting cap worn by women, often richly ornamented; a net for the hair".'

'Isn't that ridiculous. How could a baby be born wearing one of those?' asked Ellen.

'Try this,' said Thomas. '"A membrane enclosing the foetus before birth; or a portion of it, sometimes enveloping the head of the child at birth, and adadadadadada . . ."' He broke off into a mumble.

'Read it all out, Thomas!'

'. . . "Superstitiously regarded as of good omen; sought by mariners as a safeguard against drowning" . . . There you are.'

'For goodness' sake,' said Ellen. 'Good Lord above!'

'Oh, I remember something.' Thomas reached up for another book. 'D'you remember *David Copperfield*? Here it is. "I was born with a caul, which was advertised for sale, in the newspapers for the low price of fifteen guineas." There you are, Ellie. So we're doing well.'

Bohercreen,
Mooreville.
27th April 1926.

Dear Mrs Kane,

You won't know who I am, but your husband knows my husband's brother, Father Ryan. I heard from him that you were expecting a baby and may God's blessing descend on you. My own brother is a sea-captain in the Merchant Navy, sailing out of Liverpool, and he has only recently taken over a very big ship. He always has me on the lookout for a Caul, and if God blesses that your own Child is born with one, I am instructed to offer you fifty pounds for it, or we could discuss the price.

God be good to you and Master Kane and the New Infant.

Yours faithfully,
Julia Ryan (Mrs)

'I know them well,' said Thomas; 'her husband is a fussy sort of man. A great fisherman, great salmon man. They're not a family I like, they're a bit full of their own importance. He's a great friend of Uncle John's.'

'I never heard of that before,' said Ellen, 'a caul for good luck, wouldn't it be exciting? But I don't think I'd sell it.'

'You mean you'd keep it,' asked Thomas, 'in case you took up seafaring?'

Ellen swiped at him, laughing.

'No. I'd give it to them.'

'Oh, you can't do that. They have to buy it. You'd break the luck of it otherwise. You know if someone buys you a present of gloves or a knife, you have to give them a little money to preserve the friendship? This is the same principle, sort of having to purchase your luck.'

Ellen said she'd write that very moment to Mrs Ryan and say she was welcome to have the caul, if there was one, for the price offered.

=

First came *The Heather Clan*, dancing girls in kilts and bonnets and white blouses, doing sedate sword dances. Then Mrs Mac and her Mops.

Time for the main attraction. Val came out like a young thing, like a gambolling lamb, and took his bow. Dublin was never as thunderous as Cork, but they certainly knew who he was. The silver buckles on his shoes gleamed. He held up a hand and began to recite *The Roads around Rathoe*.

> *'My son has brought me over to end my many days,*
> *Amidst his wealth and comforting that meet my worn-out*
> *gaze,*
> *I'm sure the boy means well enough and the wife's a treasure*
> *too;*
> *She calls me 'Pops' and 'Popakins' and smiles with eyes of*
> *blue.'*

The applause fell a little short of wonderful, to Val's way of thinking, and would be described by next day's newspapers as 'appreciative'.

> *'Although they do their best to make me feel at home and*
> *safe,*
> *I'd rather tread this moment the brown of autumn leaf,*
> *That makes a thickened carpet along where streamlets flow,*
> *I'd rather be a-strollin' the roads around Rathoe.'*

How Val had also struggled for that third and fourth line rhyme.

In Furnace Wood, near the old lime-kiln, spring had truly become established. Under the beginnings of hard shiny little shoots, other buds were forming down near the floor of the wood; tiny wild strawberries would bloom here in August, bittersweet on the tongue. A wren had nested, its domed roundhouse in never-ending construction, with small twigs being ferried in to reinforce the moss, the wren's wings whirruping softly whenever the bird, its tiny tail indicating the sky, landed on the branch high above the protruding cloth in the earth. The woman and the girl walked through the wood slowly, looking here and there; like diviners, they prodded the ground with sticks.

Late Saturday evening: 'Am I ever allowed to write in your ledger?' asked Thomas. Ellen sat there, copying in a recipe.

'No,' she said laughing. 'Go away. All your old seeds, and potato varieties and things.'

'I have a formula for Macassar oil,' Thomas fought back.

'You never use it. Just as well, think of the mess on the pillow.'

'I know how to mix gentian violet,' said Thomas.

'The next time I get a sting from a wasp I'll send for you,' countered Ellen. 'Thomas, go and do something, will you?'

'I can't. I'm just waiting.'

'I'm the one who's expecting,' said Ellen. 'You're like a child.' She dropped a hand on his knee in affection. 'You could pick up that goosewing and dust the place.'

'Will I read to you, instead?' he said.

'All right, love,' she conceded. 'You're the dearest man.'

'What are you doing, anyway?'

LEMON CREAM TARTLETS

(from Mrs Annie Dalton, 28/4/1926)

Three eggs, I use between two and four depending on how many people I'm expecting. Separate the yolks from the whites and keep the whites to one side in a cup.

'A recipe Mrs Dalton gave me; d'you remember those lemon little tarts she had?'

'I thought you used Mrs Beeton for everything?'

'She hasn't these.' Ellen consulted the thick, black-covered volume. 'Mrs Beeton has, look – lemon-and-acid drops, lemon biscuits, lemon blancmange, lemon cheese-cakes, lemon cream, lemon jelly, lemon pudding, baked *and* boiled, lemon sauce, lemon sorbet, lemon sponge, lemon water ice, but she has no lemon cream tartlets.'

Ellen, when concentrating, never lifted her head.

> Beat the yolks of the eggs to a frothy consistency. While you're beating, keep adding nearly a cupful of sugar if it's two eggs, a full cupful if it's three eggs, and just over a cupful if it's four eggs. Grate the peel of a lemon, and add the juice of the grated lemon and the juice of another one to the mixture. Roll out enough pastry, the lighter the better, and with it line some cake-pat tins, that you have already greased every little compartment of with butterpaper.

Thomas returned with his book.

'Now,' he said, settling down beside Ellen.

'Not for just one minute, Thomas, I'm nearly finished.'

> Add about a cup of cream to your mixture, folding it in thoroughly, and then fill each of the pats on the tray with the mixture. Do not fill too full. Bake medium to hot, until the pastry is as brown as you like and the custard setting on top good and firm. Take the tins from the oven, and keeping them level(!) put them in a cool corner. Take the whites of the eggs and with two to three tablespoonfuls of castor sugar whip them into meringues. When the tartlets are cool enough, dollop the meringue on top of them, and then put the trays back in the oven, in a slow heat so that the meringues set.

'You can if you like,' Mrs Dalton had added, 'pour cream on these as well, but I only do it for the men, as I think it is too much otherwise.'

Ellen sat back. 'Good! Lovely! I'll make those the minute I come out of the nursing home.'

Thomas began. 'Now. Are you ready?'

Ellen tidied her papers, slipping back in some loose cuttings and notes not yet fixed in the ledger.

'Guess who this is?' Thomas began to read. 'Here we go. "The cuckoo, as has been said elsewhere, makes no nest, but deposits its eggs in an alien nest, generally in the nest of the ring-dove, or in the nest of the ground-lark, or on a tree in the nest of the green linnet." Any ideas?'

Ellen shook her head: she loved these book games Thomas played with her: he had covered the spine and cover with one large hand.

'I'll read on. "It lays only one egg and does not hatch it itself, but the mother-bird in whose nest it has deposited it hatches and rears it." Well?'

'No clues?'

'No. "And, as they say, this mother-bird when the young cuckoo has grown big, thrusts her own brood out of the nest and lets them perish"? You'll never guess, Ellie, in a million years.'

'Who?'

'Aristotle, you eejit.'

'You eejit yourself. Oh, Thomas!'

'What?'

'My back!'

'Here. Come on, get ready for bed.'

Thomas had bolted the back door and was winding the alarm clock to take it upstairs when he heard her cry.

'Thomas! Thomas!'

He rushed up the stairs.

'Don't come in! Don't come in! Hand me in a towel from the landing cupboard.' He handed a towel in through the door.

'Get out the car, Thomas!' Ellen called, half-flustered, half-laughing.

'Where's your bag?'

'Talk about on time, I only got it ready this very day.'

344

By then he was halfway down the stairs.

'Oh, shite,' he said, remembering something, and turned back, almost falling. 'What about the doctor?'

'We'll call to Dr Hogan and take him with us.'

He pushed the car back far enough to get the starting-handle in, and twisted: it fired first go: he reversed carefully from the garage.

'Hold on, Thomas.' Ellen dived back to the door, opened it, dipped her finger in the little brown, bakelite holy water font on the wall, blessed herself and dabbed a little on Thomas's forehead, and he also made the Sign of the Cross.

Dr Hogan's lights were on: 'I'd better get the bag.'

'He sleeps in that bow tie,' observed Thomas.

'Any pains yet?' said the doctor cheerfully.

'Just a hint.'

'Good girl. Good girl.'

'Will your coat be warm enough on you in the dickey seat?' said Thomas.

'Fire away,' shouted the doctor, once he had crammed himself in: his bag was placed inside the car, on the floor at Ellen's feet: he fought to prop himself up: the dickey slanted outwards and upwards like the lid of the car boot.

'That reminds me – I never went to see that poor Stephenson girl,' Ellen remarked.

'You can when you get out,' said Thomas. 'We'll go up there then. Show her the baby.'

Within seconds of knocking on the door of the nursing home, Nurse Cooper herself appeared, a coat over her nightdress.

'Hallo. Oh, Dr Hogan?'

'Hallo, Nurse, you were expecting Mrs Kane, weren't you?'

'You're very punctual indeed,' said Sheila Cooper. 'And what about Dr Morgan?'

'I could go and get him,' said Thomas.

'But how long would that take at all?' asked Nurse Cooper.

Thomas pulled out his watch. 'There and back, what, two and a half, three hours?' he said hopefully.

'Great God in Heaven, sure the child'll be out and up and running about in short trousers by then,' said Nurse Cooper.

Jack Hogan said, 'John Morgan can't do it, anyway, he's after getting another case of malaria.'

'You'd think a bottle of it would be enough,' said Thomas.

Ellen leaned with one hand against a wall, laughing.

'Show me your hands,' said Nurse Cooper to Dr Hogan. He put down his bag and held out his hands.

'God.' She glared at him. 'Look at the cut of those hands. In there, like a good man, and wash yourself.'

'Only the hands?' he asked. 'Is that all you're going to look at? What about the lugs of the ears, or the navel?'

Thomas asked Ellen, 'Are you all right?'

'I am, but I won't be in a minute.'

'Come on, now,' Nurse Cooper said to Ellen, 'this is your first, isn't it? I have the nicest bed in the place kept for you. Would you like a cup of tea, maybe?' She took Ellen's bag and led her upstairs, and then looked back at Thomas.

'Well, go on, what are you looking at, go on.'

'Where will I go to?' asked Thomas, who still had his hat on, most unlike him.

'Mauritius. Where d'you think? Stop standing there looking out of your mouth, and go.'

Ellen had never heard anybody speak to Thomas like that before, and she would have intervened, had a pain not hit her, the first real one, knocking her breath out, making her gasp.

Thomas stiffened, and Nurse Cooper, observing, held

346

up a hand, and spoke softly, 'Mr Kane, a bit of calm.' She nodded seriously. 'A bit of calm' – one moment, harpie: now, carer.

'But –'

'– A bit of calm!'

The women disappeared round the corner of the staircase and continued to the landing above.

And Thomas drove home in the darkness, the headlights shafting up to the night sky as he climbed the hill, and then the long white and amber beams flashing into the fields as he swung around Hogan's Bend, first lighting up little puzzled, glazed, opaque lamps in the eyes of the cattle as they chewed large and silent in the fields behind the low stone wall, and then the lights closing back in on his own eyes and straight features as he entered the tunnel of trees and high hedges.

At a quarter past six the knocking awakened him out of a deep and late-arriving sleep; then a pebble hit the window.

'Master,' the voice called. 'Are you there? Master.'

Thomas clambered over, raised the sash, and peered out into the half-light. 'It's me, Jack. Jack Hogan.' In such circumstances do people learn to drop formalities and begin thereafter to use the first names of others.

'Jack. Oh?'

'A girl. Lovely and healthy.'

'A girl?'

'Grand and strong.'

'A girl,' said Thomas, the word ending in a little gasp.

'Hold on.'

He ran down the stairs, feeling his way in the dark, not bothering with a candle, and opened the front door in his pyjamas.

'Come in, come in, hang on, I'll get a lamp.'

'No, no. I only called to give you the news.'

Ellen's hats hung on the hallstand.

'And all well?'

'All serene,' said Dr Hogan. 'She's a great girl, great girl.'

'She's all right, so?'

'Ah, grand. I mean, for a first birth, d'you see, she's a miracle. She must have been practising for years.' He laughed and so did Thomas.

'You'll have a cup of tea, come in here 'til I find the matches.'

'No, no, no. I have to be going, the wife will have heard the car passing the house, and she always has the breakfast ready if I'm out on a night call.' He left.

Thomas lit the lamp, and then set up the small Primus stove on the scullery side-table, shaking it first to check that it had enough paraffin; he made a cup of tea for himself. Blackie had slipped in while the door stood open to Dr Hogan. Mewling, she painted Thomas's shins with her tail. Two of the other cats, Jen and Soot, clambered on the windowsill and prowled against the glass, ghostly in the opening glim of day. Thomas, cold, fetched a coat from the hallstand, wrapped it around him, refilled the large cup, smiled at how fiercely Ellen would have clucked at him for eschewing a saucer. He opened the door of the range: a few embers from last night glowed; Thomas poked at them, threw in three, four, small pieces of wood, dusted the disturbed ash off the rail with the goosewing. The little timbers flared and Thomas chose two small pieces of turf, then a third, made a tiny tent of them, watched for five minutes.

'My thanks – will be inadequate,' he had said to Dr Hogan at the front door, 'no matter what I say.'

'Ach, what thanks?' dismissed the doctor.

The fire built a little, and Thomas repeated the process, first a wigwam of small firewood, hemmed in by walls of turf pieces, and within twenty minutes the blaze began to speak for itself.

Not even Ellen knew that Thomas talked aloud when alone. Had the pattern been mapped by an invisible watcher, it would have become evident that he did so only on specific occasions – when recalling an acute embarrassment; when severely troubled by a bad memory; when inordinately excited; or, as now, when flummoxed.

'I don't even know what it means. A daughter.' He put his hands between his knees and rubbed the palms together, a gesture of bemusement as well as warming himself.

'I suppose it'll be Helena?'

They had talked out names, and came to the traditional agreement: if a boy he would be called after Thomas's grandfather; if a girl, after Ellen's grandmother; a second son after Thomas's father, a second daughter after Ellen's mother; a third son after Thomas himself; a third daughter after Ellen; then, they would switch the preferences; a fourth son after Ellen's father; a fourth daughter after Thomas's mother, and so on.

'We'll be in right trouble when number thirteen arrives,' Thomas had said; Ellen scolded him.

'Helena, that's it,' said Thomas aloud. He had left the clock upstairs and had to guess the time: about a quarter to eight, he reckoned, and the grey light had begun to take over from the lamp: the cats still paced, wraiths against the windowpane.

'Sunday. Nine o'clock Mass. No post. No bus. Should I drive in and tell all the relatives? The best thing to do. Now, if I go to Mass here. I'll have to tell everyone, and might it get to the folks before I have time to tell them?'

Thomas resolved, ticking it out on his splayed fingers, to (a) Call in to the nursing home, see Ellen and the baby if possible, but anyway verify everything, see did Ellen need anything, he'd surely only be let stay a short time? (b) Get Mass in town, there's an eleven o'clock Mass, he'd get that straight away after coming out of the nursing home; or maybe get Mass first, then call to the nursing home; (c) Head for Brunswick Square; they'd give him his dinner, he could drop a note into Dr Morgan, and tell Leah and anyone else Ellen wanted told; (d) Get back in time to visit Ellen and the baby again, and be back in Deanstown, what? some time around eight or so tonight? Good.

Nurse Cooper stuck her hand out in a formal congratulation. ''Tis never easy, but this was as easy as it could ever be. In grand fettle, the two of them.'

Long-hipped and starched, she led Thomas upstairs; he smoothed his hair and stood outside the door, as candidates hesitate before an interview.

Nurse Cooper first checked her patient, then held open the door: 'Here's God the father.'

She stepped back to admit Thomas, and then closed the door behind him and went away. He stood with his hat in his left hand, and said, 'I heard the good news.' Approaching the bed, he said, 'How are you, Ellie?' and stood for a moment, then asked, 'Where is she?' Ellen, sitting up, washed and combed, pointed to the crib on her side of the bed, and Thomas stood on tiptoe to lean over.

'You and your left-handedness?' he smiled. 'How are you feeling?'

'A bit sore,' she rued. 'Glad to have it all over.'

'They said you were great.' He walked to the end of the bed and came halfway up to where the baby lay on its side, soundless, wrinkled and asleep. Again he stood on tiptoe, although he didn't need to.

'The mop of hair,' he whispered, in a slow and foolish awe.

'And no caul,' joked Ellen. 'Poor us.'

'We have luck anyway?' Thomas consoled. 'How are you feeling?'

He came around to the side and sat on the chair beside the bed, as Ellen lifted a towel to make way: his overcoat seemed huge in the room.

'D'you want to take off your coat?'

'No, I'm grand.'

'Oh,' she said, catching sight of his tie and shirt, 'you're in your very best.'

He looked down. 'Why wouldn't I be?'

He asked for no details, no account of what birth entailed, no specifics regarding soreness and its location, nothing other than asking whether Ellen had much pain, and how long did a pain last, and what was it like, was it very hurtful? Ellen gave him the weight of the baby, people would ask.

'And when you saw her?'

'At that stage, I was exhausted, and I thought, "Oh, so that's what I looked like when I was born," and then they told me she was fine in every detail, and then I thought, "Oh, what am I supposed to think?" Do you know what I mean? The doctor and the nurse were like a circus together.'

In the inner corner of Thomas's eyes, tears almost appeared, and he blinked them away. He sat erect and said, 'You're a great girl.'

'Imagine,' said Ellen, mocking her mother's tone.

They organized. He would drive on to Janesborough, and take care of all that, and then through the week call in every day after school; he would also make arrangements for exactly which day the Brunswick Square contingent would visit. Ellen said perhaps she would take up Leah's offer to visit for a while, and would Thomas make sure the spare room was made up, and then Leah could come out the day before Ellen and the baby were due home? They agreed on the following Sunday – Nurse Cooper's advice: 'a first baby needs the full week for the both of them' – and Thomas left promising to see Ellen later.

In the belled and Sunday-empty city, Dr Morgan's wife brought him Thomas's note as it fell through the letter-box.

At Brunswick Square, Jim opened the door.

'Hallo, Uncle Jim,' said Thomas, and May, ever vigilant, overheard. Eagerly they all found a place at the table for Thomas, who gave them all the details he knew, prefacing every stage of the proceedings with a time-table.

'At exactly twelve minutes past ten, she called me, I was downstairs . . .' ending, many minutes later to their agog attention, 'and the baby was born at exactly twenty-six minutes past four.'

To Leah and Herbert, the word of the new baby, safely born, might have been a personal blessing: Rachel and Sarah wanted to know what colour hair, eyes; did she have fingernails; what would she be called? Herbert gave Thomas a crown piece to press in the baby's hand; 'More than he ever gave me,' ribbed Leah, who handed Thomas a mysterious small parcel for Ellen, revealed in time as a small jar of home-made hand-cream accompanied by a note. Thomas made arrangements to meet Leah off the Deanstown bus the following Saturday.

Back at the nursing home, Ellen was receiving instruction on how to hold and feed.

'Here – you take her,' said Sheila Cooper, thrusting the baby into Thomas's arms, and he, unprepared, dropped his hat on the floor. 'I'm always trying to get the fathers involved too,' she said, 'and most of them would be more at ease holding a calf.'

Thomas sat ramrod straight, inspecting every visible fibre of his daughter.

'Oh, she does have fingernails?'

'What are you talking about?' said the nurse. 'Is it that you have none?' He laughed, and told them of Leah's little girls; he marvelled on the smallness of the baby, and the frailness, and the tininess.

'Yes,' said Nurse Cooper, 'and you should see what some people do to them, frail and all as they are.'

Thomas asked to see Helena's feet: they unwrapped the swaddling clothes and he inspected her little toes, setting their minute wrinkled redness to rest in his huge palm.

Thomas's week passed in a blur of wellbeing. He walked to school smiling: he never told the schoolchildren, but they knew. Naturally enough, the postman, knowing everything, congratulated him, as did the bus conductor, dropping off a parcel of schoolbook samples for the changed curriculum next September.

Alone in the house in the evenings when he returned from the nursing home, his solitude had a completely different texture from the life he had lived before he met Ellen. It felt almost as if he now tenanted her house: vases, empty at the moment; the mystical arrangements of jars in the pantry; the washboards fixed in ascending sizes on the left-hand scullery wall; the peremptory notes in her handwriting pinned to sundry surfaces: 'Every vessel likely to hold milk must be scrubbed severely; every bottle cleansed out by a little gravel in the water and Shaken Vigorously, then Rinsed'; '*Do not Boil* the Master's Shirts'. He brought the newspaper to the nursing home every day, and, with the exception of Wednesday, when the Morris family visited, he read Ellen the day's news, and from time to time held the baby as gingerly as if he had just landed a sacred fish. People who encountered him found an unbent and warmer man.

Ellen, in her turn, regaled him with the many details of Nurse Cooper's humour, or the characters in the other rooms. She showed him the envelope with five hundred pounds in it that Bob Morris had given her.

'Better than a caul,' Thomas commented.

Ellen struggled on with the bottle-feeding, as she did with the bathing and changing.

On Thursday when he visited, having resisted again the temptation to close the school early, and not trusting the temporary teacher, he slipped in, as had become his wont, through the unlocked front door. Ellen was not in her room. He found a maid, who found Nurse Cooper, who had a story to tell him.

'That Mrs Stapleton isn't well at all, and her child just will not take the bottle. I asked your wife would she help, and she's down now in Mrs Stapleton's room feeding the child. Would you give her half an hour and call back?'

When Thomas did, he found Ellen a little out of phase, and when he pressed, she grew embarrassed. Briefly she told him.

'Nurse Cooper said the child was even more poorly than the mother and it didn't look at all good, and she asked me would I wet-nurse for it a few days?' Ellen paused, then truly blushed. 'Actually she didn't give me any choice, she said I had enough to feed triplets. So what could I do?'

Thomas said, 'But where's the harm in it? How is the child?'

'Apparently,' said Ellen, 'there's a great recovery.' Thomas did not ask why she blushed, nor did he understand.

The month of May grew warm quickly in 1926, as hot as high summer. Leah came on the Saturday bus, to stay and settle Ellen and little Helena Sorcha in easily. That night, Thomas wrote Ellen a note and placed it in her dressing-table drawer where she would be sure to find it, perhaps when he was at school on Monday.

8th May 1926.
Saturday night.

Dear Ellen,

Do you have any idea of how I feel now? After all the things that have happened to me, all the awful things, some which were not of my creating, and worse than that, many which were my own doing?

I suppose that very few men get a chance to make for themselves a good life. I have, and it is mainly thanks to you.

Now, I have a daughter of my own, God bless her, and you have therefore given me something I have always wanted, ever since my own little sister Sorcha died, R.I.P.

All I can say is, that I will do my level best to provide for you and the baby, and any others that come along.

Thank you very much.

Your sincere husband,
Thomas

On Sunday morning, Nurse Cooper and one of her other two nurses stood at the door to see them off. Thomas had been to nine o'clock Mass in Deanstown and the entire half-parish, it seemed, waited to congratulate him. Leah had made him a breakfast so large he could scarcely finish it, and she stood at the door waving him off, and saying the house would be aired and fresh and warm for the baby, and she expected them about twelve noon, or just before.

Unaccountably, Leah then stood at the gate and watched the car climb the hill and go out of sight, then she put out saucers of milk for the cats, and cleared the table.

Halfway through the washing-up, Leah dropped the cloth in the basin, and said aloud, 'Oh, my God!' She never told Ellen this, and when recounting it to Herbert late the next week, said, still on the verge of tears, 'I don't know why, Herbert, I don't know why. But at that moment, I felt something awful, something black and awful.'

The Canon's sermon droned on even longer than usual, and when Thomas went round to the sacristy with the Collection afterwards, he could not get away from the Canon, who seemed excitable – but Jeremiah Williams never mentioned Helena's birth.

'Umpteen people, the Relihans, the Ryles, Mrs Dalton, they were all asking for you, and they all want to call and see you,' Thomas told Ellen.

'It'll be fine if they come during the day,' said Ellen.

'Now,' said Nurse Cooper, 'you've to look after yourself too, you know.'

'How will the Stapleton child be?' whispered Ellen, as Thomas prepared the car.

'He'll be fine now,' confided Nurse Cooper, 'you started him, and this morning's bottle was the best he had. Sure, the poor little fellow is getting a variety of food very young.' They laughed.

Ellen called from the doorway, 'The hood, Thomas. Put the hood down.'

He called back, 'But what about the baby, won't she get cold?'

'Oh, but such a gorgeous day,' said Ellen, and looked to Nurse Cooper for support.

'She's very well wrapped,' agreed Nurse Cooper, and Thomas lowered the hood of the car, although only to the three-quarter mark: the brass headlamps shone; he had wax-polished them early yesterday morning. The two nurses on the doorstep waved goodbye.

The Deanstown road declines as it leaves the town, and then climbs a steep hill past the cemetery, to one of the highest points for miles around: on a clear day, Thomas always pointed out the Castle, a comforting landmark. They passed a woman and her son walking on the left, going home from Mass: the couple stopped to look at the car going by, and stepped out in the road when it had passed, then toiled on up the hill; the fair-haired curly boy remarked to his pleasant and plump mother how handy it would be for them to have a car. Just before the brow of the hill, the car, as it always did, struggled a little, and, with Thomas humorously urging it on, the car made it.

The plateau of the hill runs on for forty yards or so, with a slight curve, then dips with corroborative steepness. The midday sun lit Ellen's face from the side: her hair streamed out from under her brown hat: she held the quiet baby firmly in her arms.

Ellen heard the fat and booming crack before she registered what it was: Thomas heard it too. With his experience, he must have known what the noise meant: they both saw the split second of milky-white little cracks, and then the shatter appearing on the erect windscreen. Ellen heard the second crack: she never found out if Thomas did. He swung violently towards her as if something had punched him terribly hard on the side of the head. Blood flecked her cream skirt: Thomas's left hand clawed towards her, his right hand seemed to get its elbow locked at the steering wheel. His head hit her shoulder, his hat half-squashed off. The car slewed onto the grass margin, and climbed the bank; the engine made several banging noises, and one of the white-walled spoked wheels flopped along; the car slewed on, drifted down the grassy bank, eventually being brought to a halt by the density of the earth, and by some low-growing haw bushes halfway down the hill. Green and shining in the sun, the car attempted to heel over and did so halfway and leftwards, pinning Ellen and the baby under the weight of Thomas's body.

She called out to him, and received no reply; then something final hit her on the head, too.

At the top of the hill, the woman and her fifteen-year-old son walking home from Mass had heard wild sounds, and the boy ran on ahead to see around the bend. He called his mother, who broke into a scurry. Coming from the opposite direction, a man on a bicycle saw the smoking car lying almost on its side and recognized it. He reached it at the same time as the boy. The panting woman arrived: the trio heard the baby crying: the man dispatched the boy to the nearest dwelling, a farmhouse two hundred and fifty yards from the road. From where they stood they could see the people, one, two, three, emerge from the house and, shading their hands against the sun, look from the hollow up in the direction of the boy's pointing finger, and still the baby cried.

The man with the bicycle told the woman, 'Master Kane out in Deanstown owns that car.'

'I know that. The wife had a baby last week in at Nurse Cooper's,' and they stood there, helplessly surmising that 'the Mistress would be in there so, too, and that must be the baby we're hearing.' They plucked uselessly at the green metal of the car.

From the farmhouse a horse and cart and two men, twin brothers, arrived. With great care they righted the car, found the baby safe and sound, and the woman took the child and cradled it. The men gently disentangled the two adults from the almost undamaged car. The woman was unconscious, but bore no trace of serious injury: the man bled profusely from the head, his white collar was soaked with red darkness, and nobody could think how to stop the bleeding. Both adults were laid side by side on the back of the cart.

'She don't look too bad,' said the farmer, preparing to turn the horse around in the direction back to town and hospital, 'but I'd say he's done for.'

20

Holding the baby in her arms, and sitting on the front of the cart, the woman suggested that instead of the hospital they should go to Nurse Cooper's on account of the child and its mother.

The farmer led the horse, walking beside it, trying to keep jolts to a minimum. His brother knelt on the cart facing backwards, attempting to hold steady the heads of the two unfortunate people. The journey, little more than a mile, and helped by the fall of ground back into the town, seemed to take for ever: the man with the bicycle had been detailed to cycle ahead and tell the Guards, and in the distance they saw him returning, accompanied by a cycling officer.

The policeman vacillated – between accompanying the stricken load, inspecting the car, finding a doctor or alerting Nurse Cooper: duty called for the first or second; humanity and practicality governed the third and fourth. Guard Burke resolved his dilemma by, first, sending the man on the bicycle to Nurse Cooper (who then sent him farther, to fetch a priest); second, calling to the barracks on the way (he had been intercepted on the Main Street) and requesting that one of the dayroom men be dispatched out to the car; third, by sending the boy – on the police bicycle – to find a doctor, while he walked along beside the swaying cart. He felt certain the Superintendent would endorse his decisions. (He did not: the man got a flea in his ear, and was told – albeit only when all the circumstances came to light a long time later – that he should have inspected the car, or searched the fields.)

The boy showed the greatest perspicacity: he rode the

policeman's bicycle along the back road – to the golf club, where, in the bar, he found not one, but two doctors, one of whom was Jack Hogan.

Nurse Cooper drew on all her phlegmatism learned in time of military and civil unrest: as the cart arrived, she waited on the pavement outside her door with stretchers already prepared. The horse and cart turned the corner, and she saw to her vast relief Dr Hogan's Austin Seven sweep around the other end of the short street by the market gates. The assistant nurse took the baby, and with a silent thanking nod to the woman, hurried indoors: the policeman and the farming twin brothers, under the super-vision of an untypically grave Dr Hogan lifted first, Ellen, on to a stretcher, and then Thomas. For a moment the bodies lay there on the side of the street, mute and slack, and the farmers edged their cart away a decent distance, and tied the horse to a lamp-post. The man with the bicycle returned, saying Father Herity was on his way: it felt to everyone as if those were the only words so far spoken in the activities at the nursing-home door – not the case, merely a breaking of the spell.

'Which of them first?' asked Guard Burke.

Dr Hogan's friend, Dr Dillon, straightened up and said, 'He's bleeding very heavily,' so they took Thomas in first.

'Good job that baby is on the bottle,' said Nurse Cooper to nobody. A few people had gathered, interrupting their Sunday mealtime to inspect a commotion they had sensed rather than heard.

'The room inside the door,' said Nurse Cooper, 'the bed there is empty. And take her upstairs.'

She led the way up to the bed Ellen had vacated some hours earlier: it had been stripped of its sheets and not yet remade, a detail to which Nurse Cooper now attended as if by magic, and she had a sheet spread on it before the bearers, grunting to keep the stretcher level all the way upstairs, manoeuvred it through the doorway.

Dr Hogan and Dr Dillon divided their responsibilities; Dr Hogan attending his recent maternity patient, Dr Dillon, with much more surgical experience, washing his hands in the corner of the downstairs room where Thomas stretched on the only bed. The man on the bicycle was sent on one more errand – down the street to call in Nurse Cooper's other nurse, and if not her, the Jubilee Nurse: in fact he called both.

Another car drew up outside, another doctor, a Mac-Donnell man, the word had spread fast: then Father Herity arrived on foot, and was kept waiting, not hugely to his pleasure, until a preliminary examination had taken place. He was then only granted minutes with each patient while the doctors conferred. Dr Dillon whipped off Thomas's tie, unbuttoned his waistcoat, and cut away the shirt and vest. Blood ran everywhere and he tried to wipe it away with a towel he took from a pile on a chair. He worked with deft furiousness, called one of the waiting men to get off Thomas's jacket with him, and cut at the clothes until Thomas was naked to the waist. Removing the rest of the clothes proved no difficulty: they jack-knifed Thomas softly upwards at the hips, and, having taken off his shoes, slid off his trousers, under which he still wore nothing. The strenuous actions elicited no response from the tall wiry man lying supine. Dr Dillon prised open the eyelids and then let them slip shut again.

Upstairs, Nurse Cooper and Dr Hogan found heavy bruising on Ellen's right temple, found a cut over her right eye, and very severe bruising and contusion to the lower jaw.

'No scarring,' observed Nurse Cooper.

Ellen's right hand, badly cut, bled heavily: Nurse Cooper covered her with a sheet while Dr Hogan examined her.

Downstairs, Dr Dillon sponged and sponged and sponged with his towel. Another nurse arrived, and without taking off her coat began to help him, until all the early blood had been washed away, although it still continued to pour from somewhere in Thomas's hair on the right-hand side of his head. Dr Dillon found some bruising to the left-hand ribcage, surprisingly not excessive; he located an unserious injury to the left hand; the nurse pointed out some spots of deep purple, as if caused by heavy pinpricks, on the back of the right hand, on which Thomas appeared to have broken a finger. They returned to the catastrophic injury, the substantial wound on the right temple, high up, between the top of the ear and the forehead. From here, the blood flowed: in this position it filled Thomas's ear: Dr Dillon could not yet gauge the extent of the head wound. Dr MacDonnell fidgeted from foot to foot, felt all Thomas's extremities, noting changing temperatures.

The doctors went to the hall and called Dr Hogan: the priest approached Thomas's bed, muttering prayers: the baby, sensibly, had been removed from all the agitation. Dr MacDonnell, the newcomer, opened his mouth to speak when Nurse Cooper shouted. Dr Hogan raced up the stairs again: Ellen had begun to flicker. But she subsided: Nurse Cooper rubbed the back of Ellen's neck even more warmly, then held the cold, wet cloth to Ellen's forehead. Ellen flickered again, and turned her head.

'She's coming, she's coming,' said Dr Hogan, and bent his head: the other doctors stood, urgent-looking, at the door.

'Mrs Kane, can you hear me? Ellen. You're all right. You're safe. And the baby is fine. Can you hear me? Nod your head if you can.' Nurse Cooper brought her head forward: 'Ellen, it's all right, you're safe. Everything is all right. You're all right.' She stroked Ellen's face, and continued to speak in a mixture of insistence and kindliness. 'You're all right. The baby's safe, dear. The baby's safe. Can you hear me?'

Dr Hogan whipped open his bow tie, undid the shirt button at his throat, and began to massage Ellen's fingers, kneading them in his own: all almost fell over each other at the bed: Dr Dillon went back downstairs to Thomas who had continued to bleed in the two minutes they were away.

'That man is dead,' said the priest. 'He's gone to God.'

'Not if I can help it,' said Dillon; 'will you go out now, please.'

'The Last Rites,' protested Father Herity, who had a piece of food stuck in the corner of his lip.

'Out!' said Dr MacDonnell, and the priest reluctantly drifted away: the nurse continued to sponge Thomas's face.

Ellen woke up – and lived: severely shocked, terribly sore and bruised, hysterical. She calmed momentarily when Nurse Cooper shrewdly sent for Helena, then became agitated again and tried to get out of bed when she asked about Thomas. They told her, 'He's downstairs; Dr Dillon and Nurse Lynch, and another doctor are with him. Now lie back and rest, just put your head back gently, that's it. The baby's safe, she's fine. Fine.'

The doctors, in a second hurried conference, decided to move Thomas to the hospital, as they could not staunch the blood: the hospital was only half a mile away and had more equipment than a private maternity home. No ambulance: in Dr MacDonnell's car, larger than Dr Hogan's, they could slump him across the back seat. On the way to the hospital, Thomas's head lolled over and the bleeding appeared to have slowed. They rounded the corner by the Post Office, and in the lurching of the car, Thomas's dead weight fell on Dr Hogan – who could not reach Thomas's pulse to check whether Thomas had died at that precise moment.

Dr Hogan, wrinkling his nose searchingly, murmured

to Dr MacDonnell when the car stopped, 'At least there's no evacuation of the bowels so far.'

Out in Deanstown, Leah had grown almost frantic. Too stable ever to give way utterly to unfounded alarm, she paced and paced, walked to the gate and back a dozen times. She folded her arms and rubbed them to remove the contradictory coldness she felt in the hot sunlight. Around her, not a sound could be heard; the countryside sat quietly in the orange warmth of a Sunday in May. She rearranged the flowers she had put out for Ellen's return; readjusted over and over the place settings for lunch on the kitchen table, fidgeted in a variety of disquiets, even took down the iron and began to heat it. Unlike the city, no people could be seen, and she did not wish to walk down to the village in case Thomas and Ellen arrived in her absence, or in case she gave cause for unnecessary anxiety which would be talked about: Ellen had told her how they gossiped.

Had Thomas by any chance said they would call somewhere on the way home? No: lunch had been agreed: chops rather than a roast on account of any delay in settling down the baby. At three o'clock, when they had not arrived, Leah put on her coat, locked the door, hid the key under the stone, went to the garage, took out Ellen's bicycle, walked it to the gate which she closed behind her, and mounted it awkwardly. Wobblily, she cycled the six miles to Mooreville, her red hair lifting in the breeze. First, on the hillside, she saw the car overturned and some people standing near: fearing their answers, she did not ask any questions. Next, she had to find Nurse Cooper's, and when she saw the cars and the bicycles and the people standing at the door, she knew something awful had happened. Dismounting, she walked into the sombre aftermath.

Thomas did not die. In what passed for an operation late that afternoon, they removed a small piece of metal from his head, and his pulse and breathing grew stronger, and in time normalized. Leah took some kind of charge, concentrating at first on Ellen and the baby. Nurse Cooper came into the room to call Leah out and say that a surgeon had been summoned from Janesborough, and another from Cork (who subsequently wrote a book-length account of the entire case). Ellen, in total shock, took no decisions, took no part in discussions.

The town rang agog: all three had been shot, one by one; the car had been riddled with bullets; the baby only had been shot; the baby only had survived. People cycled, or took out their pony-traps, to view the overturned Singer Roadster. The Master was dead; the Mistress was dead; the Mistress was fine and up and about; the Master and the baby were dead. Nobody knew the truth, nobody attempted to ascertain. The Guards said little; the Superintendent could not be found – he and his wife had gone to visit his wife's mother over by Pallas, a fifteen-mile cycle for the Guard who had to fetch him.

Next day, the surgeons discussed; they deliberated: no further operation – 'for the moment'. Jack Hogan hung like a schoolboy near their edges. With instructions for acute observation, they left Mooreville. One, an old colleague of hers, called to see Nurse Cooper before he departed the town; she told him Mrs Kane was sleeping and she even let him look in, and then let him see the sleeping baby who had a tiny scratch just between where her eyebrows would grow.

'There's a friend of Mrs Kane's here,' said Nurse Cooper. 'A very capable woman, a Mrs Winer,' and then whispered, 'she's a Jewess, but she seems very sensible.'

In the shadows of early Monday evening, the surgeon told Leah and Nurse Cooper in the small downstairs sitting-room, 'We have no idea how he will turn out. He's unconscious, probably not very deeply. He responds to some things, his lips withdraw from a pinch, that sort of thing. But 'tis in waves, at times he seems to lapse deeper, at other times he comes very close to the surface. What we're hoping for is some kind of steadiness.'

Leah asked, 'What is to be done?'

The surgeon replied, 'How is the wife? Will she be capable of looking after herself?'

Nurse Cooper said, 'The shock is the big thing, that's the big problem. She has only small injuries, I think she has a sprained wrist, but the shock . . .'

Leah asked, 'When you say you don't know, what do you know? Is the man going to live or die?'

'That,' said the surgeon, 'is what we don't know.'

Leah pressed, 'But how long could he live like he is now?'

'We don't know that, either.'

'What do you know?'

The man pulled at his ear and said, 'We know he has had a bad head wound, from a gun. He was shot at. We know he is not conscious. We know that he is as strong as a horse. He could recover. If he doesn't – he'll die. But we don't know when.'

Leah said, 'There is something you are not saying?'

With an embarrassed look, the surgeon asked, 'Are you next of kin?'

Nurse Cooper reassured him as to the proprieties.

Leah went on, 'What you're not saying is – he could live like this for a while?'

'Yes,' said the surgeon, 'that's the worst possibility.'

'But how could he live?' asked Leah. 'How could he eat?'

'It happens.' Surgeon and nurse spoke together. 'He will be able to swallow soft food if it's placed deep in his mouth.'

366

'But otherwise he will just lie there?' asked Leah. 'Like a living corpse?' The man nodded his head, twice.

Thomas did not recover consciousness: the same surgeon, who called several times in the next weeks, had predicted accurately. Most of Thomas's body returned to a normal physiological state, and he existed somewhere between coma and general lack of consciousness. His eyes opened from time to time but they were as blank as blindness, and flapped closed slowly again, like a dying fish. He had, they surmised, suffered irreparable brain damage, and longevity did not seem a prospect. Nevertheless, as Leah had been told, and it was not an unknown curiosity, he could swallow liquid and semi-solid food. The doctors had encountered a similar case only by repute: the patient – a Collins man, too, as it happened, and with worse injuries than Thomas – had lived for eight months, and then died of pneumonia.

In Thomas's case, who could say? He had immense vitality and physical strength. Wasn't it ironic, said the doctors, that such properties could prove a disadvantage, as now they did? All his bodily functions had to be attended to by others: he had almost no physical response of any kind other than breathing, sometimes even snoring; he took the soft runny food, provided his mouth was held a little closed after each mouthful, obliging him to swallow involuntarily. The doctors had no medical literature to which they could have had recourse: the one and only case of which they knew had not been written up, on account of the Collins connection and the attendant secrecy in the mood of those times. Dr MacDonnell said to the others one Sunday, as they stood by the prostrate bedside, that perhaps a radiograph would help, but he doubted it, and besides they did not have one; the nearest was in Dublin, he thought. Nobody mentioned radiographs to Leah, or even to Ellen when she resumed her capacities. The men

367

conferred one last time in the room where Thomas lay.

'It's a terrible bind,' said Dr MacDonnell, an unsentimental Northerner, 'that man is too strong to die.'

Thomas's room in the hospital took on the atmosphere of an oratory: people tiptoed in to see him, as to a figure lying in state, and the less charitable folk, who had disliked him, or feared him, or, since the old days, hated him, muttered things about the 'living dead': in truth, commented Jack Hogan, it described him well.

Leah stayed overnight on the Sunday at Nurse Cooper's, making sure to be in the room on Monday morning when the sedated Ellen awoke to find Leah simply holding her hand and smiling carefully.

'Helena's yelling for her bottle,' said Leah.

'You've cut your hair,' said Ellen. 'Why am I so weak?'

'You had a very bad accident,' said Leah. 'No wonder you're weak.'

Leah cycled out to Deanstown, and arranged changes of clothing for herself, then cycled back to the nursing home. Each time, she averted her eyes as she passed the askew car gleaming and brutally sad on the roadside. She walked around Ellen's room, cradling Helena, whose eyes remained mostly shut, and whose lips made endless little pink sucking motions. Leah kissed the child softly over and over.

'And Thomas?' Ellen asked again and again. 'How is he? I know something dreadful happened to us. Tell me.'

Leah said, 'Yes, but you are all alive. Thomas is in the hospital. He is unconscious; he had an operation and the surgeon was telling us yesterday about his extraordinary strength.'

On Thursday, Ellen rose, helped by Nurse Cooper and Leah, and she stood and then walked, then sat in a chair by the window. For hours on end she scarcely spoke. The

Guards removed the car: someone had stolen the rug: the car now sat in the yard of the barracks in Silverbridge, and parish ghouls came to view it.

One afternoon, Nurse Cooper, Leah and Ellen, a day before her homegoing, left the nursing home and walked to see Thomas, taking a route that avoided Mooreville's main street. At the door of the hospital, Nurse Cooper said, 'I'll wait out here.'

Leah said, 'What?' and Sheila waved a hand: 'I'm not allowed in; I'll explain to you later.'

In the hallway, people looked curiously but knowingly at Leah and Ellen: nobody came forward. The girl at the desk said, 'Wait here a minute,' and returned with the Matron who shook hands, a woman of forceful earnestness.

'He is down here,' she said, 'although how long we can reserve this room for him I don't know. The surgeon is coming in in the morning.'

'Mrs Kane is going home tomorrow,' said Leah.

Pale, diminished, Ellen walked along the corridor as if encased in glass. The Matron opened the door and ushered them in, then stood back, unveiling her exhibit. Leah knew what to expect, Ellen did not. At the end of Thomas's bed she looked at Leah, then at the ceiling, then forced a glance again.

Leah snapped at the Matron, 'Why isn't that bandage clean? When was it changed?'

Matron defended. 'There's still the occasional oozing. We can't stop it, 'tis only very slight.'

Leah threw her hands apart. 'Get a nurse to change it. Now!' Matron assessed her and left the room.

Leah said to Ellen, 'Come and hold his hand.'

'I can't.'

'Come on!' She took Ellen's arm and drew her to the head of the bed. 'Stroke his face.'

When Leah began to rub Thomas's jaw gently, Ellen did the same.

'He's so white,' she said. 'He's so white. And that's a huge bandage. Leah, what happened to him? Poor Thomas.'

Matron returned with a nurse who began to rearrange the bed, so that Thomas's bandage could be removed from his head. Matron said to Leah, 'At least they were able to get out all the lead.'

'Lead?' said Ellen, from the edge of a trance; Leah had been unable to shush the Matron.

'All the shot. It was a shotgun,' the woman blundered on: they had not yet told Ellen.

'Come on,' said Leah, 'that is enough for one day.' She did not let Ellen see the tears in her eyes as she walked from the room.

21

In Deanstown, Thomas's misfortune moved the parish as
nothing had ever done before.

'They say he'll never stir again. Never stir. He'll live for
a while. But sure . . .'

All became medical experts. 'A living death. That's it.
A living death.'

Heads shook; tongues clicked. 'Well, sure. Dlokk.
That's the way. You never know what's going to happen
in this world. And no notion of the next world. Well,
well.'

They stared into their fires, watched the pictures in the
flames. 'Do you know what it is? She'll be a living widow,
that's what? Did you ever hear of such a thing? Whoi-oi.'
They blew soundless whistles through their lips.

One evening, as if by accident, five of the men drifted
together in a farmhouse to consider whether they could
make any contribution to Ellen's new circumstances,
improve the Master's shattered life.

'Nineteen-twelve. That's when he came here. God,
wasn't he the hard man, though, when he came? All that
skelping he did to us in the school, hauh?'

'All the same a fair man. And sure, who'd be able to
read a line, sure we couldn't post a letter if he wasn't hard
on us, so we couldn't.'

A third voice said, 'Jayzes, there's many the form he
filled in for me. An' I don't want to take any of them
forms to the Canon. Or the Sergeant. The one thing about
the Master, you never knew him minding your business.'

'Oh yeh,' said a fourth, 'as silent as the grave' – at which
irony the company fell quiet.

371

John Relihan offered one last thought: it entered forbidden territory. 'He was as good a man as any of them when the time came, wasn't he? He was as good a man as Ernie O'Malley, or Sean Treacy. Or Michael Collins himself come to that.' Someone coughed on the draw of a cigarette, and the conversation changed tack.

Exactly one week after the event, several of Thomas's family came by various means to the house in Brunswick Square, and mournfully discussed the matter with Ellen's parents. May arranged cold meats and tea and cakes, apologizing all the time for the fact that she had to buy everything: 'I hadn't the heart to bake.'

To the faces whitened with shock and hurt, Bob asked a general question, 'Do the Guards know anything yet?' and received no conclusive reply. The group fragmented into several smaller groups, having quiet conversations, anxious to get off the subject as soon as possible.

Bob asked another question. 'Is there anything anyone thinks we ought to be doing?' and was answered by a few mumbling, shaking heads, and a vague, 'Sure what can we do, what can anyone do, until the doctors know one way or the other?'

Jim Morris, unusually grave, answered the door knocker and ushered in Father John Watson, who accepted May's cup of tea promptly.

'What is the latest news?' he asked through crumbs, 'and is there such a thing as a visiting arrangement?'

They told him what they knew: Thomas showed no responses; Nurse Cooper had recommended as few visitors as possible for Ellen who remained 'extraordinarily shocked, but, thank God, no injuries at all, hardly'; the baby was fine. John Watson looked around the room with a most kind expression on his face and addressed them.

'May I say just one thing? This is a dreadful occurrence, and my heart and prayers are with you all. I have little to offer you by way of practical assistance, as you know. But I have two things I can give you. One, whenever you need anyone to talk to, about anything, however worried you are, write to me and I will write back. Or call and see me: if I am teaching at that moment just wait for me, and then my time will be your time. And two, remember this. You are all decent, good people, and it is that decency and goodness that will carry you, and dear Ellen, and the baby through this dreadful thing.' He did not mention Thomas: nobody noticed.

Father Watson put down his cup of tea and spent the next hour moving through the room, talking to each individual there: May and Bob Morris, and Rina and Jim; Thomas's two sisters in their identical navy hand-knitted cardigans; his brothers who did not know where to put themselves, and who stood awkwardly near windows and doors. When the little priest had spoken to them all, and then left with a general wave, and wish, and a wipe of his hand over his wavy fair hair, the mood in the room had almost lightened.

'Ah,' said Bob Morris, when the door closed, 'isn't that man a good man?' and the conversation took such a relaxed turn, that by the time they began to leave the house, all seemed somewhat cheerful.

Just before Ellen came home to Deanstown with the baby, John Relihan and Michael Connors met by arrangement, and, collecting Tom Dalton, they drove in John Relihan's trap to Dr Hogan's, where 'that peculiar woman' let them in, and, sidelong, sparsely, told them the doctor was 'out'. They waited in the room with the palm in the pot, and just as they discussed leaving, heard his car.

Dr Hogan listened carefully. 'I perfectly agree with you. I perfectly agree with you' – and would willingly lead a delegation to the Canon on the following Sunday after Mass.

Jeremiah Williams listened to them in silence and said, 'I have to talk to the Curate.'

'Sure, what can we do?' asked the Curate.

'They want me to give her his job.'

'Ah, sure you can't do that, that has to be a man,' said the Curate. 'The Department'd be up in arms.'

'They would, they would.'

'Sure how could we do that?' asked the Curate. 'Don't Principals always have to be men?'

The Canon inspected another young apple, as the Curate followed him at a distance, avoiding the branches.

'Apparently there's a Mrs Sweeney over in Callan or somewhere,' said the Canon, 'and she got the job when her husband died, but she had only a year to go before retiring or something. And it gave her a better pension.'

'Sure this is a different case altogether,' said the Curate. 'That woman is only in her twenties.' He paused for reflection. 'And she's a fiery bit, into the bargain.'

'Hah, don't I know it?' said Jeremiah Williams.

'I know 'tis a sad case,' said the Curate, 'but sure God alone knows what trouble you'd have with her.'

'The men are saying I have to do something,' said the Canon.

'Did you try the Department?' asked the Curate.

'They say that technically she has to vacate before the school reopens, 'tis the Principal's Residence. But that, of course, I'm the Manager, and 'tis up to me.'

'Sure what can we do so?' asked the Curate. 'I mean, if she wasn't a woman . . . ?'

'D'you know what it is, Father?' said Canon Jeremiah Williams, peering at a green apple. 'These'll soon be ripe at this rate of going.'

Dr Hogan collected Ellen and six-weeks-old Helena.

'I hope you don't mind, Ma'am,' he said, as he settled

374

them in the car, 'but I have to go a small bit out of my way. I have to go out by Carrig, I know 'tisn't the straight road, but 'twill only be a few minutes extra. Glorious day again, thanks be to God.' The baby blinked in the bright light.

In the event Jack forgot to make even a pretend call, and thereby exposed his good intention of not taking Ellen past the scene of the shooting.

Leah heard the car, stood at the open door, and reached out to take Helena. 'Hallo, hallo, hallo, you little pet, you little sweet one.' She fingered aside the shawl to see Helena's face better; Helena pursed her lips.

'Will you have a cup of tea, Doctor?'

'I won't thanks, Ma'am, I have all sorts of oul' things going on. I'll skedaddle.' He turned to Ellen. 'Good luck now, Ma'am, I'll drop in and see how you're getting on, and I'll keep an eye on the boss'; he glanced resignedly at Leah over Ellen's head.

Leah led the way: on the kitchen table sat a blue Moses basket, readied for Helena who began to whimper when Leah laid her down in it.

'Ah, little puss'ms, I'll warm a bottle for you.' Leah let Helena clutch a finger. 'Oooh, your grip, already, you dear little sweetheart.'

The light caught Leah's ring: Helena tried to focus on it, still grizzling a little. Two prepared bottles and teats stood on the shelf.

'Leah, you're here again, you're a champion. What can I say to you?'

'Now, now,' said Leah, 'none of that.'

Ellen had seated herself on a chair just inside the door. Still holding the handle of her suitcase she looked around the kitchen: Thomas's chair; the book he had been reading, and the careful bookmark torn from a newspaper; the case for his spare set of spectacles on the windowsill; the calendar on the wall directly opposite his head, with all the school holiday opening and closing dates ringed – at which Ellen closed her eyes tight, notwithstanding the tears squeezing out.

Leah watched while pretending not to. Leah said nothing. Leah warmed the bottle of milk. Leah lifted Helena and began to feed her.

Ellen released the suitcase handle, turned her head away from Leah as if to look through the window, and slipped a wiping hand up to her eyes. Leah made soothing, affirming sounds to Helena, who began to fall asleep halfway through. Eventually, Ellen rose, took off her coat and hung it on the hallstand.

'Will I unpack down here, d'you think, Leah? Or should I do it upstairs?'

'Down here I would say,' said Leah, 'all that washing, you might as well.'

Presently, with shrewd management of the moment, Leah contrived to get upstairs ahead of Ellen, and carried the fed, changed, dozing Helena in the Moses basket to the stand in the corner of the bedroom. Pondering for a second – should she hide Thomas's razor, and deciding not to – she called Ellen. She called her again. And again. Then went downstairs.

'Ellen, dear, we'd better decide which corner of the room for the baby. Are there draughts? – from the chimney or the window?'

Leah went back upstairs leaving Ellen no choice but to follow her.

'See what I mean?' she said when Ellen stood in the door. 'This corner looks like the best, although it's a tight squeeze past the end of the bed. Oh, Ellen, dear.' She came and stood in front of the younger woman and took her in her arms as she would a child, sat them both on the bed and rocked Ellen gently. 'Dear God,' said Leah, over and over. 'Dear Ellen.'

=

In the following two weeks or so, little happened. Ellen's mother, having been to the nursing home and the hospital twice already, came for a day, with a note from Bob enclosing some money. He had bronchitis again – 'In weather like this?' queried Ellen.

Letters poured in. Surprisingly few neighbours came; those who did brought baked cakes, or home-made puddings, or meat from freshly-killed animals, or their own butter. All avoided the subject of the man lying still, the warm statue, in the Mooreville Hospital bed six miles away. Michael Connors, with not a word to anyone, took to leaving a can of new milk inside the gate each morning. Mrs Ryle called with tea, sugar, butter.

Miriam Hogan stood on the road, but would not enter the house, perhaps picking up the hesitancy in Ellen's invitation. She said, 'Have you a good book to read? Distraction is very useful, you know. I'll bring you something.'

The Sergeant called again, as he had to the nursing home.

'When'd be a good time to talk to you, Ma'am?'

'Now,' said Leah, 'get it over with.'

'No,' said Ellen. 'Nothing more. Only what I told you so far. All I remember was – it was very warm, and we had the roof of the car folded down, and there was a crack.'

'You mean, like a shot? You must have heard shots before, Ma'am? You know, in Janesborough, like, a few years ago and that?' The Sergeant's wife had a terrible turned eye, Ellen told Leah later, a squint that went out to the west.

'Yes, I suppose. A shot.'

'We found cartridges, Ma'am, well, a cartridge. There's a man down from Dublin, a detective. He found it inside the ditch. You see, if, if – God forbid, if the Master. If anything happened to the Master. I mean to say,

377

something is after happening to him, but if anything more happened to him.'

'You mean if Mr Kane died?' asked Leah abruptly.

'Well, sort of, Ma'am, it ed be murder, so it would.'

'Who fired the gun?' asked Leah.

'We don't rightly know, Ma'am, I mean. Ma'am, we've to be very careful. I mean did you see anyone?' The Sergeant put away his notebook. Ellen shook her head.

'Are you suspecting anyone?' asked Leah, again abrasive.

'We can't suspect anyone unless somebody saw someone, that's the way of it. Unless the Mistress saw anyone, or if anyone threatened the Master. But if nobody saw nothing, I mean to say, if there was nothing seen by anyone . . .'

At the gate, the Sergeant said to Leah as he left, 'There's'n't a thing we can do, Ma'am, and that woman here with no man in the house. You'll have to move her. Out of here, Ma'am. And the baby. 'Tisn't safe, so 'tisn't.'

Leah did not report this to Ellen. She did make a tentative suggestion that Ellen should return to Janesborough, but Ellen told Leah that under 'no circumstances, point blank' would she leave Deanstown; nor would she stay in Brunswick Square, not even for a few weeks; nor would she think of getting a job elsewhere.

'I've made my bed, I have to lie on it,' she said over and over, and did not amplify, other than saying, 'And anyway we have to wait and see . . . what happens . . .'

Thereafter, Leah directed Ellen's attentions concentratedly towards Helena, and the housework, and towards picking up the generalities of a life. Leah said, 'No, Ellen, it is not a sin to miss Mass in these circumstances, you will go to Mass when you feel able. And you can't until you have somebody to help you look after the baby.'

'Leah, what in the name of God am I going to do when you go?'

'You'll manage. You'll be surprised. Wait and see. Sheila Cooper said she'll keep on calling' – as she had done twice in one week already, arriving like a descending fowl, red-faced, the bicycle almost running on out of her grasp.

On Sunday, Leah said to Ellen, 'Right. Washing tomorrow. Blankets. All your woollen things. And Thomas's. The whole house!'

Ellen came downstairs next morning with huge armfuls. Three times Leah had to ask her to fetch Thomas's two V-neck pullovers, and his three warm, long-sleeved undervests.

Leah said, 'He's going to need these.'

When Ellen set up a wail, Leah repeated, 'I said – he's going to need these.'

She held them up to the light, inspected them for any darning needs and handed them to Ellen. 'Here. You wash them.' Leah stood on a chair and took down three of the five washboards from the scullery wall.

That evening, Ellen said, 'Whew, my back.' She stretched her upper body forward and pressed her hips with her hands.

Baby feed and change four times a day; cooking – a new recipe even; cleaning – the range had to be blacked; the women worked all week side by side, talked quietly, and sometimes silences fell; in the evenings they sat at the kitchen table and went over and over again what had happened.

'There are no reasons, Ellen, there are no reasons. All you can do now is get yourself going again; there's the new life there, the baby.'

'Leah, what about Thomas? What about Thomas?'

If she asked the question once, as Leah reported

to Herbert, Ellen asked it a hundred times.

'We can't push anything, Ellen. It has to wait. The old saying: doctors differ.'

'And patients die,' said Ellen, completing the proverb.

Standing on the road on Saturday morning, seeing the bus in the distance, Ellen said, 'Will I be all right, Leah?'

Leah said, 'You will. You will.'

Silence in Deanstown. Silence in the Teacher's Residence. Ellen Kane closed her gate, and closed her door, and at the hallstand pressed her face into the folds of her husband's good grey overcoat.

They came to see Ellen in two cars, one of them Dr Hogan's. The tall man whose name she did not quite catch, said, looking down at the Moses basket, 'Well, at least the baby is very healthy. How are you feeling, Mrs Kane?'

They sat in the parlour. By now Ellen had re-familiarized herself with all corners of the house, and had begun to address the stabs of pain at each encounter with Thomas's domestic life: his gardening cap; the old paint drum for holding the oil he drained from the car; his piles of newspapers that she had complained about – 'they're always in my way, Thomas'; the sharp brightness of the spade and shovel blades that he cleaned so assiduously with a flat mutton-bone after each use; the tray that had been his mother's, on which one of their wedding-gift tea services now sat.

'It's like this,' said the tall surgeon to Ellen. 'We don't know. He can eat soft food, mush, bread-and-milk –'

'What they call "goody", d'you see –' interrupted Hogan.

'I know what "goody" is,' said Ellen impatiently.

'`Course you do. The baby'll be on it soon.' said Dr Hogan.

Ellen said, 'My father had it for his gums when he got his teeth out, that's all he could eat.'

'Your husband can swallow that, provided he's fed properly,' said the tall man.

'Nurse Cooper showed them down at the hospital, she went over the other day,' smiled Dr Hogan, 'and read the Riot Act over them.'

'I thought she wasn't allowed in,' said Ellen.

'She reported them once for hygiene,' said Dr Hogan, 'and they barred her, but this time she forced her way in.' He laughed.

'But something has affected the brain, and that's the case as I see it,' continued the tall surgeon, who had a white triangle of stiff good handkerchief in his breast pocket.

'Will that "something" ever stop affecting it?' asked Ellen.

'We don't know,' he said. 'We don't know.' The remainder of their visit grew sombre.

The other two doctors said little, until the end. One then remarked, 'Even if he is comatose, and even if it seems that he's going to remain comatose –'

Ellen interrupted. 'Comatose? I've never heard that word? Is it from "coma"?'

'– Yes, and if it appears that he'll be comatose, then he'll need constant attention.'

'The hospital can do that, can't they?'

The doctors looked at each other and the tall man said, 'We'll watch how it turns out.'

When they stood and began to take their leave, the fourth man had yet not said a word. At the very last moment, he turned to Ellen: 'I'm a great believer in human contact, Mrs Kane, a great believer. It is also part of the medical process.'

381

'Tell me one thing?' Ellen leaned forward. 'How much life is in him?'

'A lot,' said the man. 'A lot.' The others had climbed into the cars. 'He is near enough to consciousness to have muscles that work in order to take in food. He may even flicker into some kind of awareness, and then relapse again. We don't know – that's the truth. He's taking food, as we said, so long as it can slip down his throat. His breathing is very strong and normal. God knows what will happen. We have nothing to go on.'

'Oh, isn't she grand!' Nurse Cooper wagged her face up and down at Helena. 'Grand. Aren't you, you little thing? You have her grand and clean. If a fraction of the babies I saw were as grand as that, aren't you grand?' Helena and the lightly bearded nurse beamed at each other.

'Now, my lady, let me look at you.' She led Ellen to the window, turned her face this way and that. 'That eye, is that a stye starting, or is it a bit bloodshot? You may be a bit run down, my lady, we'll have to get you a tonic, or a few rose-hips or something. What about the tummy, are you eating all right? And what about down there?' She nodded her eyes towards Ellen's pelvis. 'Is the after-the-birth over? Well, your hair is grand anyway, your crowning glory, let me see.' She drew Ellen's head towards her and fingered through the abundant hair; she scrutinized Ellen's hands: 'You should use a bit more hand-cream, the water round here isn't all that soft.'

Sheila Cooper had twice been unlucky in her life. Her training in London from 1891 to 1894 had given her a penchant for men in uniform.

'Not good,' rebuked her aunt. 'Men in uniform die.'

As did her first love, Dick Speight, descended from a Janesborough family. When Sheila met him in London, they found much in common, knew many people from entwining strands of life. He died of blood-poisoning in the Transvaal, was buried out there: Sheila lit a candle in some church she wandered into in London.

Ellen said, 'You were at the hospital?'

'I was, dear, I was. That crowd. I'd box their ears for them.'

Sheila's second love, a relationship more mature, firmer, than the first, was an officer too, posted to Ireland, and the staff car in which he was a passenger crashed not fifteen miles from the Cooper family home on its way to the aftermath of an ambush. In London at the time, she missed his funeral: he, a John Gibbs from Hertfordshire, a morose and slightly irascible man, was being taken to his grave in the opposite direction as she crossed from Holyhead on the Mail Boat. Regarding all of this, Nurse Cooper only ever made one remark. To a *confidante* she said that although everyone is supposed to have three great loves in life, she would 'never risk a third'.

'How is he?' asked Ellen.

'He's just the same. You weren't in yet?'

Ellen deflected the question, 'The doctors, they were all here.'

Ellen looked at her to gauge how the remark had been received. Nurse Cooper and she had discovered something steadfast in common: as in Ellen's family, a Protestant had married a Catholic a forebear or two ago, and although the ensuing generations were reared as Catholics, the Protestant veneer and its waxy odour had lingered refiningly.

'Well, I'll tell you now.' Nurse Cooper began to take off her coat. 'You know that young man, that young Condon man. Well. I asked him to call here today, now if you don't want him he'll go away again. He knows that. But he has the car nearly fixed, there wasn't a whole lot wrong with it. Anyway. I'll stay with the baby, to let you go in and see himself.' She paused. 'Probably you should tidy yourself up.'

When Ellen came downstairs, Sheila Cooper looked her up and down, then put aside the baby's bottle, lifted Helena to her shoulder, rose and said to Ellen, 'Come over here to the window so that I can see you' – then added, 'Haven't you something a bit brighter you can wear?'

At the hospital door, Ellen paused, looked back at the respectful Michael Condon; she had faced getting back into the car; they had driven past the scene of the incident. She hesitated again, then broached the hallway. The girl stopped her and said surlily, 'You can't go in anywhere. 'Tisn't visiting time.'

Ellen said, 'But – the Matron said – I could come any time, my husband is Master Kane.'

The girl said, 'Visiting time isn't 'til half-two. There's the notice about it there.'

A man put his head round the door: 'Eily, he's gone in, so don't let anyone –': he stopped abruptly when he saw Ellen and retreated: the girl's face reddened, and grew furtive. Suspicion flooded Ellen: she charged at the double doors and ran down the corridor after the man, all her fearful tentativeness dissolved. At the door of Thomas's room she caught up with the hurrying little porter – and found Jacks, the photographer, actually in Thomas's room setting up his 'sticks' to take a photograph of her prone husband: he had even dragged the bed into the window to get the light.

She kicked Jacks so hard that he later went and complained to the police, who did nothing. Ellen rushed back to the hallway and shrieked at Michael Condon. 'COME ON!' she screamed. 'Come on. HELP ME!'

He blinked his brown eyes and clambered from the car. 'COME ON!'

She beckoned and beckoned, leaving him no choice but

to follow her down the corridor: the girl had vanished from the hall, and Thomas lay alone in the room.

'Under his shoulder.' She directed Michael to one side of the bed, as she whipped off the thin and grubby blanket. 'Under his shoulder,' she repeated, snapping. As Michael grasped Thomas's slack hand, Ellen took the other arm and lifted it: together they raised Thomas into an upright position.

'Jesus, Ma'am. This isn't the right thing at all.'

'Shut up, will you? Lift him. I can't do it by myself.' They hauled. Amiable Michael Condon abandoned his reluctance. Swivelling around slowly, they dragged Thomas's dead weight clear of the bed, and carefully, although they could not prevent some bumping, allowed his legs and feet to crash-flop to the floor.

'Get out of the way!' she shouted to a dumbfounded maid who had materialized from somewhere. 'Out! OUT!' The girl jumped back and then ran.

As they reached the main door, the Matron appeared. 'Where do you think you're taking my patient?'

Ellen spat at her, 'I'm taking MY husband home to clean him up.'

Two panting figures; and between them a sagging, night-gowned white spectre with the beginnings of his dirty beard, stale food traces messing his chin; and a hefty woman in white with her nurse's cap and its narrow blue band: 'Look at him?' Ellen roared at the Matron. 'Look at him.'

The woman tried reason. 'There isn't a lot we can do.'

'Look at the cut of him. Look!' Ellen simply could not stop shouting. 'He's FILTHY. That man was always SPOTLESS!'

'If you're discharging him you can't get him back in here.'

'I'll discharge you if I get my hands on you!' Ellen yelled. They manhandled Thomas into the passenger seat of the car.

'Take off your coat and put it round him. How do you

385

open the dickey seat?' asked Ellen, frantically. Months later she discovered that the hospital porter had been permitting people to view Thomas like a freak at a carnival: many of the Deanstown neighbours had sneaked in.

At the house, Nurse Cooper displayed no astonishment. They propped Thomas in an armchair in the parlour. Michael Condon dismantled the single bed in the spare bedroom, and they staggered it down the stairs.

When Thomas had been stretched on it, Nurse Cooper said, 'You need an invalid bed-chair, I have a spare one, I'll get somebody to bring it out.'

Ellen asked Michael Condon to put the car in the garage.

'There's still work to be done on it, Ma'am, I'm waiting on the bit of paint . . .'

'It'll wait, and thank you,' said Ellen. 'How much do I owe you?'

'Oh, Ma'am, nothing, I mean, I don't know yet.'

He left. Ellen did not close the door; instead she turned to Nurse Cooper, who said, 'He has to walk seven miles home.'

Ellen ignored the remark and said, 'I have to be on my own now.'

'But listen . . .'

Ellen said, 'I have to be. I have to be. I have to be.'

'I see. I see. Well, look. I have to call and see the Harpers anyway, the mad brother again. I'll just take a spin over there and when you're settled in, I'll drop in on the way back. Make yourself a cup of tea now; there's a good girl, you're after a shock, aren't you?'

'I have to be on my own,' repeated Ellen. 'I have to be on my own.'

'All right so, all right.' Sheila Cooper soothed, put on her coat and wheeled her bicycle out on the road. Ellen closed the gate and padlocked it.

On her return Nurse Cooper could get no reply, not even when she shouted from the road, nor could anyone else for the next three days: the postman took the letters back to the Post Office in Silverbridge and said, 'The Mistress must be in a terrible way; we'll hang on to them here, I suppose.'

Ellen made 'goody'. She took two thick slices of white bread, boiled a large cup of milk and let it cool a little; she broke the bread into larger chunks than the ones she and Thomas fed to the birds last winter, added the warm milk and a little sugar, pounded it all into a mess as soft as porridge – and sat by Thomas, raising his head with a pillow.

Silently, in an attitude composed of morbid curiosity and numbness, she spooned the warm soft mixture into his half-open mouth. Each spoonful sat somewhere in there, and then, each time with a suddenness, his throat muscles contracted. Sometimes the food threatened to lurch back up out of his mouth; most went down his throat. She repeated the procedure again at six o'clock, and a smaller amount at nine, and even tried to pour a little warm tea into his mouth.

During Helena's chores in between, Ellen normalized somewhat. After one last look at Thomas she blew out the candle, returned to the kitchen, tidied it, folded the cloth she had been repairing, lowered the sewing-machine into its recess, heaved the table-top back up into place, clicked the machine shut, and went to bed, checking Helena's sleeping face.

Next morning, when she awoke and lay still for a moment, a procession of implications began to march by, the first and most distasteful of which were later confirmed by the smell whose source she located and understood immediately she entered the parlour downstairs where Thomas lay.

22

My dear Leah,

This is going to be the worst letter I have ever written. I am beyond the Vale of Despair. I have no idea where to turn, what to do, what to say even when I talk to myself. At twenty-six years of age my life seems to be gone as bad as a life could be. Even, God forbid, if poor Thomas had died, I would have something definite. I can't sleep, I can't cope with the day, it gives me all I can do to feed Helena – who is a little dote it has to be said. And on top of all that I am frightened – until whoever did it is caught.

Leah, I don't know what to do, or where to turn. My prayers seem to have lost their power of consolation, although I'm sure that is only temporary, and that God will come back to me. But why has He sent me this awful Trial? And what am I going to live on? The Canon is coming in the next few days, and I know he's going to either tell me I can't have the house, and if I don't agree, he'll give me the sack, because he has to find a new Principal. I can't teach children any more in this frame of mind. Then where will I live? This house is owned by the parish, and neither the Bank nor the Post Office will allow me to draw Thomas's money. I have some that Dada gave me when Helena was born, but although it was very generous it won't last for ever.

The house is grey with sadness through and through. The nurse managed to get me a kind of bed-chair for Thomas with castors on it; it came this morning, and the parlour has now become Thomas's bedroom (so that I don't even have a good room for visitors any more, which is just as well because I don't want to see anyone).

So here I am, Leah, with this man I depended my life

on, stretched out like a grey ghost in a corner of the house, silent and damaged for ever. I get up at seven or so, change Helena and do something the same with Thomas, and feed them both before I have my breakfast, which I then can't eat because my stomach is still turning. I feel I've aged twenty years. And after breakfast there isn't anything to do, there isn't anybody to talk to.

Please think of me. Remember how we used to laugh – already I think of those days as if they were dreams I had a long time ago. And please don't tell the girls too much of this yet.

Your affectionate friend,
Ellen

Leah handed Herbert the letter when he came home at one o'clock. Before he touched his food, he read it, then put it to one side, and read it again.

'What's wrong, Mamma?' asked Rachel.

'Poor Uncle Thomas isn't very well,' said Leah.

'Is he going to die?'

'No, he's not.'

'Oh, good, then,' said Rachel, and looked puzzled at her mother's sad face.

Herbert paused while eating his food and re-read the letter. He took off his spectacles and polished them.

'I think I will go out there,' he said.

Ellen was trying to dig some of the potatoes Thomas had sown at Easter. Every such task anguished her. When she stuck the spade in the ground (not knowing she should have used a fork) she found that the potatoes got sliced across uglily. Nor did she know how to stake the pods of peas on their runners. She even had to learn how to wind Thomas's old alarm clock.

Fear intensified the hopeless learning of small essential tasks. The locking-bar of the shutters was too stiff for her to manage alone, and the shutters remained perilously unlocked at night. Every noise outside the house made her jump: even when going as far as their little lavatory beside the garage she carried Thomas's heavy blackthorn stick, with its silver band.

Throughout the day, she made raids on the outside, the garden, the garage: otherwise, she kept the front and back doors bolted, and only opened the upstairs windows wide. If she heard footsteps she shouted, 'Who's there?' often waking Helena and making her cry – but never even causing a flutter in the comatose Thomas. His long body, wrapped to the throat in a white Foxford blanket, lay semi-reclined, with only the occasional rattle of a slightly caught breath – each of which in the first two days caused Ellen to run and stay there watching for any increased sign of consciousness.

As Herbert rattled the gate, he saw another figure approach from the opposite direction, a lanky, bustling man.

Ellen, hearing more clearly when the noise of the bus engine had abated, shouted, 'Who's that?' and froze among the drills of the garden.

'Ellen, me! Herbert.'

'Who?'

'Herbert. Leah's Herbert.'

She walked cautiously around the corner of the house, her hands covered with clay, the blackthorn stick in her hand.

'Leah, I wish you had seen her,' said Herbert that evening. 'No washing of the hair. Skirt was torn a little, here, just at the waistband' – he indicated. 'The jumper she had, oh, all stains. The shoes . . . and neither stockings or socks . . .'

'And she who thought out every stitch,' said Leah.

=

The hedge obscured from Ellen's view the other arrival, and he reached them just as Ellen released the padlock on the gate.

'Mrs. Mrs!' he called.

'You can't see him, Mr Vousden,' said Ellen, retreating a little.

'I know that, Ma'am.'

'And did you ever see her being rude to anyone, ever?' Herbert asked Leah late that night, as they sat before bedtime.

'A bit brisk, maybe, rude not,' said Leah.

Ellen said to Val Vousden, 'Can you go away? Just clear off.'

Val said, 'I've come down from Dublin specially. How is he?'

'He won't see you or anyone else. He's –' Ellen hesitated. 'Now will you go?' She almost barked.

Val, taken aback, opened his mouth again, and Herbert said, 'Ah, hold on.'

He spoke softly to Ellen. 'Is it all right if I correspond with this gentleman, or speak to him later?' Ellen turned on her heel and walked towards the door.

'Mr Vousden, is it? My name is Herbert Winer and my wife is an old friend of Mrs Kane.' He lowered his voice. 'The thing is, there's been an accident.'

Val said, 'That was no accident. No accident. I just want to know how the man is.'

'I wonder – will you, would you, wait around the village or somewhere, and we'll meet at the evening's bus. The Castle up there is very interesting.'

Val said, 'No need, if there's anything I can do, tell her to tell Mr Kane, that I'm doing very well reviving the band.'

'Reviving the band?' repeated Herbert.

'He'll know,' said Val, then corrected; 'she'll know.'

=

Herbert, trying to pick his way in his light shoes to where Ellen had been digging, took the bucket and moved towards the house. Not since the pogrom in Janesborough had he seen a face so troubled: the memory convinced him of the rightness of the approach he had come to suggest. They reached the scullery together and Herbert put the bucket on the floor beside the table: dishes from several rounds of meals stood unwashed, but at least there was some evidence that a start had been made on them.

'I'll give you a hand with these,' said Herbert, and Ellen fetched a kettle of hot water from the range in the kitchen. Herbert took off his jacket and rolled up his sleeves. Neither said anything: she took each cup, saucer, plate, knife and spoon from him and dried it and stacked it for putting away. He wiped his hands, turned to her and said, 'Ellen, dear. Listen carefully to me. I came out specially to say something to you. Just one thing.'

Ellen stared at him; a fixed stare.

'Before I do that, I want to see Thomas, then I want to see Helena.'

'I can't let you see Thomas.' She bit the words off. Then she paused: 'Helena's due a bottle soon.'

Herbert said again, 'I want to see Thomas.' He said it very softly and Ellen began to tremble.

'You can't. I won't let you.'

Herbert stood, saying nothing, just looking steadily at Ellen, whose lip crumpled.

'Nonononono, don't touch me!' She stepped back as Herbert moved to take her hand. She began to cry like a child, standing there, one hand leaning on the table beside the basin of dirty soapy water. Herbert, not very much taller than Ellen, in his soft brown waistcoat, put his hand on her shoulder, and said nothing.

When she stepped back and could speak, she said, 'I'm so ashamed of how he looks. And you know how Thomas kept himself. I try to clean him, and there always seems to be a smell off him, and I can't comb his hair the way he used to, and now there's a smell in the room, so what will it be like when he's here another month – or a year.'

Herbert asked, 'Has anybody else seen him?'

'No,' said Ellen. 'They come and they try. They slow down on their way home from Mass, looking in as if we were animals or something.'

'Is that why the shutters are closed?'

'I'd never let them see him like that. And the feeding is so messy.'

'What about the nurse? Leah said she's very capable?'

'I'm not letting anyone in.'

Herbert said, 'Where is he, Ellen?'

Ellen took the key from the pocket of her skirt, and before turning it in the parlour door, listened at the foot of the stairs for Helena. Then, unlocking the door, she led Herbert into the dimness of the room.

Herbert said, 'Yes, I see what you mean about the smell,' a remark which seemed to give Ellen some relief.

'Can he hear us, do you know? Thomas, can you hear us?' Herbert asked.

Ellen said, 'Even if he can, there's nothing he can say or do.'

'What do you do when someone is like that?' asked Herbert, thinking aloud. 'Do you have a conversation about them or with them, do you include them or what?'

'Doctors always talk as if you're not there,' said Ellen.

'Can I roll that blanket down a little?' Herbert asked, and Ellen helped him, until Thomas's neck came into view, his Adam's apple protruding through the growing beard.

Herbert stood away and looked at Thomas very carefully. A knife-edge of light came through the joint of the shutters. Herbert then moved himself into a position for an even better observation, and asked Ellen to wheel the bed-chair back a little. 'The room is very dark. How do you move him?'

'I don't. He's too heavy for me to shift him much. I can lift an arm or a leg, that kind of thing.'

Herbert approached the moribund, slanting figure and looked very closely at Thomas's right temple, remarking in little 'h'ms' as he did so.

'May I see his hands?'

'They've gone terribly white and useless,' said Ellen, and she drew them up, limp chalk-white stalks, from far below within the blanket. Herbert examined each of Thomas's hands in turn, and then caressed each hand and gave it back to Ellen to tuck away.

Overhead, Helena woke and began to whimper.

Ellen shrugged hopelessly. 'See what I mean?'

'Leah says she's lovely,' said Herbert. 'Can I just stay in here a minute?'

Ellen went out. Herbert opened the shutters wide, flooding Thomas with sunlight, then opened the window's lower sash; the breeze rushed in like a friend. He drew up a chair. A foul smell came from Thomas's breath, and his mouth fell a little open, as foolishly as that of somebody asleep on the bus: white slime coated his teeth. Could this be the sleek, authoritative man whom Ellen had married?

Herbert had said to Leah, when he first met Thomas, that it took a little time to adjust to someone as young and girlish as Ellen marrying such a distinguished-looking figure – but that it obviously suggested something about Ellen that they had not yet realized. Herbert now reached out and touched Thomas's forehead: it felt normally cool, if a little clammy, not in any way feverish. Not that Herbert knew anything about such things, he felt Thomas's pulse, and found it not at all unusual in any way – Herbert felt his own pulse several times a day as if to verify, as Leah used to tease, that he was 'still here with us'.

'Thomas, my friend,' he said. 'Thomas, my friend –'
but he did not pursue.

He patted the blanket back around Thomas's throat
and smoothed Thomas's hair as he heard Ellen coming
downstairs muttering to the baby.

Herbert wheeled Thomas's bed-chair forward a little
towards the open window, and left the room, closing the
door behind him. He caught up with Ellen in the kitchen
and spoke many delights over Helena, taking her in his
arms while Ellen made a bottle.

As they sat there, with Ellen feeding Helena, Herbert
said, 'It must be like having a living corpse in the house
with you, and it must be most dreadful of all at night. I
opened the shutters and the window.'

Ellen's only respite came when dealing with Helena's
needs. Even if the despair had never shown a single sign of
lifting, it became fractionally more tolerable when feeding
Helena, and even daring to play with her a little while
washing or changing her – procedures in which she still
did not feel confident.

'That's what they were calling him in the hospital,' said
Ellen. 'That's why I brought him home. "The living
dead". They were treating him like something in a side-
show. The whole country knows about it.'

'It was all in the papers, of course. Hallo! Hall-low,
sweetheart!' cooed Herbert to Helena, who puffed her
cheeks placidly on the bottle. 'It remains a mystery.'

'Nobody around here ever talks,' said Ellen.

'And no idea who did it?' Herbert murmured.

Ellen glanced at him.

'I read your letter to Leah,' said Herbert; 'she showed
it to me. I suppose this is about the worst thing that you
could imagine happening to you.'

'Sometimes,' Leah complained, 'you have to strain forward to hear what Herbert says in that soft voice of his.'

'Unless to be tortured or something?' replied Ellen, 'but

395

I can't think of anything ordinary that could be worse. I can't look at a calendar in case I have to think of what next month will be like, or next year, or ten years from now.' She spoke in a dullness of which she was once incapable.

'No,' said Herbert, 'no, I suppose not. I see you! I see you!' he cooed again to Helena, who frowned round the shoulder of the bottle.

Herbert said in a most even voice, 'The night before the pogrom in 1903, Leah's mother's brother was walking home along the banks of the Shannon and three fellows caught him and threw him in. Maybe they only meant to give him a ducking, but they didn't know there were only two feet of water there, and beneath that, several feet of soft mud. He fell on his face and never appeared again, until they dragged his body out.'

'This would be Leah's uncle?' exclaimed Ellen. 'I never heard that!'

'Too painful, even now. The following day, when those boys were arrested, because in their fright one of them talked, the pogrom began in earnest.'

Herbert spoke without bitterness of any kind.

Ellen interjected again, 'I wonder does my father know about that?'

Herbert continued, 'Leah's mother blamed herself for it, said she should never have allowed Simon out alone. I was sitting with her the day of the funeral and she kept on blaming herself, over and over.'

'Blame?'

'Well, what I really mean is that she felt responsible, or that she felt she ought to feel some responsibility in the matter.'

Ellen put the bottle down and tilted Helena over her knee: the little face grew red and bulging, then drooled a little as she belched.

'That's what kills me, Herbert. That Thomas can't

see any of this, that he can't even help with the baby.'

'I said to her, "But why do you blame yourself, he went out all the time, he was a normal eighteen-year old?" And she said to me, "Unless I can give myself a part in it, I can never understand it." I'm still trying to work out what she meant.'

Ellen heard Herbert, looked away and did not look back at him for some time, busied herself with Helena, to whom Herbert also chatted.

'By the way,' said Herbert, 'a couple of things. I can show you how to shave Thomas; my uncle was an undertaker and I know how to shave an inert figure, I watched him. And Ellen – and Leah agrees with me – you'll have to make a list of your choices. That's what I really came to say to you.'

'I don't understand you fully,' said Ellen.

'We'll talk about it later.'

Val Vousden sat in Hand's public house and had a tall glass of red lemonade, and Mrs Hand made him a cheese sandwich and said, 'I declare to God,' when he asked her for mustard.

Dreadful it was, what happened to the Master, and what was the Mistress going to do at all, surely she was only a young one? At which Val remarked, 'She seems well able to look after herself.'

To which Mrs Hand replied, 'She'll have to be, for the Canon will have her out of that house like a shot.'

Val, fishing for information, asked, 'I suppose that's the very first motor-car "accident" around here?'

'It must be,' said Mrs Hand thoughtfully, re-tying the thin strings of her crossover apron. 'I never heard of another one anywhere in these parts. Although there was military lorries and cars, the Tans and that. That Nurse Cooper, her intended was killed in one,' she said.

=

As he saw the Curate off at the orchard's little door, the Canon said that he could not confirm whether he would call tomorrow to see the Mistress, or whether he would leave it until after he came back from his two weeks in Lahinch, and anyway there wasn't time to advertise before then for a new Teacher, and the sea air would clear his head, and besides, all the teachers would be on holidays themselves, and he wondered aloud whether he might meet somebody in Lahinch who might even know of a Principal looking for a job or who might move.

The Curate said, 'I'd love to do it for you, Canon, even while you're away, but 'tis a sensitive business, and it has to be done by yourself, you're the man with the authority to do it.'

The Canon knew he had a reputation in the Archdiocese for not getting on well with his curates, but God Almighty, how could you get on with a foxy man like that?

'Well, Father,' he said with some asperity to the departing man who bent to put on his bicycle clips, 'what'll we say to the Archbishop in four years' time when we have children who aren't nearly as good as this year's crowd were?'

The Curate straightened up. 'Sure, the point is, of course, Canon, we can't get a new Principal until we have a house for them to live in. I don't know when the Mistress can move out of there. I mean she can go on teaching, can't she, if she can manage, with a small child and that man the way he is, but she'd have to move into another house, wouldn't she?'

It suddenly occurred to the Canon to ask, 'Have you somebody in mind for the job, Father?'

'I haven't yet, Canon, but I'm sure if I thought hard . . .'

The Canon watched his Curate mount the bicycle.

'The thing is, Father, what sort of Christians are we that we're not out in force trying to find the man who did it?'

'Sure, how would we do that, Canon, sure, who has that kind of information? And anyway, sure who'd want any man hanged, I mean if the Master died?'

The Canon watched his Curate, whom he did not like at all, cycle away down the short winding avenue.

When Helena had been returned to her crib, Ellen and Herbert ate a light meal, and then, at Herbert's suggestion, sat outside on the seat in the sun. Initially, Ellen jibbed at this – the seat was right outside Thomas's window, but Herbert insisted. In an atmosphere between them of increasing intensity, and in hushed tones, even though there was nobody for at least a mile around to hear them, they talked for two hours, with Ellen arguing all the time, but eventually giving way on each of the points Herbert made in a series of upraised fingers.

At four o'clock, Herbert said, 'How long 'til the bus?'

She peered through the window at the clock. 'An hour and a quarter.'

He promptly rose from the seat, and went indoors, with Ellen following. At his request she filled a basin of water, the temperature of which Herbert tested with his elbow, and he asked her to fetch Thomas's favourite razor, the stick of shaving soap and the brush. 'And the scissors.'

By Thomas's side, Herbert drew up a chair, placed the basin and shaving things on it, and then with love and care tucked a towel under Thomas's chin. Outside, a horse and cart clip-clopped past the gate.

'Now watch me very closely,' said Herbert. 'And let me just tell you one thing.' Herbert, according to Leah, believed very firmly in fixing matters to one point: if he could find one mooring, he believed, one means by which to guide or judge the matter in hand, then any man could cope with anything.

'And the one thing is this – don't be afraid of the razor. The way to defeat it is to go right against it, to oppose the thought completely. If you were shaving the baby,' he asked, 'would you cut her?'

'Oh?' said Ellen. 'I never thought of that.'

'Exactly,' said Herbert.

He clipped the heaviest hair from Thomas's face and neck. This took ten minutes or so, after which he ran his hand all around the cheeks and jaws to feel the consistency of the remaining stubble. Herbert wrinkled his nose to keep his spectacles from slipping. Next, with a vigour that surprised Ellen, he began to lather Thomas's face. He showed Ellen how to pull Thomas's cheeks this way and that, how to begin by declaring a line under the ears, depending upon the length Thomas liked to grow his sideburns, and then how to sweep down the face to the chin, holding the open razor, as it were, backwards in the hand.

'The point is,' he said, a phrase over which Leah sometimes threatened to slaughter him, he used it so often, 'the point is, that Thomas himself would never go through a day without shaving, or would he?'

Ellen said, 'Under no circumstances. He hated not being shaved. I used to joke him about it. I used to threaten to tie his hands behind his back, as a torture, to stop him shaving.'

Herbert pressed down on Thomas's lip to flatten it into a plateau.

'The thing,' he breathed, 'we are never taught is, that caring is about making the other person feel the way they want to be, not the way that will make us feel nice and good. In Thomas's case, the way he himself would want to be, the dear man.'

Ellen said, 'No wonder Leah married you.'

Herbert towelled the side of Thomas's face he had shaved, and the chin and upper lip, then said to Ellen, 'Now you do the other side.'

She flinched.

'Go on,' he said, 'I'll guide you.' He showed her how

to make the lather begin to work by rubbing it very hard on the heel of her thumb.

'If it still doesn't work, pinch the brush when it's wet, pinch it right up all the way from there, where the bristles meet the handle right up to the top, and that will bring up all the existing soap.'

She began to lather the other side of Thomas's face. On the far side of the road Val Vousden sat on the wall opposite the gate, his legs dangling: Herbert could see him through the rustling net curtains.

'Harder, harder, don't be afraid,' Herbert said. 'Did you ever watch him lathering himself? I bet he didn't do it timidly.'

Ellen took the razor from the basin, and wiped the handle.

'Hold it out like that, in front of you,' Herbert said, 'let me see. Look, your hand is perfectly steady. Now, off you go.'

Ellen began, gingerly.

'The point is – not to scrape but to sweep, an even movement,' said Herbert. 'Let me see, oh, that's ideal. Yes, yes.' He praised her.

'My hand keeps wanting to shake,' she said.

'Remember. It's the baby's face you're shaving,' said Herbert, and watched how Ellen's concentration upon the task developed.

'It's a mixture of care,' said Herbert, 'care-ing and care-ful. Good, steady. That's it.'

Ellen's hand swept steadily down Thomas's jaw; she moved back and held her head at an angle to allow better light on his face, and soon she had shaved down to the neck. She towelled the remains of the soap away.

'Now, Thomas, let me tilt your head forward,' said Herbert. Suddenly, like a man with a brainwave, he said to Ellen, 'Have you a small looking-glass, you know, that you use yourself?'

'But he can't see, Herbert, and he can't hear you,' she said, her teeth gritting in frustration.

'No matter, no matter,' Herbert said, 'get it, will you? Please.' She went upstairs and fetched it.

'Now, I'll hold his head up straight and you hold the glass in front of him. Come round here to the side, so that you can see his face in the mirror. All right, Thomas? I'll just move your head a little.'

Thomas had given Ellen the hand-glass as one of many wedding gifts, along with a comb and a hairbrush of the same set: they were backed with green glass, inside of which had been fixed the piece of lace so fascinating to little Timmy Quinn. Ellen held the glass in front of Thomas's face, and could see his lifeless reflection.

'Now,' said Herbert, 'doesn't he look better? That's how he would see himself if he had just been the one doing the shaving. What d'you think of that, Thomas?' he called, as if to an elderly, slightly deaf relative.

'No, he doesn't look better. And he can't see himself. Herbert, what are you doing, this is so stupid!'

Ellen burst into tears and flung the mirror on the floor where it shattered, the handle breaking away from the cracking rear, the glass of the mirror spreading in slivers on the floor. 'Now look what you've done; Thomas gave me that. Oh, Jesus. Now I'm going to have seven years' bad luck!'

Herbert laid Thomas's head back.

'Ellen, you'll see what I mean,' he said, 'you'll see what I mean.'

She spun on her heel and walked from the room: Herbert followed her, deliberately leaving the door wide open, with Thomas framed in it.

On board *The Princess* bus, Herbert told Val Vousden the story of Ellen Morris and Thomas Kane, ending with the afternoon's scenes. Owing to the softness of his voice, Val had to ask this odd little man several times 'What was that?' and 'I'm sorry?' and 'I beg your pardon?'

In his turn, Val told Herbert of his correspondence with Thomas Kane, and the background to it, and the dialogue they had been having, and how Thomas had embraced the idea of reviving the Deanstown Band: 'And I'm going to revive it myself, so I am.'

At home with Leah and the girls, Herbert took off his shoes immediately he sat down.

'It's my tongue that's tired out. I can't remember a day when I talked so much.'

Leah gave the girls their supper and plied Herbert with questions. Typically he frustrated her with superficial and cursory answers, and then disappeared to his home work-room with a tray, saying he would speak to her later. He always did, of course, it was just that Leah found the waiting so unendurable.

When Helena was settled to sleep, the dreadful silence fell again on Ellen and the house. Her mind failed to function at these moments. Every position in which she chose to sit or stand felt so listless. The only difference this evening was that she actually managed to wash the dishes in the scullery, and she even put most of them away: yet, she could not bring herself to face the bucket of napkins outside the back door. The cats had not been fed for days, and came hopefully to the window from time to time. A year ago, 'in Thomas's day', as she had unwittingly begun to describe it, Ellen often perched on the end of the kitchen table, her legs swinging, while he sat in his chair, his body turned towards her, and they chatted until the twilight obscured the expressions on their faces from each other.

Remembering, she said aloud, 'Tired the sun with talking. And sent him down the sky.'

And then, after a quick turn in the warm night air, to bed together, to fall asleep eventually, in silent exhaustion: 'the merry newlyweds' Thomas called themselves: next morning, as she washed at the basin and ewer, he would tangle her hair gently and say, 'And how are the merry newlyweds this morning?'

Now he lay, a grey, mansize slug, in there, across the hallway, and his pretty baby daughter, growing plump, asleep upstairs. The light had not yet gone, no need yet for the lamp: what in the name of God was she going to do in the winter? She slid the knives and spoons away in the ordinary cutlery drawer, and then searched in the other drawer for the carving-set box. As she drew it out, the box's catches caught in a ball of string which fell, unravelling, to the floor. Ellen bent to pick it up and she wound it back into its shape again. Thomas's meticulousnesses could still be seen all around the house – string, and paper, and small empty tins into which he put his nails in the garage, and the polishes for his shoes every night, and his regular oiling of the locks and window-catches.

She replaced the rewound string in the drawer, and went to the kitchen door to look across the hall. A breeze had blown the door slightly to, but she could see the blanket where it wrapped around Thomas's feet. On the wall, just at her shoulder, hung her favourite Thomas joke – his certificate from Primary School declaring him qualified at the age of seven in 'Reading, Writing and Ballframe': on the day Thomas showed it to her, she asked him for it, and then she had it framed, because she always wanted to imagine the little boy of seven, with curly hair, long before this dreadful life had come out of the fissures of the earth and foully breathed fire on him. Thomas gave her the certificate, but accused her of sentimentality. On the sewing-machine table-top stood the bag of fruit Herbert had brought, which she had not opened.

Ellen stood for a long time in thought, her eyes red

and sore from crying. She could see her reflection in the window, in outline only, not in detail, but knew that her hair seemed stringy and greasy: in the clothes she wore she could not trace her figure with any clarity, no matter how she turned.

She spoke aloud.

'I promised Herbert.' She turned back and went to the far corner of the kitchen, poked about in the bureau, found her blue tortoiseshell fountain pen, took her ledger from the drawer beneath the bureau's flap, dragged herself to the sewing-machine table-top, moved the fruit to the seat of the chair Thomas used to sit in, and sat at the table-top to write. The ledger hadn't been opened for over two months: the first thing Ellen saw was Mrs Dalton's recipe for lemon tartlets, entered before she went into the nursing home to have Helena.

Ellen spoke aloud again, fiercely: 'No, I am not crying again, I am not, I am not, I am not.' She shook her pen on her blotting-paper, verified that it contained ink, and began to write.

More or less simultaneously, Leah finished reading to the children, and Herbert emerged to sit in the living-room. A pigeon landed in the tiny yard outside. Leah had a handful of socks and things, which she left on the living-room table.

'I don't even know where to begin,' said Herbert, 'my jaw is still tired.'

Ellen, thirty-six miles away, wrote on an unlined piece of paper, using the lines of the ledger as a guide, 'I promised Herbert that I would make a list of my choices.' She stopped, sucked the end of her pen, folded the sheet of paper, tore it in four, and in the ledger, on the fresh page opposite the lemon tartlets, wrote, 'My Choices'.

Outside, on the road, unseen by her, a heavy man

stopped his bicycle, and holding it stationary by touching the road with the toe of his boot, looked in for a moment, then cranked up the bicycle again and rode off.

'So I said to her,' continued Herbert, 'was there one thing she did every day, rain or shine, when Thomas was, you know, in the whole of his health? When things were normal?'

Leah leaned forward, not missing a word, eyes as glittering as a bird's.

'Anything, no matter how trivial, but anything that was part of their life together, you know, like polishing shoes, or always putting a certain dish away in a certain way, or making a cup of tea at a certain time; this is something for herself, I meant, not something she used to do for the two of them, and that she should go back to doing that, to see if she could get herself started up in some sort of pattern. You see, this is the point. She has no pattern yet that has not been imposed on her by these terrible circumstances, and it's, what, getting on for between two and three months since the baby was born, do you know what I mean?'

'Yes, yes,' said Leah, 'go on, go on. What did she say?'

'Oh, yes, well,' said Herbert, 'actually it was very good, she said she had a housekeeping book that she put hints in, and recipes, and that, and I said, ideal. Ideal.'

'She has,' said Leah, 'her ledger. I know it.'

'And I made her promise me, because she has to promise somebody, that she'd do it, and if she promises I think she will.'

'Oh, yes, Ellen will,' said Leah. 'That's the religion in her.'

'And I put it to her that she now should use the book to write down, like she was making a plan or something, to write down what kind of life she could now make for herself, because she has to make some kind of life. She has to choose, to make some kind of choices. I mean, will she keep him there, will she stay out in that place, what? They're the choices she has to make, Leah.'

'She has,' said Leah. 'She has.'

'Well, the second thing we talked about was, that she must get Thomas turned every day, and that was very interesting,' said Herbert. 'You see the house is dirty already.'

'Oh, no?' Leah interrupted, consternation beginning.

'And untidy, and there is no nurse coming in because she had a row with her, and with the hospital, and she has also forbidden the doctor to call.'

'But that house was like a new pin?!'

'And if Thomas gets sores, and she has to call somebody in, she will be judged unfit to look after him, and maybe even unfit to care for the baby.'

'I hope you didn't say any of this, Herbert?'

'I did, I said it all.'

'You shouldn't have.'

'I should've, if we're her friends.'

'No!'

'Yes, Leah.'

'But what did she say?'

'She looked desperate, and then she told me about the house. It isn't theirs, it is the official house of the Principal Teacher, but only insofar as whosoever that may be.'

Leah put her hands over her face.

Herbert said, 'So I asked her to promise me, for Thomas's sake – that she would ask the one person she really trusted in the whole place, provided they lived any way near her, to come in and turn Thomas every day with her. She resisted that too, like she resisted everything, but eventually she said she doubted there was anybody, so I told her to find somebody. Anybody.'

=

While Herbert told Leah of his day, Ellen wrote under *My Choices*: 'I have the following choices as to what to do with my life and this predicament.' Then she stopped.

Herbert did not tell Leah the full story. He left out several of the details – such as the fact that he refused to help Ellen with what might be a course of action she could choose to make matters easier – to get Thomas into a home or a mental hospital; or that he did not minimize the greatness of the threat to her dwelling-place when the Canon eventually called. Nor did he tell Leah that against Ellen's will, he held Ellen's hand firmly in his, and told her that she had to begin pulling things together, not pulling away – as she tried to do now with her hand from his; that no matter how harsh that might be, she had to begin accepting help. Nor did he tell Leah that Ellen should find where she was to blame in the entire matter, and how he chose not to use the word 'responsibility', and even said to Ellen, 'You will understand the word "blame" from your religion. After all, you worship in a faith which is based on blame. Jesus's fame came out of the dreadful punishment of crucifixion. Therefore, you have to purge your "blame".'

He did say to Leah, 'She looked a little, what? – deranged from time to time.'

'Patchwork,' said Leah suddenly, 'she has to make something, something like patchwork, so that she can see it and others can see it, and admire it.'

Herbert said, 'I tried to persuade her to ask her mother to come and stay.'

'No,' said Leah, 'no, she won't do that, not at all.'

Lying in bed, with Leah's arms around him, her face between his shoulder-blades, Herbert asked, 'Did I do all right, Leah? Did I do the right things?'

'Oh God, I hope so, Herbert.'

Ellen wrote one letter, just a note; she had promised

Herbert and she could not renege. She did not write another word, and, despite her best intentions, cried herself to sleep again. In the morning she awoke to another day when even the summer sunlight shone grey on her face.

23

Mrs Greege arrived two days after the postman handed her Ellen's note. Ellen, upstairs, putting Helena down after her morning bath, heard the catch of the gate clicking and looked out of the window. Then, consciously for the first time in weeks, she checked her appearance in the dressing-table mirrors. Dreadful – and too late. Panicky, Ellen stood back on the landing, hands in consternation to her jaws, then had to run downstairs in case Mrs Greege's calling disturbed the drowsing Helena.

She unlocked the gate. 'Come in,' she said, and held the door open, directing Mrs Greege to the kitchen.

'She is a bitch,' Thomas said, 'and she always will be a bitch,' as he reversed the paper on the parcel of wedding-gift linen Mrs Greege had sent them, and posted it back to her. When Ellen wondered if this might not be a little extreme, he reminded her of Mrs Greege's behaviour. Now, here, the woman stood in Ellen's own kitchen, waiting as Ellen closed the front door.

'Will you sit down?' Ellen asked. The woman looked, wiped a chair with her hand, sat down, put her tall, brown handbag on the table, clearing a space for it by pushing it forward, and stared all around.

'You were a deal cleaner and tidier when you were with me.' She looked at Ellen. 'No fine clothes today, huh? What happened to all the underwear?'

Ellen said slowly, 'No, that's true enough.'

'You look a hundred,' said Mrs Greege, wading straight in. 'I thought you had better stuff than that in you. Although I never liked you.'

Ellen sat down, tentative in her own kitchen. 'No,' she said again.

'Where is he?' said Mrs Greege. 'They're all saying the hospital wasn't good enough for him, that you were too posh, too big in yourself.'

Ellen moved a breakfast plate out of the way, spilling the crumbs from it.

'There's not a lot of people sorry for the two of you,' said Mrs Greege. 'Notions, the two of you had, going up the aisle there of a Sunday morning, Lord and Lady Muck.'

Ellen, white-faced and bleary, ran the back of a hand across her forehead. This morning, she had not had even enough energy to attend yet to Thomas.

'And the two of you thought you were so popular.' Mrs Greege stared at Ellen, and gave the impression of some relish. After a slab of silence she said, 'You wrote me a note?'

'It doesn't matter,' said Ellen.

'You mean I wasted my time coming down here.'

Ellen shook her head and lowered her gaze. 'No, it doesn't matter.'

Mrs Greege reached for her handbag. Instead of preparing to leave, she opened it and took Ellen's note from it.

'There it is,' she said, 'the note you wrote me. It says here, "Please will you call to see me? I need your help. Yours faithfully, Ellen Kane." And in your writing.'

'I know I wrote it, but it doesn't matter now.'

'And I have that sort of time to waste?' asked Mrs Greege, in what Ellen used to describe as 'her whipping rhetoric'.

'No.' Ellen shook her head. Mrs Greege studied her, looked around the kitchen again, then back at Ellen, who raised her eyes and said, 'I didn't mean to waste your time. I apologize. 'Tis just that –'

411

'Just that what? That Lady Muck can command the parish?'

Ellen shook her head.

Mrs Greege said, 'My wedding present wasn't good enough for you. That mouth of a postman told everybody it was thrown back in my face. How did he know that unless the Master or yourself told him?'

'Oh, no,' said Ellen, 'I would never do such a thing,' and realized that Thomas felt so strongly about Mrs Greege anything could have been said. 'Nor would I approve of it.'

'Well, it happened,' said the widow, thin ring solitary on her long hand. 'We're decent people, and you used the biggest mouth in the parish to make a laughing-stock of us.' Another silence fell. Neither woman looked at the other.

Ellen said, 'I'll pay you.'

Mrs Greege looked at her.

'I always knew there was malice in you,' she said.

'There isn't, there isn't.'

Mrs Greege broke the silence by asking, 'What help was it you wanted, anyway?'

Ellen said, 'No, it doesn't matter.'

'You owe me for my wasted time to tell me.'

Ellen, her head down, said slowly, and barely audibly, 'A friend told me that my husband would get very ill from bedsores if he wasn't turned every day. I can't do it myself, he's too heavy, and I'd hurt myself. If he goes wrong on me, and anyone gets to hear of it, the authorities might call, the Cruelty Man or someone, I might be judged unfit to look after my husband, or to look after the baby. I'm ashamed to let anyone see my husband in the state he's in now. This friend asked me was there anyone at all I trusted completely hereabouts. That's why I wrote to you. That's all there's to it.'

Had Ellen not forgotten – again – to bring the alarm clock downstairs to its habitual daytime place on the bookcase ledge, its ticking would have dominated the silence in the kitchen. Mrs Greege, resting her elbow on the table, arranged all the fingers of one hand vertically over her mouth: the fingernails touched the grey nostril hairs of which Thomas and Ellen once joked.

The woman stood up, straight as a rifle.

'I'll be back in an hour in my overalls,' she said, 'provided you wash yourself, and provided this place starts getting cleaned. I'm not having anything to do with a house this dirty. You shouldn't be bringing up a child like this. Lady Muck is right.' Pleased with her little joke she let herself out.

She returned in exactly an hour, dressed as she did when working in her own kitchen. Hanging her coat in the hallway – Ellen, for once, had not closed the front door – she confronted Ellen, who was still washing her hair in a basin on the scullery table.

'Where is he?' and then said, 'No, I'll go by myself.'

Minutes later, when Ellen, her hair piling in a towel, entered the room where Thomas lay, the curtains blew in the breeze from the open windows. Mrs Greege, having cleared away into a pile the towels and other clothing strewn on chairs in the room, was opening the blanket down to Thomas's waist, and preparing to prop him up.

'Are you all right now there, Master Kane?'

'He can't hear you,' said Ellen, who had a look of dismay on her face.

'How do you know?' The woman seemed a little less harsh than when she first sat in the kitchen.

'The doctors . . .' Ellen stopped.

'I've no time much for doctors. Is there water on the boil?'

'No.'

'Is the fire on?'

'No.'

'Have you anyone coming in to help you here?'

'No.'

'I hear you had a fight with Dr Hogan.'

'He came to the gate and complained to me for taking Thomas out of the hospital.'

'I hear you threw a stone at him.' Ellen didn't answer.

Mrs Greege looked down at Thomas, then sucked her lip and said, 'I'll be back in a minute, Master Kane,' in a normal tone, not shouting, not slow-speaking-to-the-hard-of-hearing.

'Have you clean towels?'

'I don't know.'

'Did you do a wash yesterday?'

'No.'

'Did your mother come out to give you a hand?'

'No. I wouldn't let her.' Then Ellen, looking at Thomas, and the dried, unpleasant saliva at the corners of his lips, said, 'That's what my friend did, my friend's husband, I should say. Herbert. He talked to my husband. To the Master.'

'My husband. The Master,' Mrs Greege mimicked. 'Call him his name, can't you? And why wouldn't anyone talk to him? Isn't he alive?' said Mrs Greege, crossing the hallway to the kitchen. 'Now. Where's your turf, and where is your kindling? Do you know how to light a fire?'

'I've only seen the Master do it.'

Mrs Greege showed her how: her method was identical to that of Thomas's, tepees of sticks and coal.

'What water do you use for washing?'

'From the tank in the yard.'

'Have you rain-barrels?'

'We have. Four': one at each corner of the house, only half-full in summer.

414

'They're enough,' insisted Mrs Greege, who made Ellen fill the two large black kettles out of the nearest barrel, and set them to boil on the range.

'What do you do your washing in?'

Ellen lugged out the large and the smaller zinc baths from under the scullery mangle-table. Both had been filled with soiled clothes, mostly Helena's.

'How long is it since you did a wash in the name of Jesus Himself?' asked Mrs Greege.

Ellen started to cry, and Mrs Greege said with hissing viciousness, 'If you start that, I'm walking out the door this minute. Do you hear me? Sort them clothes into four piles – your own, the baby's and the Master's and the linen for the house. I'll get the others from the room,' and she returned piled to her chin with all the clothes discarded near Thomas's bed-chair.

'It'll be an hour before them kettles are boiled. Go and put clean clothes on yourself, and open every window in the house except the baby's room. And bring down all the dirty bedclothes.'

When Ellen returned, Mrs Greege had folded all the towels and any sheets she found, and said, 'We'll send these into the nuns' laundry. Now, tidy the kitchen to the state it'd be in if the Master was coming in for his dinner.' For the next hour she bossed Ellen, made her dust with both duster and goosewing, saw to it that every piece of crockery and cutlery was washed again and returned to its normal habitat. Mrs Greege then filled a bucket from one of the kettles and set to scrubbing the floor: 'And I'll make a better job of it than you made of mine. Now, refill that kettle. No, don't take it off,' she barked. 'Use the can or the bucket,' as if to a slow-learning child.

The kitchen began to look clean and fresh: the bow-window sashes were raised as high and open as they could be; the table was pushed back against the wall and the chairs tucked beneath it, and the top of the range gleamed;

a through draught blew its pleasant breeze from the window to the open back door.

Mrs Greege fetched two basins which she made Ellen fill from one of the boiling kettles.

'When we've finished this job, you can go and get a few flowers from the garden and put them there on the sewing-machine,' said tall, bony, sour Mrs Greege over her shoulder as, followed by Ellen, she marched into Thomas's room, 'and then we'll start on this place.'

She put the basin on the floor. 'Now, Master Kane. We're going to give you a good wash, and we're going to turn you.' Her voice was more relaxed than the tones she used with Ellen, to whom she said, 'You take the far side.' Ellen went around the back of the bed-chair.

'Now, we're going to let the back down, Master Kane,' Mrs Greege said, and to Ellen, 'the least you might do is talk to your husband.'

'Hallo, Thomas,' said Ellen, uncertain and wan.

'Ask him how he is, can't you?'

'How are you, Thomas?' said Ellen feebly.

They lowered the bed-chair into the recumbent, flat position. Mrs Greege pulled down the rest of the blanket covering Thomas, exposing the large towel Ellen had clumsily fastened on him as a napkin.

'What's this?' asked Mrs Greege, who removed without fuss or comment the filthy, noisome towel from around Thomas's groin: his thighs were covered with urine stains.

'You poor man, Master Kane, they must be stinging you,' said Mrs Greege conversationally. 'Your backside must be in an awful mess.'

Ellen, although she winced, ventured a question at Mrs Greege's deftness: 'How do you know so much?'

'I had a bedridden father and I had a bedridden husband. Aren't you the lucky woman to have me.'

It took an hour and a half, and three changes of water, to wash Thomas. They washed his hair and his genitals and his back and buttocks and feet, and almost lovingly Mrs Greege dried him, and beginning-to-be-lovingly Ellen dried him too. She did score one victory: Mrs Greege acknowledged the skill with which Ellen shaved Thomas: 'I never learned how to do that properly,' she said.

When he lay there, naked and white, and no longer, it seemed to Ellen, as grey as he had been, and cleaner than at any time since his incapacitation, Mrs Greege said, 'What clothes will we put on him? We'll have to put on a good towel until we get something better, and you're going to have to watch what food you put in his mouth on account of the other end.'

Ellen, weary, said, 'Clothes?'

'Of course clothes. Wouldn't he wear clothes if he was all right?' Her waspishness to Ellen scarcely varied. 'Get him a shirt, a pair of trousers, socks and slippers and a pullover': and they dressed Thomas.

'He looks like he's only asleep,' said Ellen.

'Tell him that,' said Mrs Greege, and left the room with her redundant basin held at her hip.

Ellen stood in front of Thomas, gazing down at him where he lay, his eyes closed, his mouth open a fraction, his breathing sound and regular. She had chosen his favourite blue wool shirt, and a navy pullover and cor- duroy trousers.

'Thomas, love, you look like you're only asleep.' Ellen bent and kissed his forehead, something she had not done since he came home. Mrs Greege, about to return, saw her from across the hallway – but moved aside out of Ellen's line of sight.

Mrs Greege's only signs of a capacity to thaw came when Helena was brought downstairs. She held the child, and cuddled her, and told her what 'a grand little bantam she was', and even murmured a half-compliment to Ellen for the manner in which Helena seemed to thrive. Other- wise, for the rest of the day, washing and hanging out clothes, and scrubbing the kitchen table, and then, in a slow tortuous way, changing the manner in which Ellen fed Thomas, she behaved in her usual curt and acid fashion.

She left at six o'clock, promising to return next day at nine, leaving Ellen exhausted in her wake, but for the first time in weeks not tearful at the end of the day. With Mrs Greege, Ellen had changed Thomas again into pyjamas, and a fresh towel-napkin for the night, and fed him spoons of warm milk with rusks melted in them. She went to bed directly after she had settled Helena down at half-past eight, and slept until Helena woke her at six.

Next morning, as Mrs Greege fastened the buttons on Thomas's shirt, she exclaimed, 'Ah, good, she's here.'

Ellen working on the other side of Thomas looked out of the open window and saw, wheeling her bicycle through the gate, Nurse Cooper in full white uniform under a blue coat.

'What?' asked Ellen.

'I sent Liam in with a note. We need an expert.'

Nurse Cooper came in and shook Ellen's hand rather formally. When Mrs Greege left at one o'clock in the afternoon, again promising to return the following day, Nurse Cooper, standing in the kitchen, put her arms awkwardly around Ellen and gave her a hug.

Ellen said, 'I'm sorry I wouldn't let you in.' From behind the curtains of the top window she had watched Sheila Cooper on five occasions try to find some means of getting past the padlocked gate; had not even opened Sheila's letters.

Now Ellen began to talk: she did not weep, she did not become hysterical.

'I realize now what has happened, that my life has been destroyed. The thing I can't manage at all is not so much the physical caring, in fact that's probably good for me in some queer sort of way.' Nurse Cooper nodded.

'The thing I can't manage is – is –' Nurse Cooper waited.

'Is the fact that none of my feelings have changed for him, that when I look at him like that, I feel exactly the same as if he was, as if he was – sitting here talking, or, if he was getting up in the morning in the room, or winding the clock as he walked up the stairs last thing at night . . .' She paused. 'In fact, if anything, I have stronger feelings for him now. Fonder of him.'

For the rest of the day, on and off, Nurse Cooper listened as Ellen talked, and told the whole story of her marriage to Thomas. Of her fears, of her hopes. Of how she had never really liked, or met seriously, any other man. 'We were always quiet at home. Mama is so bossy, Dada is so quiet, we never met anyone except our cousins.'

Of how when she first knew she felt something for Thomas; 'I got very confused, it was all lovely and it was rosy and like the magazines and books say, and yet what I liked about him was not that. 'Twas that he made me think.'

Of how when they first got married, 'I didn't know that – I didn't know, I didn't know – what marriage was like, it wasn't at all like our religion says it is. That Thomas's respect for me didn't cut across his fondness for me, or the excitement we, the excitement, I, him and me, what we felt together, I mean we didn't talk about it, except a little, but we both knew that this was lovely, and that we had such freedom, I mean, there was no having to go to Confession, or anything. I could go to Communion every Sunday, even in spite of all the – of all the, all the excitement. The being married.'

Of how Thomas's anger with others worried her. 'And I got this idea, and it grew all over me, like weeds growing inside in my head, that any children we had, especially if they were boys, that they would be violent too, and that

419

the whole thing would never stop . . . And then a priest friend of mine, he told me that once I was expecting, that Thomas and I should, that we shouldn't, that we should have no more, that we –'

Sheila Cooper cut in: 'I have a friend, they've six children, and when they had their third – she always has them with me – her husband never again talked to her during the whole nine months she was expecting, and I said to her, why, and she said she didn't know, and I knew she wasn't telling me the truth, and then eventually it came out, that on account of her condition the priest told her in Confessions she had to have no more to do with him until the baby was born.'

Ellen agreed. 'That was the same as us. I don't mean the not talking, but the rule, although I heard the opposite in Confession, from the Canon, of all people.'

Sheila Cooper said, 'Jeremiah has a mind of his own. D'you know who his closest friend is? Father Ferris, d'you know who I mean, he's always giving out about the Church, they call his sermons "Feresies", he's about ninety.' They laughed.

Ellen continued. She traced the weeks before Helena was born, their lovely peace together, the way Thomas had been about the baby.

'I remember saying it would be grand if she was born on the first of May, and he had a bit of poetry, he always had a bit of poetry –'

'– Always *has* a bit of poetry,' corrected Sheila Cooper.

Ellen continued, 'And he recited it, "May Day, delightful day". And then when she was born, not on May Day itself, that few hours after, as you know, he said to me inside in your nursing home, "Sure aren't women always late for everything?" D'you know why she's called "Sorcha"? Because he had a little sister who died, she was called "Sorcha"; as you know, that's the Irish for "Sarah", and the first time he ever talked about it, he told me, talked about it to anyone, was just before the baby was born.'

Ellen's spate of talking ended when she told how she could face nobody, had not been to Mass since she finally came home from the nursing home with Helena, and had generally deteriorated into the condition in which Mrs Greege had found her.

At half-past five, Nurse Cooper said, 'We'll have one last cup of tea before you have to feed Helena, and then I have to go. Now, these things I brought with me –' she had a small parcel of nursing equipment, including incontinence materials – 'I'm sending another parcel out to you, you'll have to pay for them I'm afraid, but I'll get them for you at cost, at the wholesale price. Now Mrs Greege is coming in every day for the time being, and I'll call out every second day for a while, and I think you should mend your fences with Dr Hogan, don't you? Jesus, Mary and Joseph, that daft wife of his.' Sheila Cooper would always make Ellen smile. 'And if you want to write a quick note to your mother I'll post it for you at the Post Office, it will go more quickly.'

Shrugging on her coat, she said, almost slyly, 'You're a remarkable girl, you know. Don't ever let anyone gainsay you that.'

In those first two weeks of August, through a combination of hard practical assistance and new emotional support, the worst rampart of Ellen's crux was thereby broken through. By talking to Nurse Cooper, she managed to regain some purchase on her life.

'Look, you might as well know,' said Sheila, 'you have a very hard time ahead of you.'

By now, they had all helped to conquer Ellen's main fear – that through lack of care for Thomas she might be judged unfit even to look after him or Helena.

Her next great anxieties, the house and the school, showed no signs of being resolved. At Nurse Cooper's prompting, she wrote to the Canon, and received a reply from the housekeeper to the effect that the Canon was on his holidays in Lahinch for a fortnight.

'Then write to the Curate,' said Nurse Cooper impatiently.

The Curate wrote back saying it was the Canon's business, and could only be dealt with when the Canon returned.

'But the school is supposed to open in three and a half weeks,' wailed Ellen.

On one of the mornings, Nurse Cooper arrived, not red-faced and glistening on her bicycle, but unfurling from Dr Hogan's car. He followed her up the pathway to the front door, and came in, not unsheepishly, his stethoscope hanging from his pocket. Ellen greeted him.

'I owe you an apology,' she said.

'Ach, what apology. Not at all. Not at all. Sure you missed, your aim is bad. And 'twasn't a big stone anyway,' and Ellen smiled a little, not just at his warm response but at the fact that he was wearing the virulent bow tie Thomas especially despised.

'It would be no harm,' said Nurse Cooper, 'if he had a look at all three of you.'

'She's not the worst,' said Dr Hogan, grinning at Nurse Cooper.

'No, then, she's not,' agreed Ellen.

Helena lay in a crib on the table, kicking her heels in the morning air. Doctor and nurse together tapped the child, looked in her eyes, listened to her little chest, looked in her ears and at her fingernails and whispered to each other, while Ellen stood at a distance, watching them, but not hearing what they said to each other, which made her nervous.

'Right, so,' said Dr Hogan as Nurse Cooper replaced

Helena. 'Well, you have her in grand fettle. She's like a thoroughbred, she's stall-fed. D'you see, if she was anyone else's child, I'd be remarking on how well they were looking after her, but in your case, all credit to you, under all the circumstances. She said –' he indicated Nurse Cooper – 'that you were a good bit of stuff.' He approached Ellen, and held out a chair. 'We'll have to look at yourself, now.'

She sat down, and took off her blouse, and he checked her breathing, her pulse, the eyes, the ears. He asked her questions about sleeping and eating, whether her body had returned to 'its monthly normal'?

She dressed again, and he sat in front of her, eyeing her carefully, and said, 'I'd say you were on your way to a good recovery. You had bad shock. And shock is a fright altogether, a fright to recover from. That's an awful time you're after being through, I've nearly not seen as bad in the war. We'll be keeping an eye on you, though.'

Then he asked to 'have a look at the man himself'. They stood beside the reclining bed, and Nurse Cooper joined them.

'Haven't you him grand?' exclaimed the doctor. 'Good God above! And you say you're only after starting to do this properly. A hospital wouldn't do him better. A nursing home would, of course,' he said to Nurse Cooper with alacrity. 'Good morning, Master Kane,' he said. 'How are you this morning?'

Ellen made no remark, accustomed now to Mrs Greege and Nurse Cooper addressing Thomas all the time. Dr Hogan examined first the location of the crucial wound. He pushed the hair aside and looked very carefully at the temple, trying to get the maximum light to bear on it by turning Thomas's inert head a little.

'Dth. Is there ever any bleeding from this?'

Ellen acknowledged that once or twice a little blood had appeared on the towel, but she put it down to her own clumsiness in washing Thomas's hair too vigorously, and perhaps rubbing the healing wound.

'No. For some reason,' Dr Hogan spoke musingly, 'that's taking a long time to heal fully, like there's something stopping it at the core.'

Nurse Cooper bent to look at it.

'If you have an antimacassar at all,' said Jack Hogan, 'put it there behind his head; it'll stop him from going bald where the head is rubbing on the pillow.'

He stood back. 'I want you to do something for me,' he said. 'I want you to start an observation pattern. Will you do that?'

Ellen asked what he meant.

'I want you to watch him, to sit here and watch his face, for long-ish stretches of time. Bring the baby in and let her kick there on the rug, or if you're having a cup of tea. Just sit here for not less than ten minutes at a time, to begin with, and then up to a quarter of an hour, then twenty minutes, and bring a notebook with you, and if you see any change of any kind at all, write it down.'

'What kind of change?'

'Anything. If he suddenly jerks his breathing, or if an eyelid even moves. I don't even know what I mean myself – yet. But write down the time it happens at.'

He began a long examination of Thomas, and said, unable to avoid a hint of despondency, 'He's as strong as an ox.'

As he took his leave, promising to call back and collect Nurse Cooper around five, he said to Ellen, 'I've another favour to ask you. A harder thing altogether. Do you think you could manage it?'

Ellen replied with the first ever hint – and it was only a small and distant vapour – of her former amused asperity: 'I can't know until I know, can I?'

'I'll tell you what it is. Poor Ernestina Stephenson up there is in a bad way. Lot of pain. But like yourself she's a great battler. Any chance you'd call up and say hallo to her some day Nurse Cooper is here to let you free?'

'I'll see,' said Ellen.

'Did he not say anything else to you?' asked Nurse Cooper.

'No. What else?'

'Well, something good. A bunch of them is putting pressure on the Canon over your case. Time the men around here got off their backsides and stood up to the priests.'

She did not add that so far they had run into a stone wall, and that the Canon and Curate were both saying Ellen was going to have to vacate the house to make way for an incoming Principal.

Although Ellen strengthened every day, her mood still dipped terribly every evening when she found herself alone. On four separate occasions she returned to her ledger, faithfully attempting to carry out Herbert's request. Nothing flowed from her pen, no list of choices, no plans, no hopes.

Her father arrived unexpectedly on the bus, carrying a big cardboard box full of meat and fruit which the conductor unloaded for him. Ellen, overjoyed to see him, also found herself flipping back to the awful greyness of those early days, when she had Thomas at home to herself and she did not know the first thing as to how she should nurse him. Five minutes after her father arrived, she went upstairs saying she wanted to change into something cleaner, but in reality seeking a moment in which to recompose herself.

Bob, to her surprise, got on immediately well with Mrs Greege, and when Ellen came back down the two were deep in conversation. He turned to give Ellen his attention.

'Can I see – himself?' he asked.

'Yes,' said Ellen.

'Thomas, Dada is here to see you,' and she arranged a lapel of Thomas's collar. She had taken to folding his hands in his lap, and even though his head lolled sideways, Thomas still seemed like somebody sleeping.

'He looks – fine,' said Bob.

'No, he doesn't, he looks grey, and older than he is – but he doesn't look dead,' said Ellen emphatically. 'Now Thomas, we'll be back later. All right? We're just going to sit on the seat outside and have a chat,' and they left the room.

'Can he actually hear you?' asked Bob.

'No,' she replied curtly.

'Do you know,' asked Ellen one day, 'the history of my relationship with Mrs Greege?'

'I got a fair idea from her,' said Nurse Cooper. 'That's one of the reasons I told you you were a remarkable girl.'

At long last, a note came from the Canon, but not with the crucial news Ellen desired: instead, he enclosed a letter of permission from the Department to postpone the opening of the school for a minimum of two weeks.

Next day, Sheila Cooper said, 'Mrs Greege has a surprise for you tomorrow.'

In this, the third week of August, the temperature climbed.

Mrs Greege, when imparting something of importance, always spoke over her shoulder, as she did now: 'There's a girl in Kilkenny, a lay sister in the Mercy Convent. She's coming over to see you, she's leaving the Convent.'

Ellen said, 'For what?'

Mrs Greege said, 'She's a great worker.'

=

426

Essie Doherty had a slightly cleft palate and the energy of a steam engine: she had been as thoroughly trained in domestic work as a human being could be.

'Another debt clocked up to Mrs G.,' reflected Ellen to Nurse Cooper.

'Not debts, Ellen,' said Nurse Cooper, 'not at times like these.'

Essie's arrival lifted huge burdens. On her bicycle, this large mild woman with her elephantine suitcase tied with a pair of leather straps, sweated under a heavy winter coat. She lugged the case up the stairs behind Ellen, and when she came down shortly afterwards she had already put on her overall. No discussion of any kind took place; no length of stay was discussed. Like a ploughhorse Essie strode into the housework, and could 'bake, sew, iron and cook', she told Ellen, who, at first, had a little difficulty understanding Essie's rather difficult speech full of the letter 'n'. They agreed terms – a pound a week and every second Sunday afternoon and evening off. Ellen stood looking at Essie, and smiled at her.

In the late afternoon, hearing voices, Ellen turned from where she sat observing Thomas – in whom she had so far not noted down a single change for Dr Hogan – and saw, on the road outside, Canon Jeremiah Williams, brown from the sun. He stood pointing out the house with his walking-stick to a man and a woman dressed in good clothes.

'Oh, Jesus, no,' she said, and went to the door: when the Canon saw her standing there, he led the strangers away, back down towards the village.

It took Ellen several hours to overcome the feelings of panic: the need to answer Essie's questions as to where she kept things, and other domestic procedures, afforded some distraction. In bed that night she lay awake for hours.

In the morning she discovered another bonus in Essie: the convent where she worked was also a retirement home for senile priests, and she had had to look after old men as if they were babies. With Thomas, Essie proved expert, and swift, and respectful.

At one o'clock, with Helena and Thomas fed and settled, and changed until the late afternoon, Ellen said to Essie, 'If I go out for an hour, will you be all right?' Upstairs, Ellen went through her wardrobe. Any summer clothes belonged to last year, and everything she touched had some memory of Thomas. She chose her cream dress, her good brown court shoes and decided not to wear a hat. She also, for the first time since last May, chose the best underwear she had, and some scent.

The most difficult part would be the walk through the village. In the event she met nobody, and she swung to the shaded side of the road and quickly down the slope to the Canon's house. A passing cyclist, or horseman, or a rare motorist would have seen a woman who looked older than twenty-six years, but would have been drawn to her presence. The slightly frizzy hair, the quick, swinging walk, the good clothes and the brown bag over her arm; not a farmer's daughter or wife, and, though not a native, a woman who had some sort of belonging to the place; and an air of determination.

'He's in,' said the hostile housekeeper, 'but he's reading his Office.'

'I'll wait,' said Ellen.

Half an hour later, the housekeeper came back. 'The Canon says he has to have his dinner yet.'

'I'll wait,' said Ellen, in the tiled hall with the spiders and the dried-out potted plant.

Half an hour later, 'The Canon says he has a letter to write to catch the post.'

'I'll wait,' said Ellen, her heart growing heavier as she sat on the hard mahogany chair, behind the stained-glass front door.

He kept her waiting two and a quarter hours. When the housekeeper showed her in, Ellen opened fire, her patience gone.

'Canon, what kind of manners have you, keeping a woman in my circumstances away from her responsibilities for over two hours? You wouldn't do it to me if my husband was up and about.'

Having arranged himself behind his table, Jeremiah rose, and immediately knocked some things over, on the table's surface, not to the floor, but it was enough.

Ellen stormed on. 'And what do you mean by showing people the house where I and my stricken husband and our baby live, without ever coming and having the manners to talk to me about my future as your employed teacher?'

Jeremiah Williams fought back. 'I hear you have Jews as friends, and that you had a Jewman calling to visit you?'

Ellen almost ran across the room, then stopped.

'My God!' she said. 'My God! I'm going to tell the world on you.'

Eyes wide, she stared at him. For a moment she touched the edge of his table, then turned, left the room and the house and walked home, where she raced upstairs and collapsed on the bed in the heat of the afternoon.

Essie called up.

'Ma'am, there's someone at the door. A woman.'

Miriam Hogan's straw hat made Ellen smile.

'I love your flowers,' she said, 'will you come in?'

'No, no,' said Miriam. 'I brought you these.' She had an armful of magazines.

'My husband will be cross,' said Miriam, 'when he thinks I've finished with them he cuts out the corset advertisements,' and she tripped away.

Next morning at half-past ten, Essie, on her way to the clothes lines, turned back and said, 'Ma'am! Ma'am!

There's a man in the garden.' She rushed in and closed the back door.

Ellen turned pale. 'What's he like?'

'A big fella. Awful big.'

Ellen ran upstairs and twitched the lace curtains in the left-hand bedroom. The Quinn man, a bucket near his feet, nonchalantly dug Thomas's potatoes, filled his bucket and strolled away the way he had come, through a gap in the Quarterground hedge. Ellen, paralysed with fear, sat on the bed.

When she returned to the kitchen, Essie said, 'Ma'am, I don't know anyone around here, but I don't like the look of that fella.'

Ellen said, 'Oh, Jesus, help me, Oh, Jesus, help me. I'll have to do something about it.' Later, after a preoccupied day, she sat at the table and wrote a letter.

'Essie, do you know the Parochial House?'

'No, Ma'am.'

'Go down the village and carry on down the hill, the big cream house on your left, there's an orchard beside it.'

'Oh, I seen it and I coming here, Ma'am, with an avenue?'

'That's it.'

Dear Canon,
   This morning at half-past ten, that man from the village came to my garden and dug a bucket of our potatoes and took them away. I don't know what to do.

                    Yours faithfully,
                    Ellen Kane (Mrs)

'Essie, just say to the housekeeper that it is urgent, but there isn't an answer required.'

When Essie returned, Ellen asked who took the letter?

'A woman who put on a holy face,' said Essie, making Ellen laugh.

Next morning, Essie said, 'Ma'am, look! Coming in the gate! With a fork and a bucket.'

Again Ellen watched from behind the curtains. It took Canon Williams half an hour to fill his bucket, then he walked to the front door and knocked.

Ellen said, 'Good morning, Canon.'

He said to her, 'This is my own bucket. If you empty the potatoes out I can take this away with me, have a clean bucket for me here tomorrow, would you?'

'Won't you come in, Canon?'

'You should be pitting them potatoes fairly soon, Mrs.'

Essie brought back his bucket and he strolled away.

He returned next morning, and dug some more, and the morning after that, and the morning after that. On each occasion he walked slowly through the village, the fork angled over his shoulder. Nobody else appeared again in Ellen's garden.

On the fifth morning, the Canon said to Ellen, 'Can you open the school for me on Monday the 13th of September. Officially.'

Autumn 1926

24

The weather continued bright and hot. The routine of the house promoted a semblance of normality, and by the end of August Ellen had analysed this mood as the shape into which things would settle, rather than any reminder of the way they once were. Essie burgeoned, a docile boon, country wife to Ellen's leadership of the home. Ellen's looks began to return when she permitted them, but despair still ambushed her – when she opened the post; or when feeding Thomas proved unusually difficult – sometimes he gagged; or in the stillness of an afternoon when a bird suddenly sang nearby; or feeling the dew on the bushes in the morning as she fetched some of 'his' vegetables or fruit, as she considered them. She had not even paused to consider how she might address the gardening problems in the coming year.

On the morning of the second Sunday in September, the day before school opened again, Ellen went back to Mass, for the first time, and most apprehensively. She expected to be stared at from the moment she stepped off her bicycle to walk the last hundred yards up the hill; she anticipated the feel of their eyes on her up along the aisle.

'I have to be as normal,' she told herself. 'As normal.'

At the point where the churchyard wall began, some twenty yards from the actual gate, a woman Ellen only knew by sight came forward. Of her, Thomas had said, 'Watch that one. She'll talk sweetly and with a big smile, and when she's gone you'll feel the sore spot where her jab landed.'

Not this morning.

'Ma'am,' she said, 'how're you off for eggs? And how are you yourself? And how's the baby? And how's the Master?' She fell into step beside Ellen, and said, 'Sure we're all praying for you.' A dozen women walked and drifted towards Ellen before she had even reached the church gate, all talking to her and nodding, mostly gravely, and wishing her well, and asking was it all right if they called to see her, and was there anything she wanted?

'Ma'am,' said one of them, 'Mrs Greege was telling me herself, out of her own mouth, what a great woman you are; she said she never seen a woman bear a burden like yourself.'

Another said, 'Ma'am, that Essie, she's a horse of a woman,' to which Ellen replied, 'Oh, she certainly is.'

From a third, 'And you have your figure back an' all, after the baby, Ma'am, isn't that awful quick, that's great.'

In a sober and concerned sorority, they virtually blocked Ellen's path, and their soft rising-and-falling voices said, over and over, 'Don't forget now, if you ever need a day's work, or a woman to look after the baby and the Master, or the blankets washed . . .'

One shy young woman who had wed into a cottage the week before Thomas and Ellen themselves married, said, 'Ma'am, I had my baby last week, and inside in Nurse Cooper's you're the talk of the place. They say you're great altogether.'

Mrs Martin Burke walked across the road and said, 'You're not to think of stirring out of that house. My Martin knows people high up, and we're related to W. T. Cosgrave. Martin is after talking to the Canon. And my nephew knows someone well placed in the Department.'

Ellen replied, 'Thanks, thanks. You're very good.'

As she reached the corner of the church wall, and began to turn towards the gate, the men standing in their habitual confabulation, thirty or so of them, straightened up in their leaning line, and one by one touched their peaks, or raised, or even took off their caps. This proved too much: Ellen lowered her head, and failed to stop the tears. By the time she parked her bicycle and reached the church door, the bell began to ring. Never had Ellen paused to consider how she and Thomas had been a nightly discussion point in the quiet homes.

But as she left the church she saw the large figure of the Quinn man standing alone, a horse's bridle over his arm, just outside the gate on the right-hand side. She looked away.

On that afternoon, with Essie on her half-day, Ellen finally managed to put into practice the first of Herbert's suggestions: she wrote a timetable for herself, and pasted it in the inside front cover of her ledger.

6.00. Rise; say my Prayers; wash: dress in housework clothes.

6.30. Breakfast.

7.00. Begin Thomas: wash, change, dress, turn and feed.

8.00. Helena – feed, change, wash (every second day a bath) and settle: play with her for ten minutes.

9.00. Change: Leave for school.

12.30. Essie to give Thomas short feed: to feed and change Helena.

3.15. Home from school: dinner: me to change and feed Thomas.

5.00. Housework: own washing and darning: bills: any school work: Progress Record, etc. school forms to fill in, etc.

6.00. Helena: long play: observe Thomas.

7.00. Thomas's last feed: settle him for the night; then settle Helena.

8.30. Rest!

10.00. Bed!

Opening the school door wrenched her: the musty smell, the clock long stopped without winding for the summer;

ink dried to the bottoms of inkwells – none of this would have happened if Thomas . . . She could have cracked apart when she saw a child posting a broken nib through the famous knot-hole in the corner of the wooden partition. The new temporary Assistant Teacher, a Miss McGoldrick, did not seem much good: Ellen took the Senior room, freezing all her emotions and concentrating on giving out new books, pencils, exercise copies, arranging chalk, ink, pens. Opening Thomas's main cupboard she saw all the supplies laid out in rows – the blotting papers, his rulers, spare inkwells.

In the afternoon, she departed the day's curriculum in order to relieve her tension and created the pleasure of a Singing lesson.

First she took them through *Curwen's Modulator* and variations:

> '*Doh, Ray, Me, Fah, Soh, Lah, Ti, Doh.*
> *Doh, Ti, Lah, Soh, Fah, Me, Ray, Doh.*'

She began a new song, teaching them the words of the opening verse:

> '*O'er the ocean flies a merry fay,*
> *Soft her wings are as the clouds of day,*
> *As she passes all the blue waves say,*
> *Marionina, do not roam:*
> *Whither, whither is your home?*
> *Come and turn us into foam.*
> *Marionina! Marionina!*
> *Come, oh, come, and turn us into foam.*'

By the end of school, the whole room, Third, Fourth, Fifth and Sixth classes, boys and girls from eight years old to just short of fourteen, had satisfactorily begun to speak the lines from memory: then Ellen briefly hummed them through the notes.

As the four pupil 'sweepers' clunked about after three

438

o'clock, she sat at Thomas's desk to finalize the Roll for the day, but childlike, could not reach up or forward sufficiently to the top of the Roll Book: she made a note to bring some cushions. Timmy Quinn was absent: he had been sent 'to live with an aunt'.

On that first Monday, Ellen came home from school exhausted, so tired that she had to look in her ledger to check what the schedule commanded next. Mrs Greege had looked in and had left word with Essie that she was going to call tomorrow after school with some stewed apple for Thomas. Helena had started taking solids – 'Not before time,' said Nurse Cooper, 'don't mind these old wives.'

'Blast,' said Ellen, more to herself than to Essie, 'that means I'll get no chance to talk to Sheila Cooper' – who was also expected.

Ellen finished her dinner, a stew she had prepared with Essie that morning, went upstairs, changed her clothes and came down to begin on Thomas. Hitherto, she had only spoken to him a little self-consciously, always stopping when Essie came near, although Essie rambled on to him all the time, and even said to Ellen, ''Tis the first time I ever talked so free to a man who never talked to me,' and Ellen managed to see the humour.

Between them they had begun to deal very efficiently with Thomas, apart from the feeding which would always be difficult. Now Ellen provided the finishing touches – some milk from a large spoon – while Essie cleared away the bits and pieces, and took the big basin out to the scullery.

Without thinking – and perhaps even thinking aloud – Ellen said, 'Thomas, dear, would you by any chance remember where the Inspectors' Reports are kept?'

So preoccupied was she, that she did not realize for a hugely absent-minded moment why he didn't answer.

'Are they in your high desk – or did you bring them home?'

Abruptly she stood up. 'Oh, God, Thomas, I'm sorry, I really am. I forgot.'

Then, hand to lips, she addressed herself aloud, 'No I am not sorry. What are you doing, Ellen?'

A new sensation began to materialize in her – an entirely different kind of loneliness, not at all like the feeling she knew when she first came to Deanstown and spent those nights in Mrs Greege's; or in those awful first days alone in the house with Helena; or during the worst times of all so far, directly after she took Thomas home from the hospital: this anguish was sharp, and the more bitter for its unexpectedness. She paced a little beside his chair, both fists flailing up and down in her small agitated beatings of the air. 'Now I see why they wanted me to talk to him – to you. Now I see it.'

Crouching on one knee, she held Thomas's fish-like hand, and said fiercely, 'From now on, my dear Thomas, I am going to talk to you every day. And every night.'

That evening she relaxed more easily than she could remember having done for months. In her ledger, on the page after the (still blank) one headed, 'My Choices', Ellen copied in the address in London from which she could get, by subscription, the *Ladies' Home Journal: The Rolls House Publishing Company, Ltd, 2, Breams Buildings, E.C.4*. She made a note to order pattern no. 5088, for *a tailored georgette dress: in navy, or any plain colour desired. Shirring at the shoulder seams in front, a slightly bloused bodice, and a gathered front section of the skirt soften the strictly tailored effect of the long tight sleeves with their flaring cuffs, and the wide flat belt that extends all around*.

Standing at the parlour door, she said, 'Thomas, I'm going to keep a record of things I know you'd like to know about eventually. Deaths, auctions, and that,' and returned to the ledger. She took a cutting from the *Irish Independent*.

Under this she noted:

Perambulator for sale (almost new); very little used; cost £8.10s. For further particulars apply to Box 115 this office.

> Monday, 13th September 1926.
> 9.00 p.m. The house is silent. Helena is asleep. Is dear Thomas asleep or awake? How can I ever tell? How long will he live for like this? How can I ever tell that either? All I know at this moment is that this is the first time since Tuesday, 11th May, that I have not felt terrified.

At which point she closed the ledger, put it away, sat in thought for several minutes, then went to bed, checking Thomas and Helena *en route*.

The new routine strengthened Ellen: the joy she found in teaching renewed her: her anguish came within her control – she became somewhat capable of her own distress. Initial problems now containable, others grew approachable – and major pieces of outstanding business needed attention. The Canon had not said one word regarding her position, or the house, or her future. In the garage, that idle, bright car tantalized her; it could prove so useful. Tax and other forms had to be filled in. Thomas's money remained a problem, although she would now have her own salary back again (it had been paid to him by arrangement from the date of their marriage). Essie did the shopping; Ellen no longer had to rely upon Mrs Greege, her sons, or the convenient parcels of meat brought by Sheila Cooper.

Four months had passed since the shooting of Thomas. No culprit had been found. Fears of further violence against Thomas, or even against herself and Helena, had abated a little, in a natural way. Sometimes, despair made a raid: however, school and home together now so exhausted her that Ellen had less time to think.

Deeper questions remained: they concerned, among other things, her own guilt at how she had 'misjudged' – as she put it to Sheila Cooper – the conduct of her own marriage. When this thought surfaced, she reminded herself that she had not yet replied to Father John Watson's two letters.

Her appearance at Mass and in front of her pupils began to give the impression that she had returned to the community, and people felt licensed to call.

To the Sergeant she said, 'Any progress?'

'Ma'am,' he replied, 'not hide nor hair.'

Softly she enquired, 'And nobody suspected?'

'Ma'am, sure how could we suspect any Christian creature when we haven't a thing to go on?'

'Sergeant, have you a conscience?'

'Ma'am, there isn't a thing in the world anybody can do about anything in all this. I mean to say, things are going very quiet around here, that's one good thing, there's a lot of guns handed in under the amnesty, and that.'

'Very well, Sergeant. I won't say another word.' He looked uncomfortable.

'Talking of conscience, Ma'am, the other thing, Ma'am, is – knowing yourself and the Master, and the way the two

442

of you are regarded, the thing people are saying, Ma'am, and now that the two of you have a little babby, they're all saying that anyone who'd do such a terrible thing, sure such a person'd feel terrible regret altogether.'

'Regret?' echoed Ellen with a note of sharp doubt, and said no more.

She pounced on Dr Hogan. 'How many times do I have to ask you? I'll ask you again. I want you to get me all the medical information you can. I know I've been trying to keep myself together, but now I have time to pay attention to the real issue.'

'But you said yourself there was an improvement in him?'

'Mild, Dr Hogan, mild. That's all. I want him cured. C.U.R.E.D. I want him to be operated on. Or whatever. It might be in Cork, or in Dublin, or in London. Anywhere. But I want it done.'

'Ma'am, I'm asking everyone. You see yourself, he's as close to conscious as you could get.'

'Dr Hogan – my husband, Thomas Kane, cannot speak. I do not know whether he can hear. Or see. His eyes are half-open, but only now and again, and when they are half-open there is no expression in them. And what will the winter do to him? Yes, I agree, his response to food in his mouth has slowly improved. But he is still, to all intents and purposes, "living dead". Now, what can you find out? And don't show your face to me at this front door until you find out something. Do you hear me, Doctor?'

By creating new arrangements with Mrs Greege and Sheila Cooper during the first week back at school, Ellen guaranteed that some reassuring senior presence came to the house every day of the week. Not for almost a month had Mrs Greege made a snide or cutting remark. Ellen began to answer the correspondence which had mounted all summer. The weather continued unusually hot.

On Thursday night she stood at the door of the parlour, *The Leader* in her hand.

'Thomas, did you ever hear this Household Hint? "Paraffin will last longer and produce a better light if a piece of salt, the size of a marble, is placed in the reservoir of the lamp." I'll put it in, I think,' and she cut it, and pasted it in the ledger.

On Friday, an Inspector of Schools arrived, to her initial dismay, as she recalled how Thomas hated them.

'They don't know our jobs, and they don't know their own,' he always said, and indeed one of his planks in the policy-making discussions for a Teachers' Union had been the formulation of a national demand to have appointed as Inspectors only those who had originally been fully trained teachers.

This Inspector turned out an angel in disguise.

'I only called,' he said, 'because someone in Dublin, a friend of a neighbour of yours – do you know a Mrs Burke? – asked high up, in case you needed a hand, but I can enter it as an official visit, which means nobody will come near you for three or four years. I'm not going to do an Inspection, or anything.'

Ellen told him the Canon had not yet resolved the Principalship, and that she had formally asked to be appointed to the position, 'given the unusual circumstances'.

The Inspector, bald as an egg, rubbed his head and chuckled. 'I know Jeremiah of old,' he said, 'I knew him when he was a Curate, and damn troublesome he was then. But he's afraid of Bishops and government departments. I'll call down and put the heart crosswise in him.'

Sheila Cooper had told her in August about Power of Attorney – how she might be able to have Thomas's money released. On Saturday she received a letter from the Bank's Legal Agent in Dublin, confirming the probability of her enquiry's success.

Val Vousden called to the school.

'Ma'am, I've great news for you and the boss. I have nearly all the instruments, bar one cornet and one trombone. I'm after tracing, you'll never believe me, eight of the original fourteen or fifteen musicians, they're some of the rest of them dead, and there's some emigrated, but out of sons and cousins and nephews, there's a chance now that I could get well a dozen, maybe, together.'

'You must have worked very hard, Mr Vousden.'

'Everyone calls me Val. I did, and Mrs Heffernan is after making a pile of uniforms for me. Blue and gold, Ma'am, they're gorgeous, with a red stripe down the trousers. She made the first one last Christmas. Now, the thing is, Ma'am, would the boss ever let us use the school for practising in?'

'He would, I'm sure, Mr Vousden. When d'you want it?'

'If we could have it of a Saturday or a Sunday, Ma'am, we'd be very careful, we're not them MacReadys.'

Four days later, the Post Office Legal Officer wrote to Ellen enclosing the Power of Attorney forms for Thomas's savings, and instructions on how to proceed. The essentials had begun to come right, and yet, hour upon hour, Thomas, pitifully supine, lay a hundred and fifty yards from the school in what had been their adventuresome parlour, its new furniture now pushed to one side to make way for the mahogany, slanting bed-chair.

Her success with the day-to-day practicalities had given Ellen's loneliness only light succour, and, as she said in an unguarded moment to Mrs Greege, she dreaded a day when she would have mastered her burdens so fully that time would hang from her hands. Her truest relief – and she resisted admitting it to herself – began slowly to materialize when she talked to Thomas nightly.

Herbert and Leah and the two girls arrived, tripping off the bus, the girls carrying posies and wearing shiny shoes and insisting they inspected everything at once, inevitably seeking the baby before anything else.

'But – on a Saturday?' asked Ellen in surprise. 'What happened to your Sabbath?'

'We are allowed to do the works of God, and that includes visiting the sick,' said Herbert, although Leah whispered to Ellen later that he had had an argument with their new Rabbi, a Cork man, who was not turning out to Herbert's liking, and that anyway, when they got home that evening, Herbert would spend an hour or two reading prayers.

'Some day,' said Ellen, 'I will ask Herbert to tell me the whole story of how he prays, and what he says to God, and where he's different from me.'

Leah asked, 'Your prayers must have stood to you in all your trouble?'

'Yes and no,' answered Ellen, surprisingly evasive, and then availed of a question from Rachel – 'Does Helena eat potatoes and meat?' – to quit the subject.

They all had a grand, busy lunch, with Leah giving Essie the benefit of all her warmth, and praising Ellen for finding her. Herbert sat at the head of the table and the children, summoned from the cats and the garden, had more lemonade than was good for them.

The adults unspokenly feared the moment when the children would tire of their distractions and forget their manners. Finally they asked. Leah and Herbert had already called in to the parlour to inspect Thomas, and say 'Hallo': the subject then slipped into abeyance during the pre-lunch bustle.

Ellen surprised them all by answering. 'Now, girls, do you know what to expect when you see Uncle Thomas?'

'Mamma says he isn't well,' said Rachel.

'Oh,' said Ellen, 'he's much more than just not well. Uncle Thomas had a very bad accident to the side of his head. Since then he hasn't spoken to us, or seen any of us, and we don't know if he can hear us. He just lies there and we care for him very much. We wash him and feed him, like a big, tall baby, and maybe you can even help.'

Hand in hand, she led the two from the kitchen to Thomas's room, while Leah and Herbert looked at each other with raised eyebrows.

'Thomas, look who's here?' Ellen called. 'I talk to him all the time,' she explained in a lower voice. 'I tell him what the weather is like, and I tell him who has written us letters, and I tell him who was bold in school today, and I tell him what's in the newspapers, and sometimes I cut things out of the newspapers for him to read when he gets better again.'

'There's a funny smell?' wrinkled Rachel, who reached out a hand to touch Thomas's bed-chair.

'Rachel is wearing a lovely yellow ribbon, Thomas, and Sarah has new black patent shoes with buttons on them,' said Ellen.

The girls stood there, holding Ellen's hands tightly and looking transfixed.

'Aren't you going to say hallo to him?' asked Ellen. 'No? All right,' she pacified, 'maybe you can come in and say hallo later.'

She led the children back to the kitchen: with relief they escaped, to Essie in the scullery, and thence to the garden to find the cats again, leaving Ellen, Herbert and Leah alone at the table.

'We were just saying,' said Leah, 'what a change, how things have improved. You keep Thomas beautifully, and Helena looks grand.'

'You must have made a huge effort to get this far,' said Herbert. 'How are you yourself?'

'I am destroyed,' said Ellen, matter-of-factly, elbows on the table. 'I feel – I feel dismantled. I keep going because I must, because I have responsibilities, but I feel destroyed inside me. From time to time I break down, and then I seem to recover some ground, and get better for a few hours, even a day at a time, but then I think – "God, this is the rest of my life I'm looking at, and no hope of it getting better." I mean the best thing that can happen to me, if you think about it, is that Thomas might die. What an awful choice.'

'What about prayer?' asked Herbert.

'I pray. But it's like it's coming out of a machine,' said Ellen.

'Any further medical ideas?' asked Leah.

'Not one. Not a single one. No hope. I keep thinking there must be someone somewhere who knows. Although I'm supposed to be talking to Dr Hogan tomorrow.'

Sarah came in claiming Leah's attention: Rachel had fallen in the clay of the garden.

Herbert said in Leah's absence, 'How did you get on with what I suggested to you?'

'Not very far. I tried. I'm going to try again.'

'If you're very angry,' said Herbert, 'that might . . . I don't know, it might open up something?'

'Angry?' said Ellen. 'I'm too busy to be angry. Angry?'

Ellen waved them off, standing in the middle of the road, watching in the white dust the small faces of the girls at the back window of the high bus. When she could see it no more, and could only hear a distant growl of the receding engine, she looked despondently at the house where in a few minutes she would begin another drudging, hauling round of feeding, cleaning and changing her two dependants. Turning her back to the house, she walked the three or four paces to the high stone stile in the wall, over which Thomas and she had climbed on the morning after their wedding night.

Only one September in living memory, in the 1880s, an Indian summer forty years earlier, compared, they said, for such golden beauty. Now, the fields of 1926 had wide patches of parched irregular patterns, as if the colour of beige straw had been dragged any which way across the grasses. Aftergrass shone brilliantly blue-green from a meadow harvested in July. Up beyond the Castle, stubble of a cornfield wore a kind of black gold. Across this glorious serenity the earliest short shadows began to fall: a dog barked somewhere very far off, rounding up, no doubt, the cows of the evening to take them home to the yard for milking. On the grass verge beneath Ellen's feet, white dust had coated the broad, bending grass and the purple shiny berry clusters fallen from an elder tree.

From upstairs, where she had gone to lift Helena, Essie drew down the sash of the window, now that the sun had moved around to the side of the house, and the room had cooled. She saw Ellen raise her arms until they rested on the top of the wall. Ellen placed her chin on her arms and stood there, motionless, in grey jumper and grey skirt. Essie chaired the baby up in her arms and, moving the net curtain back a little, pointed to Ellen and said through her half-cleft nasal palate, 'Nlook. Nlook, nthere's your'n Mamn.' The thrush that Thomas liked so much began to sing, 'Your-tea. Your-tea.' Essie and Helena saw Ellen put her face down on her forearms, then raise, shake herself and turn towards the gate.

'Ma'am, who's this coming in, look at him, an apparition?'

Ellen twisted, peering round the high back of the chair, and looked out of the window. A dapper man with a white moustache, and carrying a suitcase, walked with a bounce up the path, on the gravel and to the front door. Ellen checked her face in the little hand-mirror on the shelf, and said, 'Essie, look at me, I'm a show.'

With the front door wide open towards the cooling evening, the man was in the hall.

'G'day. Have I the honour of addressing Mrs Thomas Kane?' He pronounced it 'Kine'.

'Yes, and who are you?'

The man put out his hand; he had a white handkerchief like a set of flat triangular sails in his top pocket: one of the triangles had the letter 'J' embroidered on it in red.

'I am a cousin of your husband's. My name is Joe Johnson. I am from Melbourne.'

'Essie, was it the Lord who sent us such entertainment?' Ellen asked hours later when Joe Johnson had left. 'Although my heart sank when I saw the suitcase. I thought he was coming to stay.'

The encounter began unpromisingly.

'Oh, Mr Johnson, I don't know, I didn't know . . .'

'Never mind that, Mrs Kane, I'm on a visit to this old country and I'm tracing every cousin I can think of or find out about. And your husband is the man to meet, they tell me.'

Ellen said coldly, 'Do they now?'

'My great-grandfather was the brother of your husband's great-great-grandfather.'

'I'm afraid, Mr Johnson, that at this moment . . .'

'And that makes me your husband's second cousin once removed –'

'I'm afraid,' protested Ellen once more –

'And you know what they say,' quipped Joe Johnson, 'a second cousin once removed is very difficult to replace.'

In spite of herself, Ellen burst out laughing. 'Come in,' she said, 'only for a minute, though. And anyway, that would be second cousins twice removed.'

'Twice removed? Worse again,' cracked Joe. 'And here

I am.' He sat down at the kitchen table and accepted the offer of a cup of tea.

Ellen began to explain. 'You don't seem to have heard about my husband, Thomas.'

'Is he in clink?' said Joe. 'That is how his Australian cousins began. I hope he's not away leaving a little beauty like you on her ownio? The Kanes always liked handsome women.'

Ellen smiled and blushed.

'Or is he out on the rant, eh?'

'No. He is in the next room.'

'Oh, great, can I see him? Is he decent?'

Ellen asked, 'You don't know at all, do you?'

Joe Johnson replied, 'I know he was a handy man with a point three-oh-three rifle, I know that.'

Ellen shuddered. 'Mr Johnson, my husband, your cousin, is very ill.'

'Oh, my dear girl, I am very sorry.'

'He got – injured. And he has been – unconscious, I suppose you'd call it, since the beginning of May.'

'Can I see him?' asked Joe.

Ellen rose and he followed. The little man stood by Thomas's side, and said, 'Thomas Kane, I am your cousin, Joe Johnson from Melbourne, and the least you might do is say hallo, but if you don't – then I'll do the talking. How do you do?' He took Thomas's hand and shook it energetically. 'All the more room for me not to be interrupted, I hate being interrupted,' and like a performance, Joe Johnson began to talk.

He told them the story of his branch of the family. Convicted as felons for an attempted local conspiracy in 1797, two Kane brothers had been transported to Van Diemen's Land, now Tasmania, and even though their sentences ended within fourteen years, they were never allowed to return to Ireland. They settled and prospered, farmers first, then builders, then steel manufacturers, and now, two generations before Joe, the respectability of white collar work, owning one of Melbourne's largest insurance businesses, and getting interested in these new aeroplanes.

'They told me I'd find the house easily, you were the only ones around here with a car, typical Kane.'

He regaled them – wonderful stories of the bush, and the kangaroos, and then he said, 'I have a surprise for you.'

He moved the mahogany table behind Thomas a little to one side, then wheeled the bed-chair around: throughout, Thomas had neither flickered nor stirred. Placing two chairs side by side, as if for people awaiting a performance, he called Essie and directed her and Ellen to sit down. As they sat there, Joe went out to the hallway and they heard the clasps of his suitcase snap open. Returning, he said in a masterful way, 'Now, where's your phonograph?'

'You mean a gramophone?' said Ellen. 'We don't have one.'

'Oh?' Joe looked crestfallen. 'Bugger. Sorry, dear.'

He looked all around the room, then at the table.

'Mind if I move these?'

To clear a space on the table, he moved Ellen's empty crystal bowl and its lace doily to the top of the piano and dusted the table with his sleeve. All this time he had a mysterious flat package under his arm, which he now laid on the table, and unwrapped to reveal two packages. From the larger, square one he took out a gramophone record, with a dark red, gold-printed label, and he laid it flat on the table.

'You've seen one of these?'

'Well, we know what it is,' said Ellen, 'we're not complete goms.'

'"Goms". That's a good one,' chirped unabashed Joe, and arranged the record on the table with the same care as if it had been on a gramophone. He then turned his back, shielding the unwrapping of the second parcel from their view; he was assembling something, and also seemed to be affixing it to his arm.

'What are you doing, Joe?' called Ellen.

'The audience is getting very restless,' said Joe. 'All in good time.'

He spun around, and on the light grey stripes of his forearm sleeve, sat a wooden cut-out of a brightly coloured bird, neither parrot nor parakeet.

'Permit me to introduce you,' cried Joe, 'to the Australian native bird, the kookaburra, otherwise known as "The Laughing Jackass". And this,' he cried on, pointing to the record on the table, 'is a recording of how it sounds, but since we have nothing to play it on, I will just have to do it myself.' He cleared his throat, steadied himself like a concert singer, and held the arm with the wooden kookaburra as stiff as a falconer's. His other arm started to flap like a wing, and from his mouth came an extraordinary sound, like a guttural merry shriek.

'Oooohahahahahahaha-haghhhagh-Oooohahahahaha haha-haghhhagh-Oooohahahahahahaha-haghhhagh': he kept this up for at least a minute and a half, pausing only to take deep breaths, and stopping only when his face had become dangerously red, and then abruptly said, 'That's it.'

Essie and Ellen applauded. Joe bowed and bowed and said, 'I think that calls for an encore.'

This time, however, he did not flap the free arm as if to simulate the kookaburra's flight; instead he took a pencil from his pocket and, standing beside the gramophone record, kept describing a circular motion over it.

'Ordinarily,' he said, 'as I'm sure you know, the motion is the other way round, it's the record that goes around and around, not the needle.'

'Yes, we'd heard that,' said Ellen drily.

'Very well then,' said Joe, 'let the encore begin.'

He moved the arm with the wooden bird on it up and down, and kept the pencil going around in a circle and then began the screech again.

'Oooohaghhhagh - Oooohaghhhagh - Oooohaghhhagh.' This time, when he had ended his screeching, he made another noise as slowly his flapping bird arm came to a stop.

'Pidyp. Pidyp. Pidyp. Pidyp. Pid. Yilip.'

'What's that?' asked Ellen.

'You ignoramus,' said Joe (he pronounced it 'ignor-ih-mus'); 'that is the noise the bird makes as it settles back on the branch.'

'A good job you told us that,' said Ellen.

Joe Johnson left the house at nightfall. He hugged Ellen, and patted her cheek. 'You're a dear girl,' he said. 'G'bye, Tom, we'll meet again. G'bye, Essie.' Turning to Ellen, he said, 'My dear, y'know it is all going to be all right, don't you? 'Course it is.'

'Mr Johnson,' she said, 'you still don't understand. He wasn't injured in an accident. Thomas was shot.'

Joe looked at her. 'It still makes no odds,' he said, 'this is a house full of life, not of death.' With a new thought, he said, 'Do you know about the dolphins?'

Ellen shook her head.

'We have dolphins in Australia. Dolphins must keep moving in order to stay alive. If they stop they die. If a dolphin is too sick to move, the other dolphins get around it and keep nudging it through the water. That's all you need to have here, my dear – a bit of dolphin work.'

'Oh,' said Ellen, reflecting long after he had gone, 'wasn't that nice? Wasn't that nice? Essie, did you see how natural he was with the Master?' Then in a musing voice she murmured, 'A bit of dolphin work? A bit of dolphin work?'

25

'No. No. No.' Jack Hogan spoke firmly. 'This is a good job here, Miriam, and we're staying here. No. I don't want to move again. No, they are not all laughing at you, dear. No, they are not. Besides how could you know? You never go out and meet them.'

Miriam said, 'I'm sick of this dump, Jack, this hole of a place. All there is to do here is walk.'

'That's what you said when we were in Pallasgreen, Miriam, and you said the same when we were in Kilmacthomas. We have to settle somewhere.'

'I'm not a good wife to you, Jack, and if we were living somewhere else, I would be.'

'That's what you said before, Miriam, and you're not a bad wife.'

'Jack, stop telling lies, you're always telling lies. You pretend to people that I have your dinner ready on the table when you come home and I do no such thing. I never cook a meal for you, I'm not able.'

Jack denied that he ever said such a thing, but he coloured.

'I don't sleep in your bed alongside you, Jack, and I don't know where that's going to lead. As a matter of interest, Jack, do you care for me still?'

Standing at the cupboard, he suspended the breadknife and bread in his hands, and looked at her.

'You never asked me that before, Miriam. Not in twelve years.'

'That is because you seemed to agree with yourself about the way I was.'

'How d'you mean?'

'My mother told you I was – what?'

'"A bit of an oddity",' quoted Jack.

'So, you never tried to stop me being "a bit of an oddity"?'

'Is that what you wanted me to do, Miriam?'

'It would have meant that you didn't treat me like any old farmer's wife.'

'Miriam, I never know what new tack you're trying. If you're serious, Miriam?'

'I am serious, Jack. I hate these long walks I have to take all on my own. But I do a lot of counting, Jack.'

He looked up. 'What is it you count, Miriam?'

'I count the money you got out of marrying me, Jack.'

Mrs Greege said, 'Your friend was stocious last night by all accounts.'

'Who?'

'Who but himself? Jack. Taking the two sides of the road.'

'Dr Hogan? Drunk?'

'As a lord.'

'Are you sure?' said Ellen.

'Certain sure. Three sheets in the wind. Arthur Grant had to drive him home. Nor was it the first time, either. No wonder the wife is as odd as two left shoes.'

Father John Watson wrote a letter.

Thursday,
30th September 1926

My dear Ellen,

What can I say? I can only presume that you have been too distressed, and too frantically busy with everything: it is most unusual not to hear from you, as you are such a prompt correspondent.

I have just called again to Brunswick Square, and never
have I seen a house so transformed from lightness to
gloom. My heart and my prayers go out to you. In equal
proportions, I have heard of your misfortune and your
bravery, and all I can say at this moment is how deeply
compassionate and sympathetic I feel. We are not privy to
every part of His Divine Scheme.

I have deliberately not visited, even though in my
previous two letters I asked your permission. However, if
I may, I shall now come and visit you, and your charming
baby, and perhaps offer some spiritual aid.

My deepest thoughts go to you.
Yours faithfully in Jesus Christ,
John Watson, S.J.

Those marks Ellen saw on the windscreen frame of the
car in the garage, those small peppered dents in the edge
of the metal frame and on one section of the glass, had
the same appearance and consistency as the small black-
and-blue marks, those thick, discoloured dots, now all but
faded from the back of Thomas's right hand.

'Medium-heavy calibre,' wrote the Sergeant in the
Amnesty Receipt Book, having accepted a shotgun.

The first cartridge had struck Thomas's right hand
obliquely, bouncing some shot off the skin, then travelled
across the car, scattering into the windscreen, some of it
missing baby Helena's wrapped feet, one grain slightly
nicking Ellen's left hand which was cradling the baby.
Other shot from that cartridge exited through the open
side of the car beyond Ellen's shoulder, and spent itself
in the ditch on the far side.

'Choices. Choices. I have to make the effort,' Ellen
thought aloud. 'I wonder if I wrote to Herbert would it
help?'

She said to Essie, 'Essie, some night this week, I'm
going to ask you if you would do both the Master and the

baby, because I have to go down to the school to fill in forms and things, would that be all right? Oh, Essie, you're a trump,' she said, when the big woman beamed at the responsibility. 'That's what you are, a trump card. I'll be back about half-nine or so. I've a lot of things to do.'

'Ah, sure, yes, Ma'am.'

Miriam Hogan walked always in the same fashion: parallel to the road, for miles at a time, and when a cart or a bicycle approached, she sometimes crouched to the ground inside the ditch and watched carefully as, unseeing, they passed by. This morning she looked at Jack's untidy face at breakfast and decided. She would head west: climbing the hill past the church, and dropping down the other side, she would make for the town, which she did not intend to enter. The light rain did not bother her at all, fine. The Dispensary front door does not slam, the wood had swollen last winter and it must be forced to a gentle close. At ten o'clock, Jack talked to a woman with a child in the surgery. Miriam walked for five miles or so, always keeping close to the road, behind the high hedges, enjoying trying to identify through the bushes the occasional passer-by. Then, disturbingly, up ahead, she saw a man, just as she climbed the last slope of that steep hill to the town, and he walked as she did, in the fields, just inside the ditch. Head down, peering, searching, he had just come through the bushes from the road, and now he turned back and, as he did so, he saw Miriam, started, and returned quickly to the road. She watched his retreating shoulders as he cycled up the hill standing on the pedals to get up speed. Miriam Hogan reached the place where he had been staring, and she stood and stared too. Nothing to be seen in the field; through a gap in the hedgerow, however, she observed, as if they had been framed, the earthen weals along the far roadside bank down which the Kanes' car had slewed on a sunny morning in May. Miriam walked closer, then clambered out on the narrow road. She found the marks on the road surface where the car had first swerved: even though the heat of the summer had melted some of the tar, the wheel gouges were there to be seen. She paced it: eighteen yards, she reckoned, from the first swerve to the last tipsy resting-place. An ash sapling had been wounded in the car's lurching journey, its bark torn from the slim bole. Back and forth, back and forth, Miriam walked, looking, looking. She plucked at grass, at leaves, wiped her hands on the seat of her camel-coloured skirt. Climbing back inside the ditch, Miriam turned her face eastwards and home again, and at the last minute kicked something in the grass.

She walked past the Dispensary and kept going. Behind her, she heard the noise of Jack's car, the clattering rev he always gave it, as he emerged on the road from their pathway. He honked and drew up; Miriam flapped her hand at him in a sign he knew, and he waved cheerily and drove on. Miriam called to the school and saw Ellen supervising the children's play. She walked straight over.

'Don't wait a minute longer,' she said in her abrupt manner, always unable to look in the eye of the person she addressed, always looking down and to one side. 'Get further opinion, my husband is too feckless to manage it for you. If you don't do it I will.'

'Why do you say that? Wait, wait,' called Ellen, but Miriam had turned back and begun to leave the village: to Ellen she looked fairly unstoppable.

'Try Dr Morgan,' Miriam shouted back. 'He's all right again.'

'That's what Nurse Cooper said,' shouted Ellen; 'come back a minute, will you.' Miriam strode off.

=

The second trigger had been pulled in a reflex action caused by the kick of the gun as it jerked up after the first shot. Half of the cartridge's load went wide, above and ahead of the car's occupants: the other half, a small hard cluster of grains, hit Thomas full on the right temple in a slightly downward trajectory.

'This is the angle, look,' the detective had said, getting the Sergeant to hold a string's end at about the height of the car roof, and he climbed on the ditch to show a descending path. 'So, the assailant was standing about there, or a little farther in? I see.'

Some of the pieces of shot had been recovered in the emergency procedures by Dr MacDonnell, who, even though he had no military experience, recognized the type of metal with which he was dealing: on the Tuesday, forty-eight hours later, with the arrival of some lucidity in Ellen, they all began to agree on what had happened, though without telling her.

'I wish,' said Ellen aloud to herself, 'I could get a slap of salt from the sea on my lips.'

'D'you want these, Ma'am?' Essie interrupted the reverie, and held out a pair of small green silk sachets Ellen had herself stuffed with lavender.

'Let me smell them. Oh, Essie, are you started on those drawers already? Oh, great!' Ellen sniffed them. 'Oh, they're nearly faded,' and Essie looked down at her with all the dear bovine, inarticulate sympathy she could muster.

'Arrah, Ma'am, Ma'am,' she said, when she saw the tears in Ellen's eyes, 'there'll be a day when it'll come right. There will, Ma'am, there will with the help of God.'

'The Master got that lavender in for me, Essie. Specially.'

On the day he planted it, Thomas said, out of the blue, to Ellen, 'Tell me. How much do you believe in God?'

'Thomas! That's nearly blasphemous.'

'No. Straight question. How much do you believe in God?'

'But I believe in Him a hundred per cent.'

'What I mean is. What is the feeling like?'

Ellen held out her fingers to count. 'First thing in the morning I say my prayers. You know that. Then I start the children off with a prayer, maybe a decade of the Rosary if it is a special feast-day, like Saint Monica, maybe, and you know I've great devotion too to Saint Joseph, Thomas. If I could only persuade you to say the Rosary with me in the evening. Then I have my night prayers. And I often say a prayer to myself during the day.'

Now, she crunched the little lavender packets in her hand and pressed them to her nose.

Tuesday, 5th October

My dearest Leah and Herbert,

I need to write this letter to you, even if I never post it. [She did.] I have so many things to consider, and even now I can't easily bring to mind the most difficult of them. I have come down to the school to write this, just like Thomas used to do when he wished to be alone. I've left him washed and clean and fed. Few signs of recovery, I'm afraid, and they give me a very big problem. Is now the time to put a big effort into finding him new medical care?

In fact, I have an awful number of problems, and since you, Herbert, asked me to try and work out my life, I thought the best thing to do was to open the whole thing up and get things fixed one way or another.

I was awfully young when I married Thomas, and when I discovered he was very violent, I got terribly upset. I even wondered whether I should (a) leave him, but there wasn't anywhere I could go. And (b) Helena was on the way and I wouldn't get a job anywhere and I certainly didn't want to go back to Brunswick Square; and even though I knew the two of you would take me in, I knew too that you wouldn't have enough room for me to stay for long.

When she addressed such topics, Ellen's stomach troubled her; she broke off and, shielding the candle's flame in the mild air, went to the girls' lavatory. Returning, she stood by the door, and looked at the few lights of the village houses. Since Thomas's prostration she had avoided passing the Quinn house too closely; the day she visited the Canon she had walked each time on the far side of the road, going through the village and coming back, eyes cast down. Since school reopened, she did the same, yet had to pass the house every day, the door always firmly closed. Only in the last week she had begun to look at it directly – as she now did, at the single light in the dim window.

Do you see the kind of mistakes I was making in my thinking? Was it that I always paid too much attention to my faith and not enough to my natural feelings? I look at Helena now and think – how could such a dear little dote ever be a murderer (or murderess, I think it is called)? Then I look at Thomas and I think – I wish I had not listened so closely to my religion and had brought myself to be more of a good wife to him. The things that I thought were sins were not sins at all – and the things I thought were not sins might have been.

Dear Herbert, you said to me that there were facts it was all right to be angry about. I feel myself getting very angry now, but the writing of this letter is helping me very much. What I think I'll do is – I'll try and go back and list what you called my 'Choices', Herbert. Despite all the awfulness of it all, and my day-to-day trying to pretend Thomas's condition is some way normal (which, of course, it has become), I feel there's something building up, both in me and in the general state of all this.

I suppose this letter makes no sense at all, but I'm having to try every means I can think of to work things out. In a queer sort of way, the full shock is only hitting me now, not in any fashion that will knock me out, but in a way that has suddenly wakened me up to the fact that I have urgent things to do – and the first of these is to get something medical done very fast.

You are dear friends to me, the two of you, and

Rachel, and Sarah. Tell them the cats were asking for
them, and my warmest love to you both, and from Helena
too. (And, I suppose, from Thomas.)

> Your grateful friend,
> Ellen

P.S. Essie is turning out to be a trump of the highest suit
of cards.

As she sealed the letter, Ellen had one last thought: on
the back of another envelope she made a list:

1. The doctors.
2. The school.
3. The car.
4. Father J.W.
5. The Bad.

Placing all the correspondence in her writing-case, she
locked the school and strode home.

'I'm back, Essie!'

'Is that you, Ma'am? Are you back?' replied Essie.

'Essie's always quick on the uptake, Thomas,' remarked
Ellen quietly as she took off her coat standing in front of
him, and shook out her hair. 'I'll just get my writing-pad
and sit beside you.' She had moved the best lamp in the
house to the table nearest Thomas.

'"Dear Dr Morgan," "Malaria", Thomas, I'm writing to him, all right? "You have probably heard what has
happened and I understand you are back at work. Can
you please come and see us?" Thomas, is it "Yours sincerely", or "Yours faithfully"? I'll put "Yours – faithfully", I think, I never know which.'

'"Dear Canon Williams,"' she read aloud as she wrote.
'"Enough is enough. Unless you make your mind up
within seven days, I will organize a petition among the
parishioners to be sent to the Archbishop, and a

delegation to the Department in Dublin regarding the Principalship. It isn't good to have things the way they are."' She lifted her head, put her tongue back in her mouth and said, 'Don't you agree with that, Thomas?' She read it again and said, 'So, "Please let me have your reply as soon as possible. Yours sincerely, Ellen Kane. Mrs."' That'll soften his cough, as you'd say, Thomas. And Thomas, don't go mad, I'm going to ask Michael Condon to teach me how to drive.'

Ernestina Stephenson proved to have unusual physical durability. To her brother and all who worked for them, and the Harpers and her Uncle Henry, she manifested all summer only what Jack Hogan repeatedly called 'the symptoms of daily life'. After a few days confined to bed, she told him that bed is 'a place where people go to die', and she 'bloody' wasn't going to do that. Cyril's absorption elsewhere and the richness of the harvest for all her relatives meant that long stretches of Ernestina's day went unobserved. She could now slip into her bedroom for frequent rests unknown to anybody, and thus revitalize herself, maintaining the appearance of a normal daily round. The doctor called once a week and Ernestina told her brother, 'He's just friendly.' By the end of September, however, the spells of what she called 'tiredness' grew ever so slightly longer, as she told Dr Hogan, and came ever so slightly oftener.

'But no bleeding any more?'

'No. None.'

She covered her extending absences from the centre of the household with a tale of a project – she had embarked upon a large embroidered bedspread (indeed, she had even purchased all the essentials) and it was 'requiring all my concentration'. Her brother raised no queries, extremely pleased that his extra-mural adventures no longer seemed to whet Ernestina's harsh tongue. If she was friendly with Dr Hogan – what of it? That was her business. God knows, a farm this size caused enough problems: that damned engine: would he sell the yearling, hardly a yearling now, but coming up to prime form?

'I wish Ernestina,' he said one day, 'we could have a bit more meat. We've the roast on Sunday and we have it cold on Monday and Tuesday and Wednesday, and we have a roast again on Sunday, and we have only eggs on Thursday or something. Eh?'

Ernestina replied, 'It was good enough for us that way all our lives, what's wrong with it now?'

Next day, Cyril said, 'Ernestina, are you going to need all that space in the garden for your raspberries next year? You hardly picked any this year, and a great crop you had, and the hotel in Mantlehill will buy carrots from us. And I could put them in there. If you're not needing the space.'

'Shove your carrots in somewhere else.'

Sunday,
17th October 1926

Dear Mr Condon,

I am sorry it has taken so long to get you your money for fixing the car, but you know my circumstances and it is only now that I have been able to get the money out of the Bank where it was in my husband's name. Thank you for waiting for so long, and I notice you didn't call or send me a reminder or anything and I very much appreciate that. Also, I was very rude to you when you helped me so much, and I hope you will accept my apology, but you could see the state I was in.

I know it is a foolish question, but in a magazine my sister sent me, I saw a picture of a woman driving a car. Is it possible for a woman to drive my husband's car, and if it is, how would I go about finding out how to do so?

Thanking you again.

Yours faithfully,
Ellen Kane (Mrs)

On Tuesday morning, Dr Hogan's Austin Seven drew up outside the school, and he and a passenger hurried through the rain. Knocking sideways on the open door, he simultaneously caught Ellen's eye and she walked down the classroom, something of Thomas's magisterial-ness in her stride.

'Hallo, Ma'am.' He always had a sturdy greeting.

'The very man, when will we talk about getting some new doctors to come and see the Master?'

'We will, we will, Ma'am, I'm sorry to disturb you, but I brought this man to see you.'

'Oh, good! Are you a doctor? Where are you from?'

The stranger, raindrops on his spectacles, did not work on the land, nor did his jacket and grey trousers suggest wealth or profession.

'Indeed nor I'm not, Ma'am.'

'And who are you then?'

Jack Hogan said, 'I don't even know if you know this, Ma'am, but the time of the polio, the Master and me discussed those letters you used to get.'

'Oh?' said Ellen. 'I thought –' addressing the other man '– that you might be a doctor or something.'

'No, Ma'am, I am not,' he said.

'But you're very sober altogether,' she said.

'This man is the Postal Superintendent in Thurles, and we came here first, we're going on to see the Sergeant in a minute. Or maybe into town to see the Superintendent.'

Ellen asked, 'What? Or – why, I mean . . . ?'

'Ma'am, this man here is after tracing the person who wrote them letters.'

'No?!' Ellen exploded in disbelief.

'I did, Ma'am, 'twas easy enough, that handwriting. We compared it a lot.'

'But how did you – find out?'

The man looked embarrassed.

'Hah,' cackled Dr Hogan, 'the Post Office kettle is for more than making the tea.'

'You mean you steamed them open?'

'I did, Ma'am, but I had the agreement of the Guards. 'Tis illegal except where the Postal Authorities feel there's something wrong, and one of them letters could be construed as a threat.'

'A bad threat,' endorsed Jack Hogan.

'But does the person know?' asked Ellen.

'She doesn't yet, Ma'am, but she'll know any day now, she'll be in the barracks soon, I'd say.'

'So it was a woman?'

'It was, Ma'am, and not any old go-the-road either,' said the Postal Superintendent.

'Well, well,' said Ellen wonderingly.

'You know her, too, Ma'am; at least she knows you.'

'I couldn't even begin to guess,' said Ellen.

'She was at the same Station Mass as you,' said Dr Hogan.

'Oh, my God!' Ellen opened her mouth. 'The long woman with the bicycle; she has black hair going grey, parted in the middle,' she exclaimed.

'How d'you know that, Ma'am?' asked the Postal Superintendent.

They arranged that Dr Hogan would call for Ellen on whatever afternoon the Sergeant agreed, and take her to the police barracks to meet the woman, and decide charges.

'By the way.' Dr Hogan stuck his hand in his raincoat pocket. 'The wife gave me this for you.' He handed Ellen a lightweight packet – a brown bag folded over its own contents, tied very tight with white string and sealed with sealing wax.

'What's in it?' asked Ellen.

'Haven't a notion,' he said.

'Goodbye now, Ma'am,' said the other man, who

seemed a little disappointed at Ellen's general lukewarmth for his discovery: he waited a moment as if for gratitude, then turned and followed Dr Hogan into the rain. Ellen opened the package at Thomas's desk. Around a spent cartridge Miriam Hogan had wrapped a page of blue note-paper. 'I found this inside the ditch at the place where you and your husband had your "accident". Just before I saw it in the grass, a man was searching near the same place, and when he saw me he ran away.' No signature, no identification.

Ellen shut her eyes in fear.

Val Vousden told the man from the *Echo* of his great new project.

'I see myself as a bridge. The music-hall is an urban entertainment, and now I want to bring the countryside into it, so I'm going to revive this Band, because they were the greatest musicians in Ireland, and I want to have them on the stage with me, it will, kind of, represent the new country. And besides which they've had a terrible tragedy in their village and this will rally them. So if you put in your article my request that if anyone knows anything about the Band or its uniforms or its instruments, I'd be most grateful. I have some information already, and that's what I based my famous monologue on. And now I have eleven men, and uniforms all made and repaired, and instruments being fixed up.'

'What was that eejit talking about?' asked the Editor when the man from the *Echo* got back to the office.

On Saturday afternoon, Essie had taken Helena for a walk down the road in the pram. Ellen, diverting herself briefly from counting whether she had all her bills paid, went back to the page in the ledger marked *My Choices*, and wrote:

1. I could send Thomas into a home.
2. I could keep him here – for ever.
3. I could neglect him and hasten his death.
4. I could take Helena and disappear.
5. I could –

She paused, went back and underlined the word 'death' three times. Staring at it, she wrote above it, in tiny writing, 'revenge' – and shivered. The ledger flapped shut and she restored it to its drawer, which she locked. She checked Thomas quickly, and for a moment looked at him coolly, then got her bicycle, went to the gate and saw Essie on her way back with Helena, cycled slowly towards her and said, 'I'm just going up to the church to say a few prayers. Will you be all right?'

Essie replied, 'Ngrand, Ma'am. No hurry.'

'Hallo, sweetheart!' And Helena grinned and grinned and waved her arms, her mouth forming an 'O' as she 'uh-uh'ed.

'Hallo again, sweetheart,' said Ellen, and she poked Helena in the tummy. 'I'll steal you, so I will.' Helena gurgled and laughed. Ellen tickled her again, and Helena beamed, and then giggled.

Earlier, Ellen and Essie stood over Helena who lay naked on the towel on the table.

'Look at the folds in that little stomach,' said Ellen smiling. 'You're a disgrace, so you are. A Dis. Grace.' And she bent down and blew air right on Helena's plump navel and the baby laughed. When Ellen did it again and again, Helena laughed uncontrollably. Then Essie laughed. Then Ellen laughed; all three females rendered themselves helpless.

'Ma'am, she's like she was butter-fed,' said Essie finally wiping the tears of laughter from her eyes.

'And then I promised Dr Hogan I'd go up and see that Stephenson girl.'

'Ngrand, Ma'am.'

'Bye, bye, baby, bye-bye, Helena. Peeps? Aaah!' Ellen, leaning across the handlebars, played 'Hidey' with Helena, who chuckled, and Ellen cycled away.

Someone, the year before Ellen arrived, had painted the plinths of the Sacred Heart and Saint Patrick statues an eye-hurting puce. Built in 1860, at the height of the post-Emancipation zeal, the church's capacity amounted to three hundred people in a completely straight structure: a high, gently arched wooden roof of light oaken rafters, and six tall pointed stained-glass windows on either side, the names of the donors inserted on the glass of each one. On either wall stood two confessionals, the Canon's name above one, black letters on a piece of white card; the Curate's on the other: each confessional door had a piece of purple velvet curtain hanging from the top to waist height. Rows and rows of pews, all stained the colour of mahogany, a little cross inserted on the outside of each one, ranged back as far as the door almost, leaving an open, stone-floor space just inside the front door. In the middle of this space, stood what Thomas called 'The Corral', a new, whitewood enclosure intended for the choir, but the brand-new harmonium had as yet proven entirely unworkable: it had been shipped with part of the pedal mechanism missing; since she came to Deanstown, Ellen, to her regret, had only played the harmonium once – in Silverbridge church at the Confirmation.

Ellen, having donned the headscarf she had put in the bicycle's basket, genuflected and slipped into the place she normally occupied, traditionally the Teachers' pew in the body of the church. No sound could be heard anywhere within the building: in the distance faintly came the voices of some children playing. She changed her mind and went to a seat nearer the tall, rural-baroque white altar, like a spiky wedding-cake, with its gold-coloured sanctuary lamp and its engraved glass tabernacle door.

Identifying, as she always did now, the exact spot on which she had stood when marrying Thomas, Ellen took out her rosary beads and began:

'In the Name of the Father. And of the Son. And of the Holy Ghost. Amen.' She finished the Sign of the Cross, drew her hands together.

'I believe in God, the Father Almighty, Creator of Heaven and Earth, and in Jesus Christ, His only son Our Lord, born of the Virgin Mary, suffered under Pontius Pilate, was crucified, suffered death and was buried. He descended into Hell, the third day He rose again from the dead. He ascended into Heaven and is seated at the right hand of God, the Father Almighty. From thence He shall come to judge the living and the dead. I believe in the Holy Ghost, the Holy Catholic Church, the Communion of Saints, the Forgiveness of Sins, the Resurrection of the Body. And Life Everlasting –' Ellen stopped. She sat back in the pew, rigid, for several minutes.

Still lost in thought, she stood up, did not genuflect, walked slowly from the church, and stood outside the door. On a nearby tombstone she sat down, until the cold penetrated her skirt. She closed the church gate behind her, climbed on the bicycle, and then freewheeled down the hill. She inhaled something deeply through her nose: 'Woodsmoke,' she acknowledged.

The Stephenson stud farm may be reached by another avenue which winds up along the crest of some high fields. From half a mile away Ernestina sees the figure on the bicycle approach and is thrown into a panic. Alone in the house, she knows she does not have the energy to make tea, nor does she wish anyone other than Dr Hogan to perceive the full extent of her illness, and how awful each day now feels – and if a stranger, especially someone with authority, and above all someone with a tragedy of her own, now appears, how can Ernestina not blurt?

471

Ernestina closes the window and half-returns to bed, pressing the pain place in her back. She counts the tablets in the little white drum-box, and subtracts them from the figure on her piece of paper.

'Ba-rang.' The bell was always too heavy for the house, and what in the hell was the point of having a huge ship's bell in a farmhouse, for God's sake? We aren't a bloody man o'war, this is a stud farm.

'Ba-rang.' It can be heard in the sheds. Bloody. Bloody, bloody. She saw this Kane woman at the garden party. People spoke well of her, said she was kind, if hot-headed. Ernestina watched how the Kane woman glinted with pride for having hooked that tall good-looking man. The bloody Sinn Feiners. They could be good-looking buggers when they wanted to be. That's what Mama said, too. Ernestina has taken off her glasses, without which only she knows how blind she is, and she puts them back on, and goes to the window, opens it and looks down.

'What are you doing?' she yells, unable to see the figure who by now has come in under the eaves to the front door.

Ellen reverses a few steps and looks up and along the top storey until she finds the open window, and then sees a part of Ernestina's head.

'Hallo. I'm ringing your bell.'

'For what?'

'Dr Hogan asked me to call': Ellen shades her eyes with her hand; 'to see Ernestina.'

'I'm Ernestina.'

'I know you are. We met at your garden party. Hallo there. Again.'

'We didn't meet. We saw each other. I'm terribly busy. I have another big party coming up.'

'That can't be true. Dr Hogan told me you were very unwell.'

'When did he say that?'

'Oh, ages ago. How are you now, Ernestina?'

'I'm very busy.'

Ellen steps back farther until she can get a better look at Ernestina – who jumps away from the window, not quite fully concealing herself behind the curtain.

'I'm Ellen Kane. We have something in common.'

'We haven't. You're a Catholic.'

Ellen looks stumped. Then she calls up, 'I'd like to talk to you.'

'No. No.'

'Dr Hogan said I should.'

'I don't care.' Ernestina moves back farther as Ellen roves about below trying to get an ever better glimpse. Ernestina catches sight of her own full-length profile in the mirror: has it been a mistake to wear this satin night-gown of her mother's? A honeymoon garment – 'everything I had was in peach or pink' – and it gapes terribly at the bosom, that rotting, knobkerried bosom. She gathers the ribbons and tries to tie them, but they are so old that one snaps. Her hand falls defeated. The outline of the thick bloomers may be seen easily underneath, and particularly against this light.

Down below, the visitor, Ellen Kane, calls again.

'Lovely flowers.'

'None of your business.'

'But they are lovely.'

'Go away.'

'All right.'

A sound of footsteps: Ernestina goes to the window. She watches as Ellen Kane picks up the bicycle where it leans against a black metal *jardinière*. Ellen Kane walks away and Ernestina, still tense, stops lurking and approaches the window again to watch her. Expensive skirt, good blouse: lovely legs. That smashing dress she wore to the party. Rich for a Catholic. And only a teacher.

'Go on. Go,' Ernestina calls, but the effort, even to speak, is becoming too much. One last shout left.

'Look at you. You have everything. Look at you.'

The visitor half-turns.

'What did you say?' she asks, not unmenacingly.

'I said. Look at you. With your smart clothes and your tall teacher. How many children are you going to have, ten, I bet?'

The visitor turns fully.

Ellen shouts. 'You bitch. You dirty bitch.' She throws the bicycle down on the ground. 'You bitch. Who cares about you? Blast you.' She looks for a stone, finds one and throws it at the window, misses, jerks her arm painfully in the unaccustomed movement, holds her elbow, in a squeal and bursts out sobbing.

Ernestina goes downstairs and opens the front door. Ellen, standing there, holding her elbow, looks up and sees her.

'I only came to talk to you.'

'Come over here, then.'

'Didn't anyone tell you?'

'About what?' Ernestina lies.

'About my "living dead" husband, that's what they call him?'

'They did.'

'Thomas was hurt. He's paralysed, and he can't talk and he doesn't open his eyes. He's lying there in the house. D'you want to come and see him? I don't know what to do.'

'About what?'

'About anything.'

'I can't make you any cup of tea, so don't ask me for one. I haven't the time.'

'Is there anything you need?' Ellen asks.

'You can't get it for me.' Ernestina steps out farther. 'It would be like asking someone to go to the lavatory on my behalf.'

Ellen smiles, even though this guttural girl is perfectly serious.

'What is it? I could try.'

'I'm too busy – to do something that I liked doing.'
Ernestina paused, then her sludgy plainness surging with
a rush of trust says, 'Do you know where the rivers meet?'

Ellen said, 'I know it well.'

'I used to go there and scream. Nobody can hear you
there. And I used to take off my clothes and go in the
water.'

'It's gone a bit cold now. If I – do that, will you, can I,
call back some day soon and talk to you?'

Ernestina nods, and then she backs into the hall, and
closes the door very gently.

Ellen set off down the other, more legitimate avenue, and
cycled to the river where Thomas and she had sat, their
first 'occasion of sin', as the priest in Confession had called
it. Not a soul to be seen anywhere: she opened the field
gate and ricketed down the bumpy path to the grove, and
threw the bicycle down.

Standing on the bank of the river, by the corner of the
seat, she opened her mouth.

'Ernestina. Ern. Est. Teen. Nah.'

A quiet shout. Not good enough.

'Ernestina. ERNESTINA.' She shook her head,

'ERN. EST. TEEN. NAH!'

Birds fluttered away, and Ellen walked to the edge of
the dark water.

'ERN. EST. TEEN. NAH!' she shouted again, then again,
and again, and again.

Her body reverberated. She began to shout all kinds of
things. 'MEAT! FLOUR! SCHOOL! CURSE! ME!' Then she
let go her biggest shout. 'ELLEN!' and then shouted out
the seven sacraments.

'BAPTISM! CONFIRMATION! BLESSED EUCHARIST!
PENANCE! EXTREME UNCTION! HOLY ORDERS!
MATRIMONY!'

She moved to the water's edge, kicked a shoe off and touched the water with her toe.

'DEATH!' she shouted, and followed it with, 'LIFE!'

She began to take off her clothes. 'I AM GOING MAD!' she screamed. Only four garments: blouse first, then the light bodice: then skirt, then knickers. Her toes made marks in the little soft mud.

'FUCK OFF!' she shouted, not quite certain of the full implications of the word. 'I AM GOING MAD! PRIEST! LIFE!'

She walked into the slow green-and-black river which after the summer had not yet become again deep enough to swim in, and she stood there, water up to her hips, hands by her sides, as white as the statue of a goddess. 'ERNESTINA! YOU'RE DYING! THOMAS YOU'RE DYING! I'LL GO MAD IF I WANT TO!'

Ellen scratched at her abundant crush of pubic hair.

'DIE!' Pressing her hands to her face, her shouts began to subside; 'PRIDE. COVETOUSNESS. LUST. ANGER. GLUTTONY. ENVY. Sloth.'

She saw the face in the tall sedges, staring at her, and screamed at it. The startled boy jumped to his feet, Michael Quinn, and he ran as hard as he could.

'I DON'T CARE!' roared Ellen.

In a moment, she lowered her head and stood, both hands folded as if in duty over her groin. Then she turned and waded from the river, climbing up through the reeds and cresses. She sat on the wooden bench, her heavy buttocks leaving wet marks on the old plank.

'Thomas, my love,' she said aloud.

She could still see the boy running away across the fields towards the bridge.

'I'm all right now. I will be all right now. I'm going to be all right now. Thomas, my love, my dear love.'

=

476

In due course, Ellen dressed and rode her bicycle home, and did not get there until six o'clock. Essie met her in unusual agitation.

'Ma'am, nthere's a gngentleman here!'

'Where? Who? Is he a doctor?'

In excitement, Essie's speech defect intensified. 'Ma'am, I couldn't gnstop him. He's gnupstairs, Ma'am.'

'Oh, thank God': Ellen had a fear of anyone harming the unprotected and unprotectable Thomas. 'Who is he?'

'I gndon't know, Ma'am, gnhe says he's gcoming to stay, he gmight be a Protestant gminister, Ma'am, he's wearing a ngrey suit.'

'Oh, Father John!' Ellen lowered her voice. 'Oh, God! I wasn't expecting him so soon.'

He had heard Ellen arrive and he came downstairs, smacking his lips softly, a perennial habit. A handshake with both hands: a holding-out at arm's length to inspect: a look of deep compassion. As never before in his presence, Ellen felt embarrassed.

'Look. I'll show you. I have a letter half-written to you. You must think me terrible.'

'Look, I bring gifts, from your loving parents. From all the family. Have you forgotten?'

Her birthday. Yesterday. 'They clubbed together.' Not even with Ernestina did she recall her birthday.

'Isn't that a massive parcel?' Father John Watson S.J. smiled.

'Very like a fish,' Thomas said of him. 'A pike, those spiky teeth.'

'Open it. I am so glad to see you again, my dear Ellen, so glad we shall be able to talk.'

No time taken rolling the string.

'The bus conductor had to help me carry it in.'

'I hope he didn't come any farther . . .'

'No, no, this is a house of the sick. I told him so.'

No time to fold the paper. On top lay a silver piece of metal, with a black end to it.

'That's the handle.' A high-domed, wooden, lacquered box, with a lock. 'A gramophone, and there are records in my case.'

'But we have a gramophone record. A man brought it to us from Australia.' She rushed to Thomas's room, saying, 'Hallo, Thomas,' not pausing, as she usually did, to be arrested by the sight, and rushed back again with the record.

'I'll do it,' he said, 'I'm used to it; we have one in the Provincial's House.'

Father John Watson wound the gramophone and put on the record. The kitchen filled with the sound of the kookaburra, a dreadful laughing, eerie and hacking sound, and not at all as pleasant and amusing and warm as Joe Johnson's version.

'What is this?' asked Father Watson, not a little taken aback, especially at the fact that Ellen laughed so loudly almost in tune with the record.

'It's a bird, Father John,' she told him, 'look, it says, "From the Series of Thrilling Sounds: The Voice of True Nature." It's a bird.'

26

Long into the night, John Watson, intimate orator, addressed Ellen.

'Moments of endearment,' he murmured, retracing incidents from her childhood; 'And may I remind you of your great spiritual strength? Your natural solicitousness for Christ's will.' In his fat hand a glass of port the colour of black blood: he sipped gently: 'I advise you to recall such good times, when you were . . . when you were still, aah, ah'm? What is the word I was looking for? Still – untroubled. By this dreadful burden, yes, untroubled.' When Ellen first described him to Thomas, she said, 'His eyes. They're funny. His eyes are younger than he is, do you know what I mean, Thomas?'

John Watson now said, 'I feel it my bounden duty to warn you of one thing, dear Ellen. You must not give in to hatred now, hatred of Thomas. You must be so close to that, you must so wish to hate him. For him lying there, demanding so much of you, and proving such a burden.'

John Watson said, 'I was always a little, a little surprised – that you did marry. And indeed I often wonder whether Thomas had somehow persuaded you, against your . . . against your – it was all so rushed, wasn't it? Whereas I, who know you, dear Ellen, who know you so well, who know your soul as well, if not better, than you do, would have assumed, and I think rightly, that your prayers would have been enough for you? No?'

John Watson stretched his short legs. 'Isn't life funny? There is Thomas in the next room. Prostrate. You know, the ways of God. They're not our ways, Ellen. I was only thinking after Mass yesterday – poor Thomas. If he is lucid, is it crossing his mind – is it crossing his mind, that he himself must have rendered so many men insensible, I mean – eternally insensible? Even without a chance to make their peace before meeting their Maker? Although I do not subscribe to the vengeance theories, or the punishment theories, "live by the sword, die by the sword", sort of thing, no, no, no, this is not a vengeful God who watches over us, but at the same time . . .'

John Watson asked, 'And you, dear Ellen, how in the name of the dear Lord have you weathered it at all? I know, I know, don't tell me.' He raised a hand. 'Your prayers, your wonderful devotion to Our Blessed Lady. I know. At the same time, I sense you may have – perhaps – aged? There is a – there is a – what is the word, there is a – *glitter* about you I have not seen before.'

'Father John, do you remember the wedding here? Wasn't it a great day? Now, wasn't it?'

'Oh, Ellen, dear, the joy of that day, and the fun. So nice not to have had it at an hotel, wasn't it? Although –' He laughed and shook his head in amused ruefulness. '– I have to say, I must have eaten something that didn't agree with me. No, no.' He waved away her quick furrow of concern, 'I was fine in a few days, just the old tummy, I suppose.'

She surveyed him sitting in Thomas's armchair which the little priest had drawn out of the shuttered bow-window towards the range, and as Thomas did with a cup of tea, Father John balanced his glass of port on the edge of the kitchen table above his right elbow.

'About your age, Thomas,' Ellen had answered, 'although, wait – no, he's older, I counted, he must be, he must be . . . nearly fifty.'

'I suppose what I really want to say,' Father Watson summarized, 'is – you will probably survive better, dear Ellen, if you release yourself from memories so, so . . . I

mean, if you dwell on, or . . . No. Let me start again. If
you turn to new pastures of thought, rather than brood –
and as we know, brooding is unhealthy – if you fill your
mind with thoughts not so intimately associated with
Thomas. If you move forward from memories of your
marriage, which must now be so painful . . . and prayer,
your own great advocate, prayer. Yes. Yes. That's it.
Prayer.' He gazed into the fire.

'Where we find strength in our afflictions, Ellen, is not
always within the affliction itself. My idea is that you
should go back to – when you were yourself, as it were.
My idea is that you should seek for succour outside those
later days. Poor Thomas. So much pain and grief to you.
Do you remember our long conversations, as we walked
by the river, or out on the Ballysimon road on a Sunday
afternoon? And your dear, if I may say so, innocent
enquiries into theology? And your earnest desire to find
the right spiritual pathway?'

Ellen listened more – much more – than she talked.

Eventually, she said, 'Father John, will you say an
earlier or later Mass than the Canon? Because I think it
would be a good idea if you helped to give out Communion with him?'

Through the window Ellen could see the sharp cold smile
of a quarter-moon reflected in her dressing-table mirrors.
Around the landing, a creak and a puff: John Watson, at
last in his bed in his room, blew out the candle. In her
cot, Helena gave a tiny whistling cry, a baby dream. Ellen,
alert, waited. Snoring began; Father John, yes, remember, he even drank nearly all that second glass of port
wine.

Ellen put on the dressing-gown from Aunt Lil, and crept
down. By the light of the embers in the range, she lit a
new candle from the kitchen drawer, and melted the butt
until the candle adhered upright to a saucer. The door to

Thomas's room squeaked only when beyond halfway open: she sidled in: he lay swaddled in the dimness. Ellen placed the candle saucer on the floor, and standing at the back of the bed-chair, manipulated the two silent cranking levers raising Thomas to a shallow angle. Gathering the folds of her nightgown and dressing-gown safely away from the candle, she came around and squatted in front of him.

'Thomas,' she began. 'I am going to nail that man. Oh, Thomas, I shouldn't say that. Oh, God.' She gazed up into the insensate, open-mouthed, beloved face.

'No. I should say it. I should. I should. You would agree with me. You do agree with me. Don't you, Thomas?'

Through the blankets she fumbled until she had secured the shape of his foot, which she clasped.

'You do agree, don't you? You do. You do. I know you, Thomas. You do agree. You have never forgiven him for what he did to us. You were right. It was none of his business.'

Ellen tilted forward, from her hunkers to her knees, and clasped his foot with her other hand. 'Thomas Kane, I have changed. Oh, my dear love. This is the first day I can ever remember that I did not say my morning prayers. I said no prayers last night either. Thomas, I don't care. I do care, I do, I do, but when I say I don't care, that isn't what I mean. What I mean is. Oh, God, my head is full of wild thoughts, Thomas. What I mean is. You may be taken from me. But if you are, I won't care – provided – what is it you always said, Thomas? That your job was to keep your balance in life? Do you remember? You used to tease me – that was why we had to have six boys and six girls? Balance.'

She took her hands from Thomas's feet and pushed her hair back. 'Thomas, I have to whisper. Everyone's asleep. But I feel so wild. I'm like a fishwife telling her Confession. I haven't been good to you. I haven't nursed you well. How many things wrong? I don't know, Thomas, if you can hear me, but if you can, encourage me. Jesus Christ in Heaven, Thomas, encourage me.'

Her rhapsody gaining, Ellen went on, 'Bless me, Thomas, for I have sinned – in thought, word and deed, against YOU, my beloved husband. Through my own most grievous fault. I feared that you would breed murderers in me. I told that man, that awful man – remember you pointed him out to me, that very first foggy morning, his bicycle and his cap, I had my scarf on me still, and I had my hand on my hip, God, I remember it – I told him although I didn't mean to, that a revenge he might take against you would be understandable. "He who takes the sword" I said to him. And I knew that you knew about that McAuliffe woman's husband and where he was. And who killed him. I lied to you. About little things. About huge things. I shut you out of my bed, and I shut you out of my body. The body that I spent my days thinking about. How about that for mortifying the flesh, Thomas? Was I mad? I'm mad now, Thomas. I'm mad for you. Mad for you. And mad about you. And mad over you. Thomas. Jesus. I even contemplated suffocating you. With one of those pillows you're lying on. Or starving you, and pretending you had begun to reject food. Who would know? And d'you think Dr Hogan, that solid-gold eejit, as you'd say yourself, d'you think he wouldn't certify the cause of death? They'd all say what a mercy; what a relief! But Thomas, when I met you I knew nothing about love, and I knew nothing about what I'm like. And now I know one thing, that what I want out of life – is you.'

She laughed, hand over her mouth. 'Oh, Thomas – is that what you'd call "a turn-up for the books"? That I'm talking about the love of Man instead of spouting about the love of God?'

Ellen bowed her face until it touched his blanketed knees. The white long shape of Thomas seemed to extend and grow into her hair and shoulders. In the not over-warm room, she began to perspire.

'Thomas, I lost my way. I wasn't fair to you. I always had everything my own way. I always got what I wanted. But now, Thomas, I am going to get what I want, but I don't want it for myself, I want it for you.'

Ellen stood, her hips aching. 'Thomas, there are things I can't even speak to you about, about feelings in my body, when I'd stand in the school listening to the children recite their prayers, and I'd feel without touching what we had been doing at home, in our own privacy; this was before "Canon Law". Thomas, I asked you once – and blast you, I could never get you to talk about anything like that, you said it was "women's business" – I asked you once what we did in the night, what it made you feel, and you said to me, "Fierce", and even though I liked it, I didn't know what you meant. I know now. My dear, dear man. Fierce. Fierce!'

Ellen bent down and across Thomas, as she had to do when turning him with Essie. She moved the blankets sufficiently to expose his pyjama-ed shoulders and some of his chest, where the hair had turned quite white, and arranging her body, embraced him as fully as she could. For a long minute she half-stood, half-lay there across him. Beneath her, the breathing stroked through the body; the beating of his heart thumped on, described by the doctors as 'too strong'. Ellen lay her face on his, and whispered in his ear. 'Thomas, if I can – in any way what-soever – I am going to bring you back to life. Back to life.'

Tenderly anchoring the blankets to keep him warm, she picked up the candle and climbed slowly to bed, not caring whether the stairs creaked.

She slept as deep as a drunkard until the cracking knock on her door in the morning: she had outslept the calling Essie and the crying Helena.

=

At eight o'clock, downstairs, dressed for Mass, Ellen put in place the first phase of her revenge.

'May I surprise you, Father John?' she asked. 'Can I go to Confession to you?'

At the dim end of the hallway under the stairs, she arranged a chair for him, a kneeling cushion for herself. The priest leaned forward on one knee, a Rodin Thinker in black with a purple stole, a hand over his eyes.

'. . . For I have sinned in the . . . the three weeks,' she lied, 'since my last Confession.'

'My child?'

'Father, I spoke badly of people.'

'My child?'

'Father, I might for a moment have lost my faith in God.'

'God tries us all, my child.'

'Father, He has tried me very hard. My husband is paralysed and insensible.'

'But – look. God has given you the strength of the Sacraments, my child? This is a Sacrament you are partaking of now.'

'Yes, Father, that's true.' In the distant kitchen, Essie's voice droned affectionately at Helena.

'Father, but I am a young and healthy married woman with no husband.'

'Yes, my child.' He paused. 'What, may I ask, are you leading to?'

Ellen blurted studiedly. 'I ask God to forgive me impure thoughts.'

'Many, my child?' asked the grave, oaken voice.

'Sometimes, Father. And – they confuse me.'

'Are they specific, my child?'

'How do you mean, Father?'

'Are they, ah'm, how shall I put it? Are they, how shall I say? Directed?'

'No, just impure thoughts about . . . Just impure thoughts, Father.'

'In the abstract, my child?'

'Yes, Father. No, Father. I mean, how do you mean?'

'Or in the concrete. I ask fearing scandal?'

'I don't get you, Father?'

'Impure thoughts about, well . . . Men whom you know, my child, men with – even – wives of their own. You may be committing Scandal, in your head, admittedly, but it is the gravest, "Woe to the Scandal-Giver", the gravest sin of all. The sin of Scandal?'

'Oh, Father, I never thought.'

'Grievous Matter. Perfect Knowledge. And Full Consent. In which case, therefore. Grievous Matter, my child, and, this is. But no, this is not – Mortal. Because no Perfect Knowledge. Is that right?'

'No, Father. Not Scandal, not men with wives. He isn't married . . . I mean.' Ellen stopped. Paused. 'I haven't worked it out yet, Father, I need the grace of Absolution and Penance to help me.'

'My child, God will help you, and He will forgive you in your special circumstances. Feel sure of that. Now for your Penance say the Joyful Mysteries of the Rosary, and offer them up for this man of whom you think.'

'Thank you, Father.'

'Now, a Perfect Act of Contrition . . .'

He went back to the city on Monday afternoon. Ellen waved the bus goodbye, and returned to the house, thoughtful hand on chin. One letter; no time until now to open it.

Dear Mrs Kane,
    Yes, I did hear the bad news and I am very sorry indeed. Just as I regret that this old complaint of mine kept me from delivering your daughter, but I believe

she's a fine infant in any case. ['The handwriting as bad as ever,' she smiled.]

Perhaps Providence inspired you [Ellen grinned at the irony: 'You old atheist'] but bearing in mind the description of your husband's condition (I read the salient details in the papers and I meant to write to you but I still had the shakes), you could not have asked a better man than myself for a second opinion. I think I know the exact surgeon to get in touch with, he's a man who knows about the silent areas of the brain; but I'd like to see your husband first and I'll come out this coming Thursday, if that's all the same to you. I bought myself a car and I'm going everywhere in it, I'm even calling on patients of mine who aren't sick at all.

Yours with best regards,
J. A. Morgan

Ellen jumped to her feet, and swung Helena above her head and danced around.

'Read that, Essie! Essie, read that!' she cried. 'Weeeeeeeee!!'

Essie said, 'Ma'am, he must be hiring a spider to write his letters.'

'Read it! Read it! Weeeeeeeeee!!' Helena, rich in gums, laughed.

'Right! Helena! Your best dress and matinee coat!'

She plonked Helena on Essie and ran along the kitchen, hitting her thigh hard as she rounded the table. 'Thomas! Thomas! Dr Morgan is going to do something!' At the parlour door Ellen clapped her hands in rhythm and danced to an imaginary jig. 'Thanks be to God, Essie! The first ray of hope. The first ray of hope! I knew it! I knew it!'

Ellen took Helena for a walk and played hiding games with her over the slim marbled-pearl handle of the pram. A woman in a cottage came out to admire the chuckling, arm-chugging baby: 'She's the spit-and-image of you, Ma'am.'

An unusual feather lay in the roadside grass: Ellen gathered it, tickled Helena's little nose. That night, all chores done, Ellen lit a lamp and took it into Thomas's room.

'Now, Thomas,' she said, settling in the chair as if for a long chat with a friend, 'isn't that wonderful about Dr Morgan? I can't wait. Look, I found this feather on the road, what do you think it is from, a seagull? I've lots of news for you. Jack Carty was asking for you yesterday at Mass. The Canon complained about the Dance last week, dancing too close again. They're all bound for Hell, he says, without even a stretch in Purgatory on the way. And he was ratty about a speech somebody made at a Gaelic League meeting in Shronell. Mrs Quilty had an extraordinary coat on her, I don't know where in the name of God she got it. The Relihans were asking for you, their daughter is going nursing after all. You'll be glad to know your bosom friend, Father John W., is gone back. Essie made the grandest meat loaf ever, although I think she put in too much onions, myself. Could Helena be getting a tooth? Look.' She lifted her skirt. 'I hit my thigh off the edge of the table and it's gone black-and-blue, and even a bit yellow. Look. It nearly tore the suspender off me.'

In the kitchen, folding clothes, Essie heard the drone of the voice coming from the Master's bedside and assumed the Mistress had begun the Rosary.

The barracks did not possess a cell decent enough, in the Sergeant's opinion, 'to put a sober woman into'. She was kept in a locked bedroom of the married quarters overhead. The three callers, Dr Hogan, the Postal Superintendent and Ellen, waited in the General Office while the Sergeant fetched her.

'I'll just lock the front door now for a while,' he said.

'Wait 'til you meet the Sergeant,' Thomas said to Ellen

on her second day in Deanstown. 'He speaks as if he's saying his prayers. He's as monotonous as ditchwater.'

The Sergeant intoned, 'If anyone wants to get in they'll have to hammer hard. My wife can keep an eye on the door.'

Dr Hogan looked at Ellen: she did not laugh.

'I nearly passed out,' she said to Thomas that night, 'when he said he'd get the wife to keep an eye on the door. I could hear your voice, Thomas: "Which eye, the good one, or the one over to the west?" Jack Hogan was doing his best to get me to laugh.' Ellen's high spirits anticipated Dr Morgan's visit next day.

The woman did not return Ellen's stare.

'Her name, Ma'am, is Edel Crowe, a fine farm and respectable brothers.'

In her middle thirties, Edel Crowe wore the same black clothes Ellen had seen on her the morning of the Station Mass.

'She went to the Ursuline Convent, Ma'am, and only left school when she was eighteen. She did a Secretarial Course in Stephen's Green in Dublin.' No, the Sergeant's voice did not come from intoning prayers, it came from giving evidence. In each of his sentences many words began with capital letters.

Unworked hands, with the surprising pleasantness of freckles: Edel Crowe sat looking at nobody. In the drab green General Office with one official book and three chewed, unkempt pencils on the single table near the fire, each of the four people observed her differently.

The Sergeant saw the puzzlement of a woman from a well-off family attempting to commit a crime, with no history of any such thing in her people, and the nuisance of it was, he'd have to get the nurse in when they were taking her to the jail for the Remand. In the eyes of the

Postal Superintendent as he leaned on the counter, she had good handwriting, and he would be cross-examined in a case that would get into all the papers. Jack Hogan, his hands deep in his raincoat pockets, saw a look of Miriam about her. Ellen considered something wistful and troubled in Edel Crowe: her own aggressive shows of unconcern often concealed defiance, or fright.

'Ma'am, I haven't drafted a Charge yet, but I'll need a Statement from you,' said the Sergeant.

'Can you do without it?' asked Ellen.

'I suppose,' said Dr Hogan, getting it wrong, 'it'd be very hard on the Mistress to have to stand up in court.'

'I have to Proceed via a Statement, Ma'am.'

Ellen said, 'Sergeant, can I speak to her on her own?'

'No, Ma'am, that'd be against Regulations, leaving the Prisoner alone with the Injured Party. Sure you'd never know what'd happen.'

The Sergeant had a private thing against Edel Crowe's brother – not the one gone to England, the one farming in the home place: he did not come up with the goods when the hint was dropped regarding a free sack of potatoes and no questions about the dog licence.

'No, Ma'am, against Regulations.'

Ellen moved over to stand near him and his silver belt buckle.

'Sergeant': she looked up at his bushy face: 'I would like very much to speak to Miss Crowe alone.'

Behind Ellen's back, Dr Hogan nodded affirmation with his head and brows: the Sergeant hesitated.

'Ma'am, we'd have to remain nearby, in the immediate Vicinity of the Prisoner . . .'

'Within shouting distance, maybe?' said Ellen, 'in case I need you.'

The three men walked through a door opened by the Sergeant which led to the rear of the barracks, and there, within view of Ellen but far away, they stood between the whitewashed walls of the corridor, talking, and trying not to look back at the dayroom.

Ellen sat on a chair two feet away from the woman and looked at her.

'Now, Edel Crowe,' she said, 'I'm the woman you wrote to, and I'm the wife of the man you wrote to. As you well know. And I have two things to say to you. The first is what the Sergeant would call a Statement. This is my Statement. You're a living, lighting bitch to do what you did. I never did a thing to you that I'm aware of. It wasn't my fault if you didn't manage to get my husband before I even knew him. Nobody but a bitch would do what you did. And a right bitch at that. You frightened me.'

Ellen eased back. 'Now, I have that off my chest. Here's the second thing. Why did you do it, why did you write those letters? For all you know, I might be the sort of woman who could be a friend to you?'

Edel Crowe, for some strange reason, bore a curious resemblance to Thomas Kane. No more than a chance of life – they had no blood connection, ancient or recent, no breeding secrets, no consanguinous history. She did not answer.

Ellen softened her tone and said, 'Come on, tell me. By the way, I am not going to press charges, so there will be no court case and the whole thing will be quietened, I'll see to it. I promise, I give you my word of honour.'

The woman still did not reply.

Ellen tried one more time. 'It isn't a bargain, that, I'm not trading with you, or trying to. I'm not having charges anyway. I haven't had things easy. To look at me, you might have thought I had a lot of things that were great. Look at me now. Come on, tell me. Please. Why did you write them?'

The woman said, still not looking at Ellen, 'I meant every word I said in those letters. I had a flair for your husband.'

'Would you have it if you saw him now?' asked Ellen.

'I would. I know all about it. About what happened. I saw it in the papers. And every chance I get, I ask people about him. I hear how he is. I'd look after him.' Then she flashed, 'I'd get him proper doctors. More than you've done.' She had a voice as cultured as Ellen's own.

Ellen blushed but did not rise. 'I wish I'd known you properly,' said Ellen, 'without any of this thing happening. We might have got on very well. And if you were – sincere about the Master, why did you try and hurt him?'

'I felt hurt myself.'

'Thomas, I couldn't wait to tell you.' Ellen prattled on as she spooned the thick soup into Thomas's mouth that night. 'The thing is, she must have wanted to marry you desperately, and how can I complain? She was here before I met you. I know, I know, what you'll say, that she's a troublemaker.'

'You felt hurt?' squeaked Ellen to Edel Crowe. 'But that's the same as taking the law into your own hands.' She turned impatiently, then faced back. 'Look. I said. I'm not going to have you charged with anything. Just don't ever do anything like that again. All right? I couldn't take that sort of thing now.'

She called the Sergeant, who blustered.

'If you insist,' she said, 'I'll go to court, Sergeant, but not to charge her. It is a witness for her I'll be, and anyway I'll say I didn't want charges brought, and my husband didn't either. So you'll have to face Justice Hipwell yourself.'

'Boys, oh boys,' said the Postal Superintendent.

When Edel Crowe received her coat and made to leave the barracks, Ellen asked Dr Hogan, 'You're not going to let that woman walk home on her own in the rain, are you, it's nearly dark. She'll get her death of cold. No, no,' she said, putting down his protest. 'You can call for me on the way back. Besides, I have something else to talk to the Sergeant about.'

The Sergeant rubbed his jaw hard, the gesture of a man contemplating shaving.

'Oh, God, Ma'am. That's fierce stuff you're saying there. Oh, God, Ma'am, and it was what, May, June, July, August, September, October, we're near November. Six months ago? Whewwww!'

The Sergeant and his Superintendent had asked questions; not a shred of evidence existed – other than gossip.

'What use is another cartridge to me?' the Sergeant asked Ellen. 'Sure we have a cartridge already. Ma'am, I'm telling you. All kinds of people were questioned. The Super himself stopped people on the road. But sure what could people say to him if he started asking again now, only – "What are you asking me them kind of questions for? Are you going round asking everyone else what Mass were they at of a Sunday last May?" That's all we'd get from anybody, Ma'am.'

'So what could I do, Thomas? You couldn't move that Sergeant if you put a horse hauling him. D'you know, I nearly felt myself slipping back again to the worst times, if it wasn't for Dr Morgan tomorrow.'

Essie had gone down to the village to bring back the large seven-pound bags of sugar for making the apple jelly. For hours on end, Ellen had continued to record even the tiniest change in Thomas. Eyes open, flutteringly or lazily a slight roll of the head; anything even approaching recognition in the demeanour. Her reports all said the same thing: 'Only minute changes. Nothing you could hang a hope on.'

She fought off the voice of despondency whenever it awakened in her. 'Am I glad, Thomas, I have all these notes for Dr Morgan tomorrow? Dr Hogan never looked at them, nor asked me. But John Morgan – he's very solid, isn't he? Here we go, Thomas, don't laugh, this is the song I'm teaching them in school.

> 'O'er the fields she passes to and fro,
> By the cornstalks standing row by row.
> Poppies whisper as they see her go,
> "Marionina, little friend,
> Whither would your footsteps wend?
> Come and teach us how to bend.
> Marionina, Marionina –
> Come, Oh come, and teach us how to bend."'

Ellen bowed and straightened up, laughing.

'Oh, Thomas, look!' She raised the skirt to mid-thigh. 'The bruise is an interesting shade of yellow, don't you think.'

She whisked the skirt from side to side like a can-can dancer.

'I think it is anyway,' she said, with a laugh-seeking flounce.

'And, Thomas, the other thing about that Edel Crowe woman. I forgot to tell you, she had lovely hands – and the most beautiful scarab ring I ever saw, in a glassy sort of green stone, I wonder was it a real emerald?'

People who knew him said, 'You have to hand it to Val. When he puts his mind to something, he gets it done.'

Again, Val proved them right. He had made 'marvellous progress altogether' with the Deanstown Band.

'Ma'am,' he said to Ellen in the school yard – Val leaned across the wall while the children milled back and forth behind him during the morning break – 'the original band, I'm finding out things all the time, had up to twenty-four men and the drum-major, not fourteen, and I think I'm going to be able to get nearly nineteen fellows altogether.

Mrs Heffernan is a genius with a needle and thread and she has two more women sewing the extra tunics, she's cutting the patterns herself; the pants aren't that important, they were a kind of a dark blue colour, but really anything would do for the moment, the red stripe will unite them anyway, won't it, but the tunic was very important altogether, the blue and gold you know, and we're going to rehearse all the winter. The school won't be big enough for the morning practice, the Canon says we can have the hall.'

Ellen described him later to Essie: 'He looks like a kind of a cross between a bony old grandfather and a leprechaun and he has red cracked cheeks like a pippin apple. He's probably a very nice man, but I don't know what in the world to make of him. He talks like this –' and Ellen mimicked Val Vousden's up-and-down voice.

'Ma'am, how are things with you?' Val asked.

'Ah, sure not bad, I suppose, even though there's no sign of a change in the Master': another advance – she could now bring herself to discuss it openly with any who asked.

'What is it he has, Ma'am?' asked Val. 'Is it brain damage itself?'

'I suppose so, Mr Vousden.'

'And nothing to be done for it?'

'We're all the time making medical enquiries, Mr Vousden, but nothing yet, I'm afraid. In fact I have someone coming to give another opinion today after school.'

'Is it hard to look after him, Ma'am?'

'Oh, it is, Mr Vousden, it is. The great fear is if he catches a cold, that's the thing that worries me the most.'

Val told Mrs Heffernan that night how much he liked that Mrs Kane – 'She has a way of speaking that respects a person, a bit like yourself, Ma'am, in that respect.'

A moment later, 'Mrs Heffernan, do you think that Mrs Kane would consult a man who wasn't a real doctor? I mean, if the man didn't have the certificates, but he could cure people like?'

'A quack?'

'Well, I'd prefer to call him a healer?'

'If it was my husband, God be good to him, I'd try anything.'

Val Vousden, about to leave the Deanstown area for three or four weeks, said, 'I think I'll make a few enquiries. I've forgotten the person's name.' Mrs Heffernan broke off a piece of thread with her teeth.

'But I thought he'd nearly be here before I got home from school?' Ellen said anxiously to Essie. 'He'd never be out this late, would he, a man that age, and he's hardly used to the car yet, surely?'

Dr Morgan did not arrive on Thursday, nor on Friday, nor on Saturday – on which night Ellen had a dreadful time, a fit of weeping of a kind she had not had for weeks.

'Oh, Thomas, I'm sorry, "Weeping and gnashing of teeth" isn't that what they say we'll have to do in Hell? Ach, Thomas, I sometimes wonder which of the two of us is in "the exterior darkness"? Oh, I shouldn't be talking like this, he'll be here tomorrow or Monday; he probably had a baby to deliver, or an emergency thing or something.'

Dr Morgan did not come on Sunday; two of Thomas's brothers and his two sisters arrived in a hackney car, and stayed for their tea, distracting Ellen.

'If he comes on Monday, it will be very inconvenient,' said Ellen.

'I'm getting as fat as a fool, Essie,' said Ellen as they ate dinner, one of Essie's specials, porksteak stuffed with breadcrumbs, and peas and roast potatoes.

Around the corner of the house, they could hear the engine of the car being cranked up.

'Did you ask Michael Condon had he a mouth on him?'

Essie said, 'I did, Ma'am, but he said he's after his dinner.'

When Ellen returned an hour or so later from her first, swaying driving lesson – guided by a watchful and amused Michael Condon in a flat field, mercifully dry – she felt exhilarated.

'Essie,' she shouted, 'ESSIE! It was great. He said I was very good. No Dr Morgan, I suppose?'

'No, Ma'am.'

'I wonder what's wrong with him, maybe he's sick again, and then he couldn't write.'

'I've tea made, Ma'am.'

'Lovely! I'll have a quick read of the paper before I start the Master. Michael Condon has very bad teeth, Essie.'

Across the front page of the *Irish Independent* ran columns of close type: BIRTHS: MARRIAGES: DEATHS: Ellen scanned them expertly and turned to the general news on the next page, then the next, at the bottom of which she shouted.

'Oh, no! Oh, God, no!'

The death took place (suddenly) at his home on Thursday last (as reported in our late editions on Saturday), of Dr John Alexis Morgan, M.D. He was aged 67. A native of Landerstown, Dr Morgan was educated at Clongowes Wood, the Royal University, and Guy's Hospital in London. He served in two Colonial campaigns, and was invalided out of the Far East, suffering consequently from recurrent malaria. A widely respected and popular figure, whose medical expertise was generously available to one and all, he will be deeply missed by his wife and grown-up family, and by members of Athlunkard Boat Club and Corbally Golf Club.

Winter 1926

27

Next day, the weather bowed Ellen's head, echoing and cloaking her dejection during the five-minute walk to school. Many children and Miss McGoldrick funked the extreme rain and wind. Ellen took all classes in Thomas's room; why light two fires? When she called, in Irish, for quietness, the habituated children stood up expecting prayers.

'No. Sit down again. Fold your arms.' This departure generated expectancy.

'Since you were all good enough to come to school, and not like the cissies who were afraid they'd melt away in the rain.' They sniggered. 'Or be blown away like thread, the ninnyhammers.' They laughed. 'We'll have something nice today.' She wrote a word on the blackboard. 'Now. A penny for the first person who tells me the meaning of this word.' Ellen smiled into their thickets of blankness. 'No? All right. A penny for anyone who can pronounce it. Come on. Try.'

Lips moved without sound: they hunched their shoulders, hands over covered mouths. 'John Ryan, come on, you big fosthoock.' He coloured and laughed and shifted his hobnailed feet. 'Sheila Carroll?' Sheila went, 'Surrr. Ik. Ullem.'

'Nearly there. Nearly there. Who's next? Miss Nobody? Or Mr Nobody? All right, all right.' With the long knitting-needle she had used as her pointer since Training College, Ellen took them through each part of the word.

'Now, there are four parts in this word, or four – what?' She nodded slowly several times as only the older ones struggled to spew out the word 'Syllable'.

'There are four. Syllables. And "syllable" itself has?' She held up three fingers on her left hand. 'Three. Syllables. Verrry Good. And the first syllable is? It isn't "Surr", like you call the Master. It is "K", the "c" is like the "c" in "Cat". So it's "Kurr". What is it?'

They sang a chorus of 'Kurr'.

'Now, the second part, or syllable, is very easy. What is it?'

Several said, 'Ik.'

'That's right, it may be spelt with a "c", as you can see, "i.c.". But it is called "ik". So put the two together and what have we? Kurr. Ik. Curric. Kurr. Ik. Now the third part or syllable is only one letter and it spells –' she rounded on the most junior child in the room, a tiny Viking-blonde girl in a fair-isle cardigan. Ellen said, with a mock-fierce face and large smile, 'You!' The child jumped back, and then blushed and giggled to her deskmate. Of the room at large, Ellen asked, 'The third syllable is, simply, "u", the letter "u", so we have what?'

They ventured, 'Kurrikyou.'

'Exactly. Exactly. And the fourth syllable or word-part is – Come on. Yes, that's it.' She encouraged the tentative sounds. 'Yes. "Lum". So we have Kurr. Ik. You. Lum. All together. One syllable at a time.'

They chorused, 'Kurr. Ik. You. Lum.'

'Quickly.' She led them.

'Curriculum.'

'Good. What does it mean? The "Curriculum" –' she beat time in the air – 'is the list of things you have to learn in school. Irish. English. Arithmetic and all your sums. Catechism. History. Geography. Put all of those together and that is what the "Curriculum" is. Now today we're not going to have the "Curriculum". We are going to have something different. We are going to have some Nature Notes. Just nice things about the countryside.'

She lifted the lid of the high desk, fumbled thoughtfully

within, fetched one of Thomas's books and from it took a tree leaf he had pressed between two sheets of writing-paper. With a flick of stamp-paper, she stuck it to the blackboard.

'Now what leaf is this? This is the leaf of the – Alder tree. Hands up anyone who has seen it before?' Several hands shot up in the air.

'Good. Good. It has red berries and sometimes it has flowers, they're white or pink. Now.'

Ellen returned to the high desk and settled herself on her cushions. One hand clasped on the other, she leaned forward, relishing.

'Libate. Libate,' Miss Humphrys had cried in Teacher Training. 'Knowledge is a god, pour libations for it.'

Ellen flooded them with interesting knowledge; that it was also called 'dogwood' because hunters used to boil the leaves, and use that juice to wash the fleas and lice off their hunting-dogs: once a dog had been washed in the juice of the dogwood tree the lice did not come back for a year and a day; that before the Celts discovered how to make really hard weapons from their discovery of iron, they carved and seasoned dogwood branches into knives and daggers; that the Red Indians of North America used it as a mix to make the tobacco last longer, and they boiled it too, not to clean their dogs, but to tip into pools and lakes because the taste of it in the water made the fish drunk and made them easier to catch. At which the children laughed.

Energetically she took them through the shape of the leaf, stepping to the blackboard and running her fingers around its edges as tenderly as if tracing the boundaries of her own mouth. Together they wondered how it flew on the wind – did it flip over, did it float? She told them that several varieties had poisonous berries, that it was sometimes called 'Nightshade' and even more mistakenly 'Deadly Nightshade' which was a different plant altogether, but the berries of some alders were poisonous and the safest thing was to eat none of them. So the morning passed with Ellen teaching them to look even closer at the leaf, and the membranes, and the stem, and wondering how they might describe what the leaf was made of – skin, or leather, or hide, or what?

The postman came – late: soaked: cursing. His waterproof cape half-protected the letters: envelopes' edges caught the rain.

'Put it there on the mantelpiece so that it will dry,' said Ellen to the child who fetched the only letter.

She called a halt and bade them begin lunch: 'Tidily!' Returning the leaf to the book in the desk, she turned over the pieces of writing-paper between which it had been pressed. In Thomas's handwriting she read there a familiar quotation.

> *They told me, Heraclitus, they told me you were dead,*
> *They brought me bitter news to hear and bitter tears to shed.*
> *I wept as I remembered how often you and I*
> *Had tired the sun with talking and sent him down the sky.*

It bore a date: '22nd August 1922'.

Feeling a shiver of more than guilt at the intrusion, she returned the quotation to the book, closed the pages and flipped through the rest of the volume, *A Child's Encyclopaedia of Nature*. At the back lay a folded newspaper page; she drew it out and unfolded it, still propping the lid of the desk up with her forearms: the *Irish Independent* of 23rd August 1922 bearing the news of the previous day: General Michael Collins's assassination in the Civil War. Ellen returned to the quotation and read it again, concluded her business beneath the desk-lid and closed it.

'Essie, clear a big space. A big, big space, Essie. The Master is going to spend his days in here – in the kitchen

– from now on.' Ellen closed the school early, taking advantage of a lull in the stormy rain.

They moved the sewing-machine even farther into the deepest recess of the bow-window, and shoved Thomas's armchair with it. Essie and Ellen hauled, with Helena propped on cushions smiling when either of them coo-ed at her. The bed-chair just fitted through the doors: 'Thomas, you'd have a fit if you saw that chip off the paint, wouldn't you, love?' He had been dressed in a warm check shirt, brown corduroy trousers and thick tweed-wool socks.

'Now, Essie, doesn't he look a lot homelier? Doesn't he?'

That night, when Essie had gone to bed, Ellen went upstairs, fetched her nightclothes, soap and towel. The shutters safely closed, she undressed directly in front of Thomas. All customary modesty abandoned, albeit in this total privacy, Ellen washed in front of him, and dressed for bed. When she had finished, she kissed him on the mouth, something they once did every night except during 'Canon Law'. Although dry and unresponsive, his lips felt warm. She took his dull hand and traced it across her breasts, then, kissing the hand, replaced it inside his blankets.

'You're not dead, Thomas Kane,' she spat, 'you're not dying on me.'

At that instant, her neckhairs chilled and nausea lurched across her stomach. Footsteps on the gravel. Are the doors locked? Did Essie lock the doors? Footsteps. The lamp. Too late. Did the shutters obscure every view into the room? The footsteps stopped, ranged a little either side the front door, paused again, receded a step or two, returned, and finally receded: she heard a tiny 'ching' as the gate closed, then a fading slow clip-clop of hooves on the road outside.

'Essie,' Ellen hissed up the stairs, 'Essie?'

Essie read novels of a kind Ellen wished Thomas could observe. Lurid, on cheap paper, they bore titles such as *Her Heart was a Liar*; Essie read them far into the night, had a trunk full of them, and did 'swaps' with friends. Ellen tried giving her George Eliot, but Essie said of George, 'He's very thick to get through, Ma'am.'

She appeared at her door, looking out over the edge of the banisters.

'Essie, there was somebody here!'

'Ma'am, there surely wasn't? Not at this hour of the night, sure 'tis nearly eleven o'clock.'

'Essie, there was, I heard the step.'

Essie, seeing the Mistress's distress, clumped softly down the stairs. She wears bedsocks! If Thomas only knew!

'Essie. There were steps on the gravel. And then when he went. A horse.'

'Oh, Ma'am.' Essie looked crestfallen, but not frightened. 'Oh, Ma'am, you'll have to go to the Sergeant.'

As she walked to school next morning, bleary from the lack of sleep, and dull with a menstrual ache, a catching-up voice called her from behind. The man tipped his cap.

'Mornin', Ma'am, how's the Master these days?'

He skidded his foot to stop the bicycle, and Ellen felt her lip skin and the muscles around her mouth go flat and tight: her palate dried as if chalk-dusted.

'He's just the same, thanks.' Ohhhnn! My Jesus, Mercy. Mary Help.

'And you're keeping well yourself, Ma'am? And the babby, sure she must be gettin' big now?'

'She is indeed, grand and big, thank God.' Walk! Keep walking!

'The lad said to tell you he was asking for you, you know he's gone off to Sacramento. You know, Michael.'

'Has he a job out there, that's good?'

Ellen reached the school.

'Ma'am, wait a minute, would you?' Ellen reached the door: not a soul in sight.

'Ma'am, I called last night, but ye were all gone to bed.'

'I go to bed very early now.' Cold words. Over her shoulder. Lock. Stiff.

She did not look at him. He tried a friendly gambit, a conversational tone, her interests at heart.

'I called, Ma'am, to say to you, you should have that Crowe woman charged.'

Fingers slipped on the big school key. The Sergeant told him. The Sergeant told him. The Sergeant told him. The Sergeant told him. The Sergeant told him. The Sergeant told him. The Sergeant told him.

'You should, Ma'am, 'twould be good enough for her.'

She slammed the door behind her. He heard her lock it. In a small moan she said, 'Oh, Jesus in Heaven.' In a louder tone he said to the unhearing closed door, 'Good day to you now, Ma'am.' He wheeled away.

Ellen had reached near hysteria. She asked the Assistant, Miss McGoldrick, to send one of the children for Dr Hogan. The child came back three-quarters of an hour later to say there was nobody in.

Miriam Hogan watched the child, guessed it had come from the school, followed it, listened to Ellen, said, 'Two things, do you hear me? One – I'll go to my uncle, he's a Bishop; that will get some action out of the Superintendent, if not out of that clot of a Sergeant. Two – invite everyone you can think of to come and visit. Make sure a lot of people are seen all around the house all the time.'

The Superintendent, known to mix not at all in the community, said to Ellen, 'I assure you, Ma'am, we will keep a very close eye on you. I assure you.'

On a sudden journey to the Depot in Dublin, he asked for help in initiating a new investigation. Nothing went in his favour: the Deputy Commissioner, a friend, said that the month of May was now too far past for any fresh enquiry to have any chance of a good result.

'It isn't as if anybody was murdered,' he pointed out.

The Superintendent argued that the man 'might as well be dead', and the Deputy Commissioner suggested that a good course of action might be to start a quiet search of his own, and 'talk to everyone'.

Concerning this, the Superintendent said he had already been doing exactly that and was coming up against a 'wall of silence. Talk is one thing, witnesses or proof is another. A wall of silence.'

'Centuries of practice,' commented the Deputy Commissioner.

'Look, John,' he said, stopping in mid-stroll near the Zoological Gardens in Phoenix Park at lunchtime, 'see it two ways. See it first as a policing matter. Make sure that woman has some noticeable protection. If you have a young fellow in your division who's looking for lodgings, get him to stay in the village or very nearby. Make sure he's seen cycling past that house very often, or better still pushing his bike past it. Then just talk. Did anyone go over the ground?'

He shook his head when the Superintendent reminded him of the empty cartridge case (the Sergeant had not handed in the one Miriam Hogan found). 'Useless. Any shotgun would have it. You see – you haven't a thing to go on, only rumour. If we arrested everyone on the basis of what the neighbours say, the whole shaggin' country'd be behind bars.'

'You see the thing is,' said the Superintendent, 'supposing something happens to that woman? Where are we then?'

=

'Ma'am, there's no use in any more padlocks, sure look at the gaps in them hedges.' Essie seemed sanguine.

'What choice do I have, Essie? I have to make myself feel safe, at least.'

Ellen wrote twenty letters to all sorts of people, and asked them to come and see Thomas. When the Superintendent called, he endorsed the measure.

'That way, Ma'am, any intruder who knows the area will never know whether there's somebody here or not.'

He comforted her further by telling her that a young Guard had just moved into the village in new lodgings, 'a big strong fellow, a Mayo man, he's built like the side of a church'.

Something nagged Ellen on the Friday afternoon, just as she left the school and faced towards home. Wasn't there a letter? That wet day, the postman. Wasn't there a letter somewhere? On the mantelpiece or somewhere? Where was it?

'They are lovely, you know. I tried not to bruise them, although one or two have a little bump, if you give me a knife I'll straighten them. This is the first time I made them and I'm afraid I ate two of them before I came up.' Ellen slid the lemon tartlets, still on a tray, out of the paper bag.

Ernestina said, 'I don't eat pastry.'

'Will the men eat them? Or visitors? If I'd known that I'd have baked a nice fruit cake, a porter cake or something. Do you like caraway seeds?'

'I hate them.' Ernestina sat back on the pillows and sighed, 'I think I'll bake a Madeira cake tomorrow myself.'

Ellen silently placed the tartlets' tray on the table inside the door and came to the bed. Sitting on the counterpane, the bed so high Ellen's legs scarcely touched the floor, she took Ernestina's hand.

'Ernestina. Listen to me. I'm going to tell you

something. My life is awful. I am frightened something is going to happen to me. I am in a round of chores that would test a hospital. I am tired all the time. I have a husband but I have no husband. He's in a living death, and I have to live alongside that, and I have to look at it every day, and worse still, in a kind of a way, I have to watch a new life growing alongside, and bring up a child that will have a father but won't have a father, and a father who'll never be able to talk to her.' Ellen nodded her head for emphasis as she brought out every point. 'But it'd be ten times worse if I tried to deny everything that was happening to me.'

Ernestina closed her eyes, and then held up a hand to stop Ellen speaking further. Ellen sat there, staring down at the white face, the closed, dark-pigmented eyelids, no spectacles today, the uselessly inappropriate and ancient nightdress, all ribbons and torn lace: once it might have looked like something somebody saw in the cinema; now it had no warmth in it, and little decency.

'She came in last night,' said Ernestina, her eyes opening and phasing.

'I know, I know,' said Ellen, thinking Ernestina was dreaming aloud.

'She was down in the kitchen, I heard them laughing.' Small beads of moisture gathered on Ernestina's white forehead.

'Yes,' soothed Ellen.

'You think I'm dreaming,' said Ernestina, and subsided again. 'I never slept last night.'

Ellen said, 'This is a lovely room, you know. Would you like me to freshen it up a little for you?' and stood.

'Wait.' Ernestina called, and Ellen sat again.

'I mean it. She was. In the kitchen.' Her breath halted. 'You'd think he'd have the decency – or she'd have the decency – not to come in until I'm better again.'

'Oh,' said Ellen, realizing. 'The Merrigan girl?'

Ernestina nodded without speaking, two deep nods.

'She's working in a butcher's now.' Again, she slipped back into her white-faced, stagnant-breath tranquillity.

Ellen looked around the large room. The square-cut windows, with small leaden panes, had been made deep enough to contain a three-sided window seat, covered with long chintz cushions. On the wall between the windows, partly obscured when the curtains hung wide open, was a large regimental photograph, with a printed caption of many names in little black tiers beneath it. Tall old dried flowers, long past their attractive days, stood on a table large enough to contain an unusually big white china ewer and basin. Behind the door hung several coats, and what seemed like a man's dressing-gown: tall boots on the floor failed to stand up straight. A walk-in cupboard door stood open, all the visible clothing in complete disarray, some on the floor, some garments hanging crazily off each other. Cardboard boxes stood piled: Ellen saw the edge of an old towel peeping from one box. In the far corner of the room, arranged to catch the light from the window, stood a round mahogany table, and a chair: on the table, still in their packets, lay scattered threads, and cloths, and a half-opened brown paper parcel of what looked like several yards of excellent white linen. The remains of uneaten meals were strewn amid three teapots and a coffeepot on the same table, and propped amid the debris stood a photograph of two laughing girls in the bonnets and parasols of a summer's day: Ellen recognized Ernestina as she must have been fifteen years ago or so. Beneath the table a nest of discarded towels lay on the floor, half-covered by a bundled sheet, with some papers and documents scattered nearby.

Ernestina started awake again.

'I always doze when I haven't slept very well.'

Ellen asked, 'When did Dr Hogan come to see you?'

Ernestina replied, 'He's useless, that fellow. But he's nice, he's harmless.'

'Who makes you a cup of tea?' asked Ellen. 'I'm going to open the windows and let in a breath of fresh air.'

'What do you mean "deny everything"? What do you mean by that?' Ernestina received a sudden small charge of vitality.

'Is that your father?' asked Ellen, pointing to the regimental photograph.

'No. Uncle Henry. When young. Do you mean, I should tell my brother to get his own meals until I recover?'

Ellen said, 'Oh, we met him, at your party here, your uncle, in the summer.'

'Wasn't that the most irritating afternoon in the history of the world?' Ernestina said, and continued half-aloud, 'But if I admit to anyone.'

She stopped, and Ellen, freeing the second window-catch and pushing back the curtains even more, turned and said, 'I know what you need, you need a dose of Sheila Cooper.'

Ernestina's laugh sounded more like a gasp. 'I'm going to get up for a while. She's barred from this house. She had a terrible row with my mother. She called my mother "an old hawk".'

Ellen moved across the room quickly to help Ernestina stand upright. Ernestina said, 'Spectacles are the greatest nuisance. When you take them off, you can't see where they are in order to put them back on again.'

Ellen handed them to her from the floor, and, inspecting the standing girl, asked, 'Would you like me to get a fresh, clean nightdress for you?'

'I haven't one. Do you know what my cousin Emmerson's father is getting – a telephone, of all things. It is costing them hundreds of pounds, hundreds.'

'Where do you want to sit? Over here? Lovely fresh

air,' and Ellen walked beside Ernestina to the table by the window.

'Isn't anybody coming to clear these?' Ellen asked.

'No. I put the run on her. She was carrying stories about me.'

'Old hawk or no old hawk, it's Nurse Cooper for you,' said Ellen, and Ernestina smiled again, brightened by the light of the sun.

'"My lady",' she mimicked.

'"My lady", indeed,' mimicked Ellen.

'That will be a laugh,' Ernestina said, 'I always liked her.'

Everybody replied to Ellen's letters inviting them all to call and see Thomas.

'But it is a great idea,' said Leah, when she, typically, was the first to arrive – on a Saturday bus, without the children or Herbert. 'This is Herbert's theory, isn't it? To bring life to Thomas, bring life to where he is?'

She brought with her a cutting from a catalogue advertising a new Valor oil heater.

'Herbert said, "Why not have the world come and see Thomas?" so – hallo, Thomas,' Leah greeted. 'You're lucky to be in here out of the cold and the damp. Herbert sends you his best regards.'

'Show him your new skirt,' said Ellen, and Leah did. Alongside Ellen, she stood before the bed-chair and talked to Thomas. Essie, in the scullery, looked up into the kitchen and saw the two women standing there, one tall and red-haired, the other very much smaller, talking animatedly to the Master as if all three of them were involved in an enthusiastic discussion. Essie's face betrayed not a second's surprise at the scene: she went on wiping the saucepans dry.

'Herbert said to tell you, Thomas, that if you were up and about he would be trying to persuade you to go into politics. You know how he doesn't like any of them, De Valera, Cosgrave, Mulcahy, "the whole tainted crew", he calls them. Well, he says the only thing that would make him change his mind would be if you went in there and straightened them out.'

As they sat to eat at half-past one, Leah turned the bed-chair around so that Thomas was made to face the table, and even though his position, owing to the height and design of the bed-chair, raised him above the level of the table, at first glance he looked like no more than an invalid included among the family, sitting there ordinarily, his eyes closed, skin marbling and a little waxen.

Ellen remarked upon this to Leah. 'For a second there,' she said, 'out of the corner of my eye, I thought he was all right.' She put her fork down and lowered her head.

'Hoi!' said Leah softly. 'Not allowed any more. Come on. Chin up.'

On the other side of the table, learning to negotiate a high baby-chair, sat Helena, being spoon-fed by Essie, murmuring, 'One for the moo-cow?'

'But look,' said Ellen, in a gesture that included Thomas and Helena, 'can't you see what I mean?'

'It is still not allowed,' said Leah. 'What you are doing needs all your courage, so you have to keep your courage up.'

'Strict,' said Ellen.

'I mean it,' said Leah. 'You said – you're trying to bring him back to life. Now, come on.'

Leah had called to Brunswick Square in case the Morris family wanted to send anything to Ellen. Her mother gave Leah a leg of lamb to bring; Bob wrote a note to say he would come out for the day on the bus on Tuesday, and sit with Thomas while Ellen was at school. This fitted the first week of Ellen's jigsaw into place: now each of the next seven days would have visitors.

As she was leaving, Leah approached Ellen and spoke to her from behind. 'I wonder. I wonder, it would only be until next week or so, Ellen would you have . . . ? I mean, ten would do, or even five.'

Ellen went off to fetch her handbag, saying conversationally, 'Do you know what it is, that new hand-cream is very good . . .'

'And don't think,' continued Leah, 'that I have forgotten one penny. Or the length of time outstanding. Herbert, he doesn't know about any of this, and I really haven't enough . . .'

'My turn to shush you, now,' smiled Ellen, still permitting Leah not to look at her.

On Monday after school, Ellen marched the sixth class to the house. She pushed the bed-chair back a little to allow all eleven of them room to stand in a bunch inside the bow-window.

'Now, Master,' she addressed Thomas, who, on Ellen's instructions, had been dressed by Essie and Mrs Greege that morning in one of his good suits, 'I have to fill in the Progress Record for October, and I wanted you to hear how good they all are.'

Turning to the pupils she said, 'Now, first the poem, then the song. I'll start you off.'

Nodding her head, she spoke the opening line, and by the second line they had taken over in a full and good swing.

> *'My eyes are filmed, my beard is grey;*
> *I am bowed with the weight of years.*
> *I would I were stretched in my bed of clay,*
> *With my long-lost youth's compeers.*
> *For back to the Past, though the thought brings woe,*
> *My memory ever glides –*
> *To the old, old time, long, long ago,*
> *The time of the Barmecides.'*

The children gathered strength, and became unstoppable by the time they entered the second verse.

> *'Then youth was mine, and a fierce, wild will,*
> *And an iron arm in war,*
> *And a fleet foot high up on Ishkar's hill,*
> *When the watch-lights glimmered afar,*
> *And a barb as fiery as any I know,*
> *That Kurd or Bedouin rides,*
> *Ere my friends lay low – long, long ago,*
> *In the time of the Barmecides.'*

Ellen had chosen the poem on account of Thomas's love for it: he quoted it often: conveniently, it came within the Department's generous curricular brief. When they rolled on, to the verse which began

> *'I see rich Bagdad once again*
> *With its turrets of Moorish mould,'*

she did not even flinch at the lines

> *'I call up many a gorgeous show*
> *Which the Pall of Oblivion hides.*
> *All passed like snow, long, long ago,*
> *In the time of the Barmecides.*
> *All passed like snow, long, long ago,*
> *In the time of the Barmecides.'*

'Very good, very good.' She unclasped her hands, and from her bag took a tuning-fork. 'Now.' She banged the tuning-fork on the edge of the kitchen table and listened, then hummed, then maintained and increased the hum, checked it by hitting the tuning-fork again, then came down a key in the humming, and stopped.

'Ready? One, two, three, four.' They began.

> *'Proudly the note of the trumpet is sounding,*
> *Loudly the war-cries arise on the gale;*

Swiftly the steed by Lough Swilly is bounding,
To join the thick squadrons in Saimear's green vale.
On, every mountaineer!
Strangers to flight and fear!
Rush to the standards of dauntless Red Hugh!
Bonnaught and gallowglass,
Throng from each mountain pass,
On for old Erin,
O'Donnell Aboo.'

'One verse is fine,' Ellen said, and turning to Thomas, 'They know all the words, Master, the whole four verses, and they know the interpretation.'

She turned back to the class.

'Now, what kind of a song is that?' They all raised their hands.

'A marching-song, Ma'am.'

'That's right, a clan marching-song.'

'Which one of you knows what a "bonnaught" is?' Several hands shot up.

'A class of a soldier, Ma'am,' said a number of voices together.

'Good, good. And a gallowglass?'

In a more slender unison, three or four voices murmured, 'Another kind of soldier, Ma'am.'

'Yes, but what kind?'

'One with a heavy sword, Ma'am,' ventured one boy.

Ellen affirmed. 'Yes, a heavily-armed footsoldier,' she said.

'And who was Red Hugh?'

They all knew that. 'Red Hugh O'Donnell, Ma'am, one of the earls of Donegal.'

'And what does "Aboo" mean?'

'It means, Ma'am, "Up", it means a cheer.'

'Yes, a cheer,' she said. 'You're all very good, aren't they, Master?' and she dismissed them.

=

On Tuesday, Bob Morris arrived, climbing heavily off the bus outside the school wearing a new Homburg hat.

'But why didn't you stop at the house?' Ellen said. 'Now you'll have to walk back up the road on your poor leg.'

'I brought my stick,' he said, 'I wanted to see you first.'

'Did you bring your pipe?' Ellen asked.

'I did,' Bob answered in some surprise. 'Why?'

'I want you to have a good smoke and make sure you blow the smoke in Thomas's direction,' said Ellen. 'He used to love –' she corrected herself: '– he loves the smell of that tobacco of yours.'

On Wednesday, Michael Condon came to take Ellen for another driving lesson, and Ellen persuaded him to sit and talk with her in front of Thomas, and gradually she led him by example to include Thomas in the conversation, as she asked him all kinds of questions about cars, and the new developments, and how many cars there were in the whole county by now, and who owned them, and how many makes of cars there were altogether in the world, did he think, and was it true the Canon was thinking of getting one, or was it the Curate?

Thursday brought the results of Ellen's most successful letter. Eight people came to the house at five o'clock, followed shortly after by another three: she had written to the members of Thomas's Union committee. The Hon. Secretary wrote back, saying how clearly he had understood her letter, and what she was trying to do, found it admirable, and ended by suggesting they might hold the meeting with Thomas there, if she didn't think that was too big a crowd in the house.

'The marvellous thing, Essie,' said Ellen, 'is that it forces us to get the parlour back to rights.'

'Why was I so moved by it?' Ellen asked Nurse Cooper that night, when they had all gone. 'Was it because every single one of them behaved as if things were completely normal, and all through the meeting they referred to Thomas, telling him things that had happened since the last meeting? And they all picked up his hand and gave him a good genuine handshake when they came, and as they left. And you know, the women, they didn't bring cakes or anything, they just expected me to provide them. Which I loved.'

Sheila Cooper said, 'Now, on that account, you're entitled to shed a small tear – only one, mind you.' She then launched straight into an account of Ernestina Stephenson's condition.

'The poor girl. She isn't in a good way at all. I mean, she always had a good physique and it is standing to her, but all the same –'

On Friday, Val Vousden called by appointment.

'Ma'am, I won't be one bit taken aback, the things I've seen.'

Ellen had begun to discover that the more she spoke openly to people, the less abashed they found themselves.

Val bowed to Thomas, and said to him, 'Sir, I have very good news for you. The band, as you'll know *via* your Mrs, has started practising, the Canon is after lending us the school. And we're doing grand. Mrs Heffernan is a Trojan with the uniforms. Now, Sir,' he addressed Thomas grandly, 'a lot of that is down to you, and you haven't had a chance to hear my new monologue; 'tis famous already, 'tis called "The Deanstown Band", but I'm going to give it to you now, if you don't mind.'

Essie came to the kitchen door and leaned against the jamb of it, watching. Helena banged the table of her high baby-chair with a spoon. Val stepped up, bowed and launched into his recitation; Ellen had to stand behind him so that he would not see her trying to choke back the laughter, and when it had finished she and Essie applauded: Helena gooh-ed.

Over his cup of tea and slice of porter cake, Val said to Ellen, 'Ma'am, d'you recall a conversation I had with you outside the school a few weeks ago, and I asked you what was wrong with himself?'

'I do, Mr Vousden.'

'Call me Val, Ma'am, that's what all my public calls me. Well, I went away, thinking very hard, and I made some enquiries. And I was wondering – would you be at all interested in taking the Boss to see a man who wasn't an official doctor like, a man who specializes in curing people though, and he has a particular interest in things of the head. And the man I was thinking about is over near Doneraile, and, as I say, he's not an official doctor, like, but he has great success with the cures. I don't know for certain, but I think he might be a seventh son of a seventh son.'

Ellen wrote down the name and address.

Father Watson came on Saturday's bus, and stayed until Monday morning. Ellen asked for Confession again.

'Father, I have two grievous matters to confess.'

'Yes, my child.'

'Father, my impure thoughts will not go away.'

Ellen, with all her classmates, had marvelled when young at the inviolable secrecy of the Confessional. The holier nuns insisted that priests received Divine Grace to erase memory or identity; 'In other words, a priest could have a murder confessed to him and meet that man in the street and never know. There's Divine Grace for you.' Their more practical Sisters inclined towards a theory of mundanity and weight of numbers: priests simply forgot because they heard so much of the same from so many. In that whispered tumult, the sins of individual penitents melded, then faded. Ellen made different calculations regarding Father John's Confessional role: he did not customarily hear Confessions.

'When do these thoughts trouble you, my child?'

'In the morning early, Father, when I wake up, and at night when I lie down to sleep. Alone in bed.'

'Are they directed to any one person, my child?'

'Well, as I told you before, Father, at my last Confession, there is one man in my mind.'

It was quite improper of Ellen to breach Confession's timelessness and anonymity like that, but John Watson did not rebuke her.

'Is he known to you, my child, or is he a stranger?'

'He's a very old friend, Father.'

'Have there been any impure actions between you, my child?'

Ellen in a shocked tone said, 'Oh, no, Father, he's a very good man. A very holy person.'

'You must put impure thoughts from your head, my child. God will help you. He will understand and make allowances for your very difficult position in life. That which you once so rightly and beautifully . . . so beautifully, what's the word – enjoyed, or perhaps I should say, experienced, has been taken from you cruelly. Nonetheless, you must pray diligently and assiduously to seek to avert temptation. Now, my child, you said there were two grievous matters.'

'Yes, Father. I have been thinking of murdering someone, and I want to know would God forgive me? Not my husband, Father, someone else.'

Father Watson smiled, and even laughed a little.

'No, my child. He would not forgive you, the gift of Life is His and His alone. We may feel murder in our hearts, my child, but a good person cannot bring themselves to do it.'

He absolved Ellen, and stayed a little while in prayer after she had returned to the kitchen from the hall.

Throughout the week-end, she showed him warmth,

this cold, confident priest. One or two visitors dropped in briefly after last Mass in Mooreville; Father John hosted the parlour, leading from an armchair. As Ellen left for school on Monday morning, Father John came downstairs to enjoy a leisurely breakfast cooked by Essie. He and Ellen made arrangements that he should come and stay for Christmas.

Ellen found the missing letter: some exercise copies had also suffered dampness that day in children's schoolbags, and had been put out to dry near the fire: a child had gathered the letter up in error, and now returned it. Ellen glanced at Edel Crowe's handwriting and hurled the letter in her basket: 'Blast her, anyway.'

'Did Father John get away all right?' Ellen asked Essie after school.

'He did, Ma'am. Isn't it strange,' said Essie, 'how the priests are not good at talking to a baby at all?'

'They've no interest in them, Essie,' said Ellen.

Ellen spoke to Thomas at length every night. Sometimes she merely prattled on, sitting there as Essie did the last chores. Damping down the slack to keep the fire in; laying the table for the morning, the cups turned upside down to ward off the fire's floating smuts; preparing the oatmeal for the porridge; all tasks Thomas once did.

On most nights, Ellen waited until Essie had gone to bed. She undressed in the kitchen, standing in front of Thomas fully naked as she washed, then raising her arms high above her head to put on her nightdress. Ages ago, she had sent away to New York for a *de Bevoise Step-in Corselette* and it had arrived on Saturday: (she saw Father John take a good look at the long, narrow box which Ellen had opened and left on the hallstand shelf).

Now she tried it on, wriggling and jiggling. 'What d'you

think, Thomas?' and raised her hands above her head like a Spanish dancer.

'Thomas?' The nightdress slipped down along her body, and she wriggled to help it fall to the ground, 'I feel vicious now. I feel vicious. I made the mistakes, but you were the one who was right. I was wrong. You can do nothing about it. But I can. And I'm putting it all right. Thomas, you may live, or you may die, but your debts will be paid.'

She kissed him on the mouth every night, sometimes more than once. She kissed him now and talked on.

'I am not going to rest until I have paid back the people who hurt you. I have been well and truly paid back. Now it is our turn, Thomas, dear, and I am doing it. No wonder Father John says to me that I've changed. He'll see. They'll all see. Remember the ploughing, Thomas, "as if God had reached down with a knife and cut a furrow along the ground". Wasn't that what you said good ploughing was, Thomas? Well – that is what I'm going to do. Good ploughing.'

Michael Condon, although short, had the strength of the farmers. He also had a good suit, and he had put it on specially for the outing Ellen had requested. Between the three of them, Essie, Ellen and Michael Condon, they manoeuvred Thomas into his heavy grey coat, out of the house and into the car, which Ellen herself had polished for the occasion. With pillows and blankets they stayed Thomas in an upright position, wedging his head gently against the hood, closing the door to fix his shoulder. The mists had cleared, promising a sunny morning: Essie would take care of Helena, whose pudgy arm waved from the door.

'Will you drive a bit, yourself, Ma'am?' asked Michael Condon, of whom Leah, when she first saw him, said, 'All these good-looking men.'

'Not for a bit,' said Ellen, 'you get us started and get us away first.'

'Fair enough, Ma'am.' He secured her in the dickey seat: she pulled the wool bonnet down over her ears.

'I don't know if we're on a wild goose chase, Essie,' Ellen had said last night.

'Ma'am, sure what of it?' said Essie. 'A person should try everything.'

'The parish will know, I suppose,' brooded Ellen.

'Sure what harm, Ma'am, they'd do the same themselves.'

Ellen called as Michael opened his door, 'How far away is Doneraile?'

'I don't rightly know, Ma'am. 'Tis a bit far.'

'Do you think the Master'll feel the cold, Michael?'

'Them hot-water bottles should do the trick, Ma'am.'

Beyond Mooreville, Ellen changed places with Michael.

'Hold on to yourself now, Thomas,' she said.

It proved the best drive she ever had.

'God, Ma'am, a few more of these drives, and you won't need me at all,' said Michael at their destination.

It took them three hours exactly: they found the healer's house easily, a cottage down a long but mercifully un-rutted lane. The man came to the door to see the car. He then went back indoors, saying, 'You'll have to wait, I have a client in here.'

'Have you any hot water?' Ellen shouted after him.

He didn't bother to answer, so she took the three hot-water bottles to a farmhouse they could see a field away, and returned very quickly.

'Here you are, Thomas,' she said. 'I'm after cleaning them out of house and home, all their hot water gone.'

She felt Thomas's hands and began to warm them.

'Of course,' she said to Michael, 'I have to watch that I don't burn him either.'

'His colour is a bit healthier, Ma'am, after the drive.'

=

524

The healer's previous 'client' turned out to be a grey-hound, led away limping by its owner, after which the healer came to the car and looked in.

'I know that man,' he said.

'Do you?' said Ellen.

'Master Kane,' said Michael Condon.

'Kane. The very man. He was very well known around here, so he was. All north county Cork knew that man, Ma'am. He nearly stayed here one night. You know, in the old days, like.'

They half-carried, half-dragged Thomas into the cottage: a hen cluttered out as they entered.

'Prop him up there, now, Ma'am, on that high chair, so that the head is clear of the back of it, that's it, rest it on the spar – there.'

Then Ellen and Michael Condon were invited to sit down by the fire. When Ellen's eyes got accustomed to the gloom she found the cottage surprisingly neat, with postcards from America on the wall above the fireplace, between two orange and white china spaniels.

She gave the healer a brief history.

'They say 'tis brain damage, do they?' he ascertained.

'They do.'

The healer walked all around, peering at Thomas's head: how he could see in the dimness Ellen did not know.

'Ah, it was there it was, right.' He found the place on Thomas's temple, 'and 'tisn't long healed?'

Ellen watched with anxiety, then could stay sitting no longer, and rose to join him.

'Well, ointment is no good, that's for a fact.' The healer walked around again. 'Ma'am, he's as strong as a horse.'

'He's not as strong as he was, to tell you the truth,' said Ellen. 'I notice a bit of a failing in him lately.' She had not so far confided this worry to anyone.

'The winter does that, Ma'am. It does it to all of us.' The healer wore a stained brown leather finger protector on the index finger of the right hand. 'And the doctors say there's nothing doing?'

'Nothing.'

He bit his lip for a moment, and went out past the cottage window, returning a moment later with a heavy parcel wrapped in damp sacking.

'You'd think to look at him sometimes,' said Michael Condon, while the healer was out, 'that the Master was full alive.'

Ellen did not reply. The healer put the parcel on the kitchen table, and unwrapped from it a pair of flat wet stones, each one slightly larger than the size of a man's hand.

'What are they?' asked Ellen.

'They're the amulets,' he said. 'In my family over two hundred years. They're healing stones, Ma'am.'

'Why are they wet?' she asked.

'That's part of the whole thing, Ma'am. You could keep them stones there by the fire and they'd always be wet, winter and summer. We don't know why.'

Ellen, out of habit, felt Thomas's forehead.

The healer came forward. Standing behind Thomas's chair, he held the stones, one in each hand, and fixing his gaze on them, pressed them gently to the front and back of Thomas's head. He spoke in a language Ellen did not understand, not a chant, not a prayer, just a series of statements, spoken rather flatly, except that each one ended on a slightly dramatic rising inflection. Staring hard at them once more, he then held the stones gently to each of Thomas's temples. Ellen winced as he pressed a stone to the location of the damage, but the healer was gentleness itself.

Again the strange dialect, and this time for longer: when it ended, and he took the stones away, the healer looked drained and disappointed. He returned the stones to their parcel.

'Well?' Ellen asked.

'No response, Ma'am. It might be that something will come out of it, but usually I feel a bit of a jolt if there's going to be a cure. Now I won't be charging you for that, Ma'am.' He had a wart at the corner of his lip.

At the car, Michael Condon whispered, 'Did you hear that tongue he was talking in, Ma'am?'

'I didn't understand a word of it, Michael. The odd word of Latin maybe. Did you know what he was saying?'

'No, Ma'am, but I'll tell you what it was. 'Twas Shelta, the tinker's language, Ma'am.'

That night, preparing for bed, Ellen, as she undressed before Thomas, said, 'I know, Thomas, you would mock me from here to Kingdom Come, for going to a quack doctor; I can hear you laughing now in my head. You'd say, "that bloody old wizard", wouldn't you, Thomas? And, yes, you'd be right. And you'd say, "That fellow is the opposite of anything", wouldn't you? But you wouldn't be able to answer me this. Why is it I'm so disappointed that he didn't cure you there and then? I know I'm too sensible to believe he could have done? And why at the same time did he give me hope for the first time that you might get better one day? Thomas, the old part of me, the part that was there before I met you, sometimes tells me I'm going mad. Out of my head. But I saw that old rabbit-catcher that day after the pond, and you so young and vigorous-looking when you were skating, that is what dead looks like, not what you look like.'

Two days after, on late Monday morning, Ellen saw Essie lumber frantically towards the school window. Ellen could hardly understand what she was saying.

'The Master, Ma'am. Oh, Ma'am. I'm after having a look at him, he's looking awful bad, Ma'am; he's feeling very hot.'

Ellen told the most senior boy in the school to put on his coat and follow her to the house. She raced up the road, Essie a long way behind. She ran through the door, skidding to a stop in the hall. Thomas's cheeks had never been so red.

'Oh, Jesus Christ, oh, God.' His forehead felt scorched. 'Oh, Thomas.'

28

'You stupid woman! You stupid woman!' Miriam Hogan snapped at Ellen. 'Do you not know anything at all about medicine? A quack? You took him to a quack? Some fool in a dirty old cottage somewhere, and you thought he'd heal this man?'

'I thought . . .'

'Don't think. Act!'

'What? I mean, what will I do? Will we move him into the hospital?'

'For him to get worse? Do what I tell you!'

The schoolboy Ellen had sent to the Dispensary found Miriam alone. She led them now through a series of procedures: sealing the windows with brown paper; keeping the temperature even; instructions to bathe Thomas every four hours; never leaving his side. Hot water was to be made permanently available; wrap him in clean cool linen; the fire to be kept even with regular tiny supplies of coal. They took turns massaging Thomas's chest, bathing his forehead; Miriam showed them how to make poultices and apply them – almost too hot to bear, never to burn his skin. Miriam controlled the panic, delegated, ordered, cooled them.

Dr Hogan arrived. 'None of your airiness here, Jack. Use your brains, any you have left. Come on! How is he?'

''Tis the lad all right, the boy is on the way,' said Jack with the stethoscope, 'd'you see?'

'The lad?! The boy?! What are you talking about? Can't you speak the King's English, Jack.'

Jack, a little aggrieved, a little defensive, said, 'I'd say,

Miriam, that man could develop pneumonia. That's what I think. Or d'you want a second opinion?'

Miriam said, 'No time for that. What we need is consistency. Tell us all the correct procedures. Now!' She turned to Ellen. 'Quick. Write these down. In handwriting that we can all read.'

Jack intoned, point after point. The morning quickened into dread.

'I have never seen,' said Nurse Cooper some days later, 'a human being change so much, and I have seen a lot of things. It's like she grew a new self.'

New and harsh. Ellen, the pious and virtuous woman, the girl Thomas often teased as 'a goody-good', the girl Canon Williams called 'Miss Prim', already disappearing, vanished completely: a woman with a different nature, cold and hot and frantic and aggressive, coped with this new pressure.

The Curate called, offering prayers, Rites. 'No time for that now, Father.' She closed the door.

All the details of duty, all the well-behaved vestiges, froze. Thomas slipped and slipped. Dr Hogan and Nurse Cooper conferred.

'Tell me plainly,' Ellen's words lunged at them. 'What are the hopes of getting him back?' Exposed to one emotional atrocity too many, a soldier under fire, Ellen's courtesy disappeared.

'A thin enough chance,' said Nurse Cooper.

'I do not care,' said Ellen, 'if I never teach another day. I do not care if I never say another prayer. I do not care if my life turns me so that I have to scrub floors, but I am going to do everything in my power. I want no mouldering rabbit-catchers in this house.'

All others around her – except Miriam – suffered

530

exhaustion within that first sleepless seventy-two hours. As if hastened by demons, Ellen drove herself.

'I don't care if I collapse,' she snapped.

Miriam said, 'You're right. You're right! Go on! Go on!'

Ellen called every child in fifth and sixth class into action, and sent them out across the parish with short, urgent messages. From Dr Hogan and Nurse Cooper she demanded the clearest possible instructions on the best, and perhaps only possible, means of keeping Thomas alive, of keeping down his fever, of preventing pneumonia; she made the pair of them bring their medical books to the house, and checked everything they told her – she questioned and questioned and questioned: once, she even snapped at Essie. The house became a hushed cauldron.

When the neighbouring women whose favours she called in began to arrive at the house, she allotted each one a firm duty. They nursed Thomas, changing him all the time, out of perspiration-soaked clothes, but keeping him warm while doing so, administering such medication as the doctor had found useful, feeding him with the greatest possible care, finding, for instance, the best meat to mince and break down almost to a *purée* in order to nourish him, and they talked and talked to him.

And when each woman left to go home, worn out, Ellen, still full of fire, thanked them, ticked them off on her roster, and asked them to tell their menfolk to call and sit with Thomas. And each woman said to the other how useless it was all going to prove, but it was as well to go along with it.

Ellen slept in two-hour breaks, three sleeps in every twenty-four hours. Apart from those short periods, she did not take her eyes off Thomas for more than a minute or two at a time.

'Miriam, will you keep an eye on the baby?' she asked.
'I will not, thanks,' said Miriam. 'I hate children.'

When Leah stepped from the bus, she found an Ellen no longer intent on speaking in the right tones, or adopting the 'good posture' she had always hoped for: she saw the brusque side in full flight. No small talk, no hint of self-pity, no mention of prayer or God, or the Church or the Sacraments, no holy epithets, no morbid interests.

'A kind of furious calm, Herbert. And she's aged, she's no longer a young one.'

'Why wouldn't she?' said Herbert. 'Wouldn't anyone?'

Dr Hogan suffered daily: Ellen tore into him. 'Think again, Dr Hogan, think again. Is there pneumonia there or isn't there? Is the man going to live? You've been in the war, you've seen crisis, is there a crisis, or isn't there?'

Dr Hogan rose to it. 'No, there isn't a crisis – yet.'

Miriam said, 'There has to be somebody with that man night and day. What would you call a crisis, Jack?'

Jack said, 'I mean, what they call a crisis in pneumonia, the moment when things go either way, d'you see?'

To Bob Morris, bewildered by his daughter's newfound force, Dr Jack Hogan said, 'What I want to know is where did she come from at all? I never saw a woman with that kind of fight in her, did you? Is it from yourself or from the mother she gets it?'

Ellen said to her mother, 'Mama, I haven't time to look at your new coat, I haven't time to pay you attention.'

The Canon arrived. Ellen directed, 'Pray over him and only that, Canon. No, you may not give the Last Rites, no, you may not give him Extreme Unction, that man is half a century away from the Last Rites.'

When the Canon began to protest, she said, 'Canon Williams, did you hear me?'

Late that night, telling Nurse Cooper about the Canon,

she said, 'Can you find such a thing – anywhere in the world – as a man who isn't pig stupid?'

The Canon came back next morning.

'Ellen,' he said. She looked up at him in surprise, never having heard the word 'Ellen' from his lips. 'I'm just saying.' He faltered. 'Look. God bless you. Whatever happens, God bless you.' He turned away. The long, scratchy face of him.

'Well, thank you,' she called after him.

He turned around briefly. 'Oh, by the way, the job is all right. The Principal. Yourself.' He hurried off.

'Oh!' In spite of everything, the excellent news penetrated.

The men from the farms came each evening, slow footsteps on the gravel, and then the throat-clearing knock on the door. Self-consciously, they held Thomas's hand the way she showed them how, and within a short time found themselves relaxed and involved. Essie and Mrs Greege and Mrs Dalton and Mrs Relihan made rounds of sandwiches, and for over a week and a half Ellen Kane drew the entire community together in the effort to save her husband's life. Nobody queried the size of the effort to which they had begun to contribute: they all spoke of it in a paradoxical combination of natural acceptance and wonder.

Ellen never established – to her intense annoyance – whether Thomas had suffered pneumonia. At nine o'clock on the Thursday morning of the second week, Dr Hogan and Nurse Cooper conferred in the hallway, and calling Ellen, said they believed the worst had passed, 'definitely'. She ascertained some follow-through procedures, looked to the two women sitting with Thomas under Mrs Greege's supervision, and to their astonishment, put on her coat, collected her basket and went to school. Men came around that evening and other women, as arranged; however the word had begun to spread that the Master was out of that particular danger. On Friday, the Canon appeared at the school door just as the junior children were released at half-past two. Ellen walked to meet him: Jeremiah Williams was concealing something behind his long back. He stood in the doorway.

'You'll find these very tasty,' he said, offering a paper bag of apples. 'I have them in hay since August, it keeps them grand,' and he walked away.

Ellen tidied up the school paperwork – not much, but it had fallen behind, thanks to the useless Miss McGoldrick, still a Temporary Assistant – every applicant's letter for the job had, in Ellen's opinion, proven them unsuitable.

At four o'clock she walked home at a more rational pace than she had walked anywhere for days. Everything seemed in place: Nurse Cooper and Mrs Greege sat by the range chatting.

Ellen ate from a plate on her knee, then said to them, and to Essie, 'I'm going to sleep, see you all tomorrow,' at which they laughed. She kissed Thomas and Helena, climbed the stairs and slept for twenty-one hours.

Ellen made a pact with herself.

'No celebration of Christmas, no cards, nothing like that. Essie, there'll be you, and me, and Thomas, and the baby, and Father Watson.'

Then, a week or so after the Thomas crisis had died down, she sat alone one Saturday evening in the kitchen, listening to Essie move around in her room upstairs, as she seemed to do for hours every night before bed. Ellen had never dared to ask what exactly Essie did in that clumping time.

'Thomas.' She turned to him, laying a hand on the side of the bed. 'Tomorrow I am going to have a talk with

Dr Hogan, and I have some hard questions to ask. Oh, Thomas.' She rested a hand on his cheek.

Jack Hogan called mid-afternoon and she sat him in the parlour: he seemed relaxed enough, notwithstanding the heated way Ellen had dealt with him during the intensive care of Thomas – for which she neither made, nor felt, apology.

'In your honest opinion?' she asked.

'Only my opinion,' he defended; 'others'll tell you different.'

'Go on. I can ask others for their opinions.'

'In my opinion –' he looked uncomfortable '– what will happen is this. The sort of crisis he's just come through will happen again. And again. And again. D'you see, each one will leave him weaker than before. You realize, don't you, that what you have there lying on that bed inside in that kitchen is a medical miracle. I mean, if this was't a Catholic country, there'd be people'd say, well . . .' His voice trailed off.

'Catholic country or no Catholic country, what about life?'

'But, Ma'am, you're a great one for calling a spade a spade, you can't call that "life", d'you see. You said that yourself. I mean to say, how long can you go on keeping him alive? I mean, one day, Ma'am, you're going to have to face, well . . .'

He did not finish the sentence. Ellen twirled a finger in her hair.

'I don't know what to say to that,' she said.

'Ma'am, I'll say it again. The man is a miracle. It is miraculous. It nearly isn't natural. Since what, the ninth of May? Ninth of June, ninth of July, ninth of August –' he counted '– seven months to the day. D'you remember the day you took him out of the hospital? We all gave him six weeks to live from that day. D'you see, none of us

535

knows how you did it? 'Tis against the grain of anything we ever heard of. That's the thing you have to realize.'

'No,' said Ellen, but to herself, not to Jack Hogan. 'A force beneath the force.'

'Ma'am, that is mad talk,' said Dr Hogan, 'that is what I call baloney. Dangerous. The medical fact is that your husband suffered damage to his brain, he's in what they call a coma, and he's shown no signs of recovering and no matter what way you look at it, you can't get away from that.'

'If I keep him alive,' said Ellen, fiercely, still ignoring the doctor, 'I am certain good will come of it.'

'Well, you asked me my opinion and I've given it to you. Look, why did I ask you to go and see that poor Ernestina Stephenson? Why?'

'So that she would have a woman to talk to, to visit her, I presume?'

'That's true. But, Ma'am, you've no experience of death or tragedy, and I also thought, d'you see, that seeing her the way she is, I mean that girl is finished.'

Ellen struck the side of her chair.

'Get me some more doctors.'

'Ma'am, I got you the best doctors you'll find. The men in Cork is the best there is.'

'Get them back here.'

'They won't come.'

'Ask them.'

'What would they come for? They were here already.'

Ellen leaned closer. 'What time of the day is it?'

'Four o'clock.'

'I know it is.'

'Then why did you ask me?'

'I didn't mean what time on your watch. I meant what time on your breath?' She sniffed and went, 'Grrrrr! Don't ever come in here again with a smell of drink on you' – but Jack Hogan had an irrepressibly genial demeanour, and he left the house cheerfully. Ellen walked to close the gate after him. Across the road, in the field just inside the wall, Miriam Hogan suddenly stood up into view, like a ghost in the December twilight.

'Oh, you frightened me!' exclaimed Ellen.

'Don't you believe a word Jack says,' Miriam said.

Ellen replied, 'Well, that's not very loyal of you.'

'Oh, good,' said Miriam. 'If you ever want a companion to go anywhere with, on a walk, or out at night or anything, let me know.'

'Thank you, I will,' said Ellen. 'I won't ask you in, if you don't mind. I have an awful lot to do.'

'I wouldn't come, anyway,' she laughed, making Ellen laugh too.

'I asked Jack to get a second opinion.'

Miriam said, 'They don't like Jack very much. Where did he say they'd come from?'

'Cork again.'

Miriam laughed. 'They're very proud in Cork. If they can't fix it themselves they'll send him to London. They'd never admit to Dublin that they couldn't cure somebody.'

Two days before Christmas Eve, in the late morning, Ellen began to cry. The tears flowed silently at first, then noisily. Essie stood there, looking. Ellen stopped and blew her nose several times. The storm had lasted five minutes or so.

'Such a difference, Essie,' she sniffled, pointing to Thomas, 'between our first Christmas and our second Christmas together – and will we have a third Christmas? Where will we all be this time next year?'

'Oh, Ma'am, sure the Master's still with us, and while there's life, there's hope, they say.'

Ellen, who hated proverbs nowadays, jumped to her feet, clapping her hands.

'Right, Essie, that settles it, I'm going to put up decorations and we're going to have a Christmas candle on

Christmas Eve when Father John comes, that settles it.'

The postman arrived at four o'clock, in good and cheery fettle, having been thanked copiously in many houses for his year's work. Ellen shivered, then bristled when she saw the handwriting, and, opening the letter, quickly looked first to see whether Edel Crowe had signed it.

Dear Mrs Kane,
    You never answered my first letter. I said in it that I wrote to my brother the surgeon in London, a long letter all about you. ['I hope you signed it,' Ellen muttered.] I told him everything that happened, and all about your own misfortune. He since wrote back to me and I enclose his letter; as you can see he wants you to write to him: he is not, unusually, coming home for Christmas, which I hoped he was, so that he might be able to see your husband. Let me know your answer.

                    Yours sincerely,
                    Edel Crowe

'Essie, d'you remember me talking about those Crowe people?' Ellen asked, as she shook out the contents of the envelope, dropping the second letter on the floor.

'Them anonymous letters, Ma'am, was it?' Essie called back from the scullery.

'Yes. What kind of a crowd are they at all, remind me?'

'Oh, Ma'am, you said they've plenty of money.'

Ellen skimmed the note, fastening on the sentence, 'Please tell your Mrs Kane to write to me here. I can't do anything unless her doctor or she herself requests it.'

She called out again, 'Jesus, Essie, do you know what? Edel Crowe's brother. He's a surgeon, over in London.'

'I knew that, Ma'am.'

On Christmas Eve, at the lighting of the Christmas candle by the youngest of each household, every family murmured, in Irish, the soft, secular prayer, 'That we may be all alive at this time next year.' In the morning, at the foot of the hill in Deanstown, Canon Jeremiah Williams, P.P., rose late, steamed noisily and long and yellow into the enamel chamber-pot, parted the lace curtains and looked at the grey day, then humped himself down backwards to his cold pillows.

'Girls are always lazy to start,' said Nurse Cooper to a first-time mother. 'Boys are savages.' The baby drowsed, and Nurse Cooper laid her down in the crib, and as the young woman then drowsed, from her stiff white uniform pocket, Nurse Cooper drew a tiny green bottle. 'Little dab of perfume,' she said, placing her finger behind each of the damp mother's ears, then on her wrist pulses, and then at the 'V' of her breasts. Nurse Cooper turned down the gaslight, leaving only a mild, flickering glow, and withdrew, leaving another new mother and baby to sleep. Outside the window, the town was dark and quiet.

In the small pool of light from the candle on the windowsill of the village, Timmy Quinn looked at the moth he had captured in a matchbox. His older sister surged forward to see it and the boy grunted, then screamed and fought her off; the sister put a kind arm around him and said she was only joking.

He had a spartan room along a bare, planked corridor within a sober brick building; therein, Father John Watson, S.J., put aside his breviary. Beneath his high window, the yellow street lamp softened in the swirl of a mist off the river. Inside the glass, Father John Watson opened a drawer and for some moments looked at an old church magazine photograph of the young Ellen Morris. He put it away again, and began to polish his shoes and pack his small travel bag.

—

Ernestina Stephenson slept, therefore long-legged Miriam Hogan received no reply to her knocking and ringing, and strode home again.

In her little notebook that she kept hidden from Herbert, Leah counted the row of figures and dates of borrowings with the letter 'E' opposite them.

Mrs Greege turned over and over in her lap the exquisite piece of silk fabric the Mistress had sent to her, delivered by one of the schoolchildren; no note, nothing, just this wide grey silk.

Through dark farmland Val Vousden dozed: the bus climbed hills of steep unseen pasture by Kilworth before the last long run down into Cork, woods on the right, the gleam of dark water on his left. Val Vousden disembarked at Glanmire, met his young friend Bernard for 'one drink and one drink only'. Bernard walked with him as far as Shandon, where they parted.

Val's sister said, 'You should take off that uniform. You look like the Chocolate Soldier in it.'

Father Watson, complaining of the hazards of bus travel, brought a small box of chocolates with him, which he flourished proudly. Essie, possessed of a glance with major potential for askance-ness, said of the chocolates: 'Sure, they weren't too heavy for him to carry anyway, Ma'am.'

'I checked with the Canon,' said Ellen to her Jesuit; 'he'd be delighted to have the extra Mass in the morning. In fact he announced it last Sunday, so I'm very glad to see you.' They smiled. 'Although I'll go to Midnight Mass, myself, if you don't mind too much, it'll help the house to get on.'

'My dear Ellen,' he held both her hands. 'You are a

wonder. I heard all about the extraordinary nursing you did for Thomas's pneumonia, you rallied the whole county it seems.'

'So long as he rallied,' said Ellen. 'And it wasn't ever pneumonia.'

Ellen had placed the new Valor heater in the corner of the hallway.

'Oh, Lord, Ma'am, I won't, I couldn't go to somebody I know,' had been Essie's response to Ellen's offer that Father John could hear her Confession.

'No, Ma'am, sure I'm grand, sure I have no sins on my soul, sure where would I get the time to commit a sin?'

'Thomas,' Ellen had hissed last night. 'He's here again. Thomas, I know I am terrible to do this, but I don't care, he deserves all I'm going to do to him.'

The heater smoked faintly, but warmed the cluttered tiled hall.

'Father, since my last Confession, I find that I have become weaker.'

'Weaker? In what way, my child?' The hand fleshed the jowl, as John Watson gravely listened.

'Father, I can resist those impure thoughts less and less.' Ellen and Essie had paid Thomas greater attention today than for some days.

'He's entitled to Christmas too, Essie.'

Father Watson asked tentatively, 'Have you confined them to impure thoughts, my child?'

Ellen paused, timing like an actress. 'Yes . . . Father.'

'How often, my child?' She never took her unblinking eyes off the rotund profile.

'Twice . . . Father.'

'When, my child?'

'In . . . the last few days, Father.' No noise is heard when the deadliest traps close.

'Do you know why, especially then, my child?'

When considerate, John Watson's voice slid like satin.

'I knew I was going to see him . . . Father.' Dropped to a whisper.

'Does he know, my child, that you have deep feelings for him?'

'He knows, Father, that I regard him as my . . . deepest friend . . .'

As she walked to Midnight Mass, hat pinned tight, scarf wound firm, Ellen talked to herself half-aloud, both through agitation and the fear of the dark road. In the night sky she looked for the star that, as a child, she believed had been the guide to Bethlehem. Occasionally a quick step overtook her, then a cough, and a 'Good-night, Ma'am' reassured her.

'I'm always puzzled, Thomas,' she had said to him once on the way home from Evening Devotions. 'How do they know it is us?'

'Amn't I always telling you?' he replied, 'they know everything.'

The heels of her black court shoes rang on the road: a light frost gathered.

The church shuffled in all its hillside lights. She did not attend Communion: all right, people would put it down to not being able to organize the fasting since mid-day, on account of the Master and the baby. They came to the seat, tapped her shoulder, whispered, 'All the best for the Christmas, Ma'am. All the best now.' Ellen mouthed thanks.

In the light of the candles and the oil-lamps around the walls, her freckled face shone pale and vigorous; her 'boxer's nose' in shadow. She folded one hand over the other until it was time to pick up the Missal and find the red-printed flimsy pages with their Latin rubrics. The

Canon, mercifully, took cognizance of the lateness of the hour, and his own need to rise early, and said a short Mass. In the porch afterwards, several people waited, again to wish her well. Their bicycles and murmurs swished past her on the night air as she set off down the hill; she strained her eyes in the direction of the Stephensons' house, but no glimmer of light could be detected at such a distance.

The road's darkness thickened into Hogan's Bend. Leafless, the trees and hedges stood silent, all conversation between them exhausted for the moment; their bare branches spread beseechingly. Ellen thought she heard something and halted her step, then walked on tiptoe. The snurry of a horse as it shook itself through its nostrils. And again. No sound of hooves on the metalled road, meaning the horse had stopped. She tiptoed on. Ahead, to her left-hand side, the shape loomed: a standing horse, a figure astride. The horse's head swung around and the horseman stirred. 'Hold! Hold hard!' the voice said unenthusiastically.

'Pewarrhhlupp!' rattled the horse's vast rubber-coral lips in the dark, its head giving a gentle plunge. Ellen's eyes and mouth widened simultaneously in a soundless wail. Jesus, I'm wetting myself! Not another soul on the road; no point in going back, everybody gone. No house between here and the church. On foot, no match for a horse. She tiptoed on, as far to the far side as possible, trying to slide through the dark. The horseman did not move: the horse enjoyed another jerking shudder, shifting its weight across all four legs like a ship on a wooden sea. The horseman said in a sleepy voice, 'Ah, would you hold, would you?' Sidling, Ellen reached a soft hand to the crown of her hat and withdrew her Tara brooch long hat-pin. On an October night on this road Thomas had shown her the Pleiades, and told her the sad story of Electra, the lost Pleiad. On a night walking from the Evening

Devotions in May they had stopped to marvel at the moon . . .

Ellen bustled silently and excitedly into Thomas's room. Essie had left a lamp for her; the red Christmas candle still burnt brightly in the window; not a sound could be heard. Her cheeks glowed bright red, and she panted. She kissed Thomas passionately on the mouth and sat beside him, looking, looking. Some days he half-opened an eye; once he even showed a brief flicker of having heard something. Once, his smile half-returned – but was it merely the muscles of his mouth in some grimace of effort?

Taking off her hat, and with concentrated attention, and rapid breathing, wiping over and over and over the large Tara brooch hatpin, and then sticking it into the lapel of her coat, she said, 'Thomas Kane. If a kiss could breathe life into a human being, if it could, if it could . . . D'you remember, that you often thought how you would like to have pumped life into the growing baby?' She clutched each side of her head, and half-frantically said, 'Thomas! Thomas! Oh, God!'

In bed, Ellen stretched herself rigid beneath the sheets, her fists clenched, arms outstretched like a cross.

'Oh, how nice!' she had exclaimed the day Thomas said, 'It comes from "*crux, crucis*" the Latin for cross. So a crux is the essence, or the real trial of something. The very heart of something vital.'

In the morning she woke dry and exhausted to a passing shudder of horror and indifference to everything. Then, the sweetest sound in all the world awakened her: Helena's crowing began later in winter. Ellen went to the mirror, perused her own face and expression with minute care. She lifted Helena out of the cot, felt her bottom through the lumpy layers.

'Dry? Still dry? Who's a pet? Who's a pet?' She jiggled the baby, and climbed back into bed, tucking Helena in beside her. The baby kicked and made eager shapes with her mouth. Ellen held a hand near Helena's face: the baby grabbed it and inspected every detail roughly. Leaning on an elbow, Ellen then lowered her face as near to Helena as she could, allowing the baby to tug her nose.

'This is a great game, isn't it? Isn't it, Hellie?' She blew on Helena's face making her little hair lift from the forehead. 'Wait 'til your Daddy sees you? Ow!' Helena had reached farther than the nose and pulled a strand of hair. Ellen detached the hand and returned it to her face, allowing it to roam. She found an ear and proffered it to Helena who took it like a lifebuoy.

'Don't grab, little thing. I don't know what I'm going to do if I have boys, if they're like you.' At which Ellen stopped smiling. 'Oh, Hellie.' She sighed. 'I have no one to talk to, only two babies. You and your Daddy. Three counting Essie.' She tiptoed her fingers across the baby's fat stomach up to her chin. 'But. We have a great New Year coming, don't we?' She paused, sad. 'Dtth. Am I fooling myself, Hellie, am I? Oh, Hellie, will I ever tell you all these things, all these awful things that are going on . . . ?'

Christmas Day 1926, a damp day, in which the sun came out and went in again, passed quietly and with gentle introspection and stillness. Father John Watson, S.J., M.A., fell asleep proprietorially in front of the fire. Ellen Kane had to put ointment on the little half-moon cuts her fingernails had made in the palm of her left hand.

29

The first group of high-stepping Wren Boys called on the
morning of Saint Stephen's Day.

'D'you give them money?' John Watson asked Ellen.

> 'The wren, the wren, the King of all Birds
> Saint Stephen's Day he was caught in the furze.
> Although he be little his family's great,
> Rise up little laddies and give us a treat.'

'Ma'am, 'tis grand to see you so light in yourself,' commented Essie. Ellen laughed over-excitedly as she recognized most of the Wren Boys behind their painted faces
and women's clothes.

'Where did you get the eye-fiddle?' Ellen teased one.
'You should wear it all the time.'

'Eye-fiddle? You mean a mask?' said Father Watson.
'How interesting? I wonder if Shakespeare used that
word?'

Ellen gave them some coins and handed around a plate
of cold meat slices, from which she told them 'not to snap
the food like pigs'. After a quick moment of reflection,
she invited them in to sing for Thomas: Helena screamed
with fright at the high hats and the red ribbons fluttering
from the holly boughs they carried over their shoulders,
one of which nearly brought down a garland of the
coloured paper decorations slung across the ceiling. Their
energy reverberated in the kitchen: with mouth-organ and
concertina, two danced a reel in front of Thomas's bed-
chair. Five groups of Wren Boys called that day: each sang
for Thomas.

As they watched the departure of what they hoped

laughingly might prove the last band, Father Watson said, 'Do you think it really a good idea that they should invade poor Thomas's privacy so much?'

That night several of the Wren Boys told their parents, 'I'd say the Master won't last long.'

Essie lit the lamp as dusk began to fall: the fire in the parlour grate roared with high flames. Wren Boys excepted, they expected no other visitors.

Yet, 'Come in, come in,' they heard Ellen say; she seemed unsurprised.

Father Watson, in his self-appointed role as host, rose to greet the newcomers. The two men stooped a little through the doorway, more out of habit than necessity, as they entered the parlour: one in uniform, the other not.

''D'evening, Father.'

'Good evening, gentlemen.'

'Sorry to disturb the Festive Season, Father.'

'This is Father John Watson, an old friend of the family,' said Ellen. 'This is the Superintendent and, of course, the Sergeant.'

Father Watson said, 'May I offer you . . . ?' He indicated his own glass.

'Ooph, no, thanks, Father.' The Superintendent rubbed his hands together vigorously, 'on duty, I'm afraid, all hours, Sunday and Monday, Christmas and all.'

'Oh, too bad for you,' Father Watson nodded understandingly.

'Ma'am, we want to have a word with yourself, if we could?' said the Superintendent.

'Sit down, sit down,' said Father Watson, and the men looked from Ellen to him.

'It'd have to be private, Father.'

'Oh, goodness, of course, of course . . . unless, my dear Ellen?'

'No, grand, thanks, Father John,' said Ellen.

547

'Well, I still have some of my Office left to say,' and the priest left the room.

An hour later, Essie said anxiously to Father John in the kitchen, 'D'you think I should take them in tea, Father?'

He pondered the advantages of inspecting the various faces should he have to open the door for the tray, and then decided against it. Another hour passed, and the noise of feet preparing to depart came from across the hallway. Ellen preceded the men and reached forward to close the kitchen door, thereby sealing off the hall. Some more conversation took place, and the men took their leave.

Father Watson said, 'Good Heavens! Did they interrogate you?'

'No,' Ellen said, brittle and aggressive. 'Essie!' she called. 'You-know-who. He was found last night on the road.'

'Oh, my God, Ma'am!' said Essie, making the Sign of the Cross.

'Heavy drink on him,' said Ellen lightly. 'The horse bolted under him, and threw him.'

'Is he hurted, Ma'am?'

'He's dead, Essie.'

They all heard the ticking of the alarm clock on the bookcase, the first wheezes of a boiling kettle.

Father Watson broke the surface of this brief pool of silence. 'My dear, I don't understand the significance of this at all . . . ?'

'A man with a big houseful of children here in the village,' said Ellen quickly. 'They used to come to school to me. Essie knows, don't you, Essie?' The women's faces gazing at each other excluded Father Watson and the universe.

'Oh, thanks be to God, Ma'am. Thanks be to God.'

Essie's fervent tone of voice bypassed her cleft palate.

=

Nurse Cooper visited next afternoon, and talked to Ellen.

'Look, my dear, there is one thing. He is not getting better.'

'Sheila, stop. I didn't close an eye last night.'

'You see. Even you're worried.'

'No, it wasn't that. You heard the news, I suppose?'

'I did.' Sheila Cooper held the pause, then resumed. 'Apart from that –' she gestured again to Thomas.

'Were you talking to Dr Hogan?' accused Ellen, returning from her reverie.

'No, as it happens, I haven't seen Jack Hogan for a fortnight.'

'Sheila, if Thomas dies, he dies. I have pledged myself to do everything I can to keep him alive.'

'Girl, you know there is no medical history anywhere of anyone surviving like this; if the man wasn't so strong . . .'

'I know, I know, he'd be dead long ago . . .'

'No, that isn't what I was going to say. What I was going to say was, if he wasn't so strong he wouldn't have been able to swallow so violently. He wouldn't be able to take in food.'

'If his throat muscles are working, then the rest of him could work again one day,' defied Ellen.

'No, you're not necessarily right. You fed him, like we showed you, by using the fact of involuntariness; we all swallow involuntarily, look how difficult it is not to swallow if a fly goes into your mouth, that's what has worked with him.'

'His lungs work. And his chest? And his windpipe?'

'Pure chance, nothing else does.'

'His bowels work. I know it full well,' said Ellen, 'and his bladder.'

'But – as he fails to be fully nourished all through, he has no exercise – he will slowly slip down and down. A day could come when even that great nursing effort will no longer work. And that day might come not too far away.'

'You haven't seen him for a week. Do you see a change in him?'

'I do,' said Sheila Cooper, 'I do.'

'Look, for all we know he could be listening to every word we say. Supposing – supposing he "wakes up" one day, won't we have fine fun when he tells us he was listening to every word?'

'Ellen, he isn't *The Sleeping Beauty*. It isn't a fairy story.'

'Sheila, don't say that kind of thing to me.' Ellen yelled. 'Now, don't! If you do, we'll fall out, you and I. I've had somebody trying to say that to me nearly every day since last summer. Supposing I'd listened and let go of Thomas – where would I be now?'

'Shhhh, dear. Shhhh.'

Ellen burst into tears and howled, then lay back in the chair, eyes closed.

'But, Ellen, it is a medical fact. You cannot bring him back to life.'

'Sheila, I won't give up trying until the day Thomas is buried. Now, look. I'm doing all I can. The surgeons are coming from Cork in a few days. I have written to that man Crowe in London. I can't hurry things any more than that.'

In the next twenty-four to thirty-six hours Ellen found space to reach for her new resilience and collect herself.

Father Watson stayed three further nights, until New Year's Eve, and thereafter visited Deanstown no more, nor did he ever see Ellen Kane again.

'Now!' Ellen clapped her hands. 'Forget your little sips of port, Father John. Whiskey tonight, it's the last night of your holiday. And wine, we have some somewhere. And Essie made something special for you.'

In the scullery earlier, Essie said, 'Ma'am, I can't make you out, you're leppin' around the place like a young one.'

'My mother used to call it "rampaging", Essie,' she whispered. 'I'm "rampaging", so I am.'

Ellen, taking out some as-yet-unwrapped wedding-gift linen, cutlery and glasses, asked Essie to lay the parlour table. The priest watched the parcels come undone.

'Are we expecting company?'

'Yes, Father John. You.'

'Oh?!'

All day, Ellen, febrile still, had raced like a dervish.

'Ma'am, I never seen you get so much done,' said Essie. 'Never.'

At Thomas's final changing for the night, as Essie took the basin and soap out of the kitchen, Ellen kissed Thomas's neck so hard she left a brief red mark.

'Jesus, Thomas, Jesus.' She pushed her face into his hair.

Father John Watson came down the stairs at six o'clock with a scrubbed face, and he inspected the parlour table set a-sparkle in the firelight for two.

'I find this quite exciting,' he said.

Ellen, who had changed into the 'famous grey dress', as Thomas described it, poured him a drink and sat him down.

'No lamps yet,' she said. 'I love the look of a firelit room before the lamp comes on.'

'Like Dickens,' he said, 'just like Dickens; all we need is snow outside.'

Ellen bustled a little more, and on a quick final trip to the kitchen, she reached into the blankets and crossed a pair of Thomas's fingers, whispering, 'My lovely Thomas. Am I going mad, am I?'

She returned, and sat in the other armchair facing Father Watson in the flickering light.

'Would you like to know what we're going to feed you?' she asked him affectionately. 'Or would you like it to be a surprise?'

Essie, in a clean frock and apron, brought soup and fresh soda bread.

'There's even sherry in that soup, Father John,' said Ellen.

Dining began. Ching of spoon on plate. Breathy grunts of joy. She opened up his reminiscences.

'It must have been quite peculiar for you watching the little girl grow up, was it?'

'I think,' he said, soup on his chin again, 'I shall never forget the first day I realized you were a young woman. You were about seventeen, I suppose, and you had a blue dress with a white collar.'

'I remember it well! It was, it probably still is, one of the things I ever had that I was fondest of. As a matter of fact, I remember wearing it specially for you.'

'And you had lace gloves.'

'I did. I bought them at Cannocks. From Mrs Doran. Goodness, you remember everything.'

'And black shiny shoes.'

'Yes! Patent leather! They had black buttons like little eyes.'

Essie brought the next course.

'Oh, dear Heaven!' he said. He threw up his hands in a gesture of ecstasy at the meat on the dish.

'The best they had,' said Ellen.

'Oh, well, of course, as you can imagine we never get anything like that in the Provincial House.'

'We roasted it,' Ellen said. 'And basted it.' The long slob of fillet beef shone like a blooded champion.

'You'll carve, Father John?' and she poured a glass of wine each. They sat behind full plates, and set to work, she silently, he grunting little noises, tapping a foot.

'How come,' she asked, 'you never thought of marrying, Father John? I mean long ago, before you entered the priesthood, did you ever have a crush on anyone?'

'I think I was an idealist,' he said slowly. 'I think the theology, the laws of the Church attracted me. The idea that Man can make laws to govern what goes on in his soul – very attractive, very attractive.'

'The mind always?' Ellen nudged.

'Yes. Yes.' He paused. 'I think. I think.' He pulled a piece of gristle loose. 'Excuse me. I think – if, but you never know how life unveils itself. I think if the right opportunity –' he spoke so carefully ' – if the right opportunity could have been seen, not just come along, but could have been seen. If that had happened. What I think I'm trying to say is – that if I knew then what I know now. But isn't that the case with us all? But, anyway, I never did marry. As you know.' He chuckled sweetly.

Ellen said, 'I remember one winter. You caught a bad cold. Mama said to me that I was more concerned about you than I would have been about one of our own family. She was cross about it. That must be what, about five, six years ago, I wasn't twenty-one yet. I remember that so clearly.'

They ate on. Sooner or later one of them might have mentioned Thomas, but neither did.

'Hoh-ho! – look at that!' Father Watson applauded the sherry trifle; Essie, with a sharp knife, pared slivers from a chocolate bar all over the top. From the cupboard in the corner of the room, Ellen conjured.

'My father's trick with trifle. A glass of Madeira.'

'You are spoiling me! Spoiling me!'

John ate two large glass dishes of trifle, one after the other, and leaned forward, elbows on the snow-white cloth, twirling the almost-empty second glass of Madeira.

'I wonder whether this isn't sinfully good,' he said. 'Only joking, only joking. But that glorious food, and

553

this, this Madeira, and the most intelligent woman in the county. And one who wasn't, if I may say so, hiding behind the door when it came to good looks being given out.'

Ellen smiled.

'Thomas,' she had said one night, 'I am going to commit great sins. On your behalf. On our behalf.'

'Father John, it is so lovely to talk to you,' she said. 'Inside or outside Confession.'

Thus lit, the flame travelled slowly along the fuse.

Essie came with a pot of coffee.

'No!' he said, 'I can't believe it!'

'True,' said Ellen, 'actual coffee. Mrs Winer sent it out.'

'But I haven't had coffee for – it must be four years!'

'We'll go and have it by the fire, and let Essie finish clearing. Essie, that was lovely, truly lovely,' said Ellen.

'Yes, my compliments to the cook,' said Father Watson.

'Oh, Father, I did the whole thing myself,' contradicted Essie.

By the fireside, Ellen Kane and John Watson looked at each other warmly, then back into the fire.

Ellen, in a pitched demureness, said, 'Do you know, Father John. I had almost forgotten what it was like to have a conversation with a man. Do you know what I mean?' She laughed. 'That must sound so funny to you, because you have conversations with men all the time.' Her voice tinkled.

'Oh, I know well what you mean, my dearest Ellen,' he said.

An occasional sigh from the fire.

'Isn't that . . . weak of me?' she asked.

'I don't think so. You are a healthy young woman.' Ha! – the phrase she had used in Confession to him.

'Yes,' she said very thoughtfully, 'ye – esss.'

He gathered his shoulders.

'God forgives. You do know that?' he said. 'All our sins.'

She looked at length into his face and sadly smiled.

'Yes. Yesss.'

Behind him, Momentum tiptoed invisibly into the room.

'And which of us?' he continued, with just a little falter, 'Is not human?'

Ellen made a little haste to agree. 'And the Lord created us, Father John.'

'He did. And He knows us. And we are His children. And He forgives us.'

Thus, on 31st December 1926, at half-past nine in the evening, in the lamplit parlour of a remote country village, to whose cultivated schoolmaster he had once behaved so patronizingly – 'Fancy, my dear Ellen? The classics out in Deanstown?' – thus was Father John Watson destroyed.

'Yes, He forgives us. Indeed,' he continued. He looked down at the backs of his hands: 'Canon Law himself', Thomas called him in one particularly bitter moment with Ellen: 'when you mentioned to me your own difficulties with . . . your thoughts, and God forgives them too, my dear Ellen, and when you mentioned the "one, good man" of whom you spoke, to whom your, what's the word, your "difficult" thoughts were directed, for a brief moment, my dearest Ellen . . .'

He leaned forward, his small eyes shining, this man with a reputation for excellent, clinical Reason.

Ellen scarcely moved: an adjustment of the shoulders and jaw, no more than that.

'Father John?' Her broad, soft voice spoke the question with sad and lethal wonderment. 'But wasn't that in Confession? I mean, I thought . . .' A small bewildered pain crossed her face. 'Isn't the Seal of the Confessional . . . ?'

He put his hand to his throat, wrestling with the silk of the invisible noose there.

'Oh. My dear. Oh. Ellen. Of course, you're right, you're right. Oh. Hrumgh.' He coughed. He coughed again. Ellen fell silent.

That was all. No more took place between them. A word or two, an attempted but never completed, 'My dear Ellen, I am so sorry,' and a tentative reply, 'I suppose in the morning, Father . . . ?' – but the question was left unfinished. Both, from different perspectives, understood the precise extent of their devastating transaction. Archbishop Edward Ahern was known by all the priests in his Archdiocese to enquire into all the circumstances of the Reserved Sins he was asked to absolve, the time, the place, the number of people present, the reasons. One such confession had lasted up to two swingeingly interrogative hours.

Mutely next morning, Ellen accompanied him to the gate. She held out her hand: they shook hands. She did not wave, and he did not look back.

Indoors, Ellen bent over Thomas, and took his face in her two hands, whispering, 'You and me, Thomas. You and me. And Helena. And Essie. I promised you. I love you.'

On *The Princess* bus, a tear of condensation rolled down the windowpane beside poor Father Watson's outward gaze into the damp lands.

1927

30

'You're not as nice as you used to be,' said her mother.

'How nice do you think what I have to do is?' replied Ellen.

Leah saw the point and said, 'Fair's fair. We must, I suppose, change to meet you. But don't lose all the lovely things in you.'

'No,' said Ellen. 'I realize, though, that I never had a life of my own before. Strange, isn't it, that trying to give Thomas back his life, should bring me mine?'

'Herbert predicted it,' said Leah.

Sailing under her new colours, Ellen asked the two tall men from Cork: 'Are you competent to judge?'

Hearing their answers, she said, 'I won't forget your honesty. You don't know how decent and helpful that is. I just wish I had known it all a lot earlier.'

The taller of the two said, 'Of course, Dr Hogan is your doctor, and we can only get involved if we are called in by him.'

She told them of Maurice Crowe, and the background to his letter, and established with them his credentials. They talked on.

'We have two radiograph machines, and we have had them for some time, but we're not that happy with the results,' said the quieter man. 'What we'd like to do, if I can speak for Dermot –' he indicated his colleague '– is another physical examination now, and then write out our recommendations. And even if we're not involved ourselves, we'd like to get behind you and support you. I mean, this is a very interesting case for us altogether.'

They spent an hour with Thomas, while Ellen fretted elsewhere. When they sent their written report, they enclosed a copy of their letter to Maurice Crowe. Whereupon, Ellen wrote to her father for 'a good deal of money'. She calculated days, dates and times, and she sent for Nurse Cooper and Dr Hogan. She snuffed out Essie's excitement instantly.

'We have to stay very cool about this, Essie, very cool.' Calming herself further, she wrote a simple letter to the Canon, but withheld it until she had conferred with the doctor and the nurse.

'You have to admit it yourself,' Jack Hogan said, 'you have to admit there's a disimprovement in him.'

'I do,' said Ellen, 'but there's the letter. Look. There's what the surgeons in Cork said. The man's colleagues in London are interested. They might operate.'

'Yes, but I mean, what are they, experimenting or something?' Jack Hogan was sceptical. 'They have no real results, d'you see. Look, they even say that in the letter. "We make no promises." And how in the name of God are you going to get the man over to London?'

'This letter,' spat Ellen, 'is a lot bloody better than any medical help I've had in this county or country. All talk, that's all I get here.' She turned to Nurse Cooper. 'Sheila, if I can work out a way of getting him over, will you help me?'

Behind Ellen's angry energy, Sheila Cooper saw the fear, the last-chance terror.

'Of course I will.'

'Mad, the two of you are. He won't last as far as Holyhead,' said Jack Hogan.

Saturday, 8th January 1927.

Dear Canon,
    I have been given an opportunity to try and have my husband operated on in London. I have to ask your

560

permission to be away from school for an indefinite
period: it could be three weeks, it could be three months.
What I think will happen is that we'll get him over there
soon and he will be there for several weeks, and I should
stay with him. Then when he comes back either he'll be
in hospital in Cork or here at home, in which case I might
be able to get back to school or not. I'm sorry I can't be
more definite.

> Yours sincerely,
> Ellen Kane (Mrs)

Essie brought back a reply.

> Dear Mrs Kane,
> Thank you for your letter. Please accept the enclosed.

> Yours faithfully,
> Jeremiah Williams P.P.

The letter contained a twenty-pound note.

Maurice Crowe sent a telegram:

> Come any day from 2nd Feb. Given typical travel
> difficulties, we will hold situation open one week from that
> day. If coming no need reply. Will need patient here at
> least, repeat, at least, three to six weeks after.

Serene and forcible, and with everything in order, Ellen
made all her arrangements: a second Assistant Teacher to
run the school – my God, the value of that Inspector
calling, no inspections for four years! Michael Condon
agreed to drive to Dublin, return to Deanstown, and be
ready to come back again to meet the Mail Boat. The
county had as yet no ambulance of its own: Ellen wrote
to Dublin to find an ambulance they could use for the
return journey. The unspoken question hung everywhere:
'But will there be a return?' Thomas had faded – no doubt:
the ruddy waxiness grown grey, the hair a little coarser;

paradoxically, he showed one or two signs of rising nearer to the surface.

They decided to leave the question of Ellen's lodgings in London open to chance: the hospital would know of a place she could stay. Helena would be safe with Essie: Ellen's mother offered to come and stay, so did Thomas's sisters and brothers, so did everyone, especially Leah who brought a large, bulky envelope from Herbert. 'He says this will support you, and nourish you, but not to open it until things get looking blue as they will; you know Herbert, how cheerful he is.' They chuckled.

An overnight bed was arranged at Maryborough Hospital, halfway between Deanstown and Dublin, should they need to break the journey either way.

The night before departure, Ellen turned to Essie who was feeding Helena in her high chair.

'Oh, Essie, tell me I'm not gone out of my mind.'

Essie, from a family of fourteen children, never caressed or cuddled in her life, and never likely to be, dumped into a convent as a lay sister, in other words a labouring drone, saw the Mistress sit down in a crumple, and putting down Helena's dish where the baby could not thump it, went across and drew the most awkward arm in the world around Ellen's shoulders.

'Ah, Ma'am, sure, look – all the things you done for the Master, he'd be dead long ago only for you, wouldn't he?'

Michael Condon arrived at a quarter to nine, as scrubbed as the morning itself: the car he hired, a Lancia, seemed as big as a bus. Nurse Cooper appeared with a packed bag.

'Where are you off to?' asked Ellen.

'Guess.'

'But.'

'Shut up, my lady.'

=

562

The Mail Boat left at a quarter to nine that evening: Essie's sandwiches proved invaluable. Three times at roadside houses, people heated Thomas's food, thinking it for a baby: Ellen's practised skills prevented them from coming out to see the deathly passenger. At the dockside as they wheeled Thomas up the gangplank in a bath-chair, Nurse Cooper holding his head straight, a familiar voice said 'Hallo' in Ellen's ear – Miriam Hogan.

'Where are you going?'

'With you.' Ellen did not have time or concentration to spare on resisting.

At Holyhead they were told, 'No trains to London. A strike.' Enquiries only yielded, 'No telling how long it'll last, no telling, could be a day, could be a month.'

Miriam Hogan said, 'A cab to Liverpool. A boat to London. I had to do that last year, big strike then.'

'In this fog?' said the shipping line official.

Liverpool had no fog. 'Good omen,' said Miriam Hogan, who startled Sheila Cooper and Ellen by her efficiency and merriment.

'I can't actually bear to be at home with Jack. I mean he's the greatest eejit, with his "d'you see", "d'you see". If a dog bit Jack he'd say, "D'you see" – "Juicy Jack", I call him to myself. And to his face.'

Later, she came into the cabin. 'You might as well know this,' she said. 'If there is fog in London, we won't get up the Thames until it lifts; they'll just wait in the fog. Maybe for days.'

Sheila Cooper and Ellen were feeding Thomas, and stopped in their tracks.

'But, butbutbut –'

Miriam stopped Ellen's anxious budding query: 'I got the Captain, men will do anything for you if you have a good pair of legs, to send a wire to Surgeon Maurice Crowe, and I told him,' she said, 'in your name, "Mrs

Ellen Kane", exactly what we were doing and why, the name of the ship and if we were delayed, what the reason might well be. It cost four pounds of Jack's money.' She waved a hand and sang in a little song. 'Or, should I say, my money. Or, should I say, my dear departed Daddy's money.'

Maurice Crowe checked the shipping lists, and the weather, and sent an ambulance to Tilbury docks. Within two hours of his arrival, four days after leaving Deanstown, grey Thomas Kane was in a silent and antiseptic ward, under the most intensive professional care he had ever received. Ellen was given a bed; the other two slept sitting upright on benches in corridors; the universal sorority of nurses brought them tea and blankets and consideration.

'You're very like your sister,' Ellen said to Maurice Crowe, who flicked her a sidelong look.

In the morning, Ellen was interviewed at length by three distinguished-looking men, called 'Mr', not 'Doctor', in whose company Maurice Crowe seemed an equal. They noted down everything, returning again and again to 'the circumstances of the injury'.

They asked, 'Do you know how many of these "pellets" were removed?' They asked, 'Do you know whether his wound was aggravated by anything that happened in the collision? By which I mean – did his head hit any part of the car?' They asked, 'To what extent did he show any signs of consciousness; was there ever a moment when you thought he might come round? Did the doctors who attended after the event, did they say he regained even partial consciousness?'

Which had always been the most puzzling part, because that was exactly what Dr MacDonnell said; he said 'despite the bleeding he seems to have woken up a little, but he hasn't come the whole way.' At the end, one, an Indian gentleman in an immaculate grey suit, asked Ellen why, in her opinion, her husband had stayed alive against the medical experience of two or three similar cases. Ellen blushed, unable to answer.

As she walked down the corridor later to join Miriam, who waited, the Indian gentleman called her, and she stopped.

He said, 'I could see I embarrassed you. But it is a very important question.' He stressed the last syllable in 'important' – he said 'impor-*tant*'.

She said, 'I would have felt very foolish giving the only answer I knew. You're all so –'

'So what? We're only highly trained. I want to know your own answer.'

She said, 'I tried to give my husband life; I tried to bring life into him.'

'How?'

Ellen told him – the talking, the schoolchildren singing, the whispering, the 'normal' life going on around him, the meeting, even, of the Teachers' Union group in the kitchen, the buying him new shirts and holding them under his nose in case he could smell the fabric.

'Did you ever feel foolish doing all that?'

'No, not really. I feel a bit foolish telling you.'

'You shouldn't. If you lived where I came from, it would be the thing everybody thought was the most natural. The impor*tant* thing is – it was what kept him alive. In my opinion.'

'Mine too,' she said. 'What's going to happen next?'

He said, 'We have a suspicion that he has suffered some membrane damage. There are silent areas in the brain. They can suffer damage that does not damage life. Your husband would have been killed outright by a single, heavy-calibre bullet. Shotgun pellets don't often penetrate as deeply. We're going to radiograph him and see is there anything to look at. There may be something pressing on something else. If there is, we may operate.'

Ellen could not stop herself asking the one question she did not want to ask. 'What are the chances?'

The man blinked his brown eyes: 'Very difficult to say.'

Hospital Administration directed the three women to a bed-and-breakfast in Goswell Road, a ten-minute walk from the hospital. Immediately thereafter, Ellen spent five of her worst days ever. The men found something in the radiograph – they would not specify – and decided to operate. It would take two days or so, to judge whether they could operate immediately or whether his strength needed to be built up. They had to gamble, Maurice Crowe said, between Thomas's obviously deteriorating condition, and whether he still had enough strength to endure major surgery. The journey had sapped: a bronchial noise had been detected: they had to wait to ascertain its strength or possible departure before they could be sure.

Miriam Hogan provided compensation, in the form of an opulent flat rented for at least a week: she became adjutant and quartermaster all in one – and morale-raiser, irritating Nurse Cooper with her firm assurances that Thomas would recover.

'But you have no medical evidence,' hissed Sheila Cooper to her in the kitchen of the flat.

'My nose tells me,' said Miriam Hogan.

'Ah, you and your nose.'

Ellen's despondence told a different tale. She drifted here and there, taking in little, or briefly achieving animated interest, then lapsing into silence again. On the third evening she urged the women forth to enjoy themselves. When they had gone she took from her bag the bulky envelope Leah had given her. It contained a little card painted by the girls, a man in a hat with a big smile and a message, 'Get better, Uncle Thomas, with love from

Rachel and Sarah'; a card from Leah: 'Dearest Ellen. We will be thinking of you night and day.'

The third item, in Herbert's handwriting, ran to several pages of foolscap, and had a note from him attached.

Dear Ellen,
    I don't know if you ever read the *Song of Solomon* or the *Song of Songs*. It is my favourite piece of anything in the whole world, better than an ingot of raw silver, and although all the scholars say it was written by King Solomon himself, it feels to me as if it was written by a woman. It is about a husband and wife, or, to be precise, about a bridegroom and a bride, and all their friends and neighbours who observe them. It might be useful to you in the coming times.

        Good luck,
        Herbert

Ellen read the opening lines copied in Herbert's clear hand:

O, give me the kisses of your mouth,
For your love is more exquisite than wine . . .
Your perfume has a delicious fragrance –
Your name is to me as sweet as the finest perfume . . .

Too much, too much. She folded the pages away.

Nobody felt it a good idea that Ellen should hang around the hospital throughout the long, long surgery. Except Miriam Hogan. In the cab taking them there, Ellen said to her, 'You're a dark horse. Why are you never like this at home?'

She replied, 'If Jack can't pity me, he'll collapse altogether and drink his head off.'

'But,' asked Ellen, 'when you go back . . . ?'

'I might not go back. And then I might.'

Ellen had to fight to be allowed to Thomas's bedside: 'The fear of infection,' they said.

'Let her in,' said the Indian surgeon.

'He seems unchanged,' she said in a very small-voiced whisper, observing the acres of bandages.

'No, he is still sedated.'

'When or how will we know?'

'If he is still alive in the morning, that is a first step. Do you want to know what happened? We found some things pressing.'

'I thought so.'

'We have to tell the police.'

Ellen said, 'The police at home know.'

'We have to tell the police anyway.'

'Yes, good. People should know. How long before we have any idea of the long-term chances . . . ?'

'Two days, three days. If he is alive in the morning. There will be some change. If. But do not expect too much.'

All three women sat up all night in the flat, playing cards. When Ellen fell asleep they covered her in her armchair with a blanket and sat there with her.

Thomas was alive in the morning, and Ellen haunted the hospital, night and day. When, on the third afternoon, she saw Thomas move his mouth slightly in what looked to her like a non-involuntary way, she sat perfectly straight until she saw it again, a moment later, no mistake, infinitesimal, maybe, but he did it, by himself.

'I'm here, Thomas, if you can hear me.' She put on her best accent, the one he called 'posh' for best occasions. 'I'm here.'

Friday, 25th March: Michael Condon drove from Deanstown to Dublin and met the Mail Boat. With Sheila Cooper and Miriam Hogan in the car, he followed the ambulance bearing Thomas and Ellen to the Richmond

Hospital, where Thomas was looked at briefly by the renowned Mr Adams McConnell, and Ellen was given an overnight bed in an adjoining room. Thomas did not speak; nor did he exhibit acknowledgment.

'He will be weak,' said Mr McConnell. 'You can expect that.'

'What else can I expect?' asked Ellen.

'Impossible to say,' said Adams McConnell kindlily.

They set out at half-past eleven on Saturday morning, driving as slowly as a funeral, Michael Condon ahead. Exhausted by the slowness of the journey, Ellen, despite herself, dozed in the back of the ambulance, and when she woke each time with a head-jerk, wished that Thomas did not still have to be sedated. They availed themselves of the hospital bed overnight in Maryborough. Miriam Hogan grew impatient and caught the Cork train; she reached Deanstown late on the Saturday afternoon.

The Canon announced at nine o'clock Mass on Sunday morning that Master Kane was 'coming home today after his major surgical operation over beyond in London; would everybody please offer up their prayers for his recovery. He is to be in Maryborough overnight; he'll be back among us around twelve or one o'clock, if it please God.'

March was going out like a lamb again, balmy and bright. After the Canon's announcement, most of the congregation never went home after Mass, they made straight for the village, and stood there waiting for Thomas: the children played with water splashed from the pump. Women in the ochre houses handed out mugs of tea. Mrs Hand asked the Sergeant did he mind if they 'gave out a few drinks'? He trapped her into untypical generosity by saying she wasn't breaking the law if the drink was free.

His friend Bernard said to Val Vousden much later, 'I s'pose, Val, 'twas as good as any opera house, was it?'

Val said, 'Bernard, 'twas, boy. 'Twas. I think, I think – 'twas my finest moment. Bernard, the sun was splitting the heavens.'

Just before half-past twelve, two of the boys raced up the hill.

'Coming! Coming!'

Through the trees beyond the Parochial House, they saw first the gleam of the Lancia car driven by Michael Condon at a slow pace, followed within a few seconds by the white ambulance. They surged forward from the village walls; Mrs Hand leaned out the upstairs window, her Sunday hat still on. The Sergeant began to count – what, sixty, seventy people? Canon Williams emerged from his avenue and began to hurry ahead: hatless he strode up the hill, his long coat flapping. The car and the ambulance slowed down to change gear for the steep incline.

Children jigged about: Bob Morris walked forward and stopped, leaning on his stick, stroking his moustache: Rina and Jim and May broke from their little group of three and began to walk nearer the pump. At the other end of the village, Dr Hogan's car drew up near the Master's house, and out got Miriam and Jack and walked forward quickly, like people hurrying to a fair. Mrs Greege sat in her trap, her sons either side of her, her severe face turned back towards the Dublin road. Between the trees on either side of Thomas's gate, Essie peeped out, then rushed in to put something warm on the baby.

A stranger might have imagined these people had gathered for a football game, or to observe a passing celebrity, as their forebears had for the Prince of Wales: men put out their cigarettes, broke off their conversations and lined the road from the pump to the pub: children climbed and sat on the demesne wall. The old, rivalrous joke came true: 'All to one side like the village of Deanstown'.

Then, everyone turned in astonishment from the approaching car and ambulance as, from behind them, clanged a blare of sound. Up out of a lane from the houses at the rear of the blacksmith's forge, up through the muck, daintily high-treading the ankle-deep cowdung outside Hanafin's farmyard, came Val Vousden waving a baton; his gold-braided tunic sparkled in the noon light like the breastplate of a quirky Ruritanian god. Behind him, in their blue-and-gold tunics, all made by Mrs Heffernan, marched the new Deanstown Band, their trumpets and cornets and cymbals glinting and blazing and clanging. Val held his baton aloft and waved it as if he had suddenly found it to be a magic wand.

Not perhaps all playing at precisely the same tempo, they swung into the road and marked time there to the metallic whisper of the cymbals. Then, playing 'O'Donnell Abu' with a fabulous rush of energy, they moved aside to let Michael Condon pass in the Lancia with the white-walled tyres. Outside the school, the band formed up in front of the ambulance, causing it to slow down and stop briefly.

Led by Val and his baton, the Deanstown Band, the ambulance, and the people of the village in their Sunday suits diffidently paraded the one hundred and fifty yards from the village to the Master's house.

Inside the ambulance, Ellen, unable to keep back the tears, said to the inert, white Thomas, 'Thomas love, if you can hear. They have the new Deanstown Band; your friend Val, they're all put in the county colours of blue and gold, and they're marching ahead of you. They're playing you home.'

The villagers marched too – and the strangers: Bob Morris could not see because his eyes were full of tears, and if he blinked the tears would fall; and Leah Winer and the girls in their little white anklesocks, and Herbert.

===

Had anybody thought to look off to the right, up through the high fields in the sunlight, they would have seen, away in the distance, on the upper road, a small, dull procession. A hearse-horse with a single, rather tatty black plume strolled in front of one car and a handful of people. They walked down an avenue that connected with the upper road, and then to the main road along which Thomas's ambulance had just driven. Ernestina Stephenson was being buried in the family plot, beneath the rooks in their cypresses and elms, in the Protestant churchyard near the river at Silverbridge. Uncle Henry, walking behind, observed Ernestina's last request. He read aloud from this dear, clumping, loveless girl's favourite text:

> *'Look, the winter is past*
> *And the rains are over and done with.*
> *Flowers have begun to appear on the earth;*
> *The time of the singing-birds has come*
> *And the voice of the turtle-dove*
> *Shall be heard in the land.'*

31

On leaving the hospital, Ellen had been given two sets of
instructions, one formal, the other informal. The first said
that Thomas needed absolute quiet except for the domestic round – no callers, apart from those essentially closest to him, no intensive activity, no pressure of any kind.
The second directive was delivered by the Indian surgeon,
who said to her, 'Whatever you were doing before,
redouble your efforts.'

He did not enquire what she meant when she murmured, 'Dolphin work.'

At Deanstown on that Sunday afternoon, she had to
control the numbers of men who wanted to help with his
stretcher. As those nearest saw his appearance, their
minds recoiled. That night the fireside talk all flowed on
the same current.

'There isn't any way a man looking like that is going to
pull through.'

'Did you see the face on him? Like a ghost.'

Thomas safely indoors, Ellen came out again and said
in general, 'I can't give you tea or anything, you'll understand.' In particular she said, 'Mr Vousden, how can I
thank you?'

Then, she answered the only question in which anyone
had any interest.

'I don't know any more than you do how he'll be. There
wasn't any point in keeping him in London, or in hospital,
even. The doctors had done all they could for him. It's all
up to – up to what, I don't know now. But he has to get
peace and quiet.'

'Is he awake, Ma'am?' one woman asked.

'No. He's asleep,' she said, an acute deflection, and thanking them again went indoors.

Leah, Herbert, the children and Bob had come in a hired car, and when their driver had been fetched from the pub, they left. Jack Hogan took out his stethoscope but Miriam forbade him to examine Thomas. 'He has to rest, Jack. For goodness' sake! He's not a toy of yours.'

Miriam, Sheila Cooper and Ellen herself undertook the routine of preparations laid down by the hospital: the observation charts; the slow reduction of sedatives; the methods of judging whether they could begin to exercise Thomas's arms and legs; the minute inspection for any sign of consciousness; the counting of any hand or eye movements over specified periods. Sheila Cooper measured out the first allocations of medicines, the iron, the calcium. They bathed and changed Thomas, who seemed to Ellen far less pliant than before – 'Maybe it is because I haven't handled him for nearly seven weeks,' she fretted.

When he had been settled for the night, Ellen took time to renew acquaintance with Helena: 'You're so big, you've grown as big as a house!'

'Look, Ma'am,' said Essie, pulling back Helena's lips.

'Oh, oh – teeth, teeth, teeth!' squealed Ellen. 'You'd swear,' she whispered, when she joined the girls for a cup of tea at the parlour table, 'that Essie grew the teeth herself.'

As Miriam and Sheila left, Ellen shook their hands and said simply, 'Thanks, girls. Thanks.'

With a new household roster established after a week, Ellen returned to school. She sent out word-of-mouth to reinforce her message of that Sunday arrival – that for the moment the Master was allowed no visitors. This was taken as confirmation of their suspicions: Michael Condon was reported as saying that when he himself took the car to Dublin and climbed into the ambulance, he thought the Master, 'if anything, worse-looking'.

'Anyone who goes to hospital – sure they never come back,' said the pessimists, always in the majority.

'The Canon wants to say a special Mass for the Master,' reported Jack Hogan.

'No. No,' said Ellen. 'I have to put a stop to that,' and she wrote a note saying, 'Not for the moment. It gives me too much of a requiem feeling,' and Jeremiah abandoned the plan.

Back at school, Ellen gave another *Nature Notes* class, illustrated with drawings of 'the birds you see in the fields'. They identified the robin, the thrush, blackbird, sparrow, wagtail: 'What's different about the wagtail? This is what's different. All the others hop, but he runs. What does he do? He runs.'

Crow, pigeon, pheasant, yellowhammer, plover, swan, waterhen: they sang out all the names as Ellen revealed the pictures, and they baulked only at the different breeds of finch: 'This is the goldfinch. Some people have them in cages as songbirds. The goldfinch has one thing about it different to all the other birds. It has a very strong beak and can even crack open the stone of a cherry.' She gained their most concentrated attention from two birds they never saw: the owl and the cuckoo. 'The first thing about the owl is – the owl is a lot smaller than you'd think. And the owl has maybe the softest feathers of all the birds. Why? Because the owl hunts at night and the soft feathers on its wings make it easy for the owl to hunt at night.'

When it came to the cuckoo, Ellen said, 'Hands up anyone who has seen a cuckoo?'

Several of the older boys raised their hands.

She asked of each, 'And what colour was it?' One said

red, another blue, a third red and blue, a fourth yellow with black spots.

Asked Ellen, 'And did any of you ever see a cuckoo with a little silk green waistcoat and a tall hat?' They all laughed.

'The thing about the cuckoo is – everybody thinks they've seen the cuckoo, but very few people ever see it, it is one of the shyest birds of all. The cuckoo is a brown bird, not red or yellow or blue or green.' They all laughed. 'And it is quite big, as big or bigger than a thrush, and it depends on not being seen, because it gets into other birds' nests while they're out, and lays its eggs there, and when the young cuckoo is hatched, it heaves all the other little birds out of the nest and keeps all the food for itself.'

All Ellen's routines changed.

'A funny thing,' she said to Sheila Cooper, 'everything about my system, you know, since the baby, d'you remember I told you how irregular everything was, it all seems to be getting back to normal again since Thomas's operation.'

'I wonder why that is, my lady?' said the raised eyebrow.

With the house organized into rotas, Ellen said to Essie, 'Would you take over the baby completely until we see how everything will turn out.'

The mornings alternated between Ellen and Sheila Cooper; Ellen and one of Sheila Cooper's young nurses; and Ellen and Mrs Greege. One of those women then stayed near Thomas while Ellen went to school. In the afternoons and evenings the roster reversed, with Miriam Hogan – who could never promise an early morning – joining in: Ellen reserved the evenings almost exclusively for herself.

Sheila Cooper found the demands unexceptional, and relished the care required of her. Mrs Greege remained contradictory: snide and forbidding to Ellen – yet capable of great tenderness towards Thomas. The young nurse had fallen for a young man not far away whose name she would not divulge, adding spice to their daily proceedings, as they tried to winkle his identity from her.

With the exception of her daily presence at school, Ellen vanished from local view. She did not appear at Mass; the gate to the Teacher's house remained firmly closed: the helping women had their lips sworn tight.

'Just give me this last one favour,' she asked them. 'While it is still touch-and-go – say nothing to no one.'

Mrs Greege said, 'You didn't take long to learn, did you?'

When Essie went shopping, people plied her with questions, but Essie had long ago learned the value of appearing stupid as a means of keeping out of trouble, and she drew on it now to the full.

Mrs Hand reported nightly to her customers on any visible activity near the Master's house.

'There was a big car there today, and two men got out of it, I thought they was there before, they had suits on them, but they weren't the same men at all, they had English accents and 'twas a Dublin car, not a Cork car . . .'

And, 'I seen Dr Jack go in there twice, but there isn't a word outa him, sure he doesn't even come in here now, only for the odd minute now and again, and all you'll get out of him is, "All serene."'

And, 'The Mistress herself, she's looking like she's in a hard bind, I mean to say, she's looking like she's, oh, up against it altogether. And the house itself is gone like the grave, I mean they've the gate shut and the front door shut, and the clothes on the line, 'tis all sheets and towels, and there's smoke outa the chimney day and night; they must be spending a fortune on coal. She wouldn't let the Canon in the other day, nor the Curate either.'

And, 'I heard that friend of hers, that priest, the small, fat fellow, I heard he's gone off on the Foreign Missions somewhere, Africa, or something. I wonder what happened there, eh? . . .'

On Easter Sunday morning the Canon asked the congregation for a Decade of the Rosary there and then, 'for a full recovery to health by the Master,' adding tactlessly, 'in case the news isn't very good from that quarter.'

Ellen needed not to know the parish's speculations. Thomas's weight loss before, during and after London had been dramatic: she now began each day with porridge for him, milky, runny porridge into which she added the gold from the fresh honeycombs. After every feeding of Thomas, Ellen stood back and surveyed him.

'If looking at him could cure him,' said Mrs Greege, 'he'd be back to rights long ago.'

Leah arrived with a new mincer, and they minced bacon and beef and mutton.

'He's in a deep sleep at the moment,' said Ellen, 'and due to wake in about an hour or so, so we won't go in to see him yet.' When they did, Leah was only permitted a brief glance from the doorway.

Herbert rubbed his hands together that night very hard, very slowly.

'Ach!' he said, 'that does not sound good. No, that does not sound good.'

Leah described the Thomas she found: very drawn and with a pallor she had not seen before; the long jawbone accentuated by the plaster not yet removed from his temple; as yet no word, no sound, no recognition.

'What did Ellen say?'

'Very little. The nurse, that marvellous Cooper woman

– she told me a lot. She said the London doctors told her privately that there was hardly as much as a half-and-half chance. What happened was that something hit a part of his head but didn't affect the brain directly, it pressed on something pressing on the brain. They got everything out, they think, but he was so damaged for so long. If only, they said, she'd brought him to them last August or September.'

Herbert said, 'Ah, she wasn't able for anything like that then.' Then he asked his wife, 'What do you think?'

Leah thought, then answered. 'I think. I think – that if by any miracle she gets him on his feet, or even smiling, she'll have a good chance. But I don't know . . .'

To the two surgeons who made the trip from London – not, alas, including the Indian consultant – Ellen reported, 'One day he's up, the next day he's down. The mouth is working a little, and the other day he moved his fingers – like this': she made a motion as if removing something stuck on the tips of her fingers; they asked her to repeat it: 'Right hand or left hand?' they asked.

'Left hand' – which excited them a little, though not nearly so much as it had excited her when it happened: she had just settled Thomas's pullover about him, and laid his hands on the arms of his bed-chair, when she saw the fingers move. With dread, the dread of hopes again dashed, she lifted his hand carefully, re-settled it – and the fingers moved again. She shouted to Essie, and the two of them stood there gazing at Thomas's whitened bony hands, sightseers at a natural phenomenon. In school, Ellen taught that day with a giddy heart – and then had to endure a week when no further movement was detected.

She took the surgeons through the charts one by one: food intake; bowel movements; sleep patterns; eye movements. They stayed for three and a half hours, accepting only a cup of tea.

In the hall she asked, 'What do you think now?'

The one she did not like said, 'I'm encouraged. Although I have to say – even if there is a noticeable improvement, and we have to record what you have told us as improvement – you must remain aware that it could go either way. And that is, in my view, the only way to look at it. In fact, you could say – it has to go either way. In fact, there are four possibilities. If he does not regain full consciousness, he cannot live for ever like this. If he does regain full consciousness he may be impaired for life; in other words, he may never be the same vigorous man mentally or physically, although he will be able to look after himself. Or he could make a full recovery. The fourth possibility is – he could die very quickly and quietly, in his sleep, and quite soon. The body gives up, you know. My guess is, from all you've told me about him – if he gets at all active again, he will make a complete and total recovery. But it's a big "if". If he doesn't, well, no woman could have done more for any man . . .'

At the school, a sudden and heated row broke over Ellen's head. Mrs Hand knocked on the door, supported by Mrs Leamy.

'Ma'am, I'm going down this minute to report you to the Canon, so I am.'

'What?'

'I'm going down to the Canon this minute.'

'What's wrong?'

'Ma'am, the things you're putting in them children's heads. And you're not teaching them hardly any prayers.'

'I beg your pardon, Mrs Hand,' said Ellen with asperity. 'You're the very woman who came here to me, here at this door, two years ago and told me I was teaching the children too many prayers. And with all due respect to you, I'm the one paid to teach the children, not you.

Indeed, if you spent a little more time cleaning up your children, they'd be a bit better served.'

As she began to close the door, Mrs Hand inserted a foot.

'You're not supposed to be teaching the children the things you were telling them here yesterday. That's not what the Canon pays you for.'

Mrs Leamy said, 'Them things are none of your business.'

'The Canon doesn't pay me. The Department does. And that's none of your business. And if you don't mind, I want to go on doing what I'm paid for, so move your foot out of the way please.'

'I will not! I will not!' Mrs Hand pressed at the door: Ellen resisted: Mrs Leamy pressed, and the air was filled with grunts and rattles of the latch. The months of lifting Thomas had made Ellen muscular: she succeeded in closing the door and bolting it. Mrs Hand rapped the window so hard a pane cracked tinily. After some minutes the hefty women moved outside the wall of the yard and stayed there. In an hour, they went away.

On the previous afternoon, Ellen had begun: 'What is a Treaty?'

Faced with the usual vagueness, she answered her own question. 'A Treaty is a signed agreement by the two enemies in a war that they will stop fighting. The Irish and the English signed a Treaty in 1921 and that gave us the Twenty-Six Counties and gave England the Six Counties. Now what happened after the Treaty?' No hand rose.

'I'll tell you what happened, because this is part of the history of your own country. There was a Civil War. A what?' She made them repeat it. 'A Civil War,' they sang.

'Now what's the difference between a Civil War and any other kind of war? A Civil War is a war between people who are friends and neighbours, or who were friends and neighbours. Some people say that a Civil War

581

is the worst kind of war. Now – there were some people in Ireland who didn't want the Treaty signed, and there were some who did. A lot of people around here, for example, did not want it signed; a lot of people in other places did. In some cases, one brother wanted it signed, another didn't. Or a father agreed with it, but a son didn't. So a Civil War broke out and it was very bad because people who were friends fell out with each other, and they even killed their friends and neighbours and relatives.'

Ellen told Mrs Greege about the altercation with Mrs Hand and Mrs Leamy.

Mrs Greege looked at her. 'You haven't learned everything yet. Keep your mouth shut about them things. Go back to the prayers.'

'I will not.'

'You should,' said Mrs Greege. 'People don't want to be reminded. Isn't that right, Master Kane?' she called to the bed-chair across the kitchen. To Ellen she said, 'If the Master was alive, he'd tell you the same thing.'

'Alive?' Ellen shrieked. 'He is alive!'

'Thomas,' she said that night, 'that's the first bit of embarrassment I ever knocked out of Mrs Greege, and d'you know what? I don't care. The children should know these things. What surprises me is the priests don't tell them. It should be part of their Catechism class.'

Obviously, they got at the Canon. A note from him said that in a fortnight's time he would conduct a short Catechism examination. Ellen said to Thomas, 'I suppose I'd better cave in a bit. But it won't change the way I feel.'

At the end of April, with all medical and nursing practices running smoothly, Ellen sat down late one night beside Thomas in the silent house.

'Thomas dear,' she began, 'I don't know if I have it in me, but I'm going to go flat out now. I don't know if this

582

is going to be the last all-out effort I can make, but I don't know either what else I can do after this. Thomas, please, please, give me something. If you're in there and if you can hear me, show me. Show me. Give me something. I'll even tell you what I'm going to do,' and on her splayed fingers she ran through a list of her intentions. At the end she said, 'And after that I'm finished, Thomas, "bunched" as you'd say.'

She continued, 'Thomas dear, do you remember the first time we really and truly walked out together? You said to me, "Are you by any chance going home to Janesborough this week-end? Because if you weren't," you said, "there's a new hotel opened by a past pupil of mine who went off to England and made money." And you said you were going to go over there on Sunday.'

Ellen recounted and re-lived the outing.

They drove up along a high wooded avenue on the mountainside to a large house with tiny wooden eaves.

Ellen said, 'A lovely place.'

They looked out over the valley, with the river in the distance.

'Do you know those Encyclopaedias of Knowledge, Thomas, with the pictures of ancient Greece and all of that, ruined temples, or artists' impressions of what it must have been like?' Pointing out of the window, she had said, 'This view reminds me of that, the groves of childhood, that kind of thing, the trees in the distance, the river, and so on.'

Thomas had remarked, 'The owner – he won't take a penny. He won't let me put my hand in my pocket.'

'I heard him,' said Ellen, and smiled. Frost had made the air clear and sparkling, and Ellen wore her burgundy-coloured paisley dress and her maroon cardigan.

Thomas fumbled a little and poured a glass of milk from the jug on the table. A man stood at the door, saw them, came over and said, 'Hallo, Sir,' to Thomas and shook his hand, and went out again.

'Mikie the Lady,' Thomas whispered, 'he's a bit girlish and that's what the boys around christened him. He's a spoiled priest, did six years, and cut before he was due to be ordained, but he's very holy.'

Mikie the Lady came back, contrived to get an introduction to Ellen, and told her, 'The Master taught me in the third, fourth, fifth and sixth book. I'd never have passed *Pons Asinorum* if it wasn't for him.'

When he left them, Ellen asked Thomas for a translation, 'being from the city,' she said, with an arch, teasing smile.

Thomas told her that 'book' meant 'class', that 'third book' meant 'third class. Classes were formed by a philosopher called Duns Scotus. *Pons Asinorum* means "the bridge of asses"': she interrupted tartly, 'Well I knew that' – and he continued, 'Euclid's fourth theorem: if you couldn't get across that, you remained an ass for the rest of your life.'

Ellen smiled. 'I never asked you how did you get into teaching?'

'I didn't want to be, although I wanted to do something for the country, I wanted to be in the law or something. But my father died when I was sixteen, nearly seventeen, and even though I had a King's Scholarship I couldn't take it up, because there was no money coming in. The youngest was only two, and all my mother had was my father's pension of two shillings a week, you couldn't feed a bird on that. So I had to forget about school and go and work for the farmers, and I worked for farmers during the day, thinning beet and hoeing drills, or in parts of the year lambing and calving, and then in the nights I worked in a pub, and I did that for eight years until enough of the family were working to bring other money in.'

Chops with gravy; jelly with custard; a cup of tea and

biscuits: Ellen had never ceased smiling all through the meal. As they left, the owner made a fuss of her, too.

'This man is a genius,' he said, pointing to Thomas.

In the car Thomas said, 'And I couldn't get one ounce of information into his skull. 'Twas like trying to teach the wall.'

'Did you go to night school, so?' asked Ellen, trying to pick up the thread again.

'Oh, it is a long, long story,' said Thomas.

'Thomas,' she said now, 'you are entitled to your long story, and you should be free to live it again and to remember it. I came out here, to this village, thinking I was educated, and then I found myself having to fight like an animal for my life and yours. Thomas, I don't know any more what education is. But I didn't know what love was, not even when I married you. By God, I do now.'

May Morris wrote, in a letter in which Bob enclosed money, 'When Rina's holidays start, will I send her out to keep you company? She's very useful now.'

Ellen's brief note thanked her all the same but, no.

'You're a pagan, I'd reckon,' Ellen said to Miriam Hogan next day. 'What do pagans do?'

'Why? Do you think it is paganism will bring him back?'

Ellen looked at her but said nothing.

'Pagans take off their clothes and dance,' continued Miriam.

'I can't see Essie and Mrs Greege doing that,' said Ellen.

Miriam whooped with laughter.

'Get him flowers,' she said, 'and bring him young animals to see, and hold perfumes in front of his nose, and sing to him. That's what the Greeks would have done. That's what we'd do if we still lived in a tribe. Cast spells for him. Show him the moon when it comes out. Wash his face in cold rainwater that you catch yourself in a basin. Let the baby rub his face. Bring in a clump of grass with dew on it. Did you ever shave your legs? Well, then shave your legs in front of him. Let him smell your armpits. Rub your clothes to him. Put your skin near him. Read him love stories. Put the cats on his lap.'

Ellen interrupted, 'They climb up there anyway, Blackie is always there, we nearly have to pull her away, he's nice and warm for them.'

'Get him a dog. But above all, rub him, put your fingers to his mouth, rub your chest to his face, show him yourself.'

Ellen, for all her new feistiness, had a shocked expression on her face.

'Miriam! How do you know all this?'

'I daydream all the time, you know all those times I'm walking the fields? I think a lot. Jack forgets how well educated I am. He thinks I truly am what my mother told him, "an oddity". I think about things all the time and I link them to what I see out in the fields. Rain is a wonder, people don't realize that. And what do you think all that out there is for, the grass and the sky and the mountains and the clay? Look –' She held her arms above her head and twirled slowly. 'I often do this when I'm at home, when Jack is out. I take off all my clothes and I dance in front of the long mirror. Jack isn't intelligent enough to look at me or touch me the way I want to be seen and touched. When I saw how unintelligent he was about me, I nearly tore myself apart, I tried to mutilate my body so that he wouldn't want to come near me.'

'Miriam Hogan, do you know something? I think you are gone a little mad.'

'A little soft in the head?'

'Not the full shilling.'

'A bit empty upstairs, maybe?' Miriam winked in slow motion.

'And Miriam, do you know something else? I think you're right to be that way. I'm beginning to think it is the only way to be.'

'For a woman, anyway,' said Miriam.

A horse and cart drew up outside the gate.

'It's all right, Essie, I'll go out,' said Ellen.

'Hold the rope, Ma'am, hold the rope,' said Dan Allen. 'Don't let him buck.'

'I'll have him back to you in a few minutes,' Ellen called over her shoulder.

To the toddling Helena's squeals of delight, her Mamma led a black-and-white calf right into the kitchen. Ellen held the calf's neck tight on the halter; the creature wobbled and buck-kicked a little: inside the house the calf looked large and highly amusing. Taking Thomas's hand, Ellen guided the calf to his fingers; the calf nosed around, then swinging its head gave a cry, then nosed again, then began to suck. It left a sweet milky scum on Thomas's hands. It then licked Helena's hand and she squealed in delight and fear.

'Oh, Ma'am,' said Essie, 'there'll be scutter all over the floor.'

Ellen took Thomas's palm and rubbed it on the calf's rough back, and back up to its ears and around its jaw, then led the calf back out.

'I haven't an iota why she wanted it,' said Dan Allen that night to Mrs Hand behind the bar. 'She only had it in there five minutes, and she led it out again, and thanked me and wanted to pay me.'

Next night, Ellen said to the departing Nurse Cooper, 'Don't. I'll lower him later.'

Although prepared for bed, Thomas continued to sit upright. Just before midnight, Ellen approached and said, 'Here, Thomas, here, look.' Slowly she took off her cardigan, then unbuttoned her blouse. 'Oh, Thomas, to think

I wouldn't do this if you were in the whole of your health?'
She lowered the straps of her slip and stood above him
naked to the waistband of her skirt. 'Here?' She raised
each arm and thrust each armpit into his nose. 'Smell me.'
She then lowered her breasts and drew them across his
face, slow, warm, pliant brushings across his eyes, nose,
mouth, cheekbones, chin, down into the cradle of his
neck.

On Saturday morning, she went into the garden with
one of the large brown kitchen bowls used for eggs, or
cake-batter. Essie and Sheila Cooper said to each other,
'What in the name of God is she doing now?' Ellen
stooped and gathered handfuls of clay; from the gooseberry and blackcurrant bushes she broke little twigs; in
the kitchen she held them close to Thomas's nose,
crumbled the clay in her fingers as if it were snuff.

Rainwater, just a little basinful collected during a heavy
shower, the smell of the honeycomb, the underclothes she
was changing from, the newly ironed linen – all of these
Ellen applied to Thomas's senses, usually held under his
nostrils. Once, and once only, the desperation broke
through. Late at night, with Essie upstairs on her clump-
ings, Helena asleep, Ellen undressed and began to shave
her legs.

'Look, Thomas, you never saw me do this before, look.'
Slowly she drew the razor down along her shins, holding
the leg up to inspect it, and rubbing her hand along it,
from the inside ankle to the outside thigh.

Not for days had there been any vestige of encouragement by way of a new flicker of life from him, not for
days, and Ellen sat back in the chair, wrapped her arms
tight around her naked bosom, moaned in frustration,
held one foot yet in the basin of water, and could not
summon the energy to shave the other leg.

'I think,' said Nurse Cooper that week, 'she's getting a little frantic. I'm worried.'

'Leave her alone,' said Miriam Hogan, 'leave her alone.'

'Come on,' said Ellen. 'Think of a song.'

'What about this one?' asked Miriam. 'Hey, big man, big man,' she said to Thomas. 'Do you know this one?'

> *'I have a song to sing-oh.'*

Ellen joined in.

> *'Sing me your song-oh.*
> *It was sung to the moon by a lovelorn loon*
> *Who fled from the mocking throng-oh.*
> *It's the song of a Merryman moping mum.*
> *Whose soul was sad and whose glance was glum,*
> *Who sipped no sup and who craved no crumb,*
> *As he sighed for the love of a lady.*
> *Hey-de, hey-de, Misery me, lacakaday dee.*
> *He sipped no sup and he craved no crumb*
> *As he sighed for the love of a lady.'*

'Oh. "Sipped no sup, craved no crumb" – not entirely the best choice of words in all the circumstances,' said Miriam and they roared with laughter.

In the third week of May, with Easter well behind them, the people of Deanstown slowly became aware that the silence surrounding the Kane household had intensified even further. Those self-appointed watchers from behind the lace curtains of the village reported Mrs Greege's increased visits; Nurse Cooper's hurried arrivals, almost daily, then daily; Dr Hogan's extended stays; Mrs Hogan 'never left the place'; the Mistress's dark frowns as she raced to and from school; the children reported her as 'different, she don't laugh as much'. Ellen wrote brusque letters cancelling all who would call. The house had completely withdrawn into itself: the villagers, picking up the mood, talked and talked, paying gloomy compliments. 'Well, the one thing is, you can't say she didn't fight for him, that's for sure.' They shook their knowing heads. 'D'you know what it is. The Mistress wasn't at Mass this nearly five months.' Prayers continued for the Master.

'Any day now,' said Mrs Hand, 'you'll see Mrs Kirwan there': the local midwife who also laid out and washed corpses and acted as the undertaker's agent. Mrs Hand continued, 'Did you see his brothers were over? Two of them cycled over on Sunday and they were there no time, and they left with faces as long as a Tuesday on them. Mr Vousden, what do you think?'

'Well,' says Val, 'the Band is going to play there Sunday, outside the door, whatever? Sure 'tis the least we can do.'

'Thomas,' said Ellen. 'I have a good one to tell you. You know those Gannons, don't you, over there near Mullinahone? Miriam Hogan was telling me: the Gannons have cousins in America who were home recently, and one of them was standing with that Gannon man, you know the man with the brown hat on him always, and the sun was going down. And the Yank, the American cousin, said, "That sure is a lovely sunset." And d'you know what the Gannon man said? He said, "I s'pose 'tisn't bad for a small place like Mullinahone." Isn't that a scream?' She laughed – and subsided.

She called, 'Essie, bring in that cake, is it fresh out of the oven?'

Ellen cut into the fruit cake. 'Blast you, Thomas Kane, you're going to eat this whether you like it or not, you used to love it. Will anything get you back to life, will anything?' and when she crammed the crumbs into his mouth, he gagged a little and jerked his head.

=

That night she took out Herbert's long handwritten piece of paper, and began to read, first to herself and then, as she warmed to the text, aloud to Thomas, skipping forward as she found the most beautiful passages.

> 'Like an apple tree
> Among the trees of the forest
> Is my love among all other young men.
> I love to sit in the shade of him
> And the fruit of him is so sweet
> To the taste of my mouth.'

She looked up at Thomas's face and then down at Herbert's handwriting.

> 'He has led me into the banqueting hall
> With his banner of love waving over me.
> Feed me cakes with raisins in them.
> Refresh me with apples,
> For I am fainting with love.'

The light from the lamp shone half-across Thomas.

> 'Look, the winter is past
> And the rains are over and done with.
> Flowers have begun to appear on the earth;
> The time of the singing-birds has come
> And the voice of the turtle-dove
> Shall be heard in the land.'

Ellen jumped to her feet and read with one arm held out dramatically.

> 'My beloved is mine and I am his.
> He feedeth among the lilies.
> Until dawn breaks and the shadows melt away,
> Turn to me my love
> And be like a swift gazelle
> Or a young stag on the mountain of spices.'

Ellen slammed the paper down on the table, ran to the

hall door and opened it. The May moon had risen long ago and now coasted high to the due south. She rushed back in and scrabbled at the locked shutters, breaking a fingernail, which she sucked.

'Thomas, look!' and sang, 'The young May moon is beaming, love. The glow-worm's lamp is gleaming, love.'

She doused the oil-lamp, whirled the bed-chair around, until the moon through the window shone in his face like a torch.

'Look,' said Ellen, 'you can see the cities there. Look. It is his face I can see. The man in the moon. When I was a little girl, when I saw the moon first, I asked my father to get it for me. Thomas, I want you to be able to show Helena the man in the moon. Thomas, you know the prayer I taught you, *Saint Patrick's Breastplate*, don't you? Whenever I think of that time, of you, out there in the fields on the run under the moon, with your gun in your bad, your evil, killing times – I know you won't ever talk to me about that, you never would, you must have been ashamed, or something – I used to think, what if *Saint Patrick's Breastplate* wasn't a prayer but a kind of suit of armour, and that my dear Thomas might have been able to wear it. The words of it, Thomas?' Ellen recited, 'Christ before me, Christ at my side . . . all that part?'

Ellen continued, urgency increasing, 'Well, there's another part, a part that's never said as often. One of the lines in it is, "The whiteness of the moon at evening". It is my favourite part. Thomas, make me a promise. Promise me you'll live, promise me you'll get better, promise me that on the whiteness of the moon, will you?'

And so, night after night, week after week, her solitary impassioned colloquies continued, and she drew the household into an ever tighter and frenzied circle about her and her man, Thomas Kane. Only one person outside the circle ever saw that chalk-white, supine Thomas Kane

again, as he lay in that now dreadful chair-bed, and that
was Val Vousden. The band gave what Val called 'a
recital' on the gravel in front of the house. Ellen permitted
it, and opened the door and the windows.

'Can I see him itself, Ma'am?'

'On one condition,' she said, 'and this has to be a
solemn promise.'

'Val is always as good as his word, Ma'am,' he said.

'You mustn't answer any of their questions about how
he is.'

'Fair enough, Ma'am,' said Val, 'I won't even tell Mrs
Heffernan,' and he never uttered a word.

The gate rattled early, just after eight o'clock. Ellen
looked out of the window, and saw a curious figure, a man
with a bicycle and what looked like a pedlar's tray across
the handlebars. Propping the bicycle against the wall,
he called through the bars of the gate. 'Anyone?! Anyone?!' She opened the bedroom window and put out her
head.

'What do you want?'

'Is this the Kanes' house?'

'Yes.'

'I want to see Master Kane.'

'He's not here. Go away.'

She closed the window. The man shouted on. Ellen
opened the window. 'I told you! He isn't here. Go off with
you.'

The man tried to climb the gate, but could not negotiate
the spikes.

Ellen opened the window a third time. Where the blazes
was Sheila Cooper? She's usually here by now when it is
her morning on.

'If you don't go away I'll call the Guards!' She lowered
the sash again, and stepped behind the long lace curtains.

The man abandoned the gate and disappeared: then she

saw him climb the wall and crash through the high laurel hedge, Thomas's pride and joy.

'Jesus!' said Ellen. She opened the window yet again.

'Where are you going? Get out. Get out. I'll send for the police, I will.'

The man ran across between the apple trees, prancing high to avoid the wet grass, and hurled himself against the front door, rapping the knocker so hard the frame of the door jumped. Ellen raced downstairs and opened the parlour window a fraction beside the front door.

'Who do you think you are?' she shouted.

'Who are you?' he asked, the white teeth flashing in his dark skin.

'What do you want? I'm not buying anything.'

'I've something here for Thomas Kane. Master Thomas Kane.'

'What is it? I can take messages for him.'

He dug into a large pocket and pulled out a small brown paper packet.

'This. But I want a reward.'

'How much? And a reward for what?' He came to the window and handed it to her. 'Judge for yourself.'

Gingerly Ellen took the packet and felt it. Small, soft: so insubstantial there might be nothing in it. Sheila Cooper appeared at the gate, had a key to the padlock. Ellen closed down the window, stepped back into the parlour, but kept the curtains apart so that she could keep an eye on the man. She turned the packet over in her hand.

He rapped the glass hard. 'Open it, I haven't all day.'

She unfolded the packet as slowly as ever Thomas might have done. Inside sat a twist of newspaper which she also unfolded. Grubby, a little twisted and slightly green, lay her gold cross, the one ripped from her neck on her wedding morning. She disappeared from the man's view, and he heard her open the door.

'Where did you get this?' she demanded, unharshly.

'Ask me no questions, and I'll tell you no lies.'

'But you're not the same man who took it?'

'No, but I know the scoundrel.'

'Wait 'til I get my bag.' Ellen returned with her handbag, took out her wallet and handed the man a five-pound note.

'I didn't mean that much,' he said.

'I do,' she replied.

He looked at the money, then at Ellen. 'Is there anything else you lost that you'd like me to go looking for?' She shook her head.

Sheila Cooper said, 'What are you doing with yourself buying from a pedlar?'

Ellen showed her the cross, told her the story.

32

Ellen exhibited the missing treasure to sleeping Thomas, and to Essie: by now Ellen knew how to tell Essie a story: much detail, lurid where possible, adjectival, with mimicry: Essie gasped satisfyingly: 'A n-miracle, Ma'am.' Helena jig-stumbled about in red dungarees, crashing into doors, climbing on chairs, pursuing Soot who got away easily, if a little furred and miffed.

Notwithstanding the brightness of the morning and its startling event, Sheila Cooper wore a tight expression, as when about to raise a difficult matter.

'D'you remember when he was threatened with pneumonia? And you sent out for everybody from around the place to come in and help? Well, they're all anxious to know how he is, they're asking me every hand's turn I take, and I can't tell them a mortal thing – because that's the way you said you want it?'

'Sheila, the only reason I wanted a bit of privacy –'

'Secrecy, it is –'

'– All right, "secrecy", the only reason I wanted nobody to know anything was to give us a chance to get him right.'

'Why didn't you go to the other road? You saw the way it worked before?'

'What other road?'

'Get everybody in. Say, instead of us standing him up, propping him up to see if he can flutter a bit more into – into normal . . . the men could do that, couldn't they, a couple of big tall men like Michael Connors – or the Canon, come to that?'

Ellen reflected, forefinger between teeth.

'Yes. Yes.'

'Yow! Yow!' Helena squealed as Blackie pounced tail-high slowly across the doorway.

'No. This is why,' said Ellen, opting for authority. 'I know how . . . how particular – Thomas is. He's very, what? He's very, I don't know, not fastidious, that isn't the full thing I want to say. He'd be put out, he'd be . . . Look. Supposing I asked the same thing again as we did at the pneumonia, and supposing Thomas, you know – "woke up" suddenly, and it was somebody holding him he maybe didn't even like very much. No.'

Ellen grew firmer. 'I see your argument, Sheila. But I'm after coming this far. And if there's any fraction of a chance – I want to be the one who's there. What I'll do if you like, is, I'll write to everyone and tell them, that's what I'll do.'

'All right,' surrendered an unsatisfied Sheila Cooper, 'but you'll be writing an awful lot of letters. You can start this morning with Mrs Stack, Mrs Hanafin, Mrs John Looby and Arthur Grant's wife. And that's only yesterday's crop.'

Dear Mrs Stack,

Nurse Cooper was telling me you were enquiring and I can't tell you what your interest and sympathy mean to us all. The Master is much the same, although lately we have been seeing, I think, and I hope I'm not imagining it, signs of improvement.

The doctors told me in London what would happen is, we should pay him the greatest possible attention in the greatest possible calm. So we stand him up every day and we exercise his arms and his legs, that's all to get the circulation going, and we rub his cheeks, and we rub his head carefully, and his shoulders.

They said I should be on the watch all the time, because as the brain heals itself, the last stages of healing can happen quite suddenly. It is, of course, all very tiring, but that is the way things are, and I hope I'll have more news for you soon.

She said to Sheila Cooper, 'Will that do?'

Sheila read carefully, and said with sympathy, 'Ah, well,' recognizing that Ellen had omitted the despair, the always-frustrated eagerness, and the crucial information that things might very easily slip the other way, that Thomas could likely die in his sleep or, as Sheila put it to Mrs Greege, 'sigh off to eternity in front of our two eyes'.

When she returned from school every afternoon Ellen asked Essie and anyone else who happened to be near, 'Any news?' in the same way her mother had used the phrase with pointed coyness in the months directly after Ellen's marriage: both questions had similar meaning: 'Any new life?'

Once, the young nurse told Ellen, 'I know one thing, Ma'am, the way he opened the eyes this morning wasn't the way they fall open, d'you know that old fish sort of a way; this was like his eyelids had their own muscles again' – but nothing further, nothing at all.

Ellen's private nocturnal colloquies continued throughout late May into the fluctuating weather of early June. One hot, thundery night, she unbuttoned Thomas's pyjama jacket and sponged him gently with a cool cloth, then towelled him with tenderness and allowed him to lie for some minutes open-chested.

'Oh, dear man – if only you'd snore or something, some sort of noise.'

33

The framework of the old village may still be traced very clearly and easily. Admittedly, prosperous bungalows have replaced all but two of the ochre, estate cottages, and smaller farms have been bought over and merged into greater acreages. The Castle has largely disintegrated: crusts of old stucco may be stumbled across, embedded in the earth. Only a corner of the brick kitchen garden wall lingers; the greengages have disappeared, and the Castle pond has dwindled to a tiny marshy fen. A headstone of bland marble in Silverbridge Protestant churchyard bears the legend,

Ernestina Stephenson
1894–1927
Erected by her loving brother, Cyril
AND THE VOICE OF THE TURTLE-DOVE SHALL BE
HEARD IN THE LAND

Stands of lime trees have grown in many fields; myxomatosis once eliminated the rabbits – they have returned to the blue-green grassy banks; and the mountains still look near when it rains. In the new school, glowing white on the edge of the village, summer holidays remain the same: closed in mid-July until the last week in August or, more usually, the first week in September.

On the Friday of the second week in June 1927, Ellen decided she would revive Thomas's custom of having a sweet giving-out on the last day of the holidays, and she sat at the high dais writing a note to Newey's in Mooreville 'for delivery in plenty of time, a wide assortment of toffees, chocolate toffees, liquorice and fruit drops, six lbs in all'. In the bright sun of the morning, she had risen well, early, breezed down the stairs to Thomas, ahead, unusually, of Essie. She opened the shutters and approached that first dread moment – the daily test of checking Thomas's forehead and breathing to ascertain that he had lived through the night.

Next, Ellen opened wide the front door and the back door: because she was so early, she could make a start on Thomas and with Essie's help have him finished before she left for school – he too would have a lovely fresh beginning to the day.

Kettles on, in a moment she heard the rabbiting and chattering and thumping and little singing, meaning that Miss Helena was on her busy way down the stairs, bumping her bottom on each step, and then bursting with self-praise when she made it to the hall without misfortune. Helena put her head around the door, and grinned, and stood up. Ellen grinned back and laughed at little Miss Comical, steadier on her pins each day.

Essie's great noises began shortly after, step by thudding step. Did she have somehow to visit and re-establish each corner of the room before braving the day? Essie descended, and soon came her inevitable opening words.

Ellen whispered one night, 'Thomas, d'you know what it is? If Essie found me sitting on the chamber-pot, she'd say, "Sure I'll do that for you, Ma'am."'

This morning, Essie took the porridge saucepan handle from Ellen, and said, 'Sure I'll do that for you, Ma'am.'

Ellen had finally assembled her school basket.

'Ma'am, what'll I put on the baby?'

'Is it going to be sunny?' pondered Ellen. 'She'll be out again, I suppose? Are her red dungarees still clean enough?'

'And, Ma'am – will I bake a fresh cake of bread, say another white?'

'Yes, that'd be great, Essie.'

Thomas looked fine, clean: Essie and Helena walked to the gate to say goodbye to Ellen: much waving took place between mother and baby daughter. Eventually, by the time Ellen reached the village, Helena could just about be persuaded by Essie to return to the house: Helena always closed the gate with a resounding clang: Essie always tried to coax her in before one of the carts passed by on the way to the creamery, delaying matters a good five minutes more.

Essie had entered the convent straight after her unnoticed years in the primary school. No question ever of her taking Vows: in ways He knew and saw and appreciated, Lay Sisters supported the work of the convent, served God, His 'special flowers' in their plainer, coarser habit – the first clothes Essie ever had, she told Ellen once, 'that weren't somebody else's, Ma'am.' Cleaning proved her initial *forte*: windows, walls, the wood in the oratory: Reverend Mother told her she had achieved a reputation for floor polishing.

Helena went, 'Unh! Unh!' – a sign she wanted something: Essie handed her down the coloured tin they kept the dishmop in. Ellen worried recently to Leah whether the 'Unh!' sound was natural to a baby that age, or whether Helena had picked it up from Essie's cleft palate.

'You know, I suppose,' said Sheila Cooper, 'that the Boss here will probably have to learn how to speak again?'

'Oh, God, Sheila – and Essie with him all day,' retorted Ellen, and the women rolled about with kind laughter.

Essie could not find the cream-of-tartar, went to the pantry to open a new packet. Bending down, she backed her enormous rump into Helena, who whacked her.

'Nah, now, n-babby, are you n-beating Essie?'

Helena continued whacking, in thorough enjoyment.

Essie returned to the scullery, and with vast hands drew the flour in from the high rims of the bright tin basin. She took the brown jug and heaved forth a little of the thickening sour cream, watching the dribble of thin curd complete with the white clots.

'She is very cheerful, isn't she, very?' commented Mother Angela, 'always in good humour.'

'Do you want to do anything about the singing?' asked Sister Mary Cecilia diplomatically.

Mother Angela smiled, her hands in the folds of her deep cuffs, shivering a little as they crossed the cold yard. 'Only not to let her into the choir, I suppose.'

Essie sang 'Slievenamon' as she baked, a sound that matched the scraping of the knife on the tin of the basin. Essie dabbed Helena's nose with a little flour: Essie then wiped the flour from her own hands on her elephantine hips. After a moment or two, when the baking had become uninteresting, Helena scrambled down off the chair Essie had placed adjacently, and wandered off. Essie, too concentrated on the basin by now, stopped singing and moved the chair out of the way.

'Yee-yee-yee. Yee-yee-yee!' Helena paused. She did her emphatic jump, relishing the sound of her heels banging on the kitchen floor. Essie heard, paid no attention. Helena chuckled, a chuckle that rose at the end, signifying surprise and delight. Again she chuckled, with a sense of some enquiry: 'Yee-yee-yee? Yee-yee-YEE?' Then 'Ahh-be. Be. Bu. BE?' This was a conversation: Essie turned her head, hands still deep in the cloggy mixture.

She could see Helena in the space between the kitchen table and the end of Thomas's bed-chair: something had caught the child's attention: and gold, dazzling sunlight drenched the kitchen.

Helena bounced again, and then crouched: she was

playing a game, one which puzzled her, but did not threaten – but with what? Had the cat climbed up on the Master's bed?

Essie, holding her hands carefully akimbo, moved to one side, and when she took in the full view, suddenly reached for a cloth. Wiping her hands she moved forward along the scullery, up the step, past the open pantry door which she drew closed out of habit (leaving flour on the doorknob) and into the kitchen doorway. Helena again said, 'Be. Bu. BE?' and chuckled and smiled and poked Thomas's leg.

Essie stared. Helena looked at her, then back at her own father, and pointed and chuckled. Essie, her hands still in the dishcloth, backed carefully, back, back, to the scullery, dropped the cloth, slipped out of the back door and lumbered under full and rapid thick-legged sail around the side of the house to the gate. Three carts approached in their typical convoy, returning with the skim milk from the creamery, churns slopping water from the pump. She stopped the first one and asked him to turn around straight away and go down to the school and get the Mistress quick; she'd go herself only she couldn't leave the child in the house on her own.

'I will walk slowly,' Ellen told herself toughly. 'I will walk slowly, I mean my normal walk.'

The carter had only said, 'You're to come real quick, Ma'am, the servant-girl said.'

'Quietness, now,' she told her children. 'Delia, you're in charge,' and she then opened the door of the Juniors and said to her Assistant, 'I have to go up home for a minute.' The carter offered her a lift and she smiled her refusal.

'Ma'am, I hope you won't kill me for sending for you.' Essie waited just inside the gate under the evergreens. 'Oh, Ma'am.'

'Essie, what is it? You're never like this. Essie! What's up? Are you all right?!'

'Oh, n-Ma'am, the n-Master.'

'Essie! Come on. What is it?' Ellen's own face was turning red, and then patchy white. Essie could not say. Ellen ran along the gravel, crashed through the front door. Nothing.

Helena grinned, and ceased pushing a chair around, held up her arms to be lifted. Ellen ignored her, turned back to the hall to greet Essie.

'Essie, what in the name of God . . . ?'

Essie, who could see Thomas behind Ellen, pointed, growing even more agitated. Ellen turned and caught Thomas's faint smile. Essie leaned back, in shock, against the jamb of the door into the hallway . . .

Thereafter, Ellen scarcely slept; for the next two nights, she sat by his bed and held his hand. One day weeks later, Ellen sent Essie down to the Parochial House with a very private note – to ask Canon Williams whether he had a walking-stick or two she could borrow: he had, but told Essie he 'wouldn't lend them to Saint Peter himself'.

In summer, they never closed the outer doors of the church, only the wood-and-glass inner ones. On Sunday, 14 August 1927, the Canon arrived at a quarter to nine, and as usual, five minutes later, the bell rang. The altar-boys reported, 'They're all in, Canon'; the two oldest lads, deputed to light the tall candles, came back with their long-poled tapers, leaned them into the corner of the sacristy, and formed up with the others in soutanes and surplices in front of the Canon.

The sacristan said, 'How much wine will I put out, Canon?' He asked the same question every Sunday, and he always received the same answer.

'A good drop.' At which point the Canon always asked,

'Have we anything after?' – meaning a child for Baptism, or a woman for Churching, the ceremony of purification after birth, or a blessing of Holy Water.

'No, Canon, the fine weather drags them all away quick.'

Jeremiah Williams dipped his hand in the water-font at the sacristy inner door and added the Holy Water drops to the sweat-beads forming on his brow. He yanked at the right shoulder of the tall, homelily opulent chasuble.

The leading boy looked back: the little procession moved off. It rounded the rear of the altar swiftly and emerged swerving across the polished floor of the Sanctuary. The congregation rose, a muted shuffling sound, with the usual coughs, even in high summer. They sat down again as Jeremiah bowed to the Blessed Sacrament in the tabernacle. He climbed the steps, placed the covered ciborium with the gold-embroidered *I H S* in the middle of the altar-table, and turned to his right to find his spectacles and the card bearing the opening prayers.

As he descended the steps, all the acolytes genuflected with him and the entire congregation sank to their knees; standing, he spread his old hands and cleared his throat.

A large, alarming noise halted him, a hard, metallic clang from the yard, and a loud, revving engine noise. At the back, the men nearest the door, farm boys and labourers, down on one knee, their caps dangling from their hands to the stone flagged floor, started in suddenness, pulled mouth-ish faces of enquiry. Outside, the green Singer car, reversing, hit the wall of the church again, not as seriously as the first clang, and not at all dangerously.

'I'll tell you one thing,' they had been saying for several months, 'the Mistress, she's a wild woman in that motor-car. Do you know what it is? She have no aim.'

The first men to reach the door saw the Mistress pull the car forward a bit, then cut the engine.

'Her face,' they said afterwards, 'it was only fierce,' and they mimicked her jutting jaw. They saw her jump out, the brown cloche hat clipped firmly to her head, scurry round the car and look at the metalwork to see whether her appalling 'aim' had caused any damage. No: she opened the passenger door.

The hood was closed, so it took a moment or two to register that it was the Master she was helping out of the car. He stood upright, 'more or less of his own accord', as they later said, and put out a hand to steady himself on the car.

'He had his good bodycoat on,' they reported. 'A big, heavy grey coat. And the day sweltering.' Ellen chose the right-hand door: a man's rough hand from inside held it open for her.

She paused in the porch, reached up to adjust Thomas's lapel and collar. She removed his hat, placed a drop of water from the font on his forehead. Steering Thomas by the elbow first, then holding his hand, and then grasping him firmly by the arm, she walked slowly up along the aisle at his side. He looked straight ahead as he always did; he moved slowly, he moved stiffly: but the austere severity of his public face, the straight-edged mouth, had almost returned in full.

The Kanes reached the Teachers' pew a third of the way back from the altar. Thomas did not genuflect, although Ellen did, still reaching up to hold on to his arm. The Canon had watched their progress all the way.

Thomas encountered a little difficulty negotiating the entrance to the pew, a little stumble at the step; Ellen eased him down just inside, where he always sat, and she then stepped high over his feet and knelt by him. Thomas moved as if he would kneel but Ellen, looking at him, put out a restraining hand. He turned his head – 'A bit stiff, only,' they all said afterwards – and gave her a small, soft, slightly rueful smile.

Canon Jeremiah Williams surveyed Thomas, and Ellen, then Thomas again, and nodded. He turned back to the altar, and spreading his mottled hands once more, intoned, '*Introibo ad altare Dei*.' Those whose Missals included English in black print alongside the crimson lettering of the Latin, read, 'I will go in unto the altar of God.'

Ellen held the Missal over to her right for Thomas to share the page with her. The altar-boys responded, '*Ad Deum qui laetificat juventutem meum*,' as the Master, the Mistress and the parish of Deanstown read in silent unison, 'Unto God who giveth joy to my youth.'

Frank Delaney

A Stranger in Their Midst

INNOCENCE IS NO DEFENCE . . .

In village Ireland of the 1950s, Thomas and Ellen Kane's daughters, Helena and Grace, are gullible young women. Then, into their lives slinks Dennis Sykes, a brilliant and driven man, with a secret history of emotional mayhem and scandal. The Kane girls, lovingly close in fear of their disturbed father, have no defences against this sexual terrorist. As the decades roll forward, the outside world comes to Deanstown. Rural electrification, intended to illuminate the land, brings instead a tragedy as dark as Thomas Kane's moods.

Using great dramatic themes – the drowning of traditional houses in an ancient valley to build a dam, the destruction of a family's inner life – Delaney draws you in deep, into a time, and place, and family, in a novel that will keep you thinking long after you've finished reading.

'*A Stranger in Their Midst* is a dramatic novel. Written in clear, dry prose, it seldom loses its conviction.'   *The Times*

'Blast Frank Delaney. With his devious, seductive writing he keeps story addicts from their sleep.'   *OK Magazine*

'Frank Delaney's *A Stranger in Their Midst* is excellent.'
Woman and Home

'A powerful story vividly told.'   *Choice*

'A good old-fashioned tale of simple Irish folk doing battle with the future.'   *Evening Standard*

ISBN: 0 00 649318 1
(Published in paperback in May 1996)